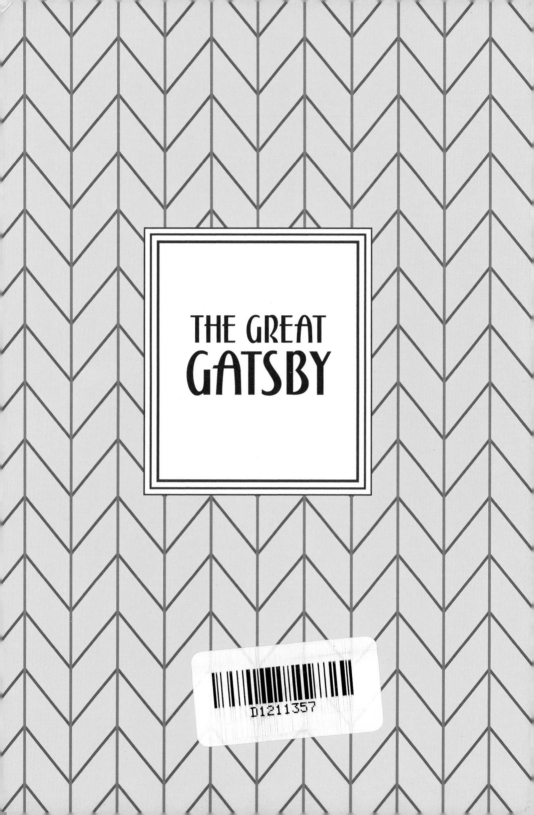

THE GREAT
GATSBY

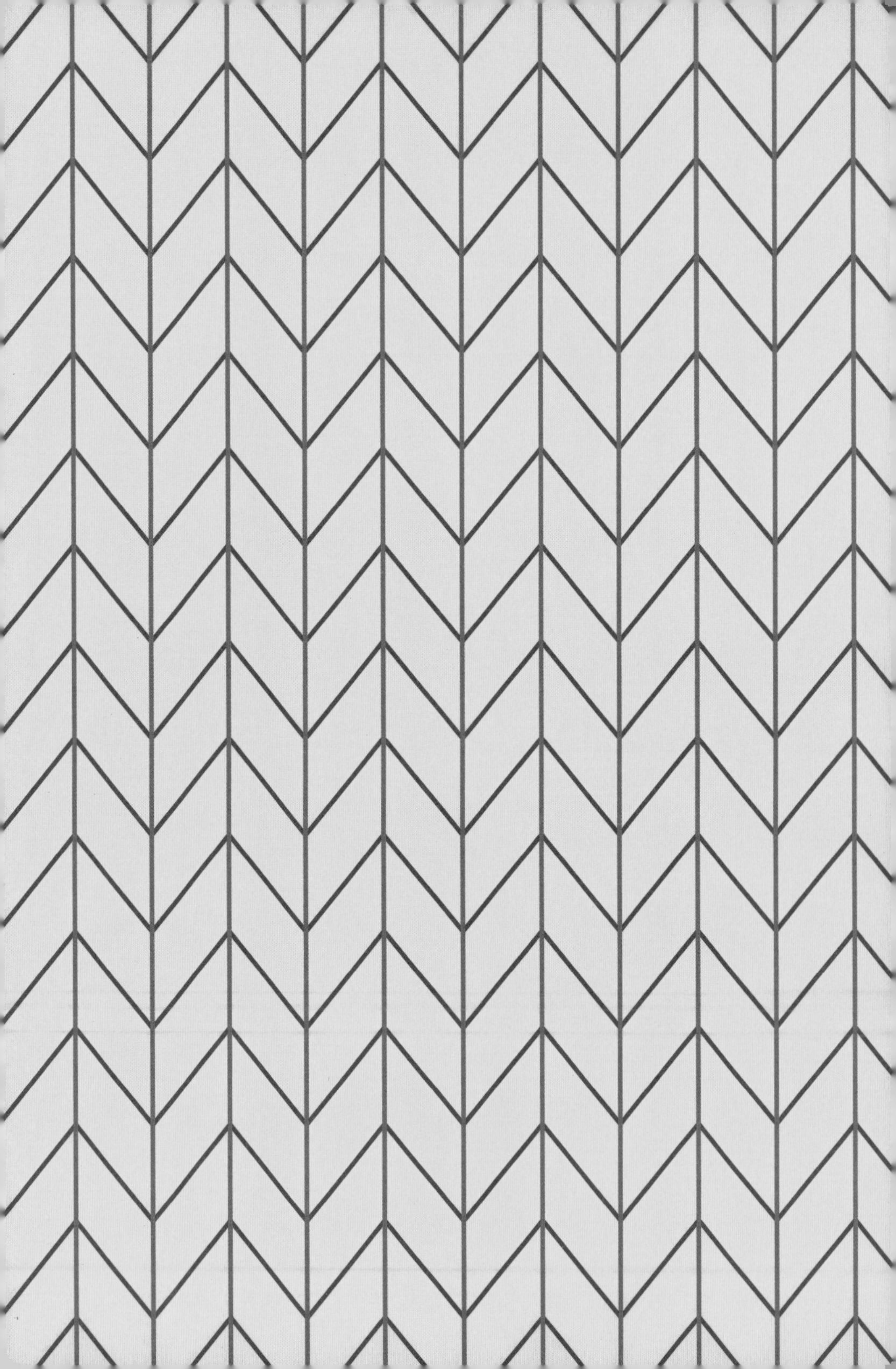

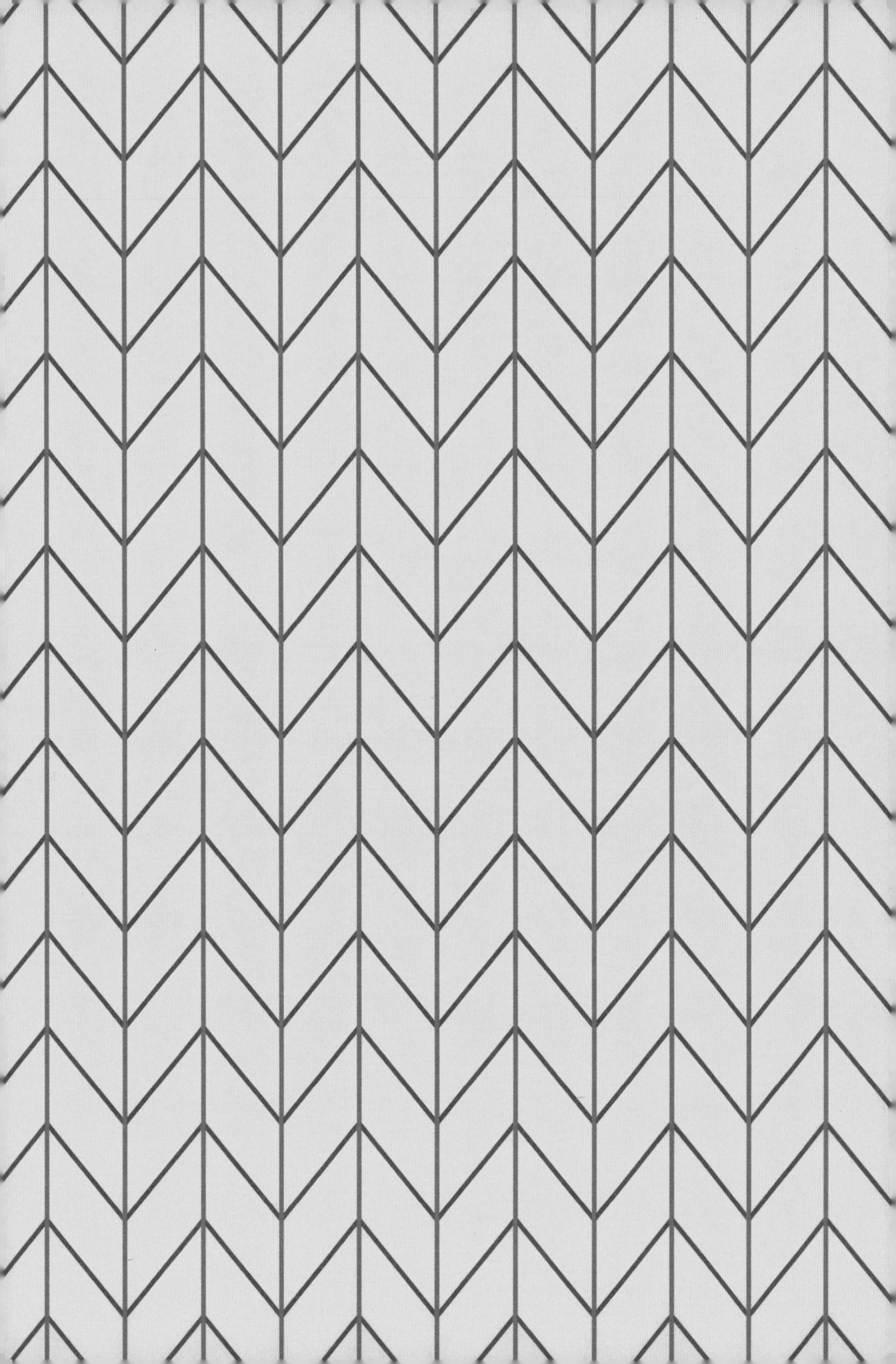

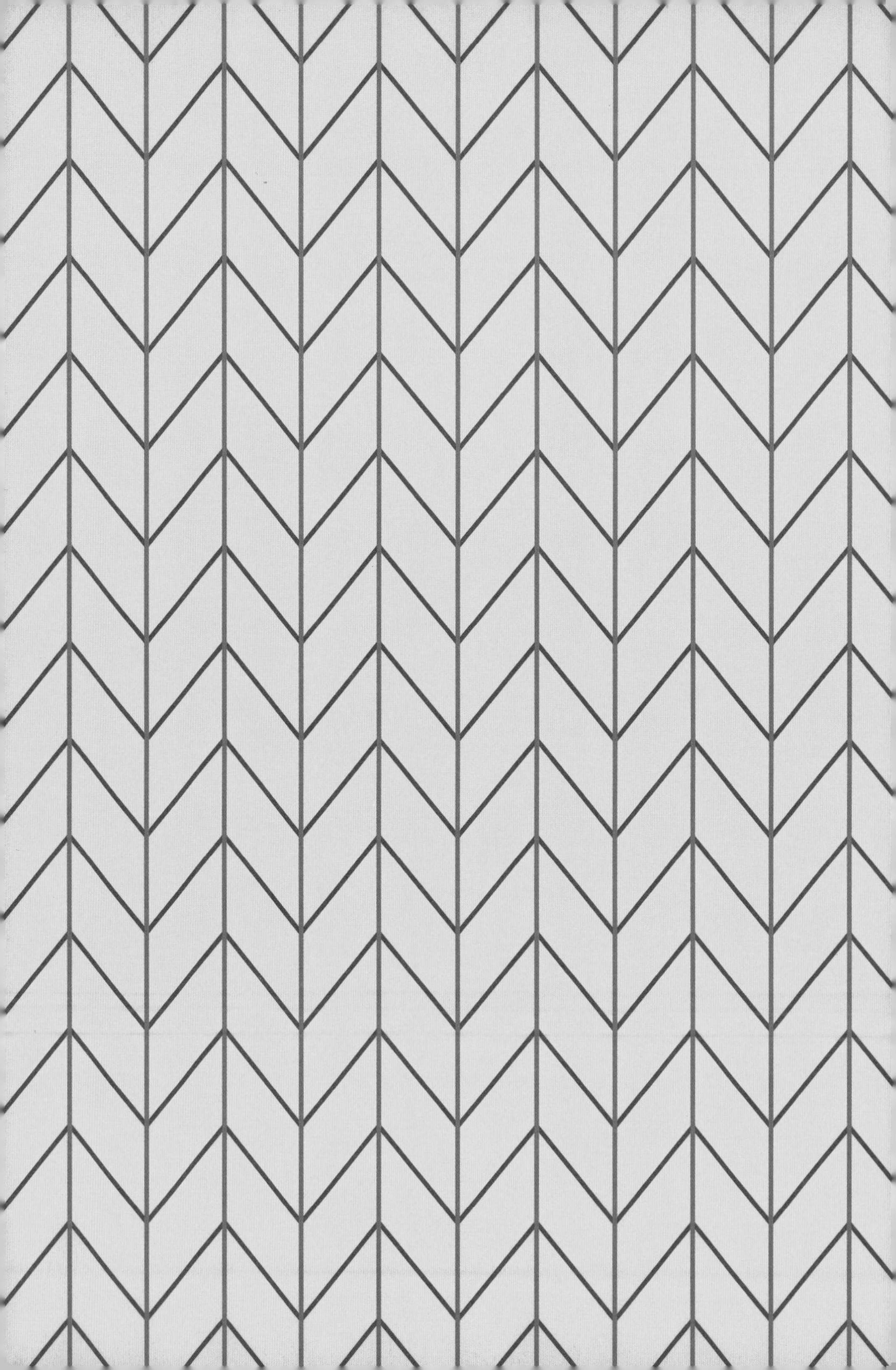

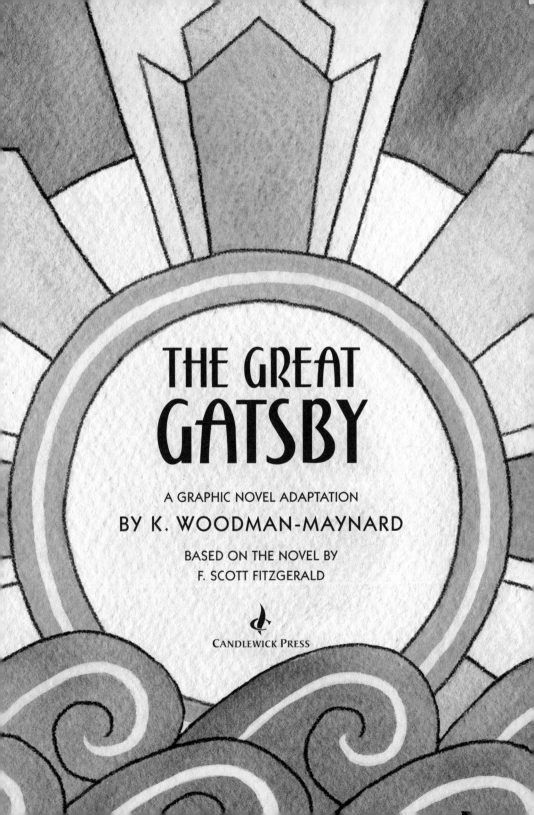

THE GREAT GATSBY

A GRAPHIC NOVEL ADAPTATION
BY K. WOODMAN-MAYNARD

BASED ON THE NOVEL BY
F. SCOTT FITZGERALD

CANDLEWICK PRESS

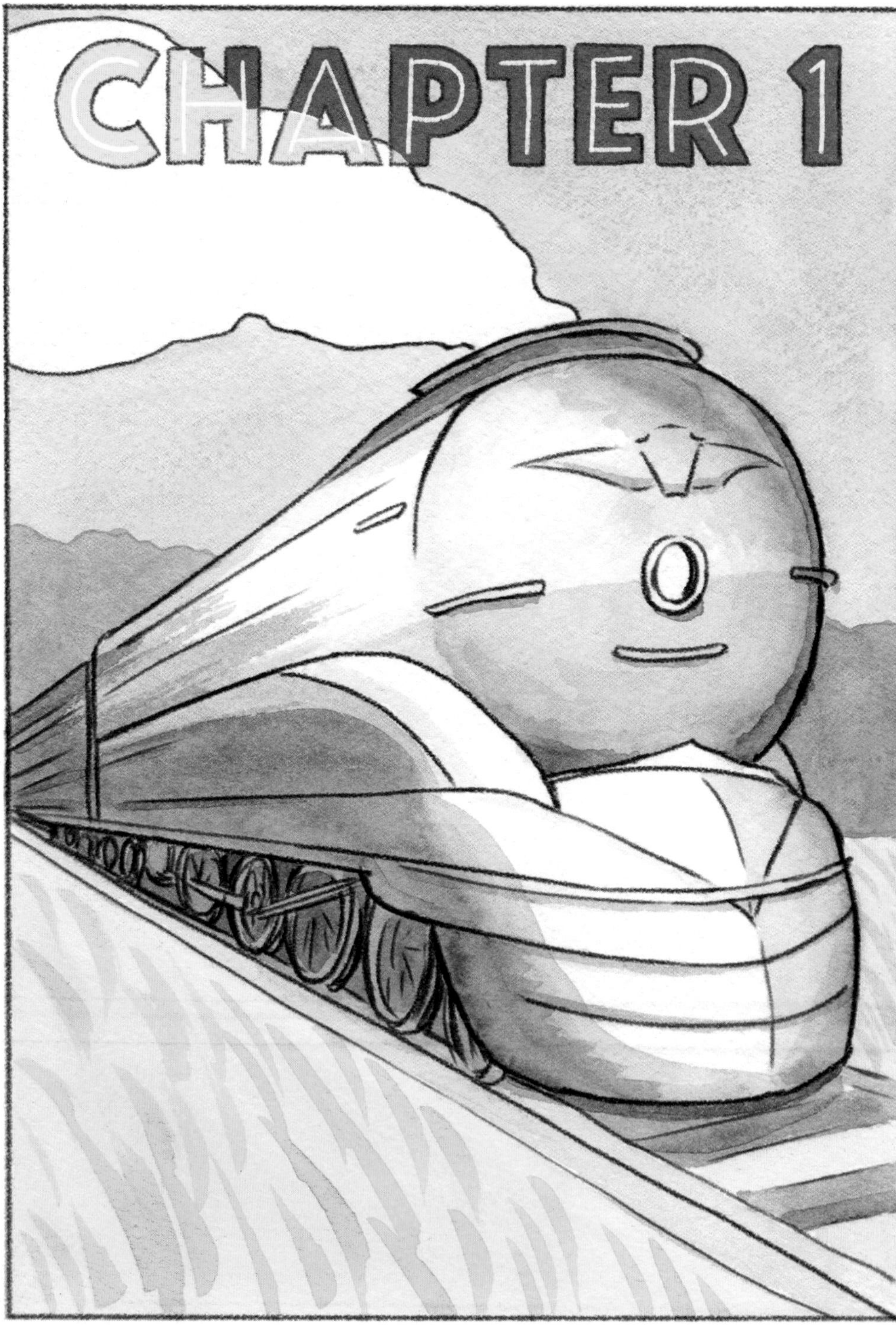
CHAPTER 1

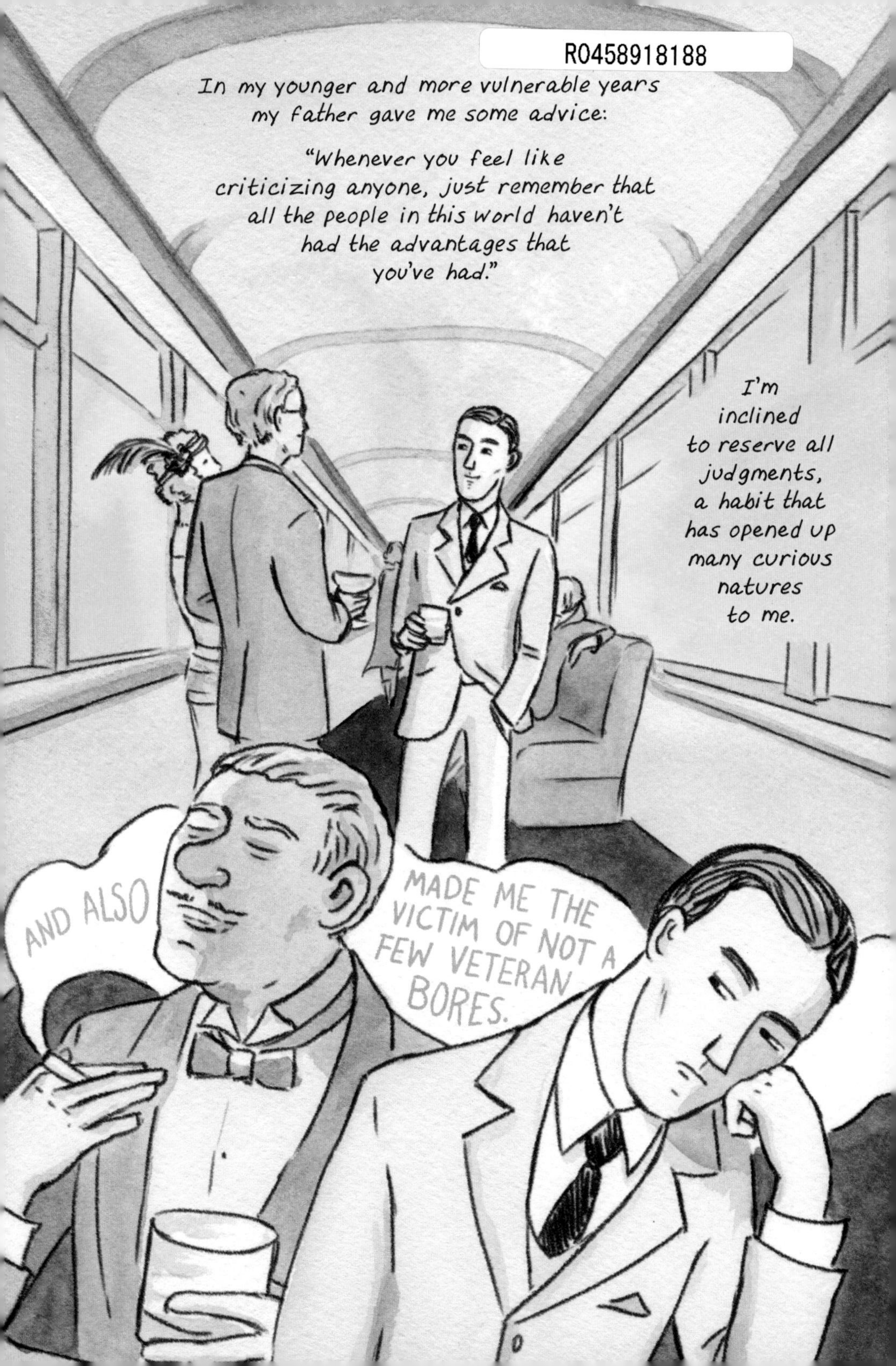
In my younger and more vulnerable years my father gave me some advice:
"Whenever you feel like criticizing anyone, just remember that all the people in this world haven't had the advantages that you've had."
I'm inclined to reserve all judgments, a habit that has opened up many curious natures to me.
AND ALSO
MADE ME THE VICTIM OF NOT A FEW VETERAN BORES.

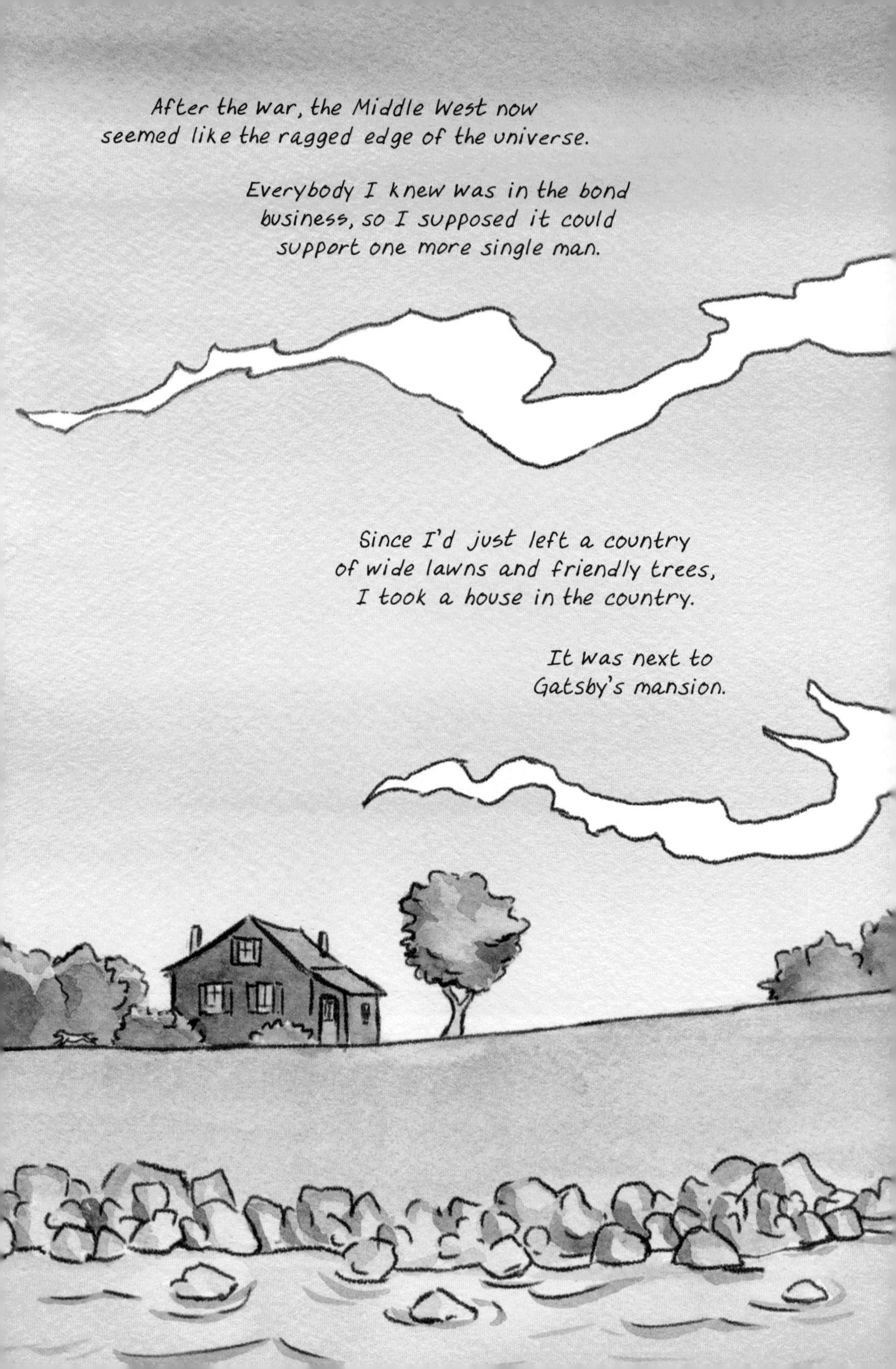
After the war, the Middle West now seemed like the ragged edge of the universe.
Everybody I knew was in the bond business, so I supposed it could support one more single man.
Since I'd just left a country of wide lawns and friendly trees, I took a house in the country.
It was next to Gatsby's mansion.

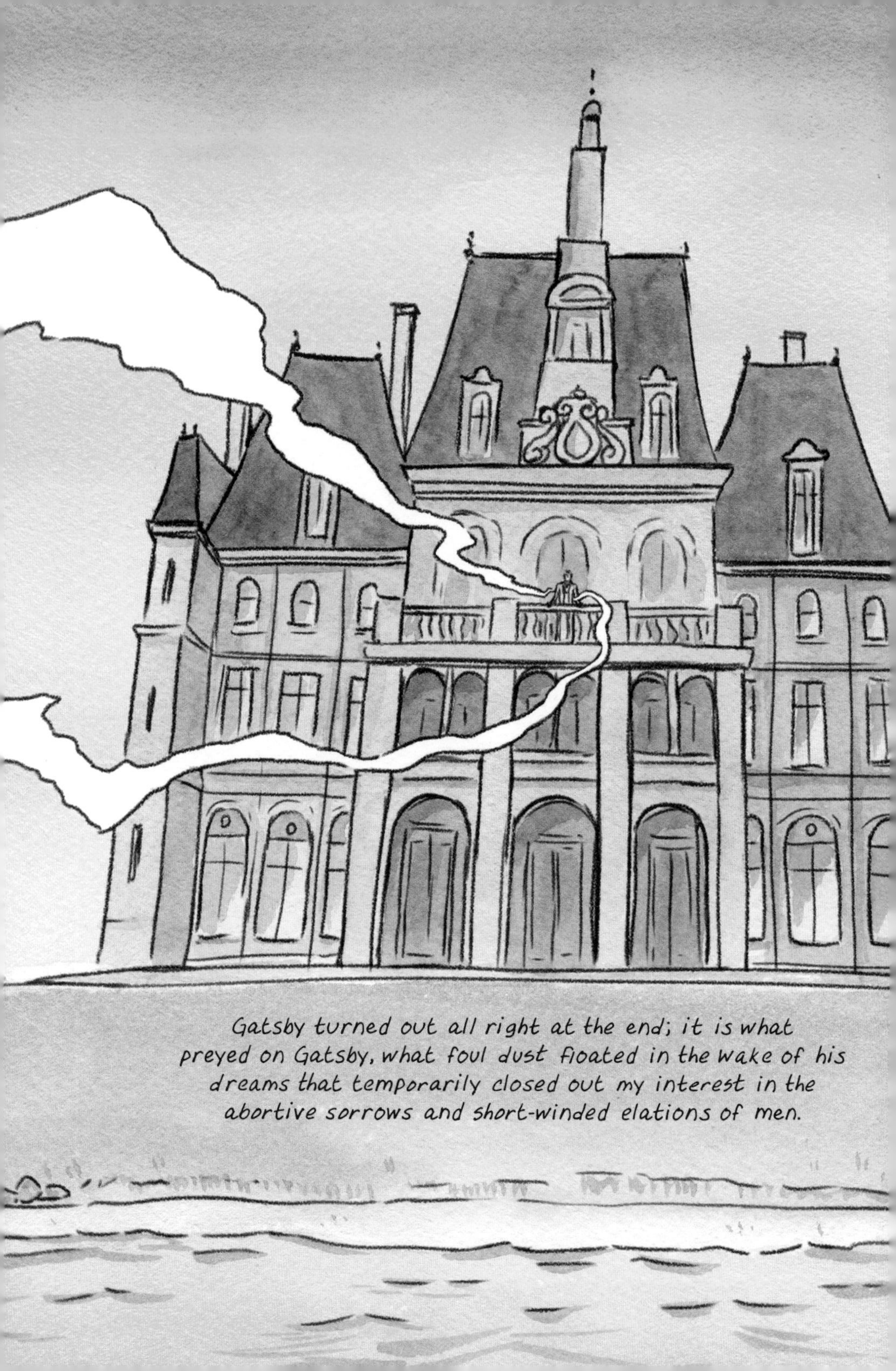
Gatsby turned out all right at the end; it is what preyed on Gatsby, what foul dust floated in the wake of his dreams that temporarily closed out my interest in the abortive sorrows and short-winded elations of men.

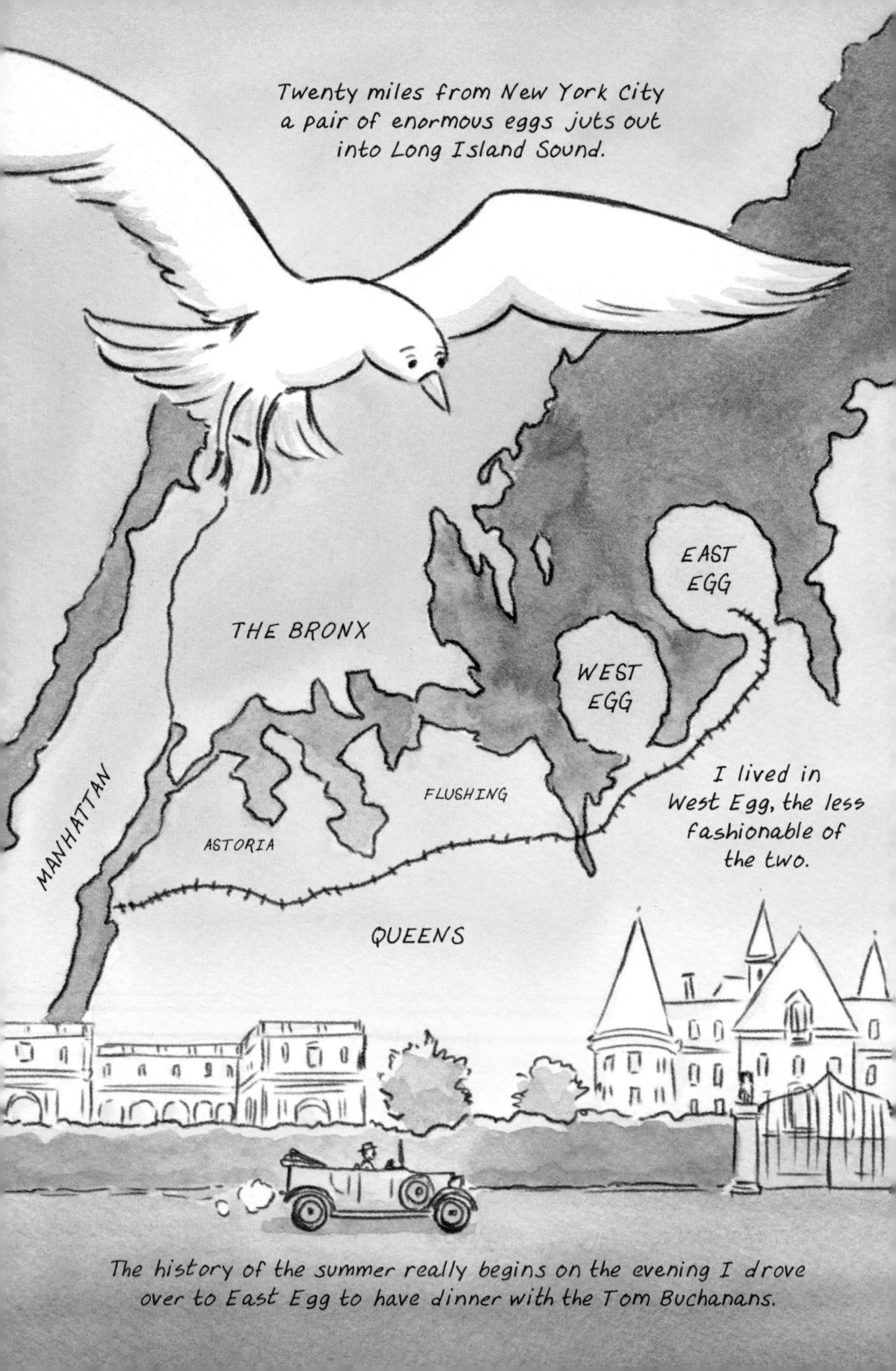
Twenty miles from New York City a pair of enormous eggs juts out into Long Island Sound.
EAST EGG
THE BRONX
WEST EGG
MANHATTAN
FLUSHING
ASTORIA
I lived in West Egg, the less fashionable of the two.
QUEENS
The history of the summer really begins on the evening I drove over to East Egg to have dinner with the Tom Buchanans.

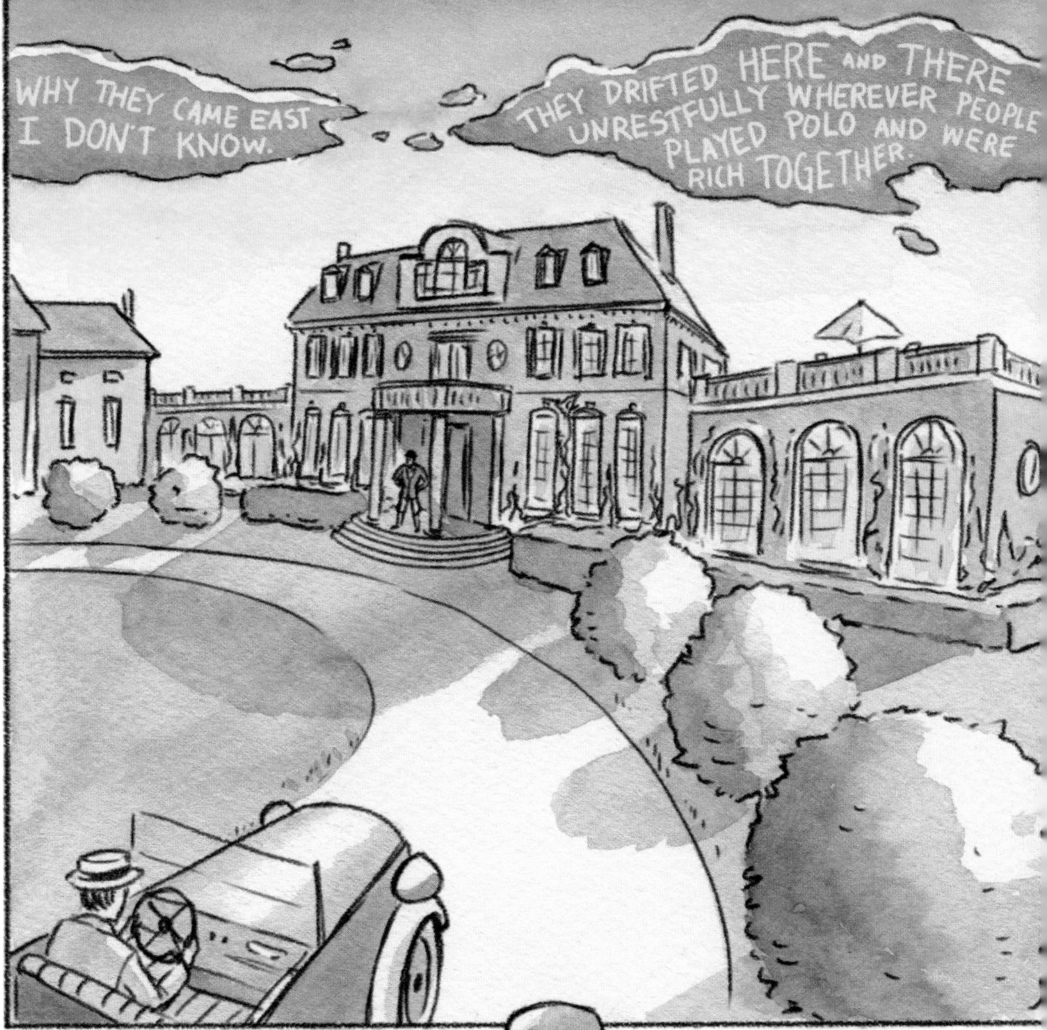
WHY THEY CAME EAST I DON'T KNOW.
THEY DRIFTED HERE AND THERE UNRESTFULLY WHEREVER PEOPLE PLAYED POLO AND WERE RICH TOGETHER.

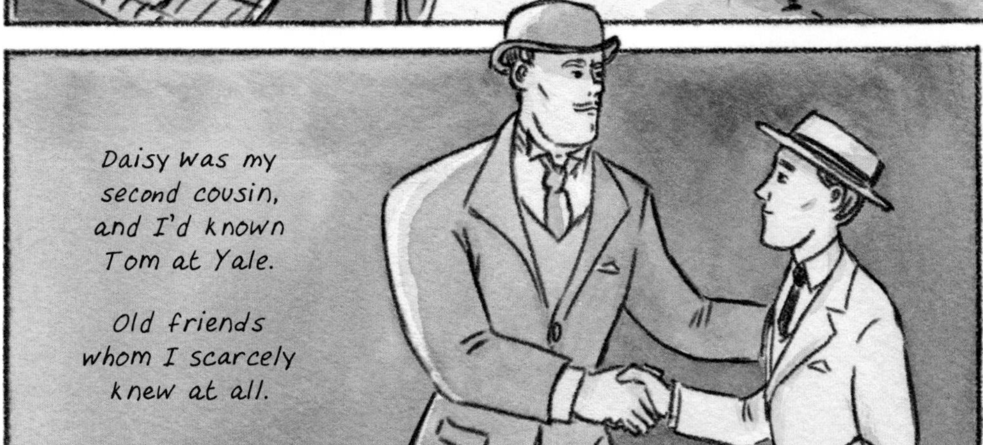
Daisy was my second cousin, and I'd known Tom at Yale.
Old friends whom I scarcely knew at all.

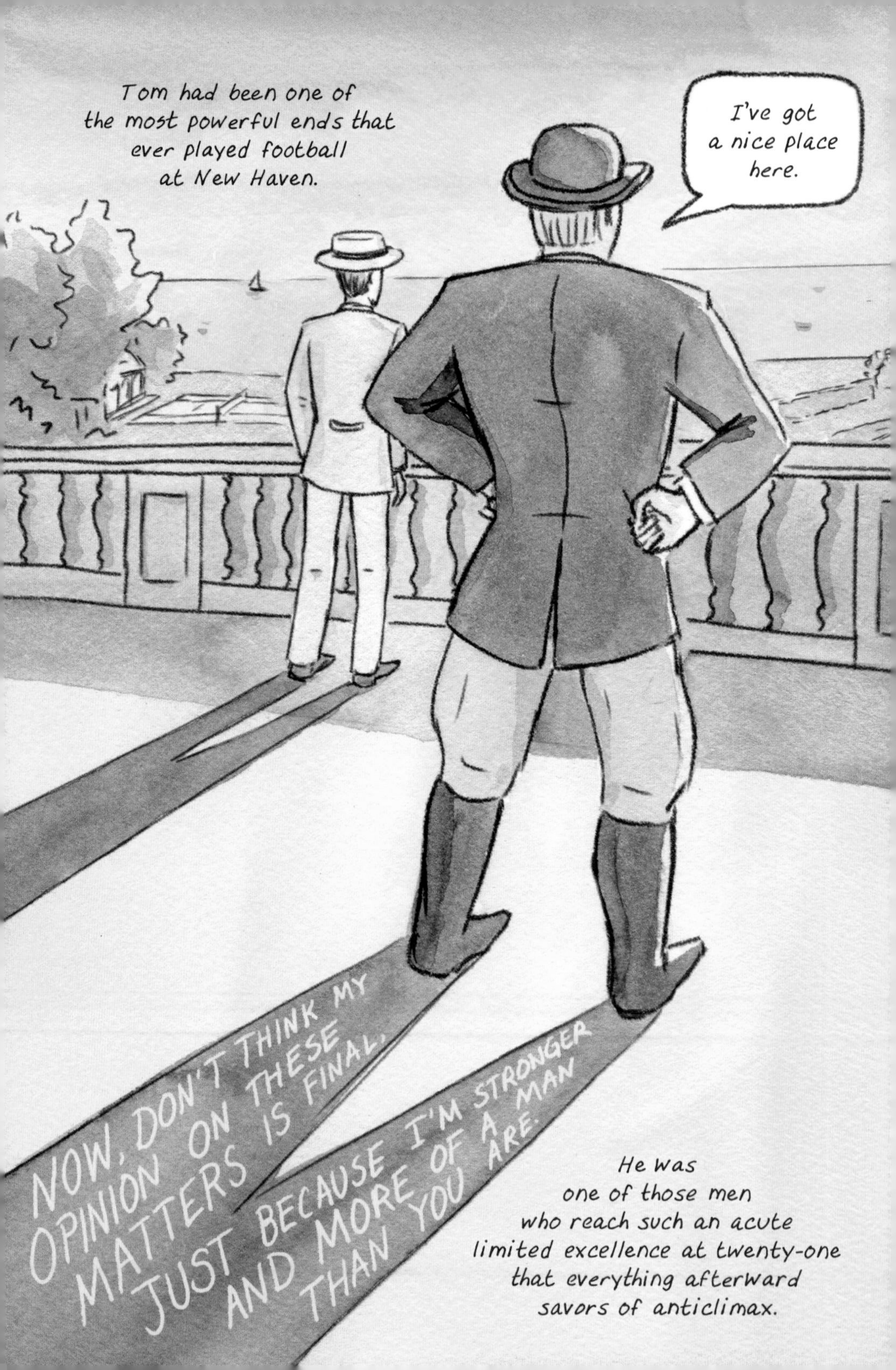

Tom had been one of the most powerful ends that ever played football at New Haven.
I've got a nice place here.
NOW, DON'T THINK MY OPINION ON THESE MATTERS IS FINAL,
JUST BECAUSE I'M STRONGER AND MORE OF A MAN THAN YOU ARE.
He was one of those men who reach such an acute limited excellence at twenty-one that everything afterward savors of anticlimax.

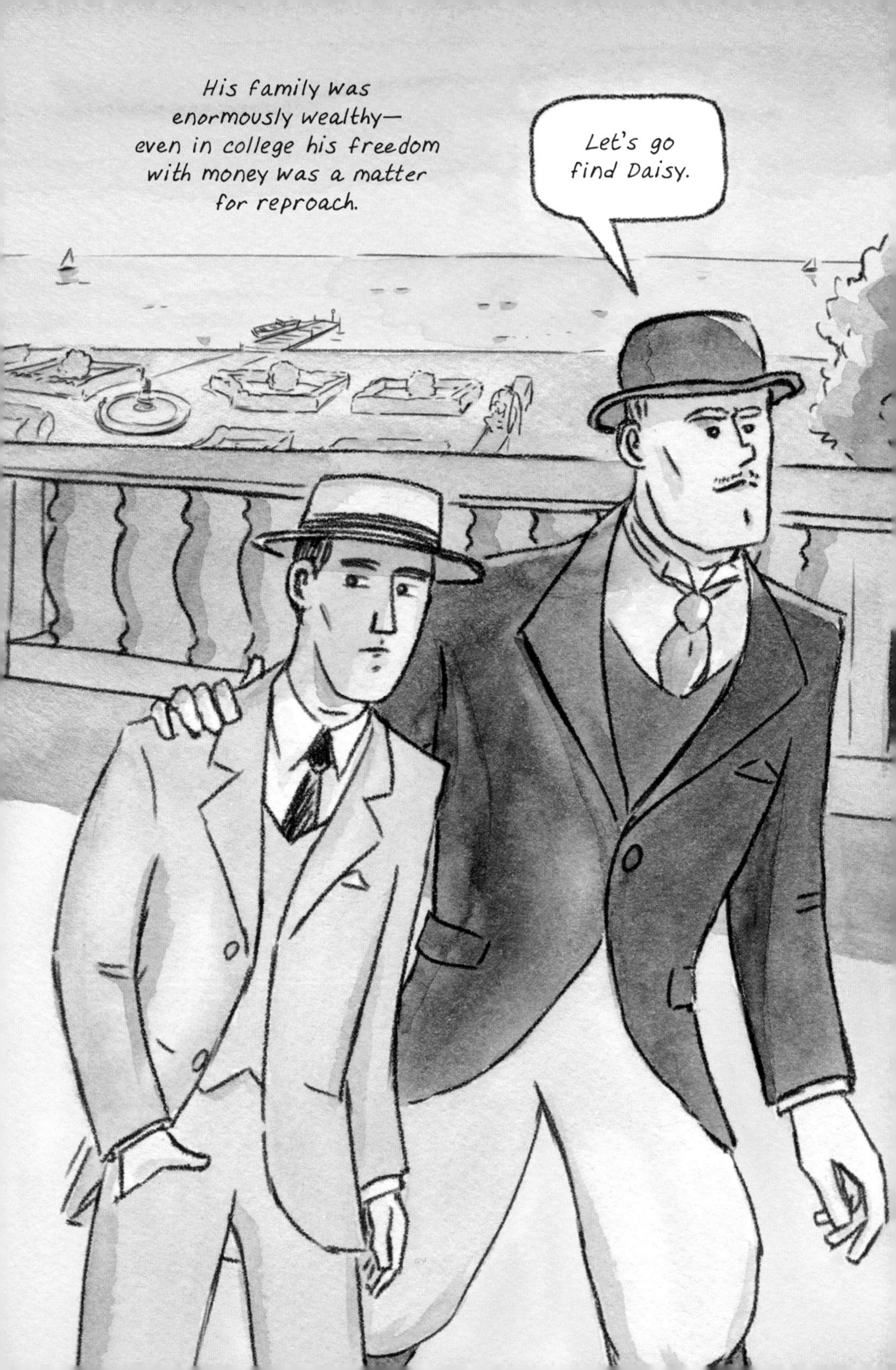
His family was enormously wealthy— even in college his freedom with money was a matter for reproach.
Let's go find Daisy.

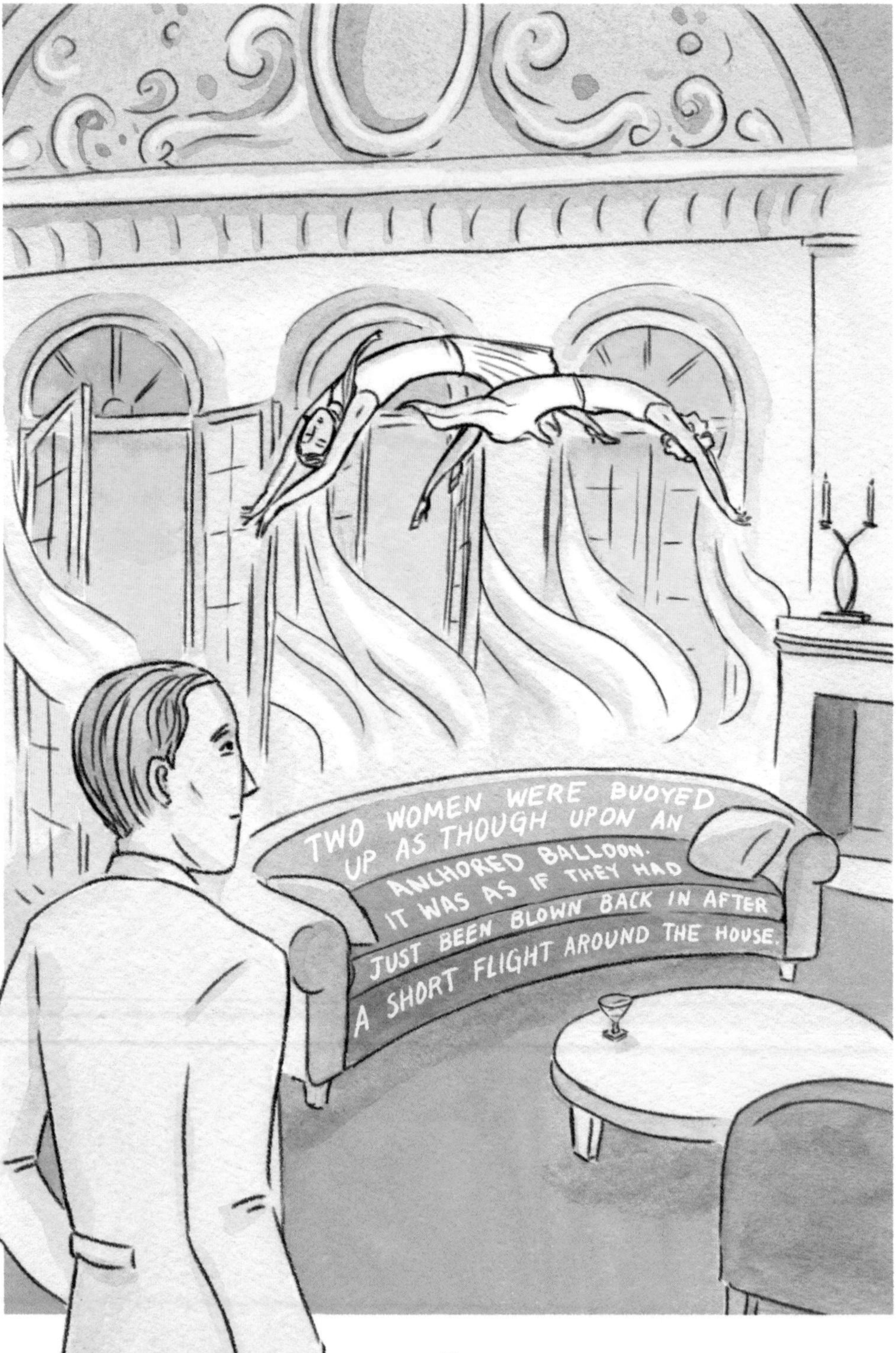
TWO WOMEN WERE BUOYED UP AS THOUGH UPON AN ANCHORED BALLOON. IT WAS AS IF THEY HAD JUST BEEN BLOWN BACK IN AFTER A SHORT FLIGHT AROUND THE HOUSE.

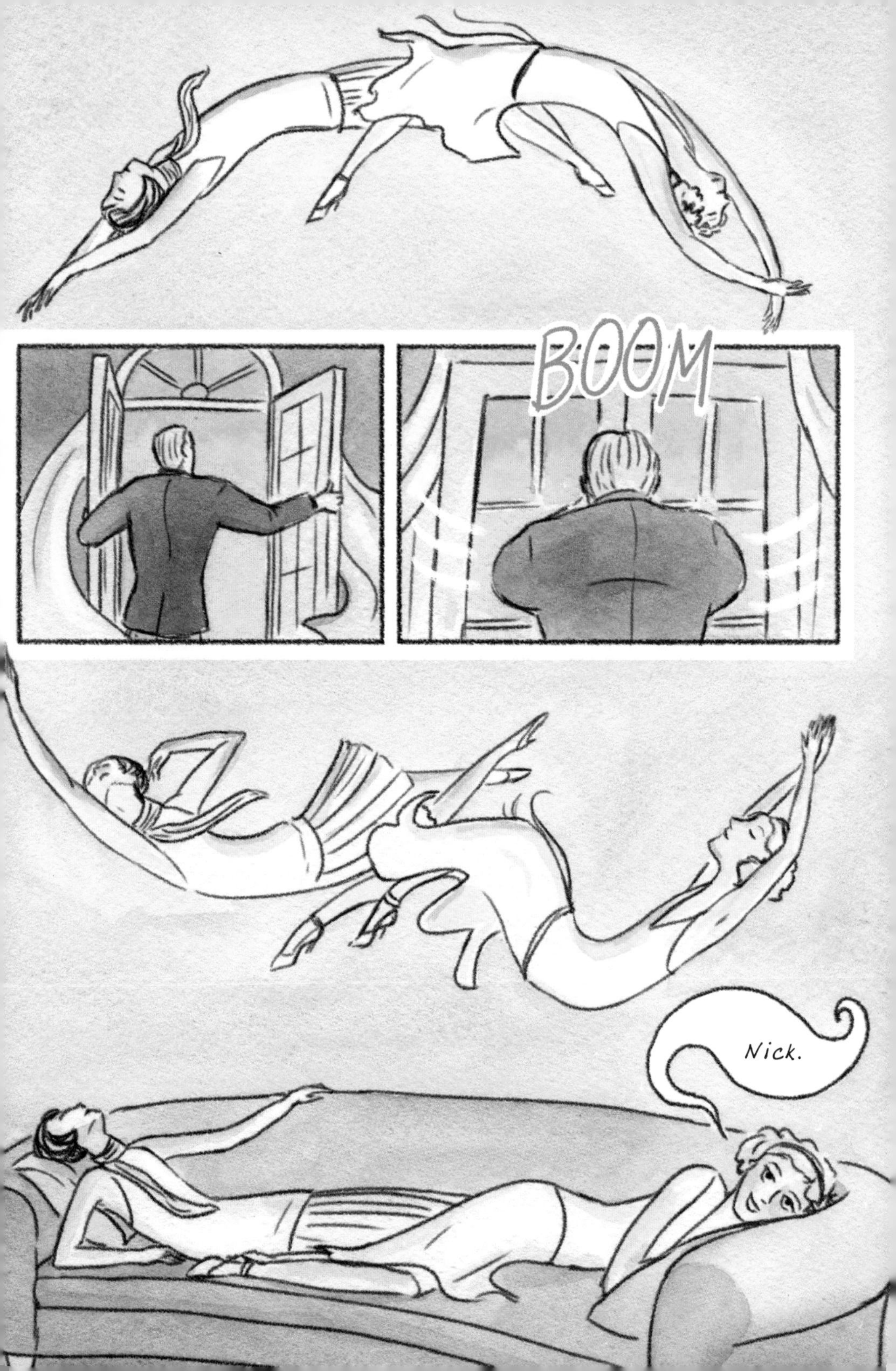
BOOM
Nick.

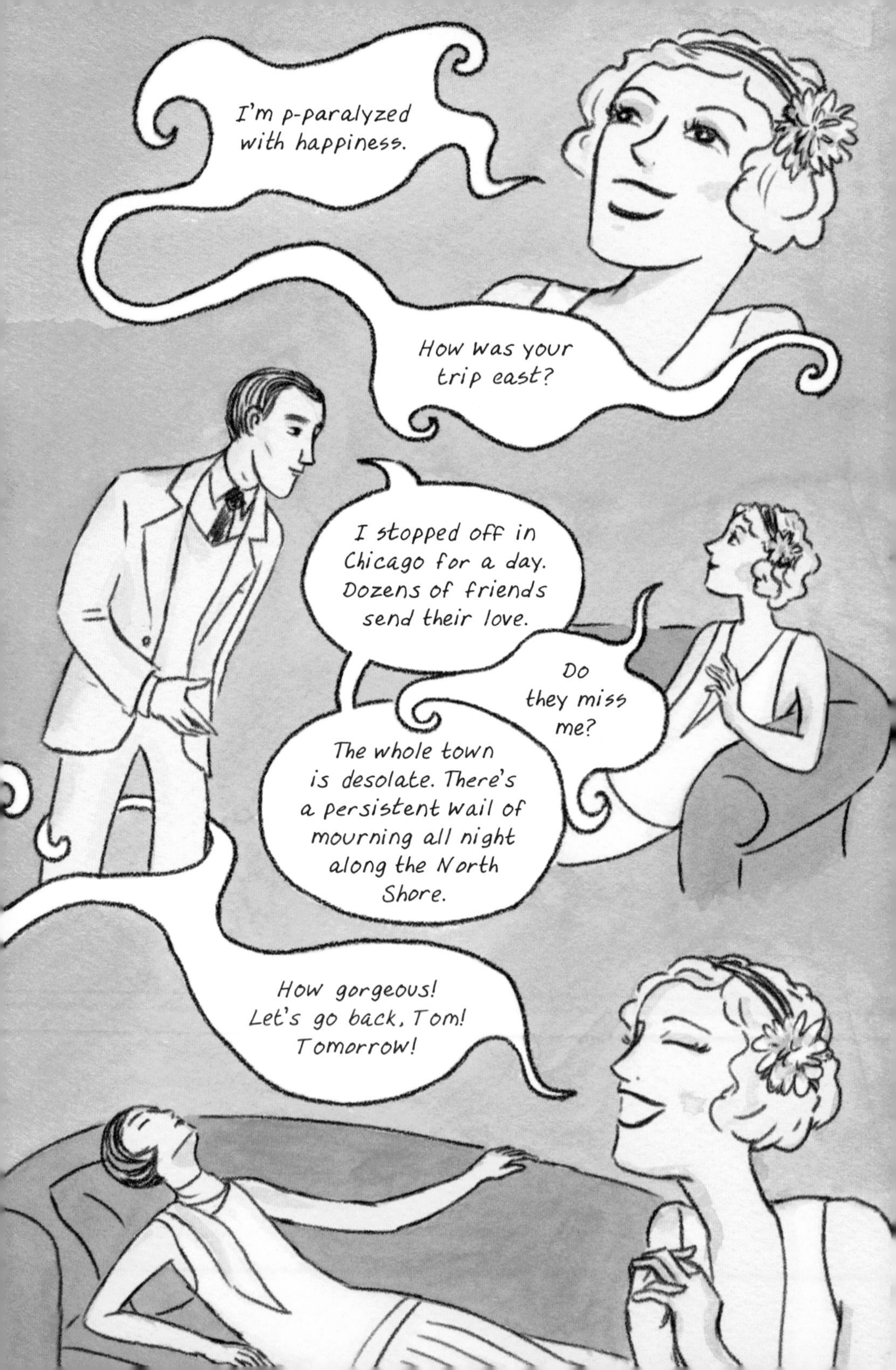
I'm p-paralyzed with happiness.
How was your trip east?
I stopped off in Chicago for a day. Dozens of friends send their love.
Do they miss me?
The whole town is desolate. There's a persistent wail of mourning all night along the North Shore.
How gorgeous! Let's go back, Tom! Tomorrow!

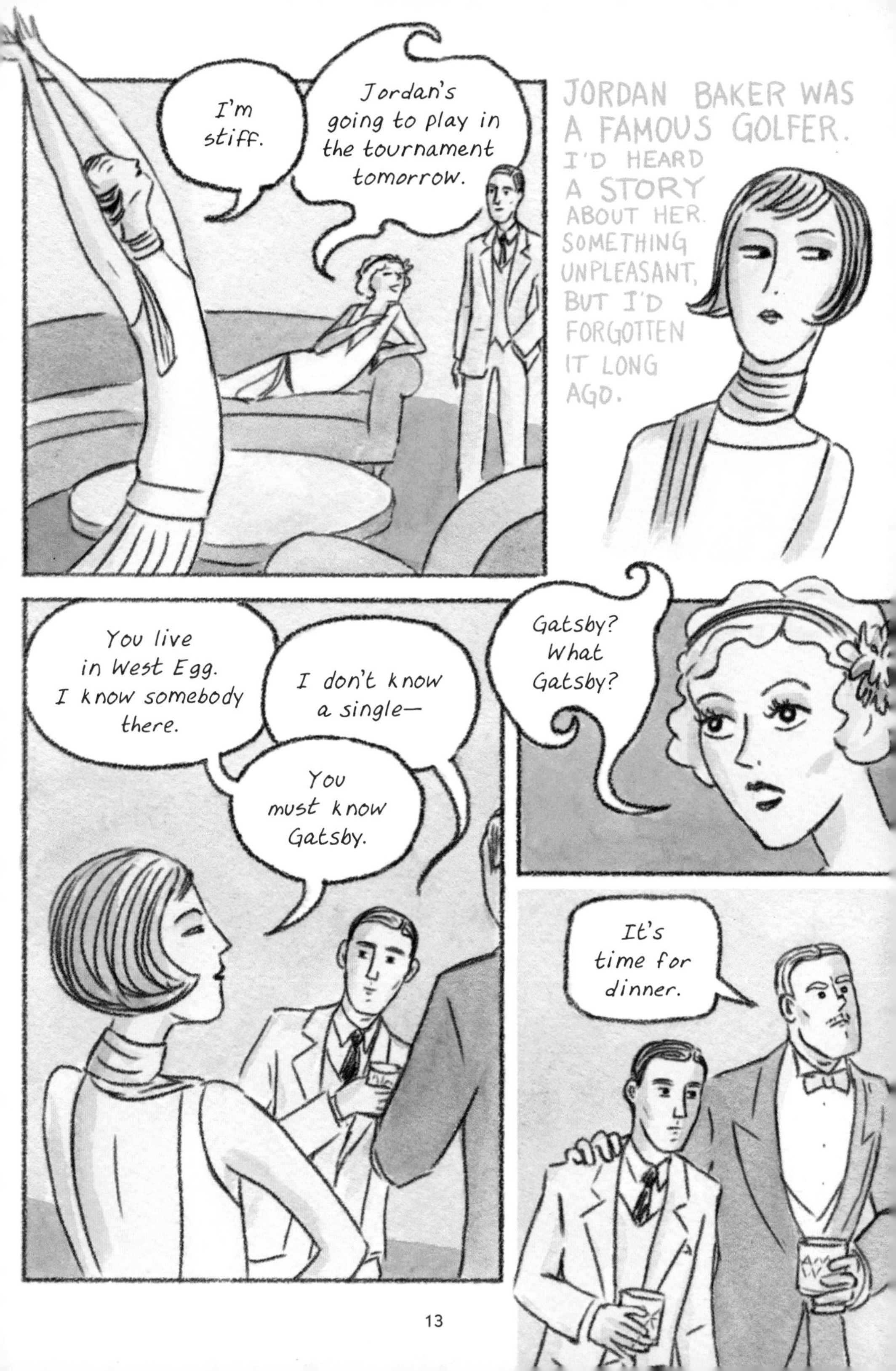
I'm stiff.
Jordan's going to play in the tournament tomorrow.
JORDAN BAKER WAS A FAMOUS GOLFER. I'D HEARD A STORY ABOUT HER. SOMETHING UNPLEASANT, BUT I'D FORGOTTEN IT LONG AGO.
You live in West Egg. I know somebody there.
I don't know a single—
You must know Gatsby.
Gatsby? What Gatsby?
It's time for dinner.

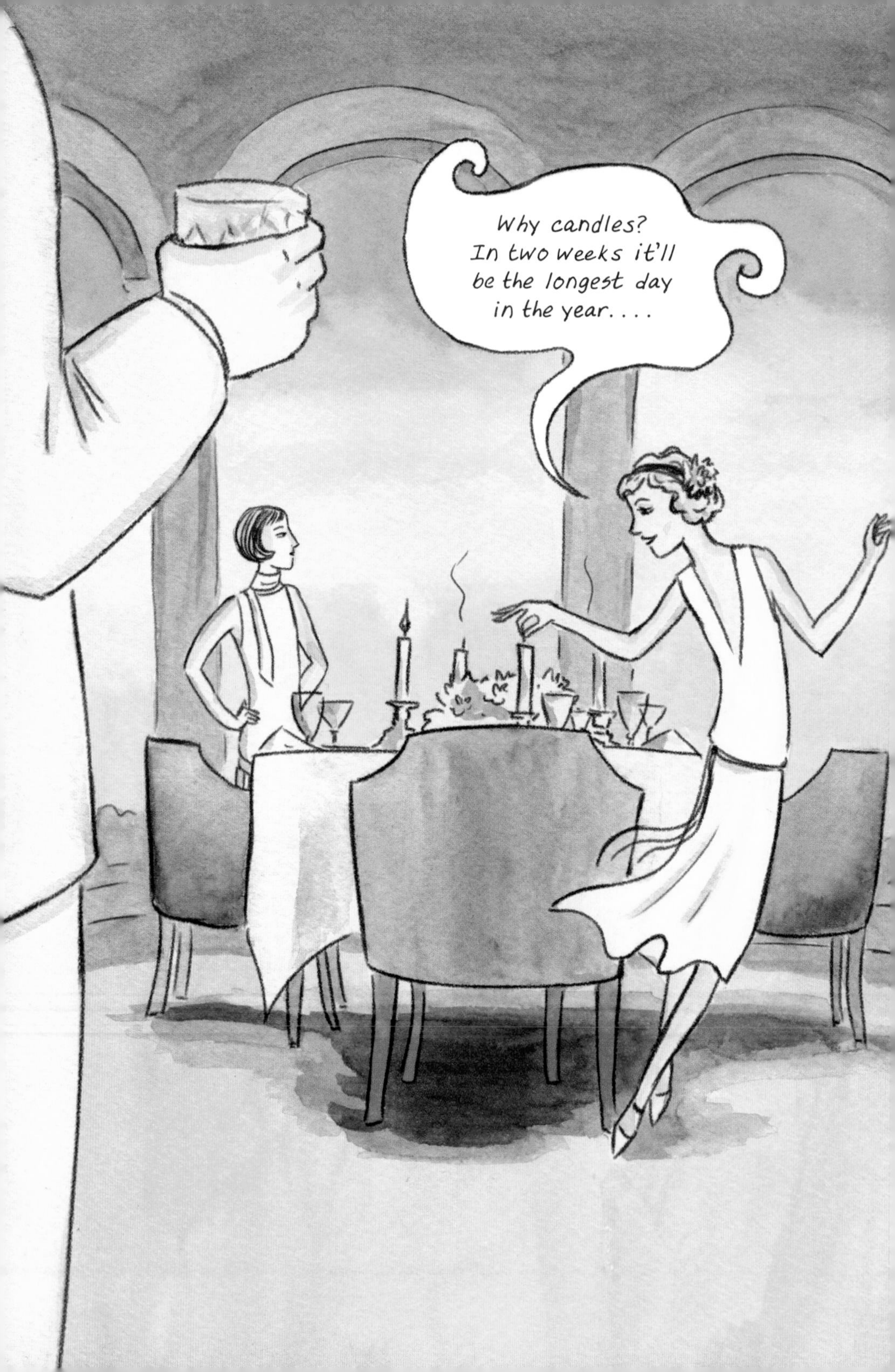
Why candles? In two weeks it'll be the longest day in the year. . . .

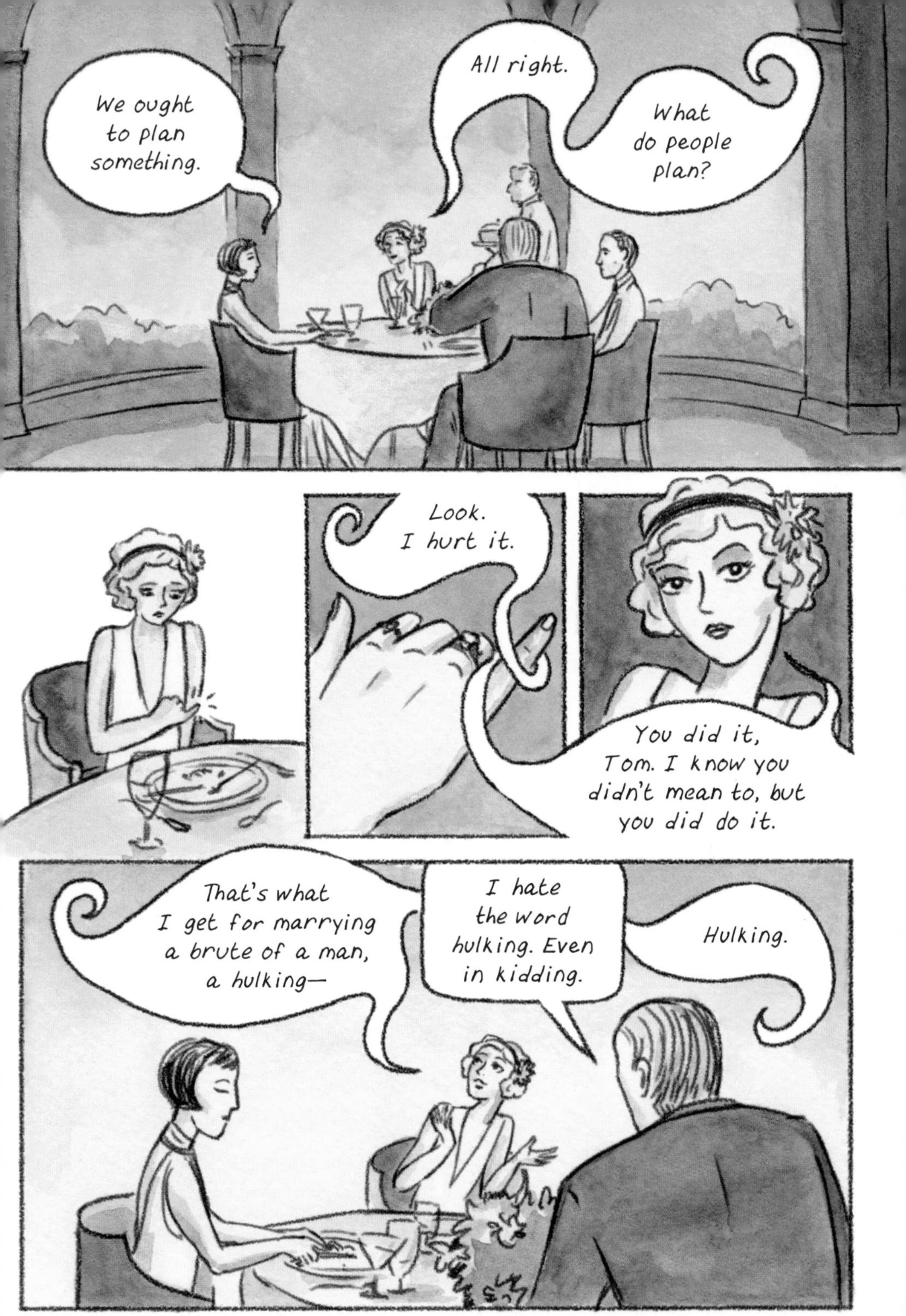
We ought to plan something.
All right.
What do people plan?
Look. I hurt it.
You did it, Tom. I know you didn't mean to, but you did do it.
That's what I get for marrying a brute of a man, a hulking—
I hate the word hulking. Even in kidding.
Hulking.

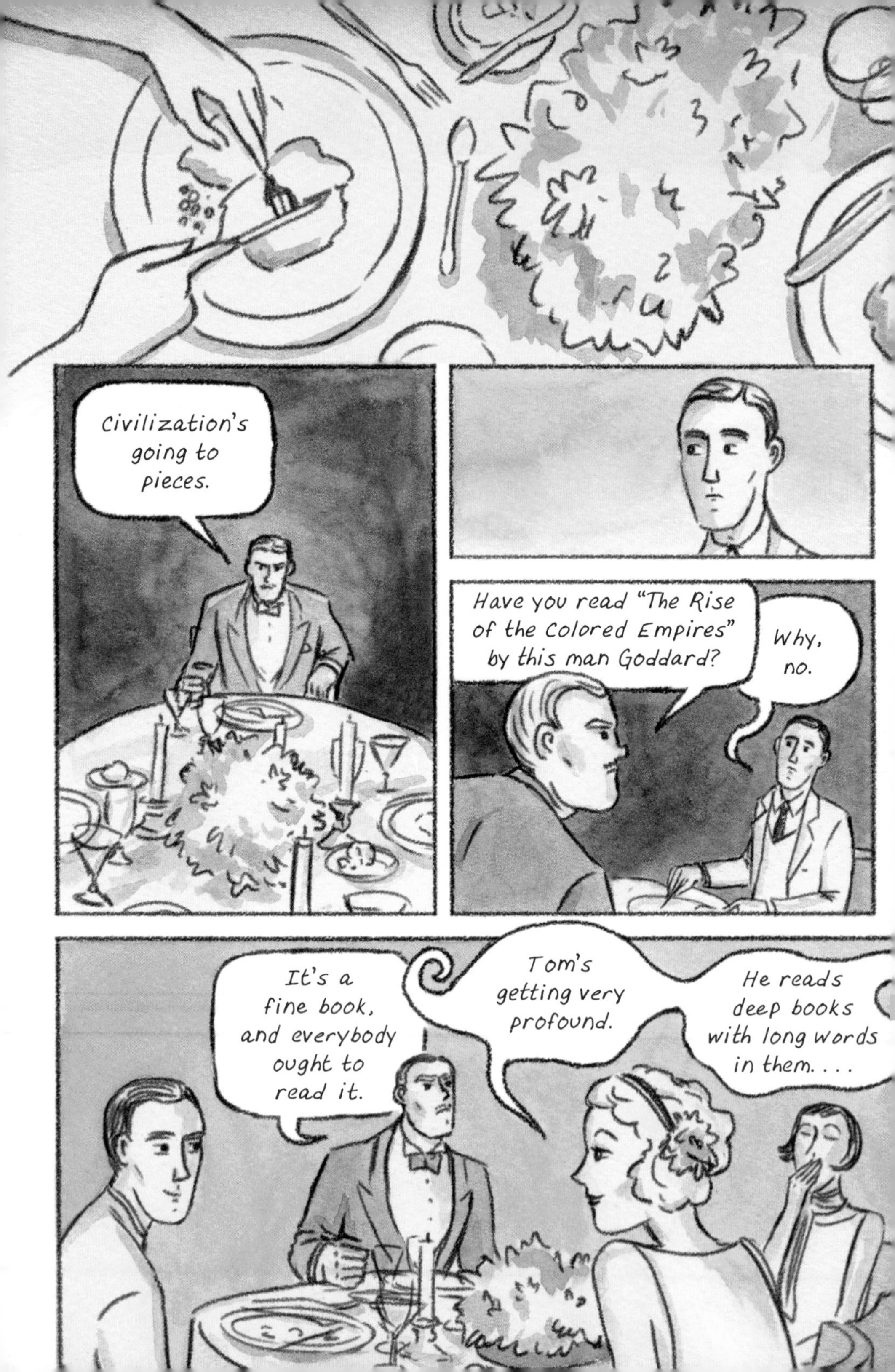
Civilization's going to pieces.
Have you read "The Rise of the Colored Empires" by this man Goddard?
Why, no.
It's a fine book, and everybody ought to read it.
Tom's getting very profound.
He reads deep books with long words in them. . . .

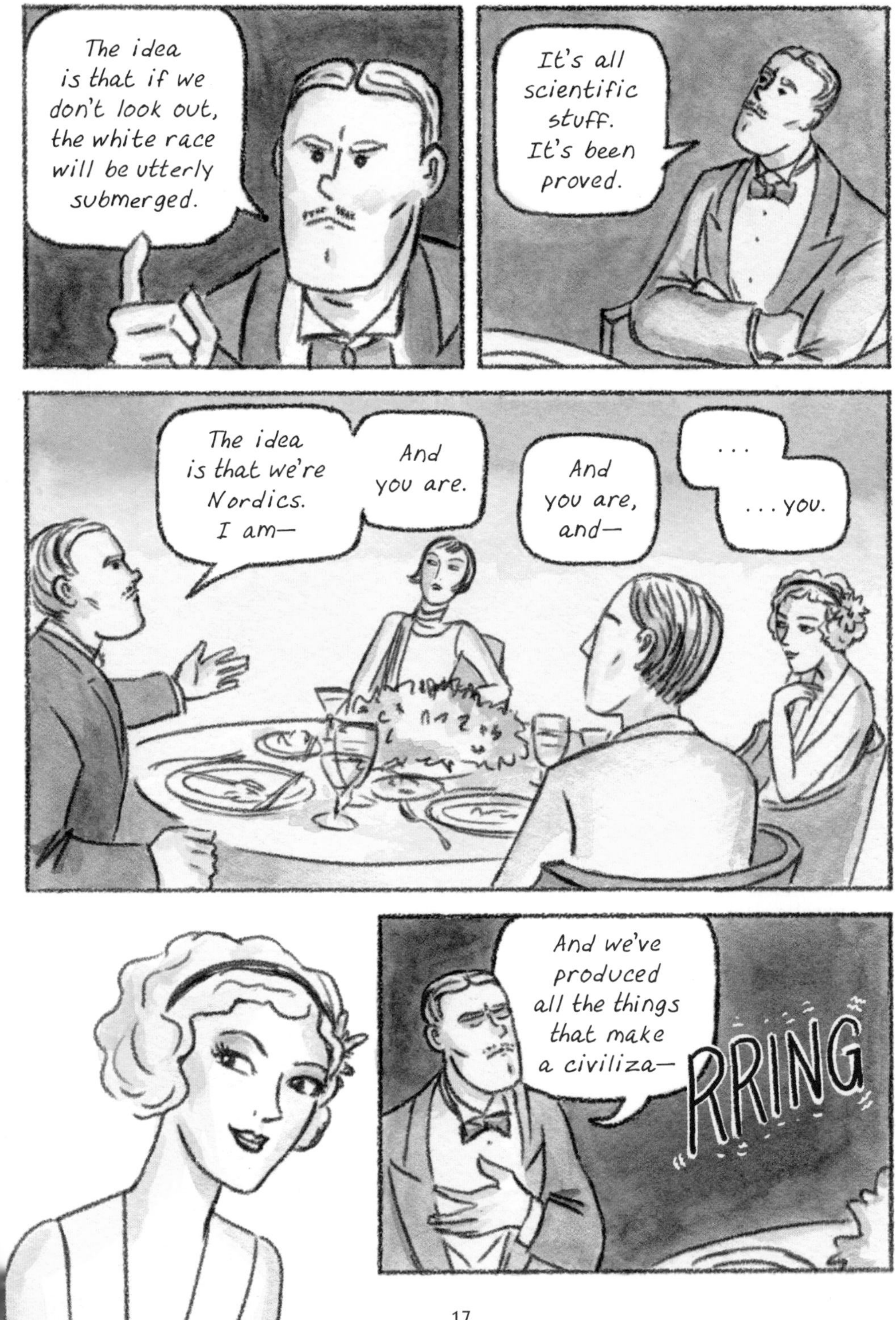
The idea is that if we don't look out, the white race will be utterly submerged.
It's all scientific stuff. It's been proved.
The idea is that we're Nordics. I am—
And you are.
And you are, and—
. . .
. . . you.
And we've produced all the things that make a civiliza—
RRING

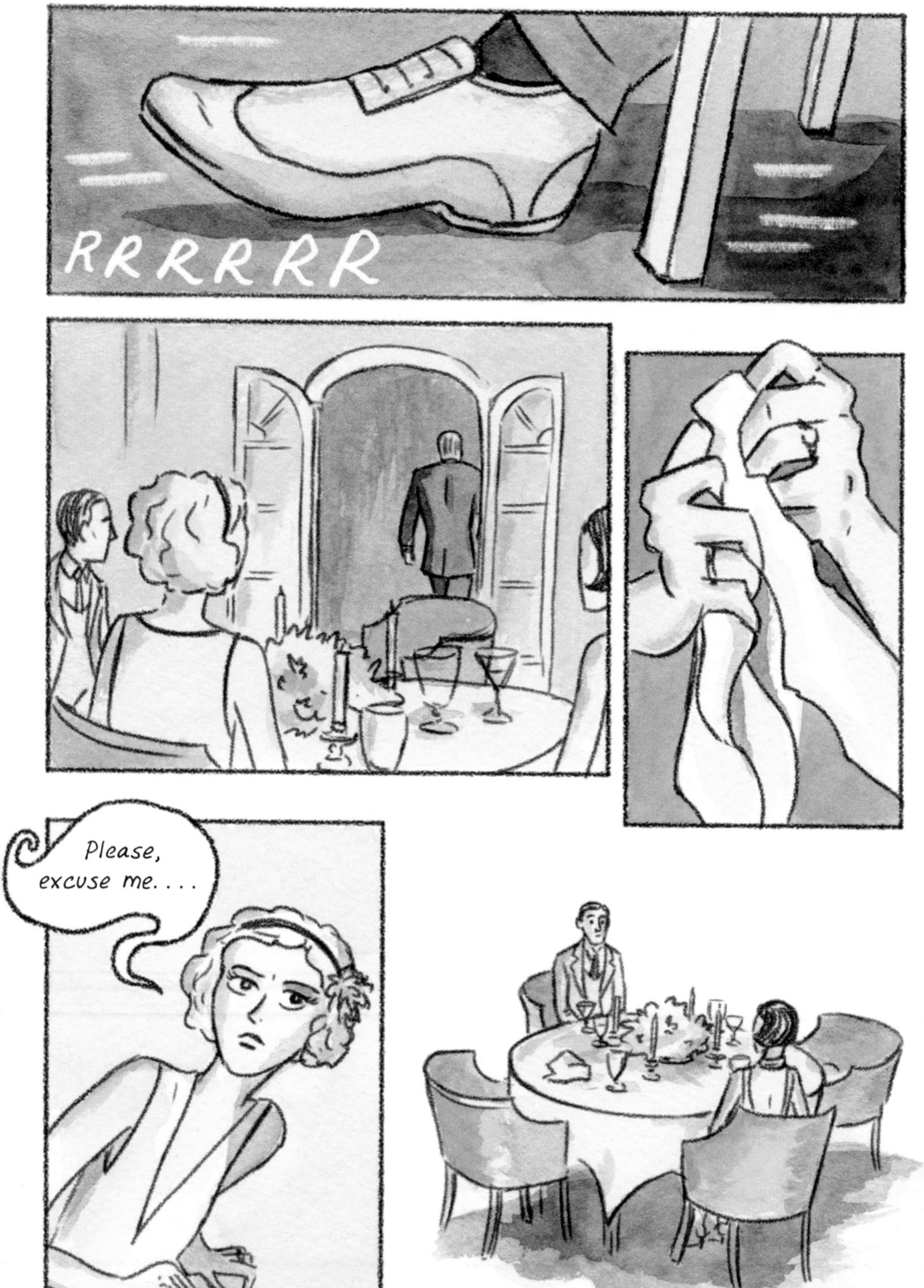
RRRRRR
Please, excuse me. . . .

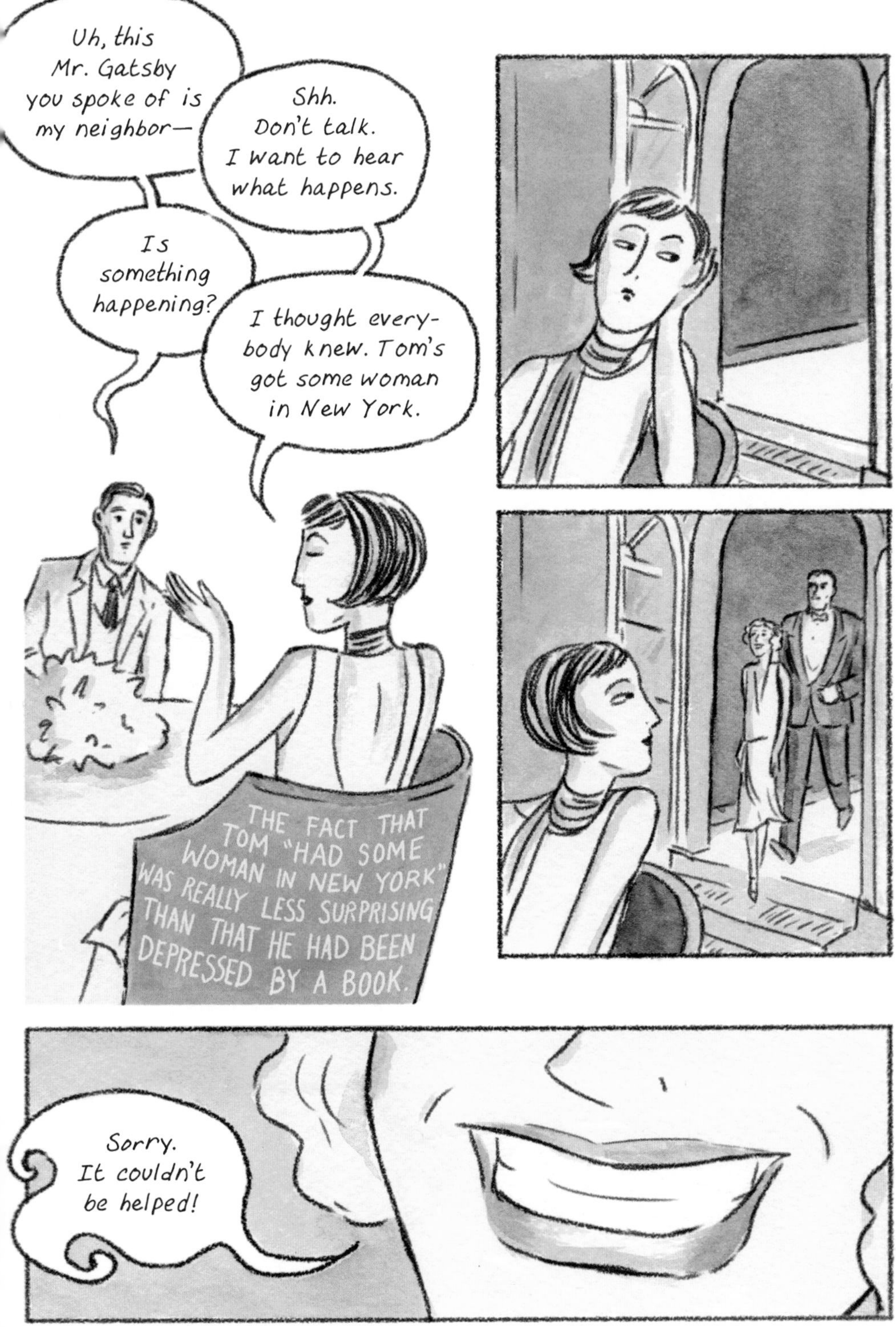
Uh, this Mr. Gatsby you spoke of is my neighbor—
Shh. Don't talk. I want to hear what happens.
Is something happening?
I thought every-body knew. Tom's got some woman in New York.
THE FACT THAT TOM "HAD SOME WOMAN IN NEW YORK" WAS REALLY LESS SURPRISING THAN THAT HE HAD BEEN DEPRESSED BY A BOOK.
Sorry. It couldn't be helped!

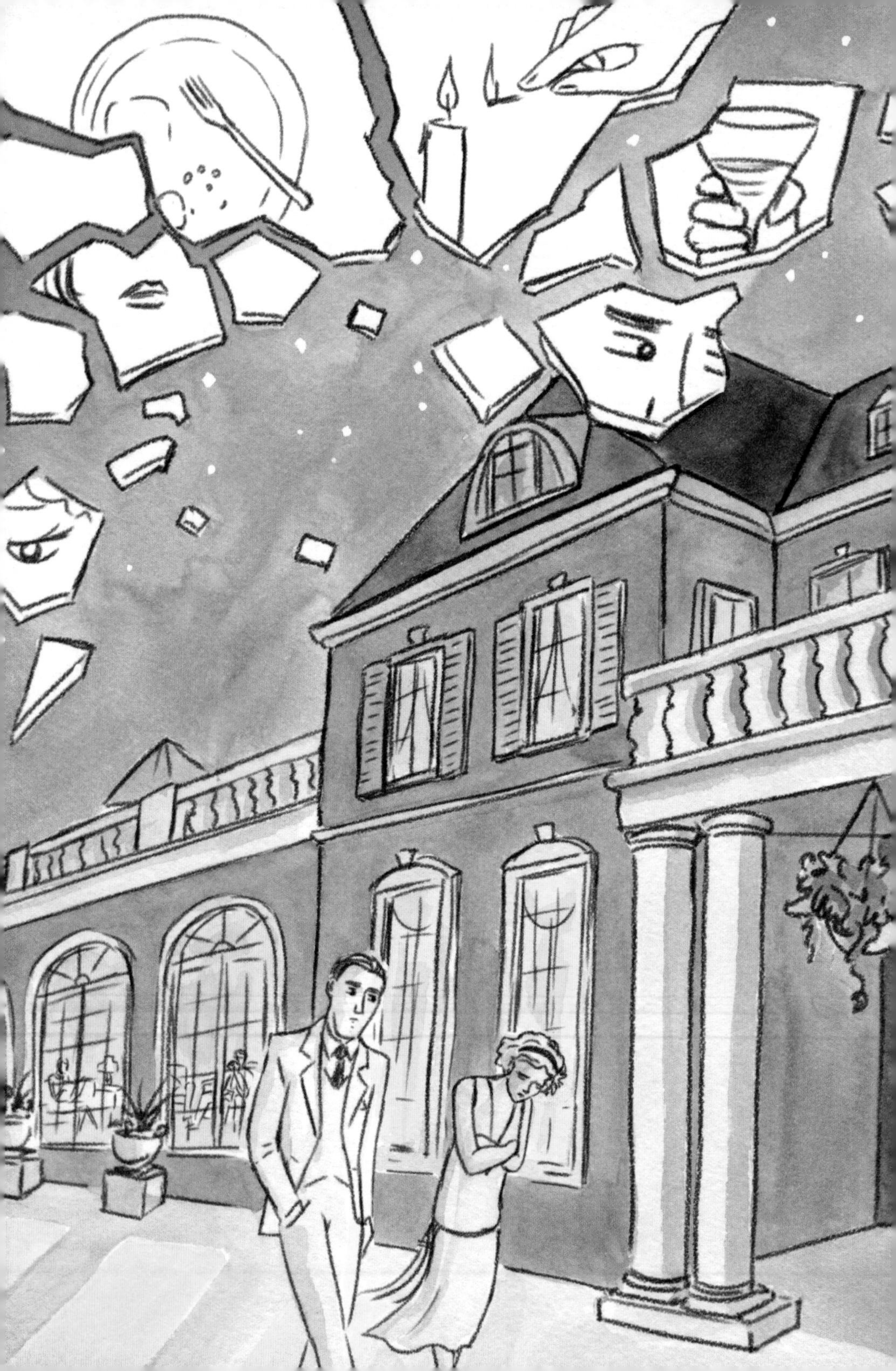

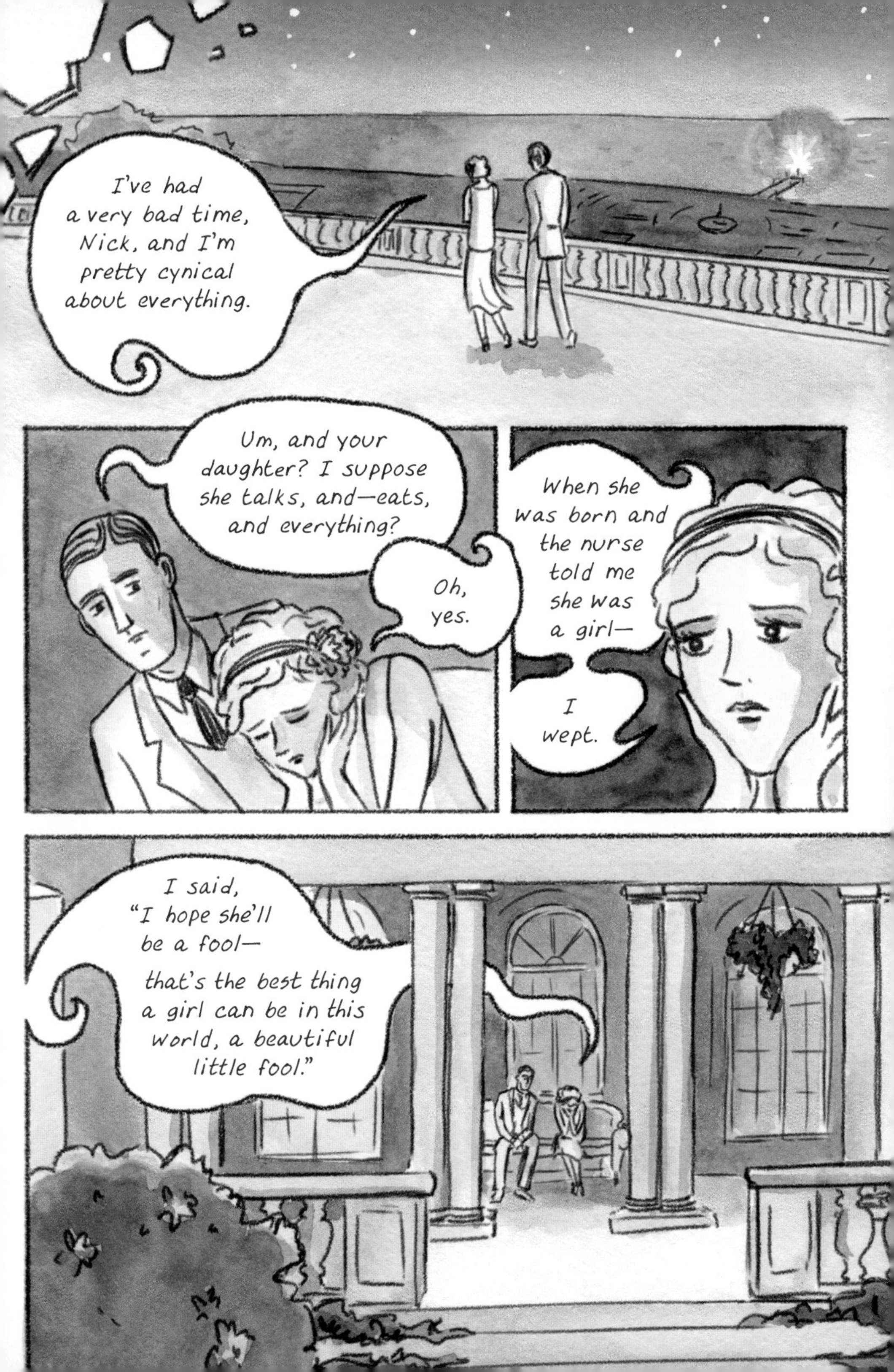
I've had a very bad time, Nick, and I'm pretty cynical about everything.
Um, and your daughter? I suppose she talks, and—eats, and everything?
Oh, yes.
When she was born and the nurse told me she was a girl—
I wept.
I said, "I hope she'll be a fool—
that's the best thing a girl can be in this world, a beautiful little fool."

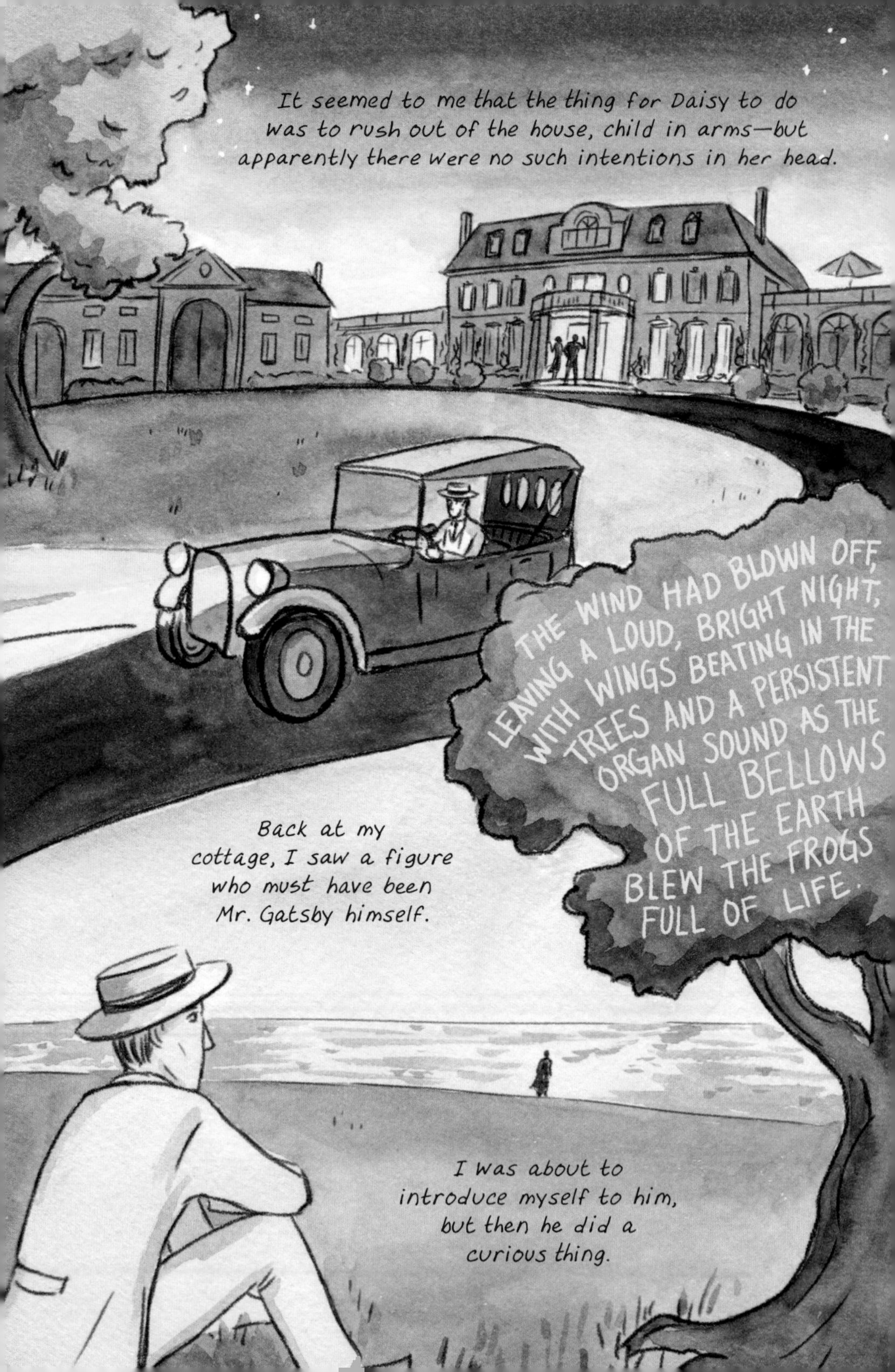
It seemed to me that the thing for Daisy to do was to rush out of the house, child in arms—but apparently there were no such intentions in her head.
THE WIND HAD BLOWN OFF, LEAVING A LOUD, BRIGHT NIGHT, WITH WINGS BEATING IN THE TREES AND A PERSISTENT ORGAN SOUND AS THE FULL BELLOWS OF THE EARTH BLEW THE FROGS FULL OF LIFE.
Back at my cottage, I saw a figure who must have been Mr. Gatsby himself.
I was about to introduce myself to him, but then he did a curious thing.

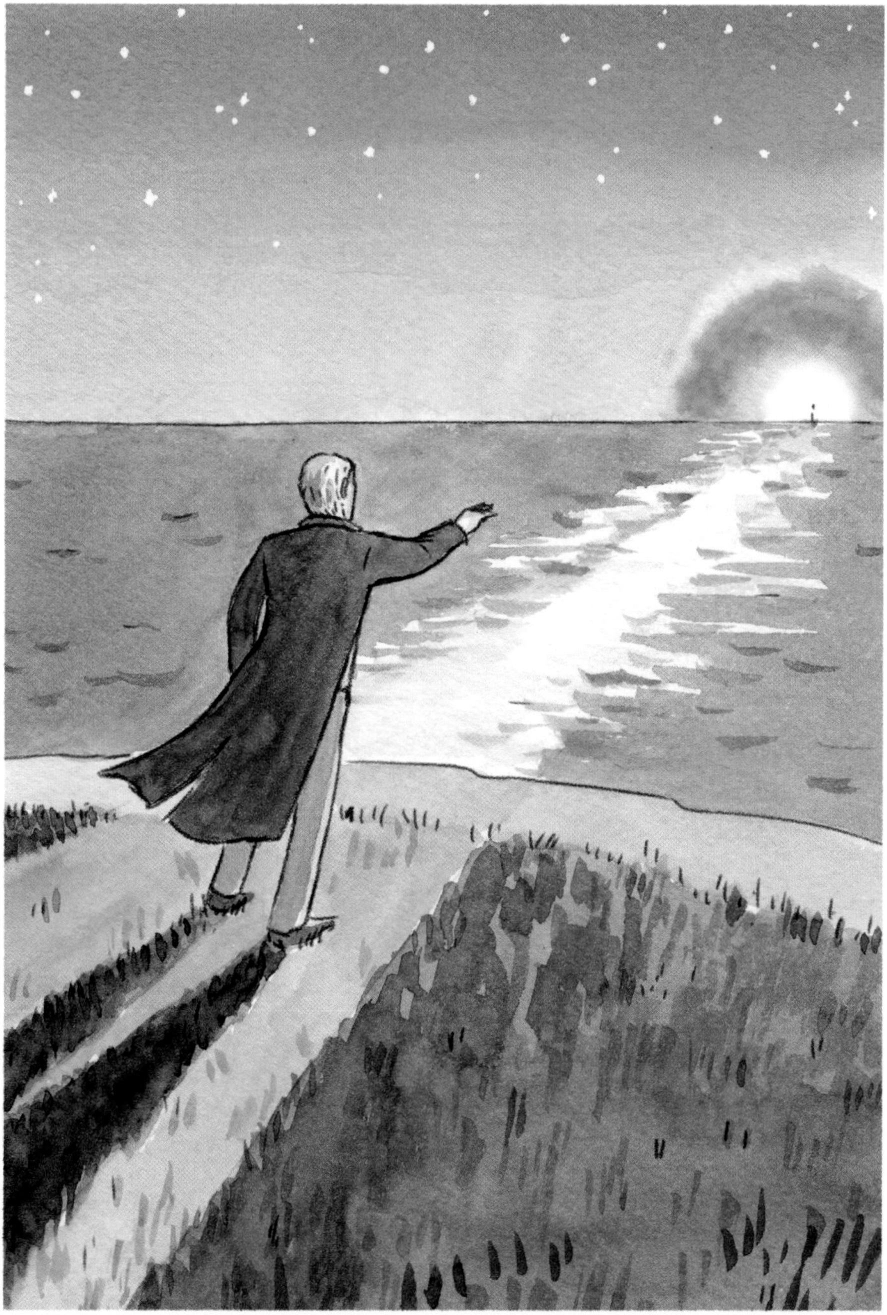

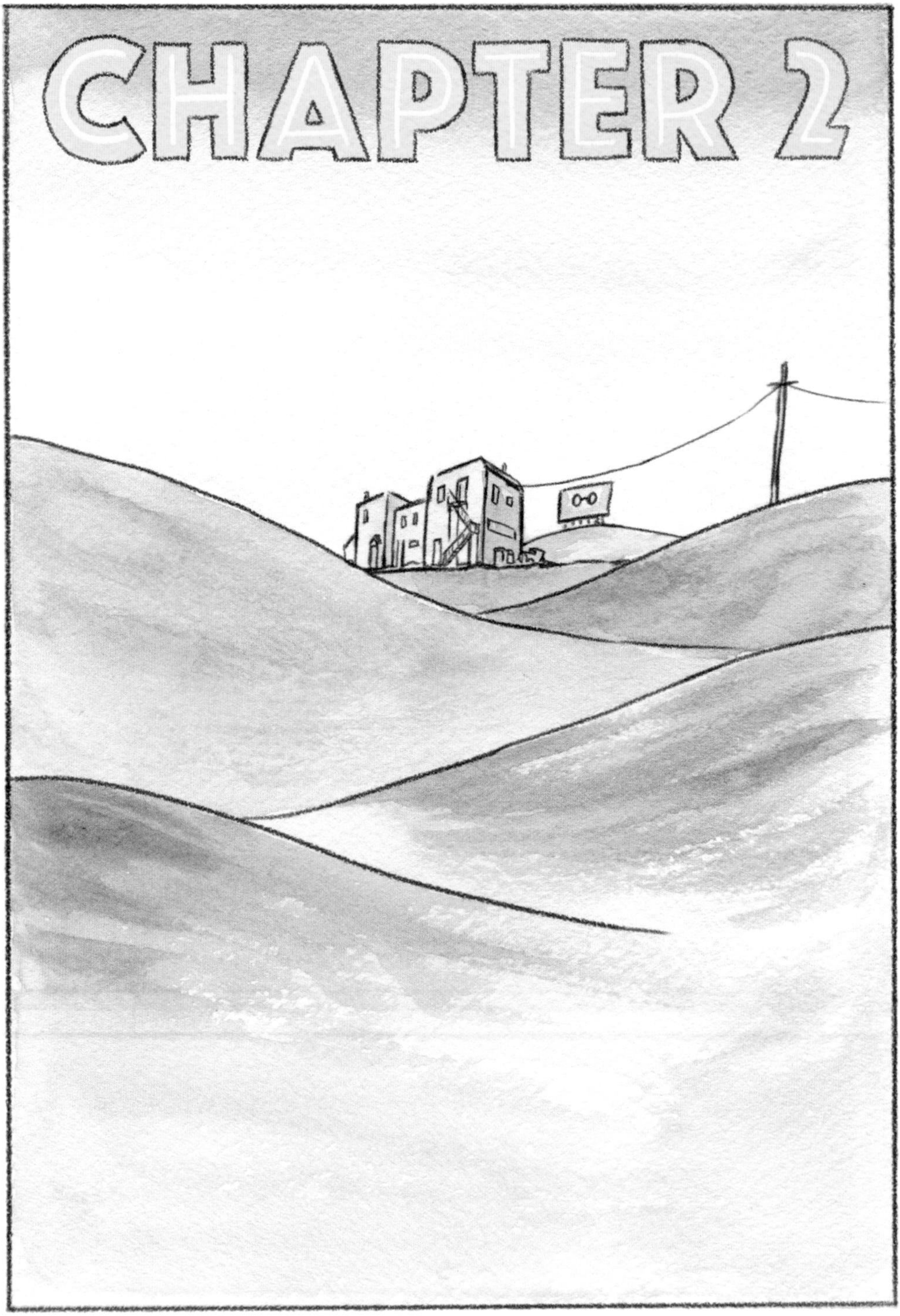
CHAPTER 2

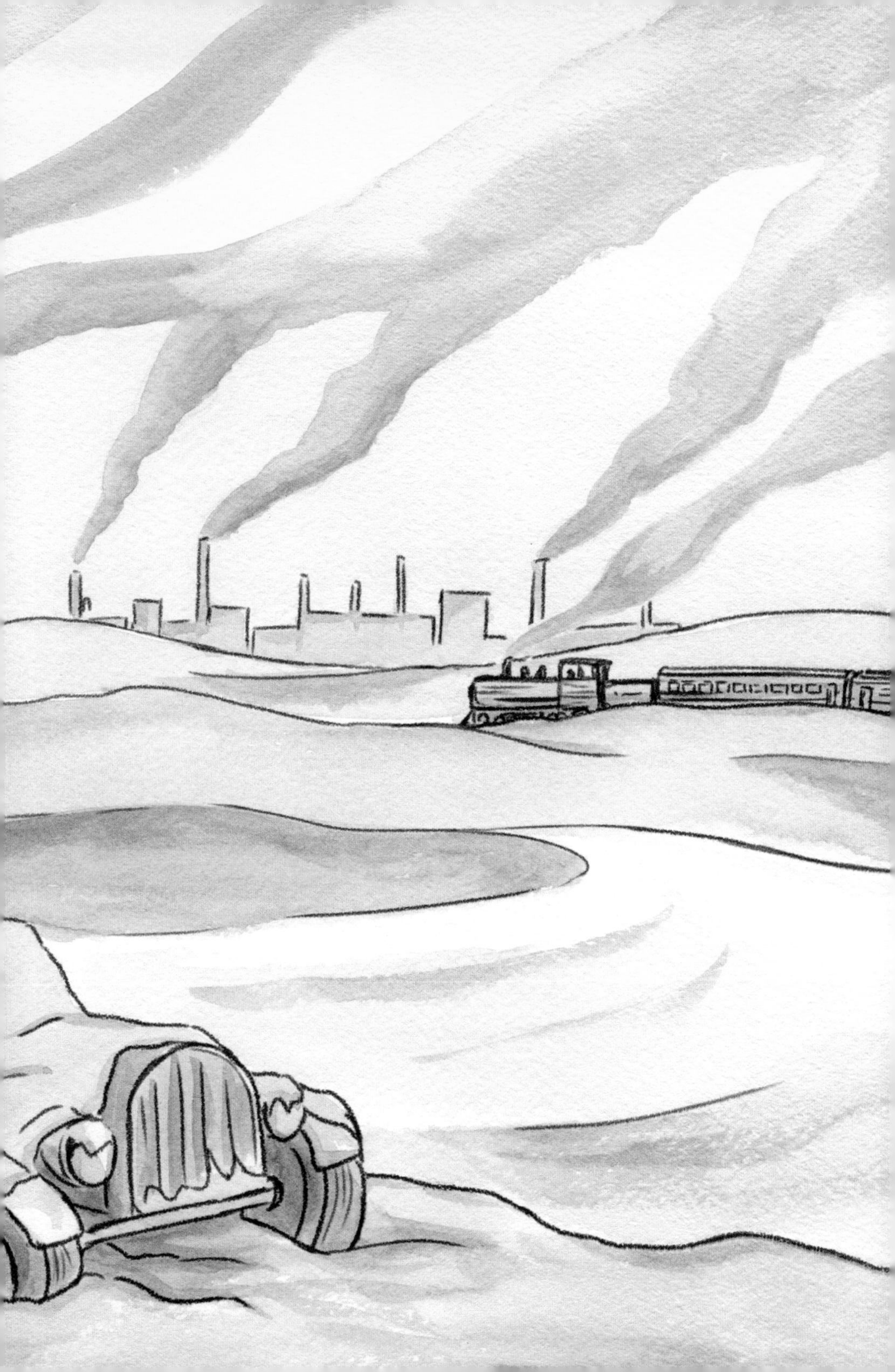

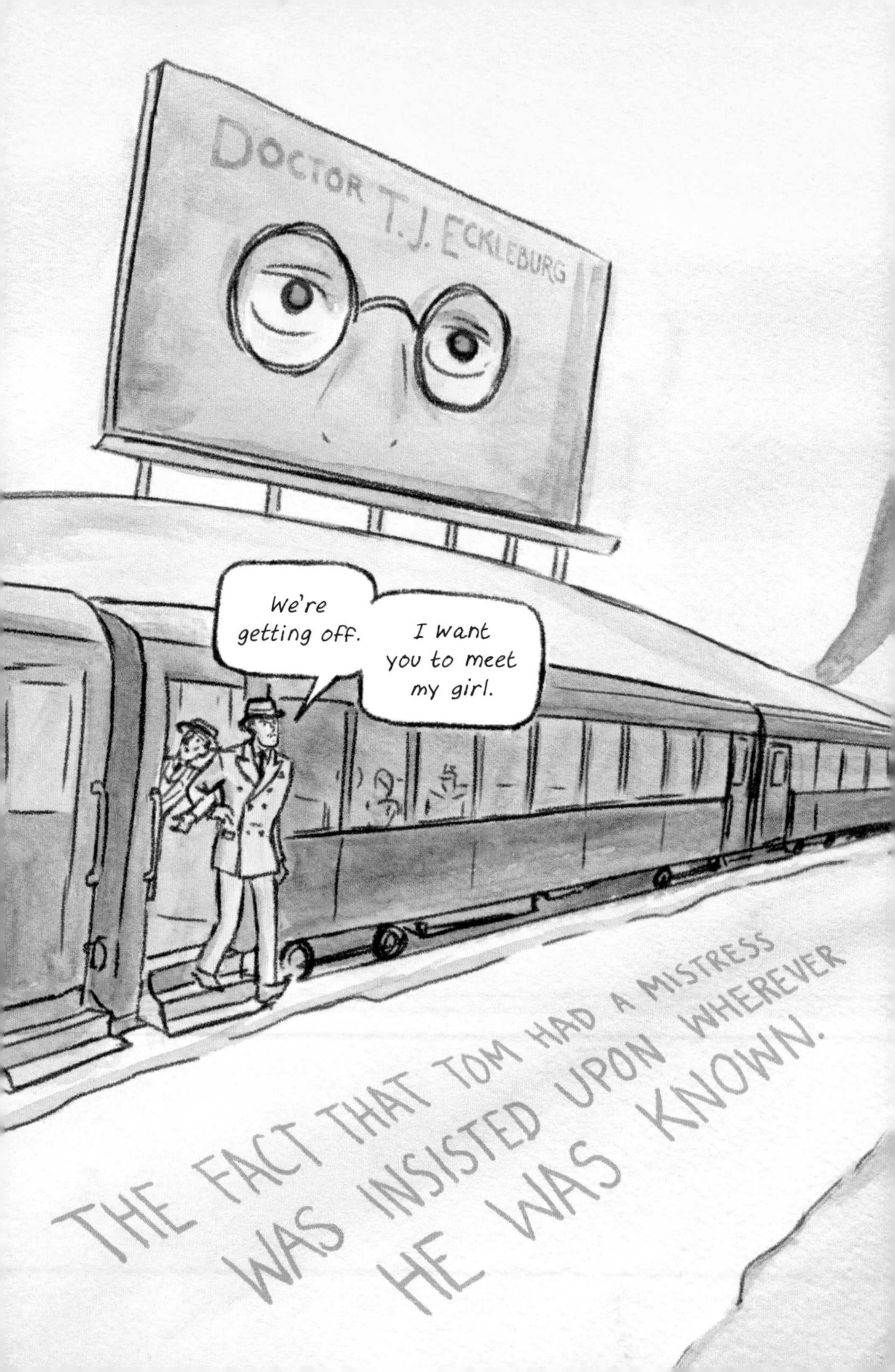
DOCTOR T. J. ECKLEBURG
We're getting off.
I want you to meet my girl.
THE FACT THAT TOM HAD A MISTRESS WAS INSISTED UPON WHEREVER HE WAS KNOWN.

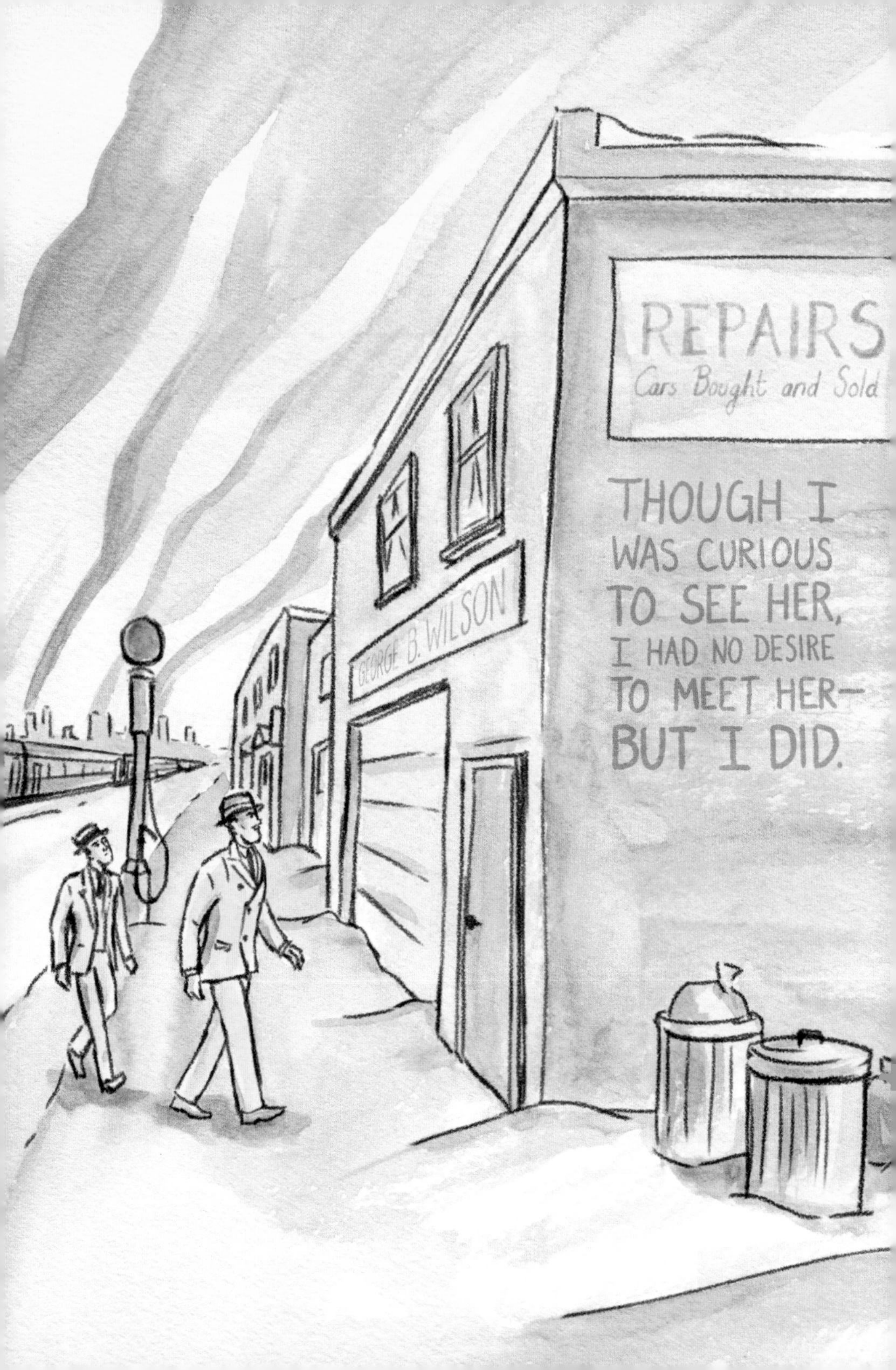
REPAIRS
Cars Bought and Sold
GEORGE B. WILSON
THOUGH I WAS CURIOUS TO SEE HER, I HAD NO DESIRE TO MEET HER— BUT I DID.

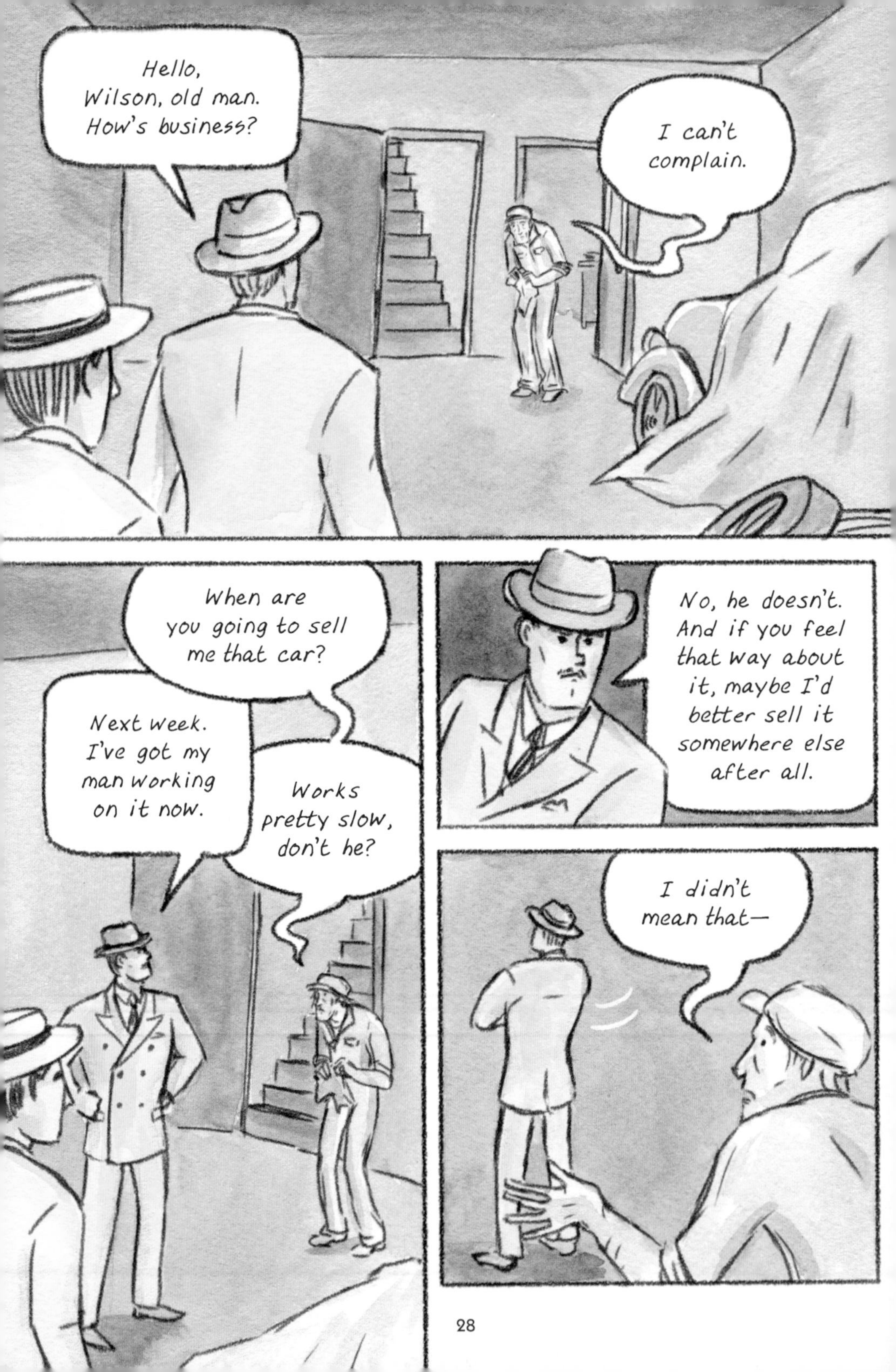
Hello, Wilson, old man. How's business?
I can't complain.
When are you going to sell me that car?
Next week. I've got my man working on it now.
Works pretty slow, don't he?
No, he doesn't. And if you feel that way about it, maybe I'd better sell it somewhere else after all.
I didn't mean that—

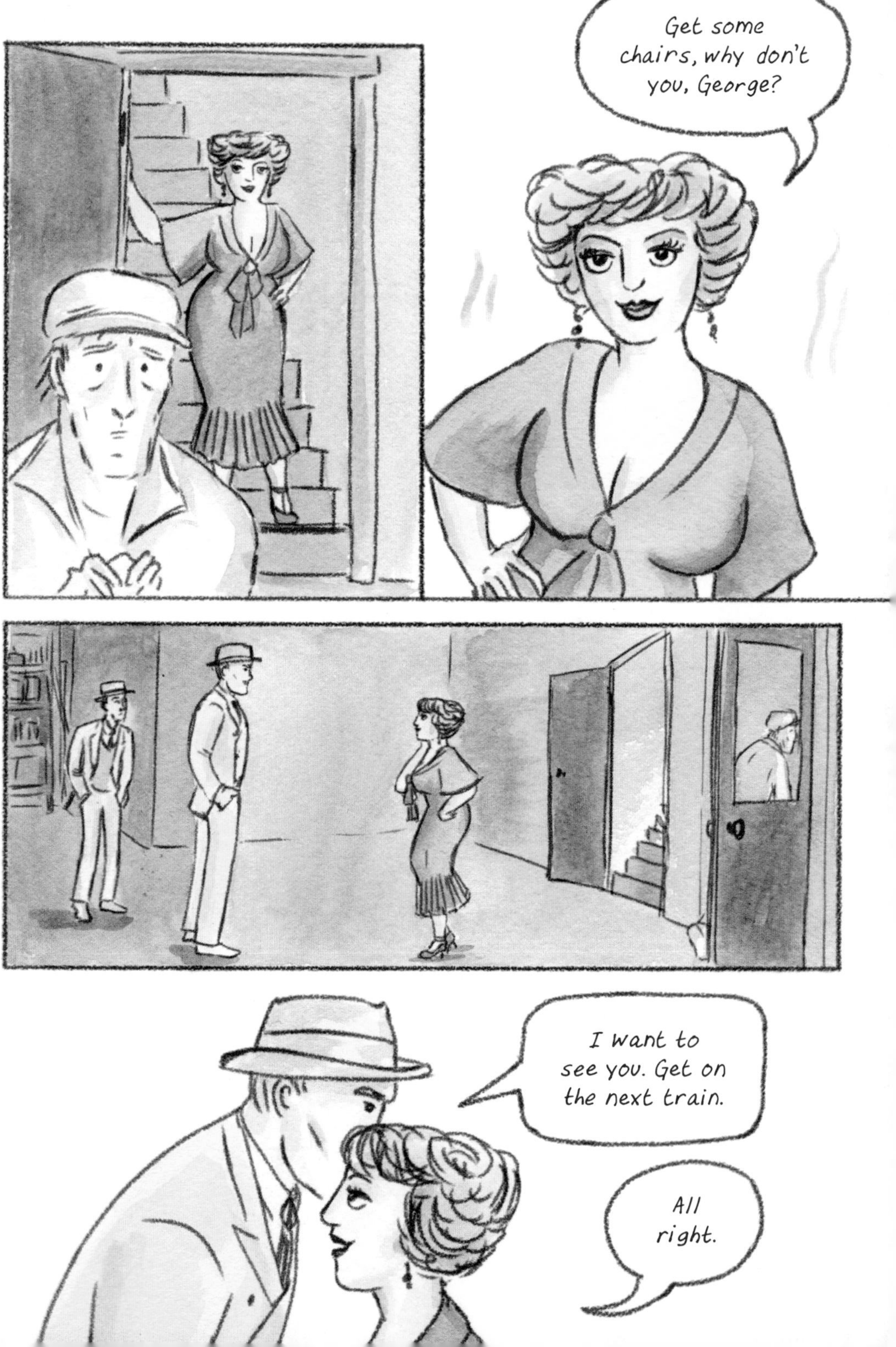
Get some chairs, why don't you, George?
I want to see you. Get on the next train.
All right.

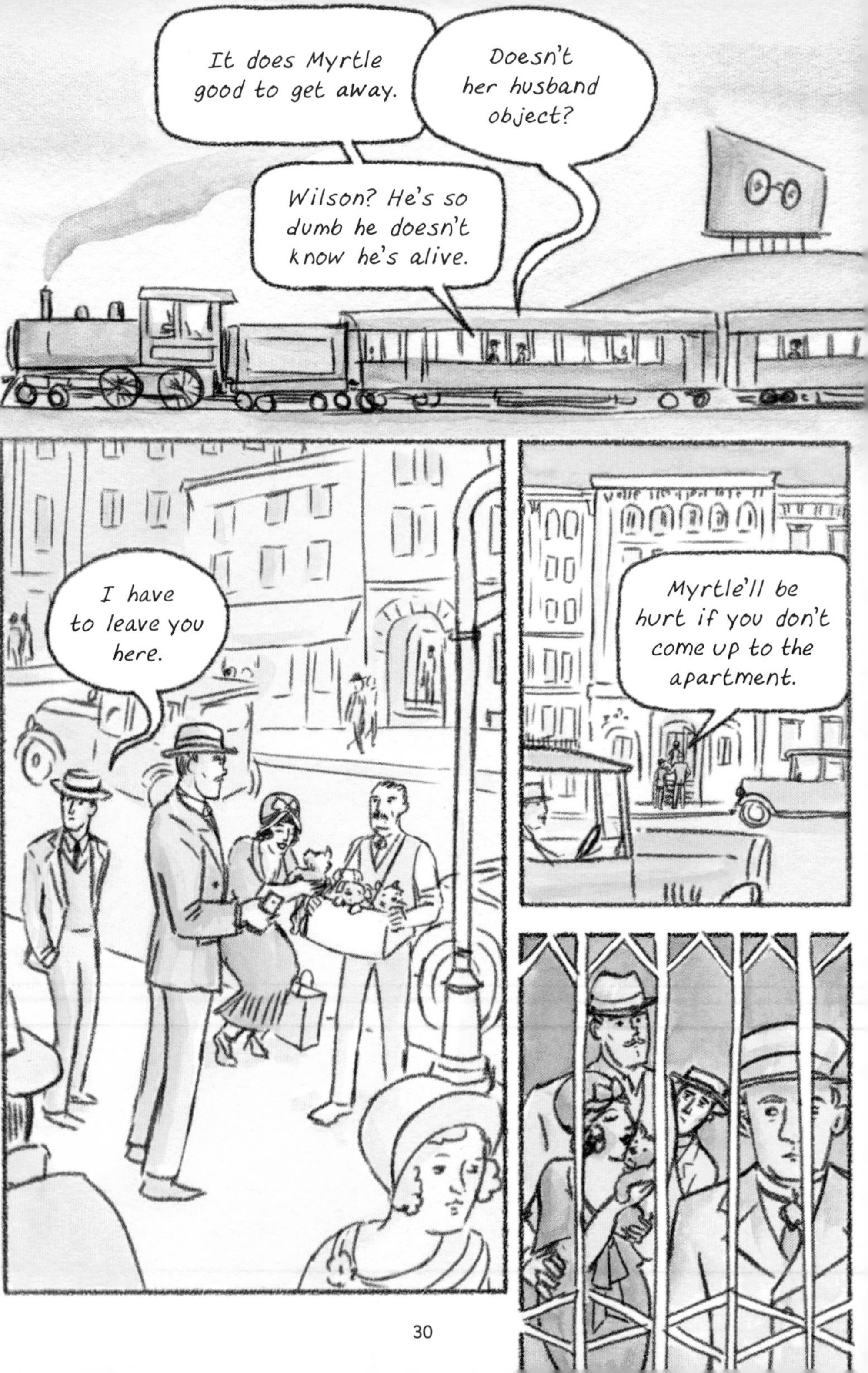
It does Myrtle good to get away.
Doesn't her husband object?
Wilson? He's so dumb he doesn't know he's alive.
I have to leave you here.
Myrtle'll be hurt if you don't come up to the apartment.

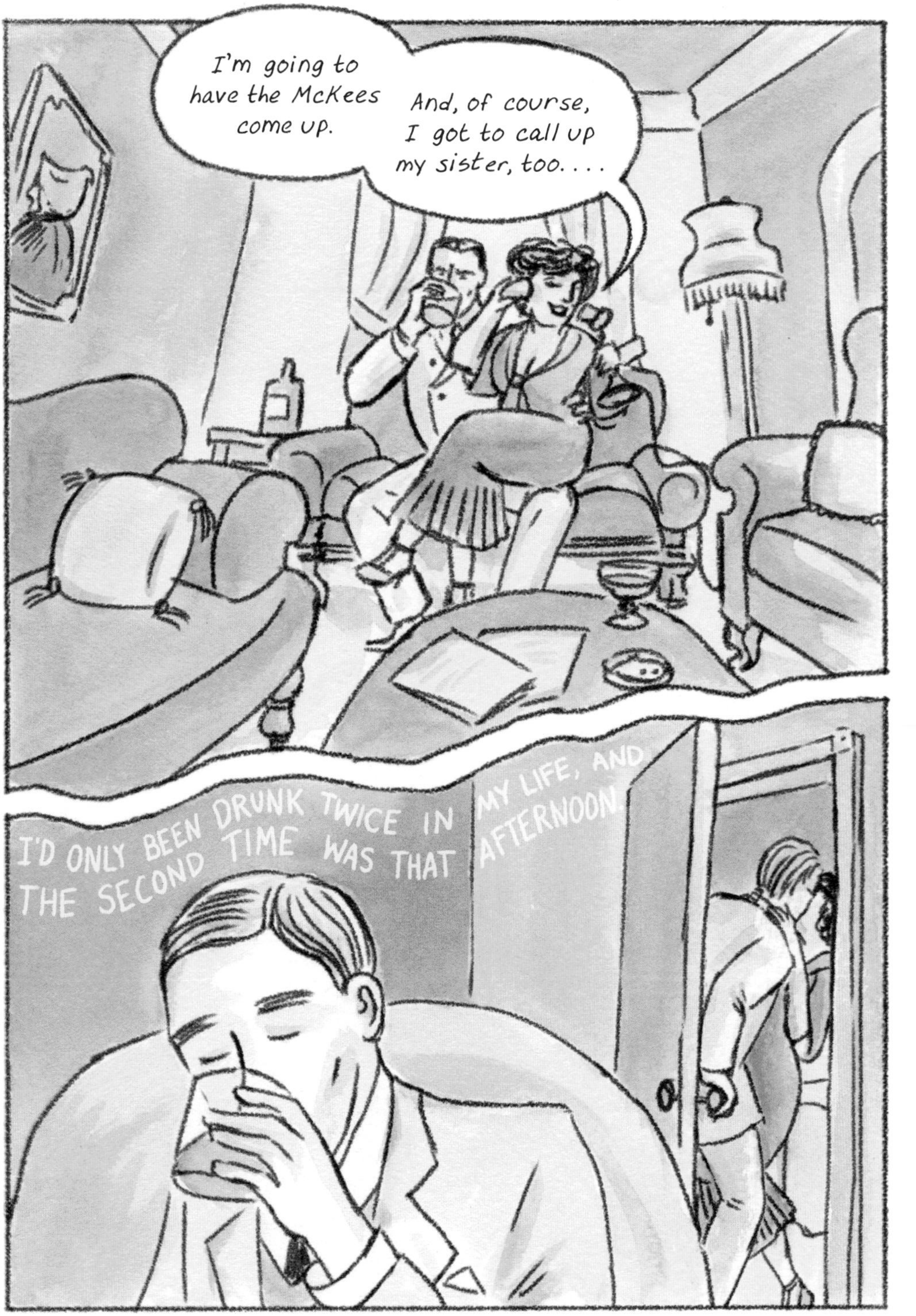
I'm going to have the McKees come up.
And, of course, I got to call up my sister, too. . . .
I'D ONLY BEEN DRUNK TWICE IN MY LIFE, AND THE SECOND TIME WAS THAT AFTERNOON.

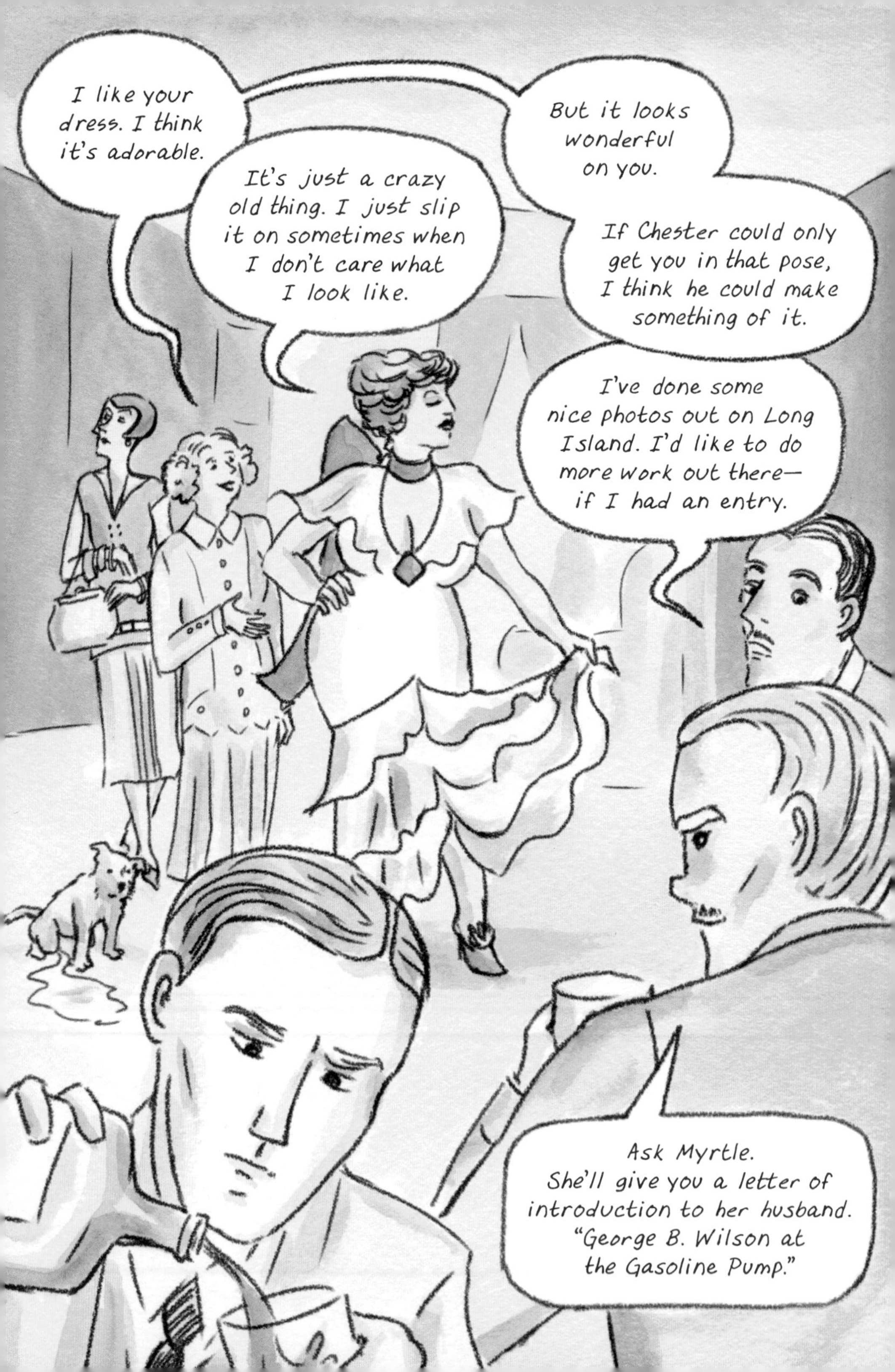
I like your dress. I think it's adorable.
It's just a crazy old thing. I just slip it on sometimes when I don't care what I look like.
But it looks wonderful on you.
If Chester could only get you in that pose, I think he could make something of it.
I've done some nice photos out on Long Island. I'd like to do more work out there— if I had an entry.
Ask Myrtle. She'll give you a letter of introduction to her husband. "George B. Wilson at the Gasoline Pump."

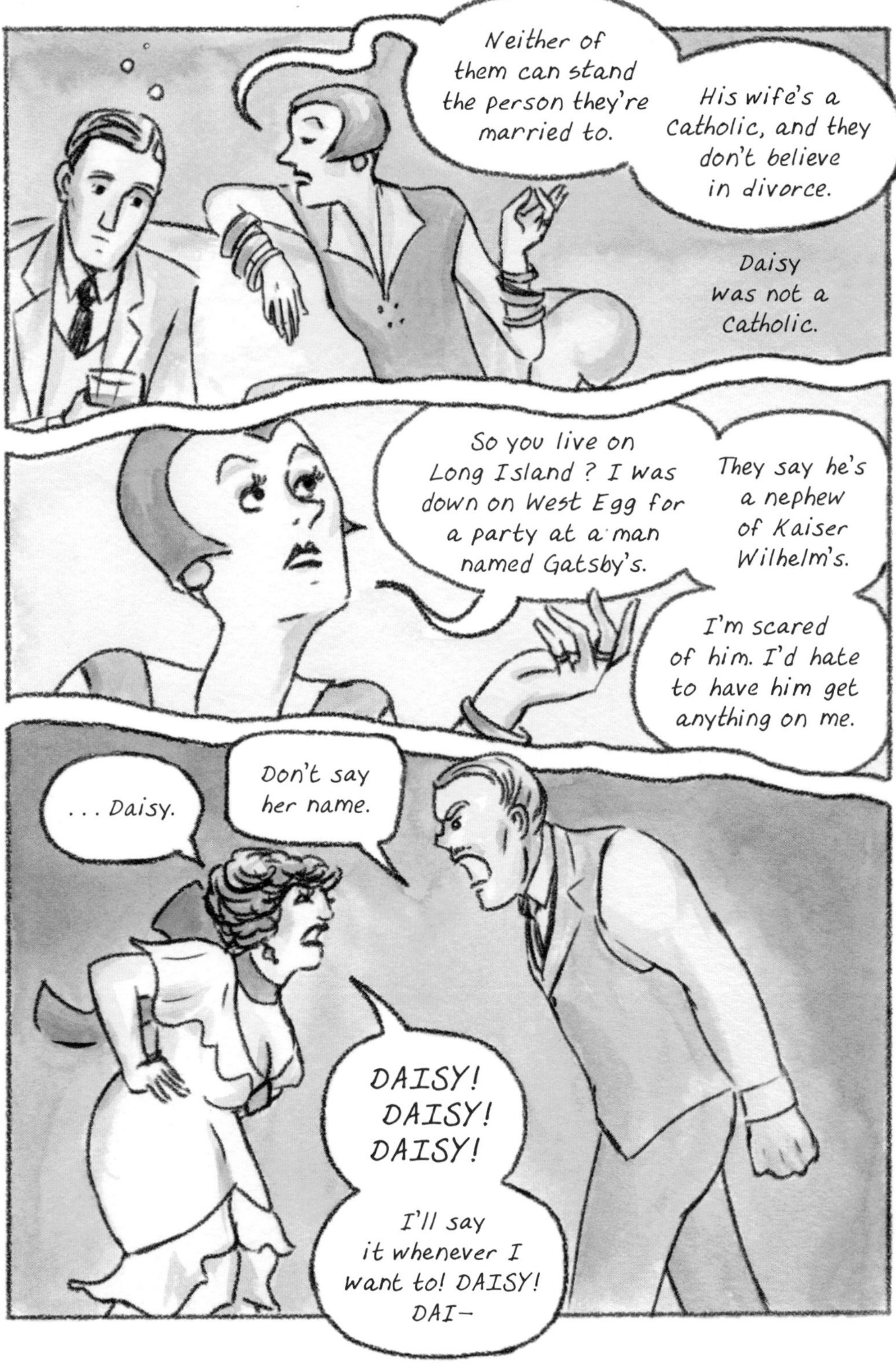
Neither of them can stand the person they're married to.
His wife's a Catholic, and they don't believe in divorce.
Daisy was not a Catholic.
So you live on Long Island? I was down on West Egg for a party at a man named Gatsby's.
They say he's a nephew of Kaiser Wilhelm's.
I'm scared of him. I'd hate to have him get anything on me.
. . . Daisy.
Don't say her name.
DAISY! DAISY! DAISY!
I'll say it whenever I want to! DAISY! DAI—

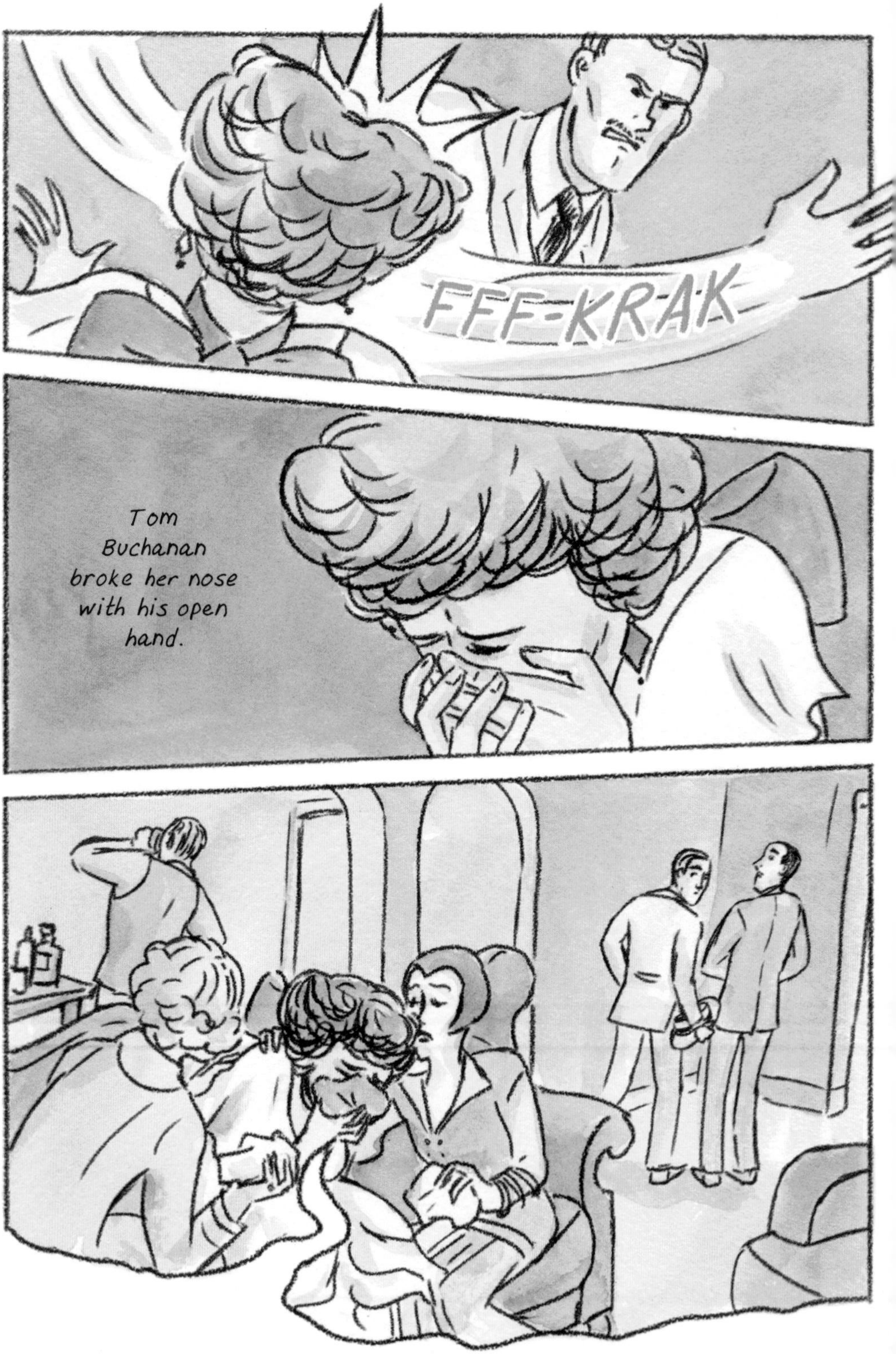
FFF-KRAK
Tom Buchanan broke her nose with his open hand.

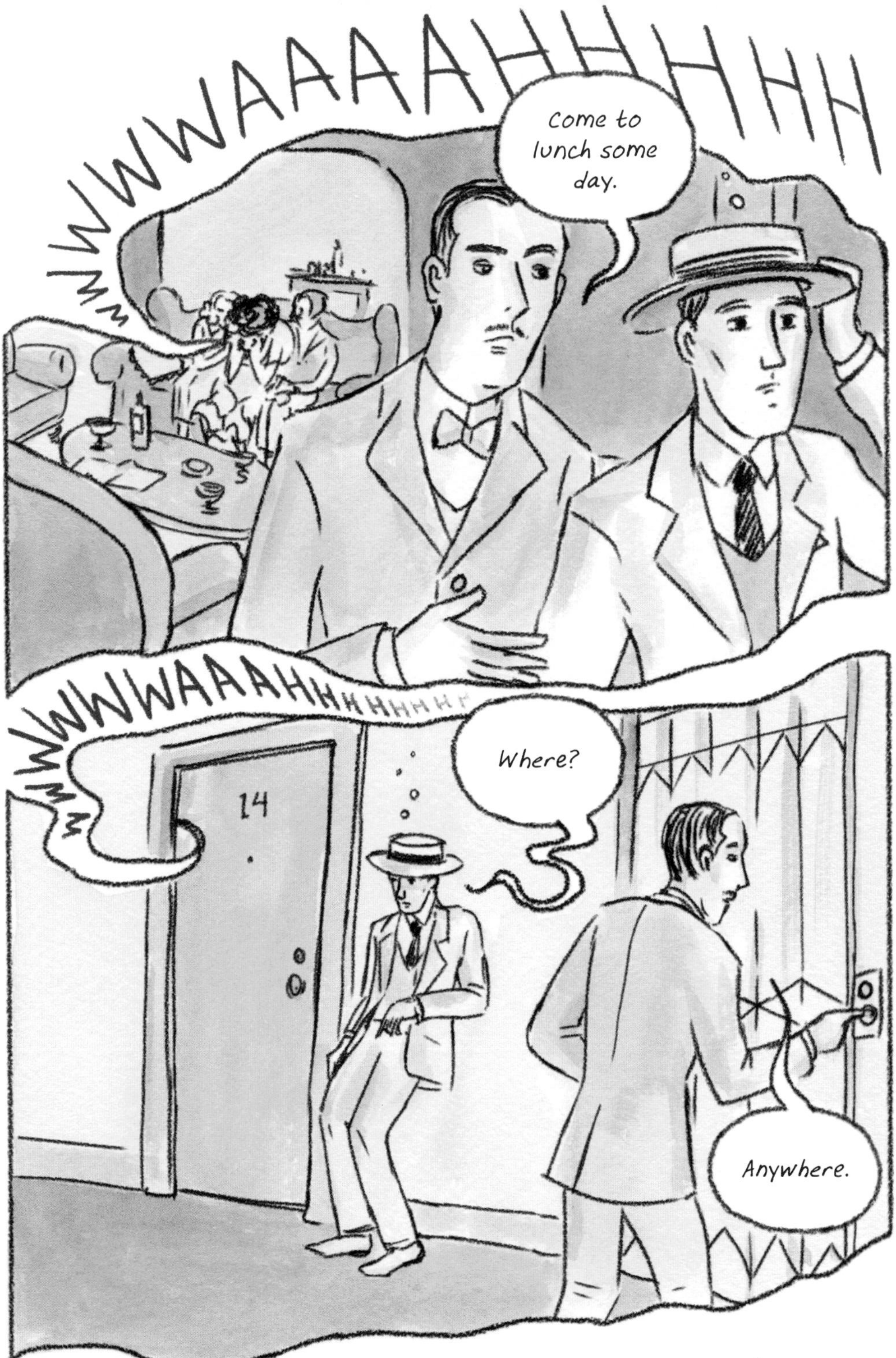
WWWWAAAAAHHHHHHH
Come to lunch some day.
WWWWAAAAHHHHHHHHH
14
Where?
Anywhere.

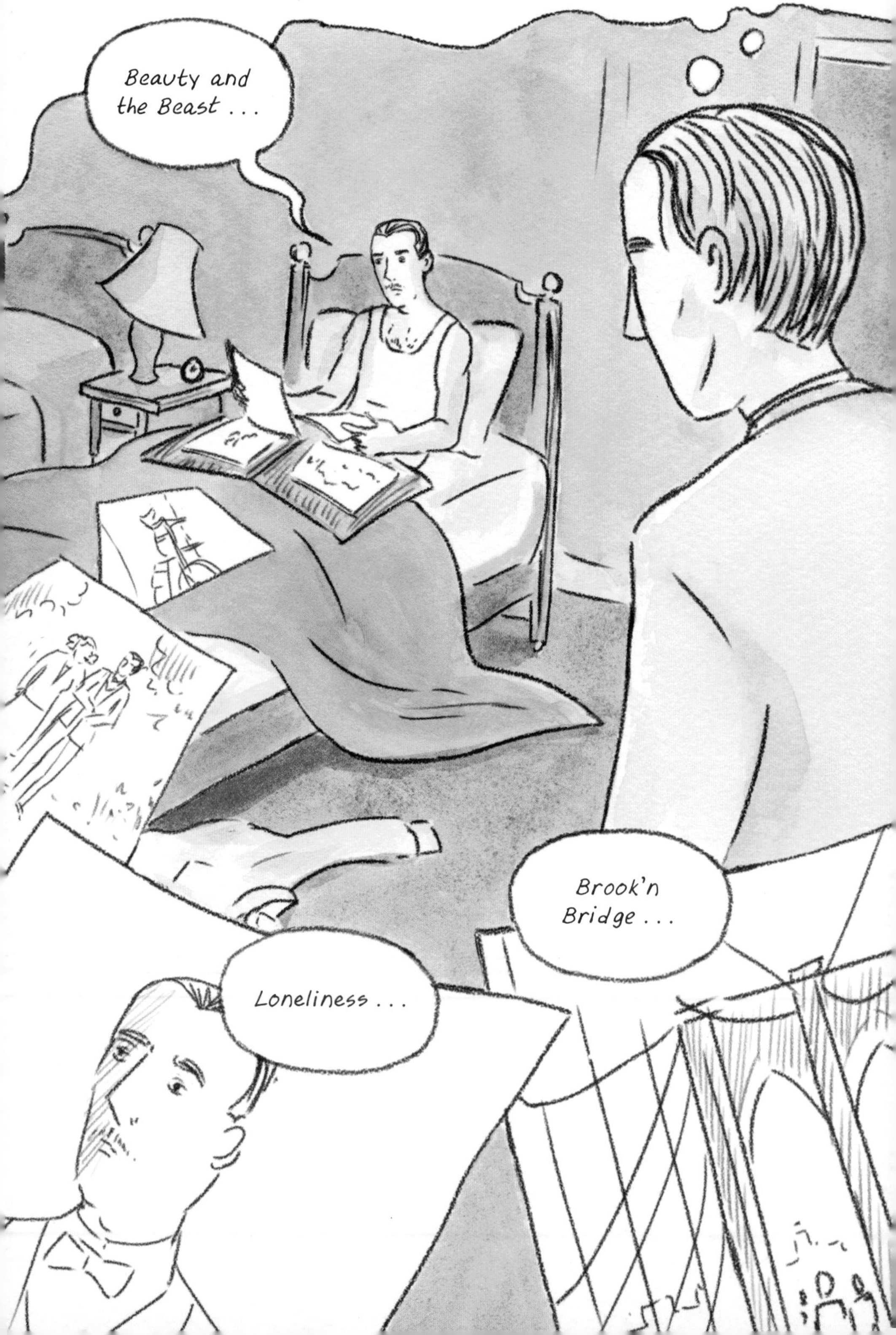
Beauty and the Beast . . .
Brook'n Bridge . . .
Loneliness . . .

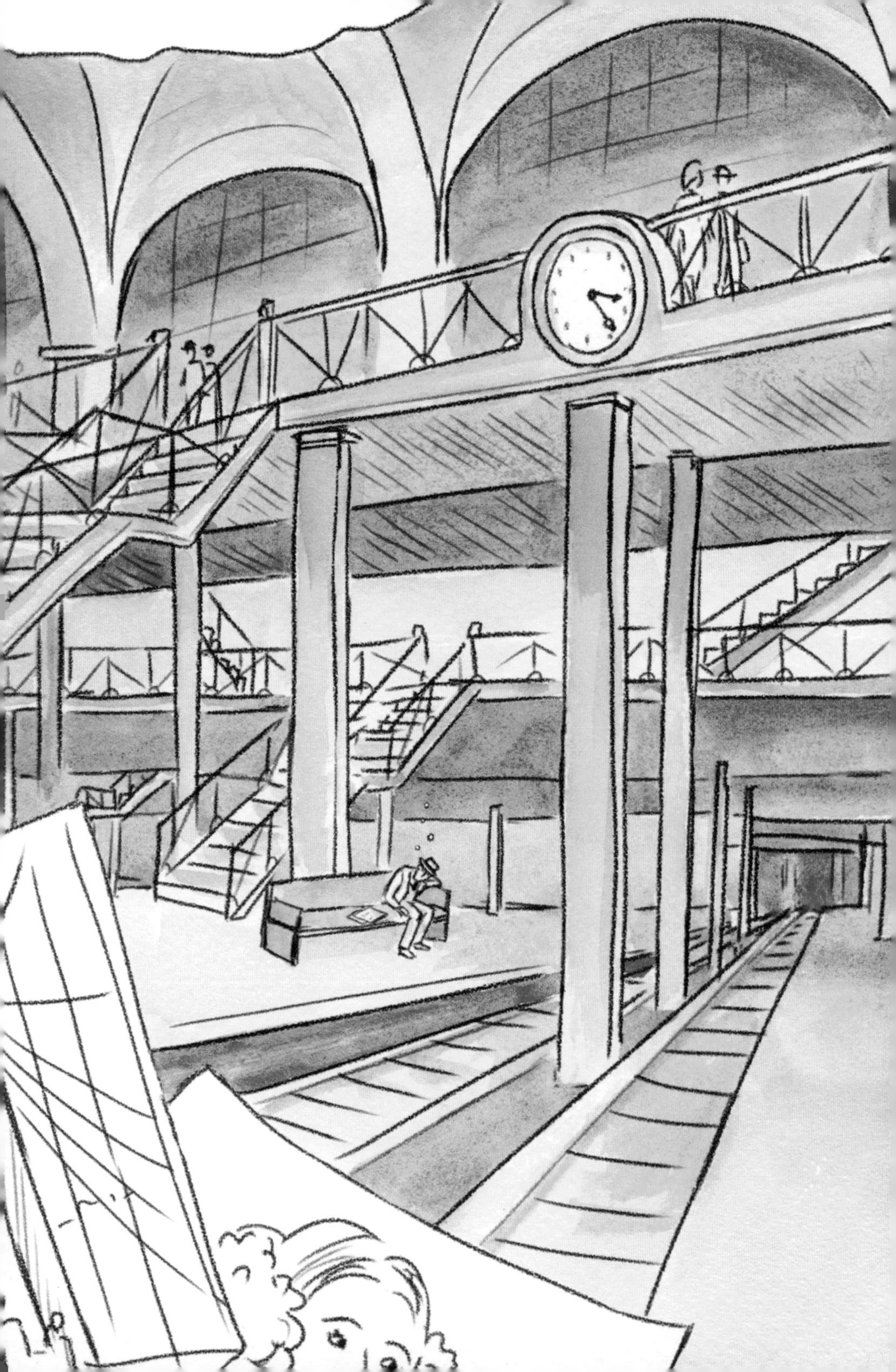

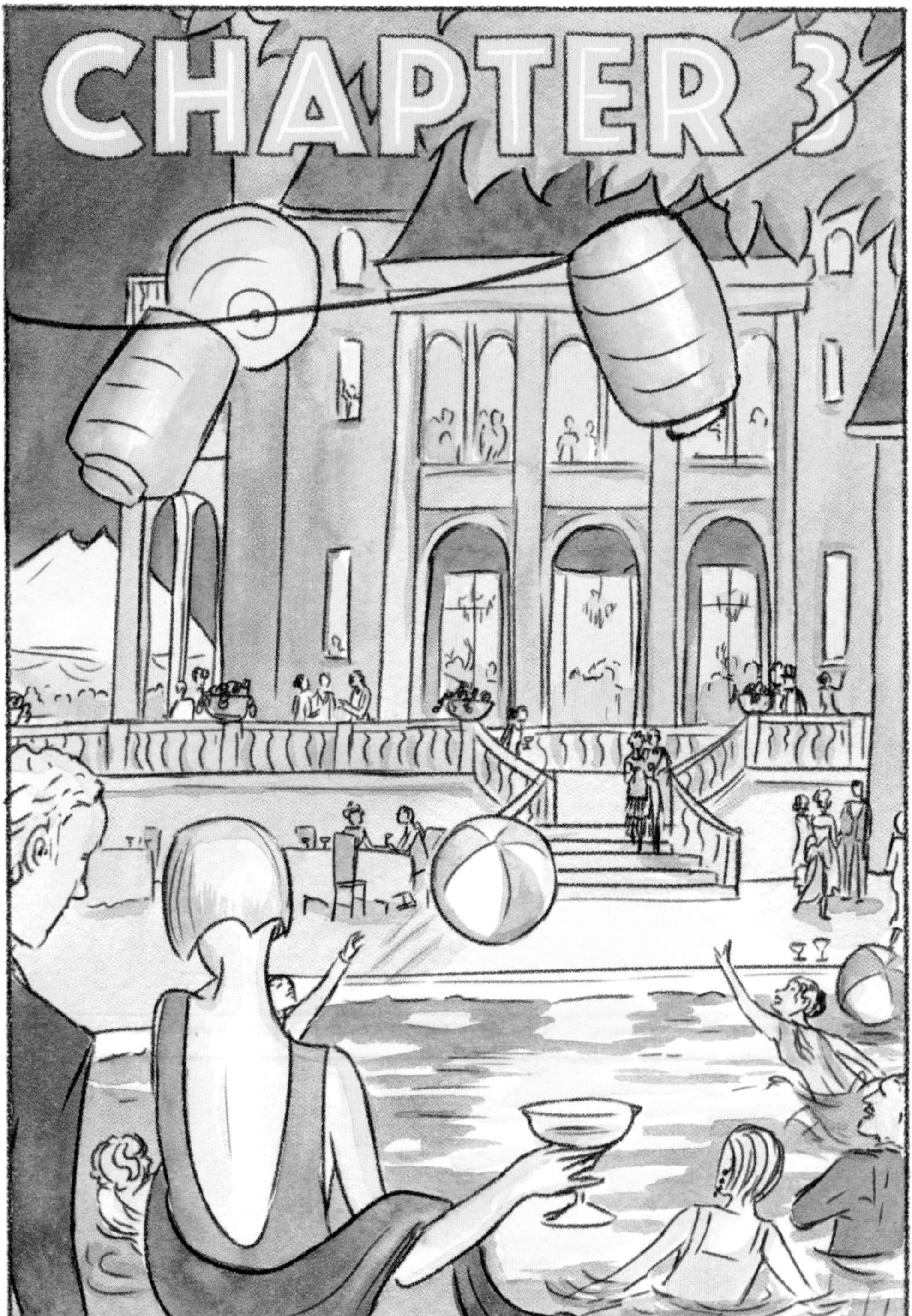
CHAPTER 3

THERE WAS MUSIC FROM MY NEIGHBOR'S HOUSE THROUGH THE SUMMER NIGHTS.

ON WEEKENDS

His Rolls-Royce became an omnibus, bearing parties to and from the city.

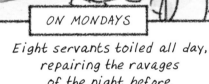

ON MONDAYS

Eight servants toiled all day, repairing the ravages of the night before.

EVERY FRIDAY

Five crates of oranges and lemons arrived from a fruiterer in New York.

EVERY MONDAY

These same oranges and lemons left his back door in a pyramid of pulpless halves.

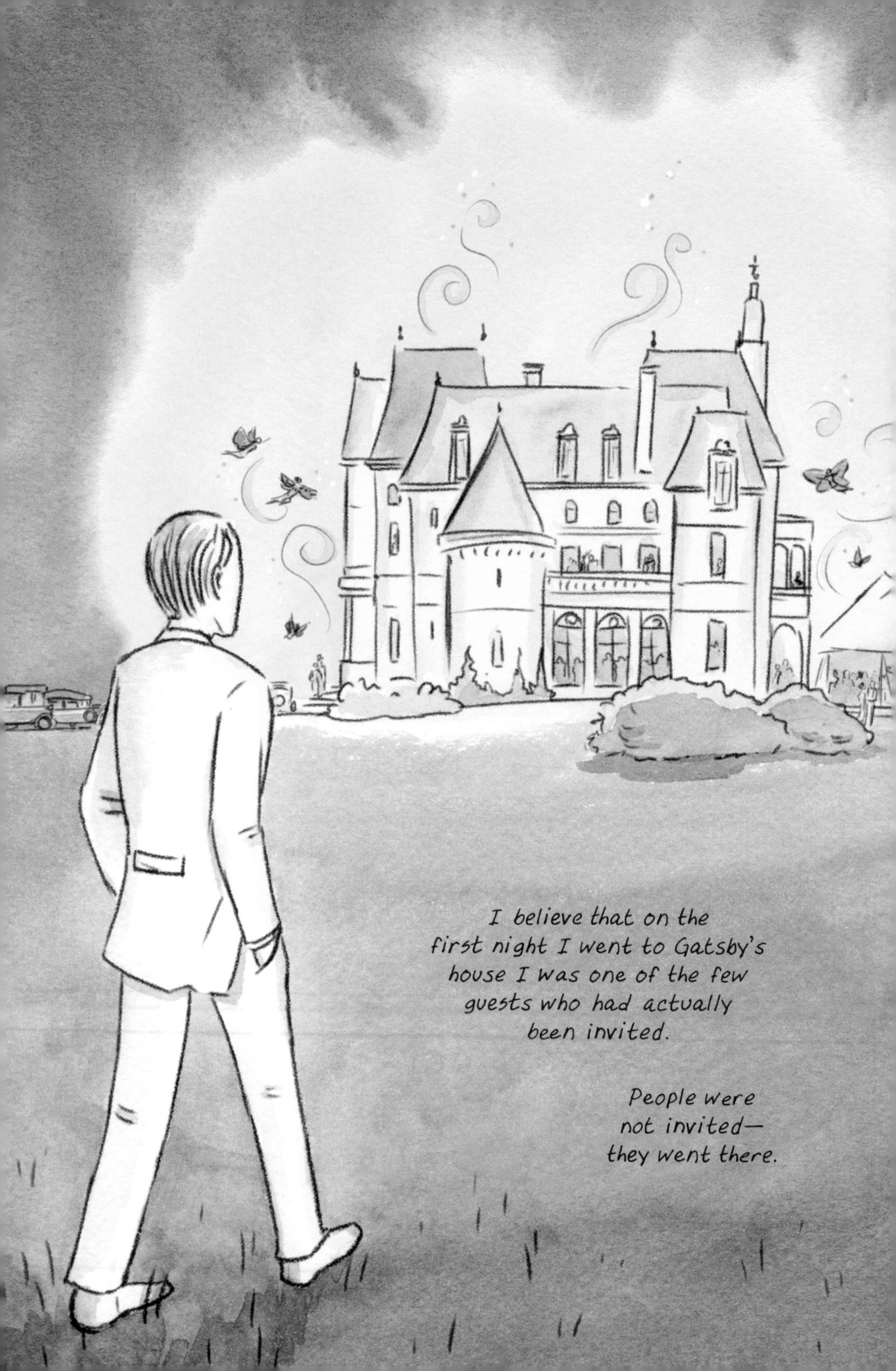
I believe that on the first night I went to Gatsby's house I was one of the few guests who had actually been invited.
People were not invited—they went there.

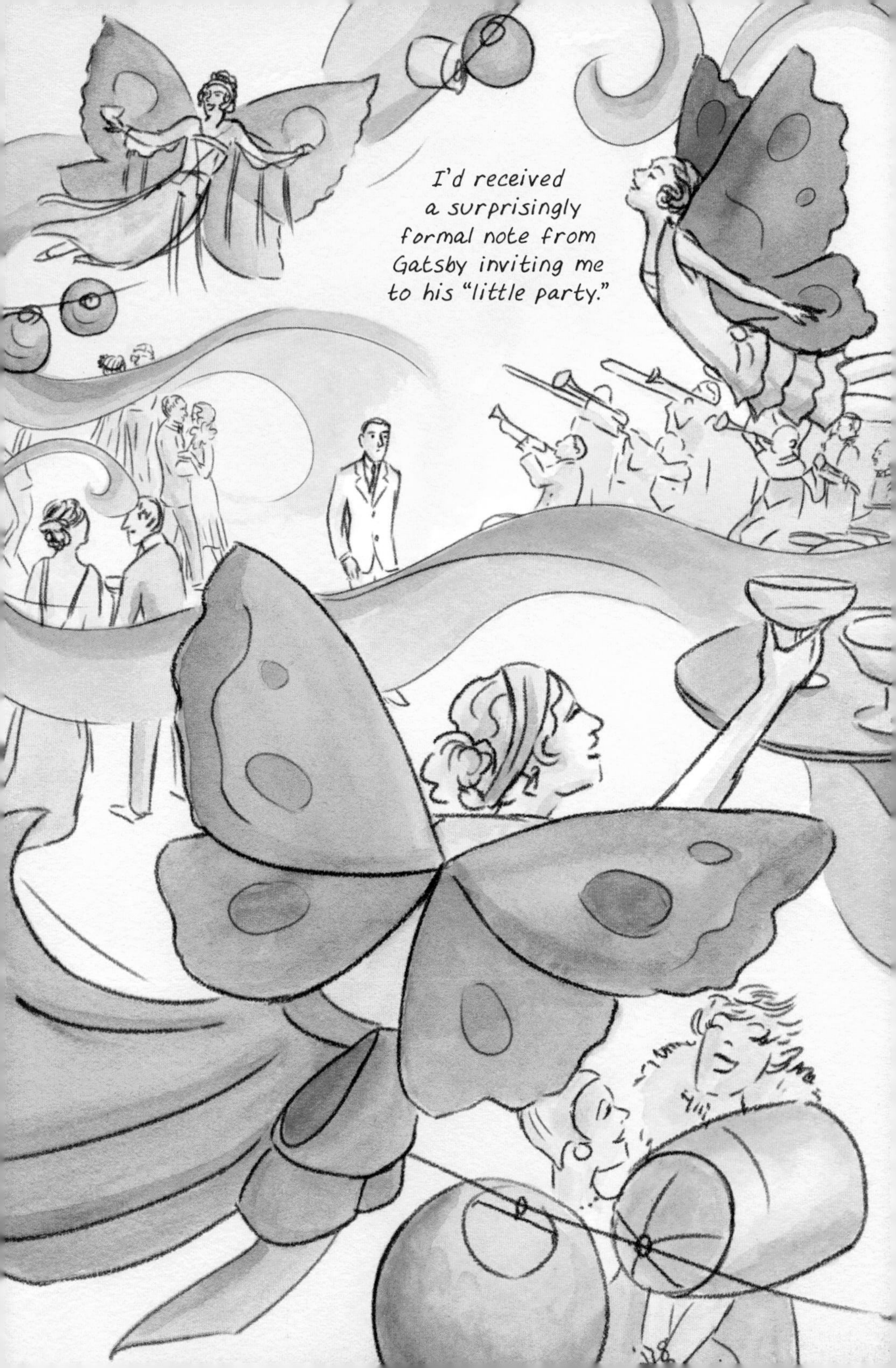
I'd received a surprisingly formal note from Gatsby inviting me to his "little party."

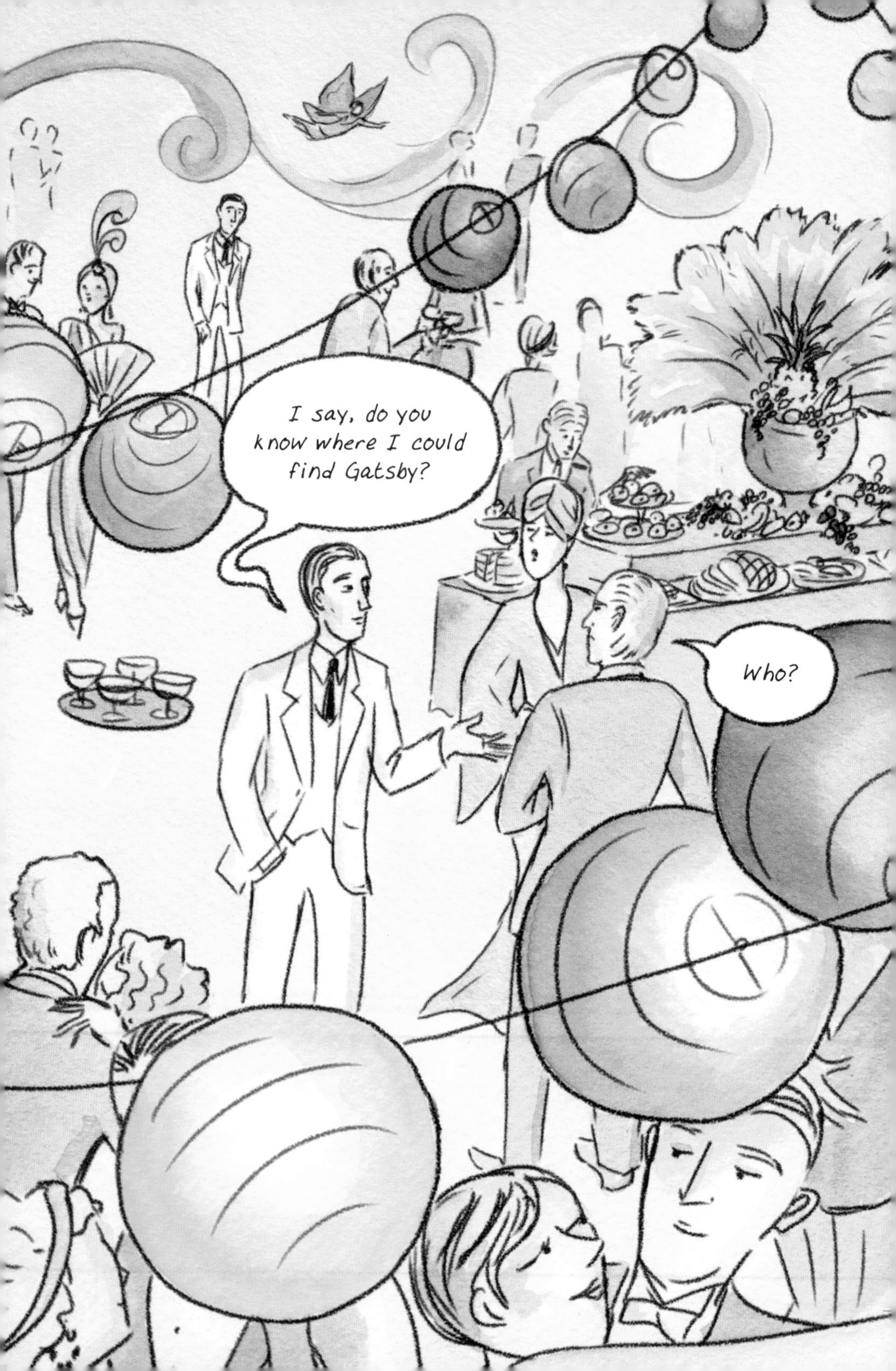
I say, do you know where I could find Gatsby?
Who?

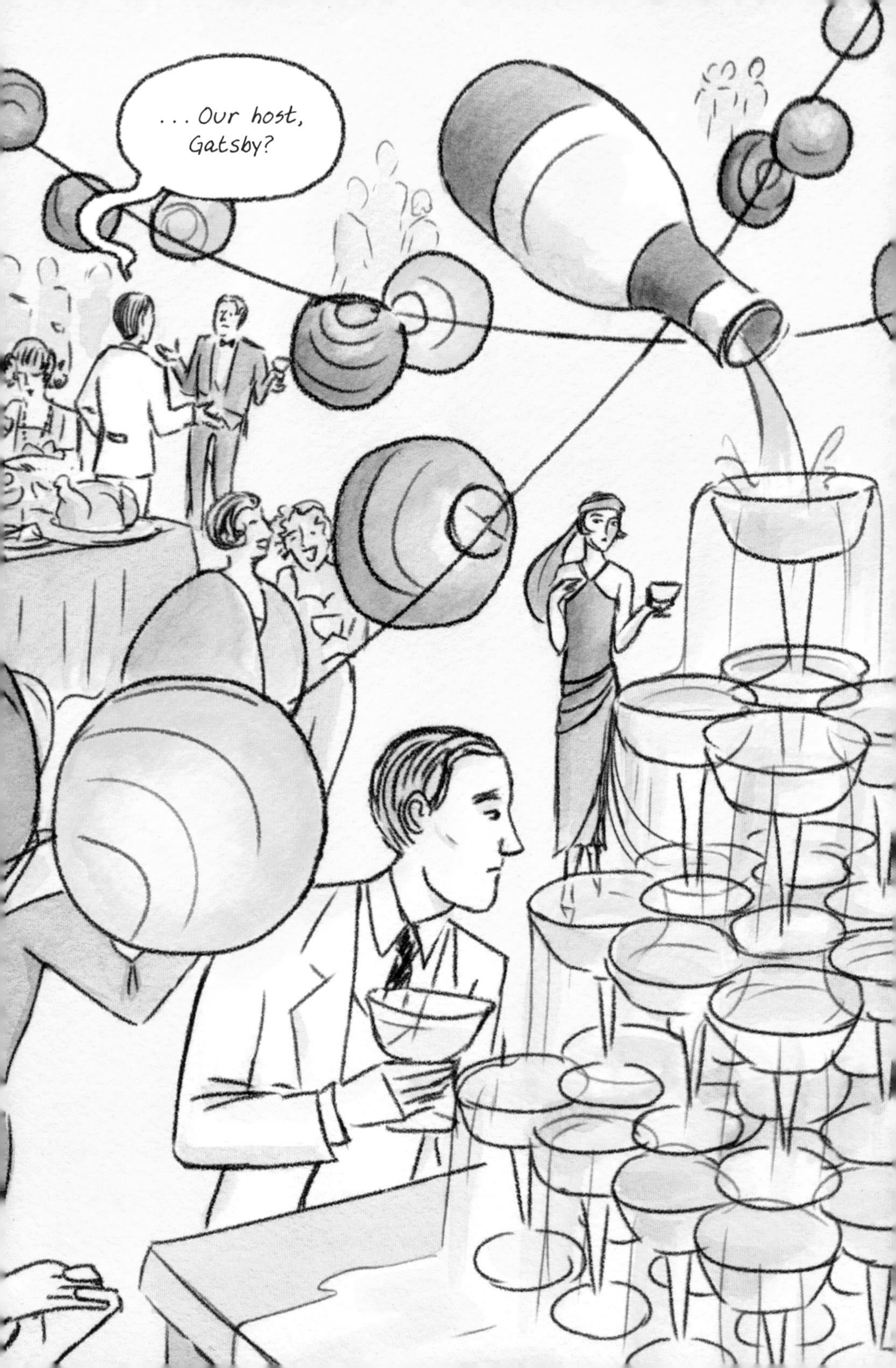
. . . Our host,
Gatsby?

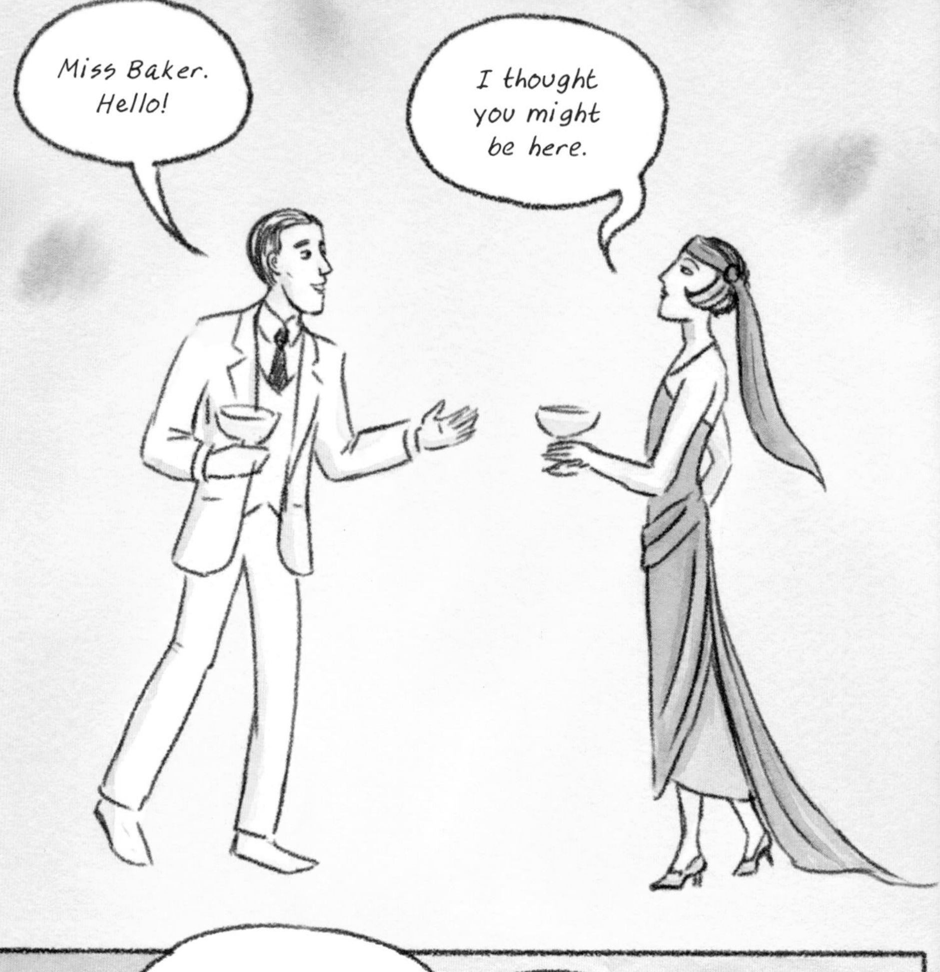
Miss Baker.
Hello!
I thought you might be here.

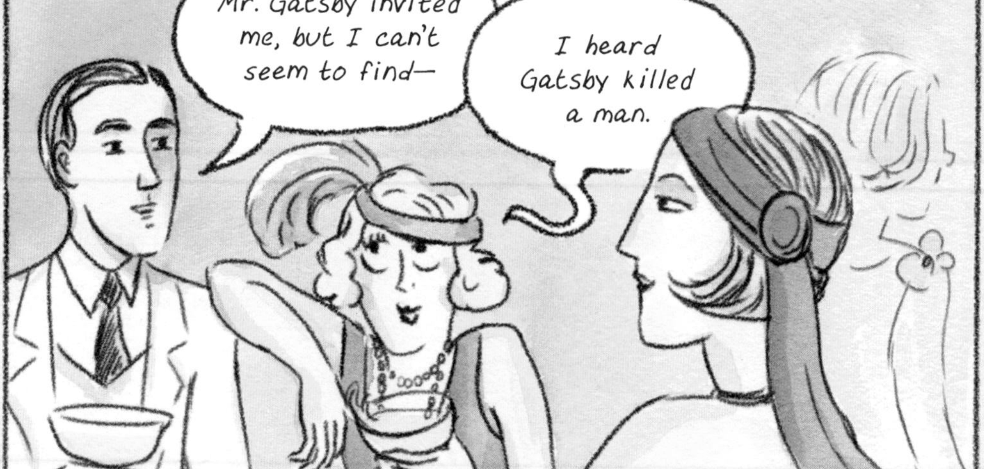
Mr. Gatsby invited me, but I can't seem to find—
I heard Gatsby killed a man.

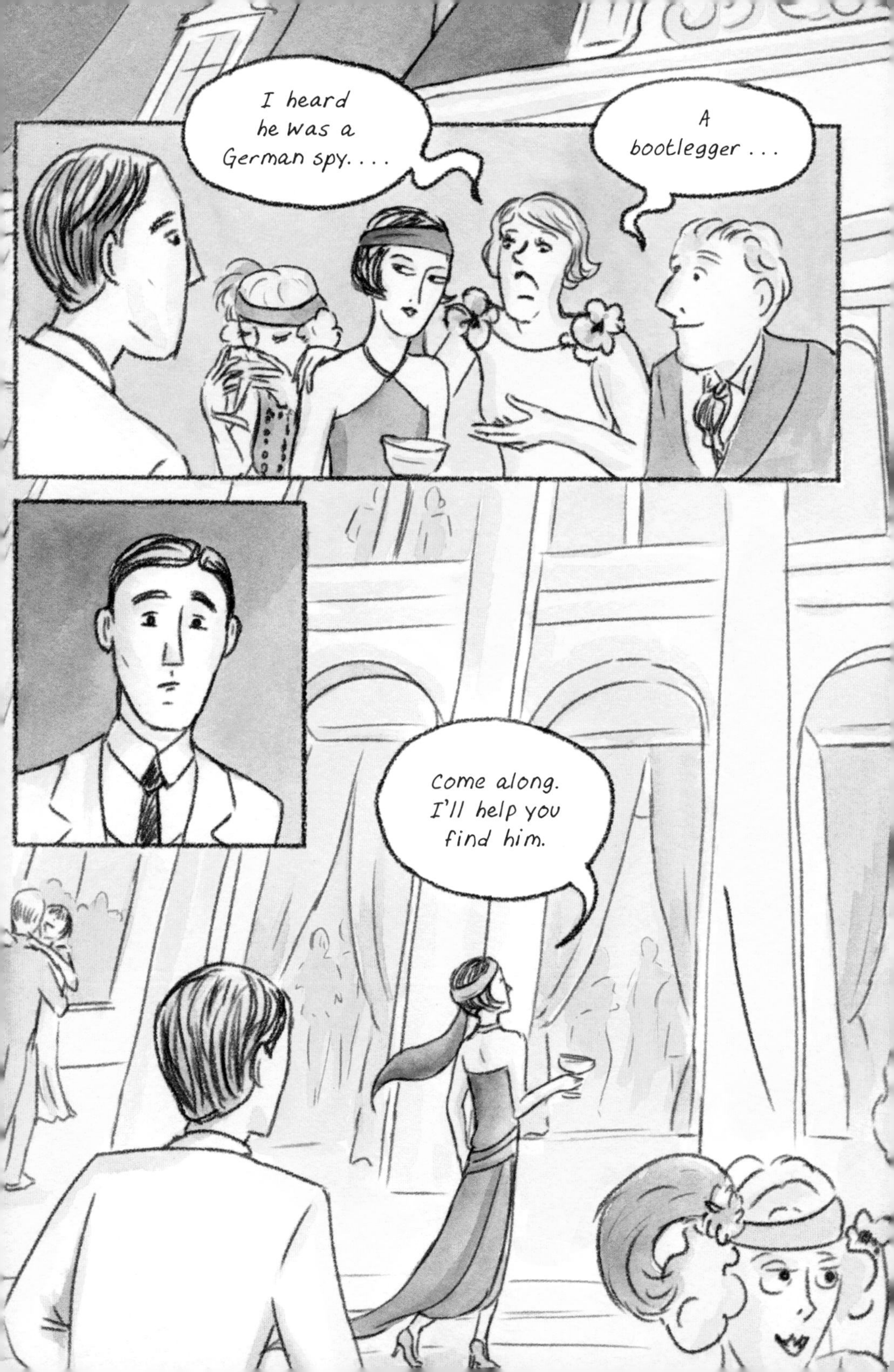
I heard he was a German spy. . . .
A bootlegger . . .
Come along. I'll help you find him.

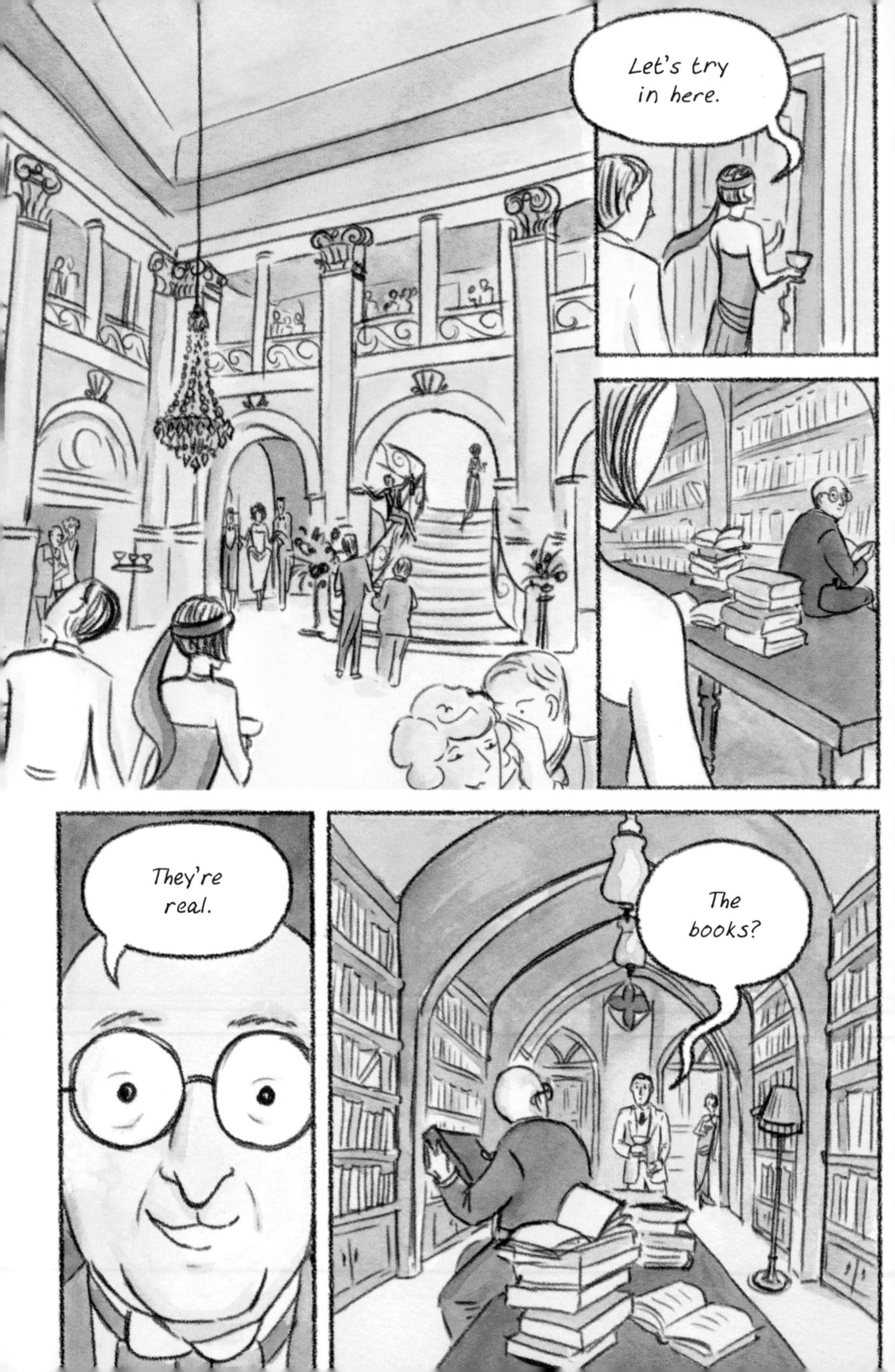
Let's try
in here.
They're
real.
The
books?

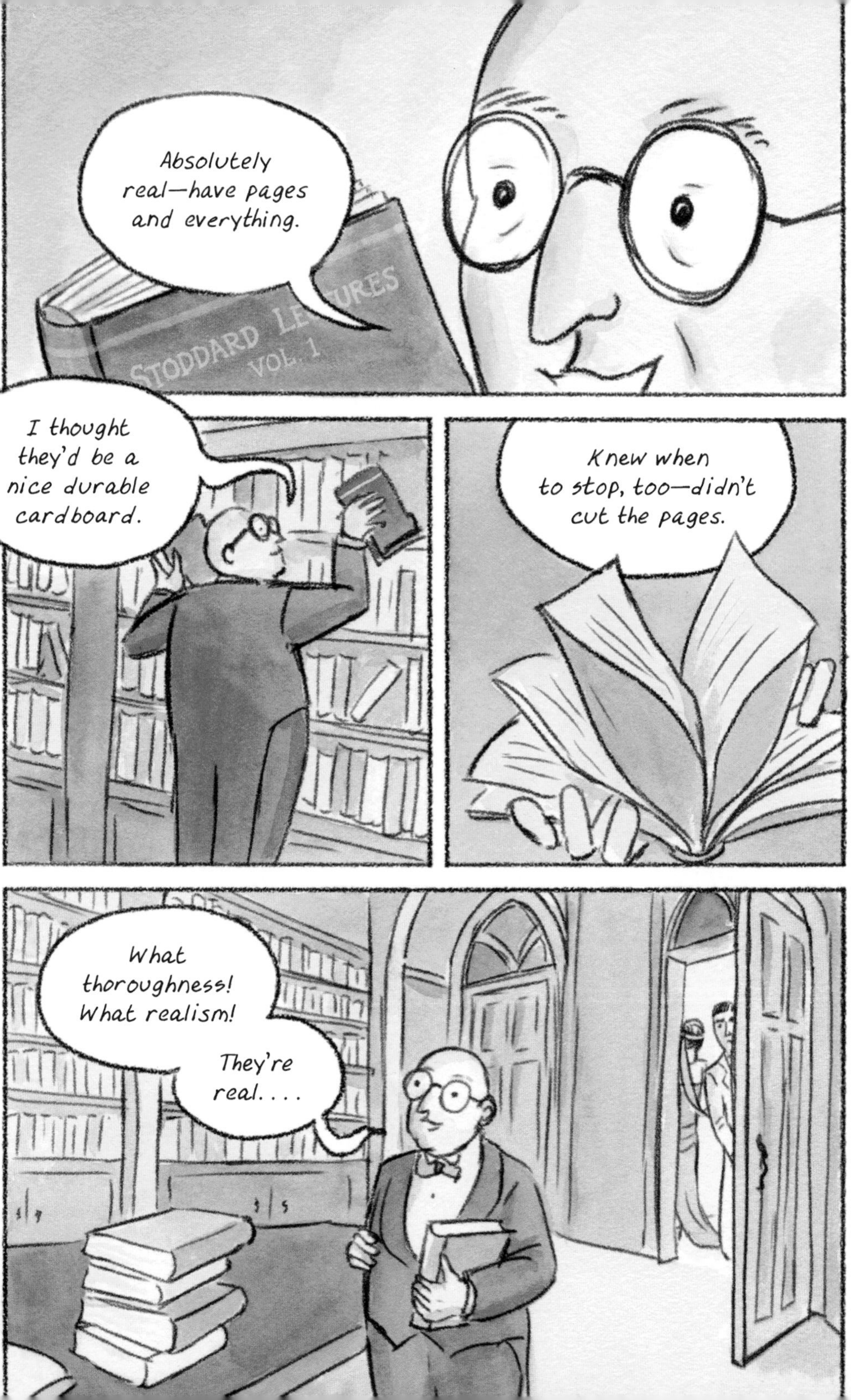
Absolutely real—have pages and everything.
STODDARD LECTURES VOL. 1
I thought they'd be a nice durable cardboard.
Knew when to stop, too—didn't cut the pages.
What thoroughness! What realism!
They're real. . . .

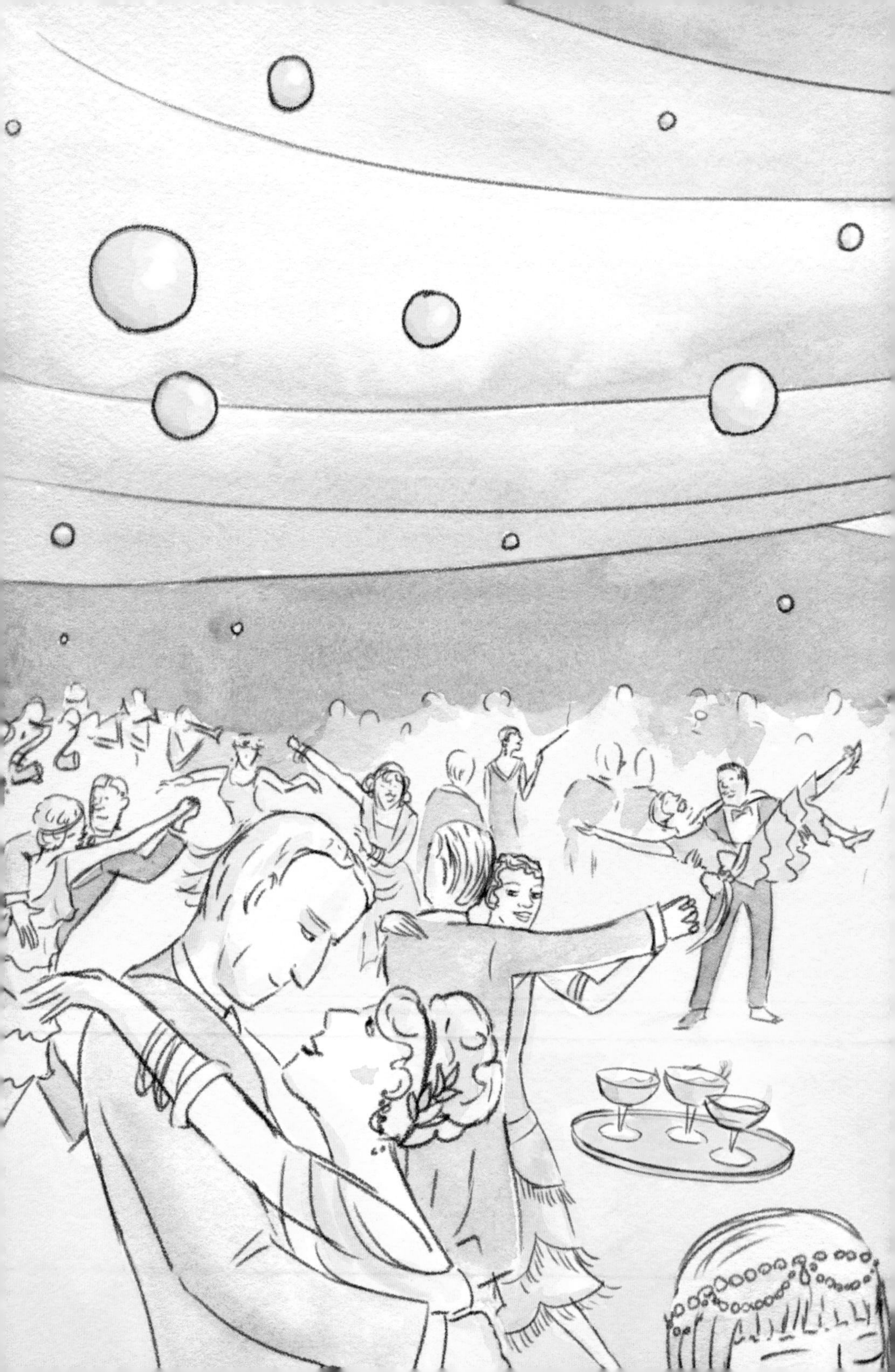

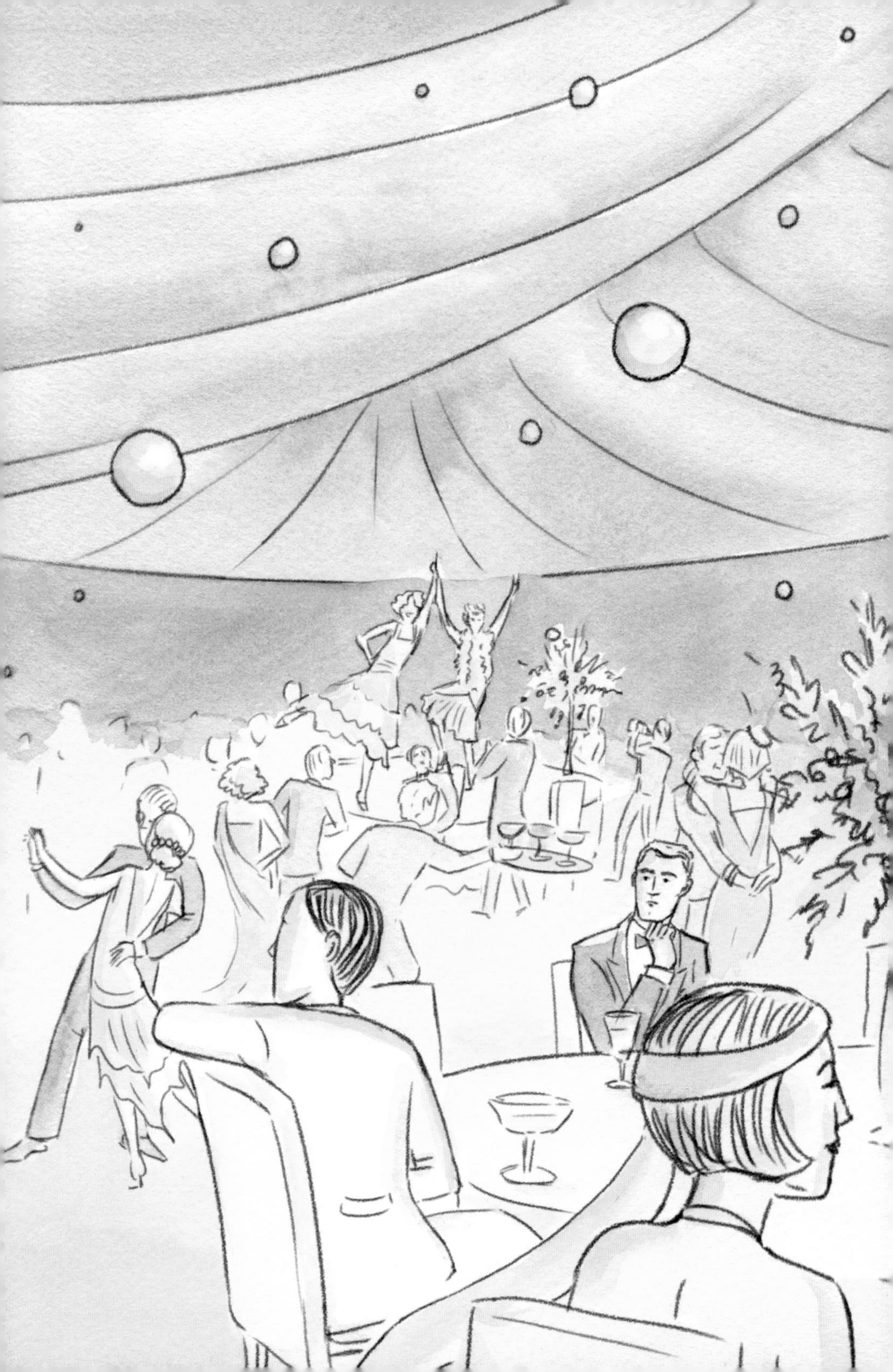

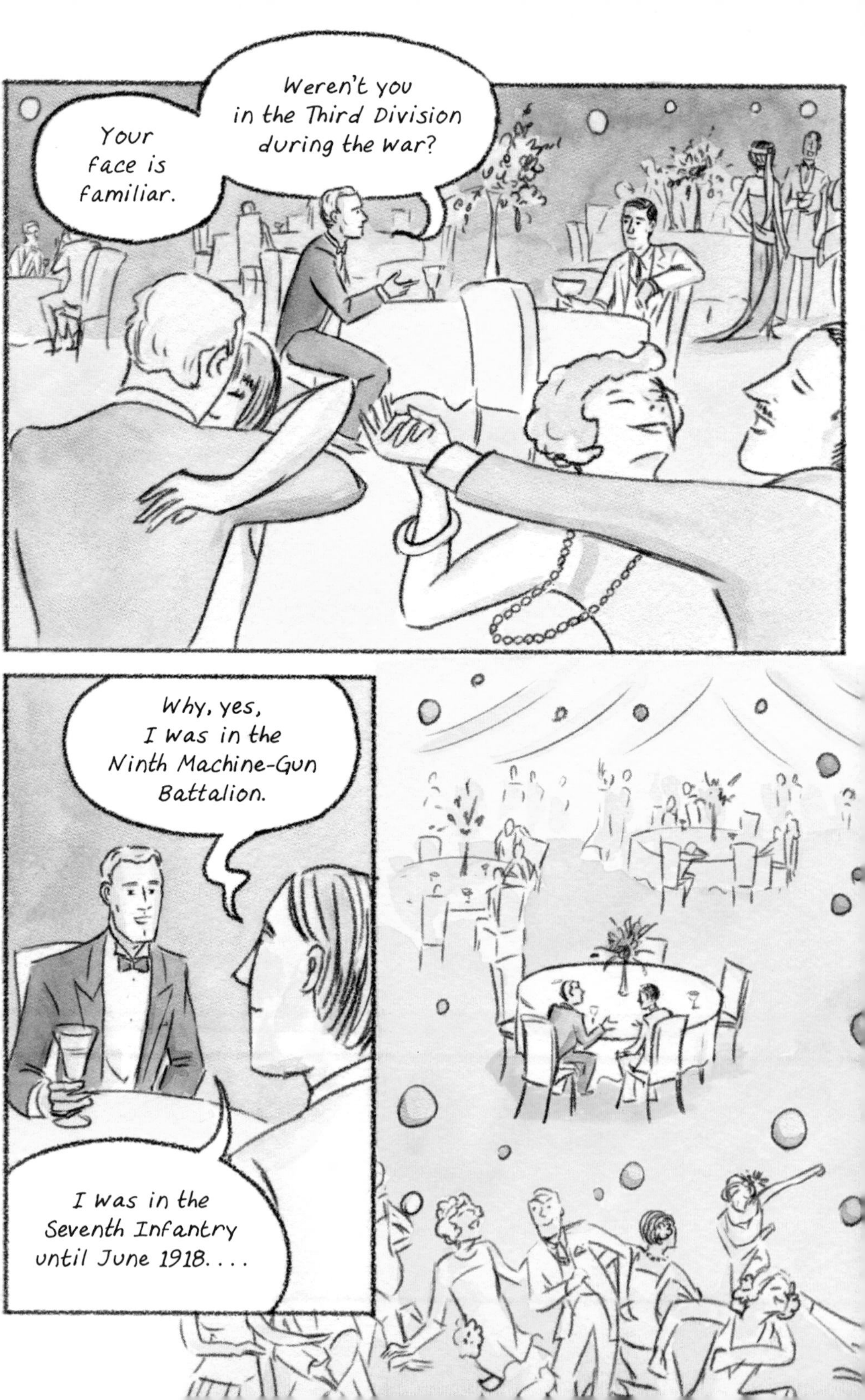
Your face is familiar.
Weren't you in the Third Division during the war?
Why, yes, I was in the Ninth Machine-Gun Battalion.
I was in the Seventh Infantry until June 1918. . . .

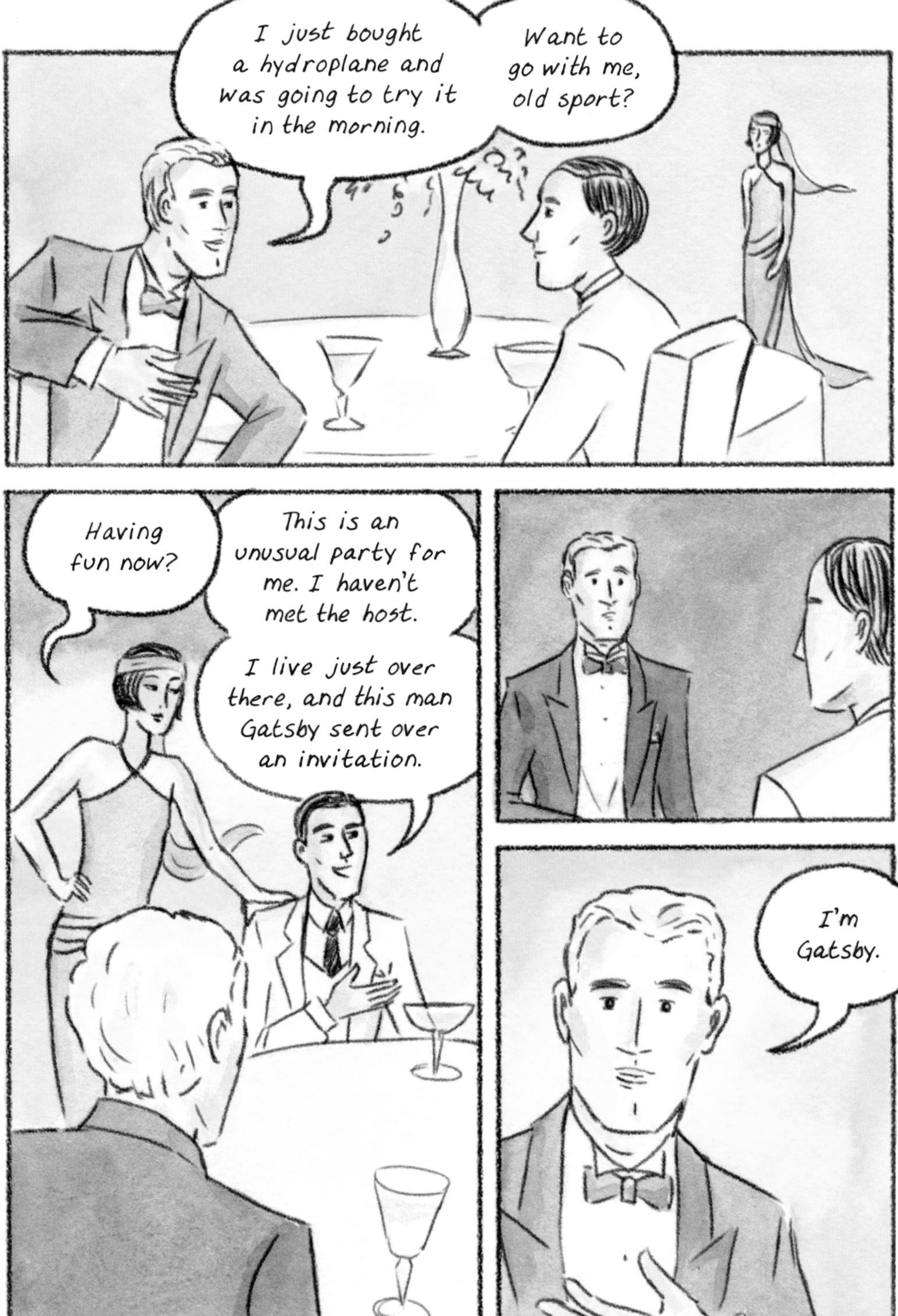
I just bought a hydroplane and was going to try it in the morning.
Want to go with me, old sport?
Having fun now?
This is an unusual party for me. I haven't met the host.
I live just over there, and this man Gatsby sent over an invitation.
I'm Gatsby.

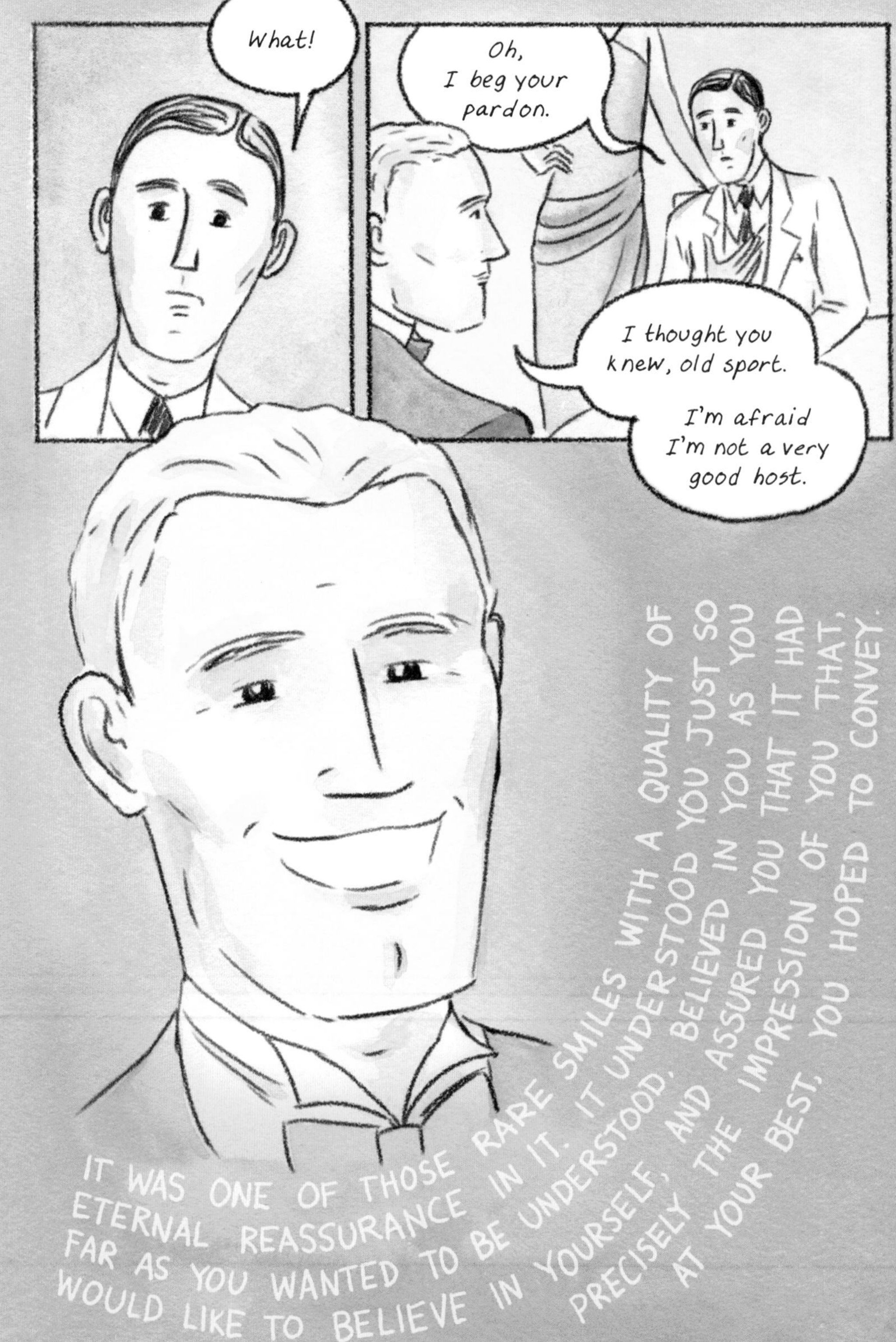
What!
Oh, I beg your pardon.
I thought you knew, old sport.
I'm afraid I'm not a very good host.
IT WAS ONE OF THOSE RARE SMILES WITH A QUALITY OF ETERNAL REASSURANCE IN IT. IT UNDERSTOOD YOU JUST SO FAR AS YOU WANTED TO BE UNDERSTOOD, BELIEVED IN YOU AS YOU WOULD LIKE TO BELIEVE IN YOURSELF, AND ASSURED YOU THAT IT HAD PRECISELY THE IMPRESSION OF YOU THAT, AT YOUR BEST, YOU HOPED TO CONVEY.

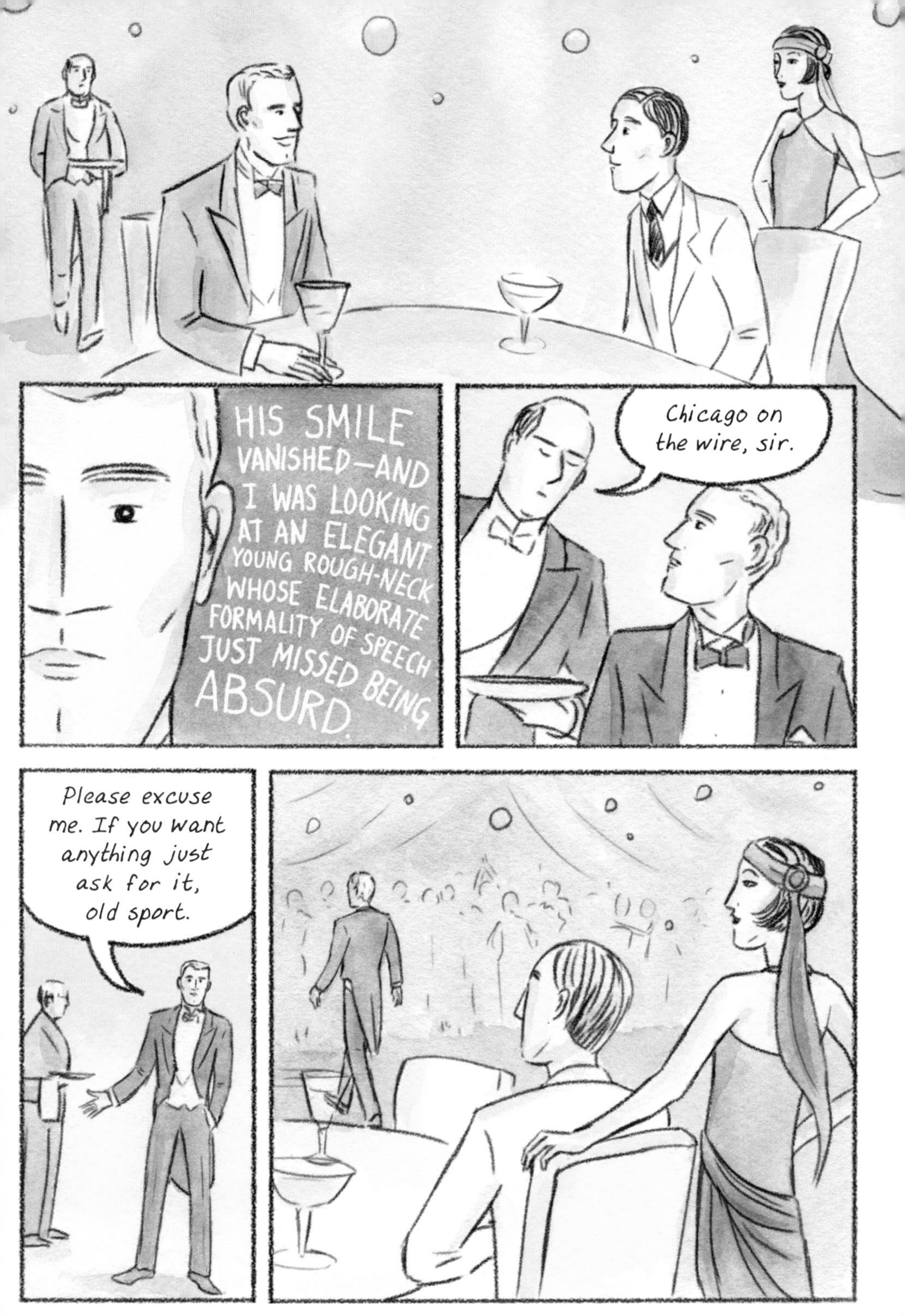

HIS SMILE VANISHED—AND I WAS LOOKING AT AN ELEGANT YOUNG ROUGH-NECK WHOSE ELABORATE FORMALITY OF SPEECH JUST MISSED BEING ABSURD.
Chicago on the wire, sir.
Please excuse me. If you want anything just ask for it, old sport.

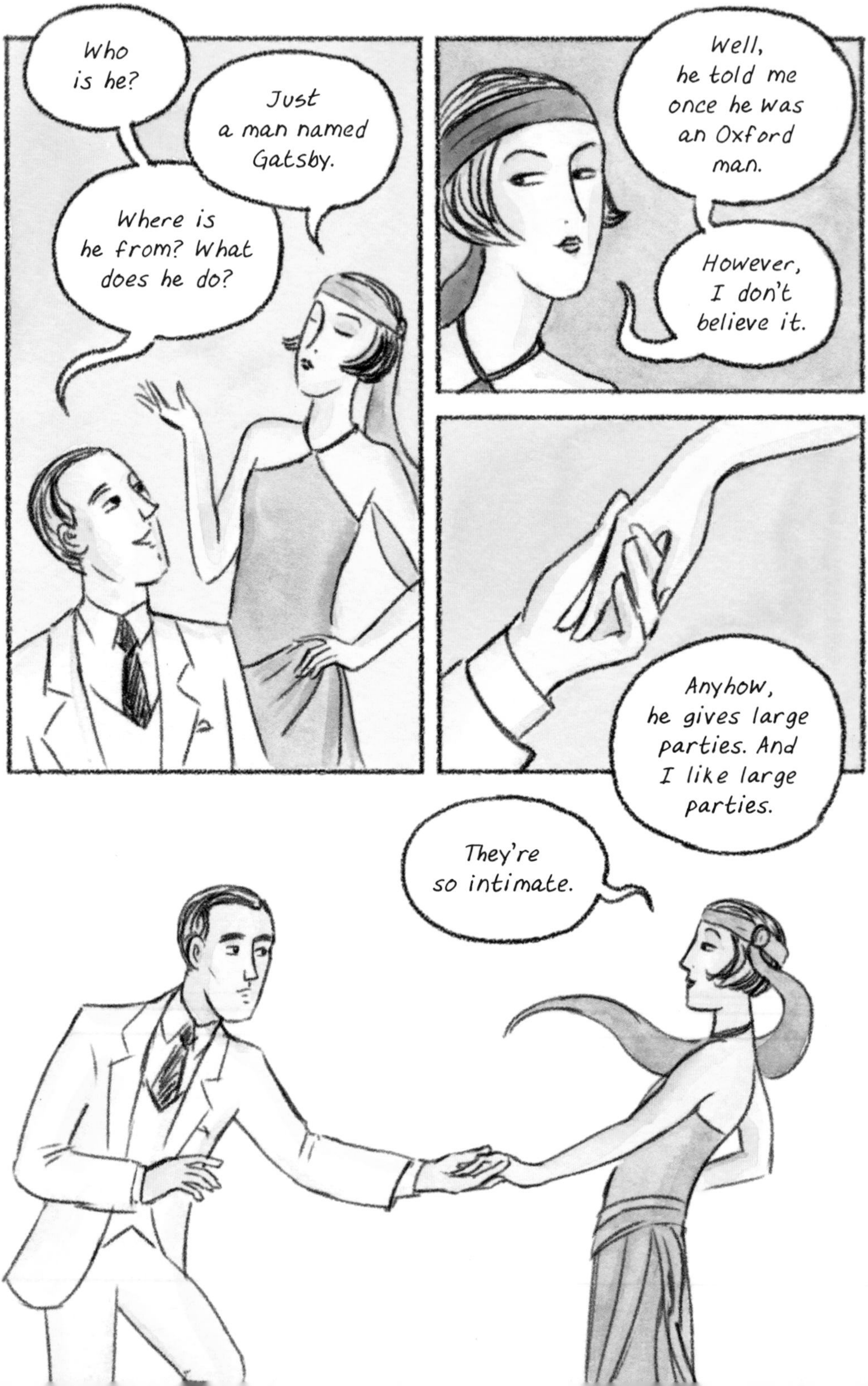
Who is he?
Just a man named Gatsby.
Where is he from? What does he do?
Well, he told me once he was an Oxford man.
However, I don't believe it.
Anyhow, he gives large parties. And I like large parties.
They're so intimate.

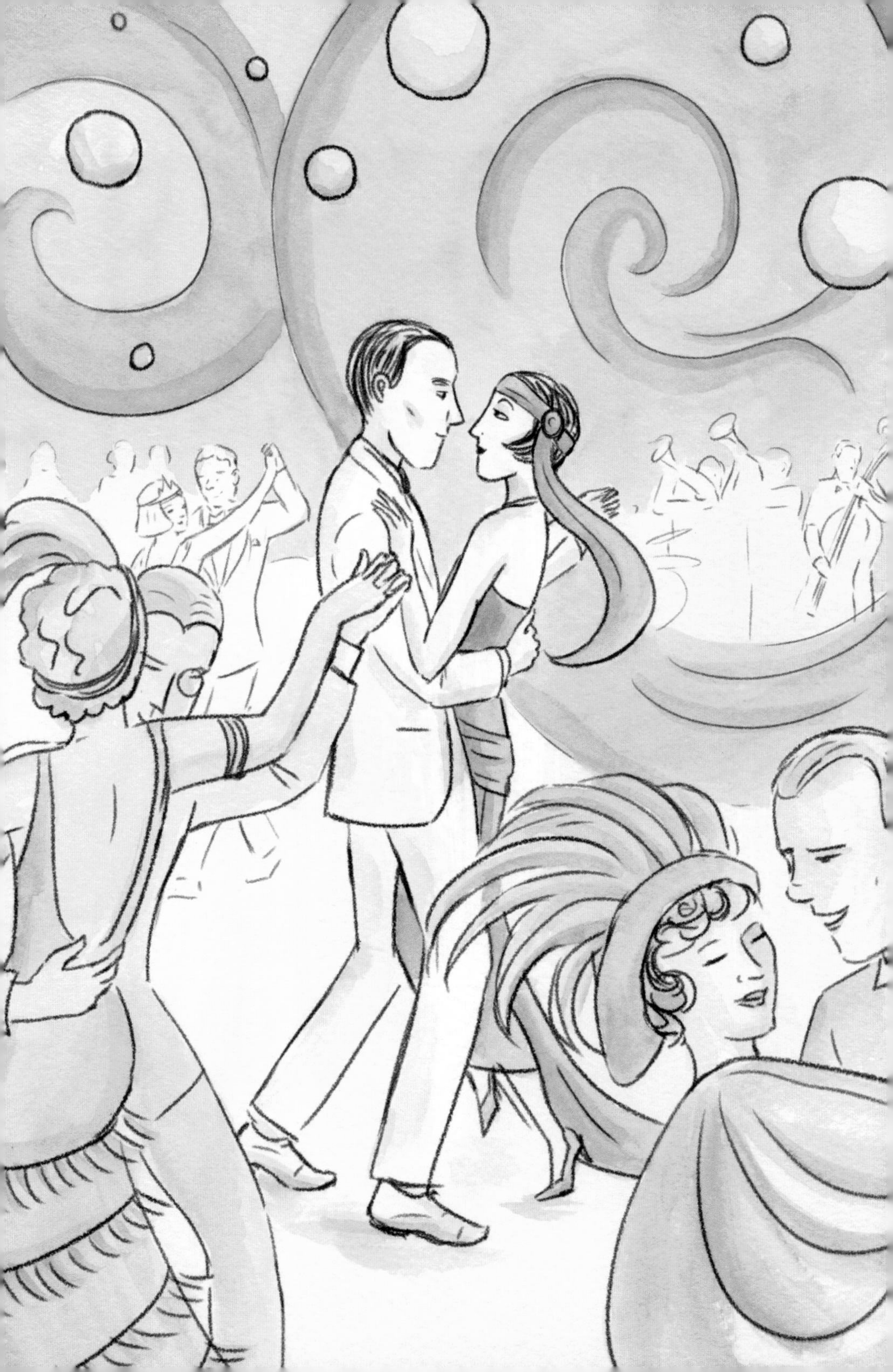

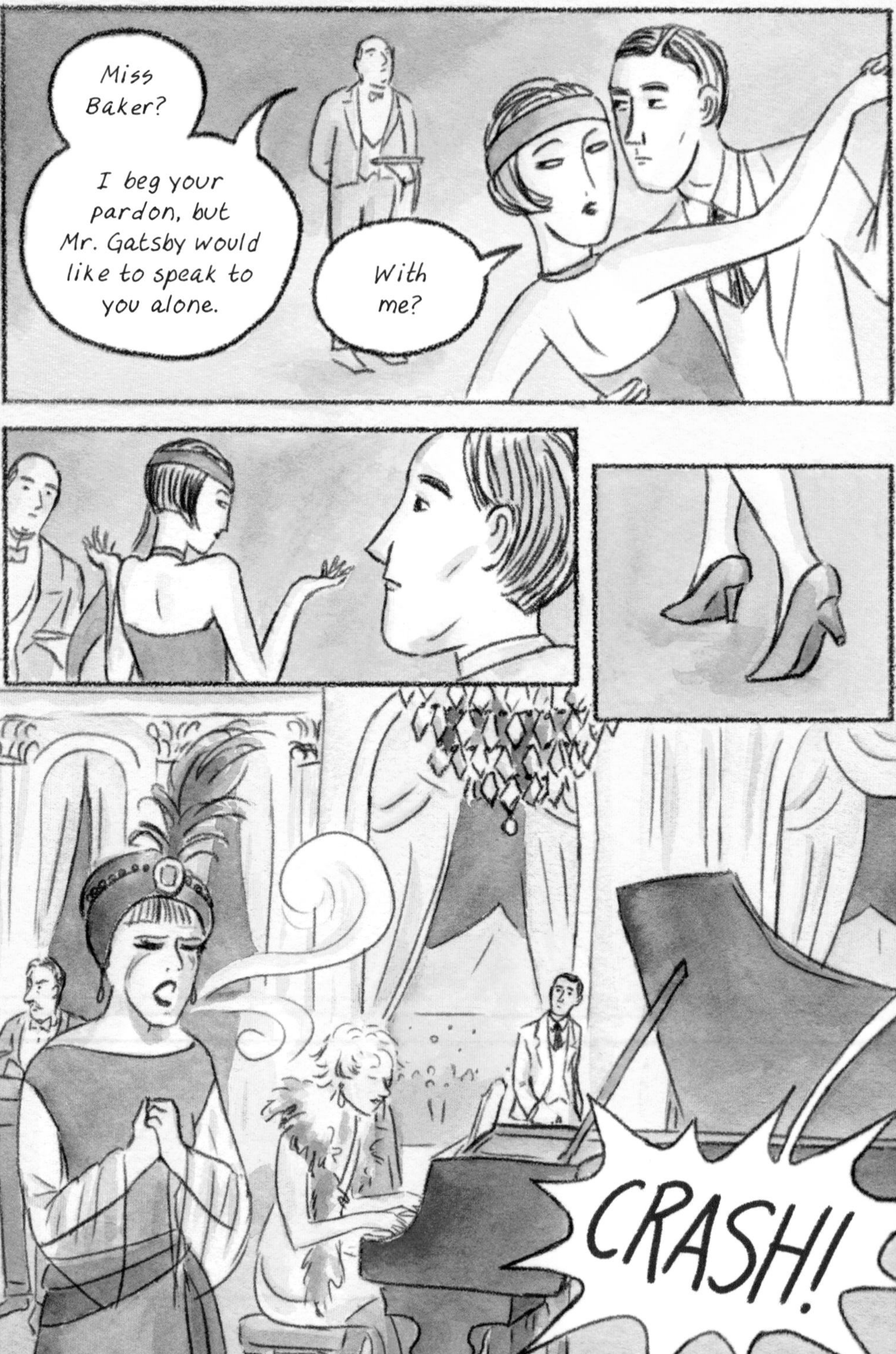
Miss Baker?
I beg your pardon, but Mr. Gatsby would like to speak to you alone.
With me?
CRASH!

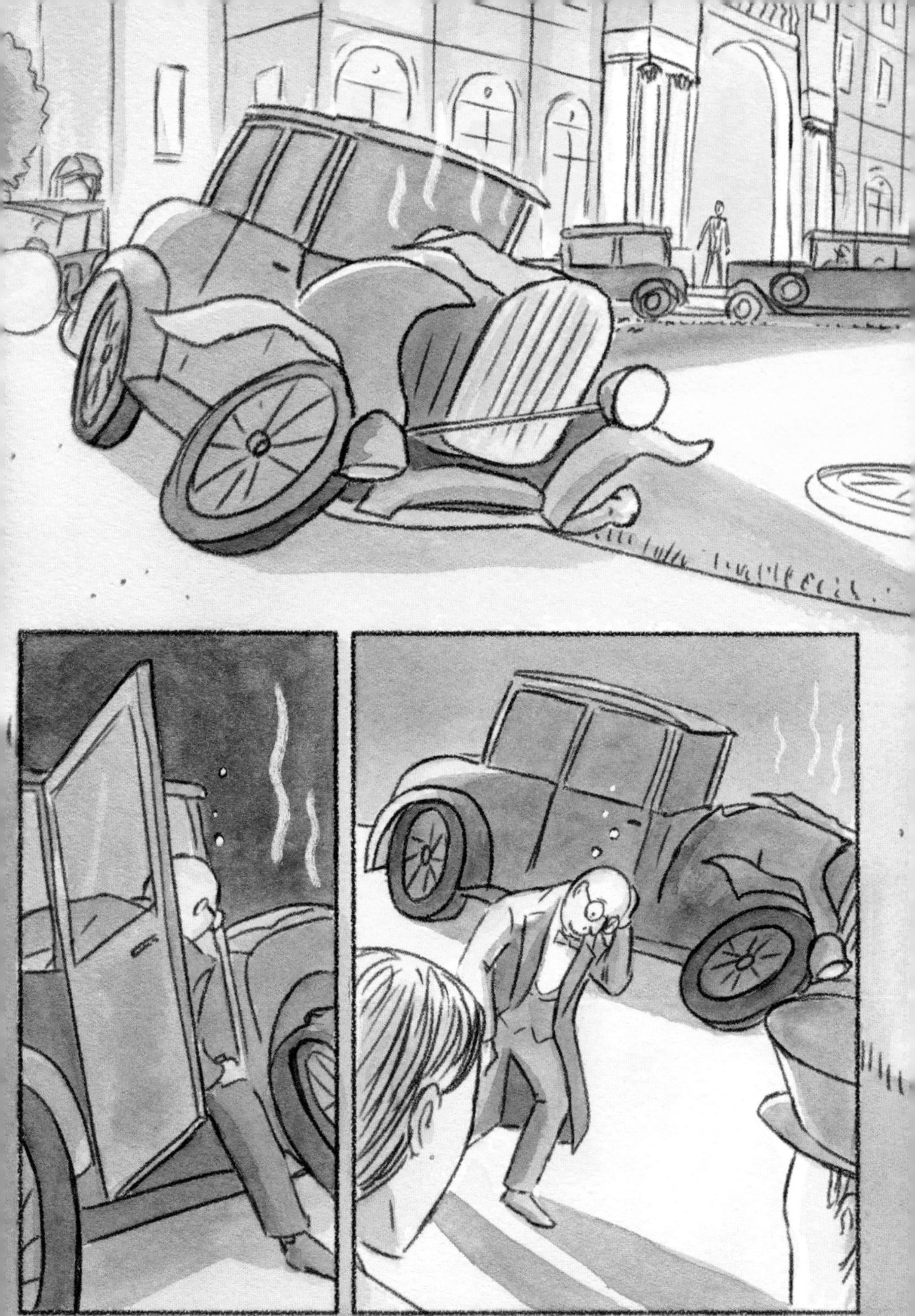

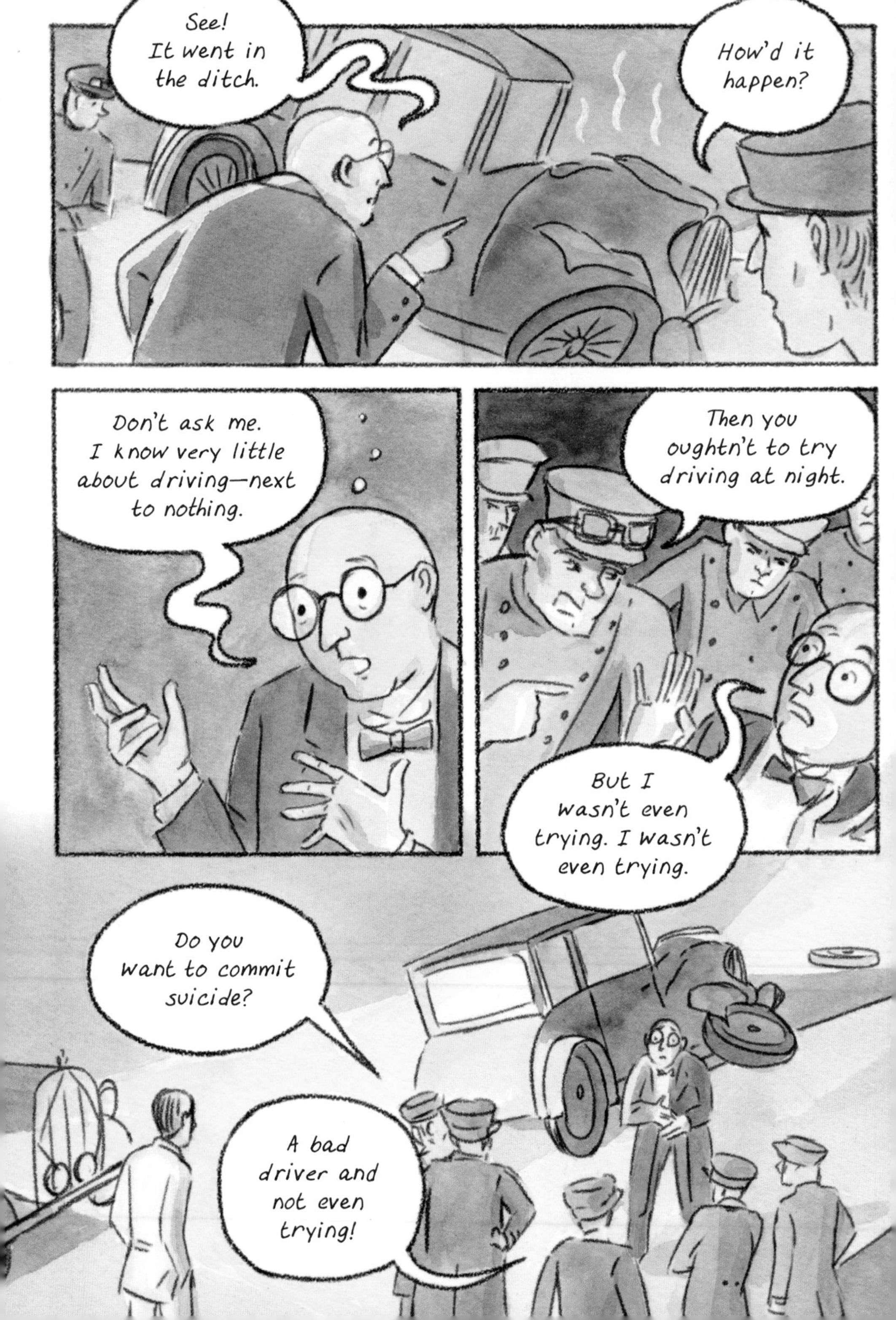
See! It went in the ditch.
How'd it happen?
Don't ask me. I know very little about driving—next to nothing.
Then you oughtn't to try driving at night.
But I wasn't even trying. I wasn't even trying.
Do you want to commit suicide?
A bad driver and not even trying!

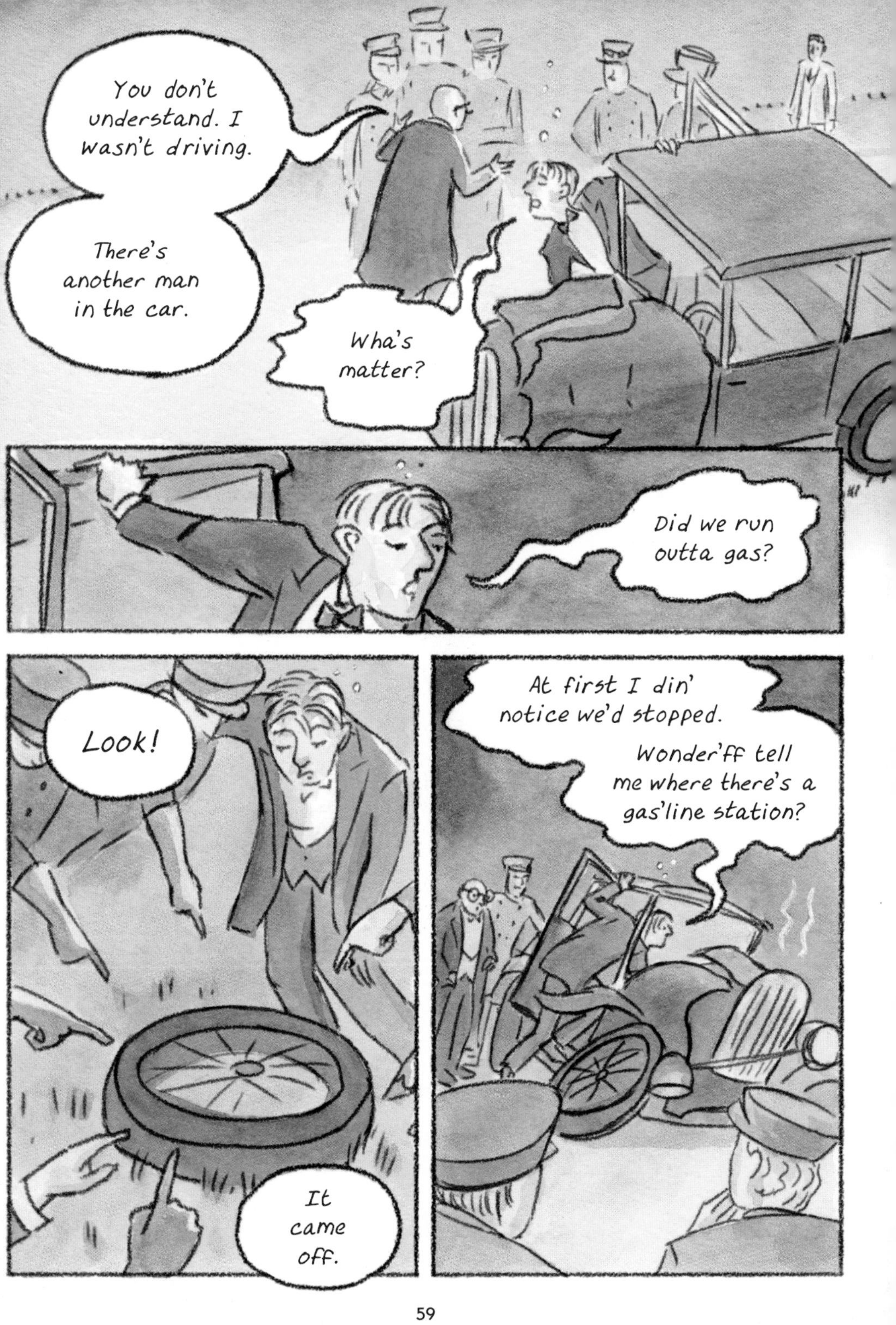
You don't understand. I wasn't driving.
There's another man in the car.
Wha's matter?
Did we run outta gas?
Look!
It came off.
At first I din' notice we'd stopped.
Wonder'ff tell me where there's a gas'line station?

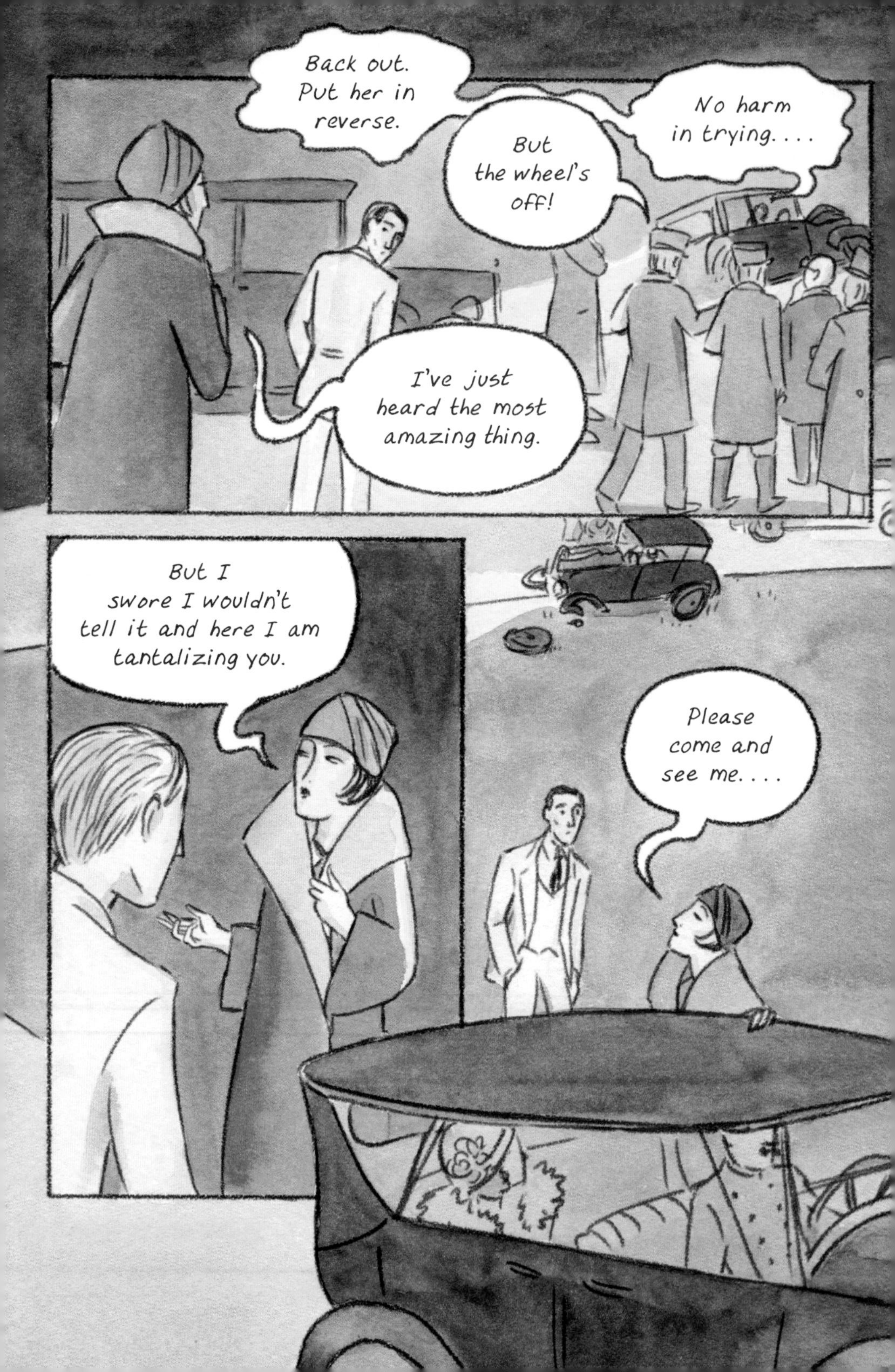
Back out. Put her in reverse.
But the wheel's off!
No harm in trying. . . .
I've just heard the most amazing thing.
But I swore I wouldn't tell it and here I am tantalizing you.
Please come and see me. . . .

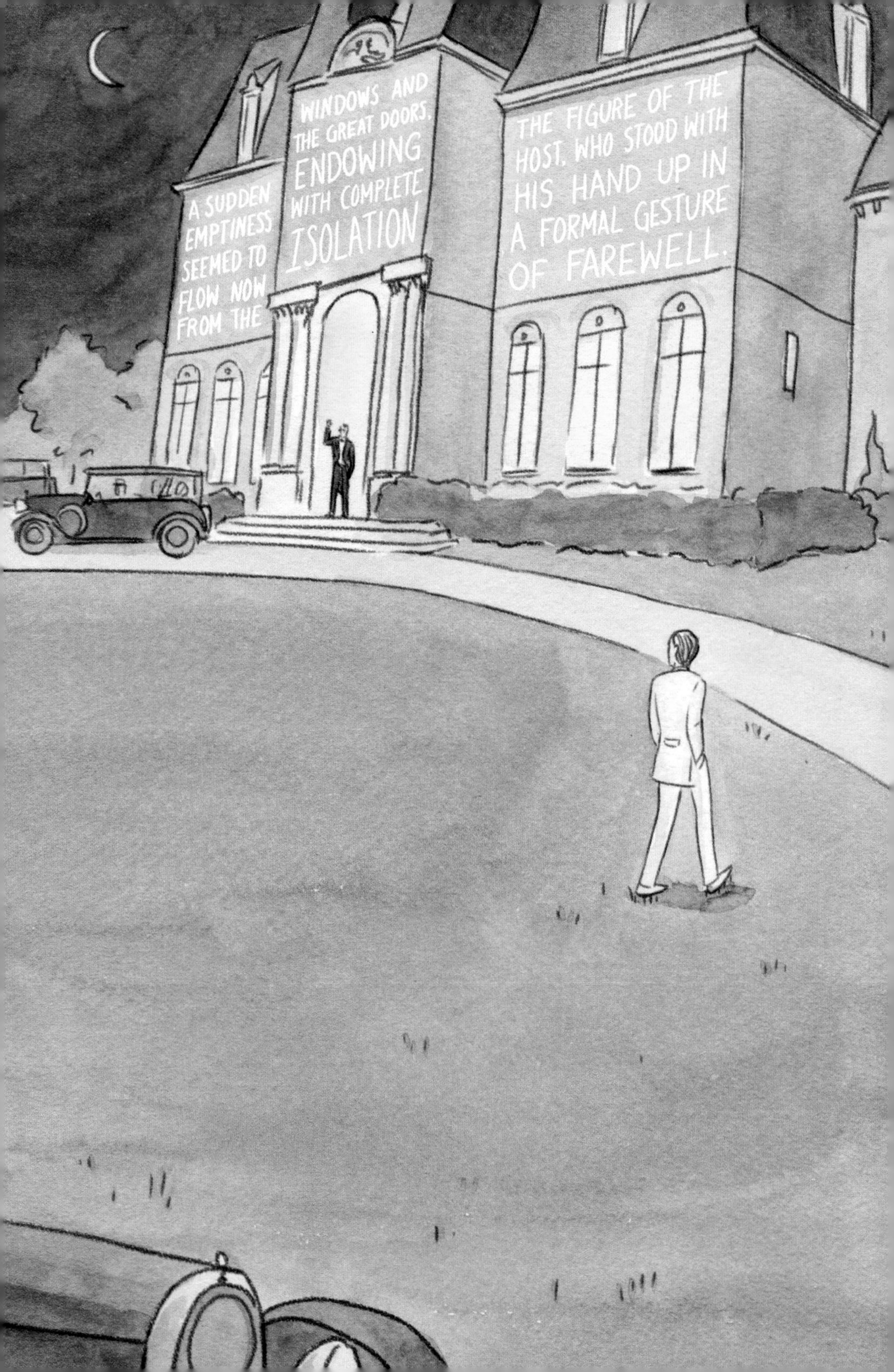
A SUDDEN EMPTINESS SEEMED TO FLOW NOW FROM THE
WINDOWS AND THE GREAT DOORS, ENDOWING WITH COMPLETE ISOLATION
THE FIGURE OF THE HOST, WHO STOOD WITH HIS HAND UP IN A FORMAL GESTURE OF FAREWELL.

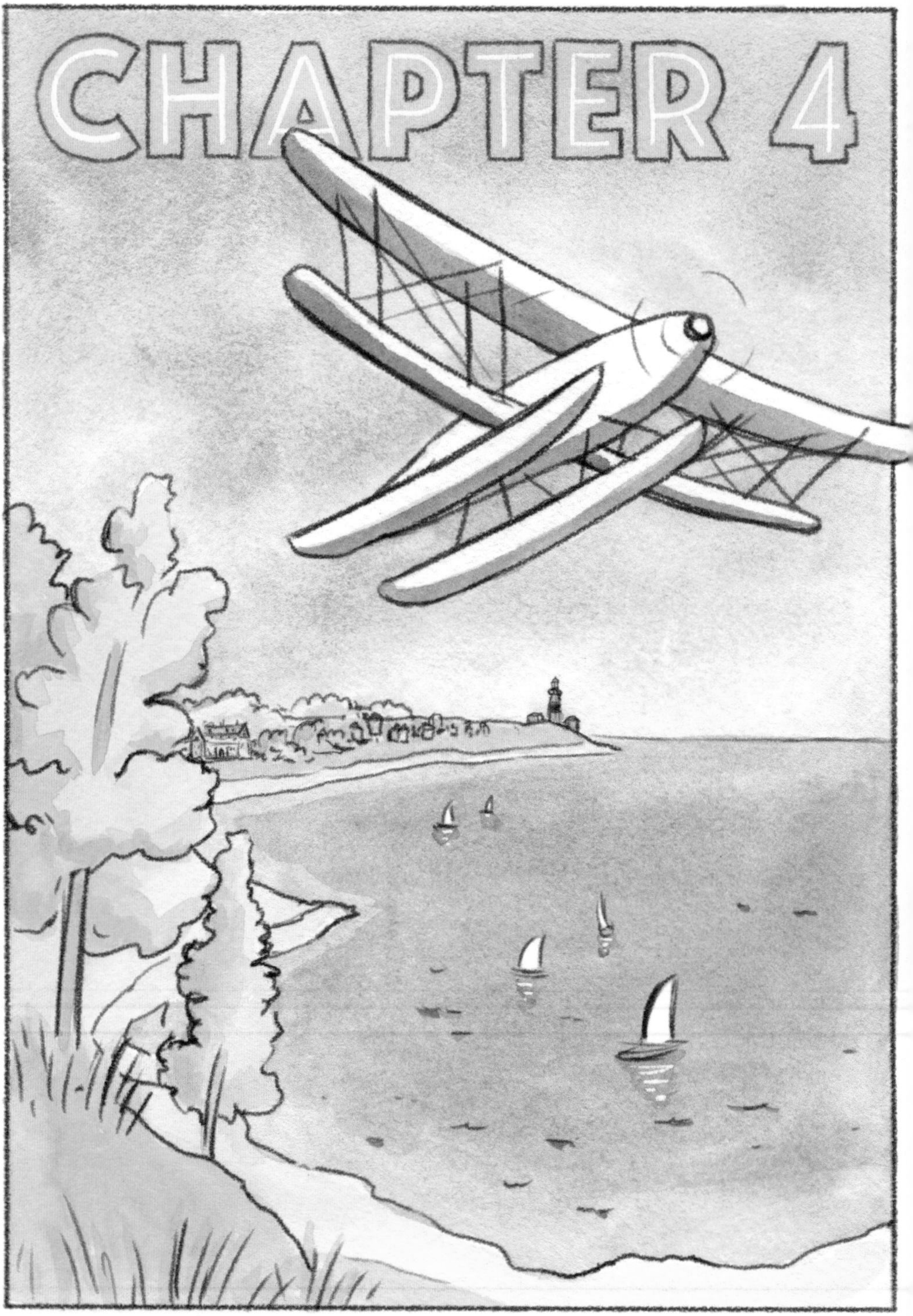
CHAPTER 4

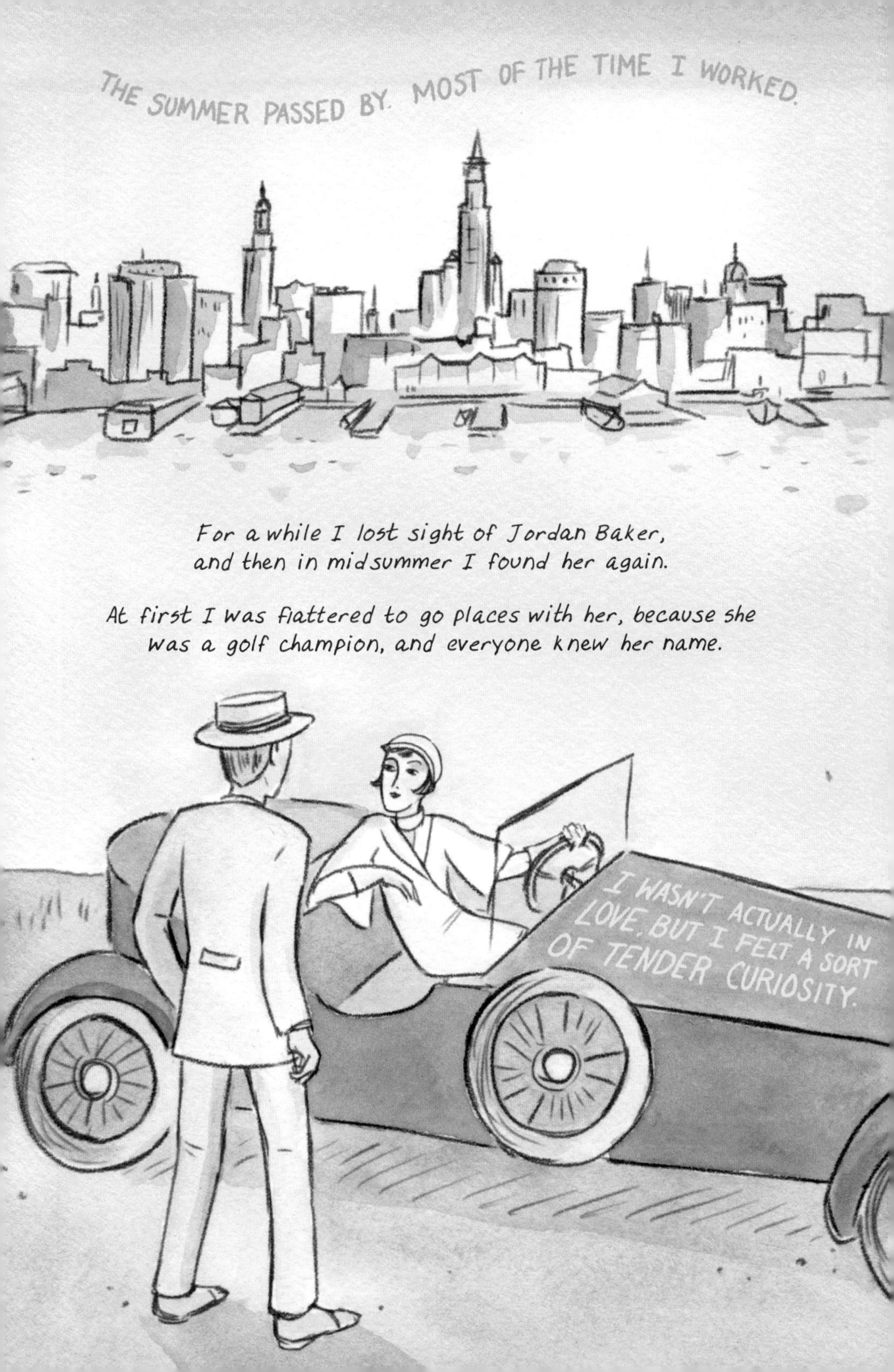
THE SUMMER PASSED BY. MOST OF THE TIME I WORKED.
For a while I lost sight of Jordan Baker, and then in midsummer I found her again.
At first I was flattered to go places with her, because she was a golf champion, and everyone knew her name.
I WASN'T ACTUALLY IN LOVE, BUT I FELT A SORT OF TENDER CURIOSITY.

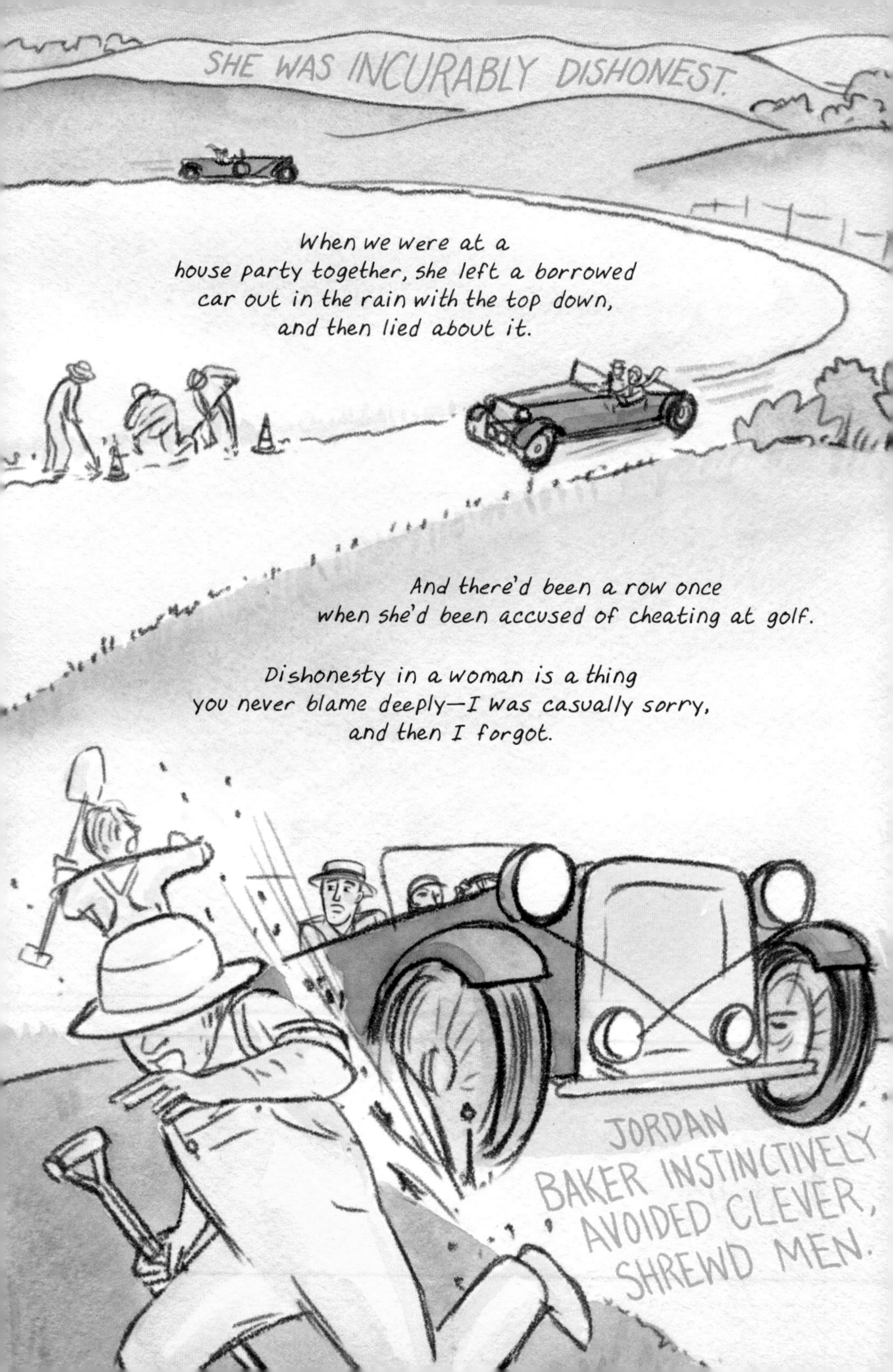
SHE WAS INCURABLY DISHONEST.
When we were at a house party together, she left a borrowed car out in the rain with the top down, and then lied about it.
And there'd been a row once when she'd been accused of cheating at golf.
Dishonesty in a woman is a thing you never blame deeply—I was casually sorry, and then I forgot.
JORDAN BAKER INSTINCTIVELY AVOIDED CLEVER, SHREWD MEN.

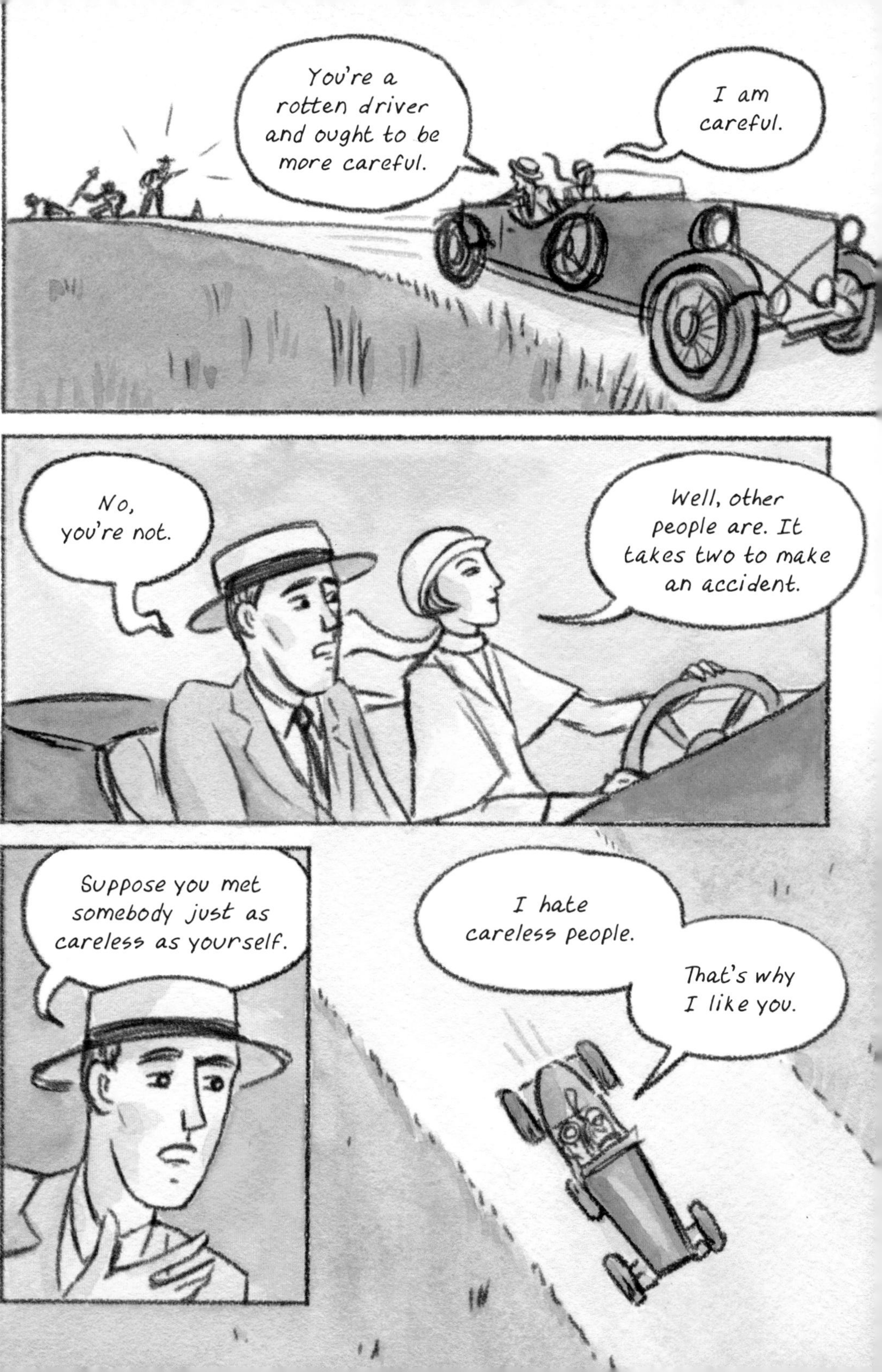
You're a rotten driver and ought to be more careful.
I am careful.
No, you're not.
Well, other people are. It takes two to make an accident.
Suppose you met somebody just as careless as yourself.
I hate careless people.
That's why I like you.

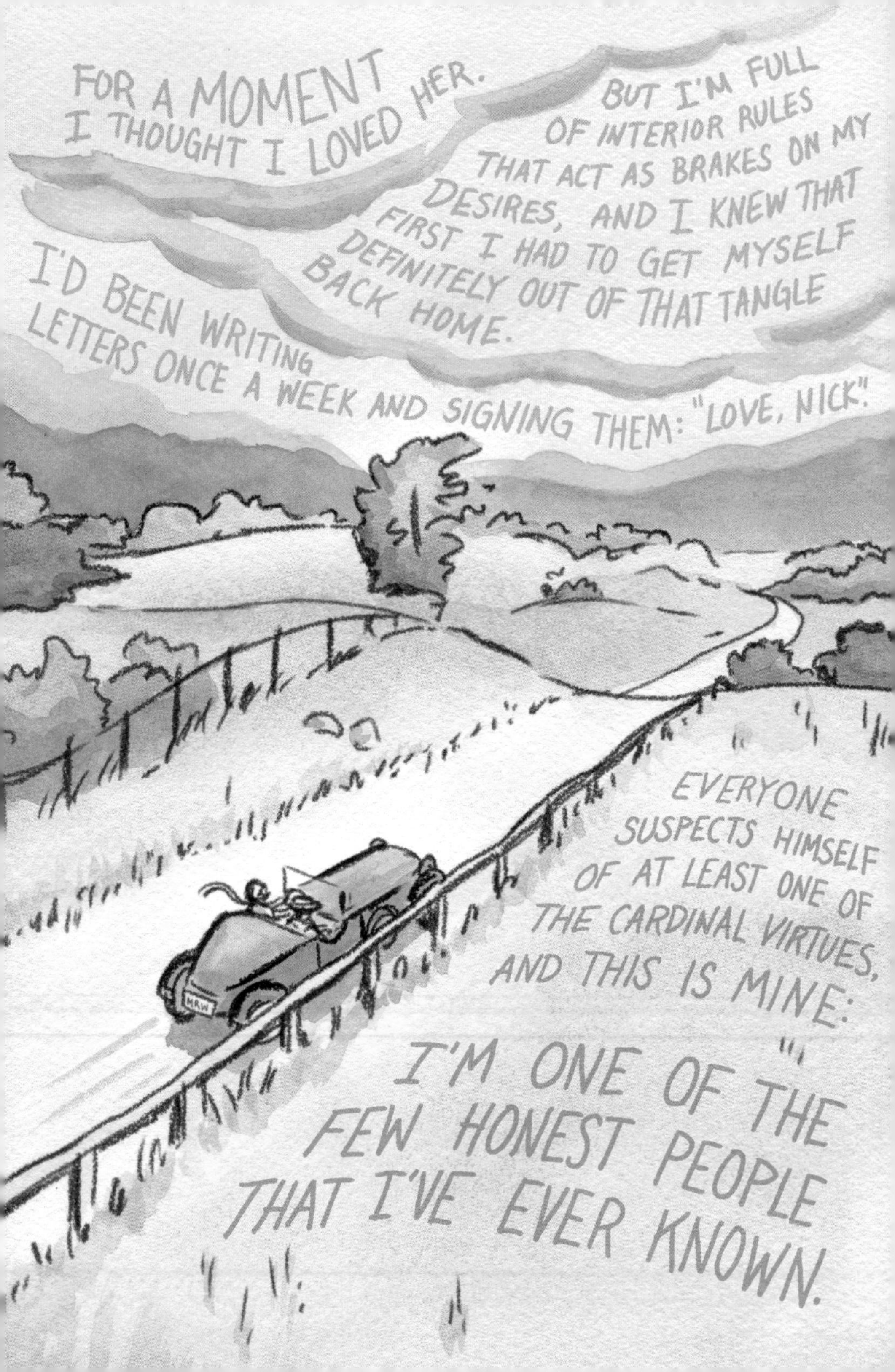
FOR A MOMENT I THOUGHT I LOVED HER.
BUT I'M FULL OF INTERIOR RULES THAT ACT AS BRAKES ON MY DESIRES, AND I KNEW THAT FIRST I HAD TO GET MYSELF DEFINITELY OUT OF THAT TANGLE BACK HOME.
I'D BEEN WRITING LETTERS ONCE A WEEK AND SIGNING THEM: "LOVE, NICK."
MRW
EVERYONE SUSPECTS HIMSELF OF AT LEAST ONE OF THE CARDINAL VIRTUES, AND THIS IS MINE:
"I'M ONE OF THE FEW HONEST PEOPLE THAT I'VE EVER KNOWN."

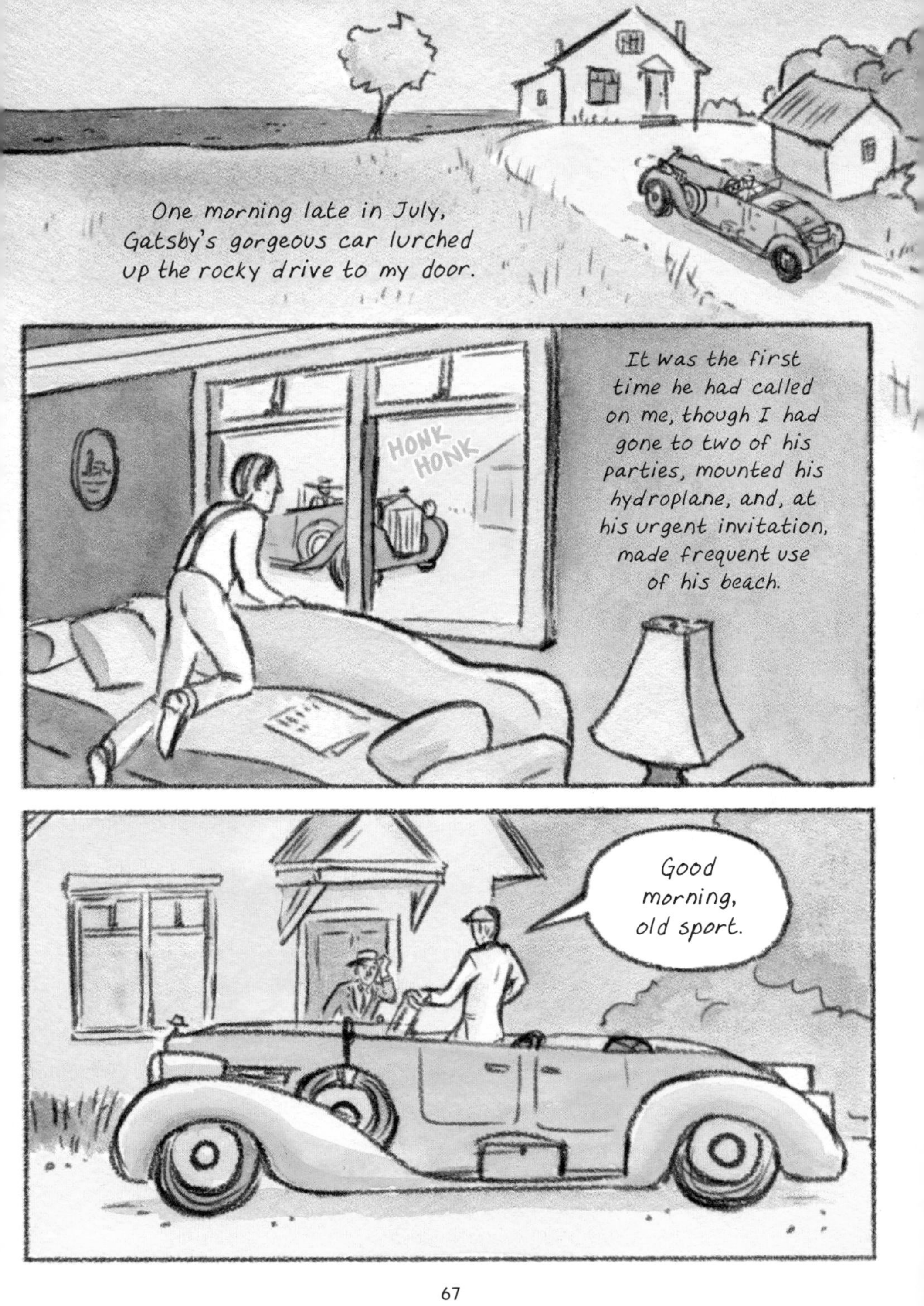
One morning late in July, Gatsby's gorgeous car lurched up the rocky drive to my door.
It was the first time he had called on me, though I had gone to two of his parties, mounted his hydroplane, and, at his urgent invitation, made frequent use of his beach.
HONK HONK
Good morning, old sport.

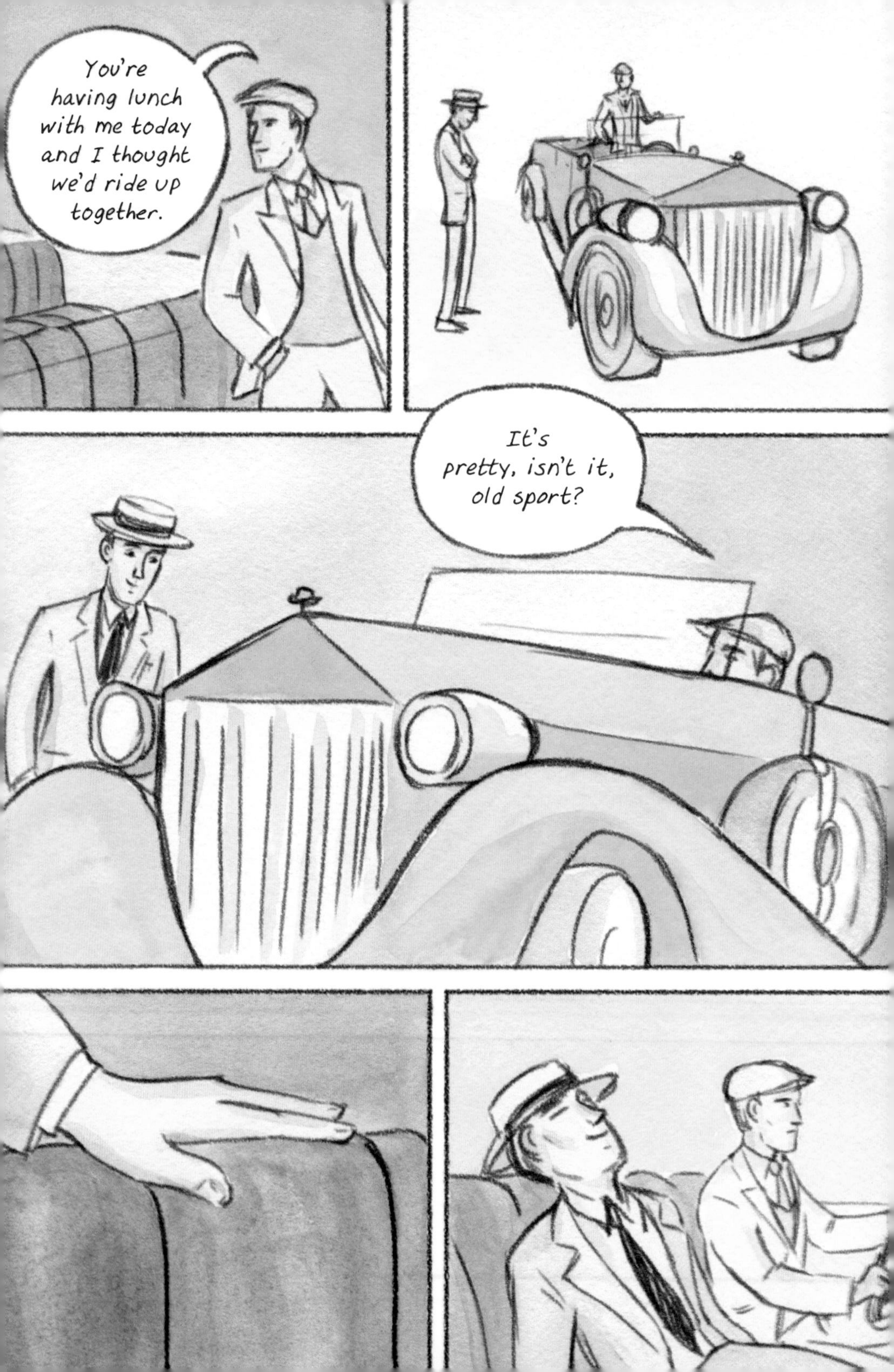
You're having lunch with me today and I thought we'd ride up together.
It's pretty, isn't it, old sport?

I HAD TALKED WITH HIM PERHAPS HALF A DOZEN TIMES IN THE PAST MONTH AND FOUND, TO MY DISAPPOINTMENT, THAT HE HAD LITTLE TO SAY.

HE HAD BECOME SIMPLY THE PROPRIETOR OF AN ELABORATE ROADHOUSE NEXT DOOR.

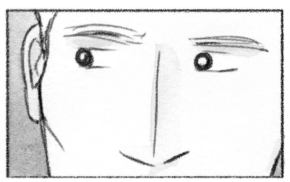

Look here, old sport. What's your opinion of me, anyhow?

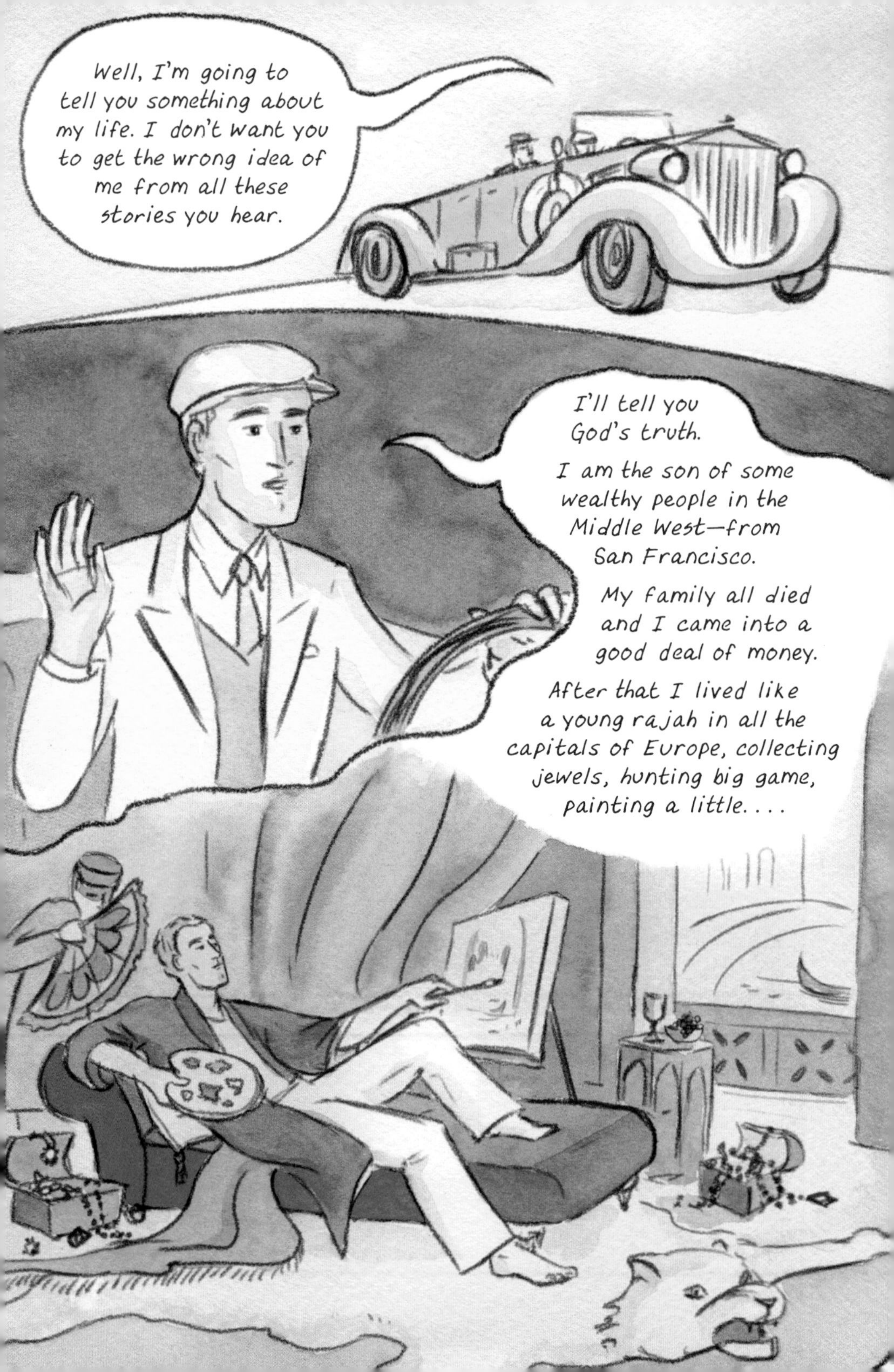
Well, I'm going to tell you something about my life. I don't want you to get the wrong idea of me from all these stories you hear.
I'll tell you God's truth.
I am the son of some wealthy people in the Middle West—from San Francisco.
My family all died and I came into a good deal of money.
After that I lived like a young rajah in all the capitals of Europe, collecting jewels, hunting big game, painting a little. . .

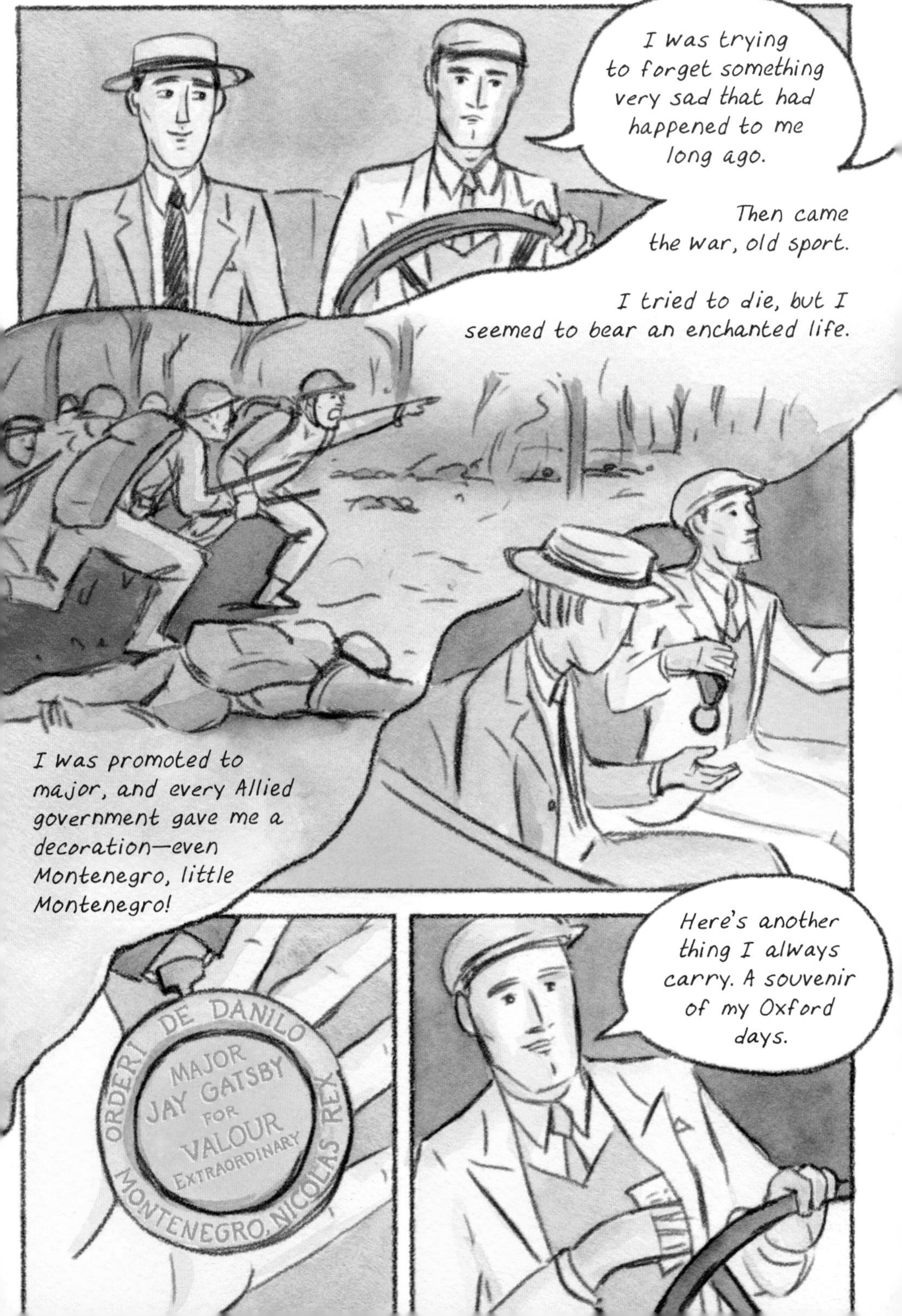
I was trying to forget something very sad that had happened to me long ago.
Then came the war, old sport.
I tried to die, but I seemed to bear an enchanted life.
I was promoted to major, and every Allied government gave me a decoration—even Montenegro, little Montenegro!
ORDERI DE DANILO MONTENEGRO, NICOLAS REX
MAJOR JAY GATSBY FOR VALOUR EXTRAORDINARY
Here's another thing I always carry. A souvenir of my Oxford days.

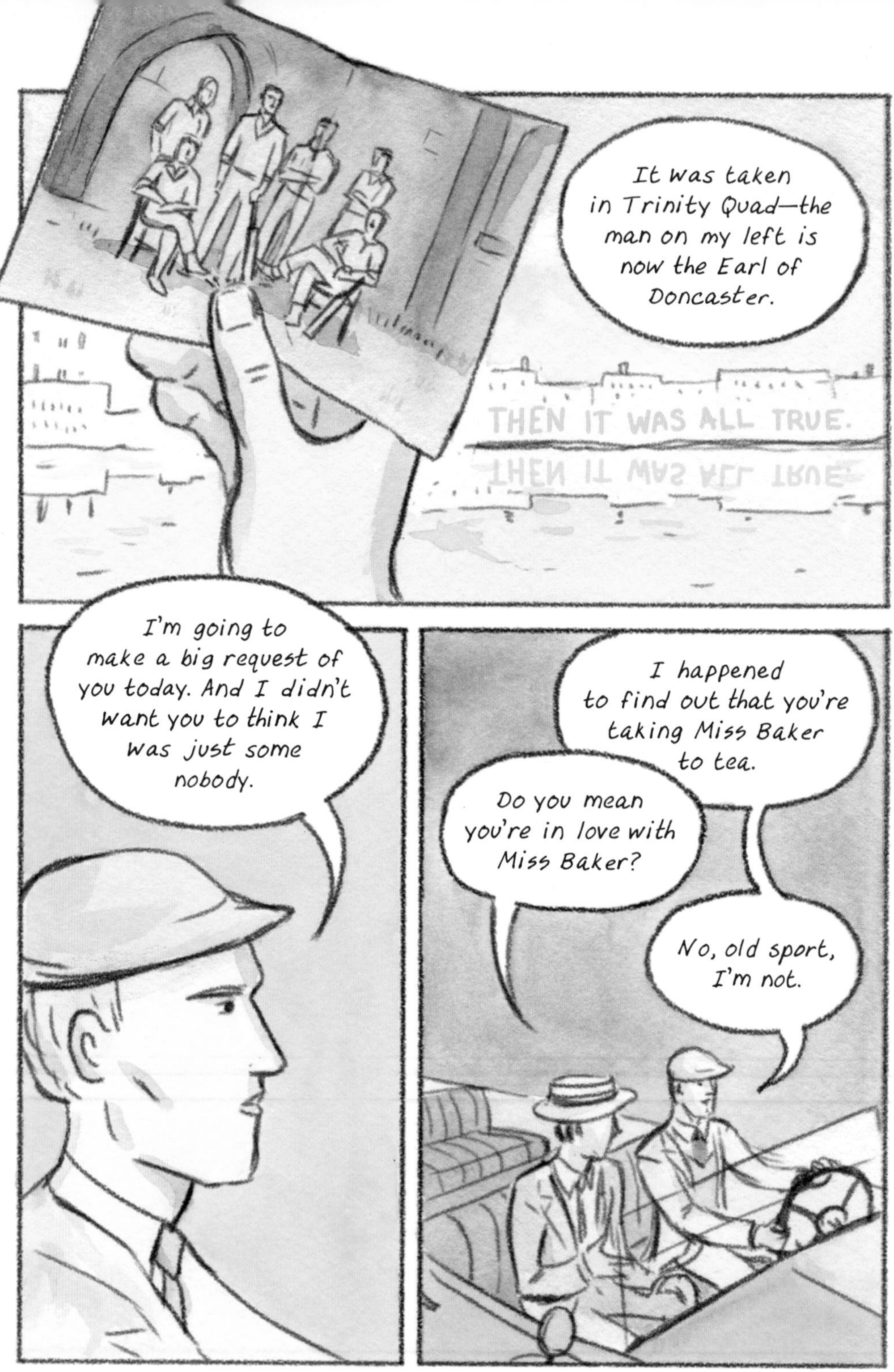
It was taken in Trinity Quad—the man on my left is now the Earl of Doncaster.
THEN IT WAS ALL TRUE.
I'm going to make a big request of you today. And I didn't want you to think I was just some nobody.
I happened to find out that you're taking Miss Baker to tea.
Do you mean you're in love with Miss Baker?
No, old sport, I'm not.

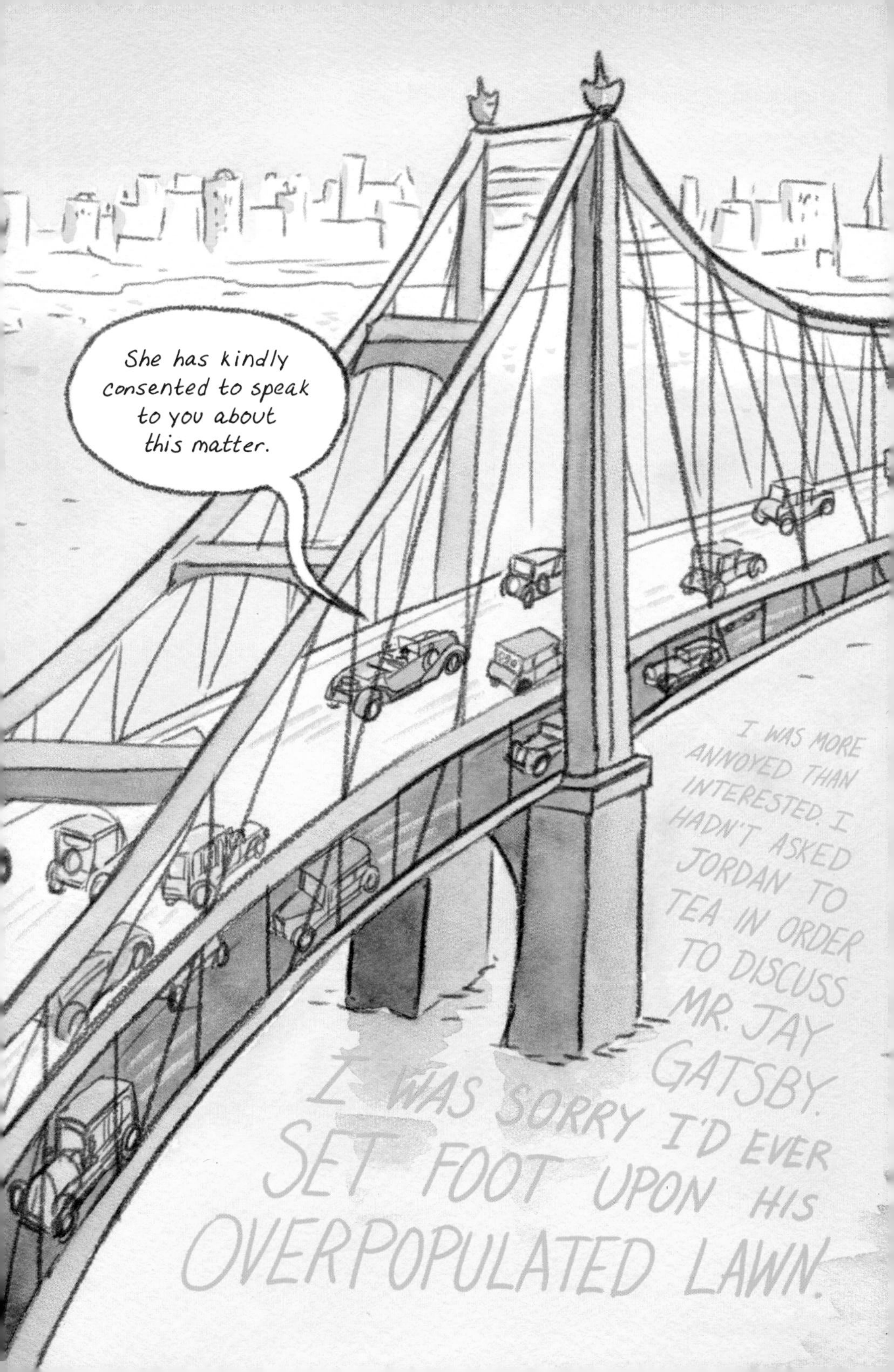
She has kindly consented to speak to you about this matter.
I WAS MORE ANNOYED THAN INTERESTED. I HADN'T ASKED JORDAN TO TEA IN ORDER TO DISCUSS MR. JAY GATSBY.
I WAS SORRY I'D EVER SET FOOT UPON HIS OVERPOPULATED LAWN.

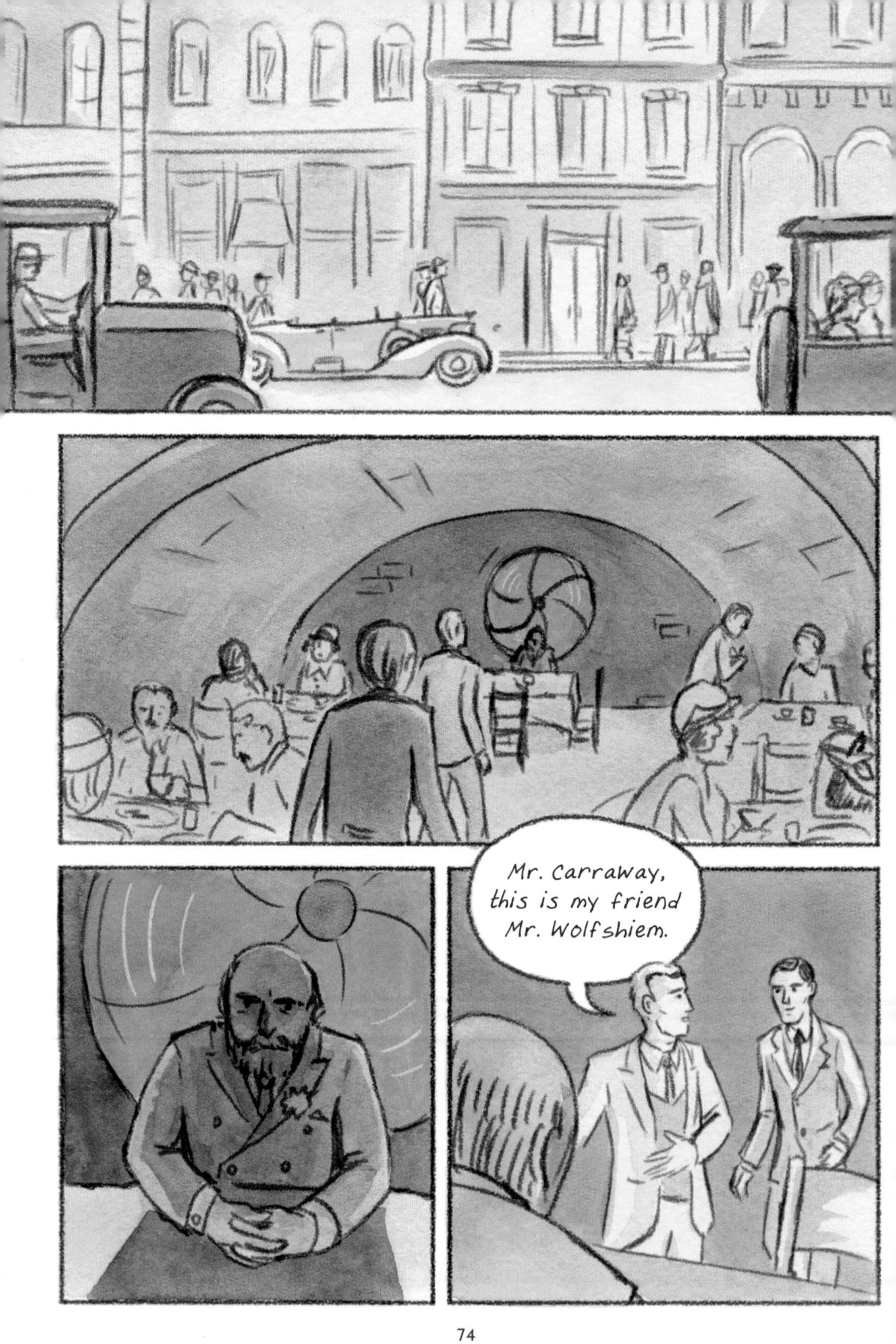
Mr. Carraway, this is my friend Mr. Wolfshiem.

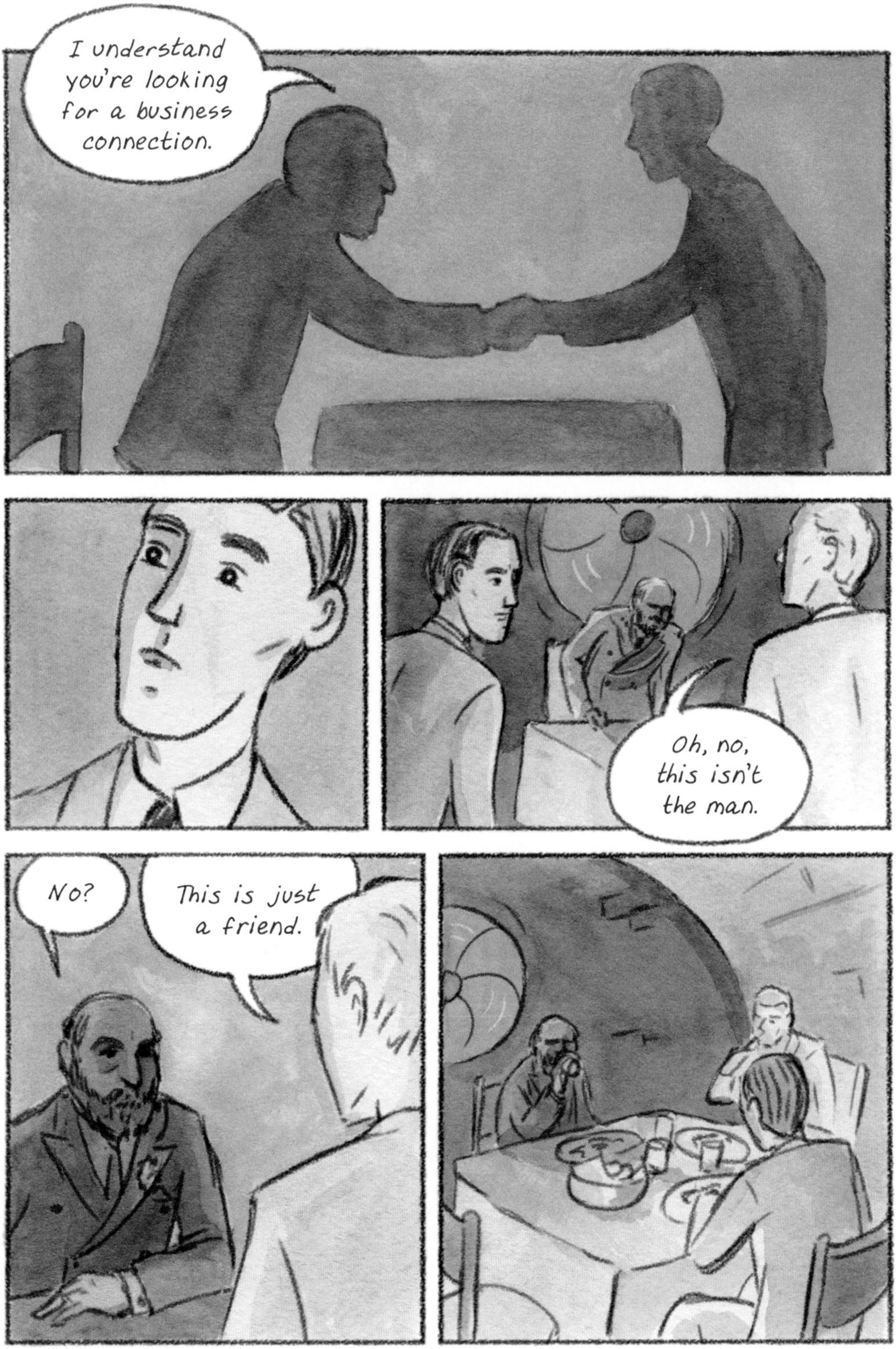
I understand you're looking for a business connection.
Oh, no, this isn't the man.
No?
This is just a friend.

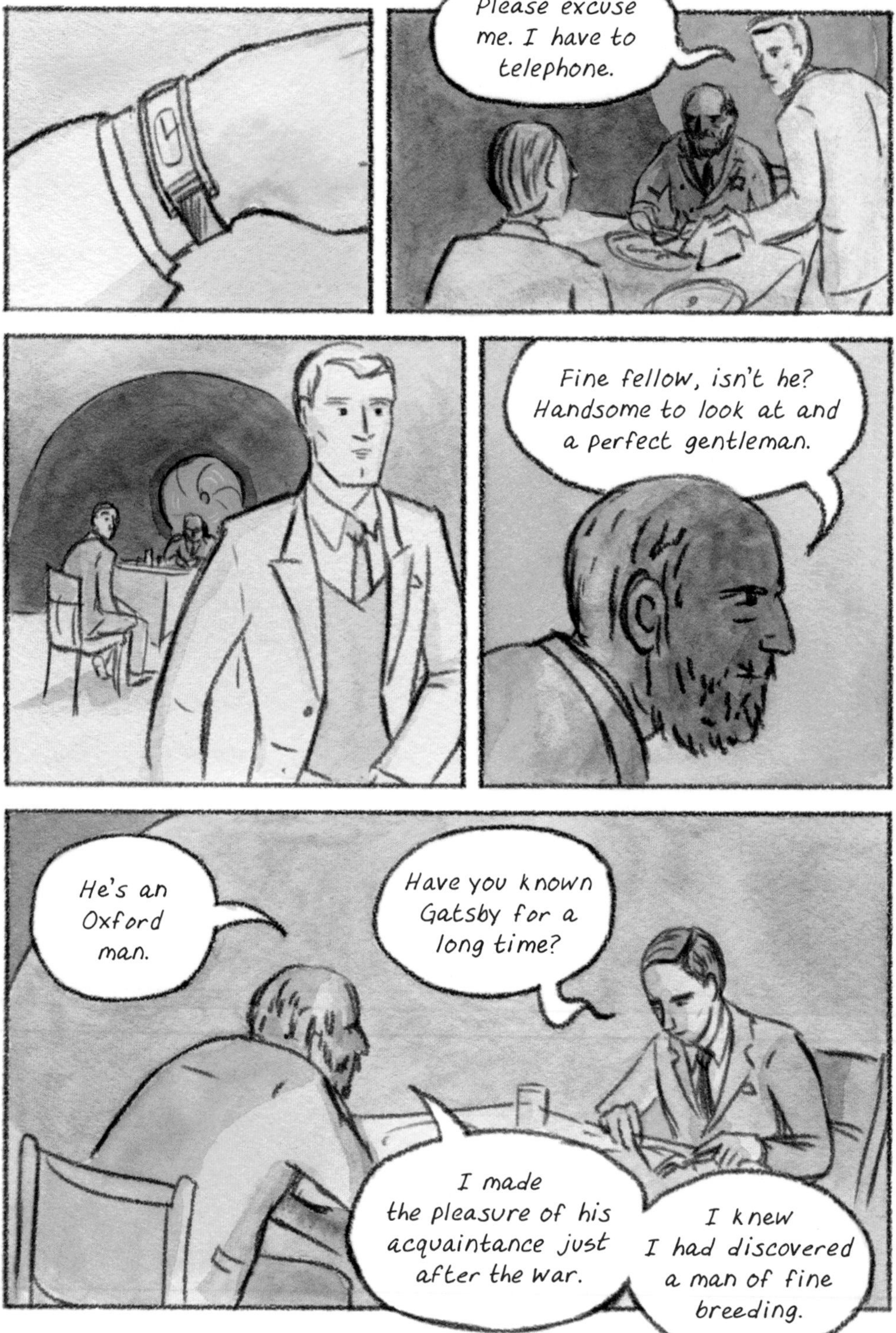
Please excuse me. I have to telephone.
Fine fellow, isn't he? Handsome to look at and a perfect gentleman.
He's an Oxford man.
Have you known Gatsby for a long time?
I made the pleasure of his acquaintance just after the war.
I knew I had discovered a man of fine breeding.

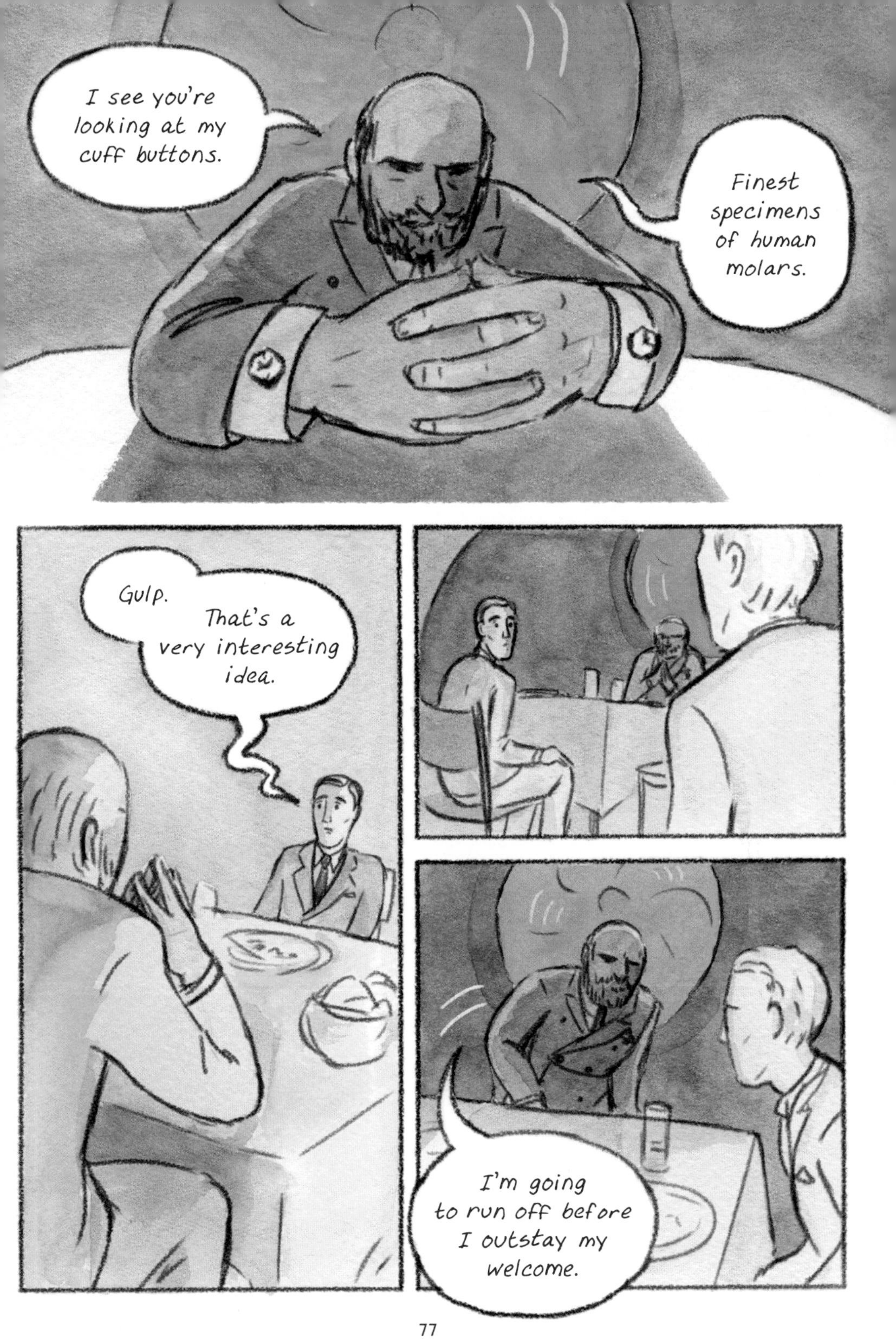
I see you're looking at my cuff buttons.
Finest specimens of human molars.
Gulp.
That's a very interesting idea.
I'm going to run off before I outstay my welcome.

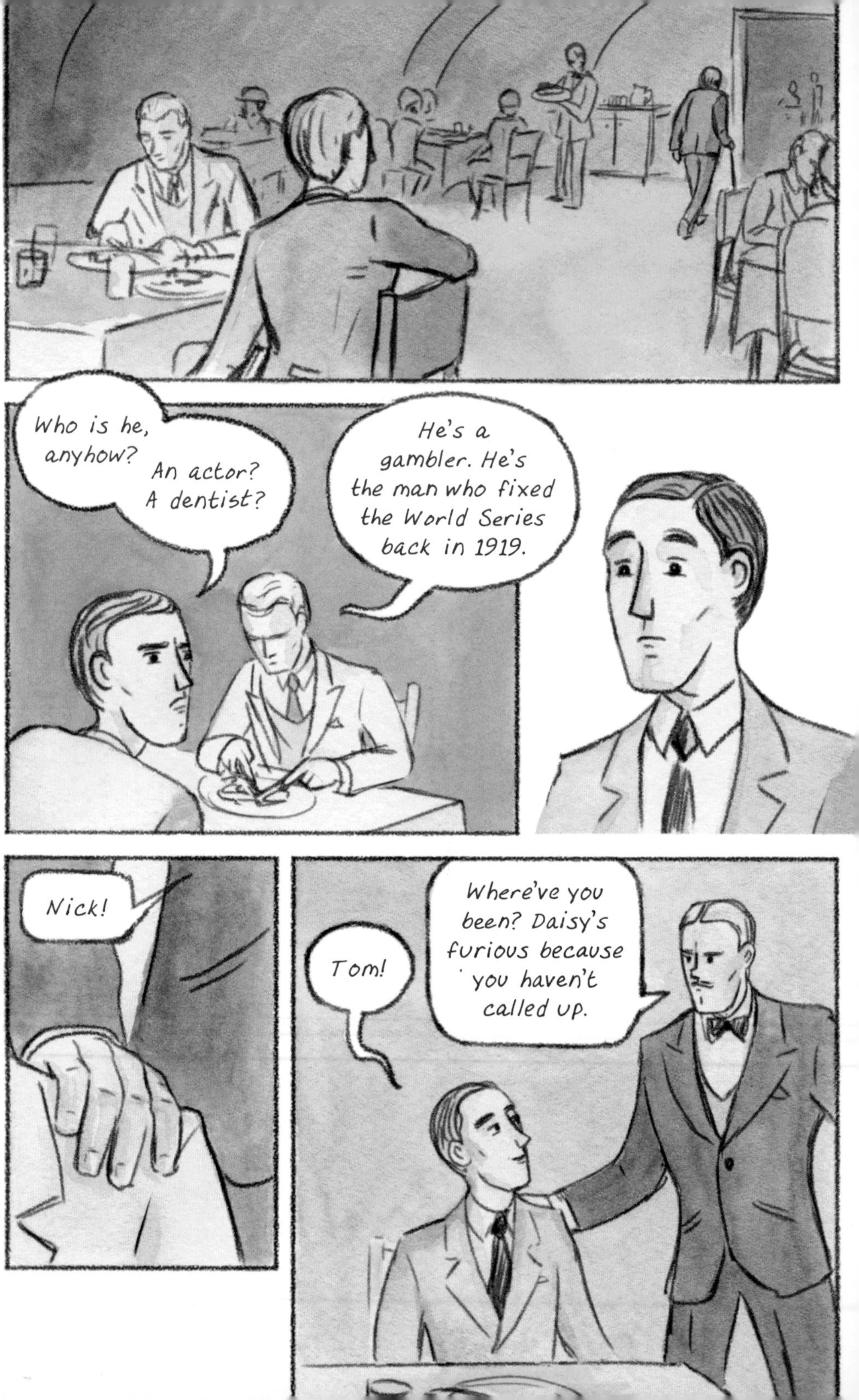
Who is he, anyhow?
An actor? A dentist?
He's a gambler. He's the man who fixed the World Series back in 1919.
Nick!
Tom!
Where've you been? Daisy's furious because you haven't called up.

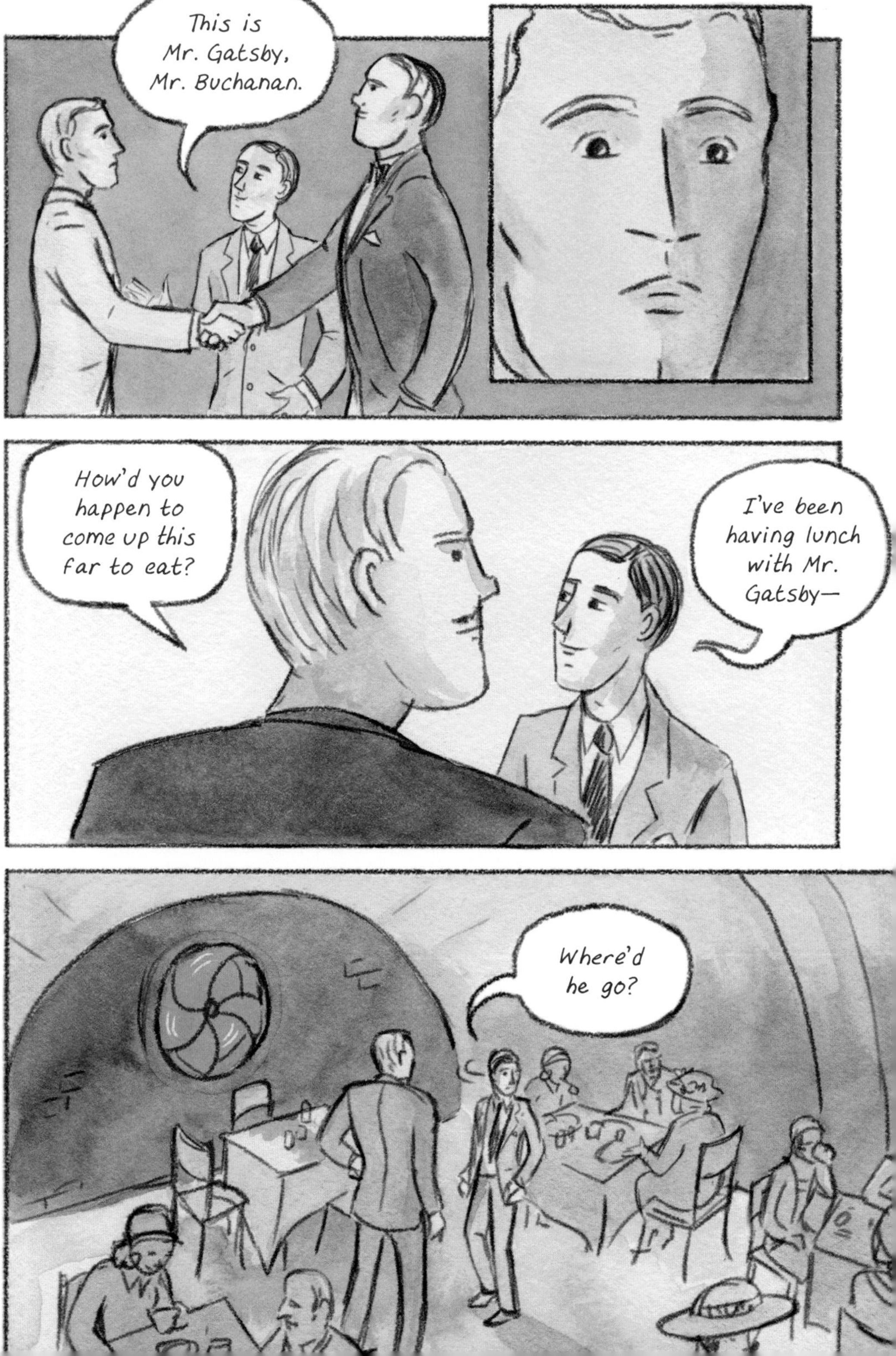
This is Mr. Gatsby, Mr. Buchanan.
How'd you happen to come up this far to eat?
I've been having lunch with Mr. Gatsby—
Where'd he go?

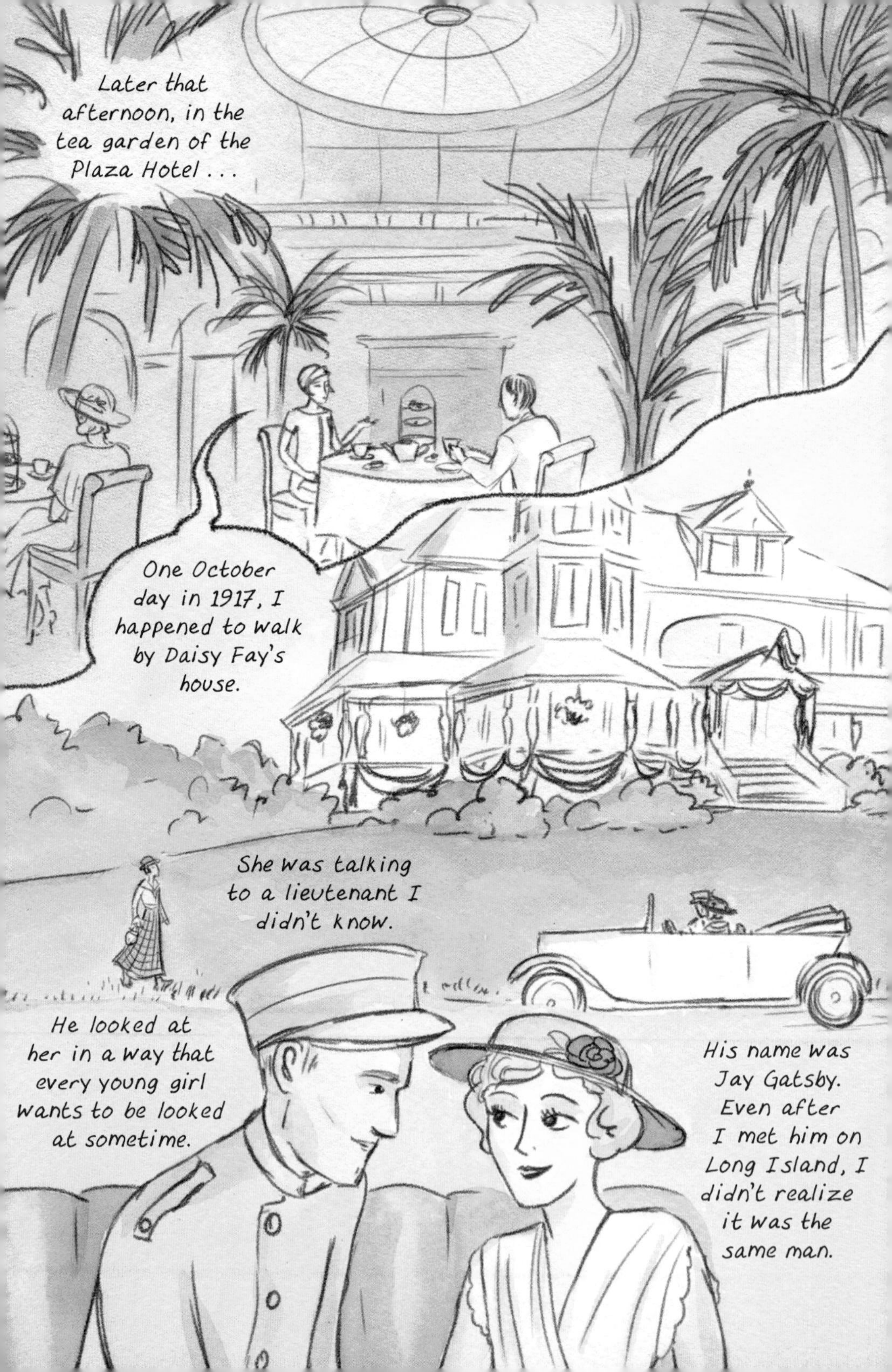

Later that afternoon, in the tea garden of the Plaza Hotel . . .
One October day in 1917, I happened to walk by Daisy Fay's house.
She was talking to a lieutenant I didn't know.
He looked at her in a way that every young girl wants to be looked at sometime.
His name was Jay Gatsby. Even after I met him on Long Island, I didn't realize it was the same man.

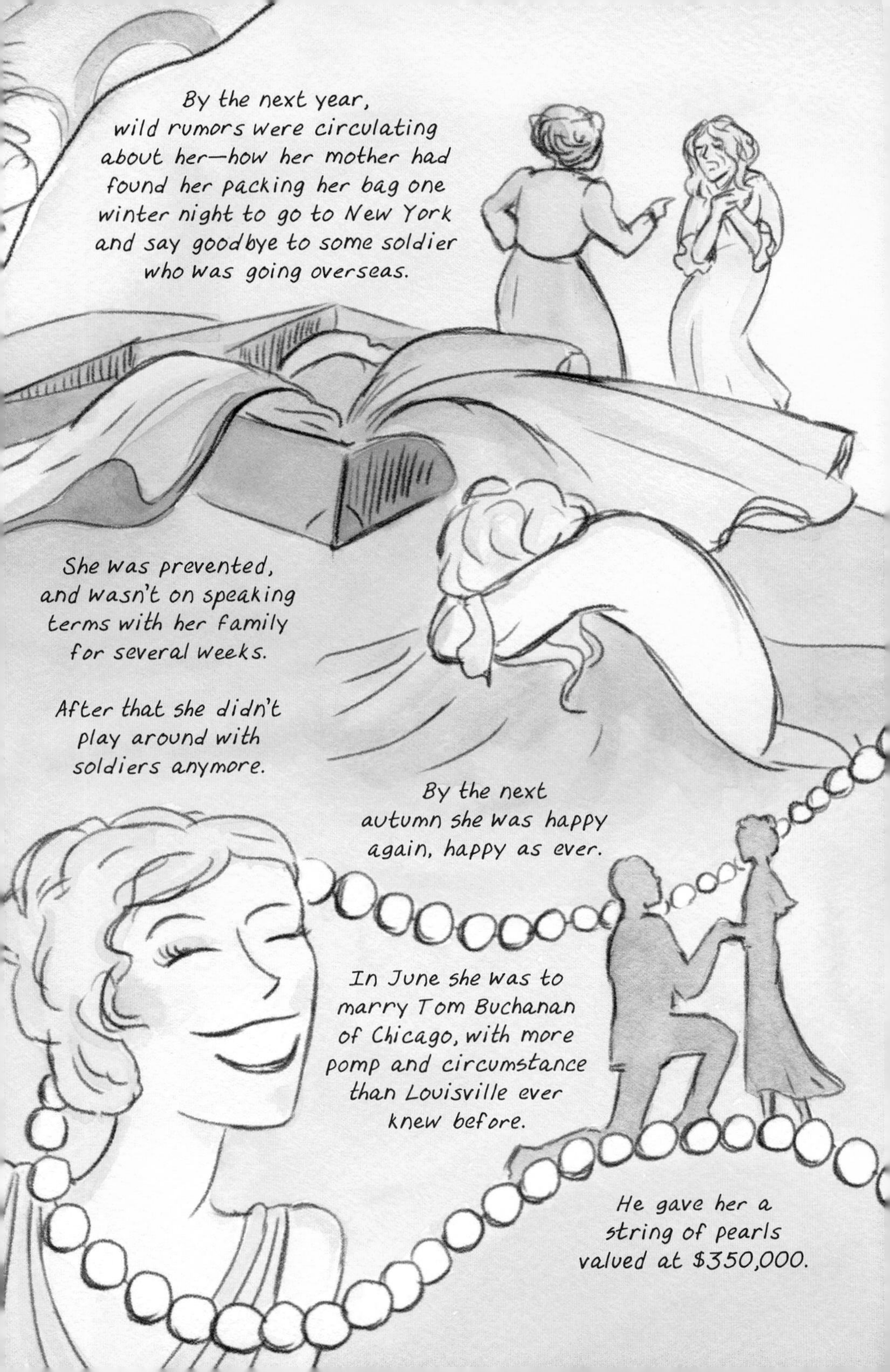
By the next year, wild rumors were circulating about her—how her mother had found her packing her bag one winter night to go to New York and say goodbye to some soldier who was going overseas.
She was prevented, and wasn't on speaking terms with her family for several weeks.
After that she didn't play around with soldiers anymore.
By the next autumn she was happy again, happy as ever.
In June she was to marry Tom Buchanan of Chicago, with more pomp and circumstance than Louisville ever knew before.
He gave her a string of pearls valued at $350,000.

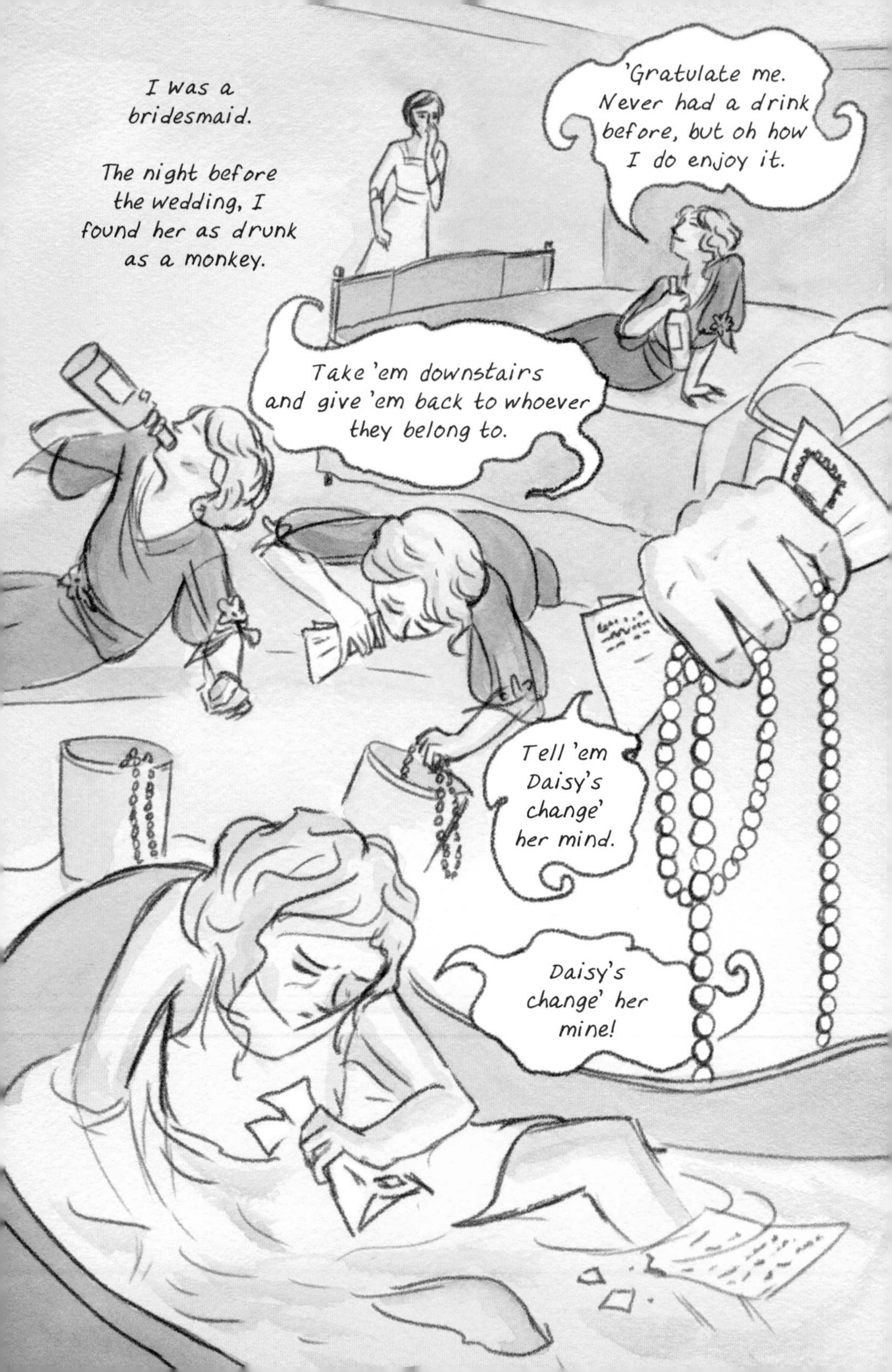
I was a bridesmaid.
The night before the wedding, I found her as drunk as a monkey.
'Gratulate me. Never had a drink before, but oh how I do enjoy it.
Take 'em downstairs and give 'em back to whoever they belong to.
Tell 'em Daisy's change' her mind.
Daisy's change' her mine!

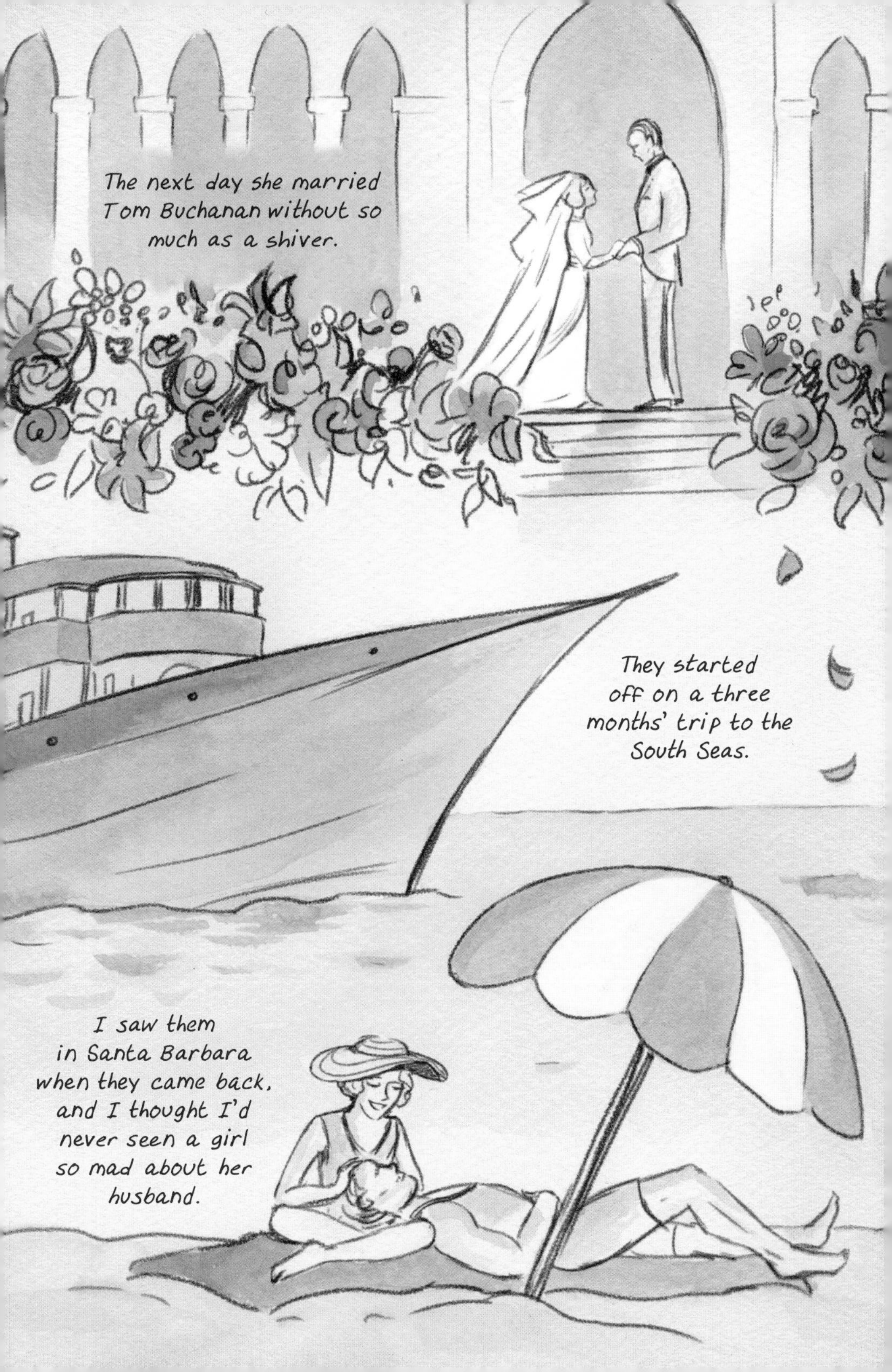
The next day she married Tom Buchanan without so much as a shiver.
They started off on a three months' trip to the South Seas.
I saw them in Santa Barbara when they came back, and I thought I'd never seen a girl so mad about her husband.

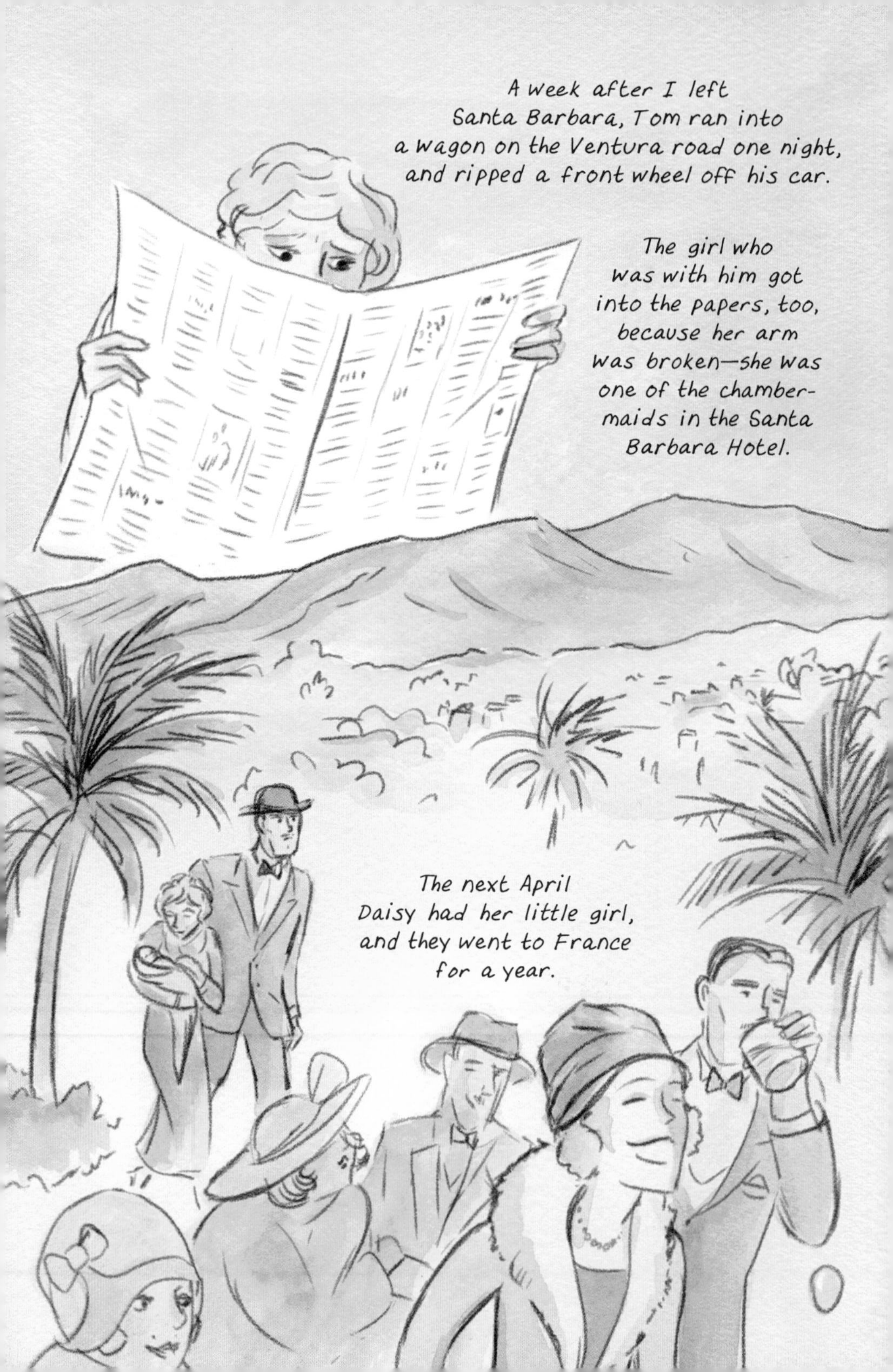
A week after I left Santa Barbara, Tom ran into a wagon on the Ventura road one night, and ripped a front wheel off his car.
The girl who was with him got into the papers, too, because her arm was broken—she was one of the chamber-maids in the Santa Barbara Hotel.
The next April Daisy had her little girl, and they went to France for a year.

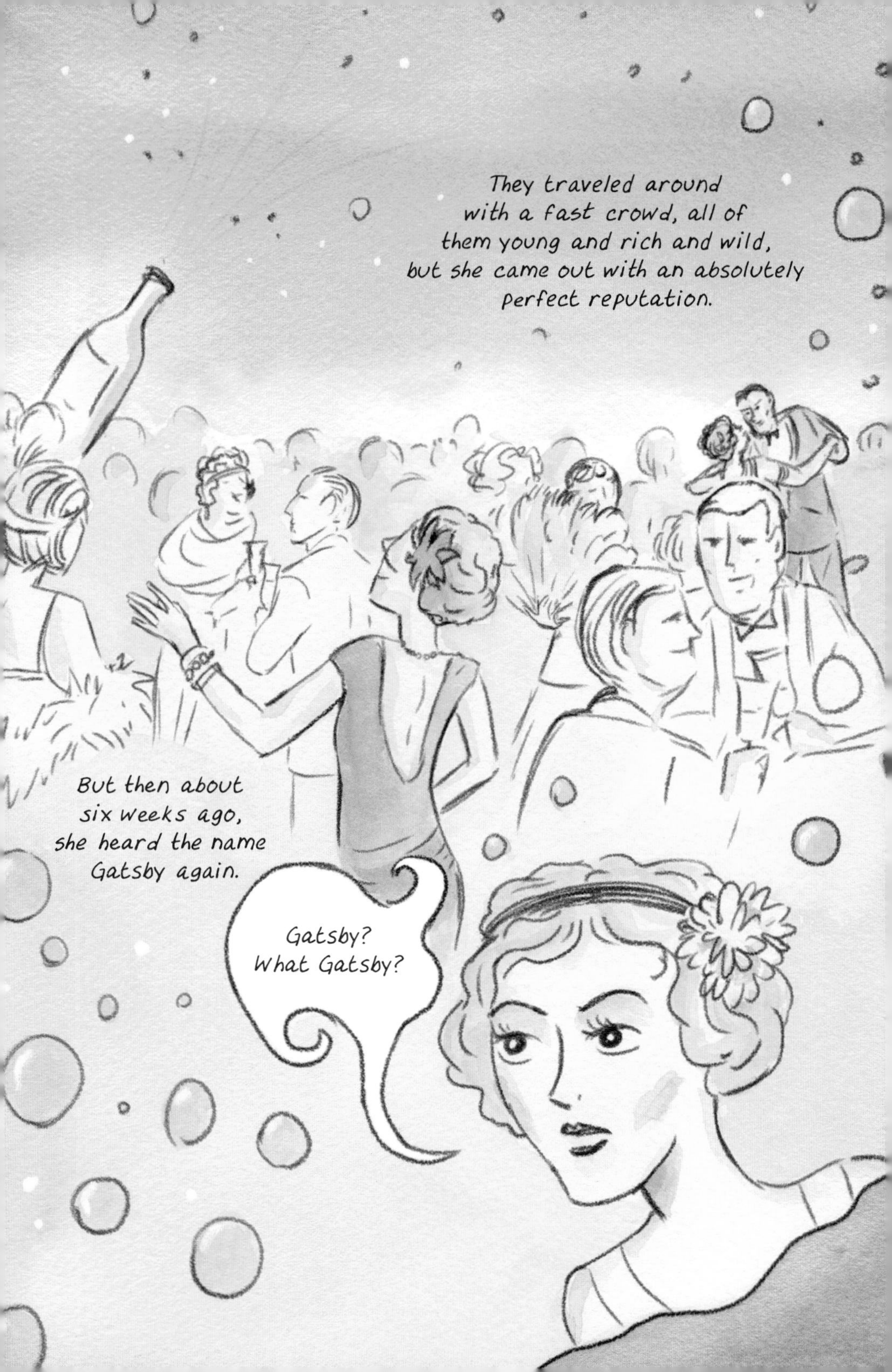
They traveled around
with a fast crowd, all of
them young and rich and wild,
but she came out with an absolutely
perfect reputation.
But then about
six weeks ago,
she heard the name
Gatsby again.
Gatsby?
What Gatsby?

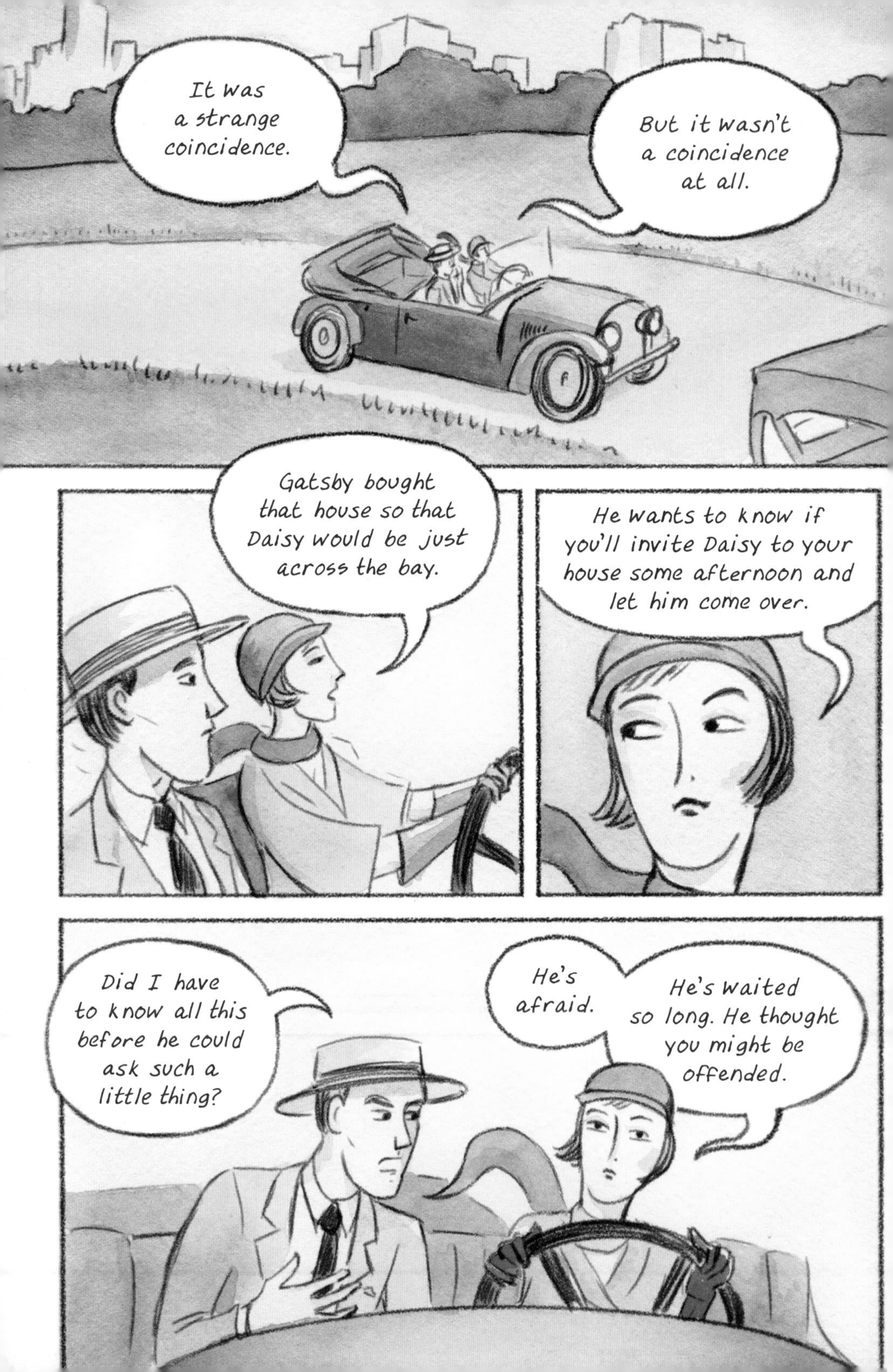
It was a strange coincidence.
But it wasn't a coincidence at all.
Gatsby bought that house so that Daisy would be just across the bay.
He wants to know if you'll invite Daisy to your house some afternoon and let him come over.
Did I have to know all this before he could ask such a little thing?
He's afraid.
He's waited so long. He thought you might be offended.

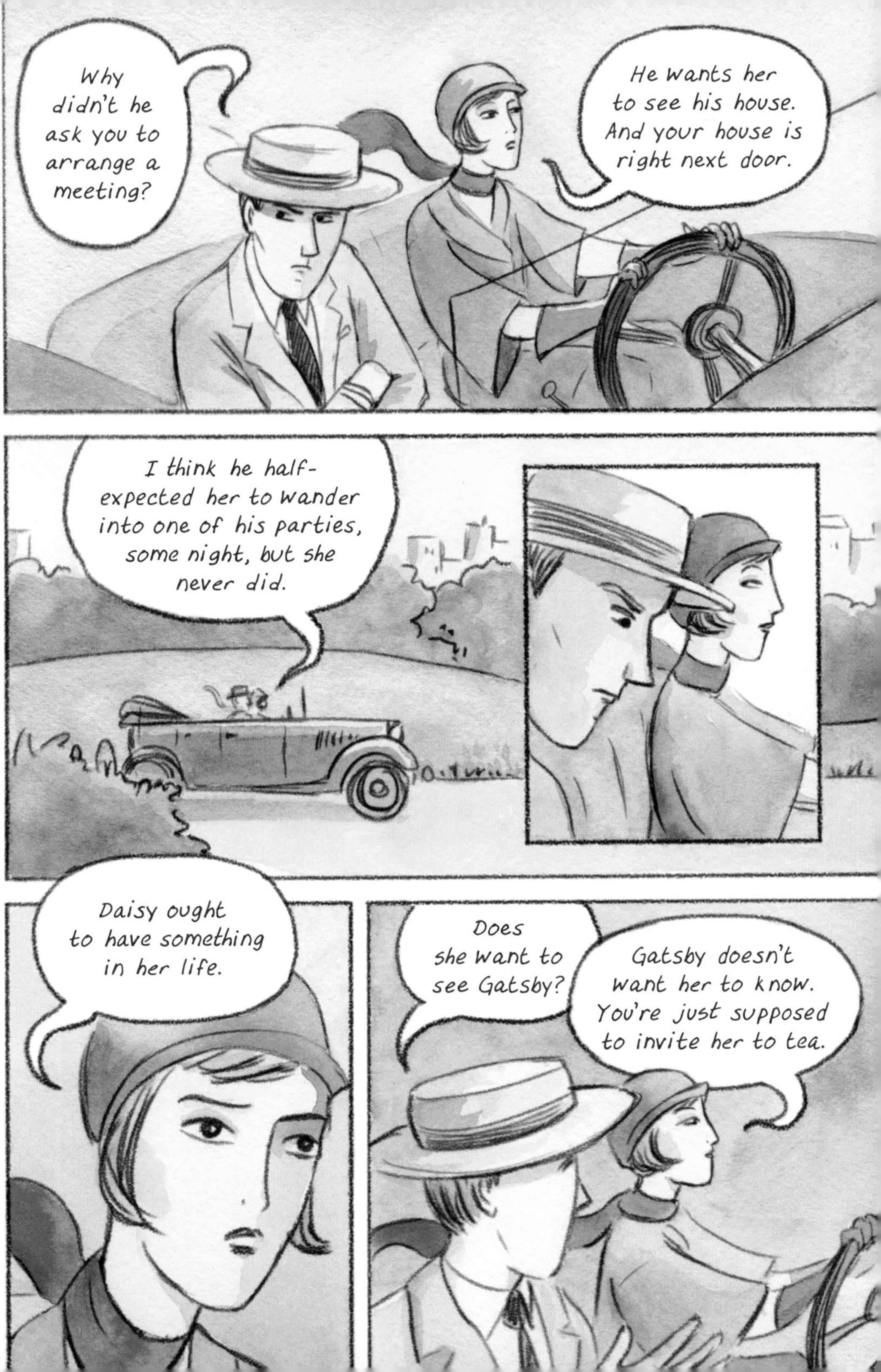

Why didn't he ask you to arrange a meeting?
He wants her to see his house. And your house is right next door.
I think he half-expected her to wander into one of his parties, some night, but she never did.
Daisy ought to have something in her life.
Does she want to see Gatsby?
Gatsby doesn't want her to know. You're just supposed to invite her to tea.

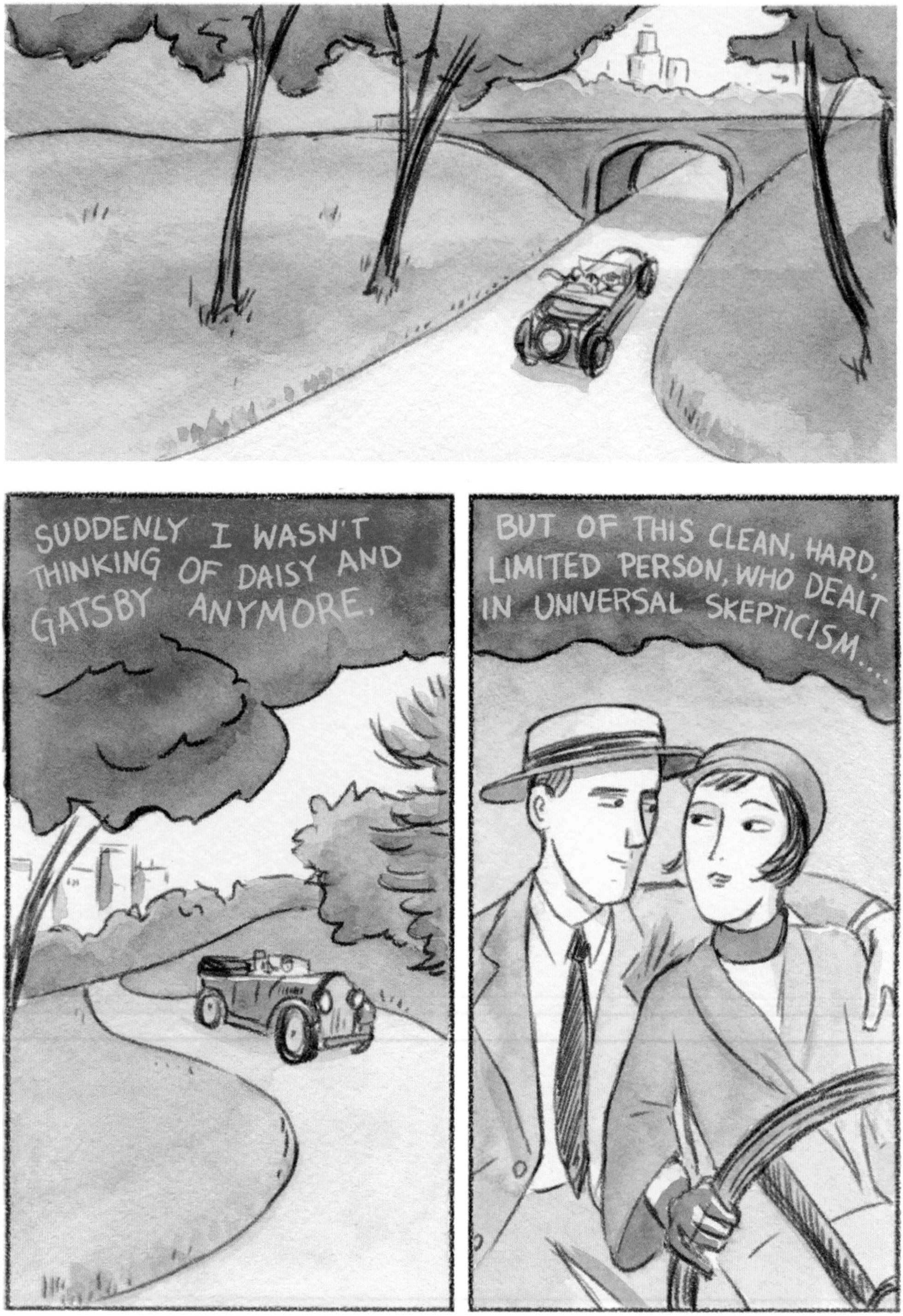
SUDDENLY I WASN'T THINKING OF DAISY AND GATSBY ANYMORE.
BUT OF THIS CLEAN, HARD, LIMITED PERSON, WHO DEALT IN UNIVERSAL SKEPTICISM....

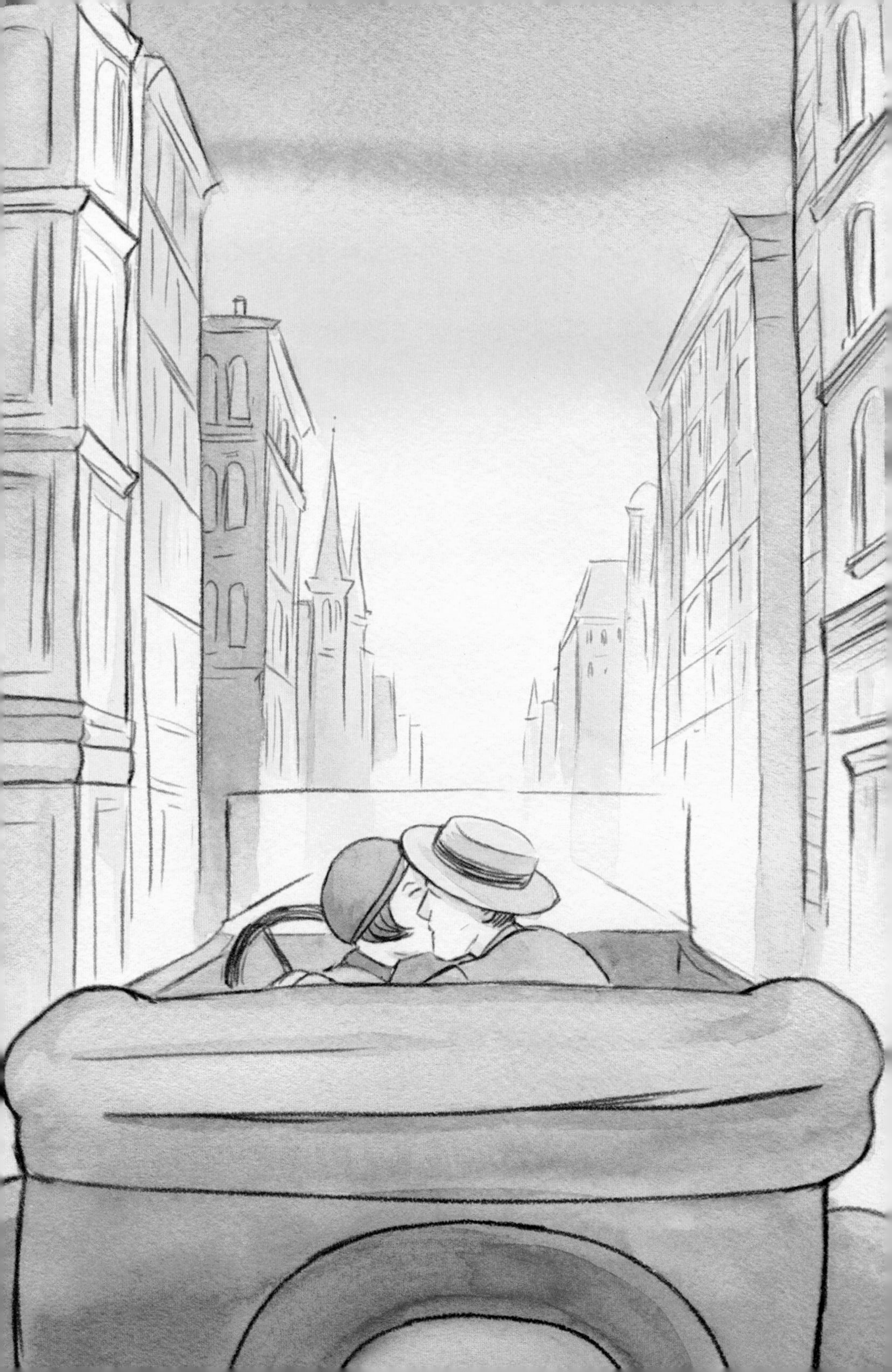

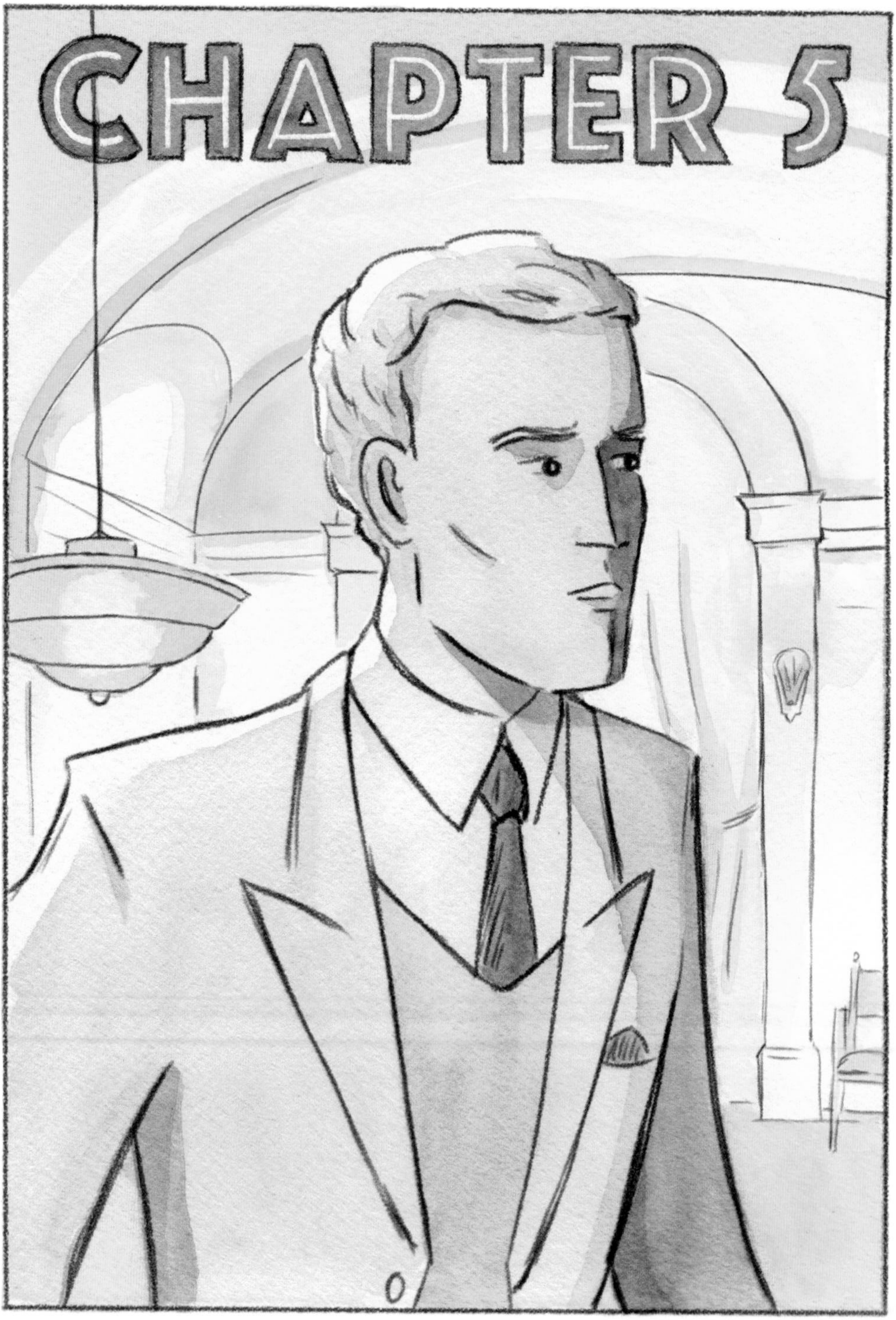
CHAPTER 5

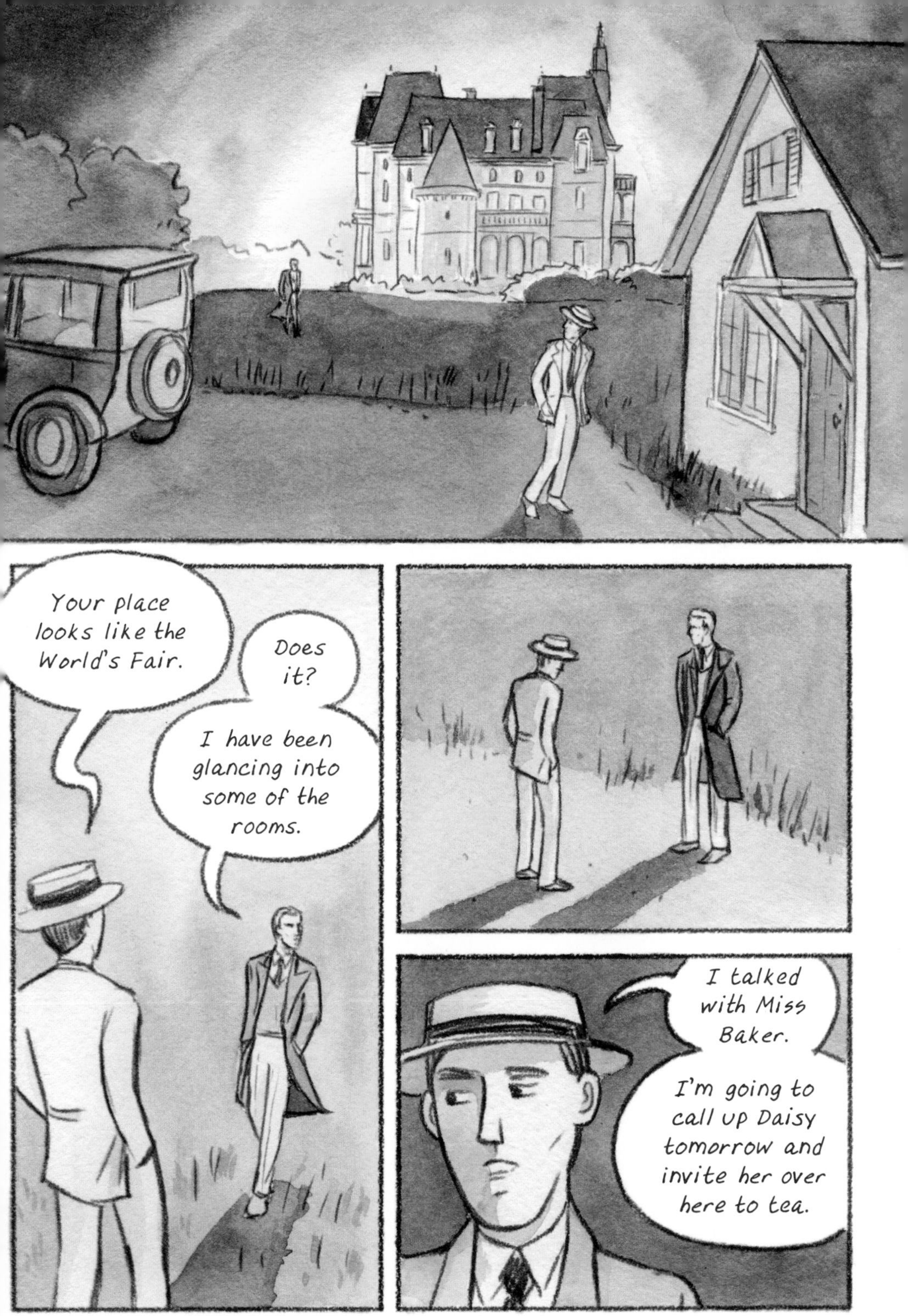
Your place looks like the World's Fair.
Does it?
I have been glancing into some of the rooms.
I talked with Miss Baker.
I'm going to call up Daisy tomorrow and invite her over here to tea.

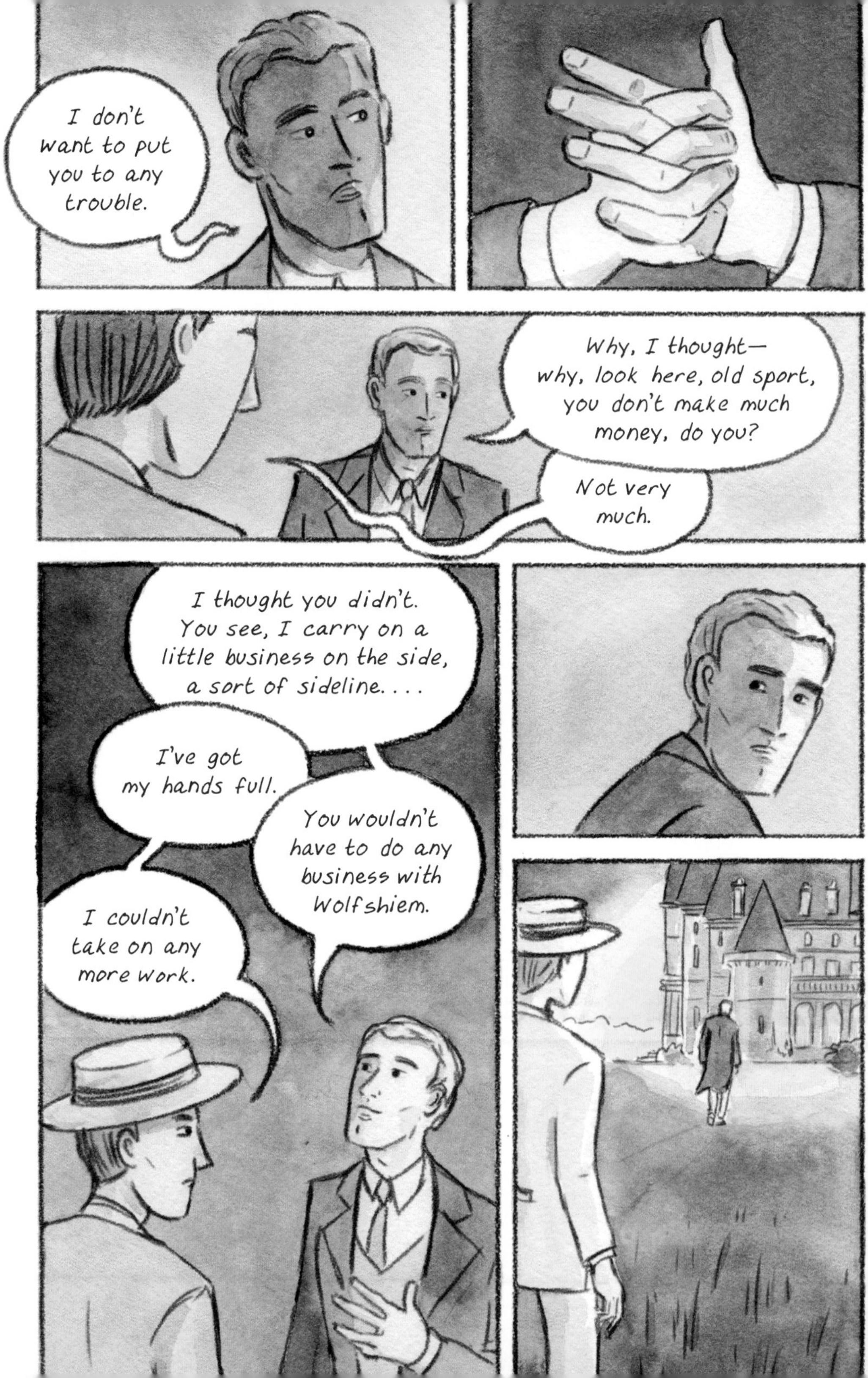
I don't want to put you to any trouble.
Why, I thought— why, look here, old sport, you don't make much money, do you?
Not very much.
I thought you didn't. You see, I carry on a little business on the side, a sort of sideline. . . .
I've got my hands full.
You wouldn't have to do any business with Wolfshiem.
I couldn't take on any more work.

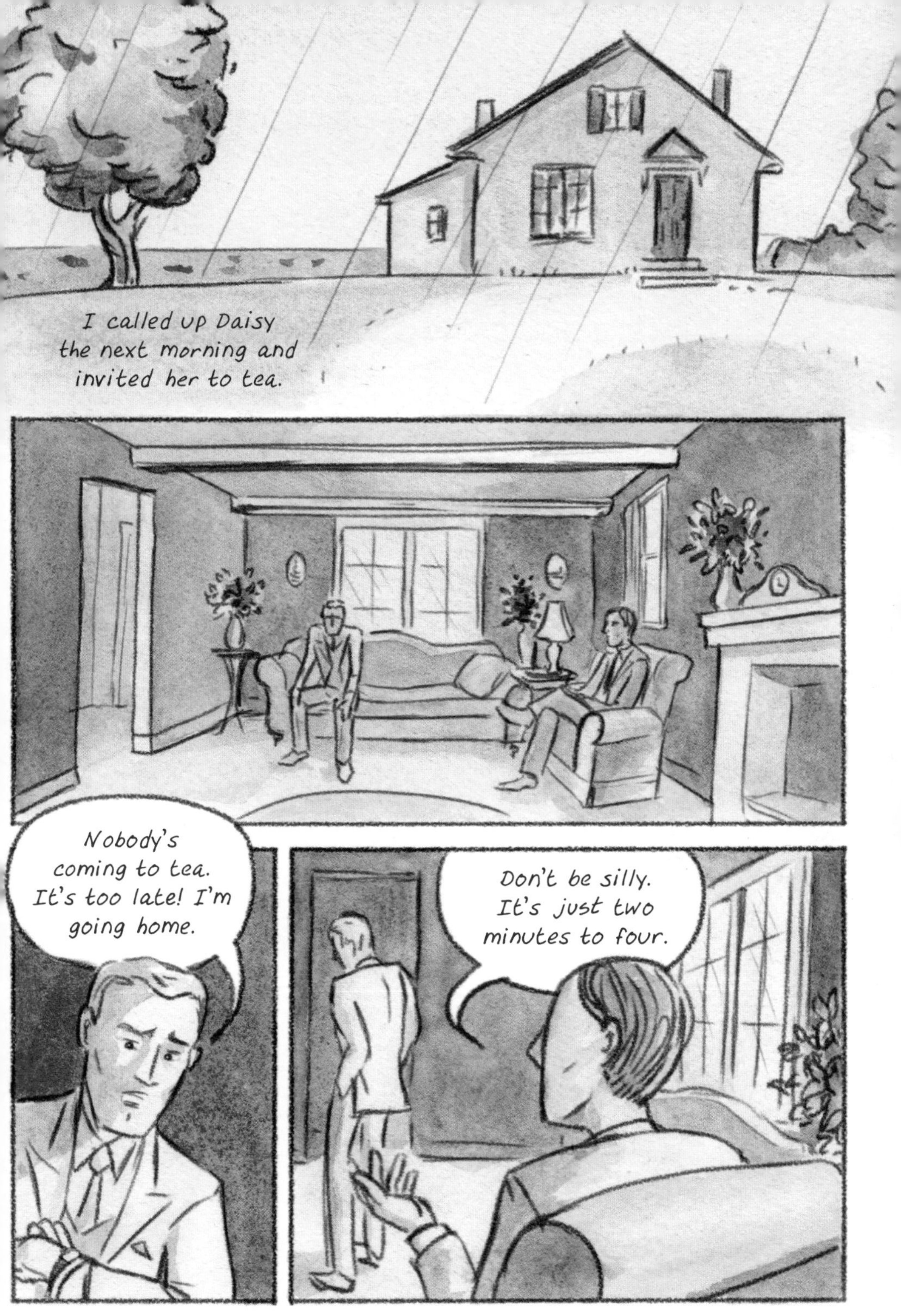
I called up Daisy the next morning and invited her to tea.
Nobody's coming to tea. It's too late! I'm going home.
Don't be silly. It's just two minutes to four.

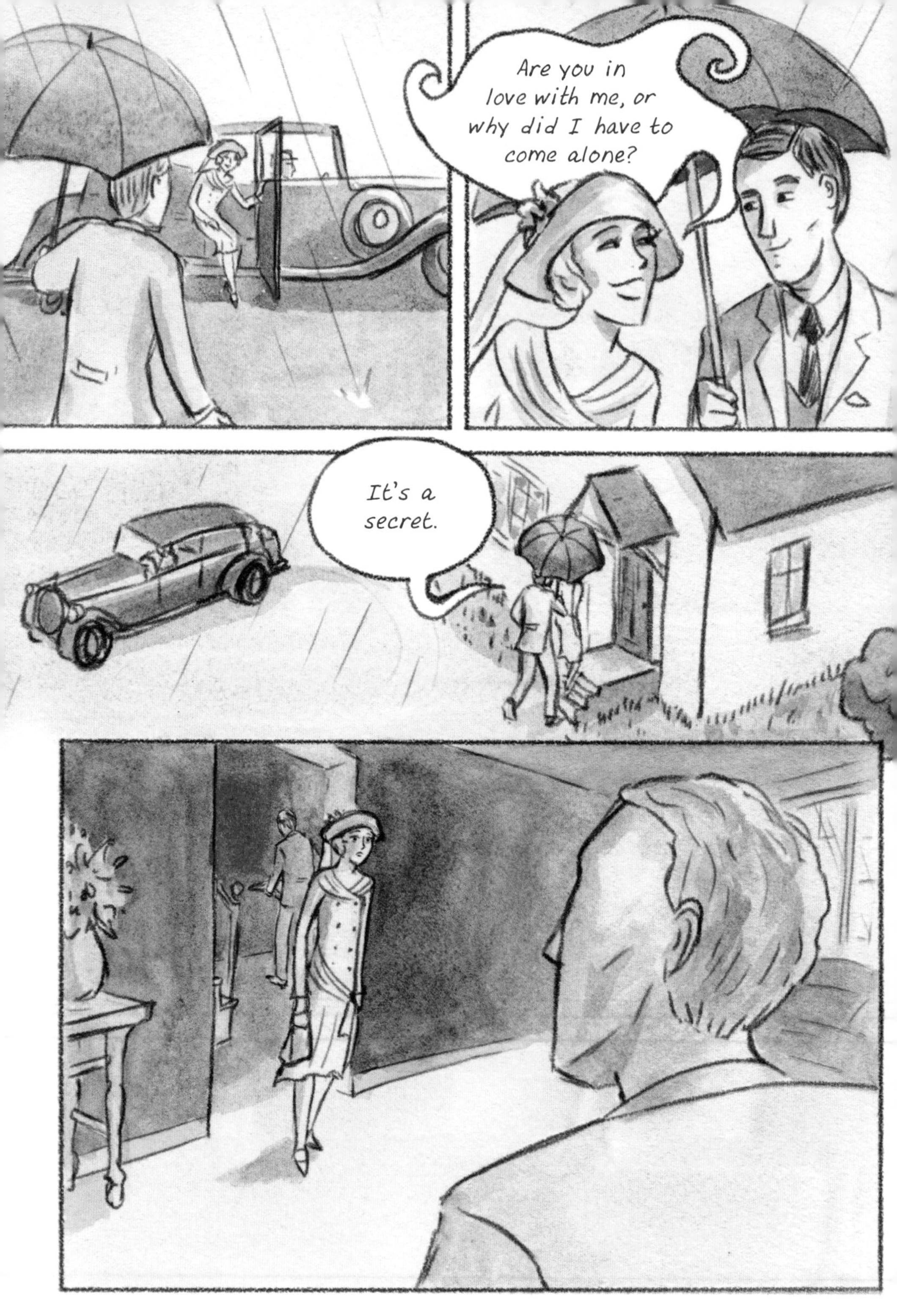

Are you in love with me, or why did I have to come alone?
It's a secret.

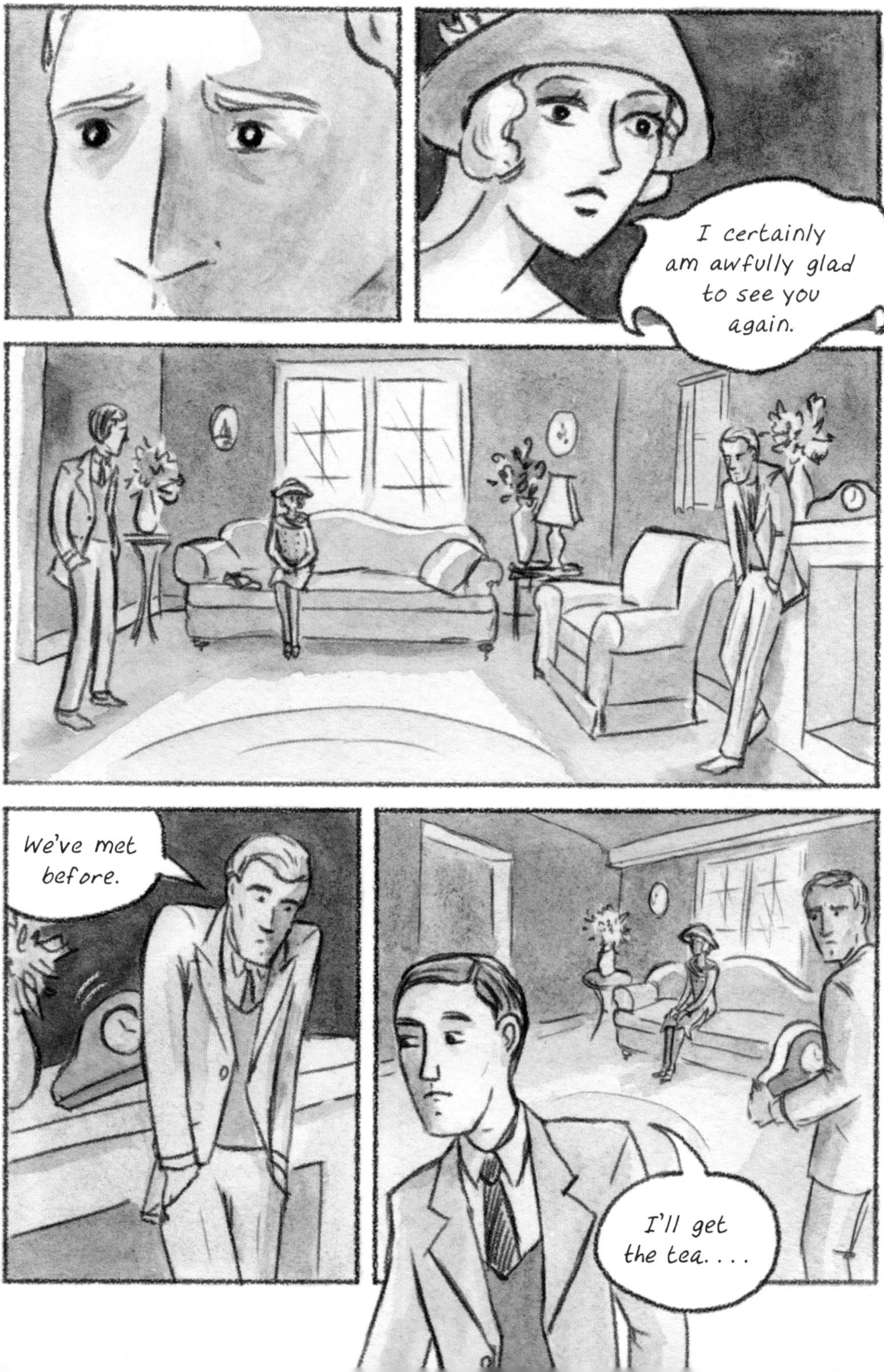
I certainly am awfully glad to see you again.
We've met before.
I'll get the tea. . . .

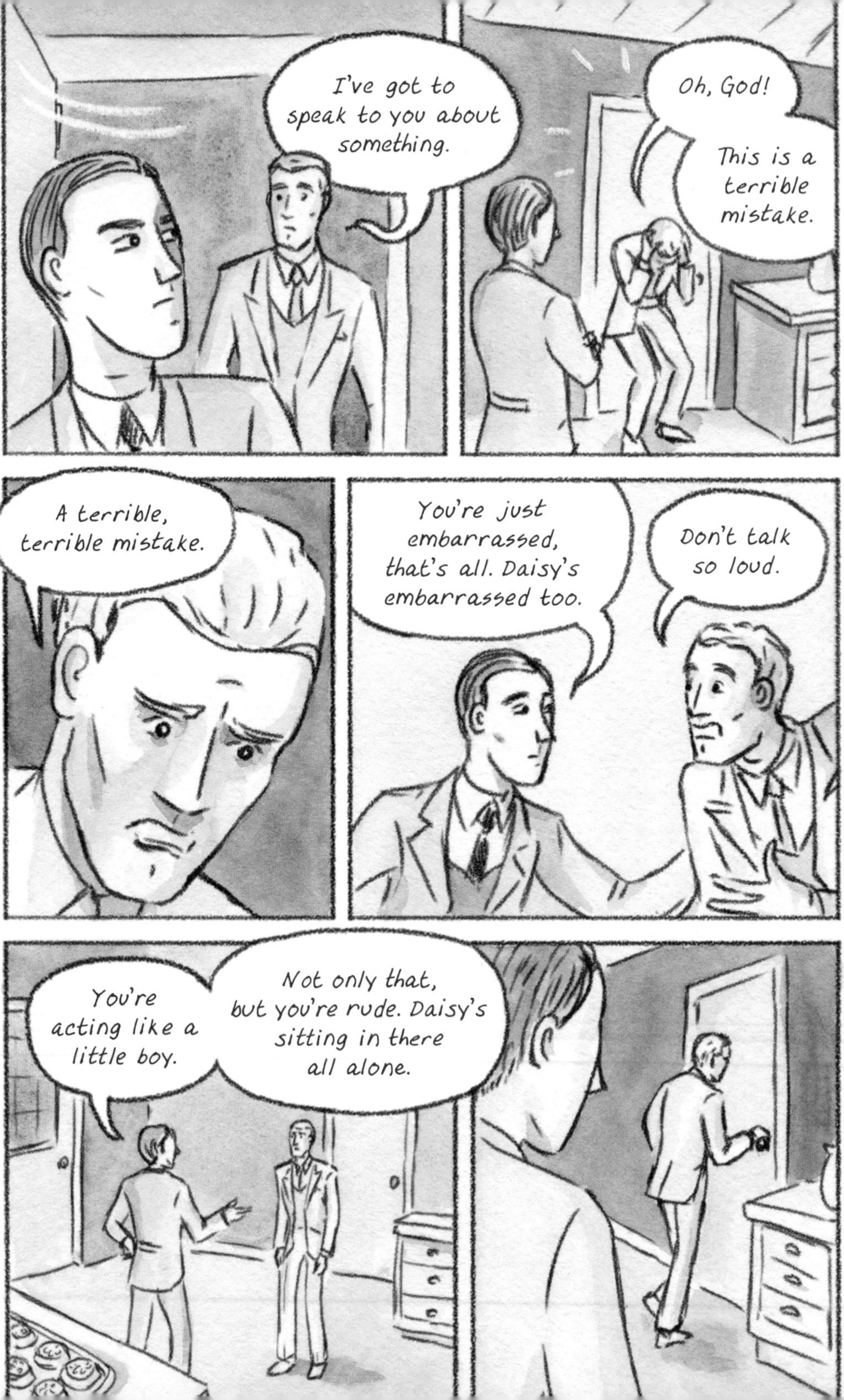
I've got to speak to you about something.
Oh, God!
This is a terrible mistake.
A terrible, terrible mistake.
You're just embarrassed, that's all. Daisy's embarrassed too.
Don't talk so loud.
You're acting like a little boy.
Not only that, but you're rude. Daisy's sitting in there all alone.

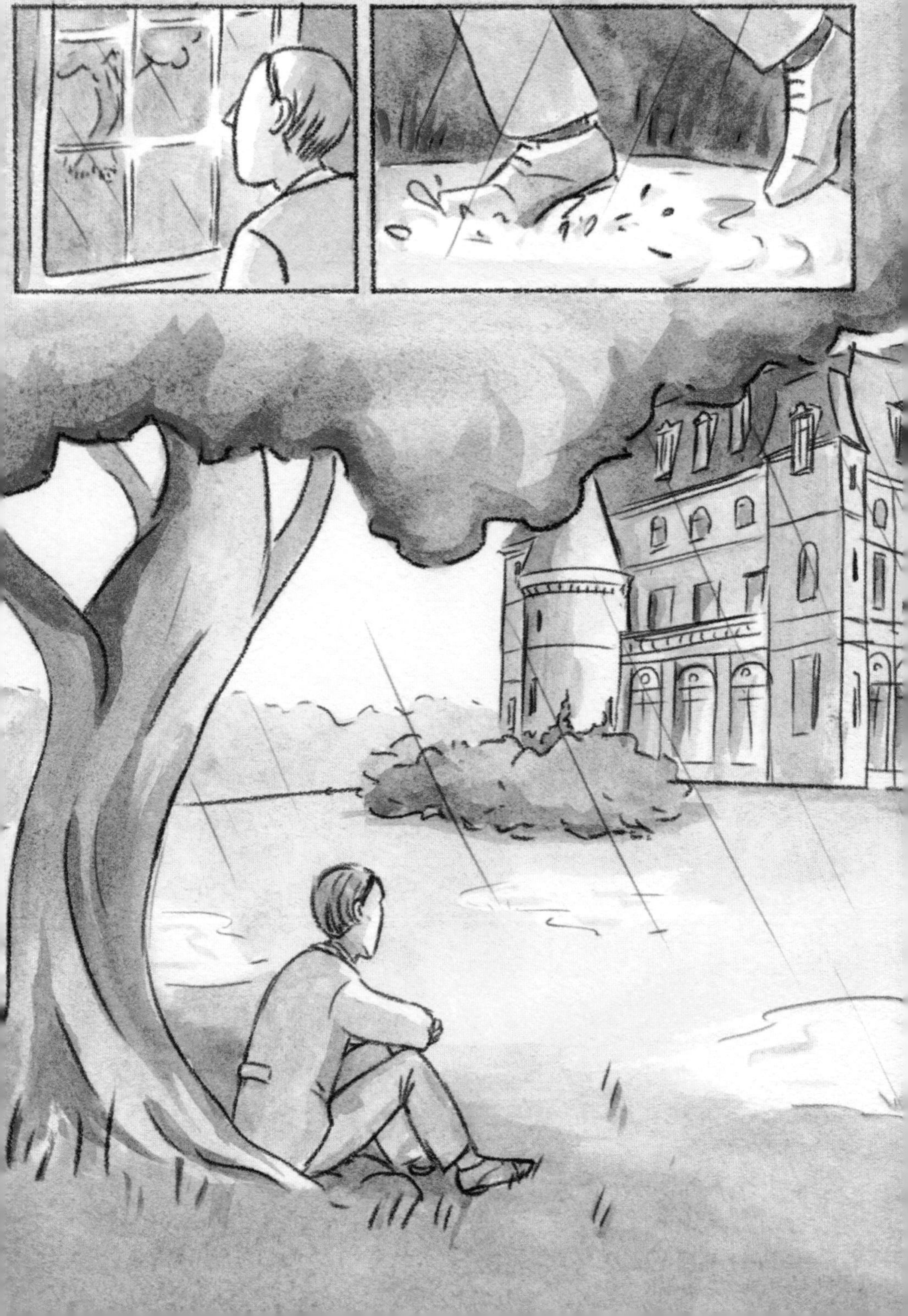

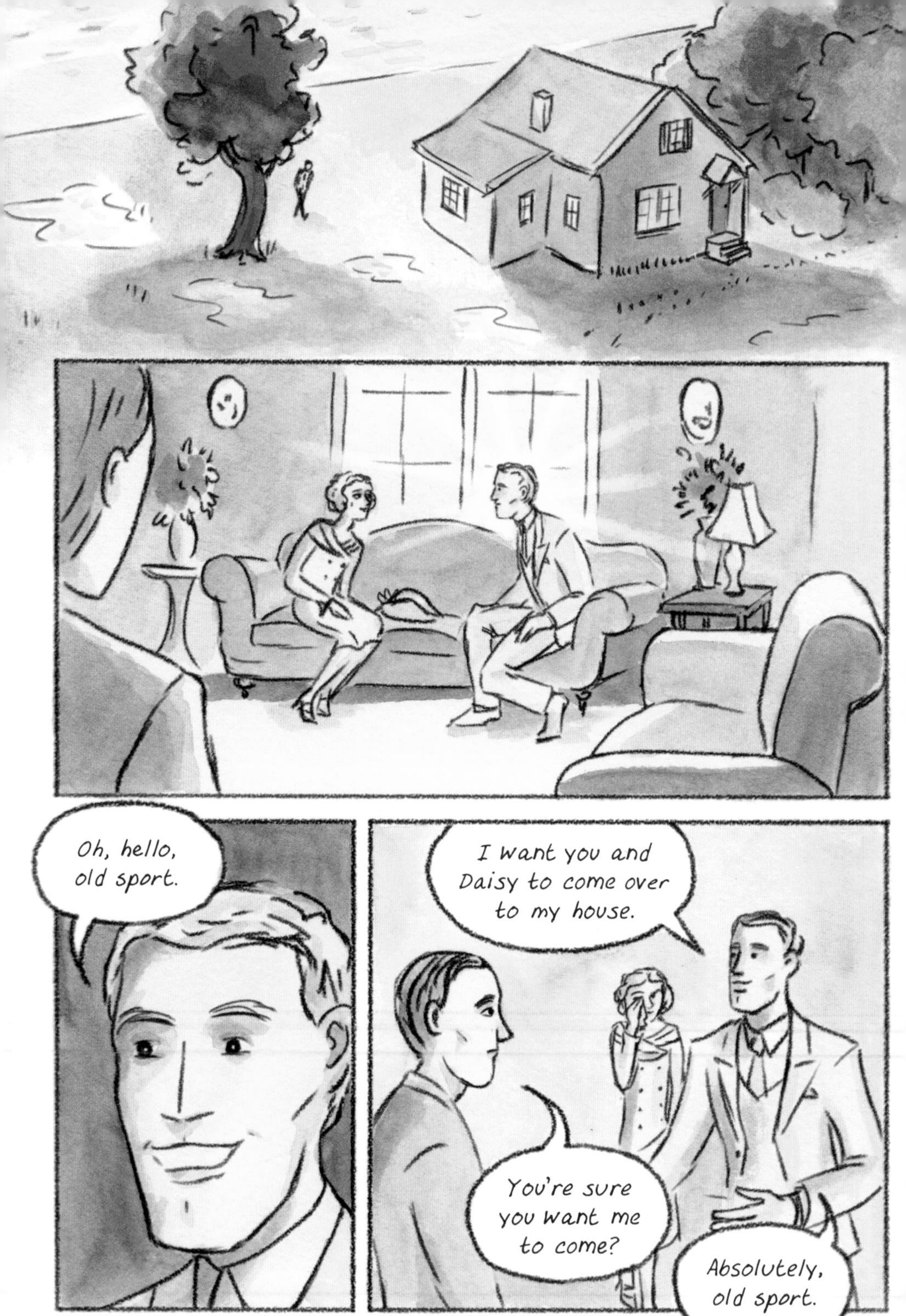
Oh, hello, old sport.
I want you and Daisy to come over to my house.
You're sure you want me to come?
Absolutely, old sport.

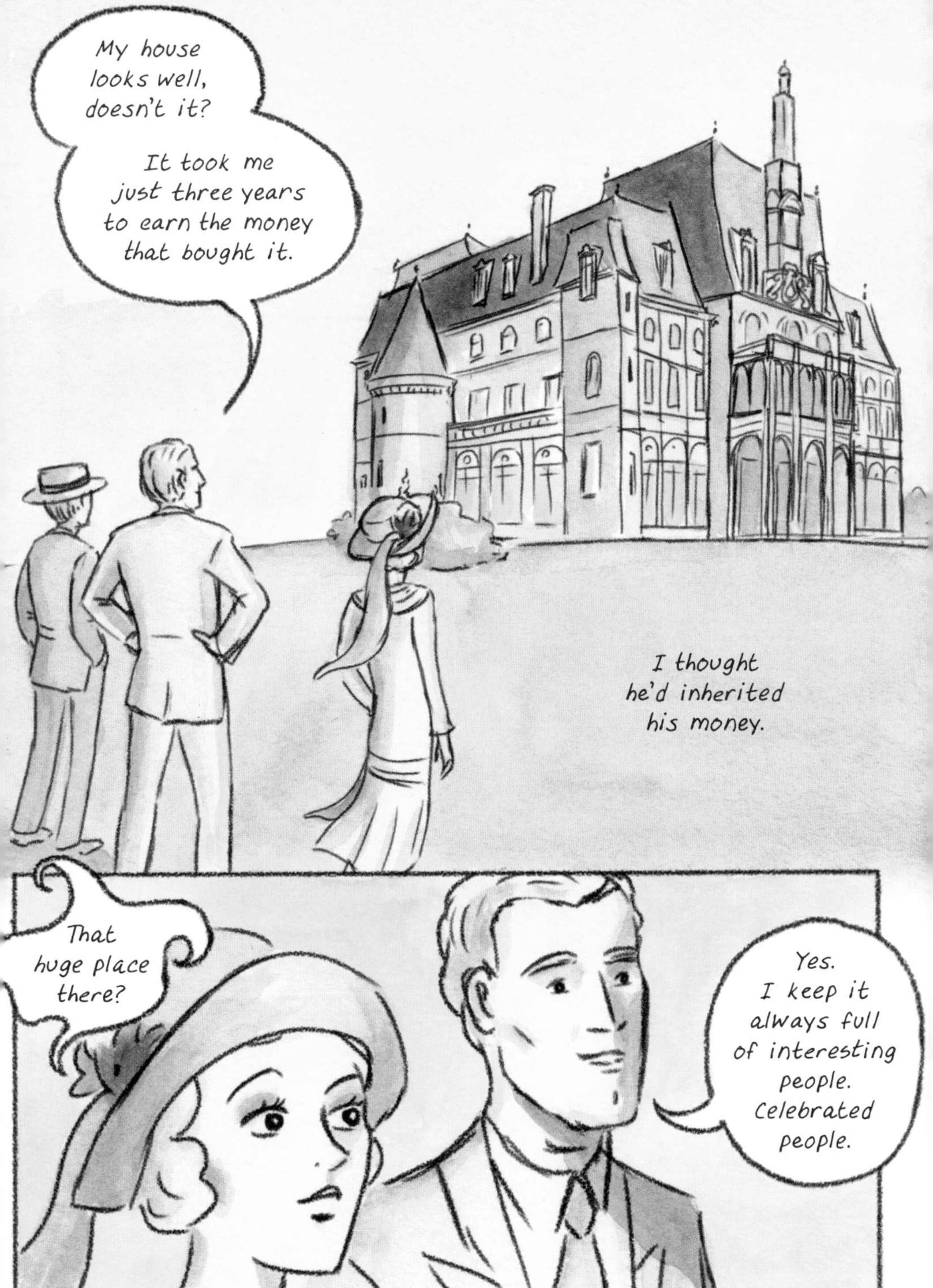
My house looks well, doesn't it?
It took me just three years to earn the money that bought it.
I thought he'd inherited his money.
That huge place there?
Yes. I keep it always full of interesting people. Celebrated people.

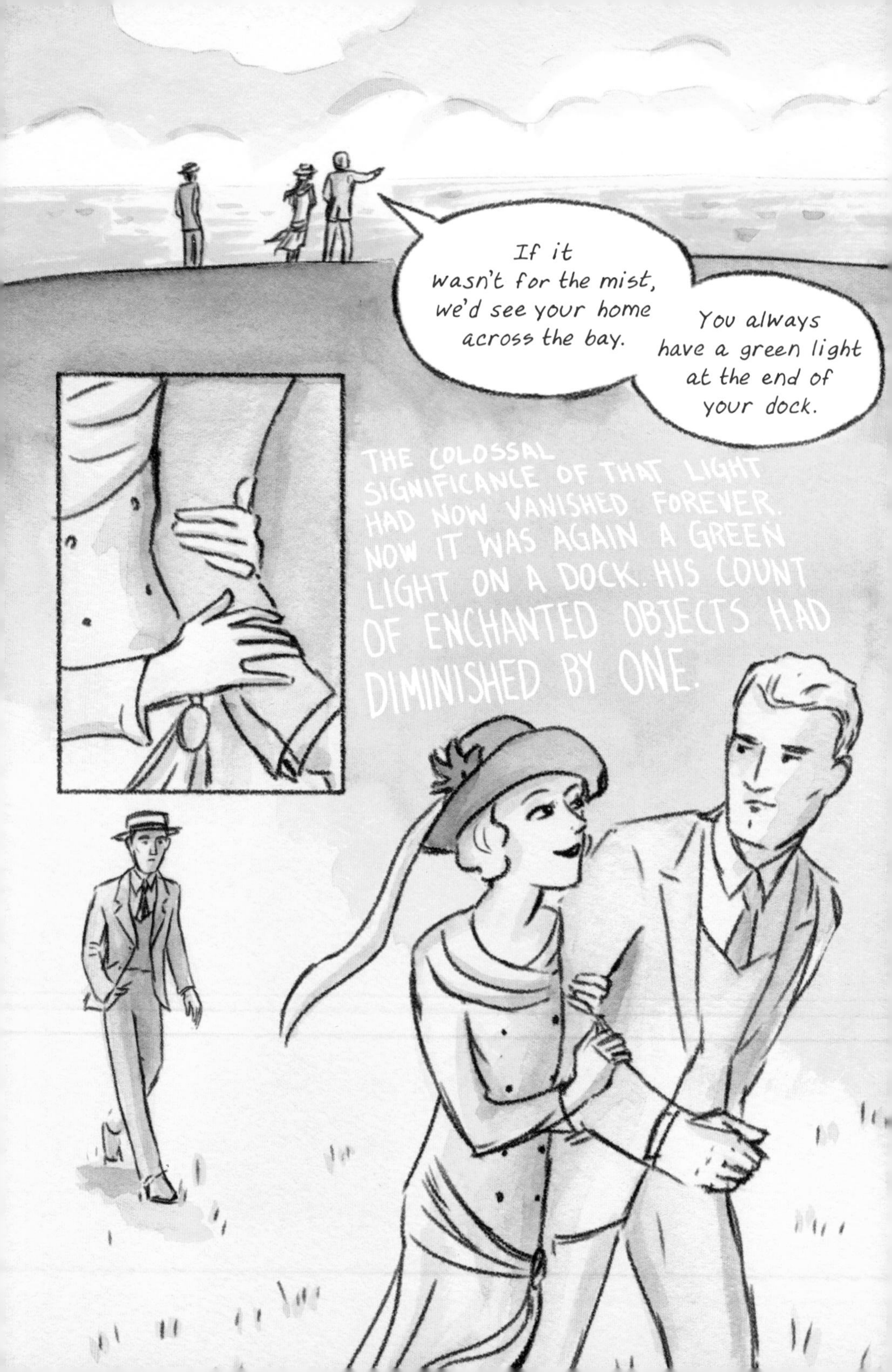
If it wasn't for the mist, we'd see your home across the bay.
You always have a green light at the end of your dock.
THE COLOSSAL SIGNIFICANCE OF THAT LIGHT HAD NOW VANISHED FOREVER. NOW IT WAS AGAIN A GREEN LIGHT ON A DOCK. HIS COUNT OF ENCHANTED OBJECTS HAD DIMINISHED BY ONE.

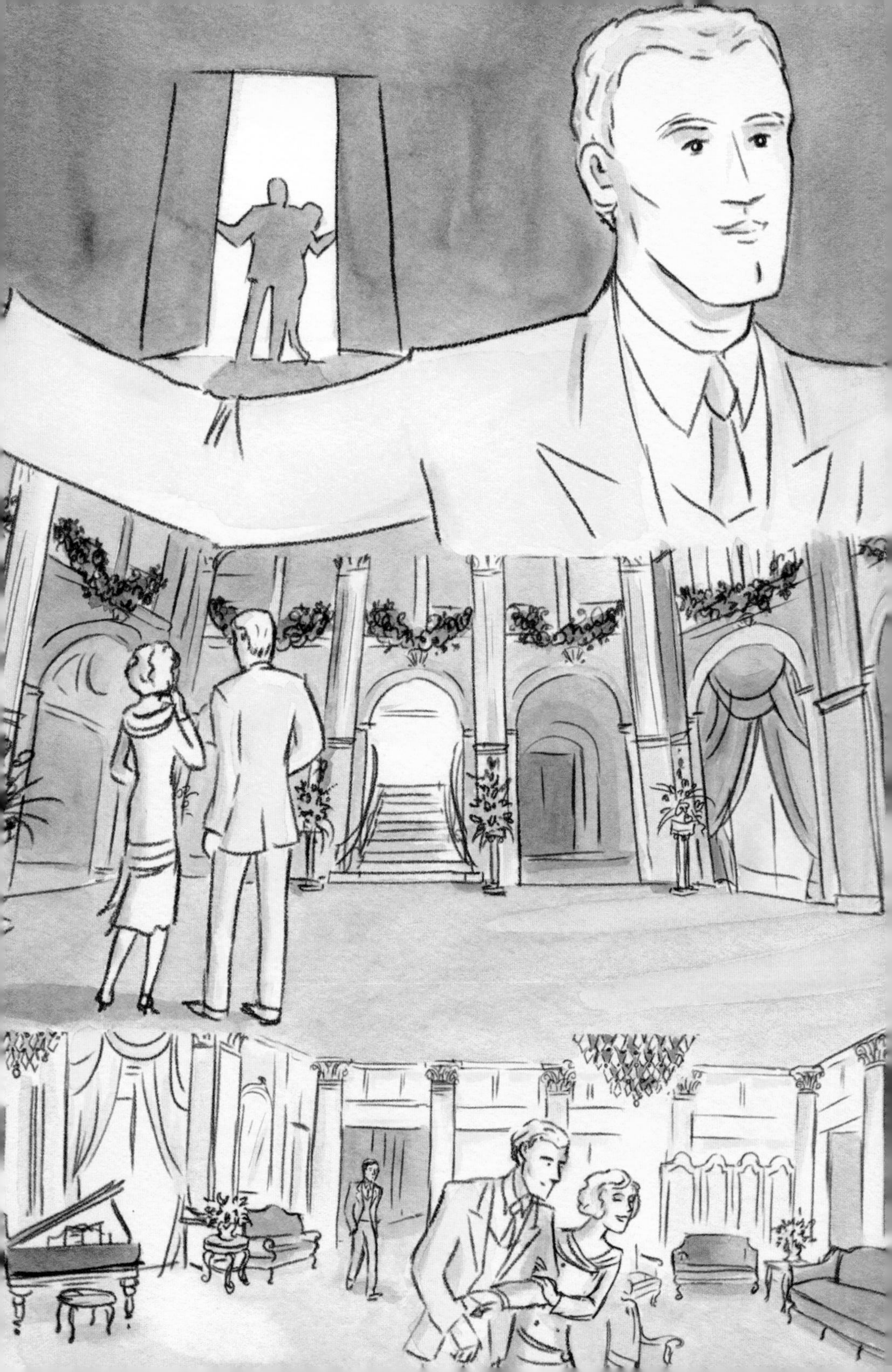

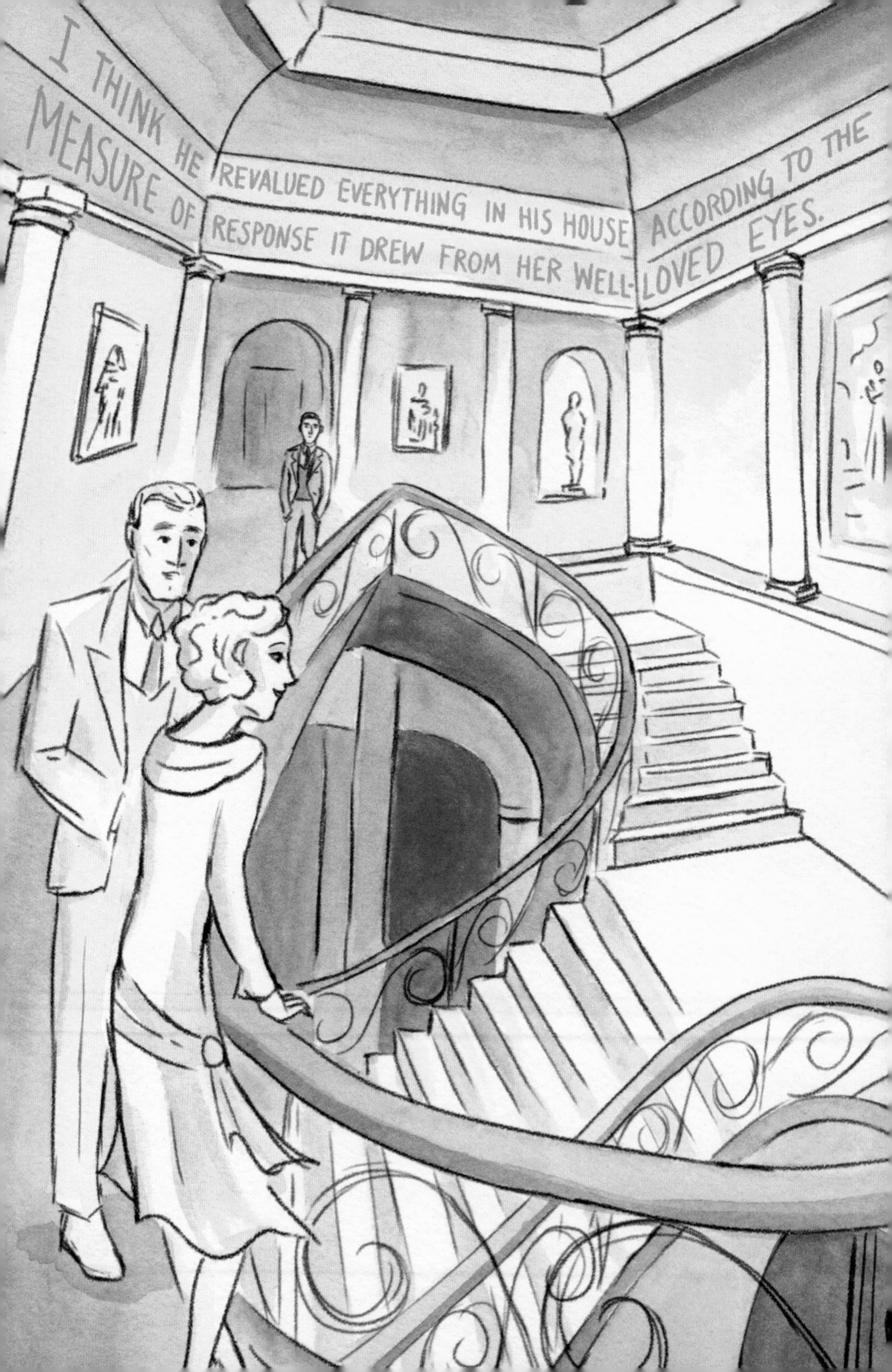
I THINK HE REVALUED EVERYTHING IN HIS HOUSE ACCORDING TO THE MEASURE OF RESPONSE IT DREW FROM HER WELL-LOVED EYES.

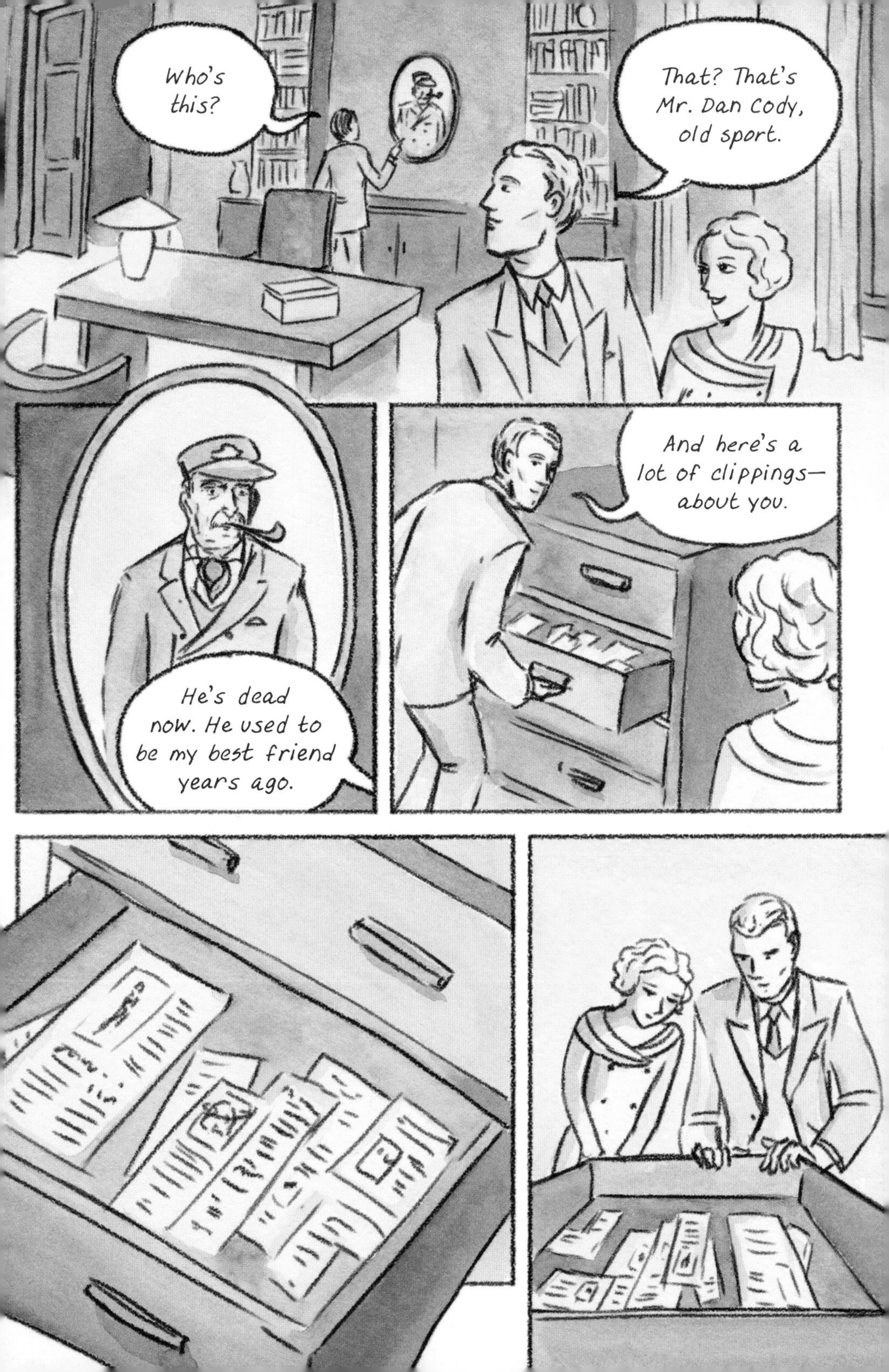
Who's this?
That? That's Mr. Dan Cody, old sport.
He's dead now. He used to be my best friend years ago.
And here's a lot of clippings—about you.

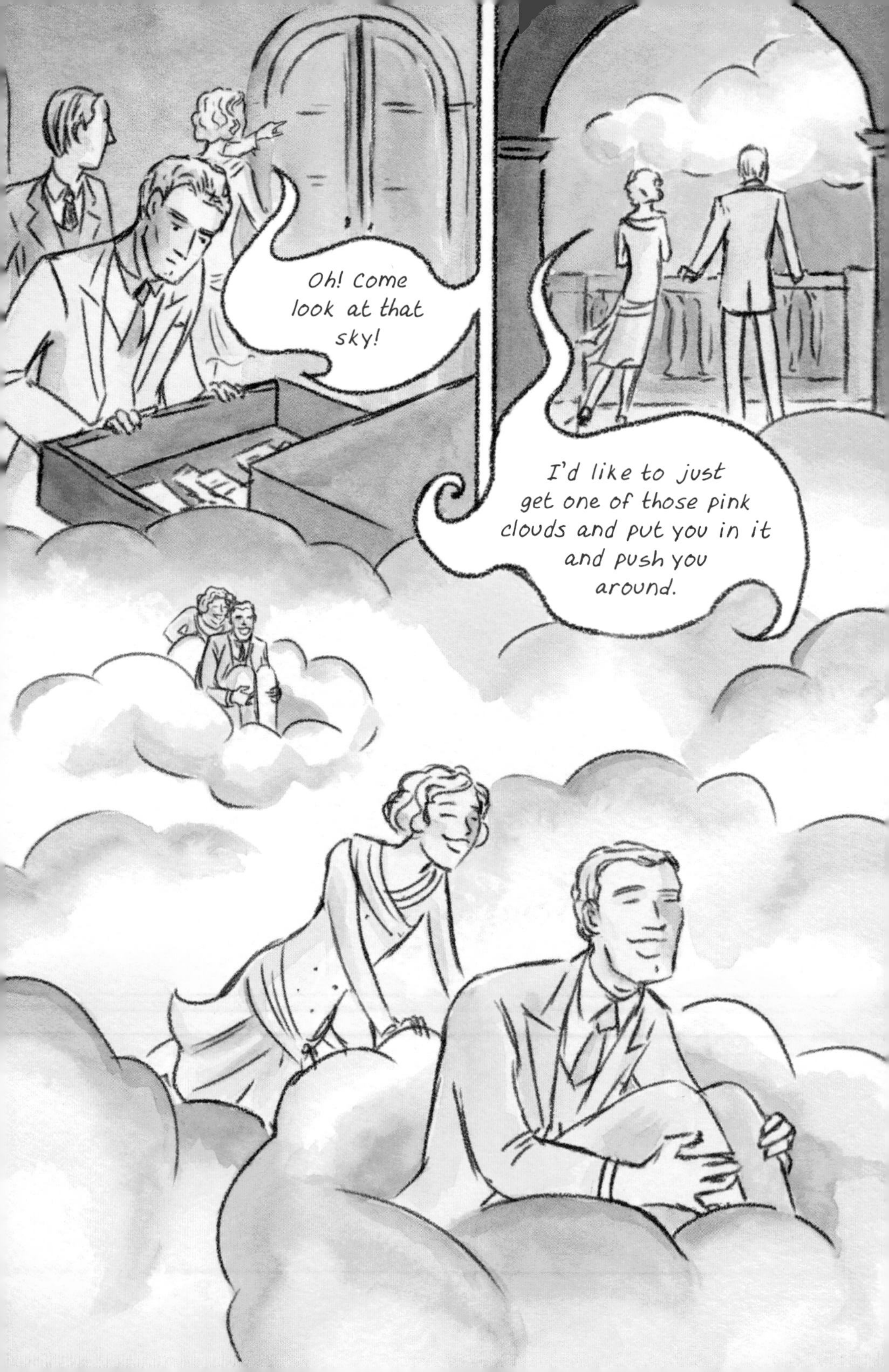
Oh! Come look at that sky!
I'd like to just get one of those pink clouds and put you in it and push you around.

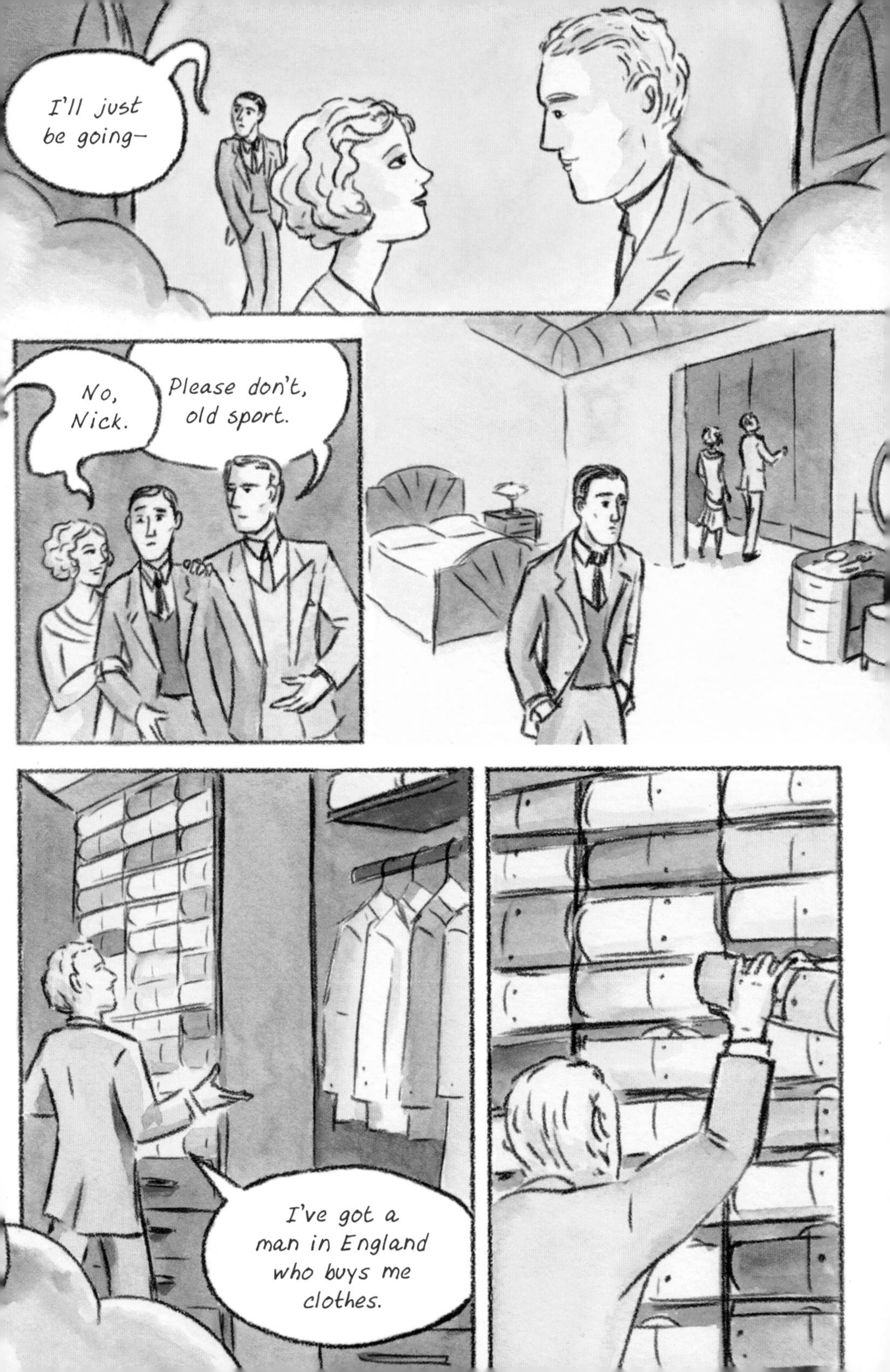
I'll just be going–
No, Nick.
Please don't, old sport.
I've got a man in England who buys me clothes.

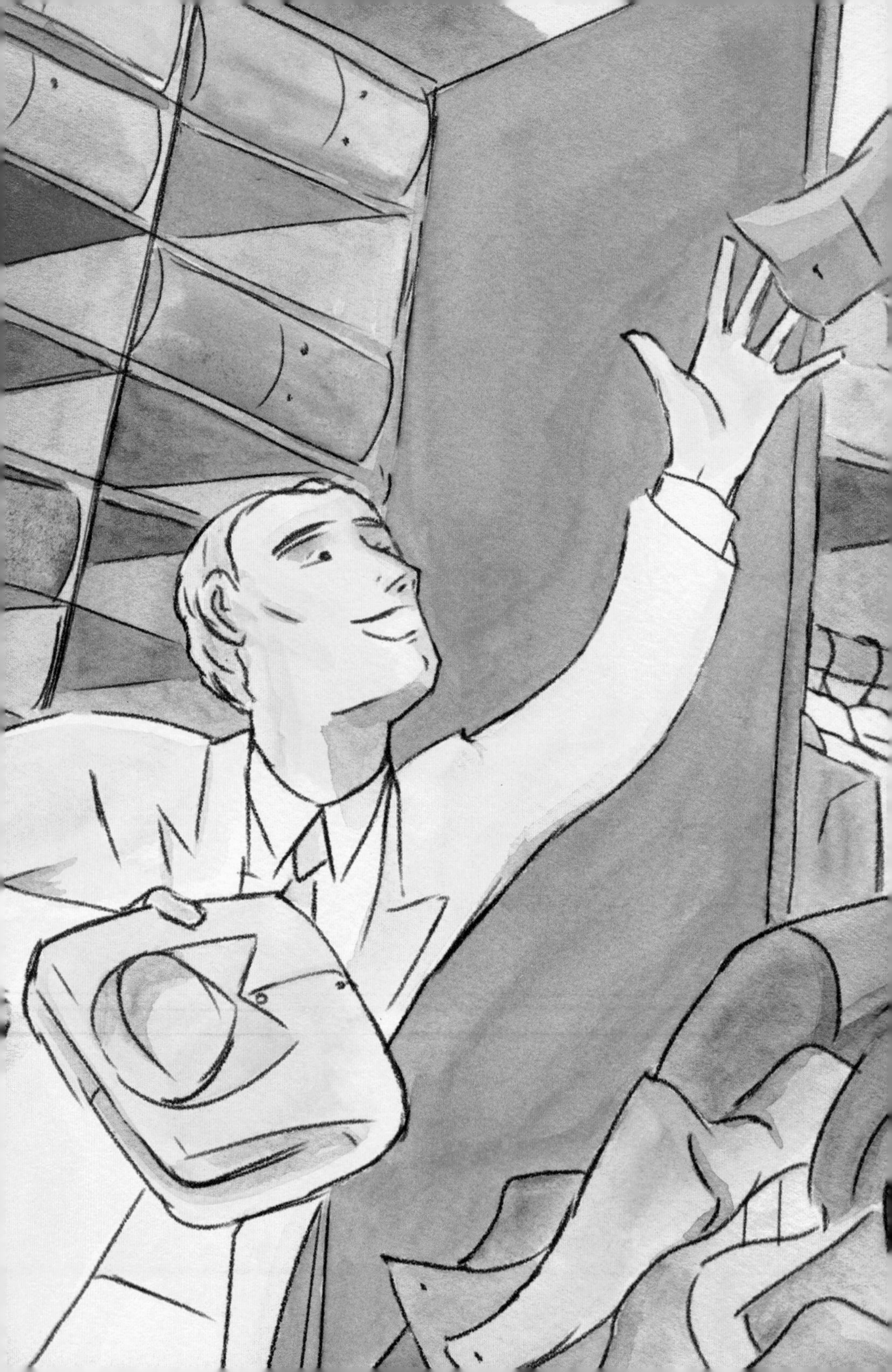

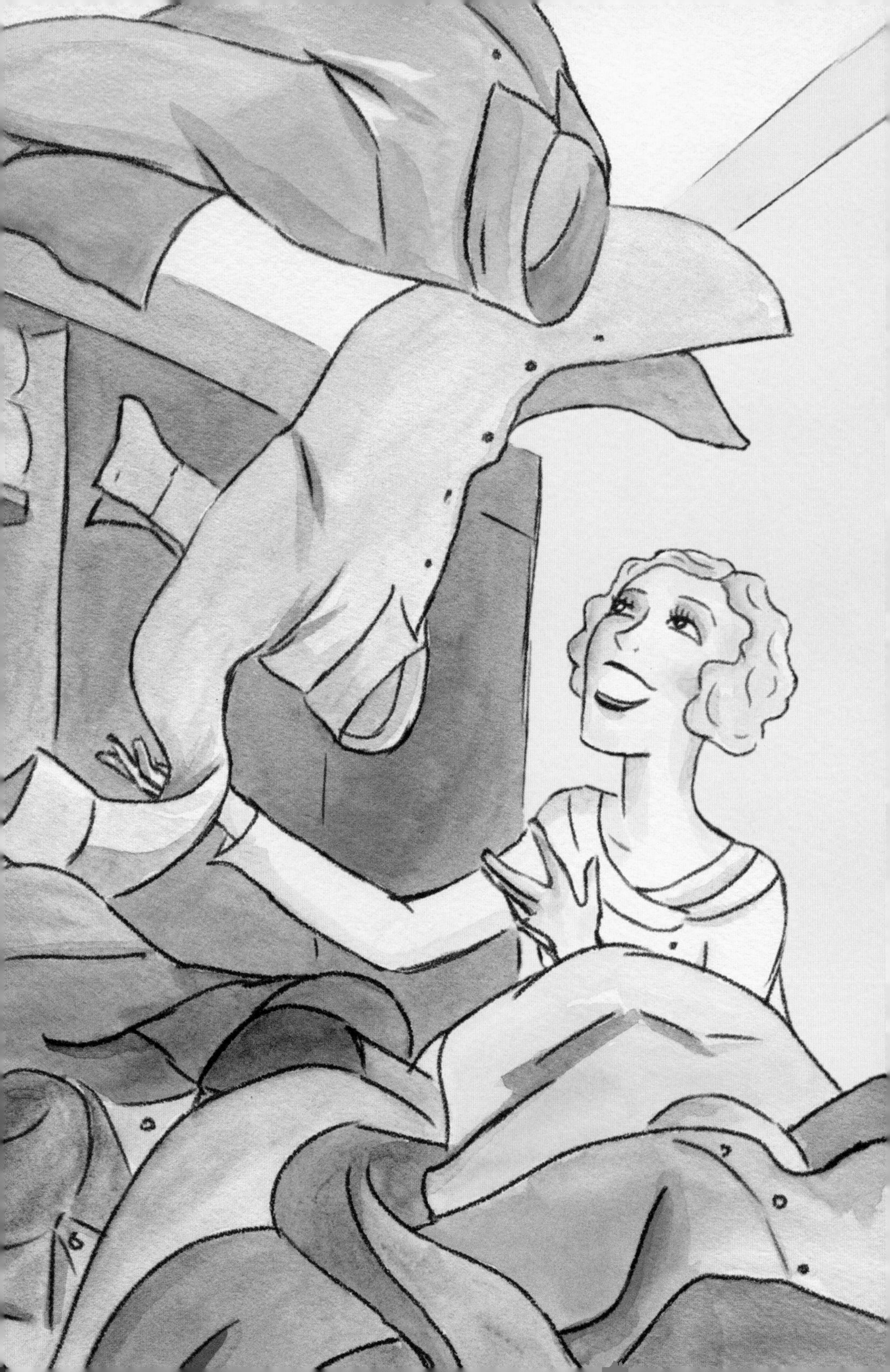

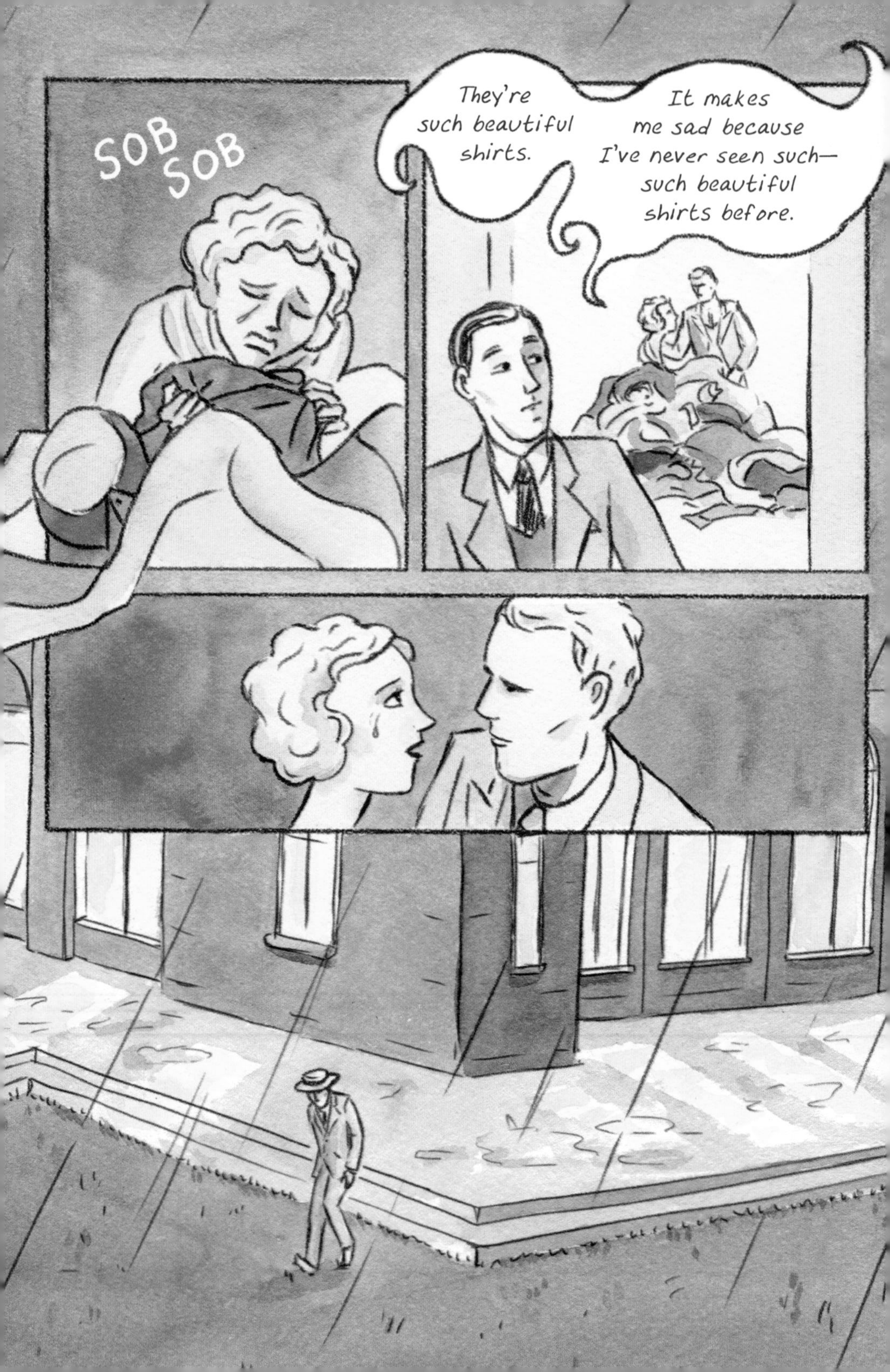
SOB
SOB
They're such beautiful shirts.
It makes me sad because I've never seen such— such beautiful shirts before.

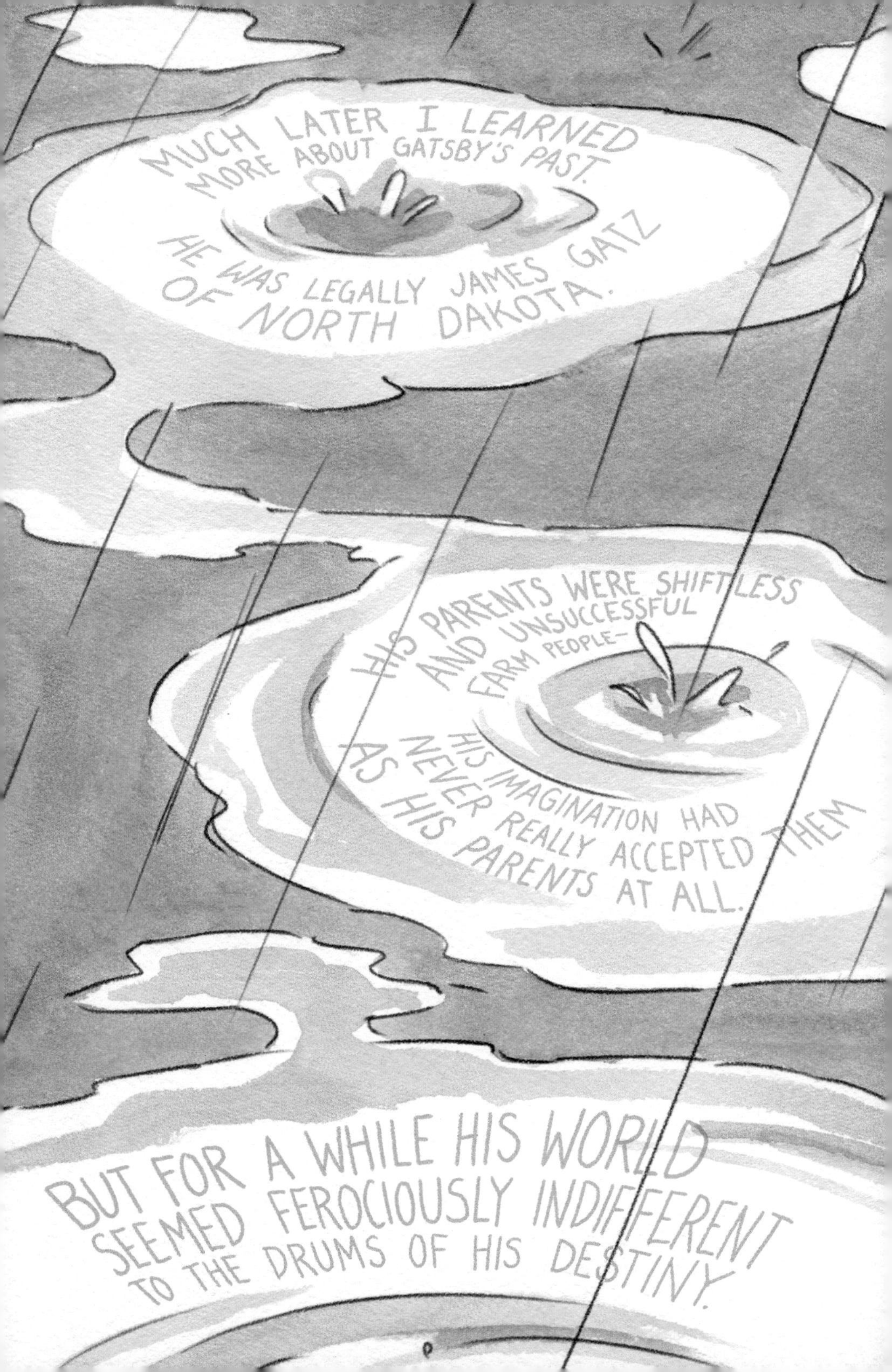
MUCH LATER I LEARNED MORE ABOUT GATSBY'S PAST.
HE WAS LEGALLY JAMES GATZ OF NORTH DAKOTA.
HIS PARENTS WERE SHIFTLESS AND UNSUCCESSFUL FARM PEOPLE—
HIS IMAGINATION HAD NEVER REALLY ACCEPTED THEM AS HIS PARENTS AT ALL.
BUT FOR A WHILE HIS WORLD SEEMED FEROCIOUSLY INDIFFERENT TO THE DRUMS OF HIS DESTINY.

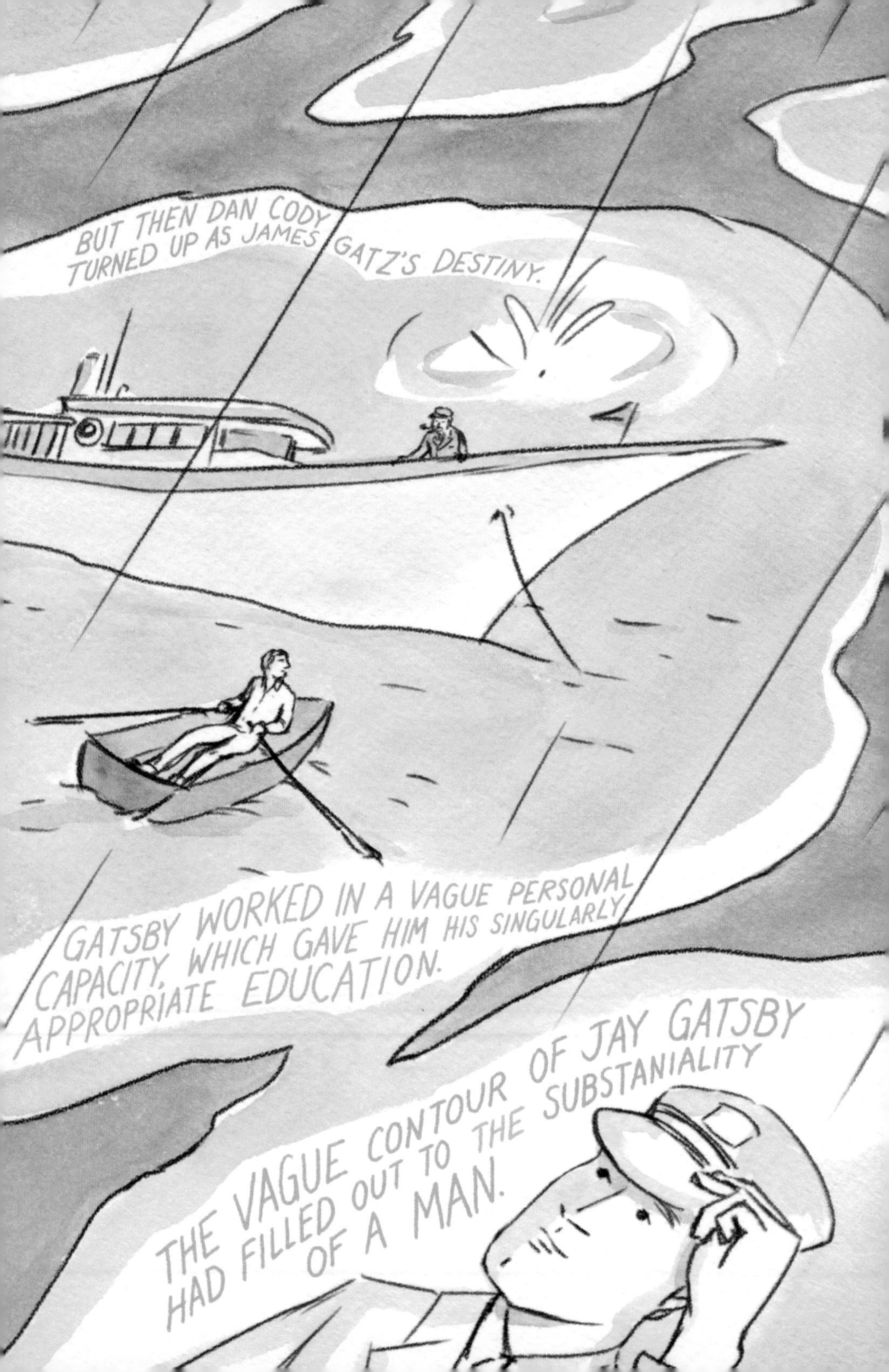
BUT THEN DAN CODY TURNED UP AS JAMES GATZ'S DESTINY.
GATSBY WORKED IN A VAGUE PERSONAL CAPACITY, WHICH GAVE HIM HIS SINGULARLY APPROPRIATE EDUCATION.
THE VAGUE CONTOUR OF JAY GATSBY HAD FILLED OUT TO THE SUBSTANIALITY OF A MAN.

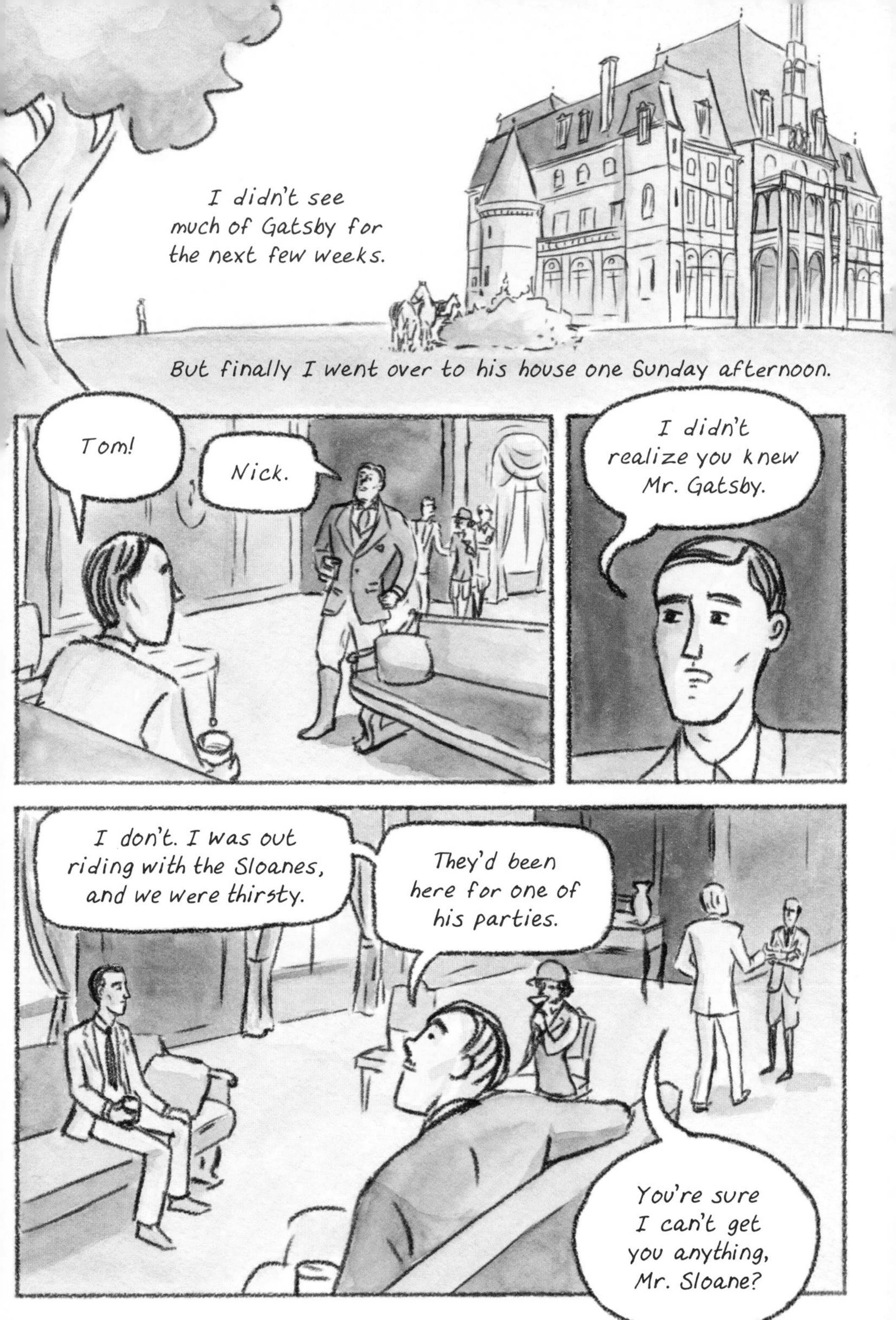

I didn't see much of Gatsby for the next few weeks.
But finally I went over to his house one Sunday afternoon.
Tom!
Nick.
I didn't realize you knew Mr. Gatsby.
I don't. I was out riding with the Sloanes, and we were thirsty.
They'd been here for one of his parties.
You're sure I can't get you anything, Mr. Sloane?

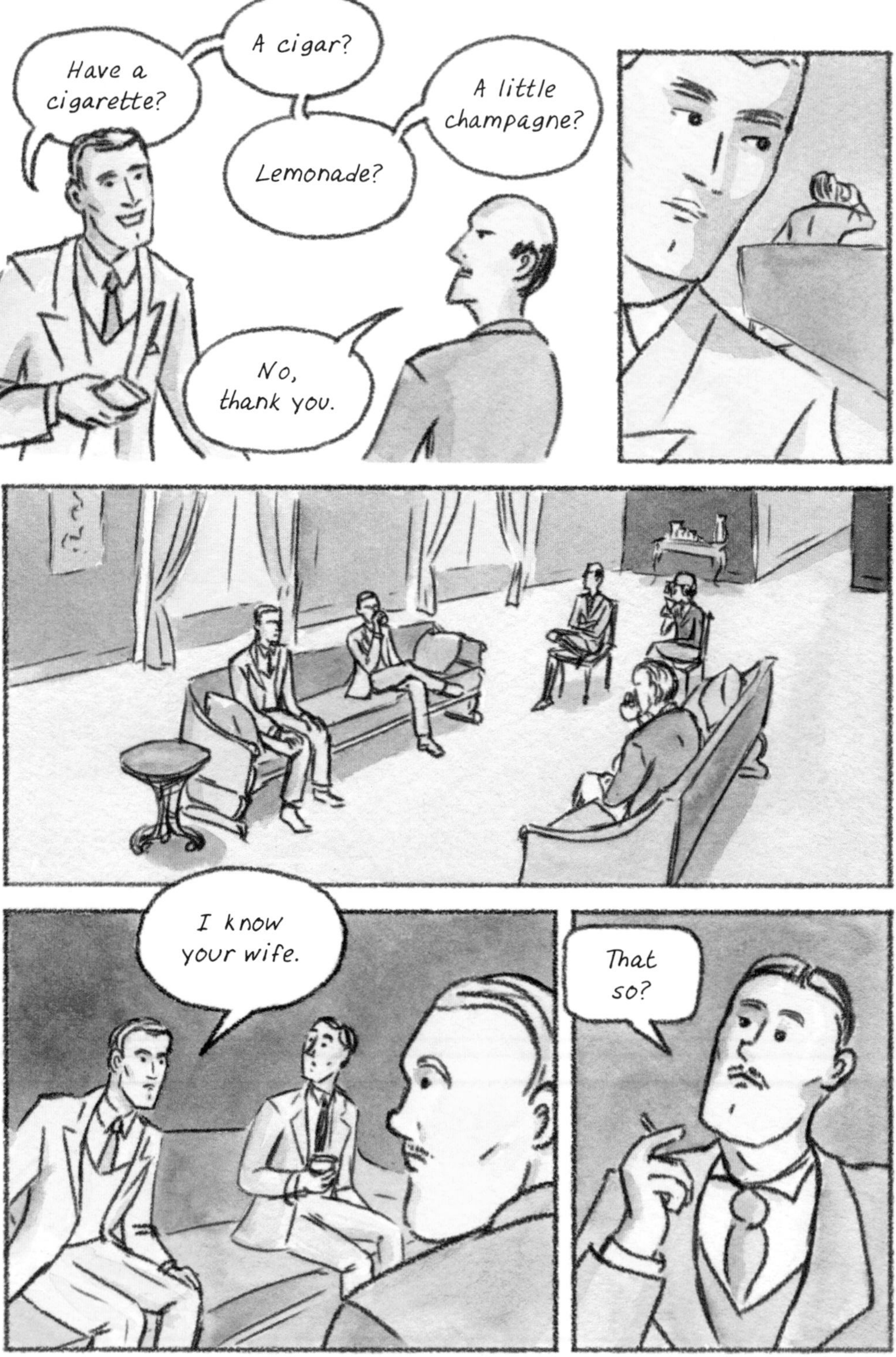
Have a cigarette?
A cigar?
Lemonade?
A little champagne?
No, thank you.
I know your wife.
That so?

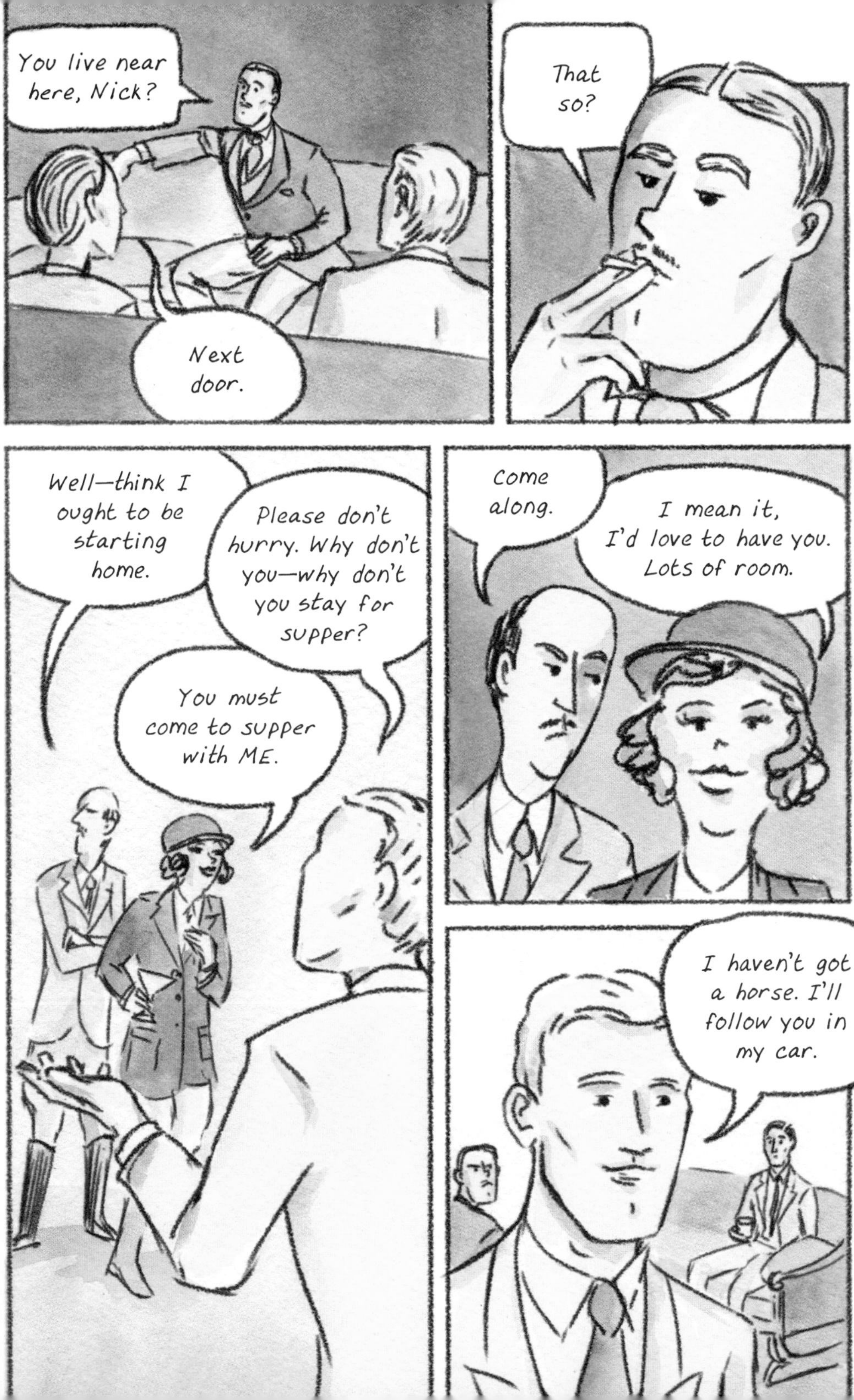
You live near here, Nick?
Next door.
That so?
Well—think I ought to be starting home.
Please don't hurry. Why don't you—why don't you stay for supper?
You must come to supper with ME.
Come along.
I mean it, I'd love to have you. Lots of room.
I haven't got a horse. I'll follow you in my car.

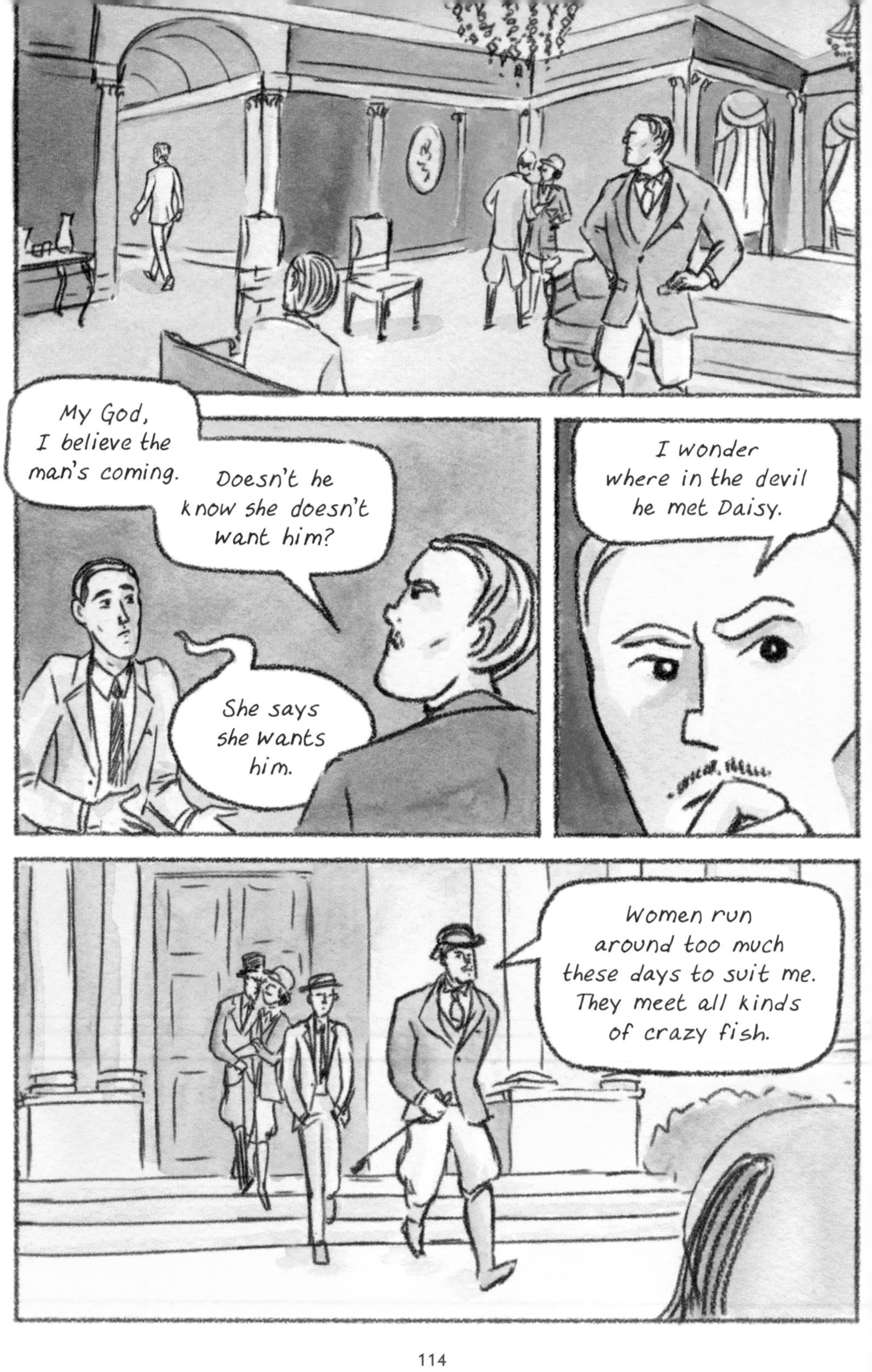
My God, I believe the man's coming.
Doesn't he know she doesn't want him?
She says she wants him.
I wonder where in the devil he met Daisy.
Women run around too much these days to suit me. They meet all kinds of crazy fish.

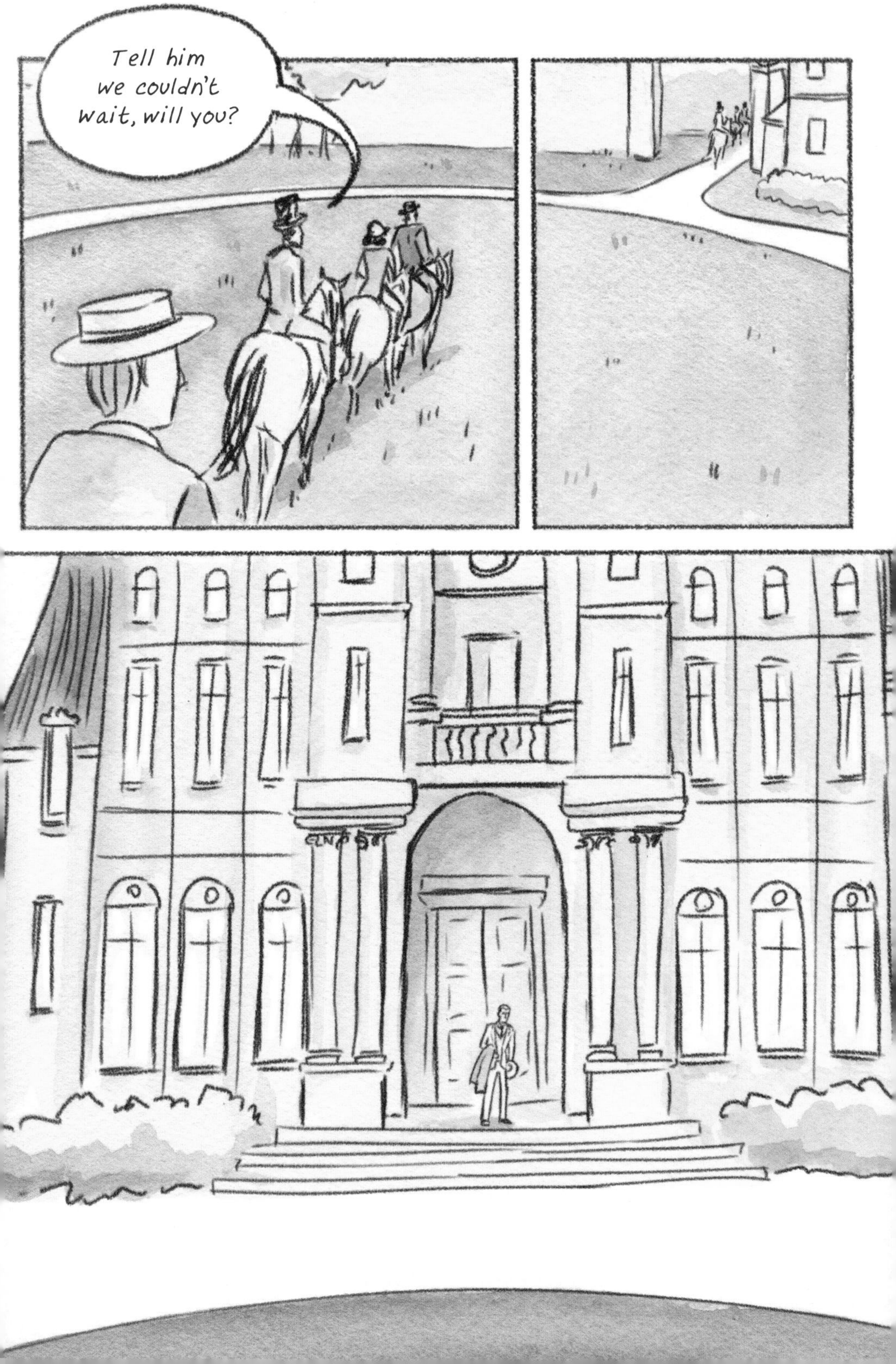
Tell him we couldn't wait, will you?

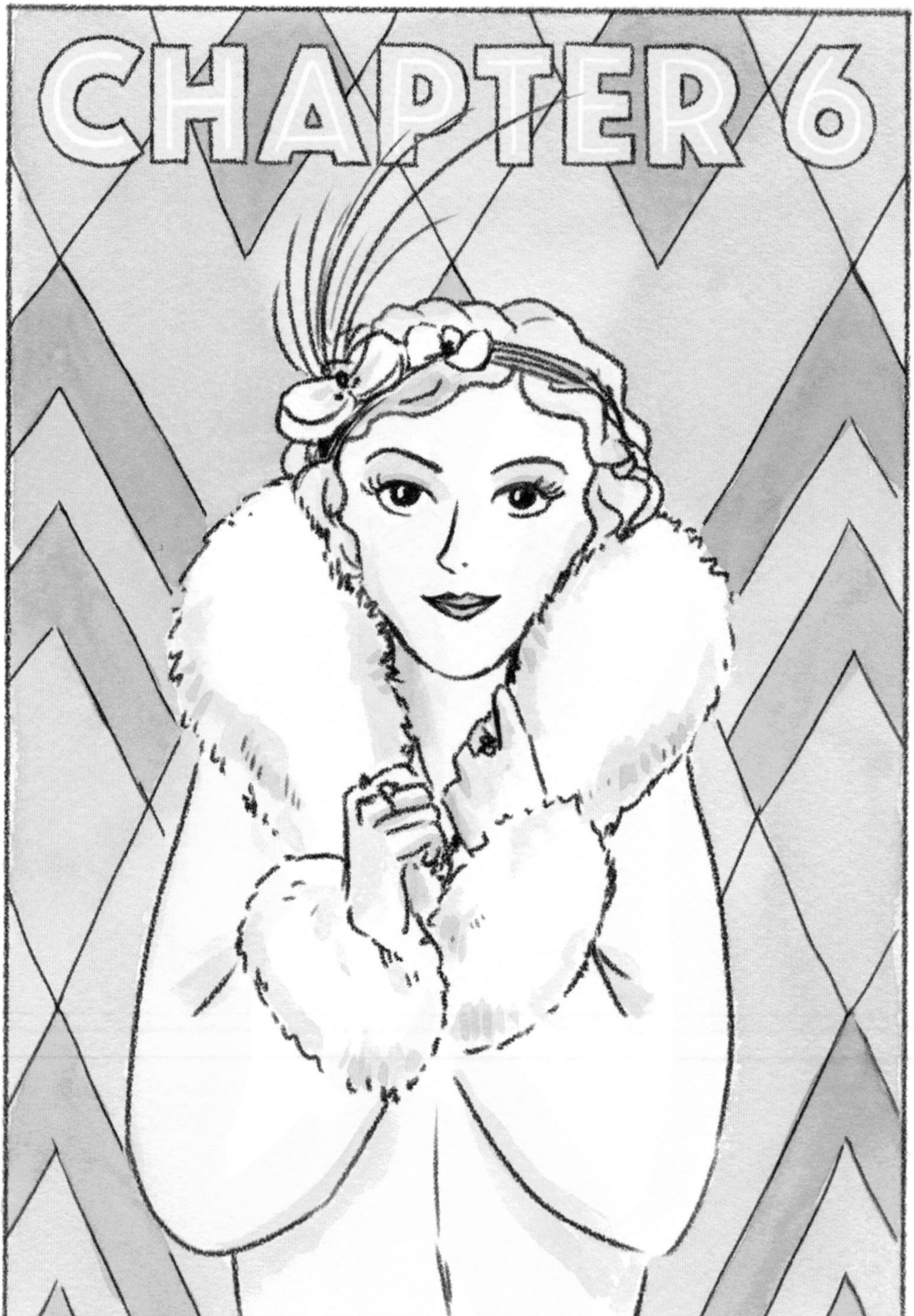
CHAPTER 6

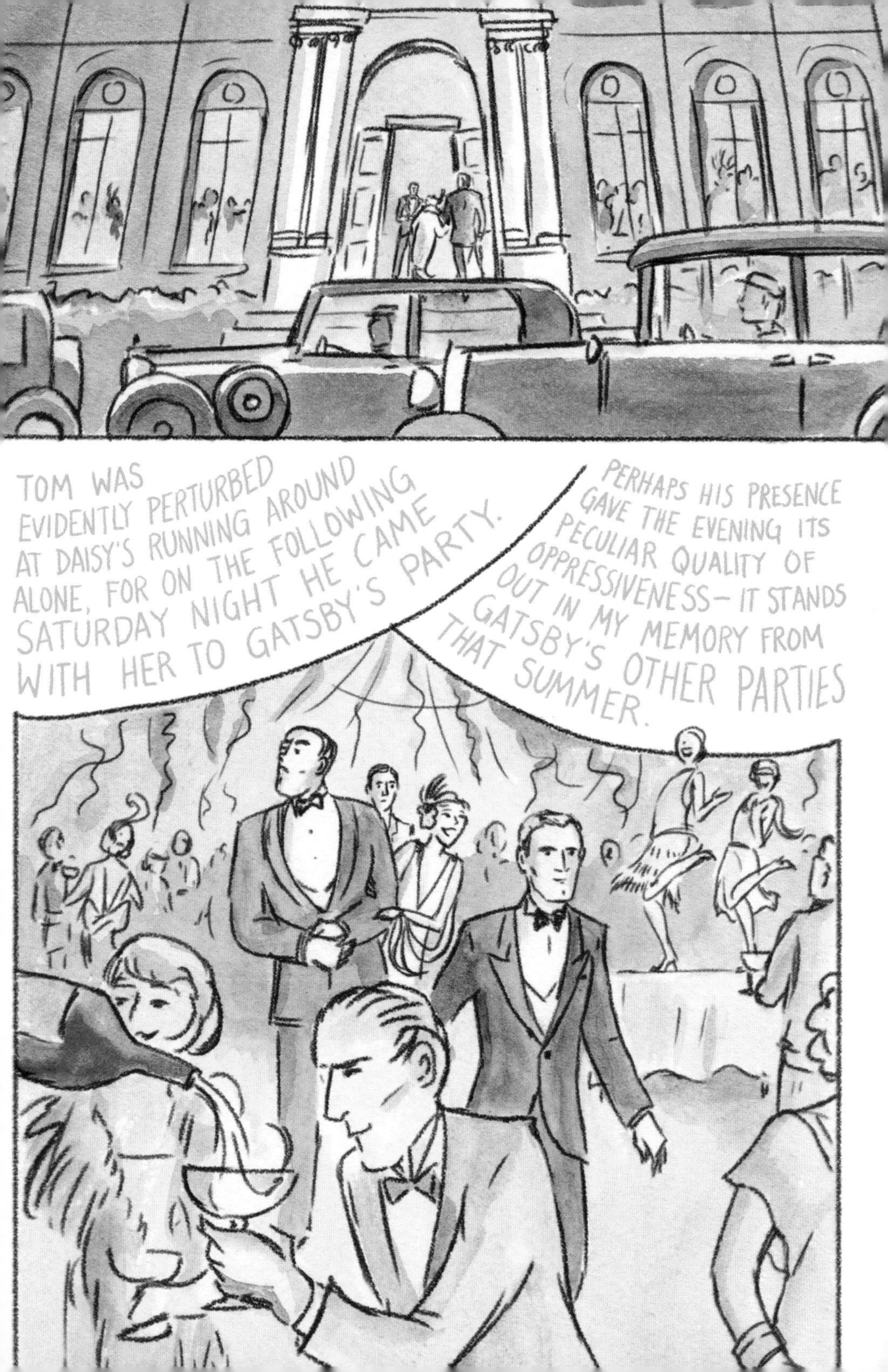
TOM WAS EVIDENTLY PERTURBED AT DAISY'S RUNNING AROUND ALONE, FOR ON THE FOLLOWING SATURDAY NIGHT HE CAME WITH HER TO GATSBY'S PARTY.
PERHAPS HIS PRESENCE GAVE THE EVENING ITS PECULIAR QUALITY OF OPPRESSIVENESS— IT STANDS OUT IN MY MEMORY FROM GATSBY'S OTHER PARTIES THAT SUMMER.

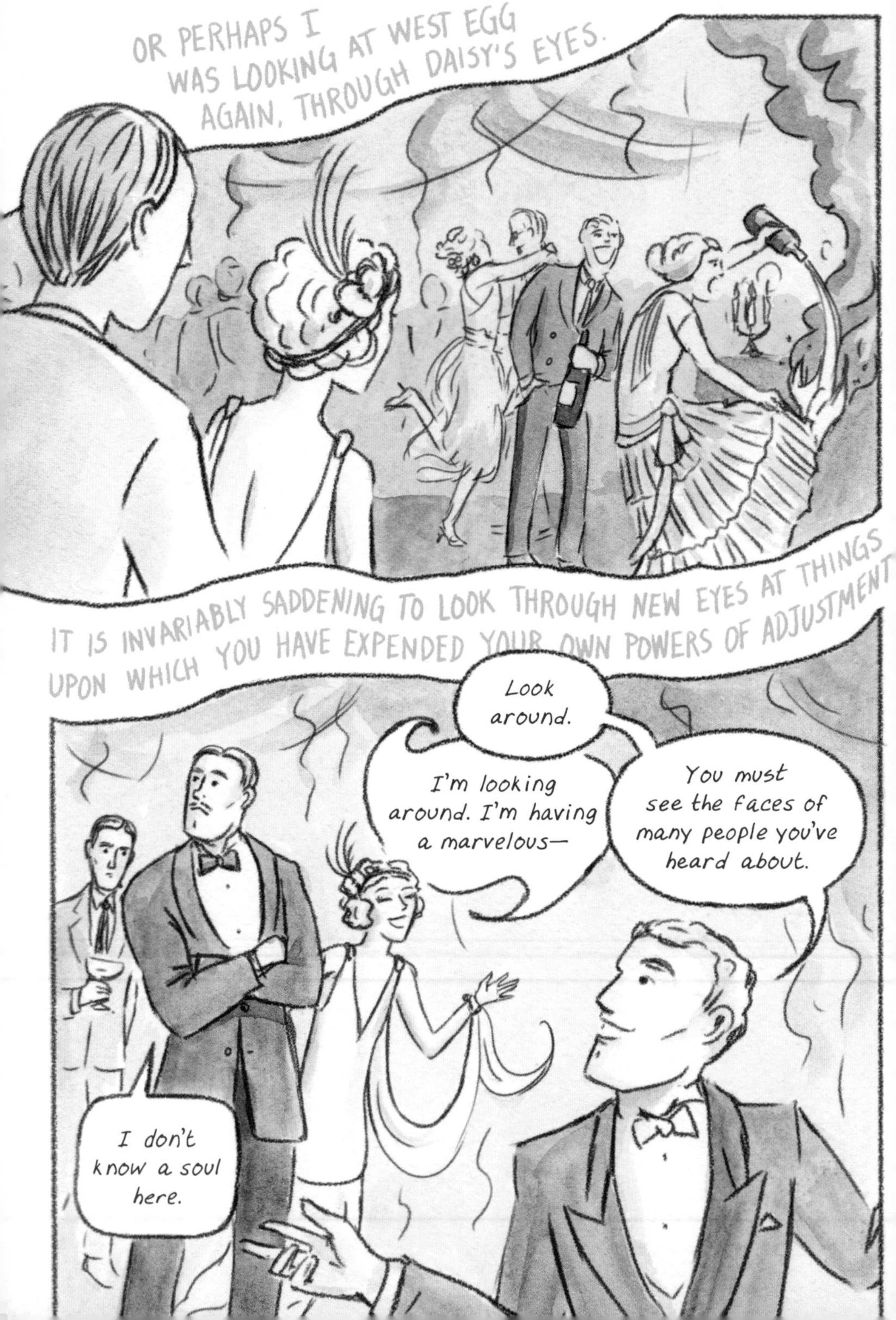
OR PERHAPS I WAS LOOKING AT WEST EGG AGAIN, THROUGH DAISY'S EYES.
IT IS INVARIABLY SADDENING TO LOOK THROUGH NEW EYES AT THINGS UPON WHICH YOU HAVE EXPENDED YOUR OWN POWERS OF ADJUSTMENT.
Look around.
I'm looking around. I'm having a marvelous—
You must see the faces of many people you've heard about.
I don't know a soul here.

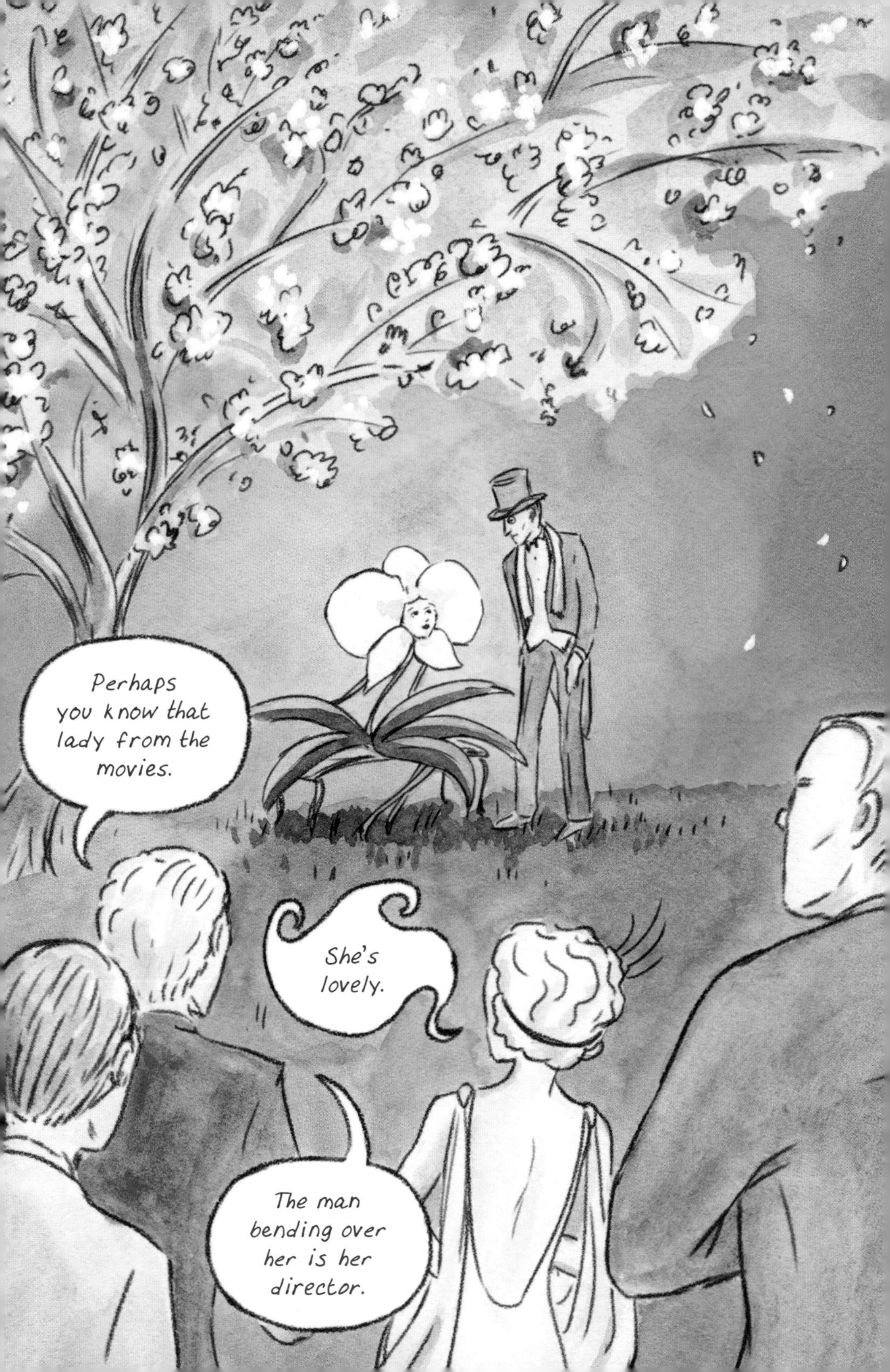
Perhaps you know that lady from the movies.
She's lovely.
The man bending over her is her director.

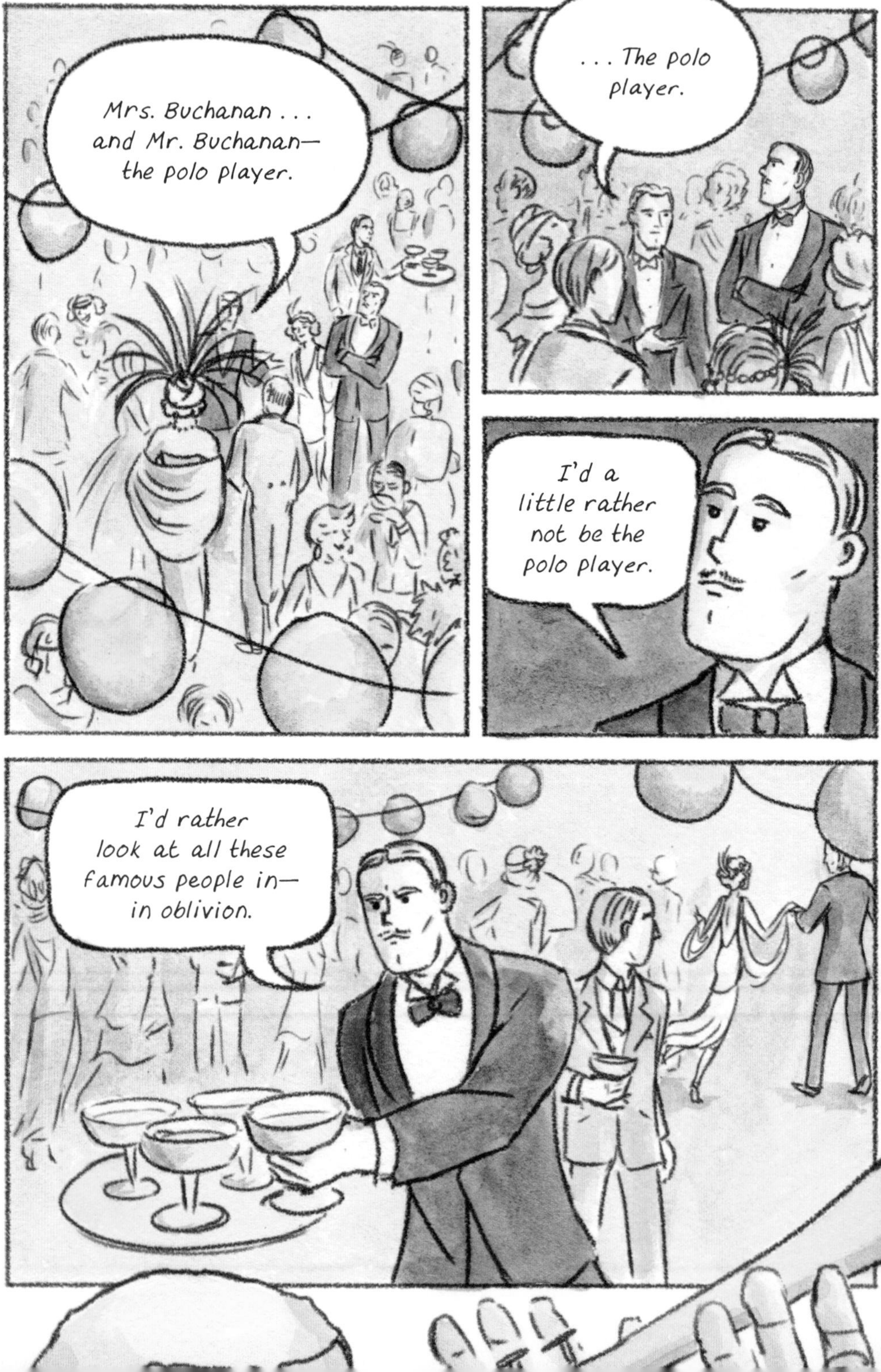
Mrs. Buchanan . . . and Mr. Buchanan— the polo player.
. . . The polo player.
I'd a little rather not be the polo player.
I'd rather look at all these famous people in— in oblivion.

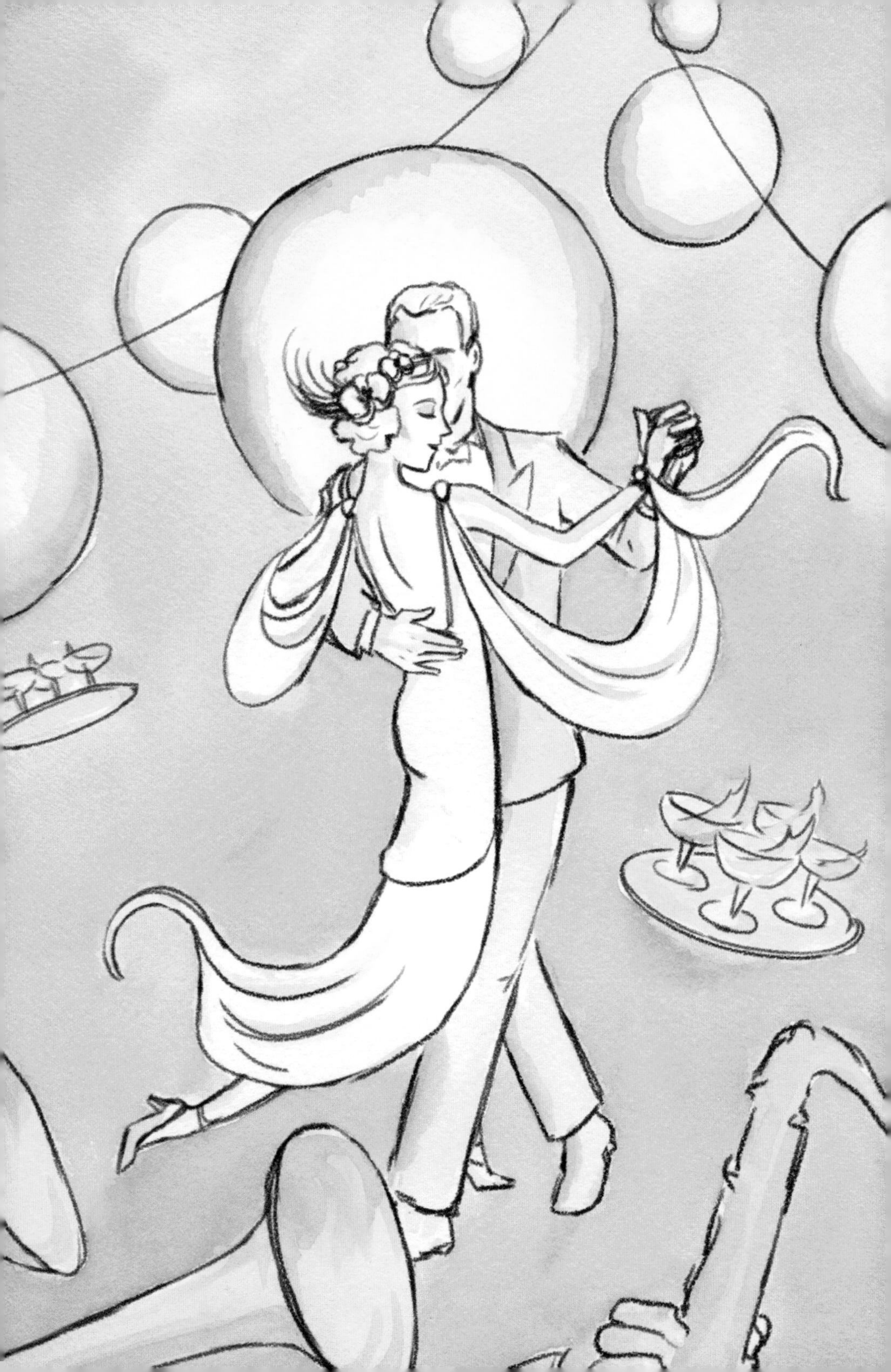

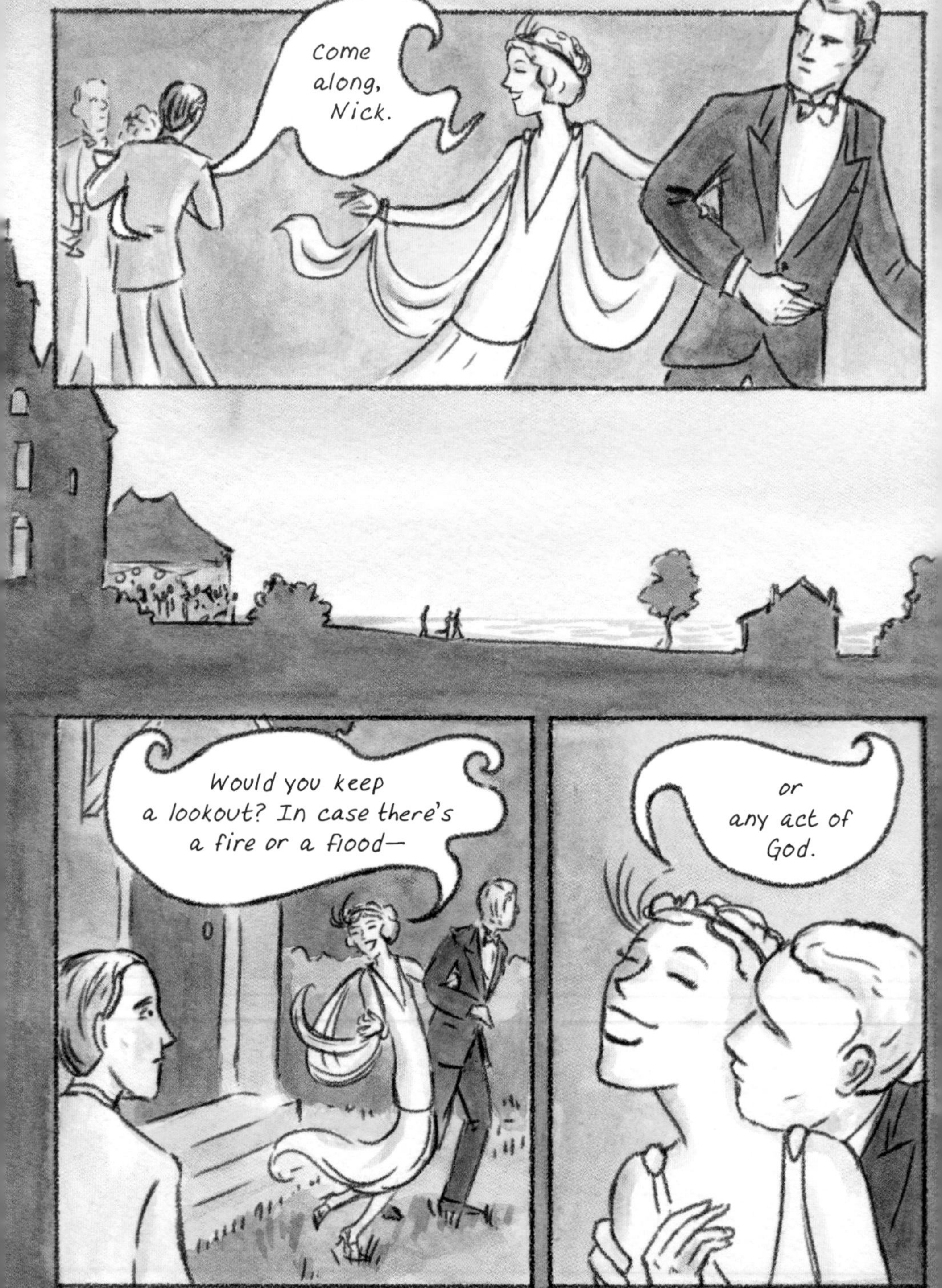
Come along, Nick.
Would you keep a lookout? In case there's a fire or a flood—
or any act of God.

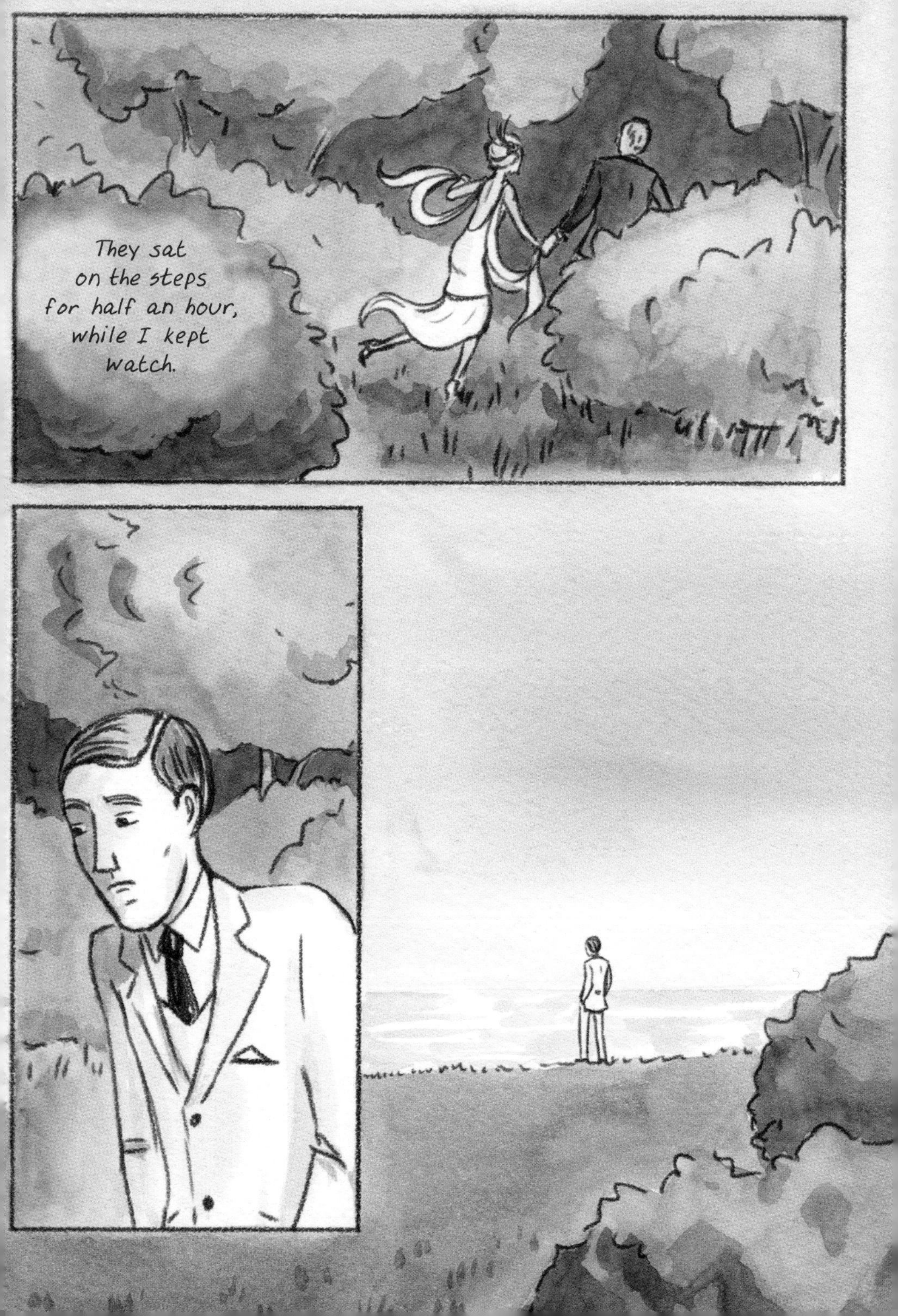
They sat on the steps for half an hour, while I kept watch.

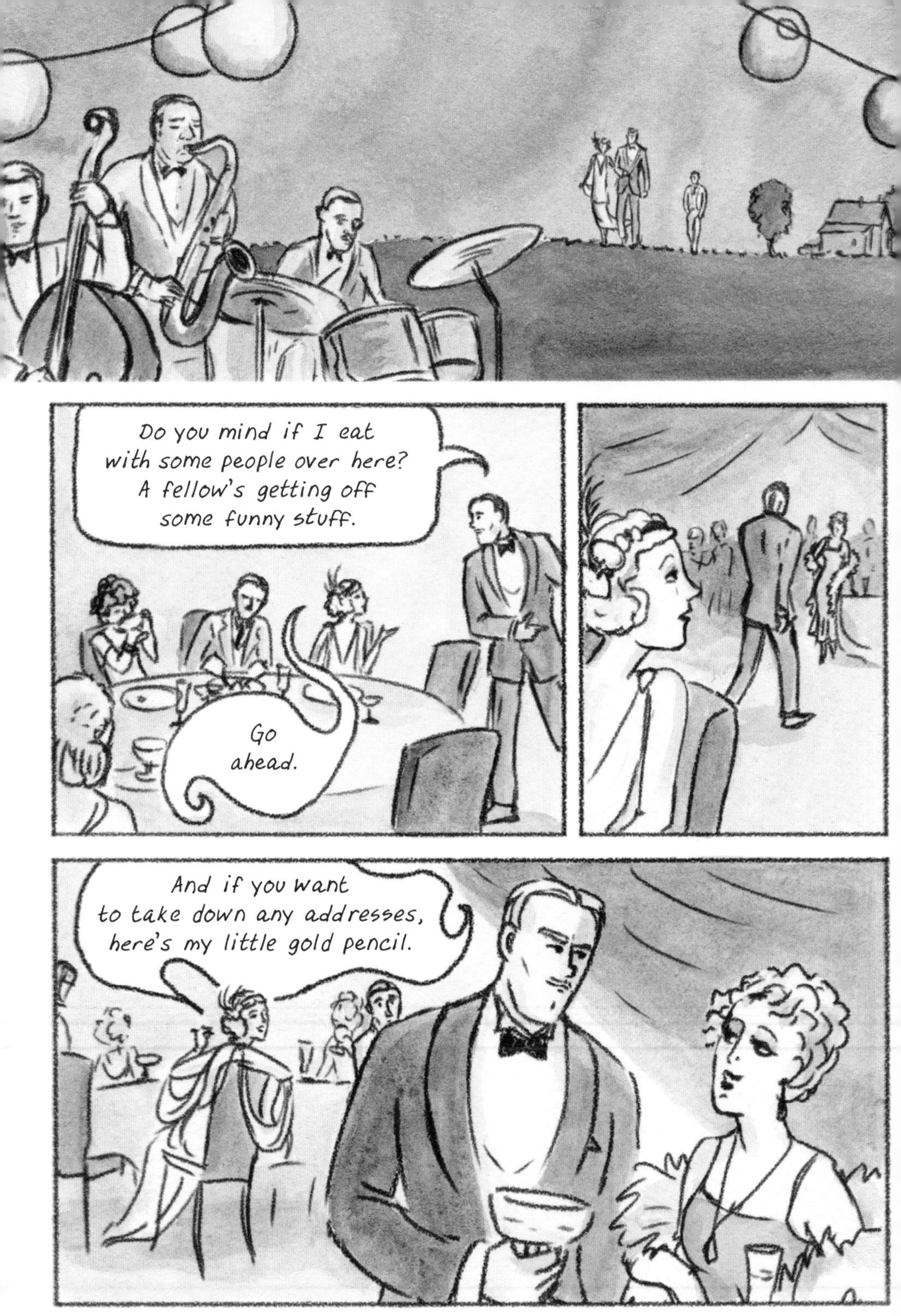
Do you mind if I eat with some people over here? A fellow's getting off some funny stuff.
Go ahead.
And if you want to take down any addresses, here's my little gold pencil.

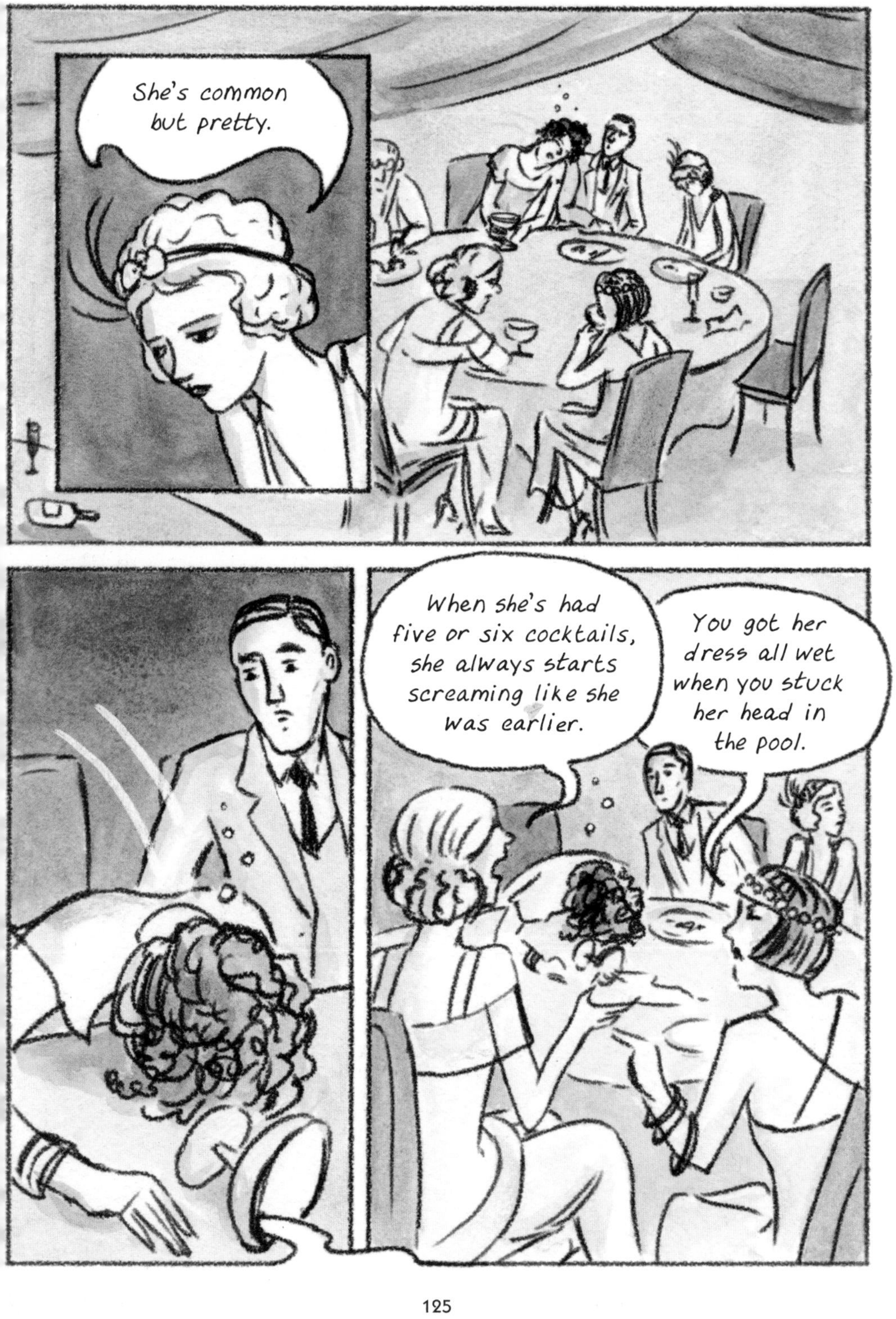
She's common but pretty.
When she's had five or six cocktails, she always starts screaming like she was earlier.
You got her dress all wet when you stuck her head in the pool.

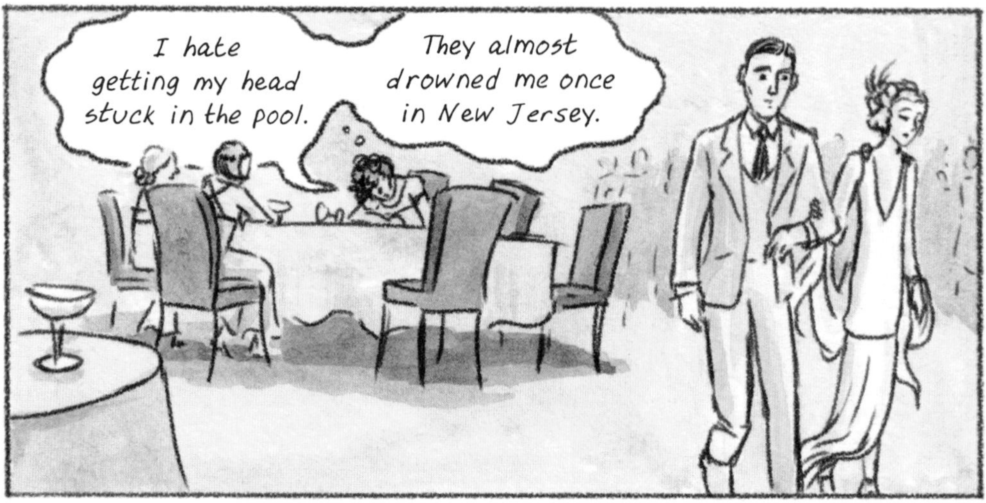
I hate getting my head stuck in the pool.
They almost drowned me once in New Jersey.

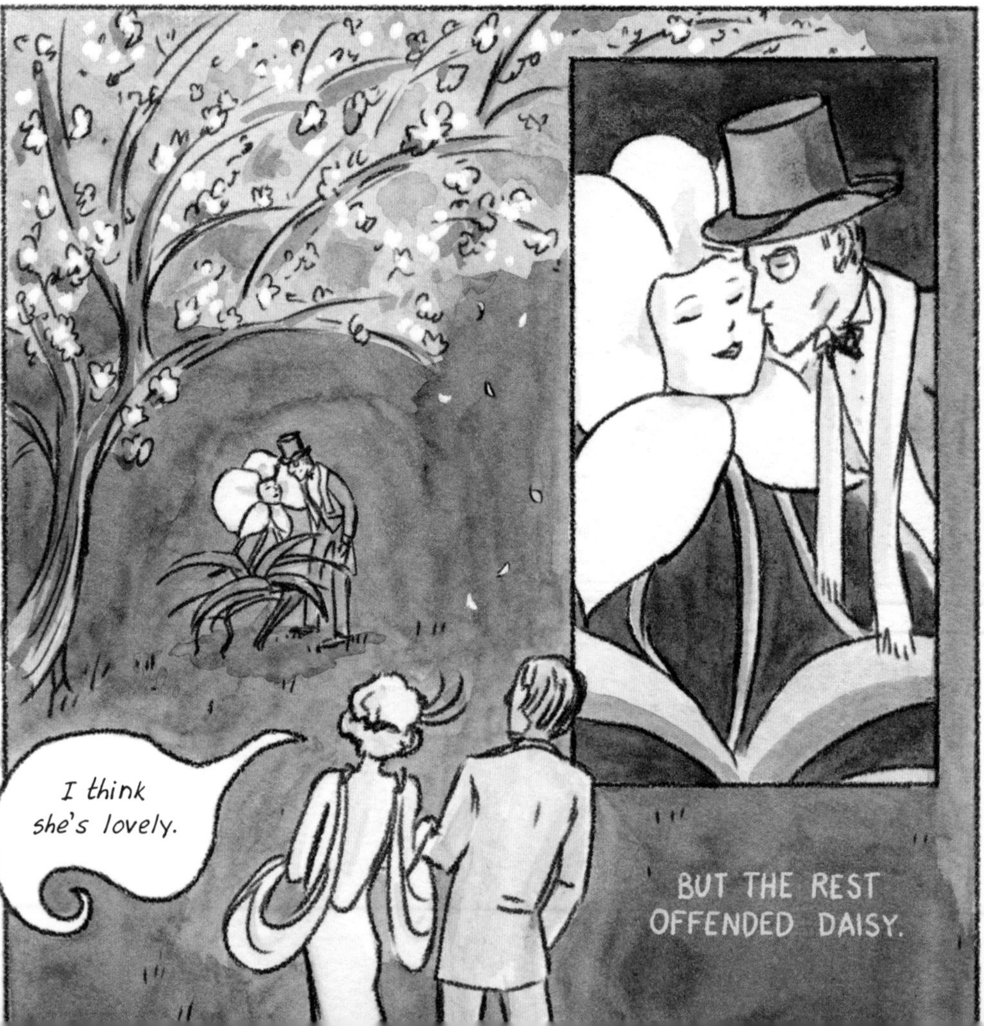
I think she's lovely.
BUT THE REST OFFENDED DAISY.

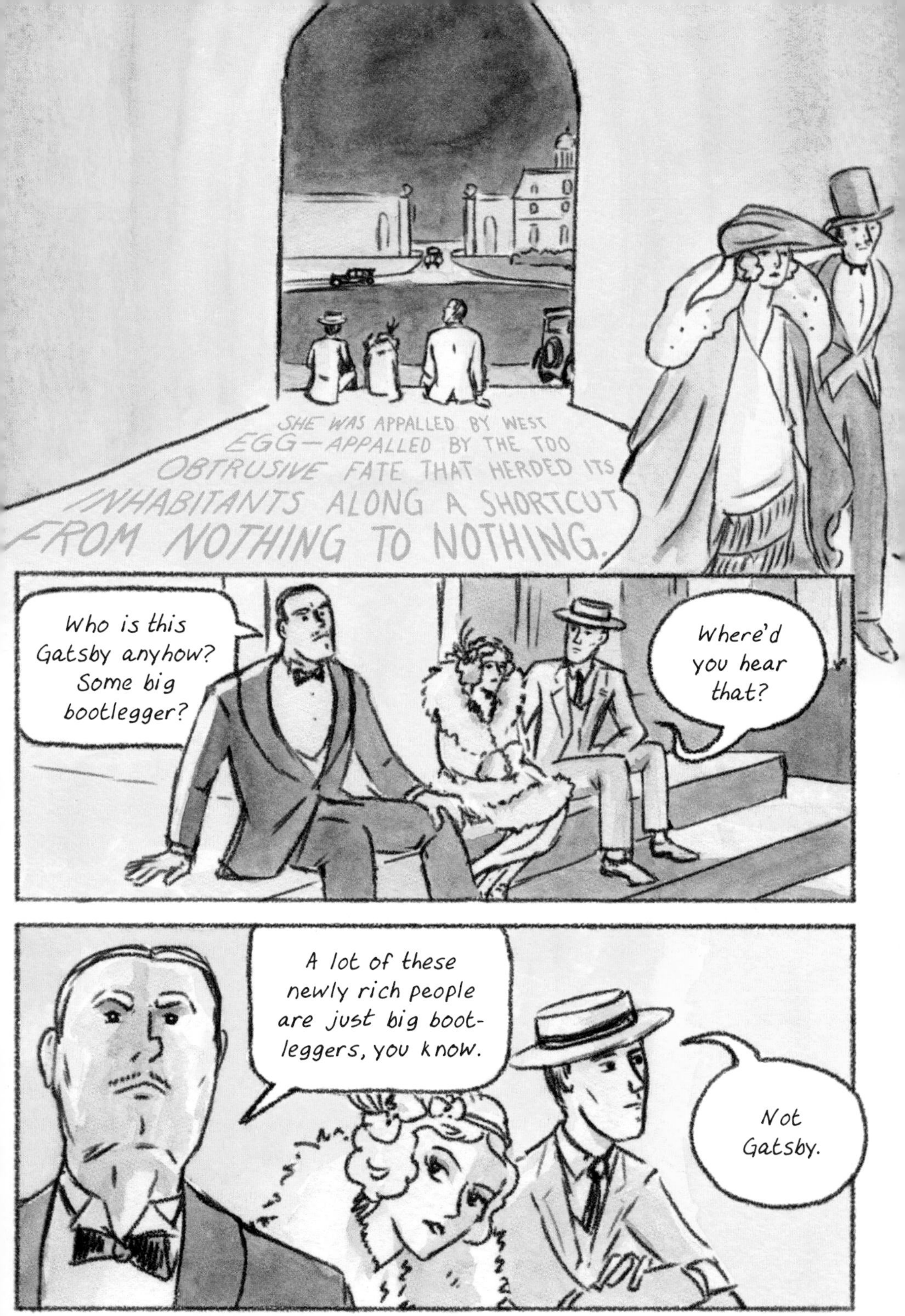
SHE WAS APPALLED BY WEST EGG—APPALLED BY THE TOO OBTRUSIVE FATE THAT HERDED ITS INHABITANTS ALONG A SHORTCUT FROM NOTHING TO NOTHING.
Who is this Gatsby anyhow? Some big bootlegger?
Where'd you hear that?
A lot of these newly rich people are just big bootleggers, you know.
Not Gatsby.

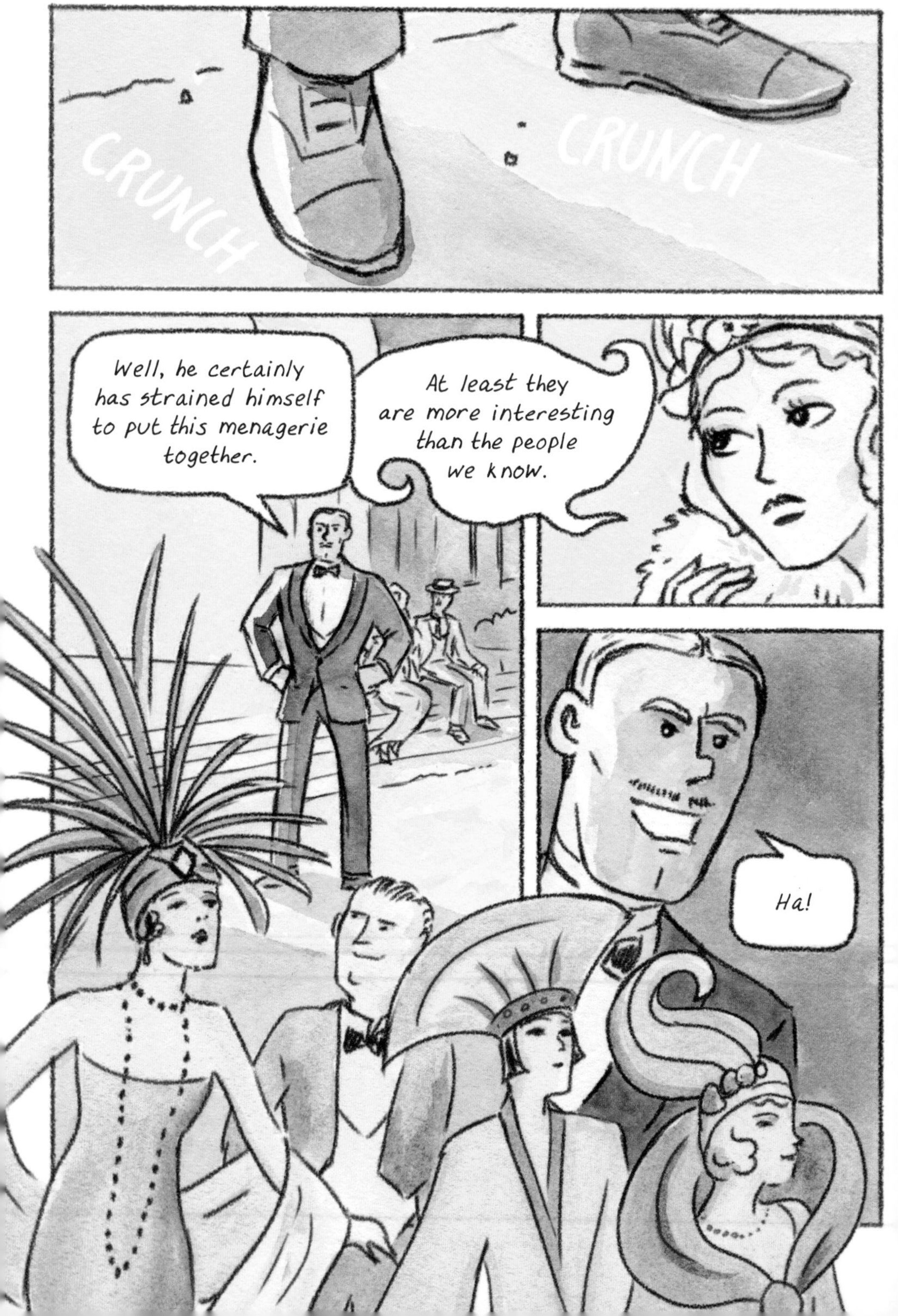
CRUNCH
CRUNCH
Well, he certainly has strained himself to put this menagerie together.
At least they are more interesting than the people we know.
Ha!

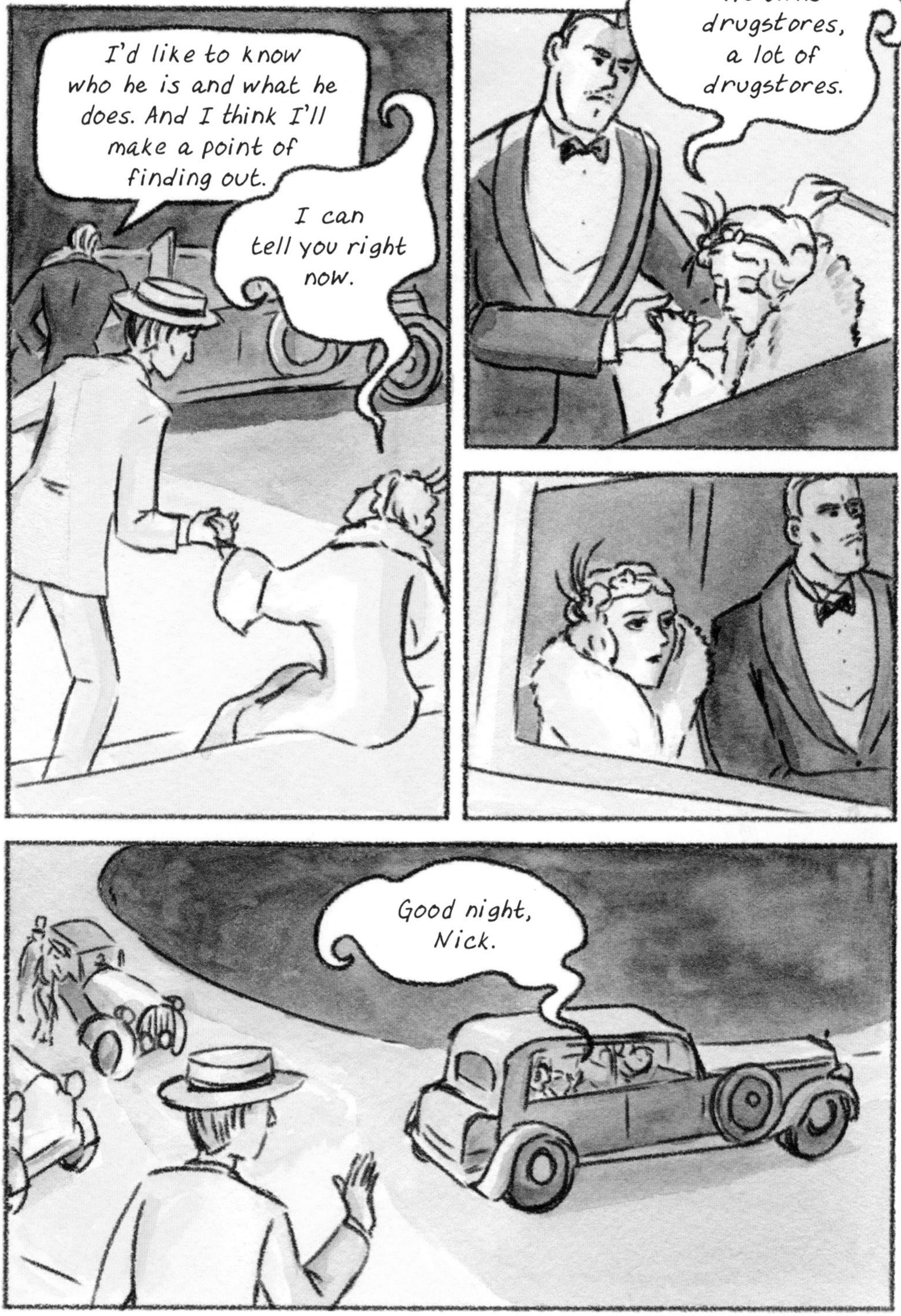
I'd like to know who he is and what he does. And I think I'll make a point of finding out.
I can tell you right now.
He owns drugstores, a lot of drugstores.
Good night, Nick.

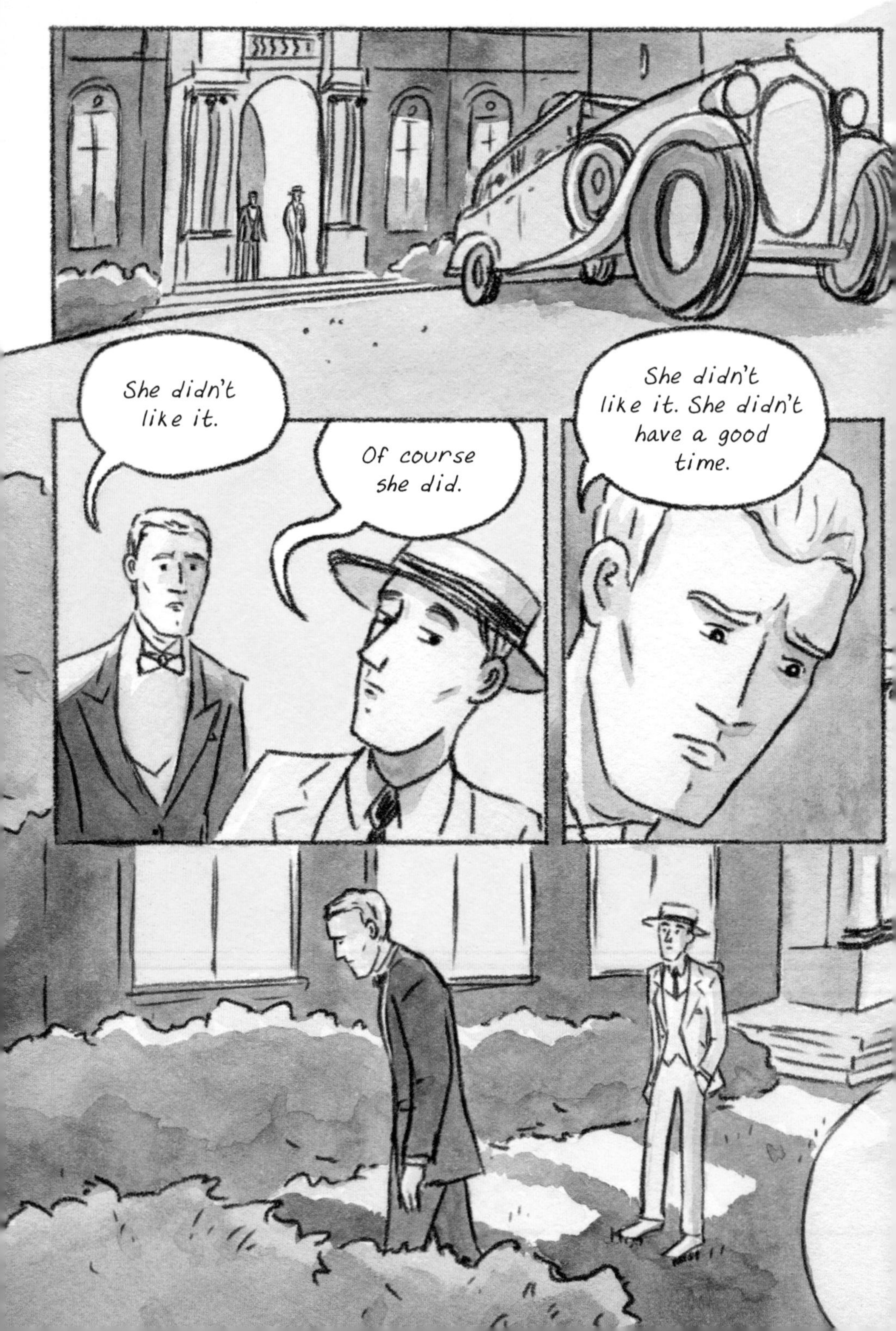
She didn't like it.
Of course she did.
She didn't like it. She didn't have a good time.

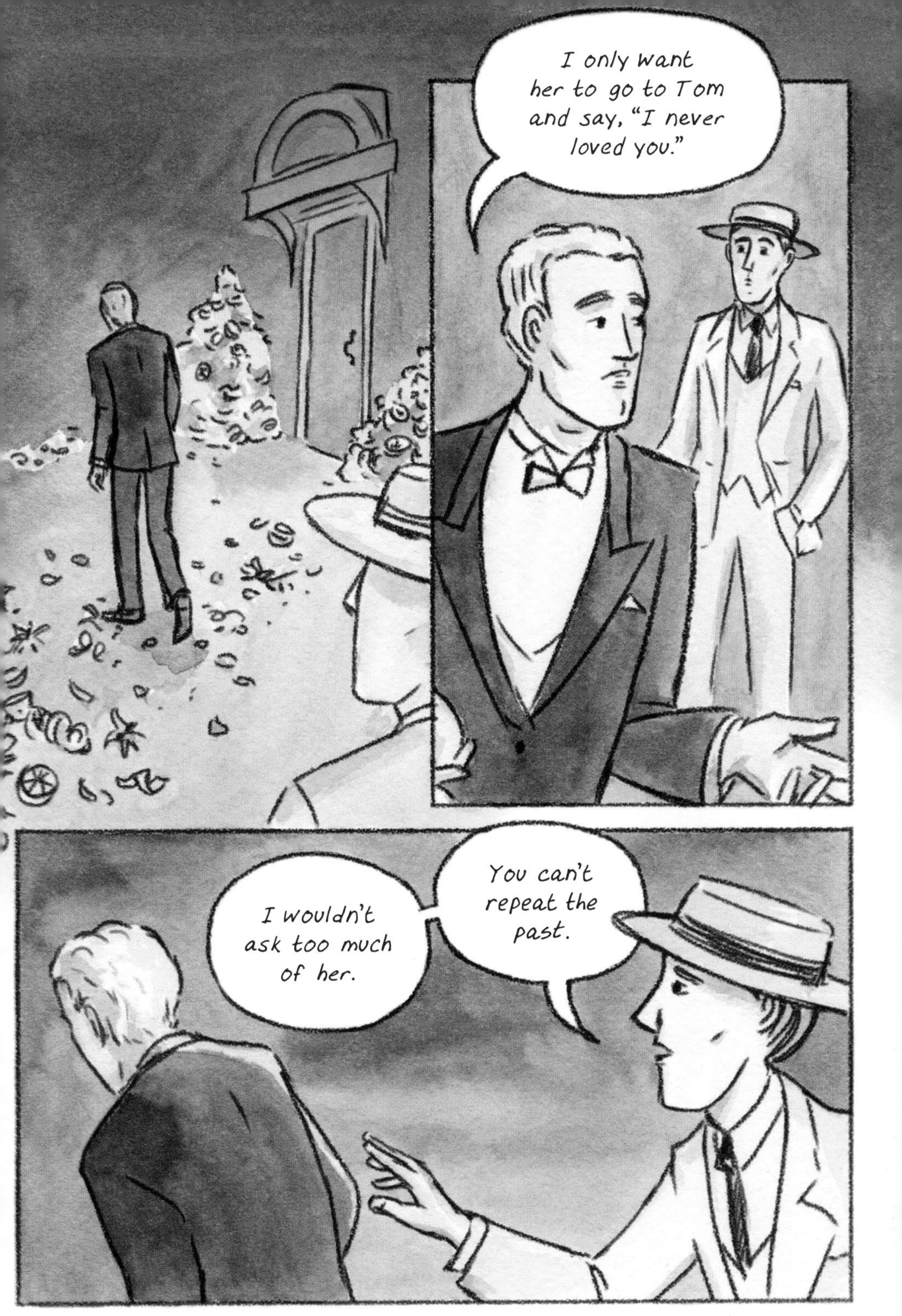
I only want her to go to Tom and say, "I never loved you."
I wouldn't ask too much of her.
You can't repeat the past.

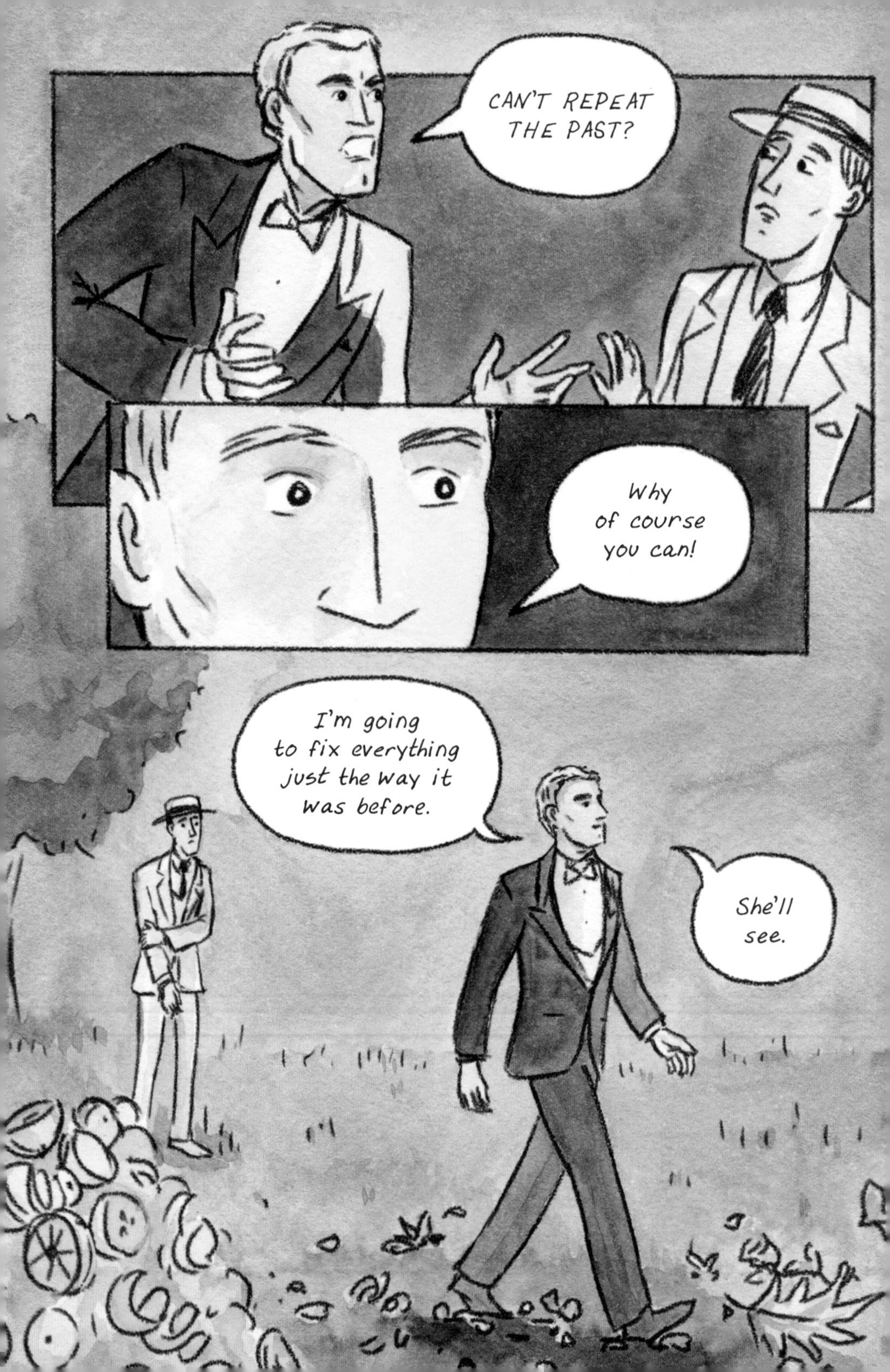
CAN'T REPEAT THE PAST?
Why of course you can!
I'm going to fix everything just the way it was before.
She'll see.

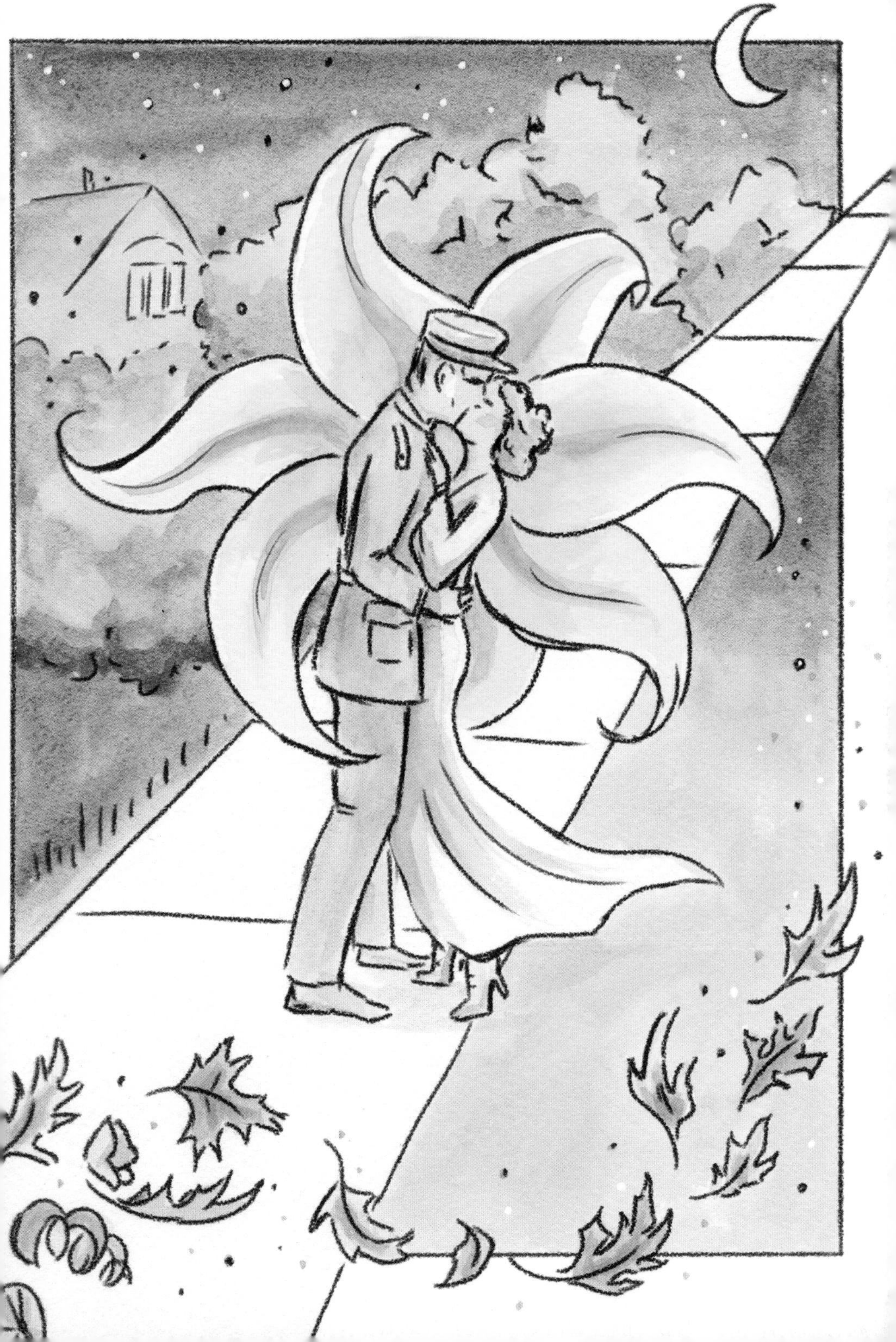

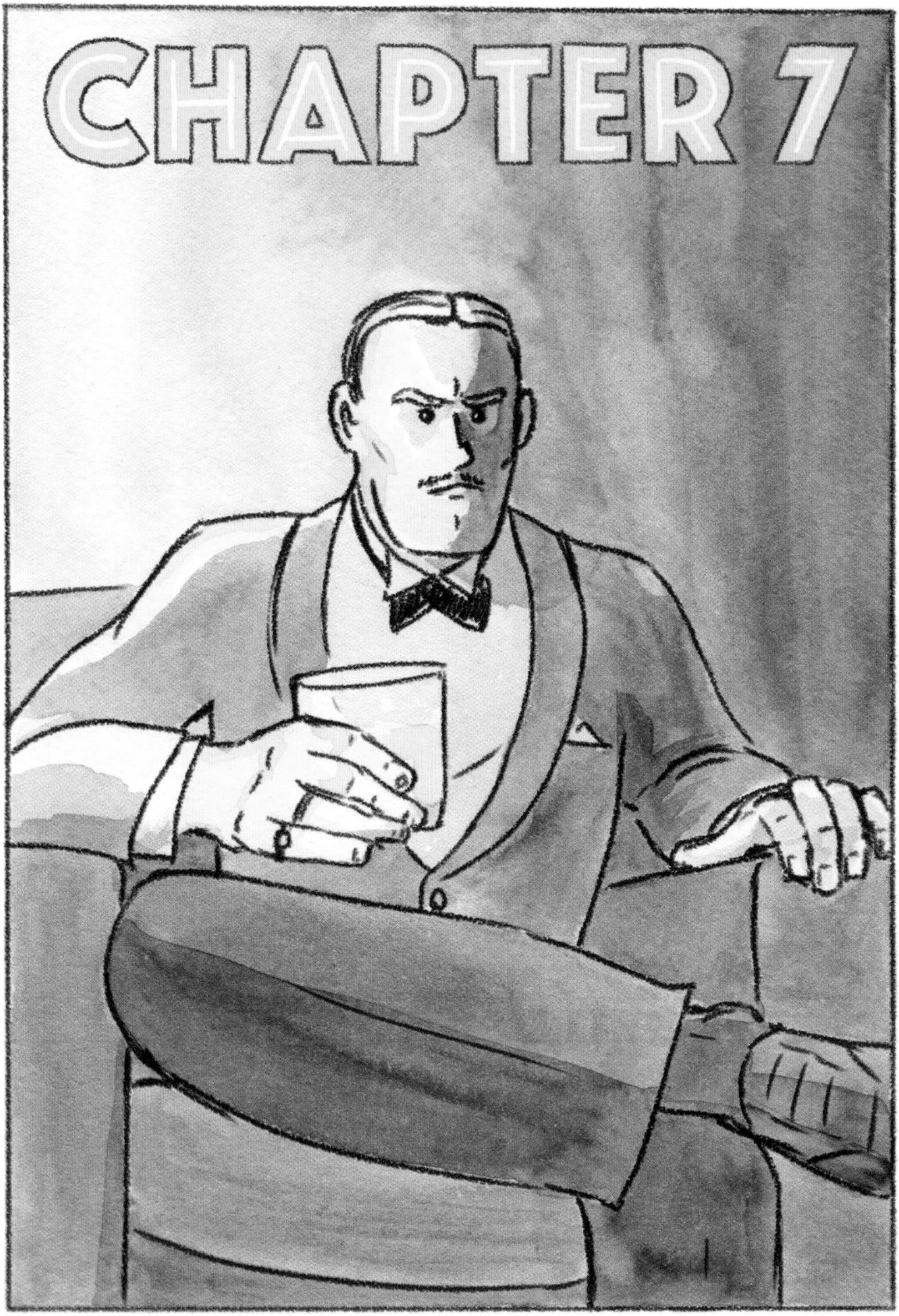
CHAPTER 7

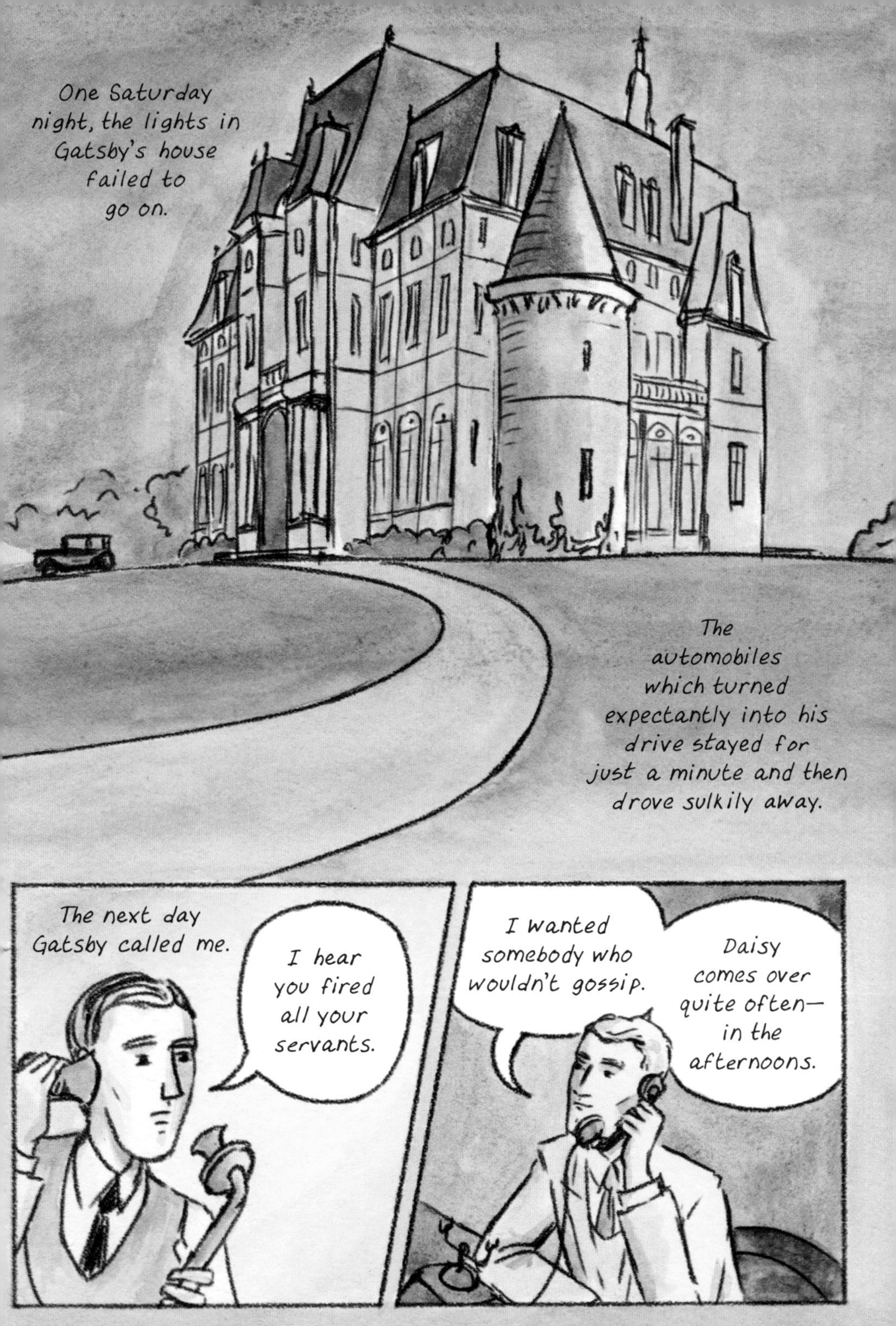
One Saturday night, the lights in Gatsby's house failed to go on.
The automobiles which turned expectantly into his drive stayed for just a minute and then drove sulkily away.
The next day Gatsby called me.
I hear you fired all your servants.
I wanted somebody who wouldn't gossip.
Daisy comes over quite often— in the afternoons.

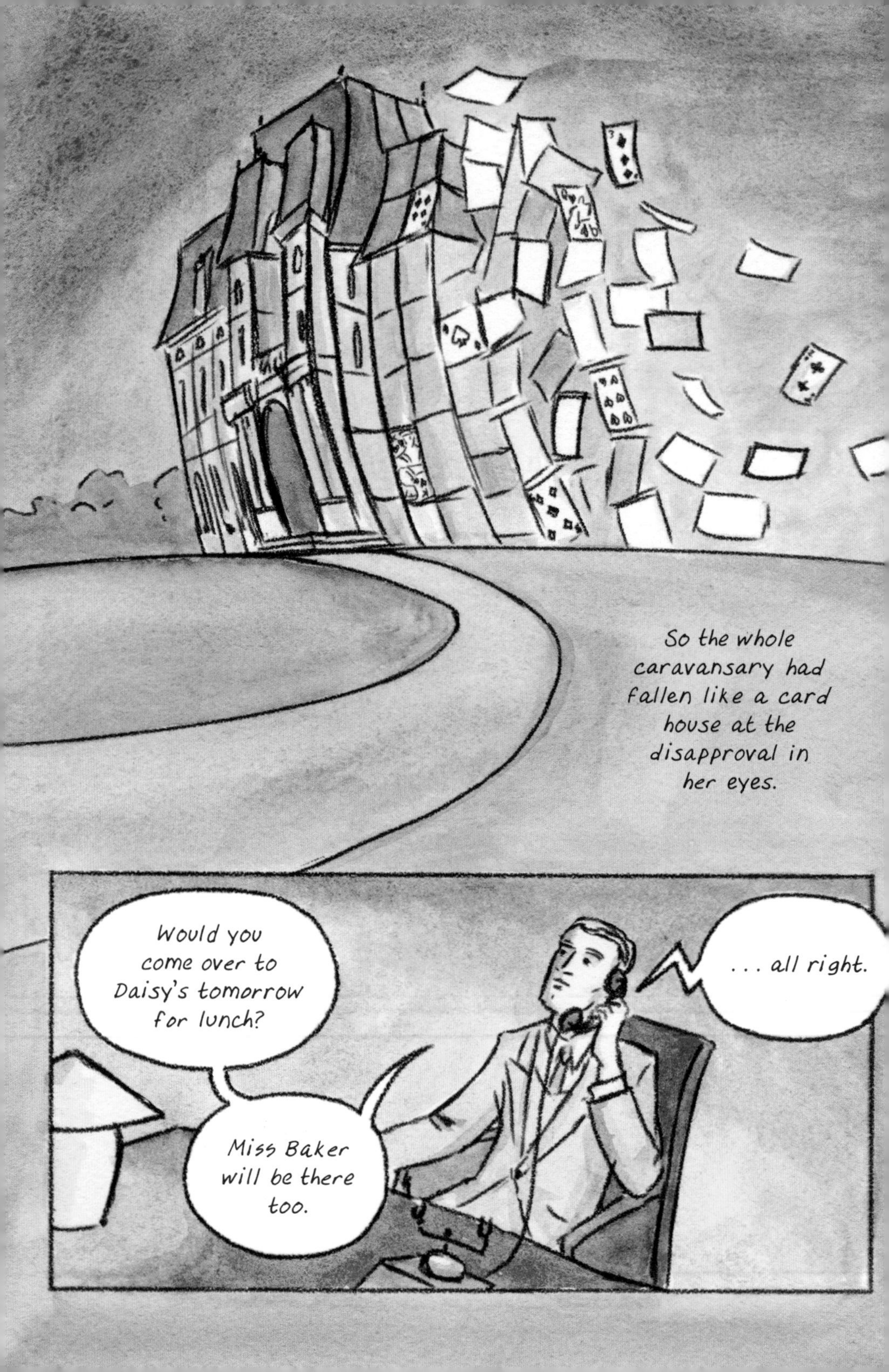
So the whole caravansary had fallen like a card house at the disapproval in her eyes.
Would you come over to Daisy's tomorrow for lunch?
Miss Baker will be there too.
. . . all right.

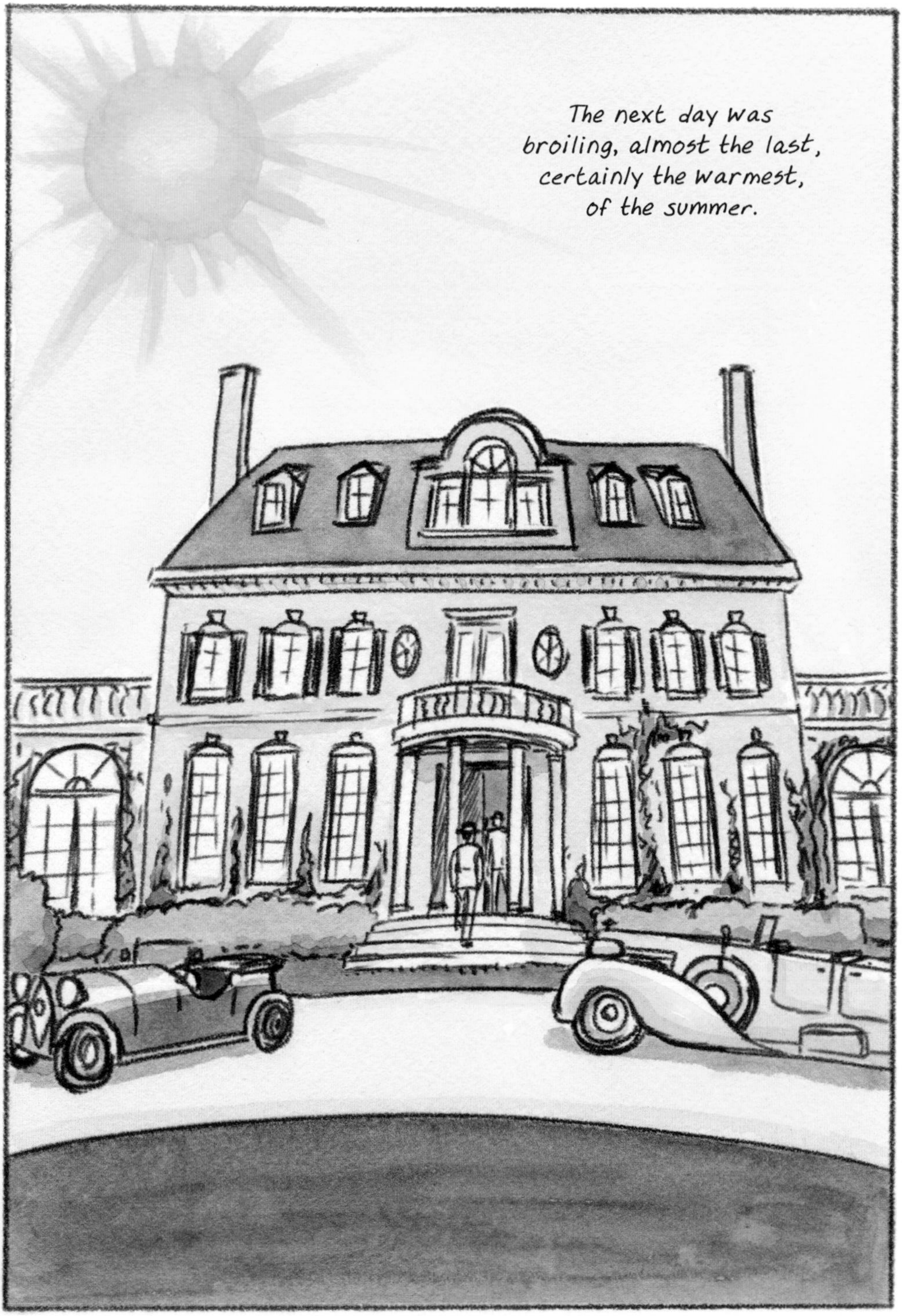
The next day was
broiling, almost the last,
certainly the warmest,
of the summer.

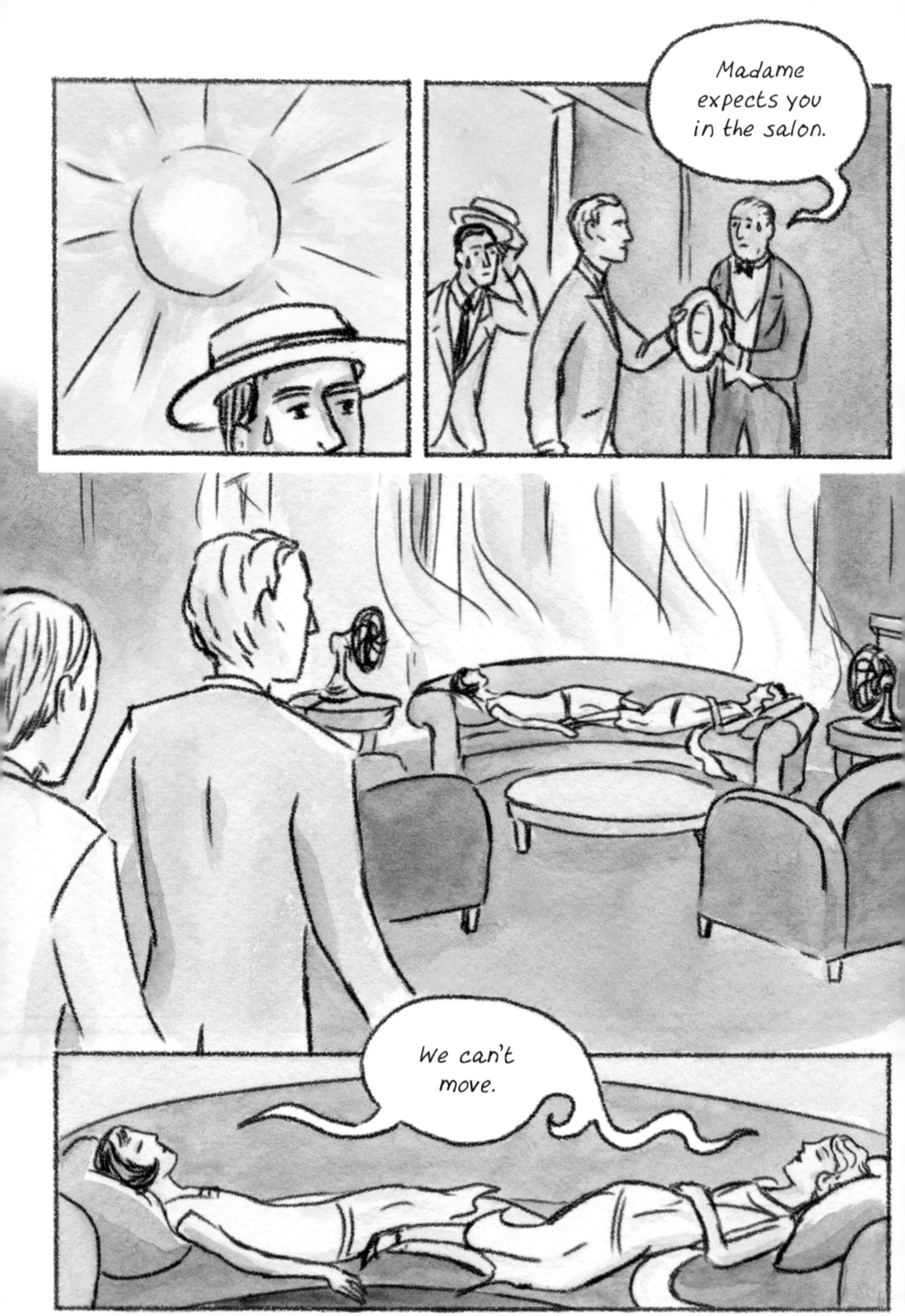
Madame expects you in the salon.
We can't move.

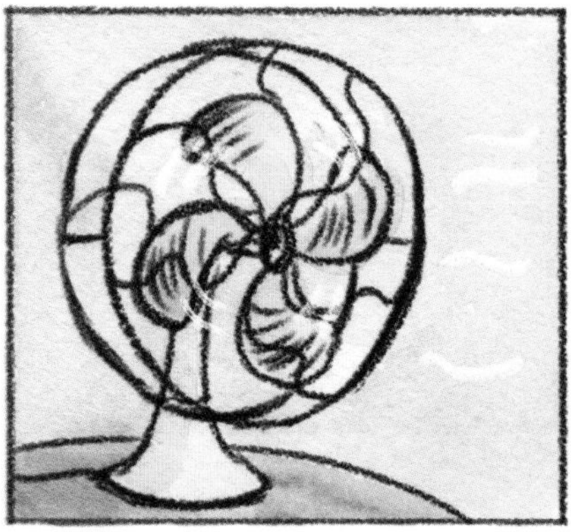

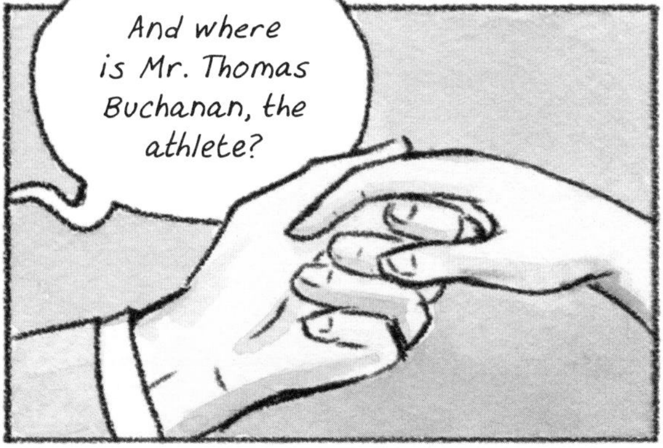
And where is Mr. Thomas Buchanan, the athlete?

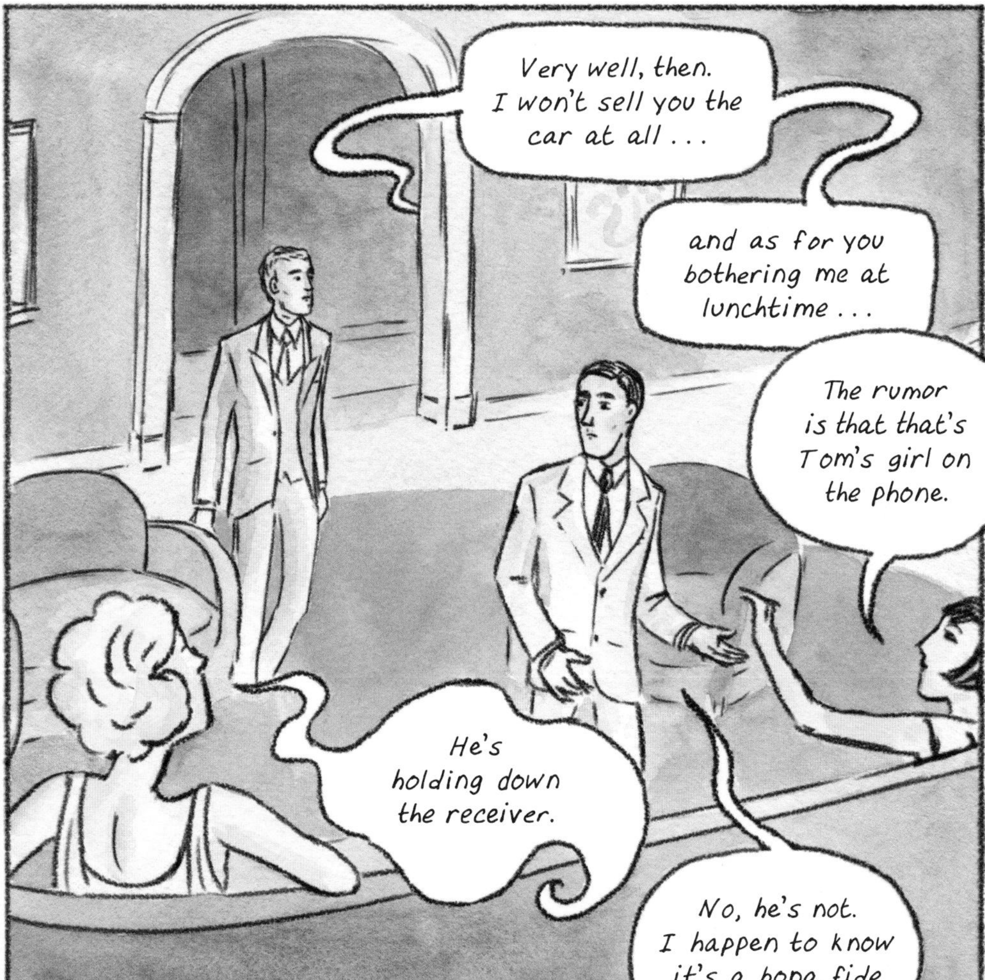
Very well, then. I won't sell you the car at all . . .
and as for you bothering me at lunchtime . . .
The rumor is that that's Tom's girl on the phone.
He's holding down the receiver.
No, he's not. I happen to know it's a bona fide deal.

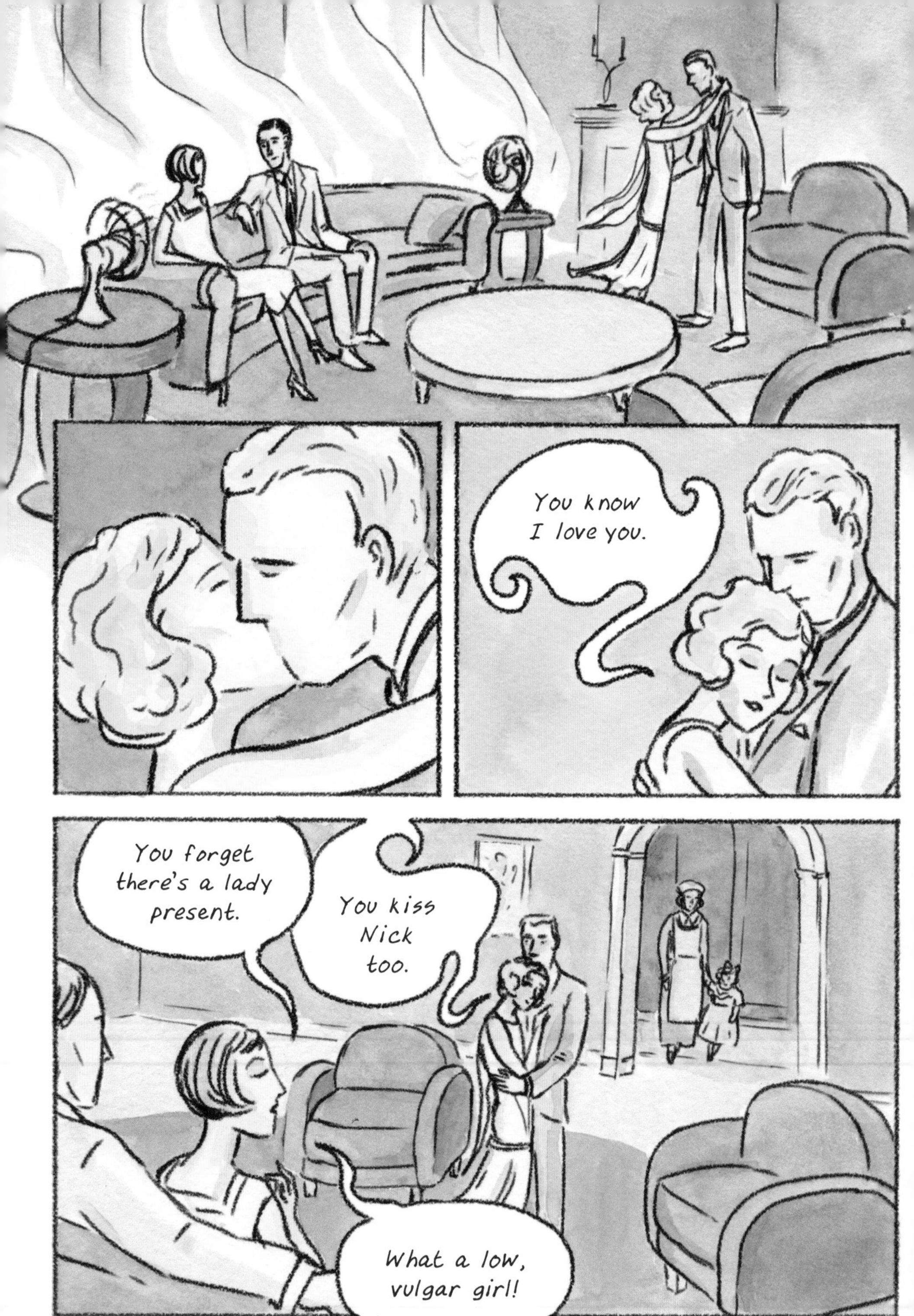
You know I love you.
You forget there's a lady present.
You kiss Nick too.
What a low, vulgar girl!

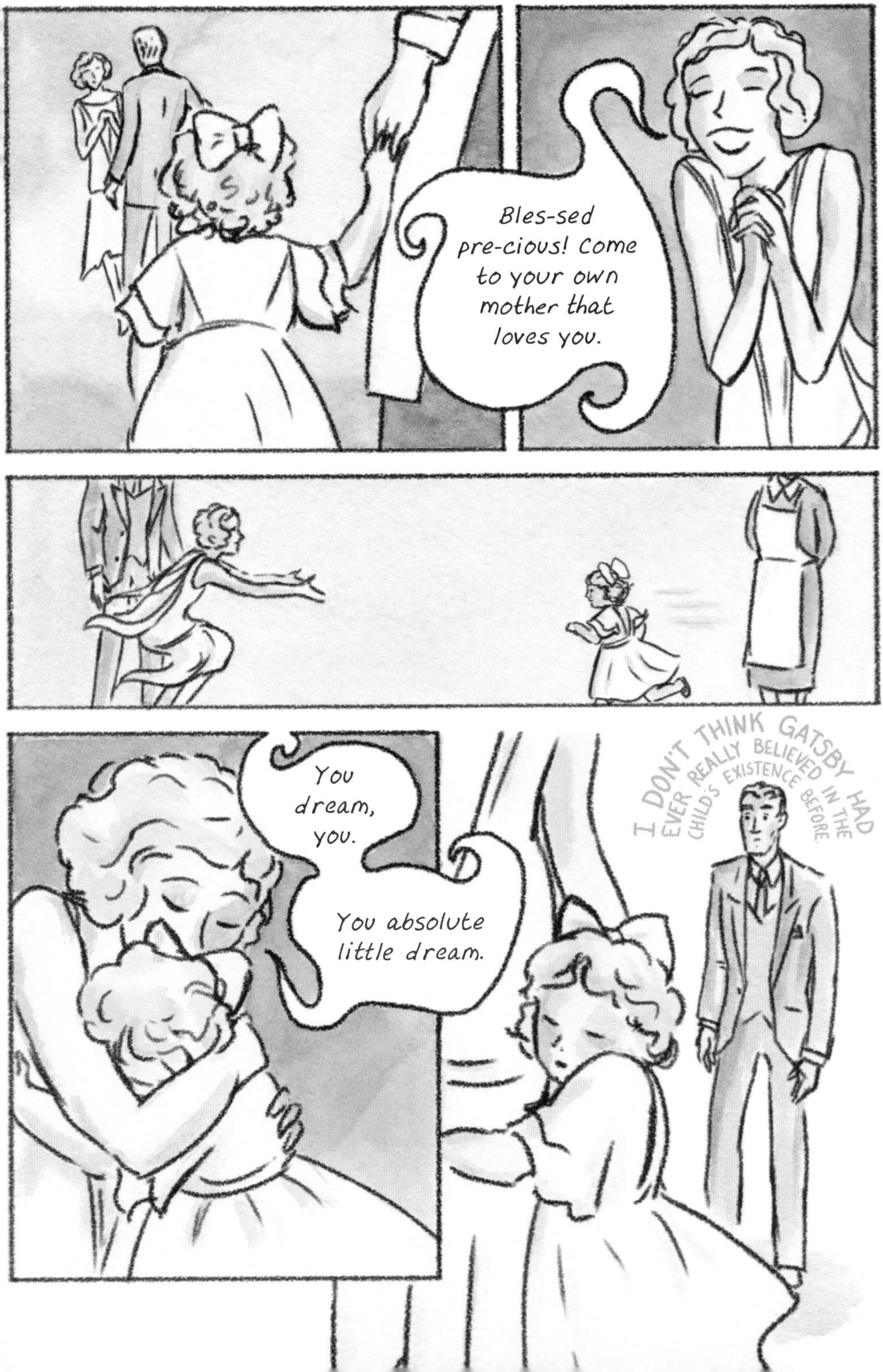
Bles-sed pre-cious! Come to your own mother that loves you.
You dream, you.
You absolute little dream.
I DON'T THINK GATSBY HAD EVER REALLY BELIEVED IN THE CHILD'S EXISTENCE BEFORE.

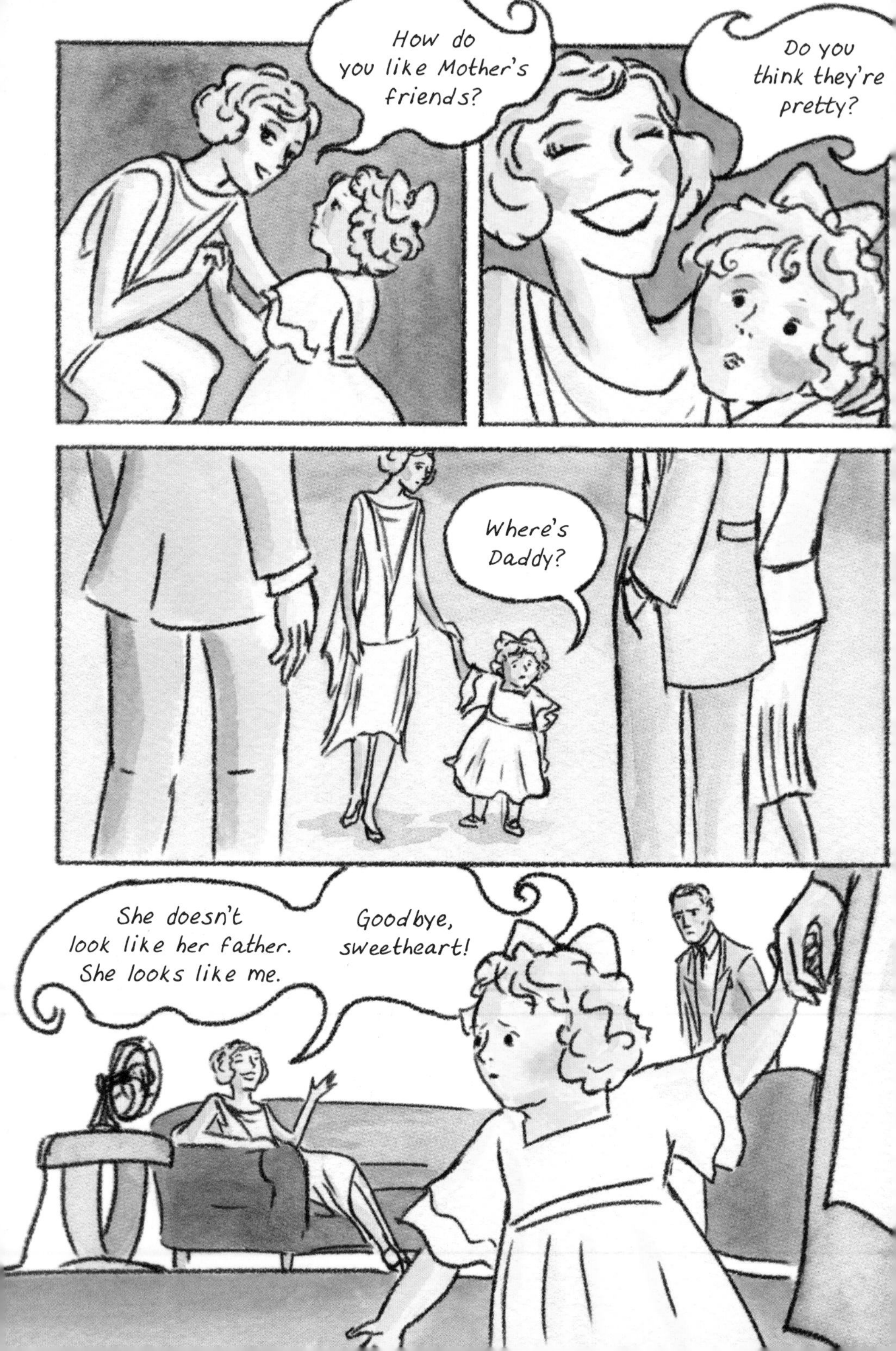
How do you like Mother's friends?
Do you think they're pretty?
Where's Daddy?
She doesn't look like her father. She looks like me.
Goodbye, sweetheart!

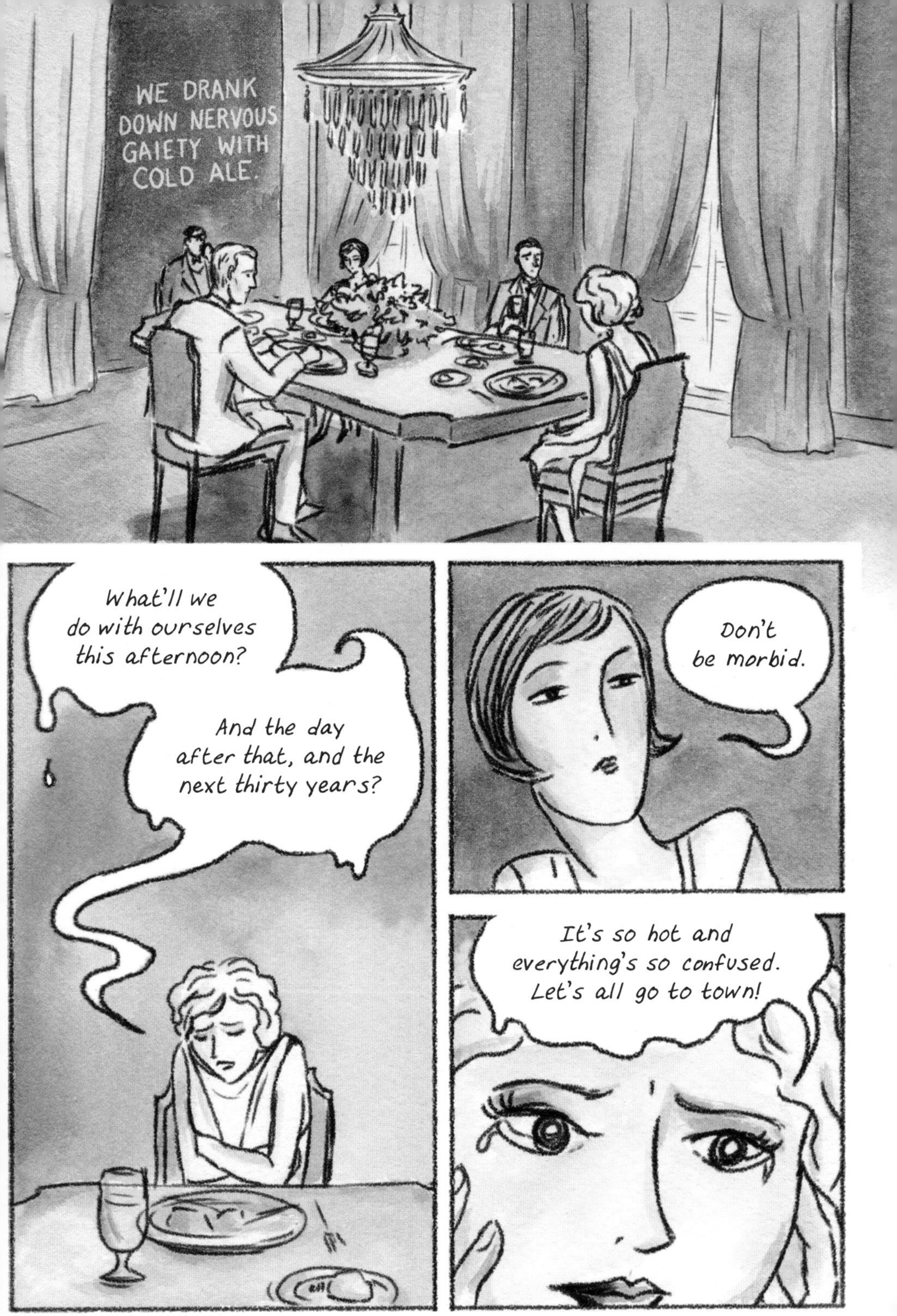
WE DRANK DOWN NERVOUS GAIETY WITH COLD ALE.
What'll we do with ourselves this afternoon?
And the day after that, and the next thirty years?
Don't be morbid.
It's so hot and everything's so confused. Let's all go to town!

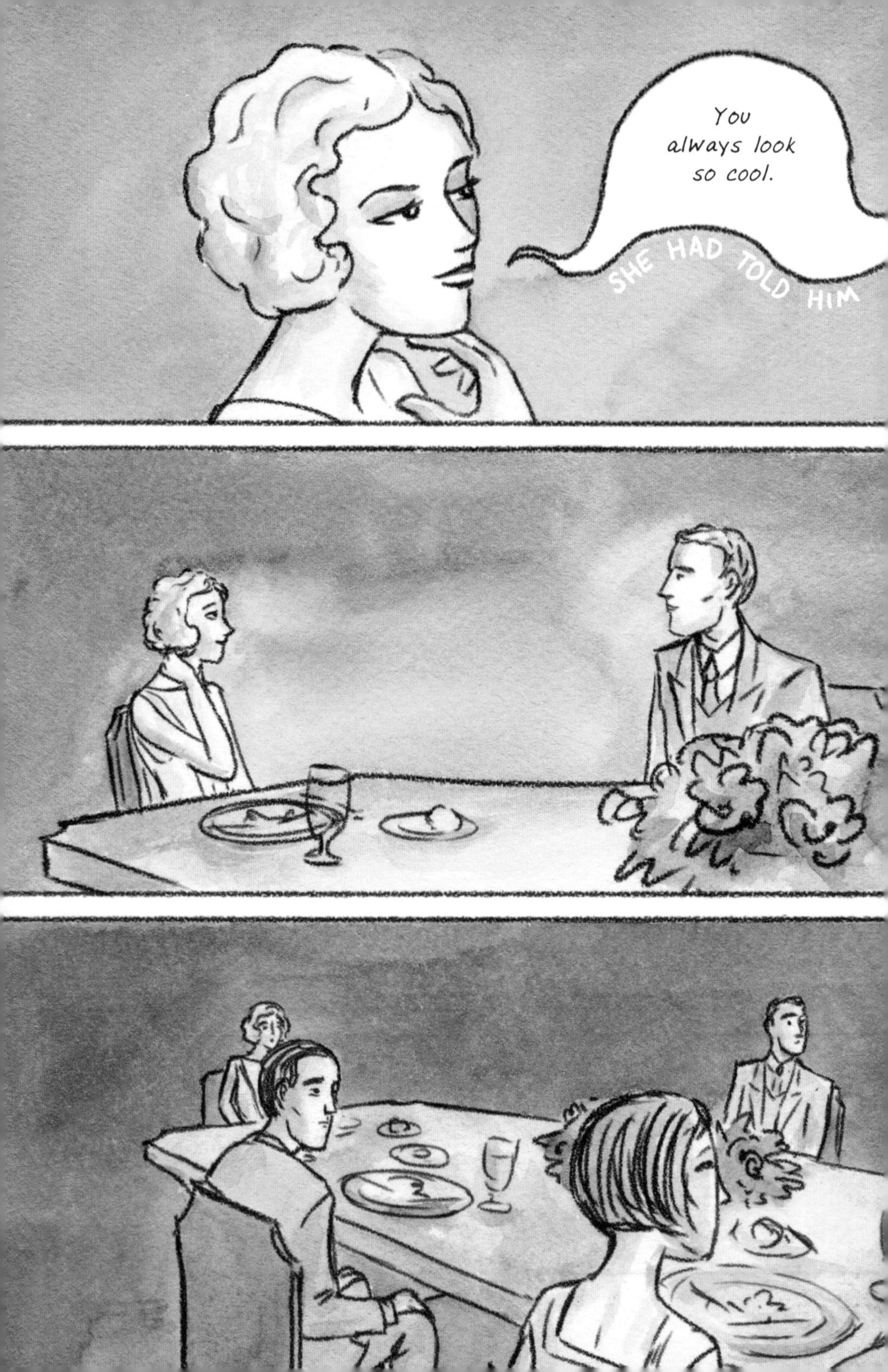
You always look so cool.
SHE HAD TOLD HIM

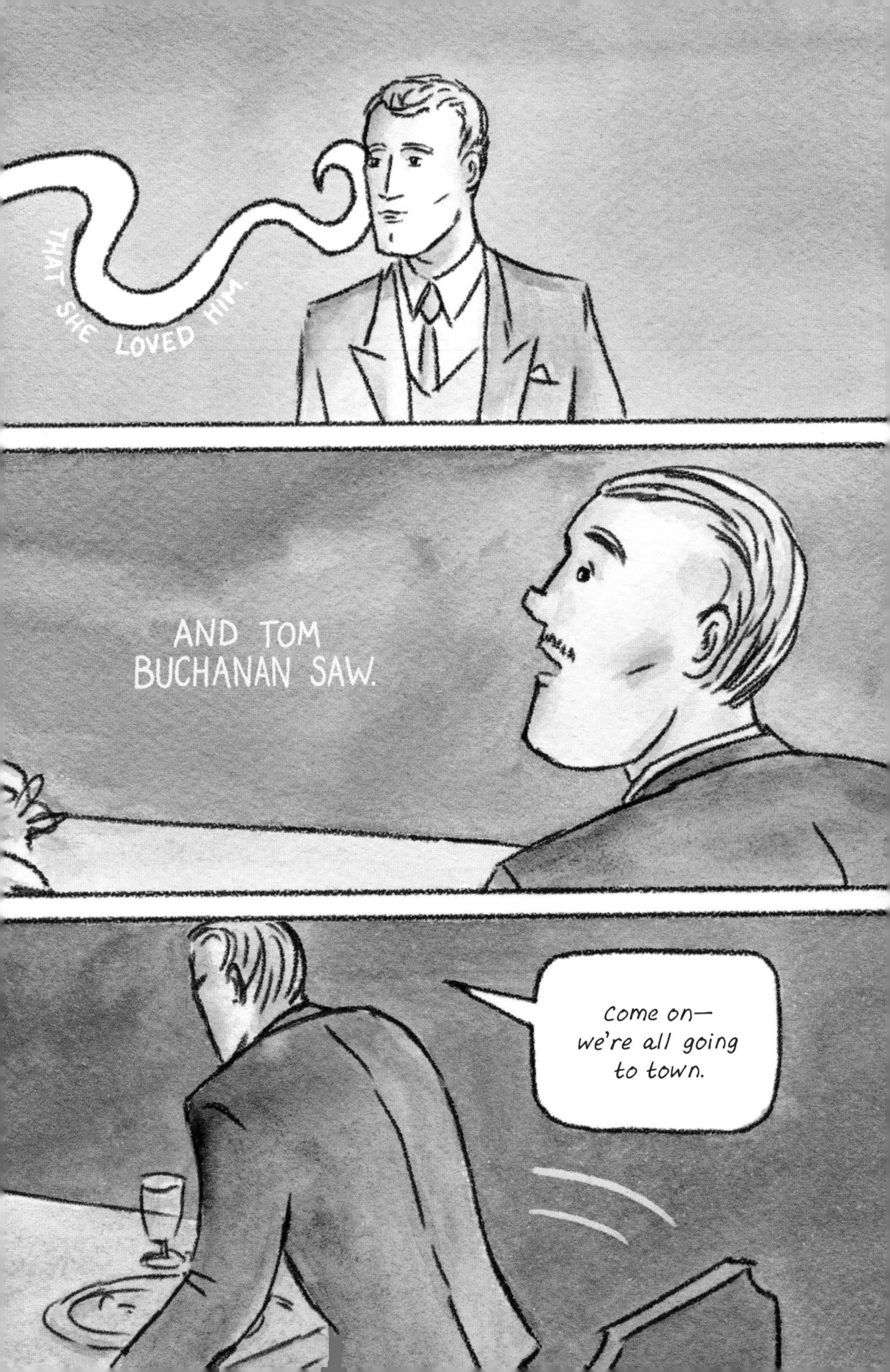
THAT SHE LOVED HIM.
AND TOM BUCHANAN SAW.
Come on— we're all going to town.

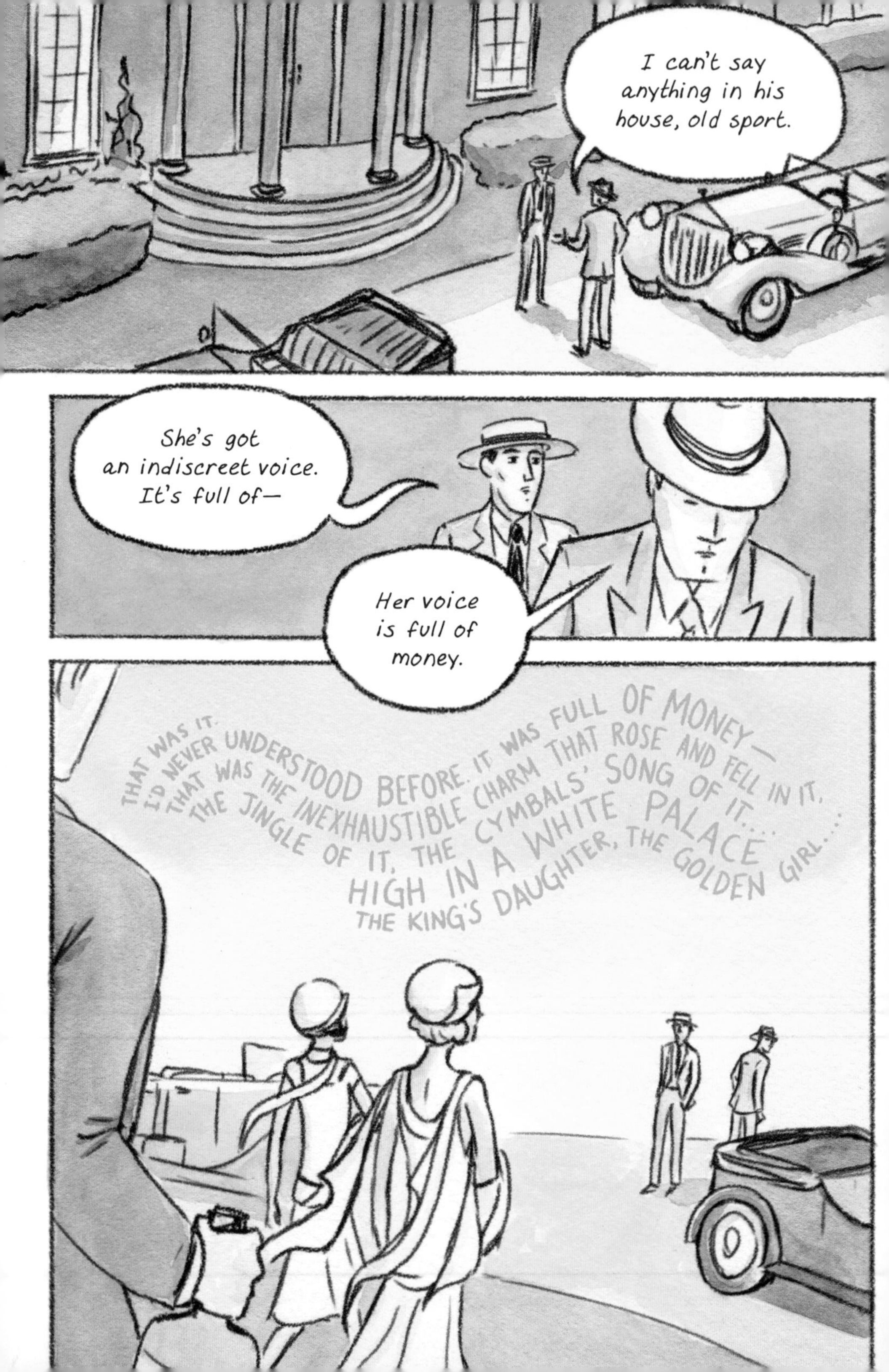
I can't say anything in his house, old sport.
She's got an indiscreet voice. It's full of—
Her voice is full of money.
THAT WAS IT.
I'D NEVER UNDERSTOOD BEFORE. IT WAS FULL OF MONEY—
THAT WAS THE INEXHAUSTIBLE CHARM THAT ROSE AND FELL IN IT,
THE JINGLE OF IT, THE CYMBALS' SONG OF IT....
HIGH IN A WHITE PALACE
THE KING'S DAUGHTER, THE GOLDEN GIRL....

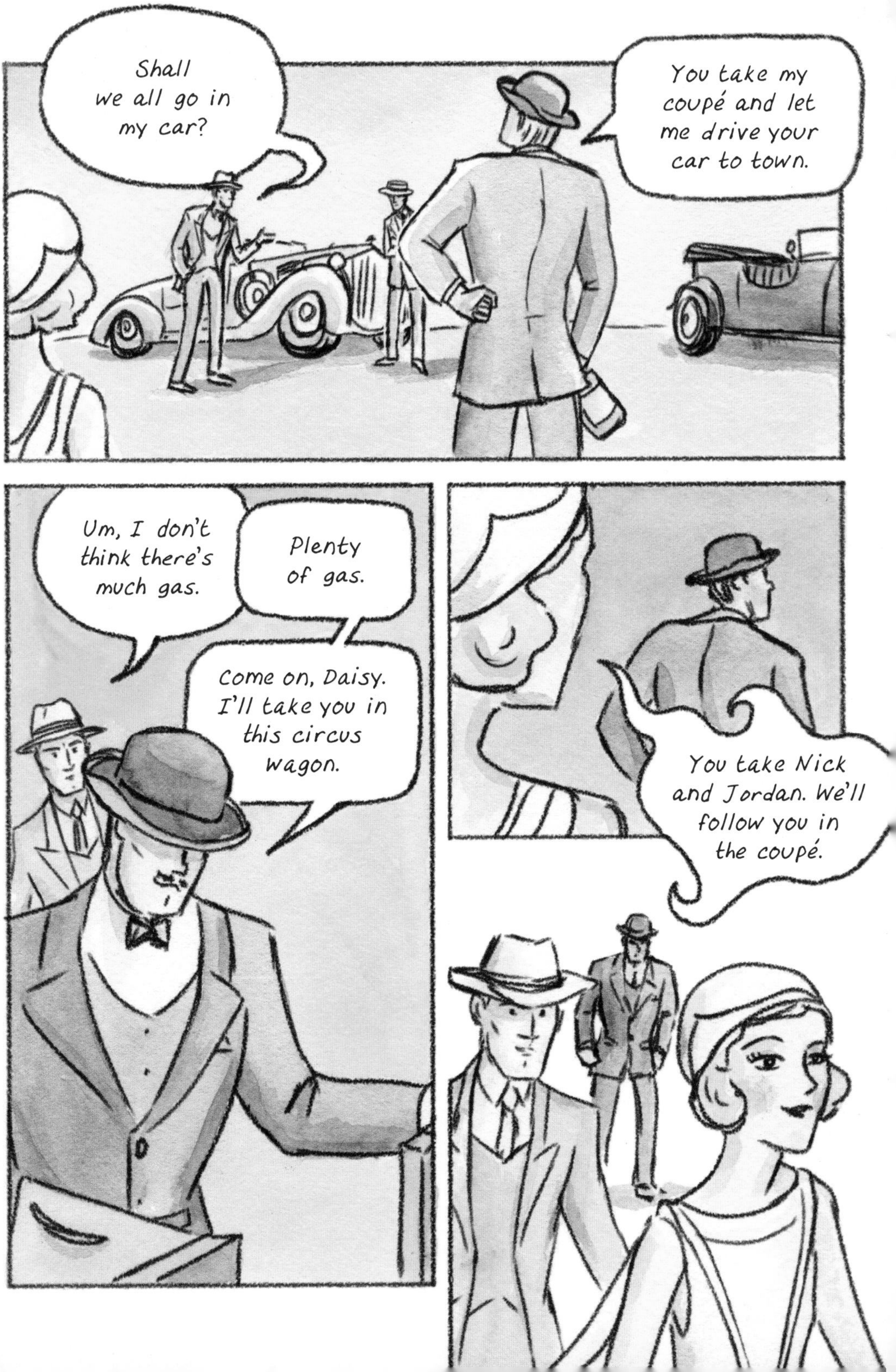
Shall we all go in my car?
You take my coupé and let me drive your car to town.
Um, I don't think there's much gas.
Plenty of gas.
Come on, Daisy. I'll take you in this circus wagon.
You take Nick and Jordan. We'll follow you in the coupé.

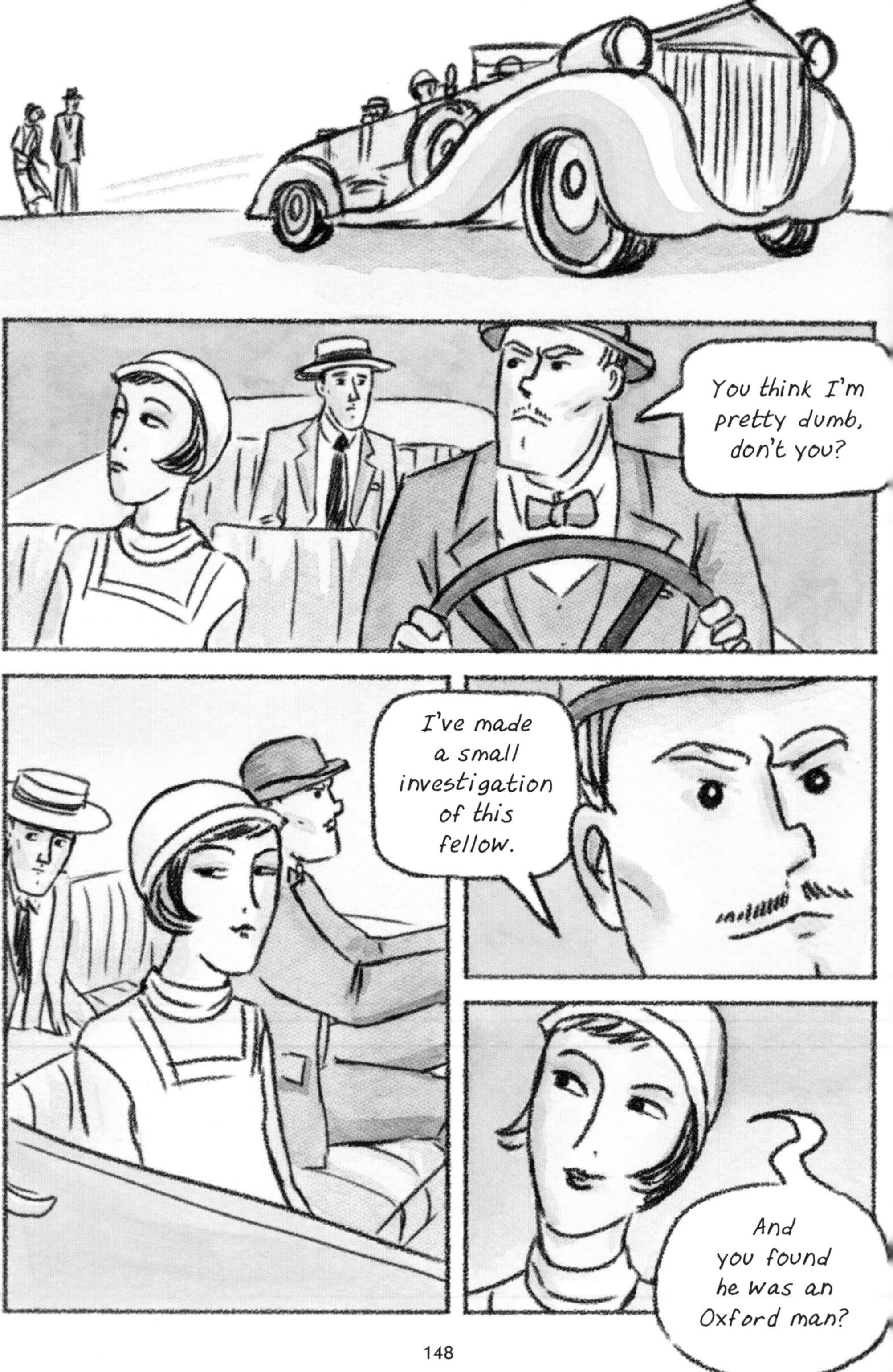
You think I'm pretty dumb, don't you?
I've made a small investigation of this fellow.
And you found he was an Oxford man?

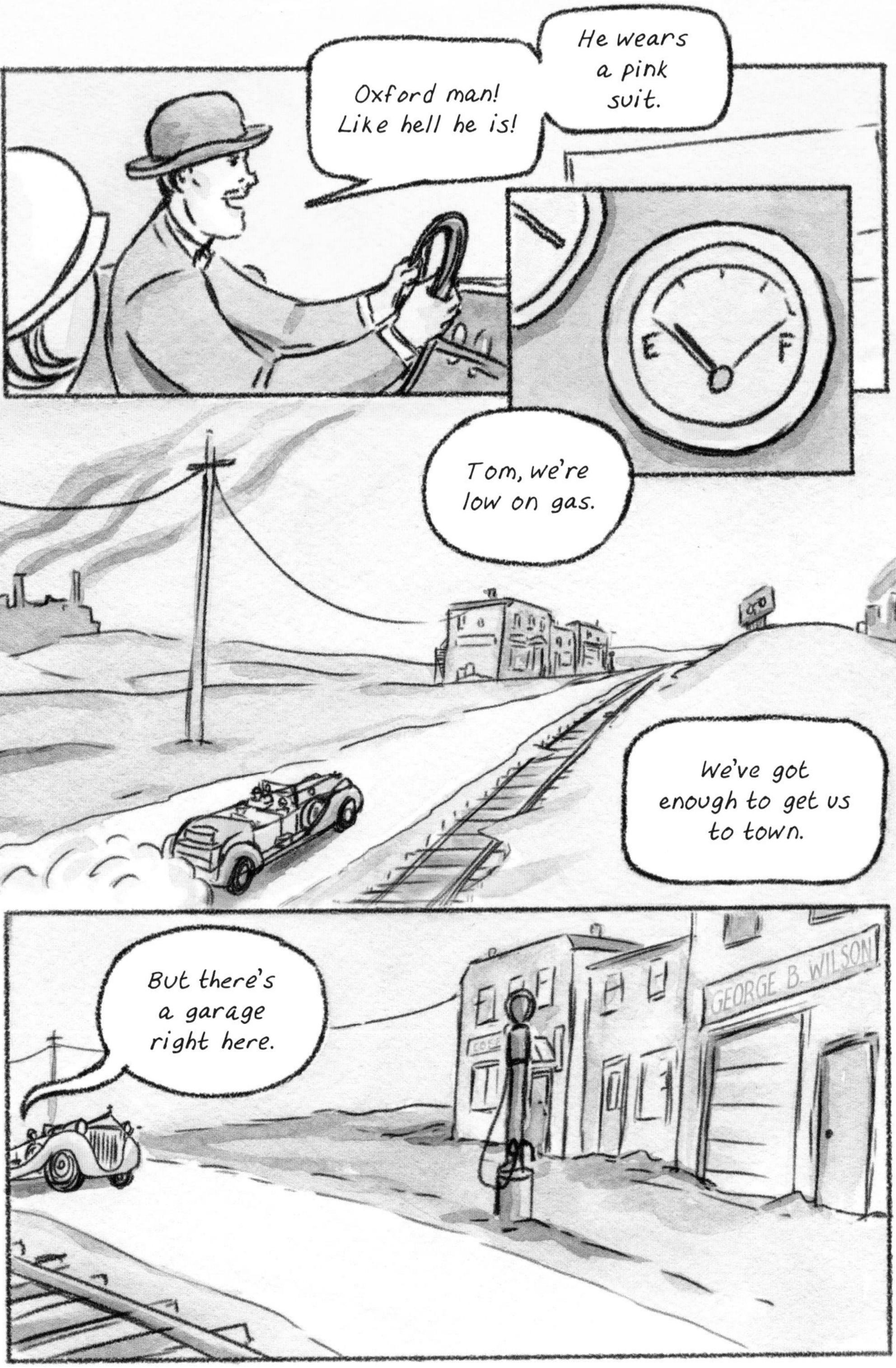
Oxford man! Like hell he is!
He wears a pink suit.
Tom, we're low on gas.
We've got enough to get us to town.
But there's a garage right here.
GEORGE B. WILSON

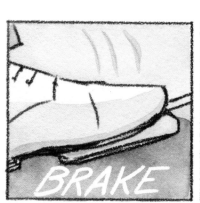

BRAKE

Let's have some gas!

I'm sick. Been sick all day.

You sounded well enough on the phone.

I didn't mean to interrupt your lunch, but I need money pretty bad.

And I was wondering what you were going to do with your old car.

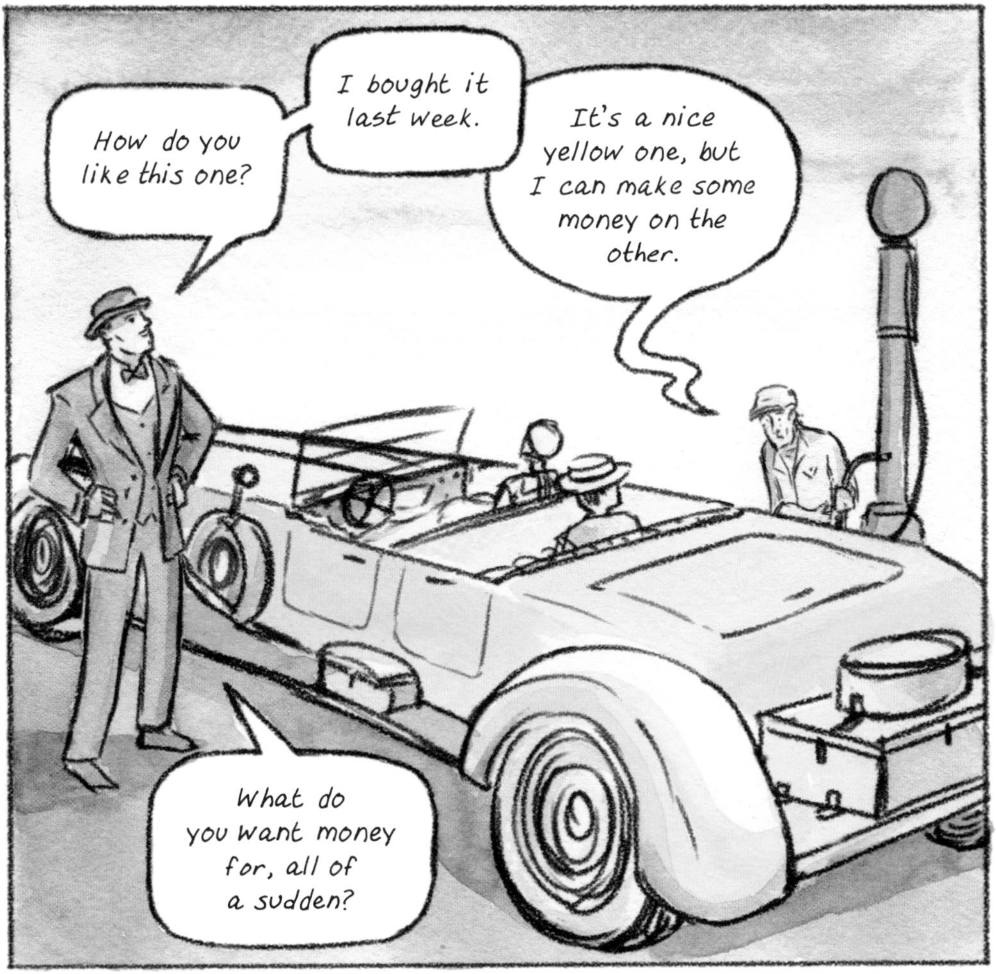
How do you like this one?
I bought it last week.
It's a nice yellow one, but I can make some money on the other.
What do you want money for, all of a sudden?

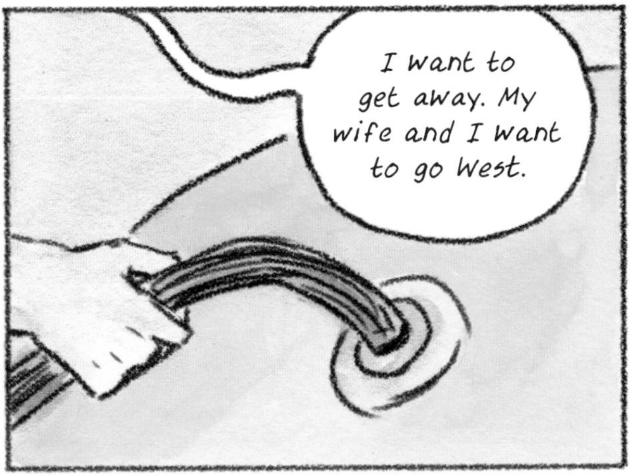
I want to get away. My wife and I want to go West.

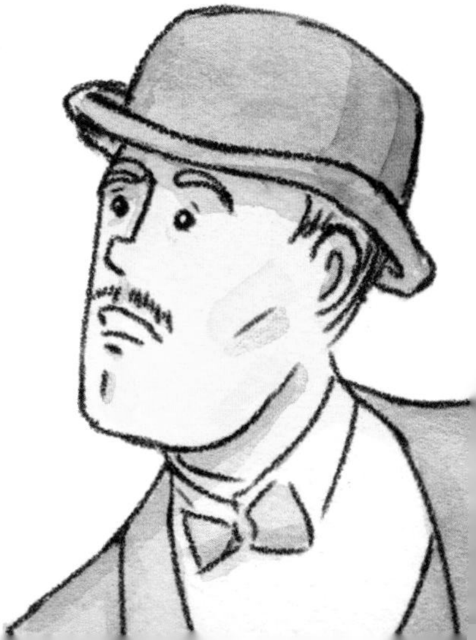

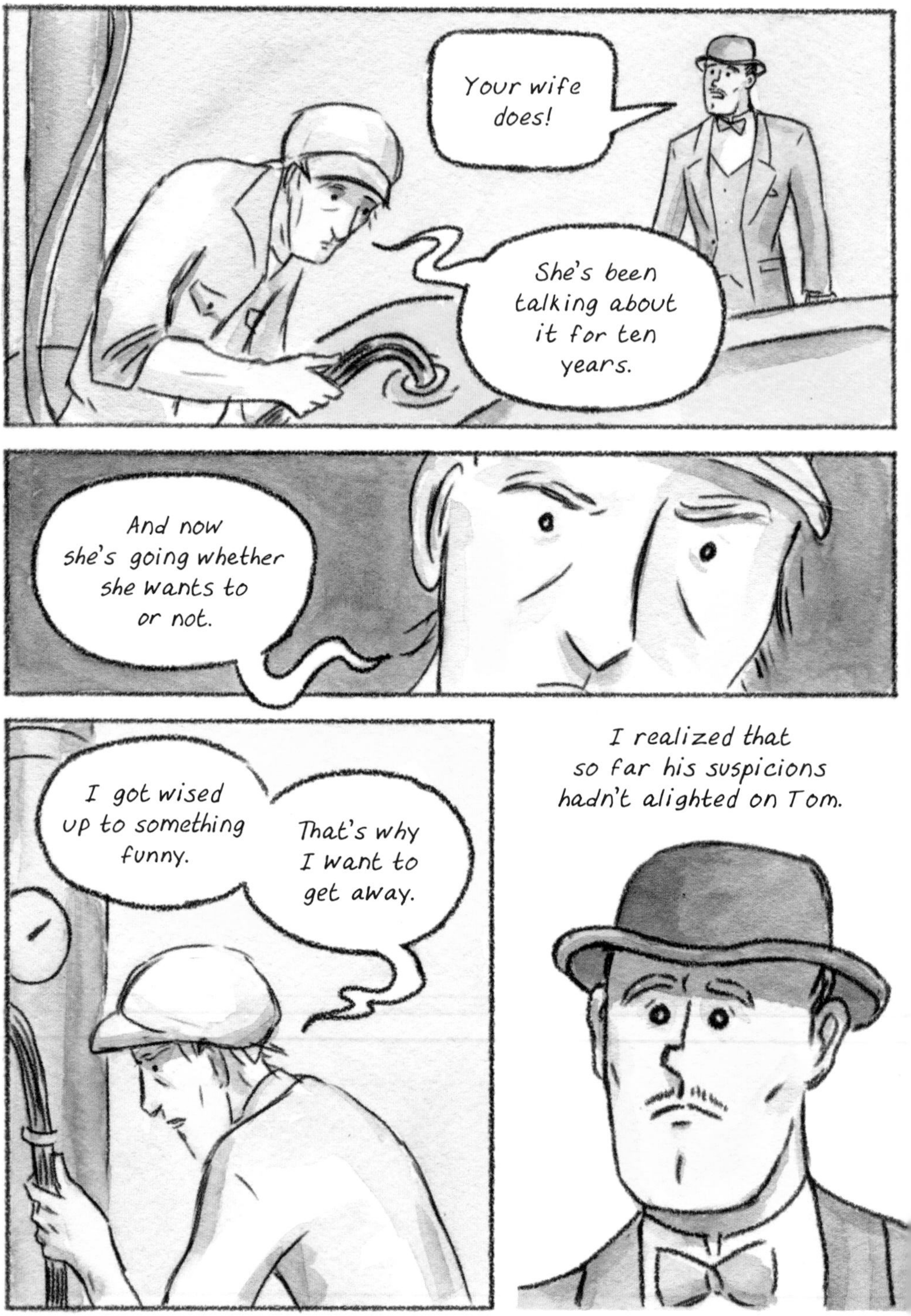
Your wife does!
She's been talking about it for ten years.
And now she's going whether she wants to or not.
I got wised up to something funny.
That's why I want to get away.
I realized that so far his suspicions hadn't alighted on Tom.

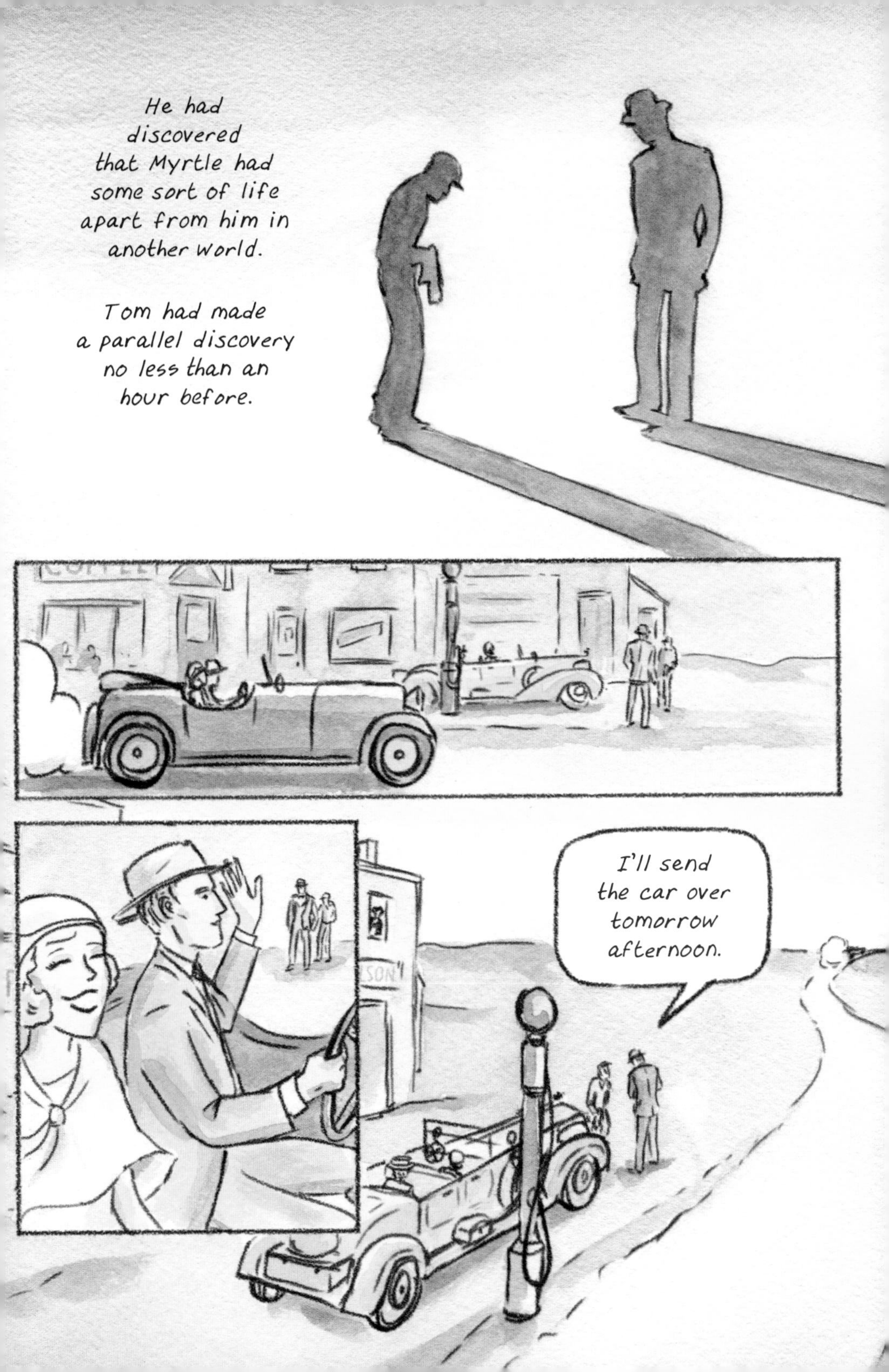
He had discovered that Myrtle had some sort of life apart from him in another world.
Tom had made a parallel discovery no less than an hour before.
I'll send the car over tomorrow afternoon.

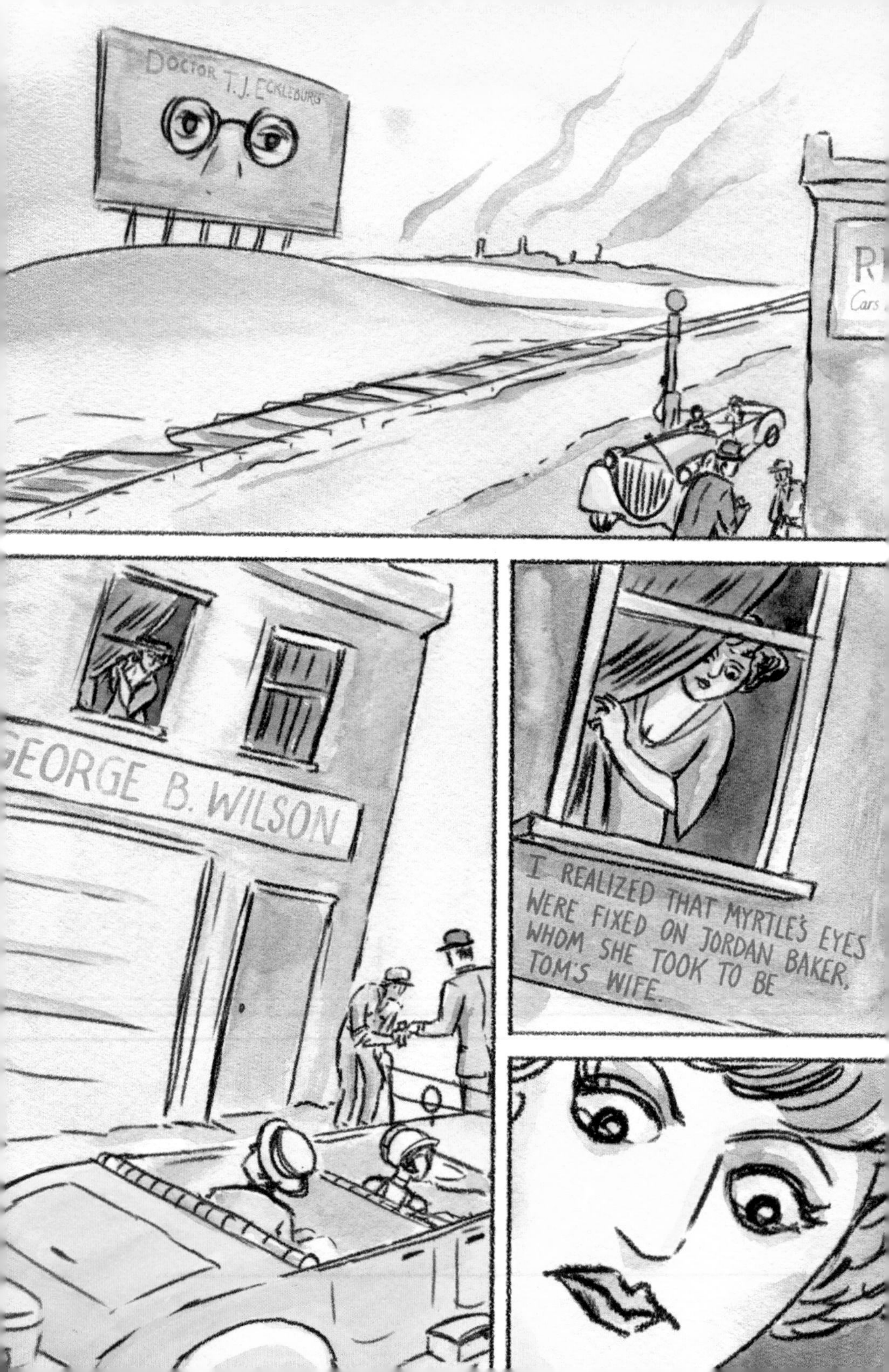
DOCTOR T. J. ECKLEBURG
GEORGE B. WILSON
I REALIZED THAT MYRTLE'S EYES WERE FIXED ON JORDAN BAKER, WHOM SHE TOOK TO BE TOM'S WIFE.

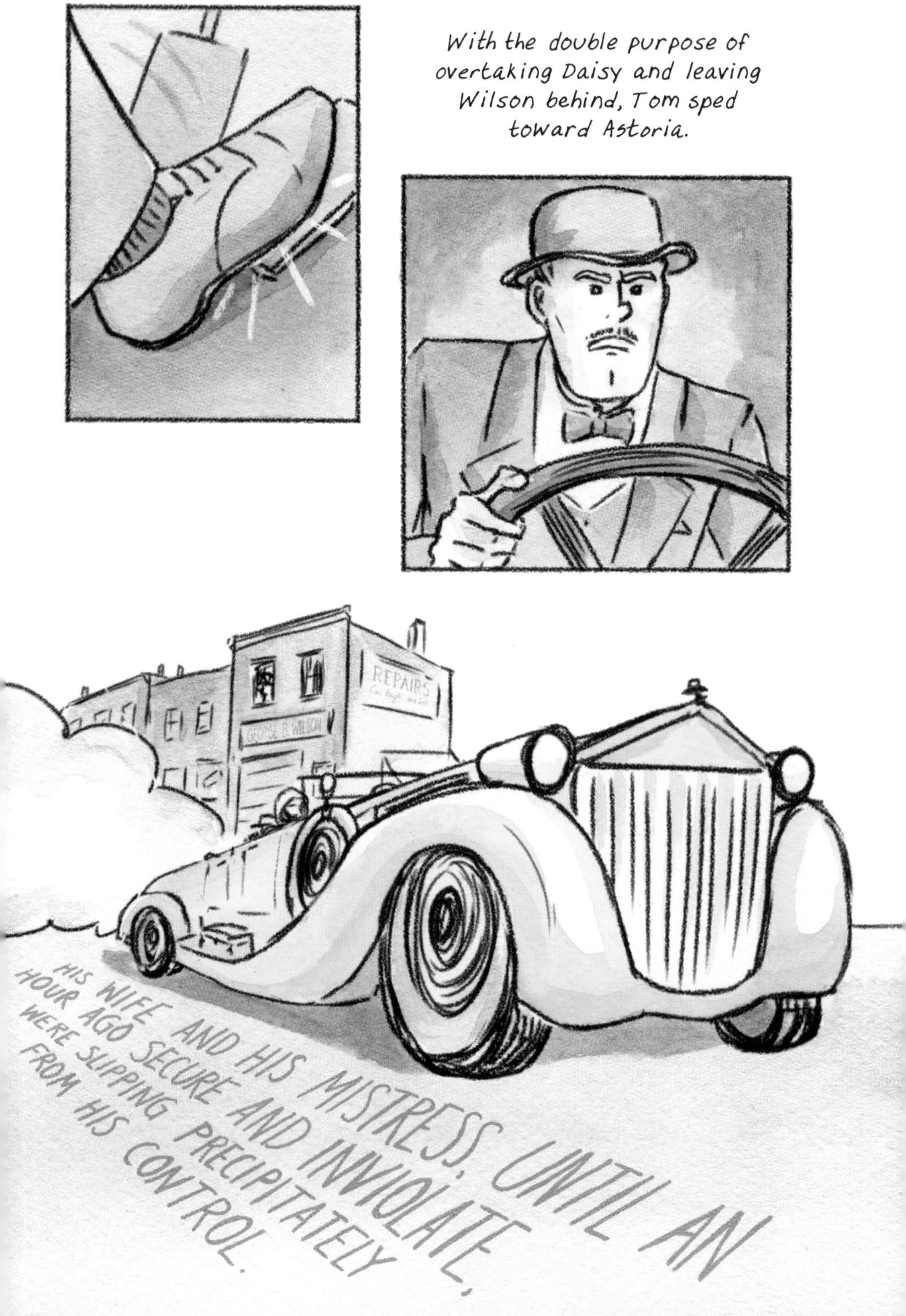
With the double purpose of overtaking Daisy and leaving Wilson behind, Tom sped toward Astoria.
REPAIRS
GEORGE B. WILSON
HIS WIFE AND HIS MISTRESS, UNTIL AN HOUR AGO SECURE AND INVIOLATE, WERE SLIPPING PRECIPITATELY FROM HIS CONTROL.

CHAPTER 8

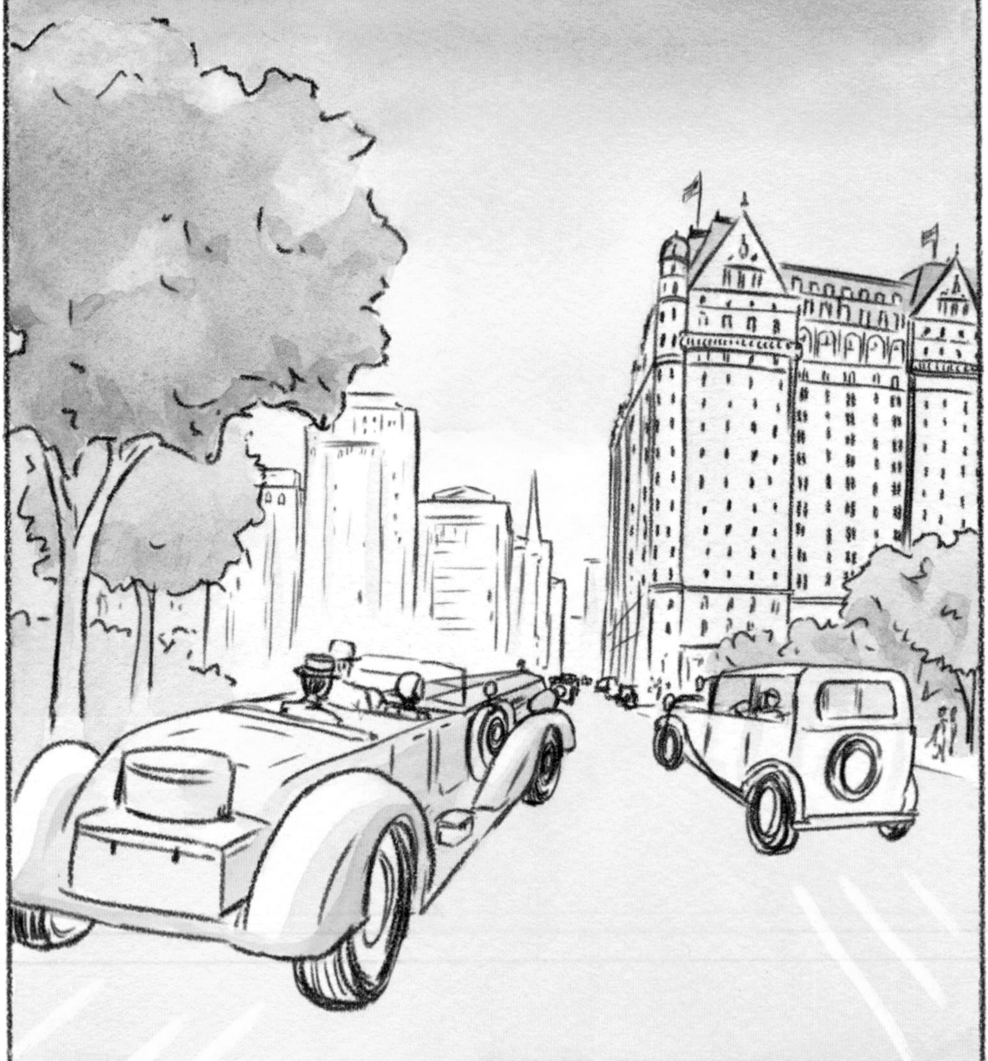

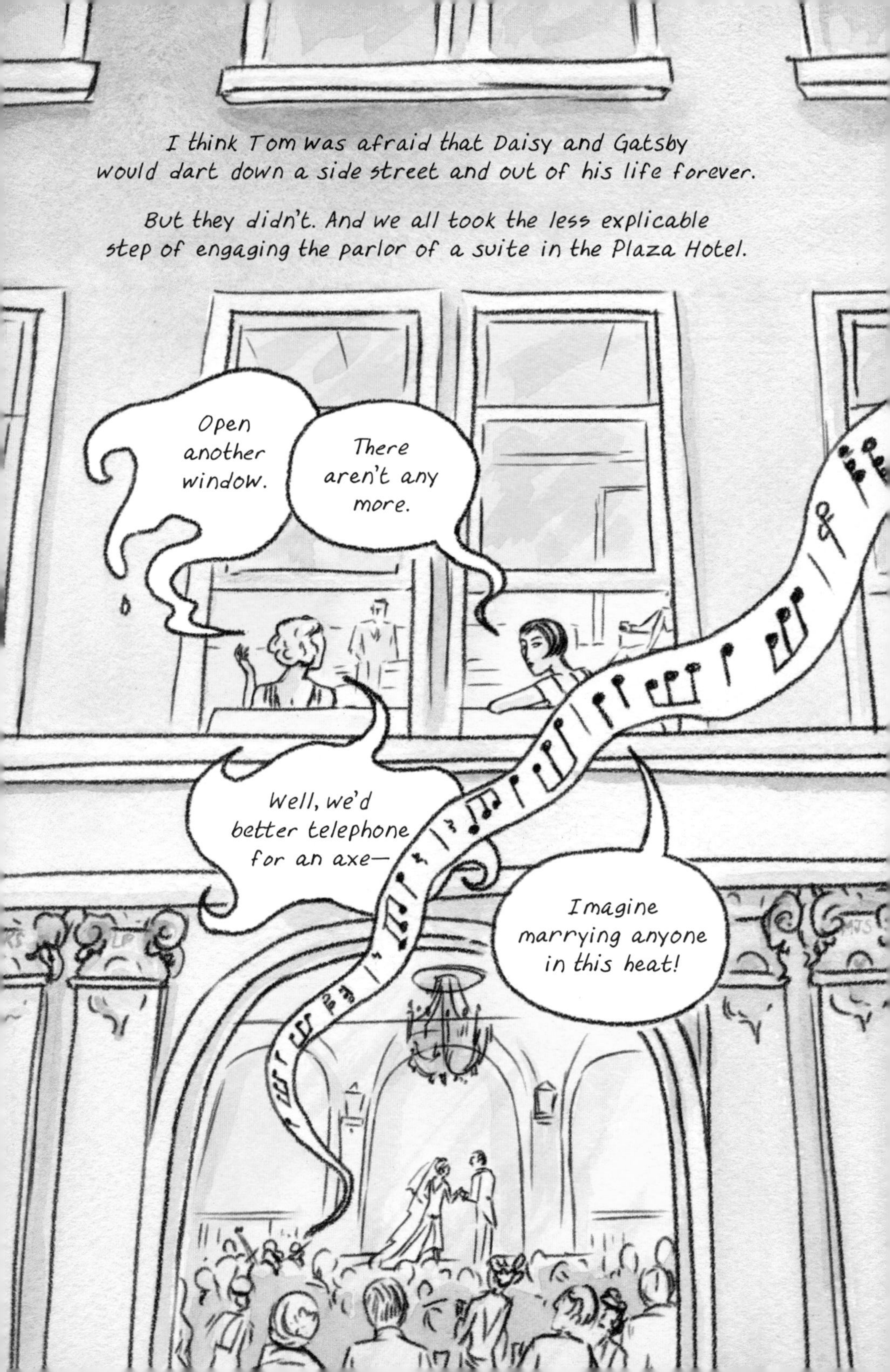
I think Tom was afraid that Daisy and Gatsby would dart down a side street and out of his life forever.
But they didn't. And we all took the less explicable step of engaging the parlor of a suite in the Plaza Hotel.
Open another window.
There aren't any more.
Well, we'd better telephone for an axe—
Imagine marrying anyone in this heat!

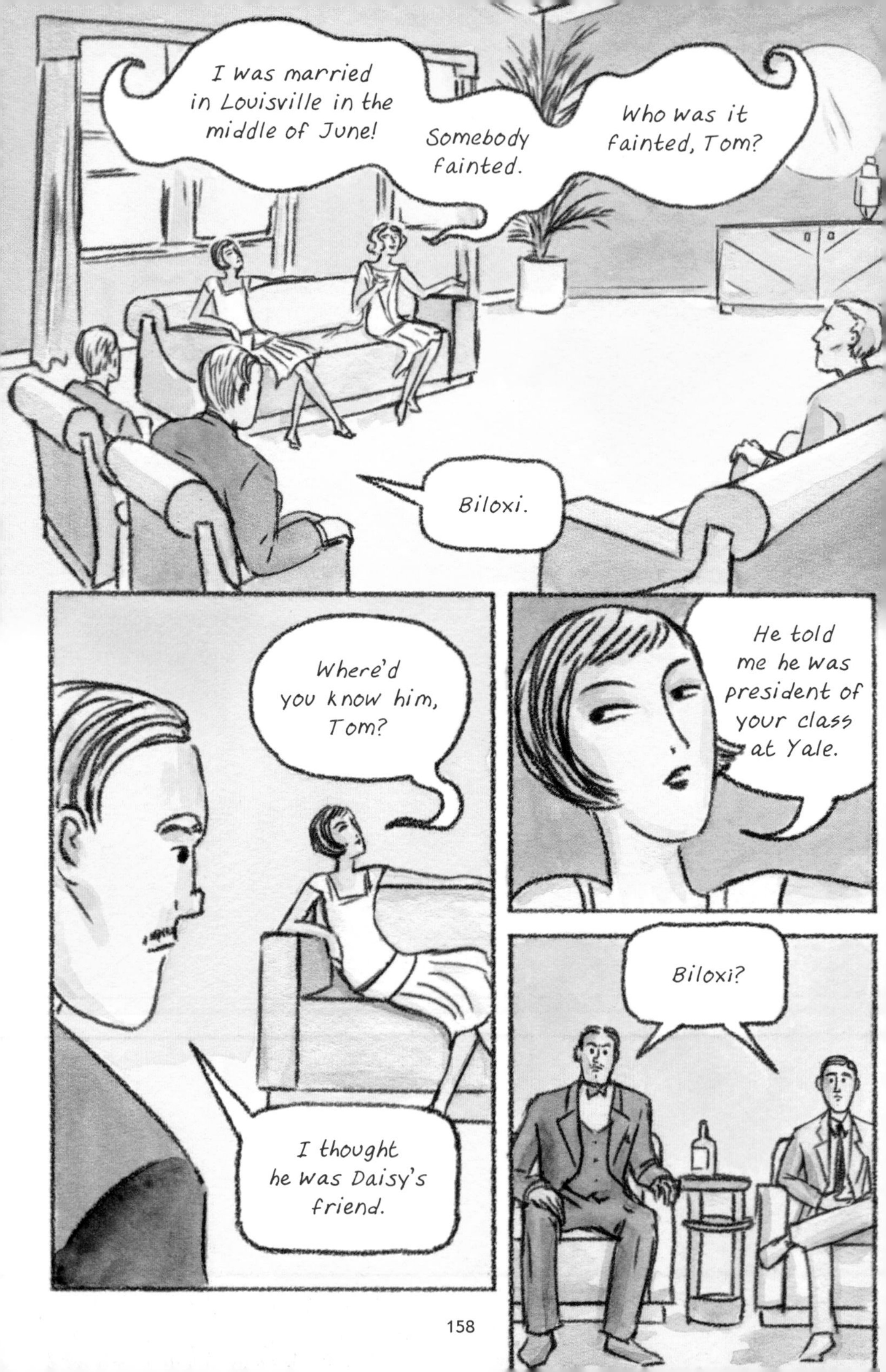
I was married in Louisville in the middle of June!
Somebody fainted.
Who was it fainted, Tom?
Biloxi.
Where'd you know him, Tom?
I thought he was Daisy's friend.
He told me he was president of your class at Yale.
Biloxi?

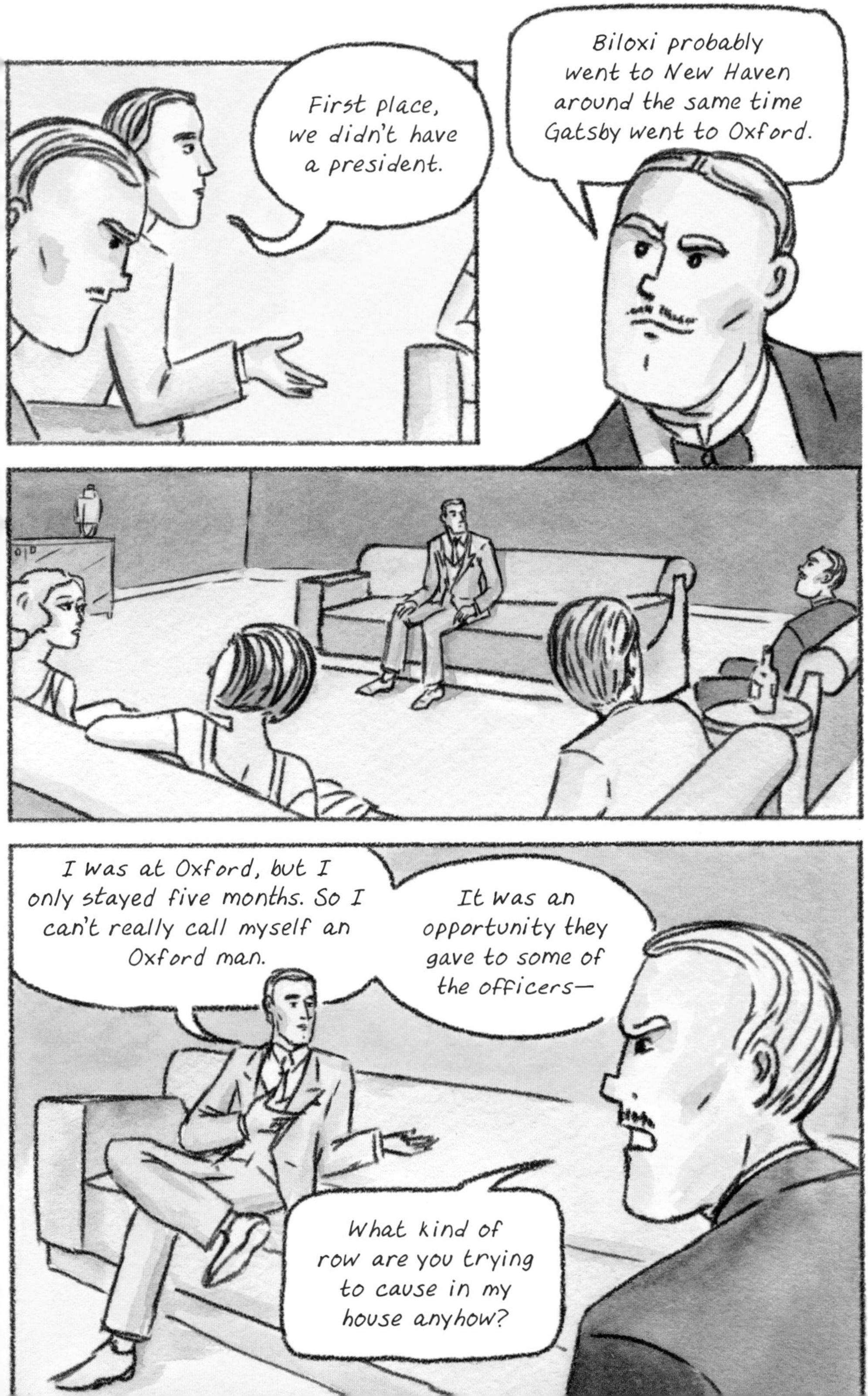
First place, we didn't have a president.
Biloxi probably went to New Haven around the same time Gatsby went to Oxford.
I was at Oxford, but I only stayed five months. So I can't really call myself an Oxford man.
It was an opportunity they gave to some of the officers—
What kind of row are you trying to cause in my house anyhow?

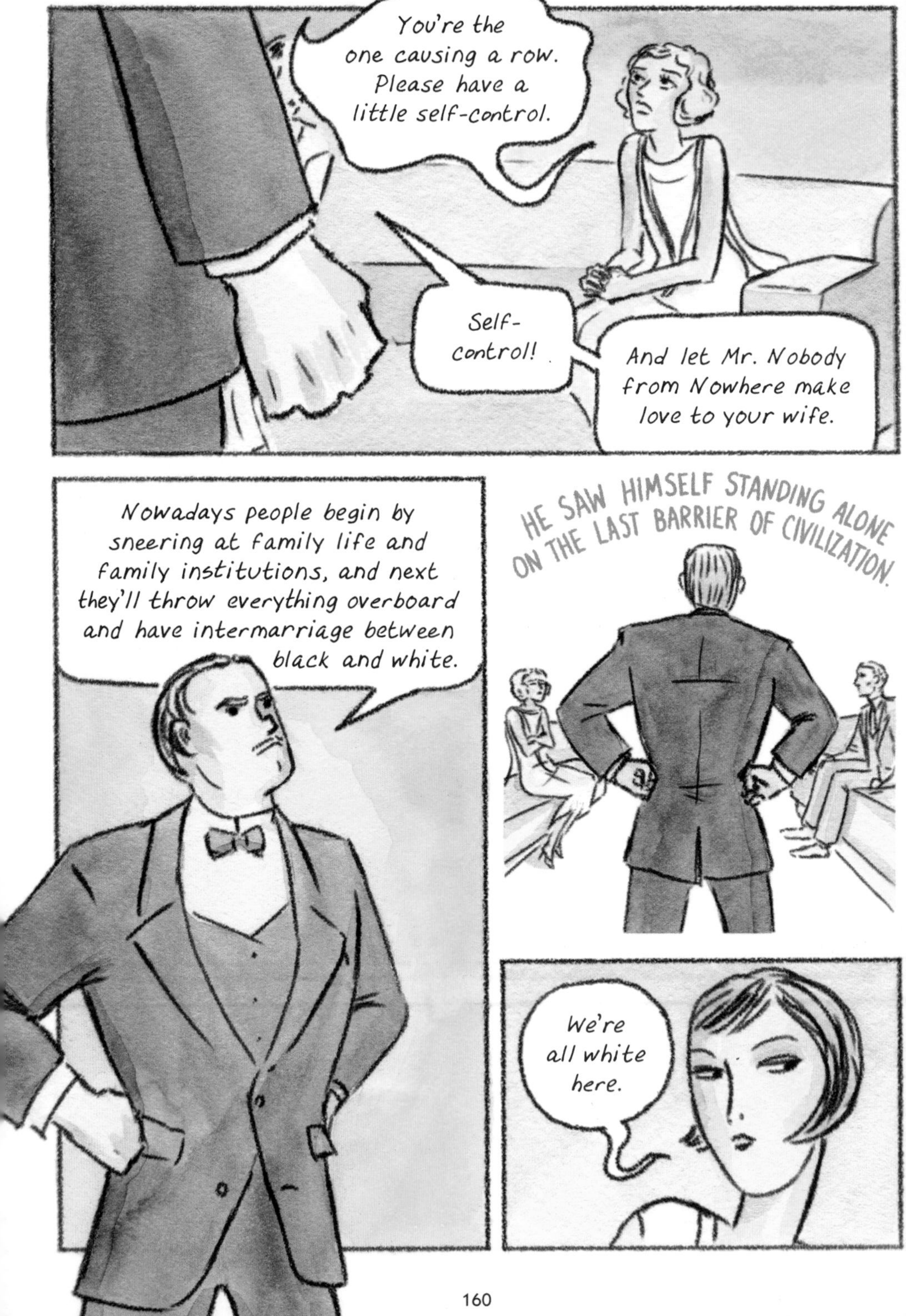
You're the one causing a row. Please have a little self-control.
Self-control!
And let Mr. Nobody from Nowhere make love to your wife.
Nowadays people begin by sneering at family life and family institutions, and next they'll throw everything overboard and have intermarriage between black and white.
HE SAW HIMSELF STANDING ALONE ON THE LAST BARRIER OF CIVILIZATION.
We're all white here.

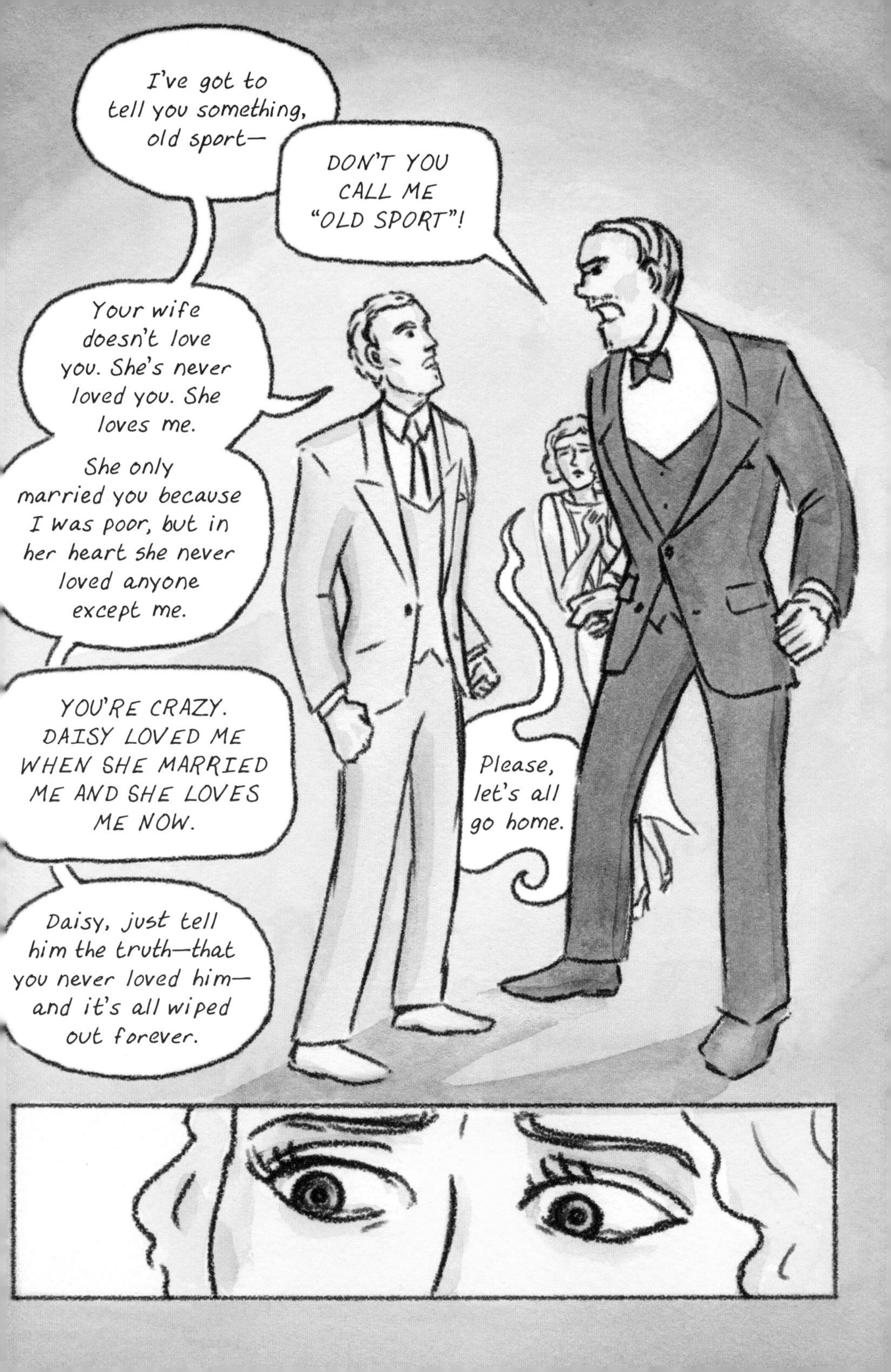
I've got to tell you something, old sport—
DON'T YOU CALL ME "OLD SPORT"!
Your wife doesn't love you. She's never loved you. She loves me.
She only married you because I was poor, but in her heart she never loved anyone except me.
YOU'RE CRAZY. DAISY LOVED ME WHEN SHE MARRIED ME AND SHE LOVES ME NOW.
Please, let's all go home.
Daisy, just tell him the truth—that you never loved him—and it's all wiped out forever.

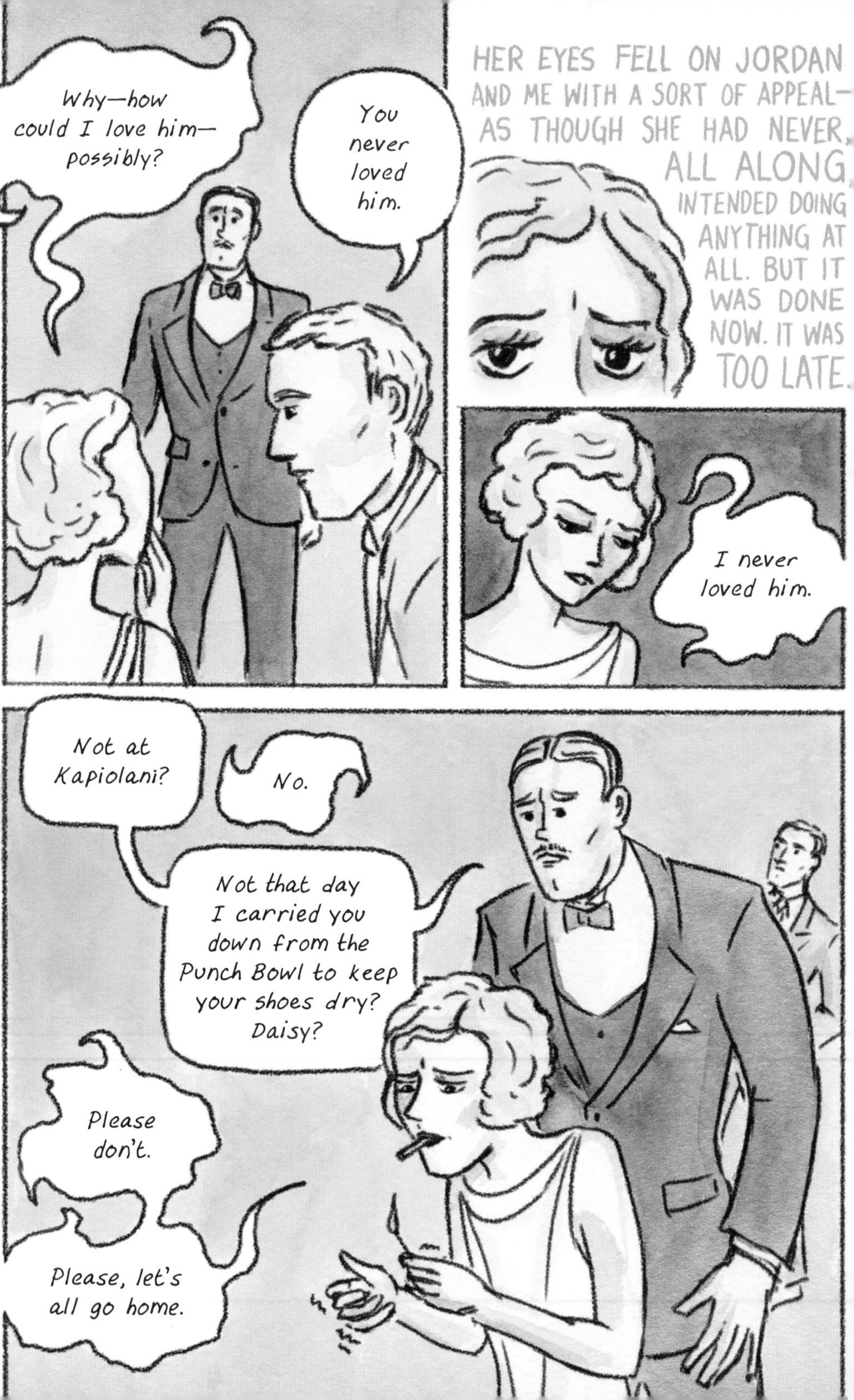
Why—how could I love him—possibly?
You never loved him.
HER EYES FELL ON JORDAN AND ME WITH A SORT OF APPEAL—AS THOUGH SHE HAD NEVER, ALL ALONG, INTENDED DOING ANYTHING AT ALL. BUT IT WAS DONE NOW. IT WAS TOO LATE.
I never loved him.
Not at Kapiolani?
No.
Not that day I carried you down from the Punch Bowl to keep your shoes dry? Daisy?
Please don't.
Please, let's all go home.

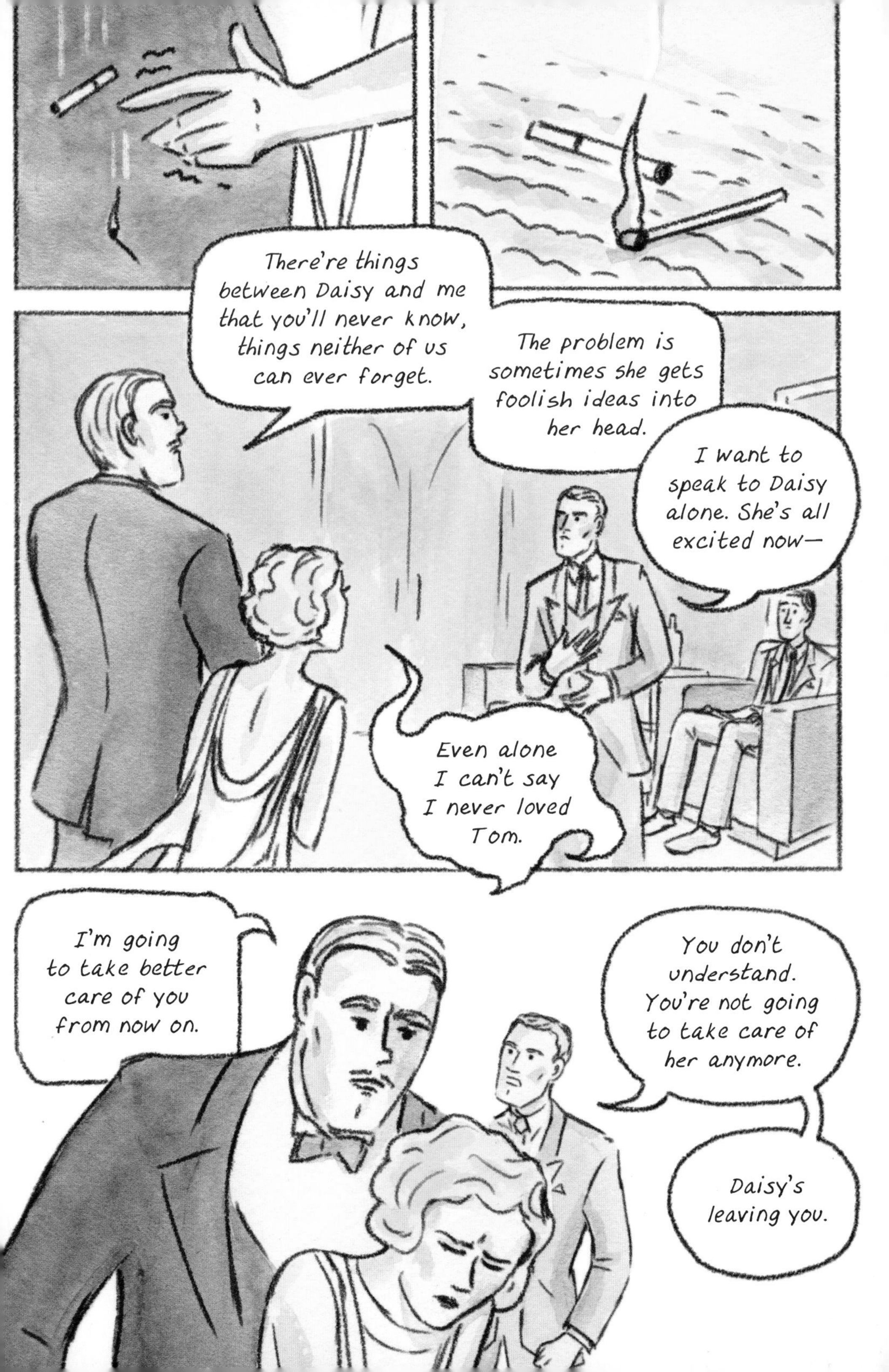
There're things between Daisy and me that you'll never know, things neither of us can ever forget.
The problem is sometimes she gets foolish ideas into her head.
I want to speak to Daisy alone. She's all excited now—
Even alone I can't say I never loved Tom.
I'm going to take better care of you from now on.
You don't understand. You're not going to take care of her anymore.
Daisy's leaving you.

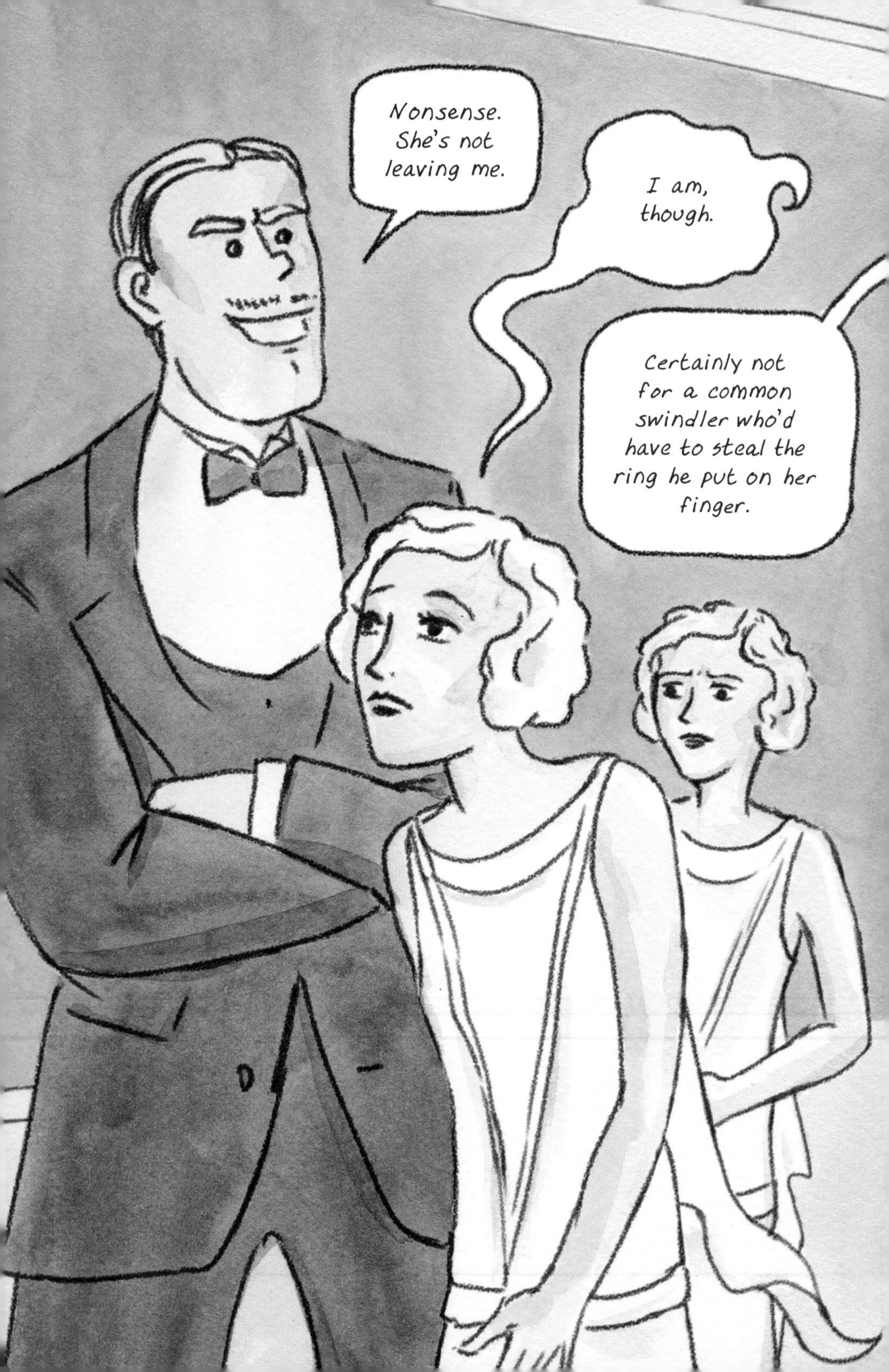
Nonsense. She's not leaving me.
I am, though.
Certainly not for a common swindler who'd have to steal the ring he put on her finger.

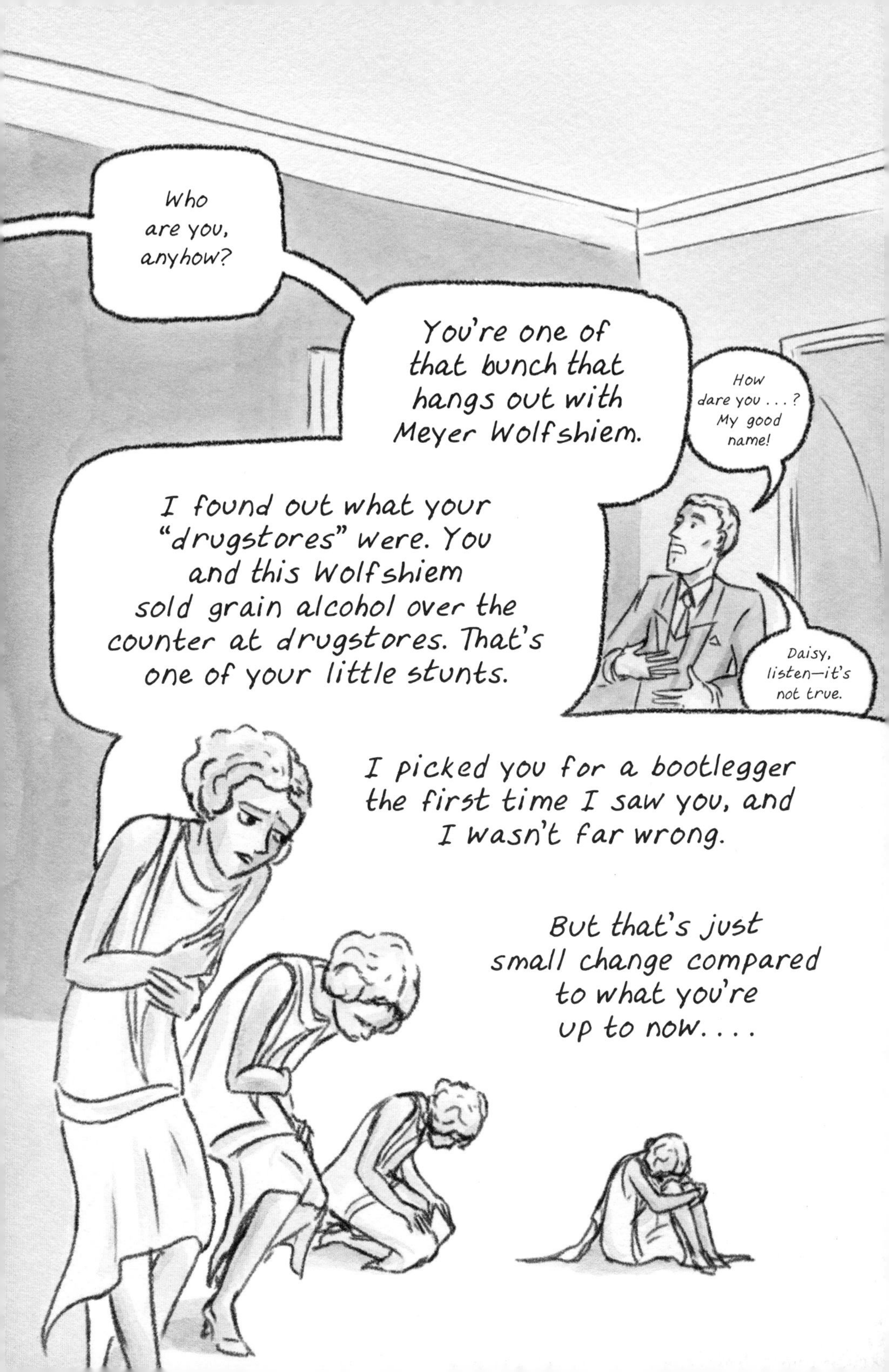
Who are you, anyhow?
You're one of that bunch that hangs out with Meyer Wolfshiem.
How dare you . . . ? My good name!
I found out what your "drugstores" were. You and this Wolfshiem sold grain alcohol over the counter at drugstores. That's one of your little stunts.
Daisy, listen—it's not true.
I picked you for a bootlegger the first time I saw you, and I wasn't far wrong.
But that's just small change compared to what you're up to now. . . .

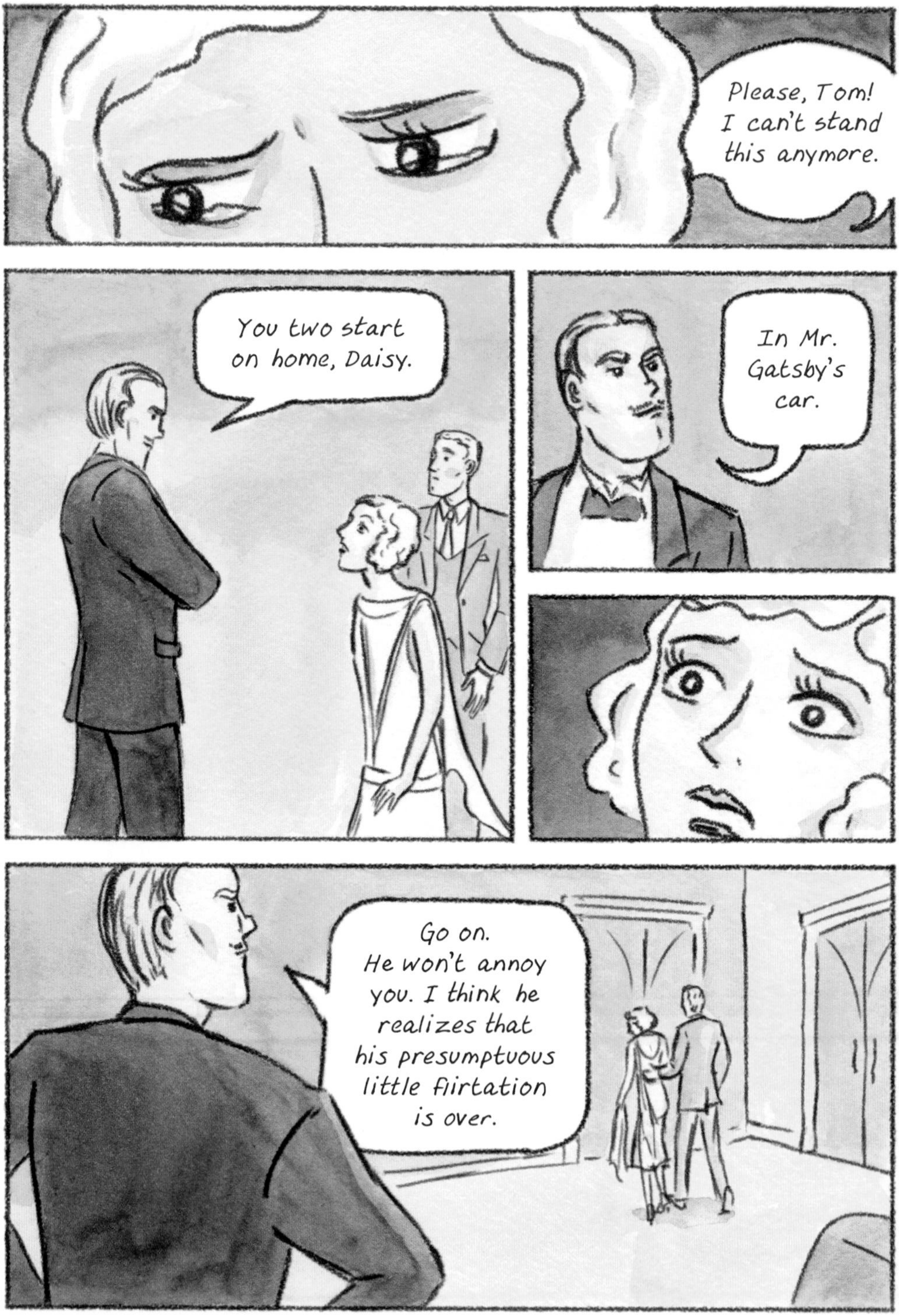
Please, Tom! I can't stand this anymore.
You two start on home, Daisy.
In Mr. Gatsby's car.
Go on. He won't annoy you. I think he realizes that his presumptuous little flirtation is over.

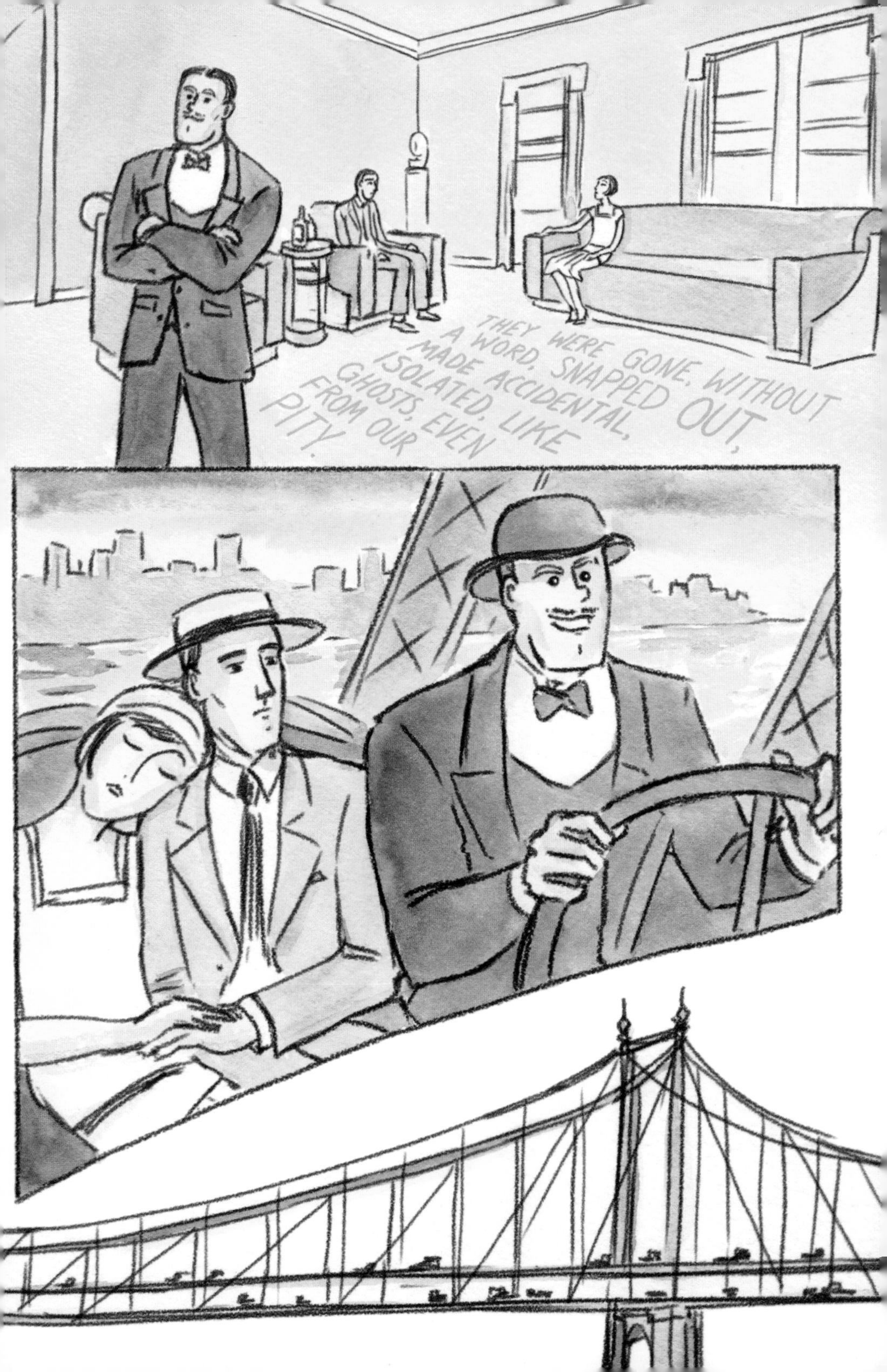
THEY WERE GONE, WITHOUT A WORD, SNAPPED OUT, MADE ACCIDENTAL, ISOLATED, LIKE GHOSTS, EVEN FROM OUR PITY.

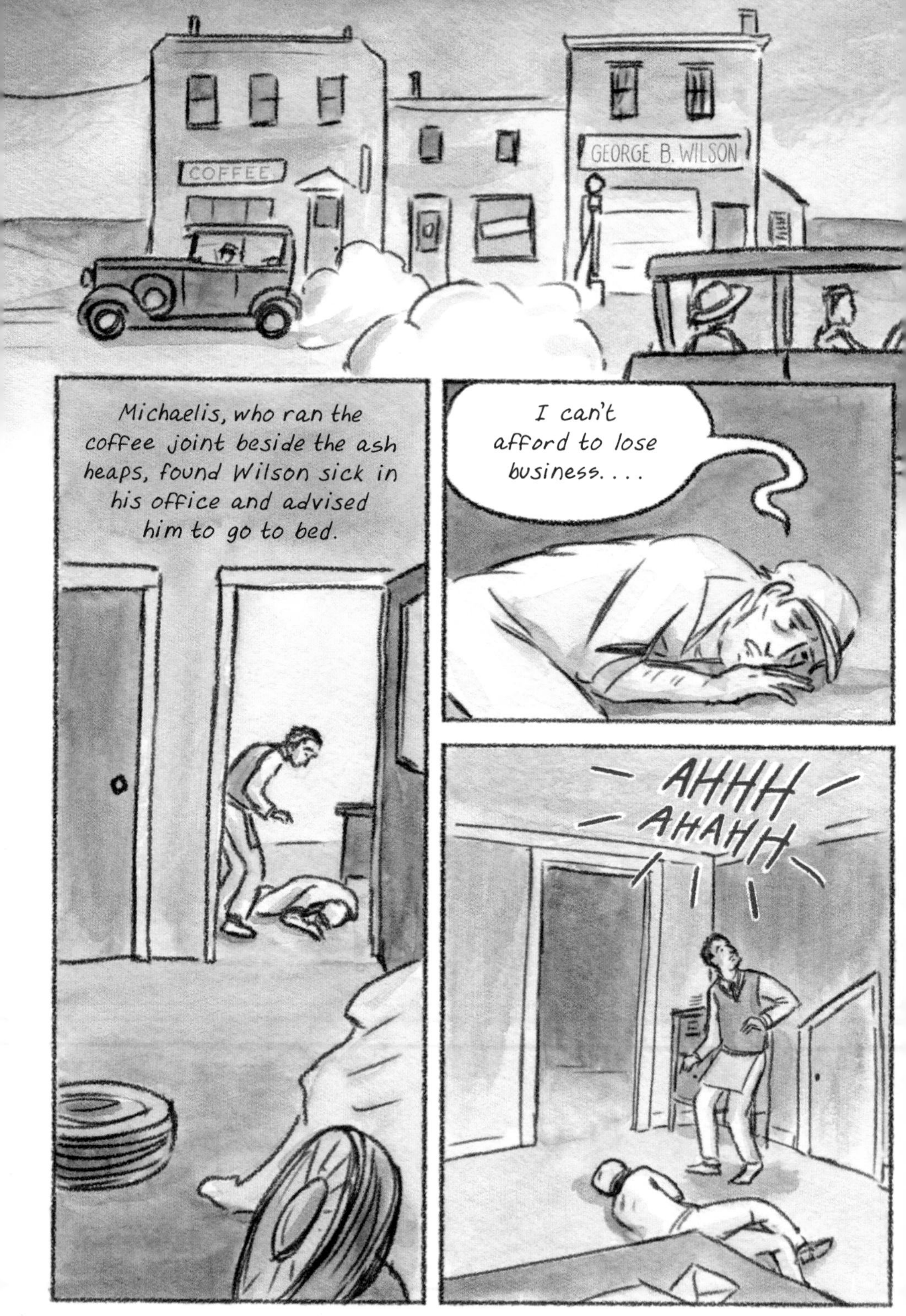
COFFEE
GEORGE B. WILSON
Michaelis, who ran the coffee joint beside the ash heaps, found Wilson sick in his office and advised him to go to bed.
I can't afford to lose business. . . .
AHHH AHAHH

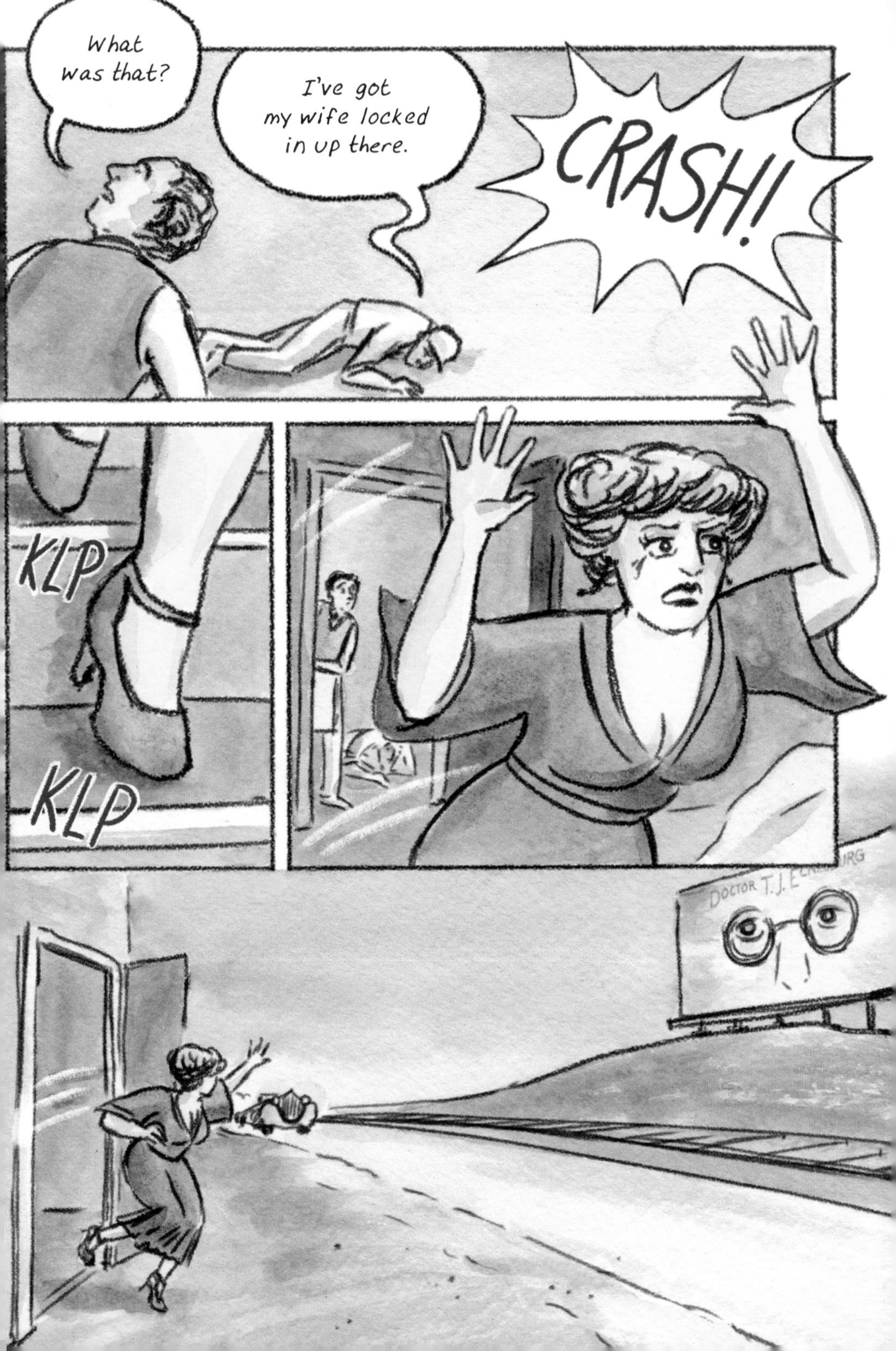
What was that?
I've got my wife locked in up there.
CRASH!
KLP
KLP
DOCTOR T. J. E

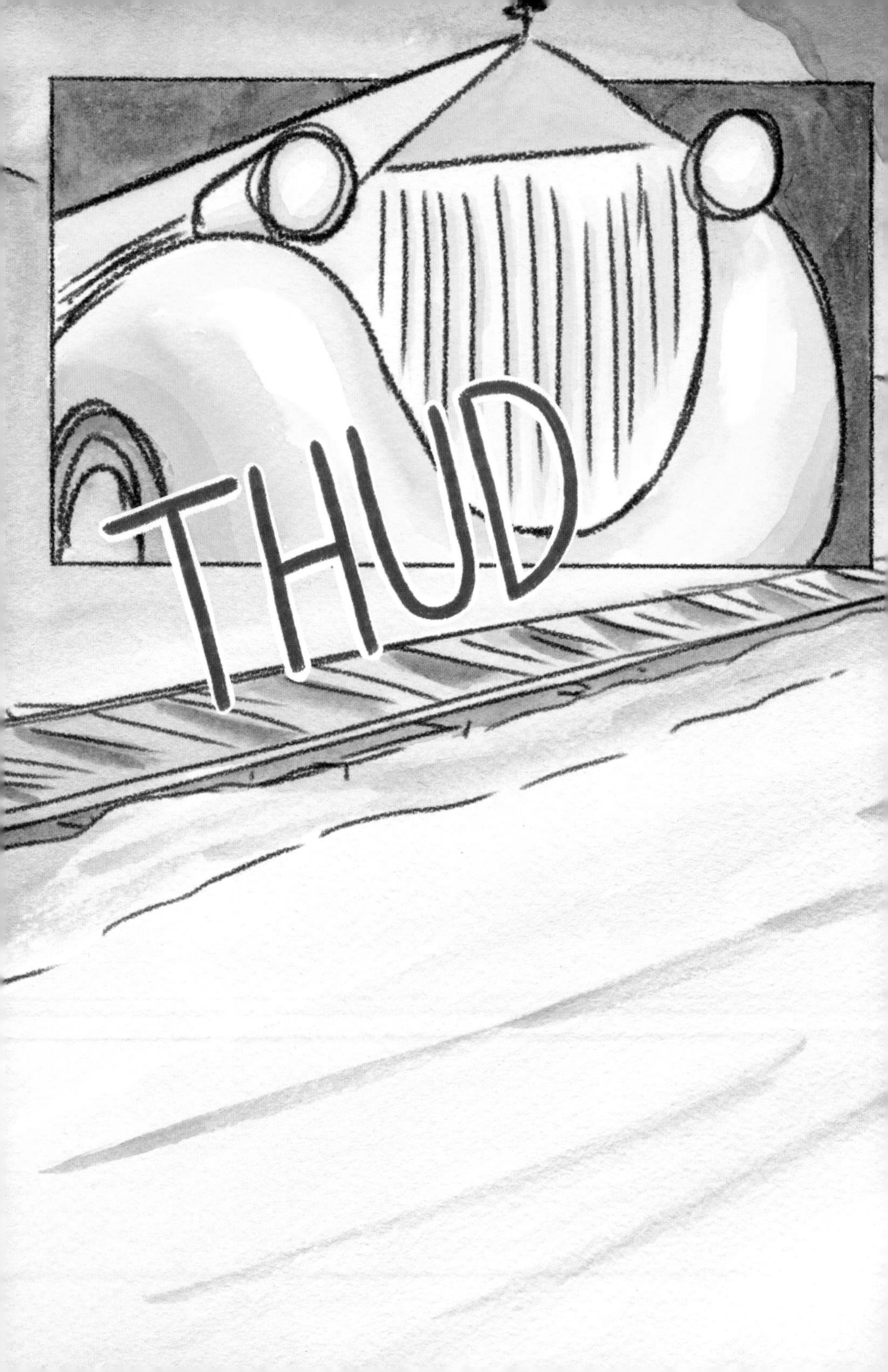
THUD

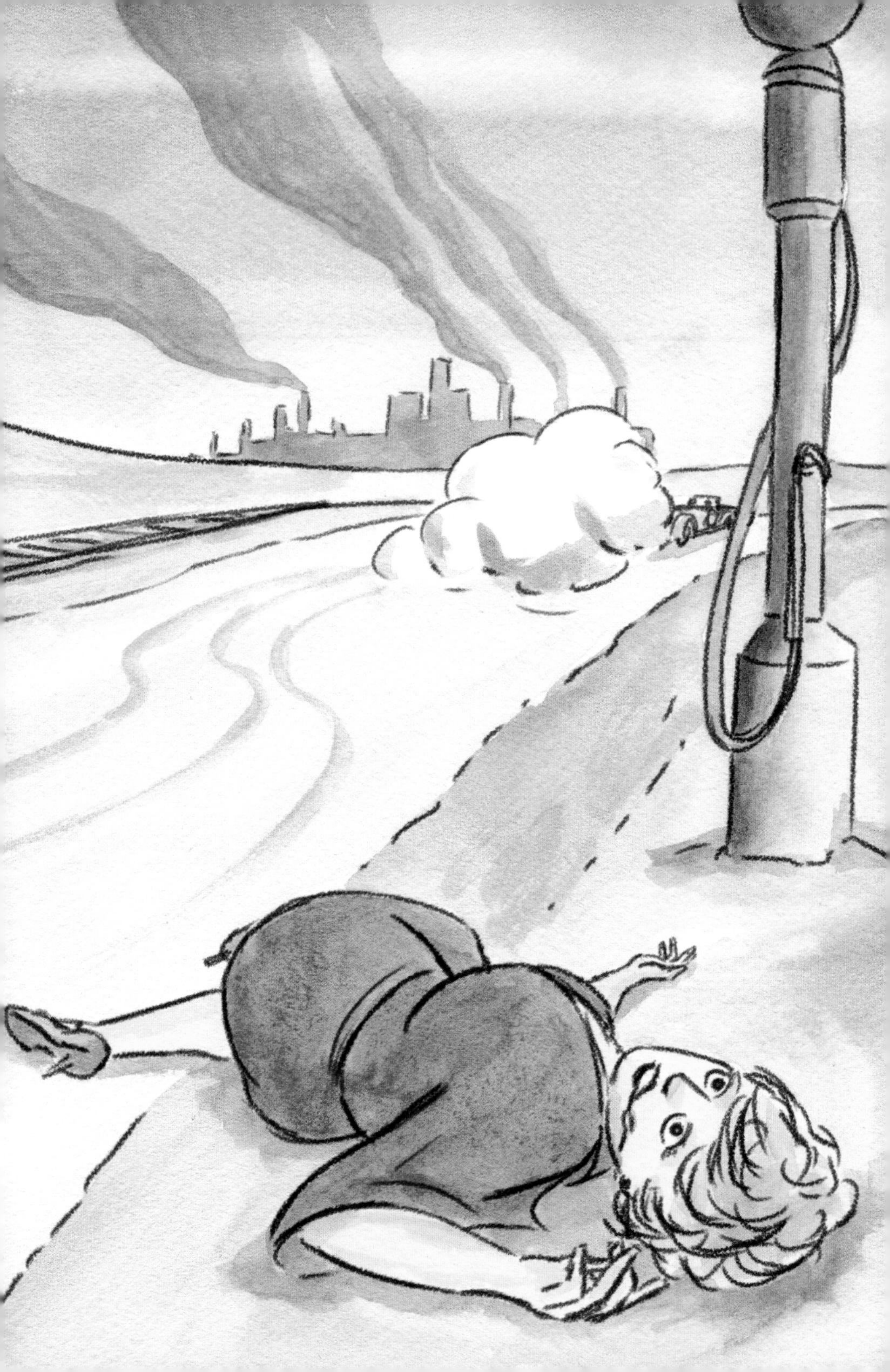

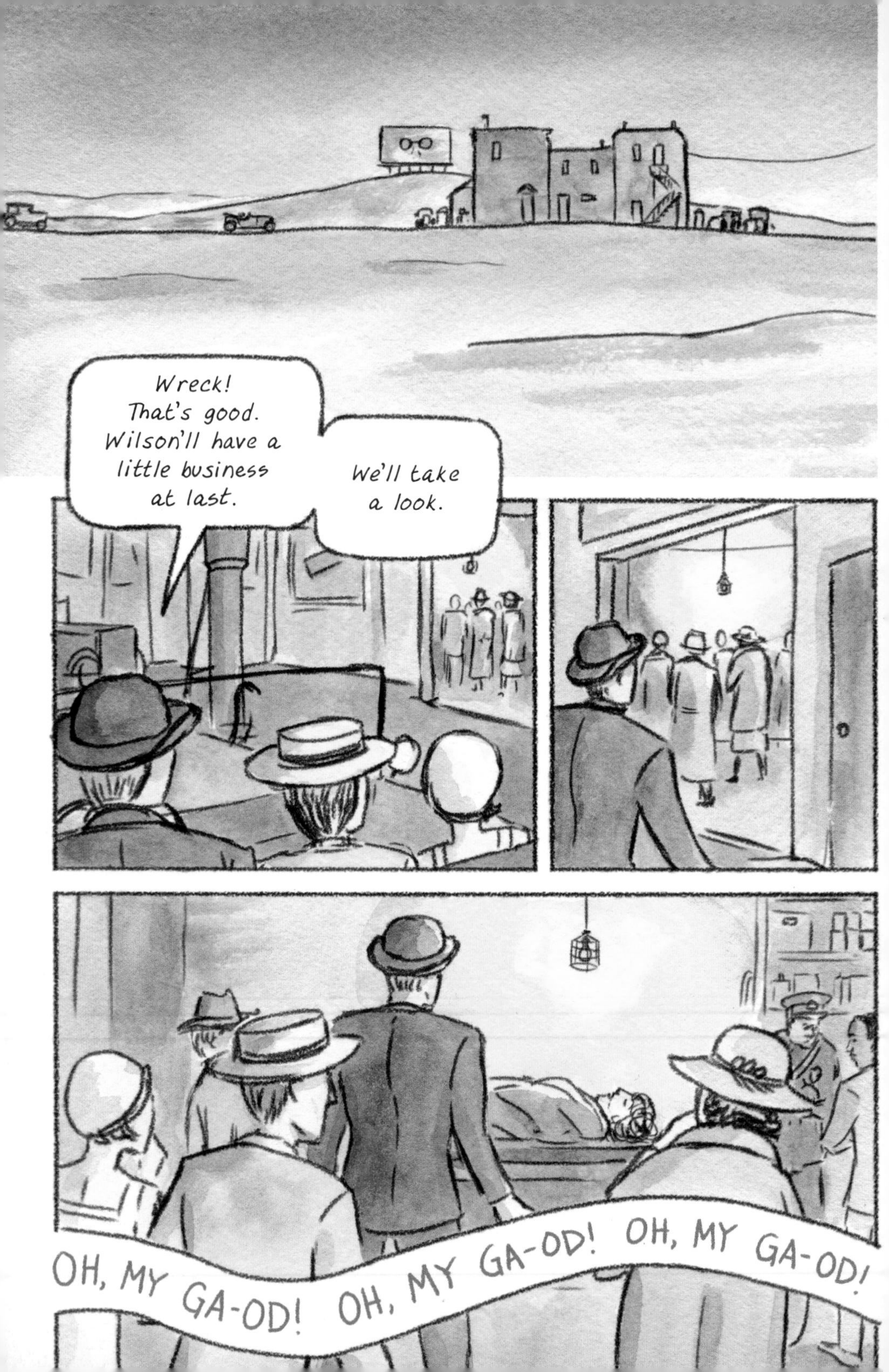

Wreck! That's good. Wilson'll have a little business at last.
We'll take a look.
OH, MY GA-OD! OH, MY GA-OD! OH, MY GA-OD!

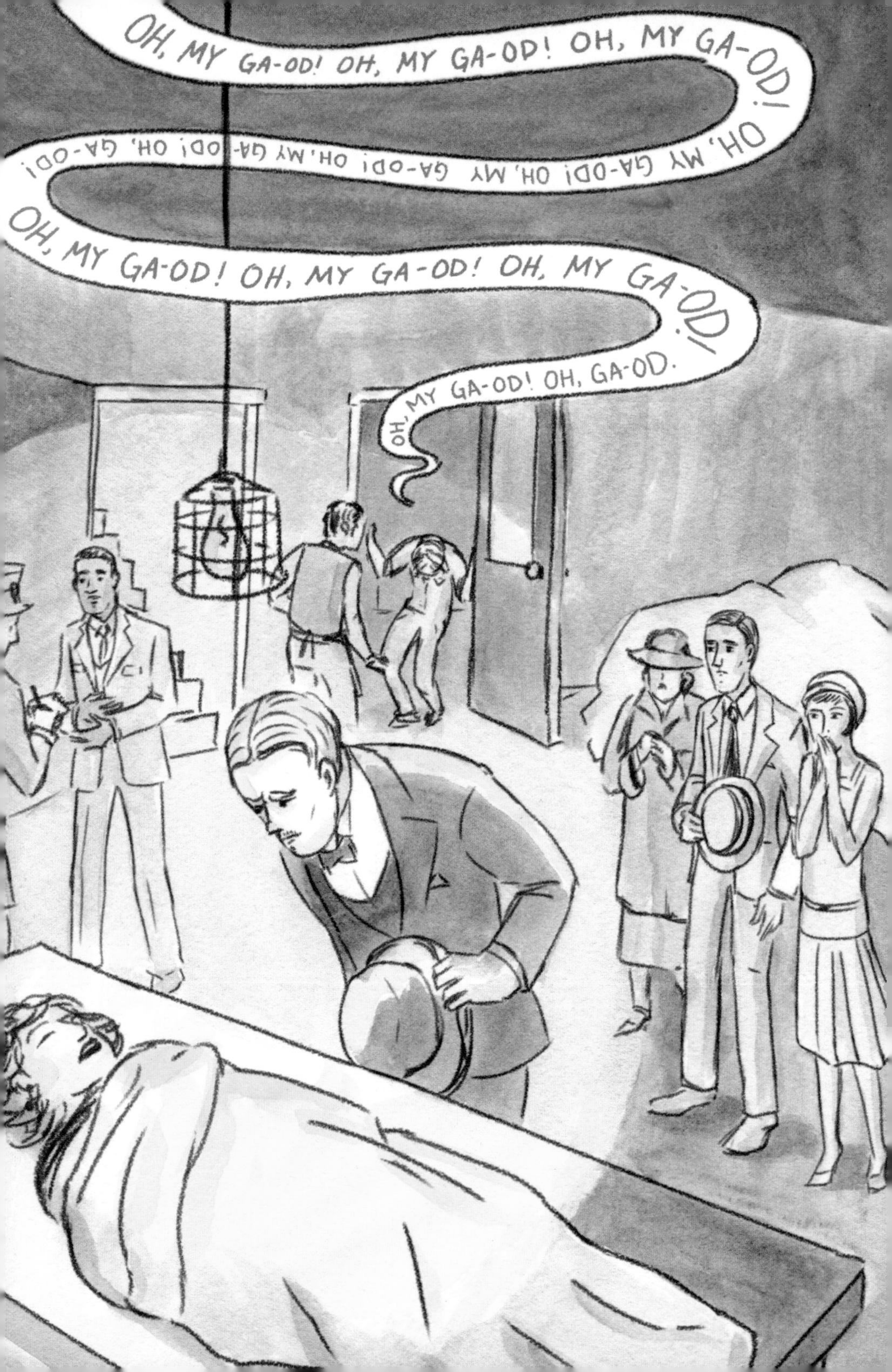
OH, MY GA-OD! OH, MY GA-OD! OH, MY GA-OD! OH, MY GA-OD! OH, MY GA-OD! OH, MY GA-OD! OH,MY GA-OD! OH, GA-OD! OH, MY GA-OD! OH, MY GA-OD! OH, MY GA-OD! OH, MY GA-OD! OH, GA-OD.

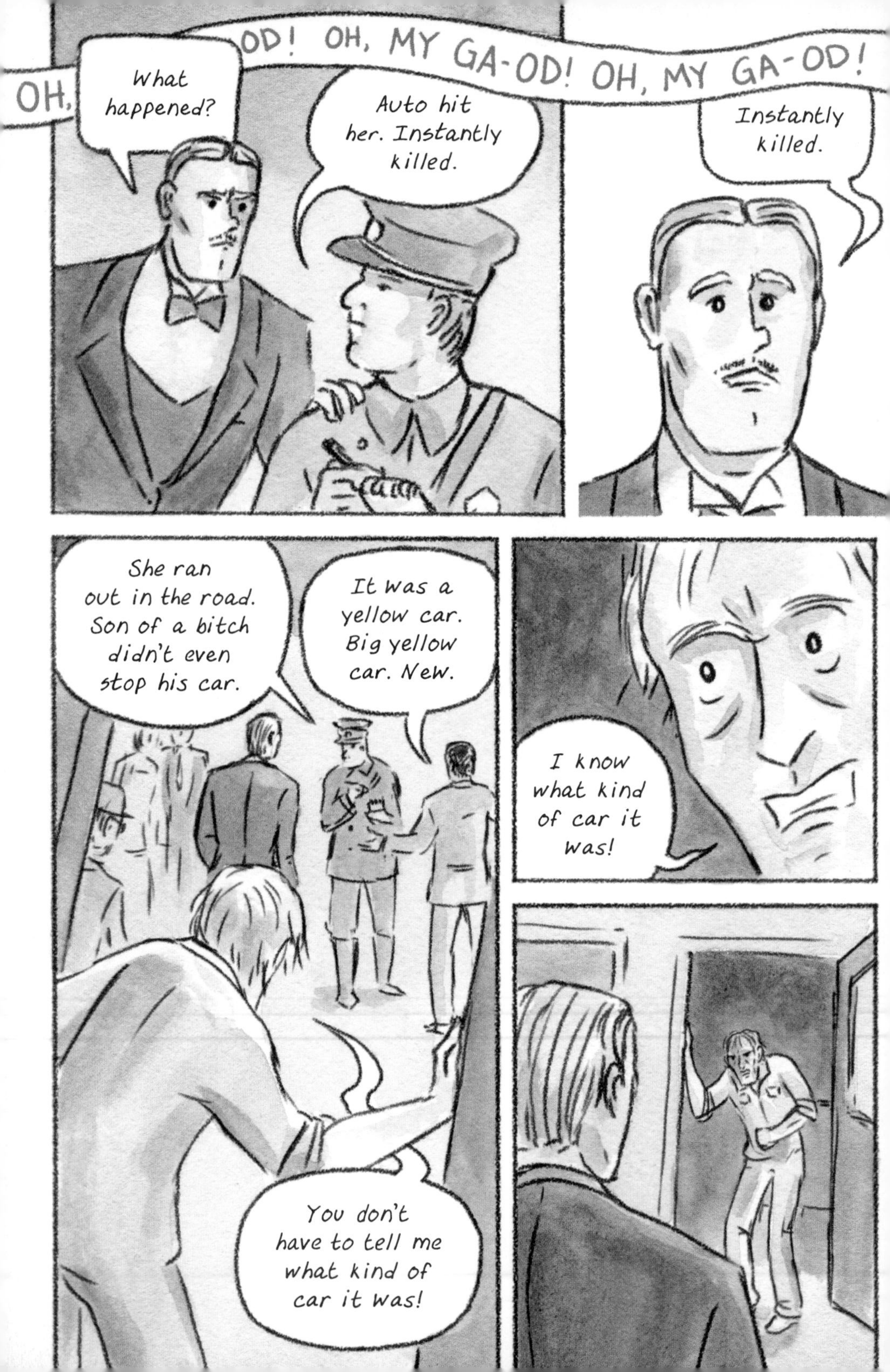
OH, MY GA-OD! OH, MY GA-OD! OH, MY GA-OD!
What happened?
Auto hit her. Instantly killed.
Instantly killed.
She ran out in the road. Son of a bitch didn't even stop his car.
It was a yellow car. Big yellow car. New.
You don't have to tell me what kind of car it was!
I know what kind of car it was!

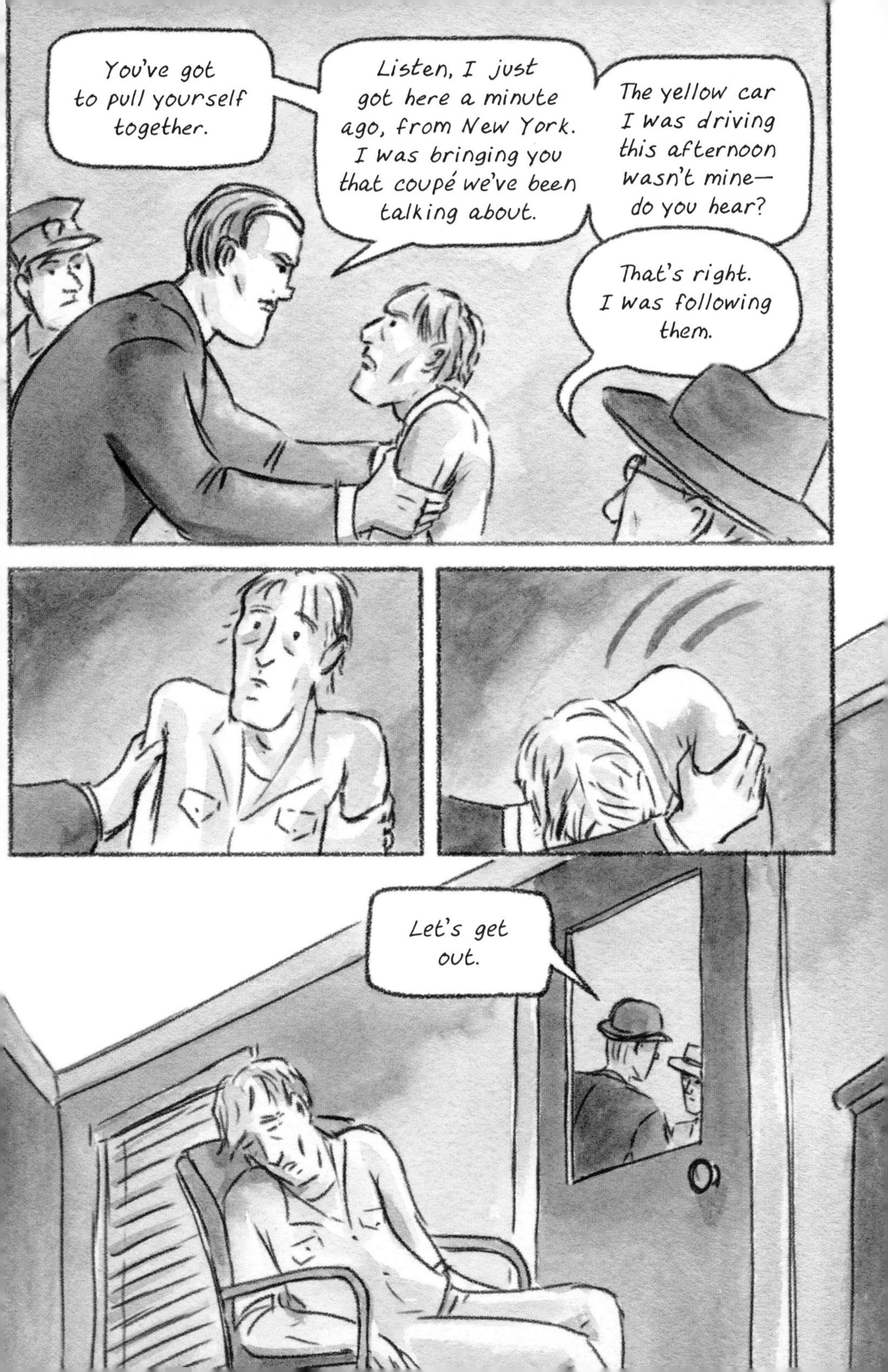
You've got to pull yourself together.
Listen, I just got here a minute ago, from New York. I was bringing you that coupé we've been talking about.
The yellow car I was driving this afternoon wasn't mine— do you hear?
That's right. I was following them.
Let's get out.

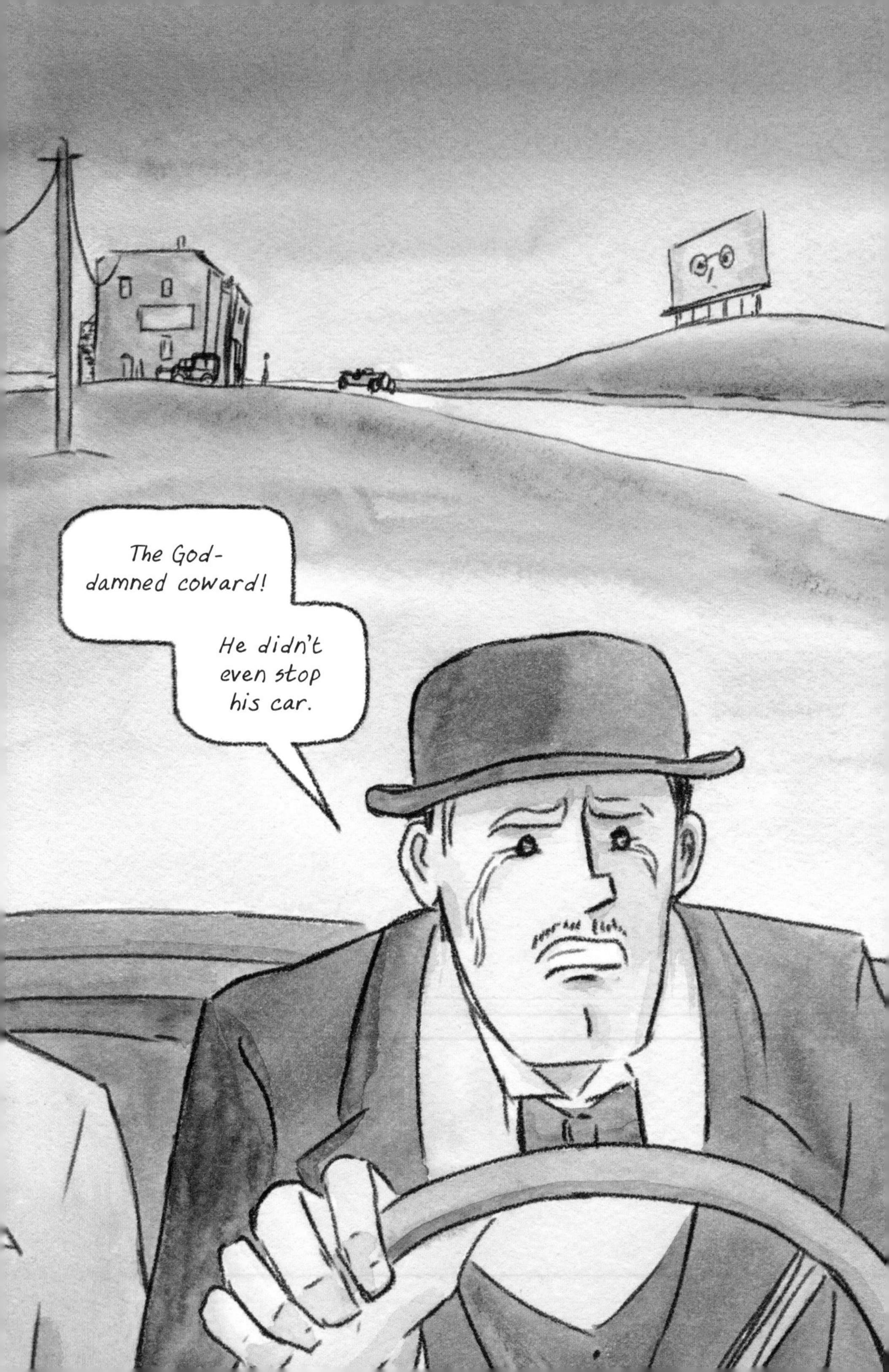
The God-
damned coward!
He didn't
even stop
his car.

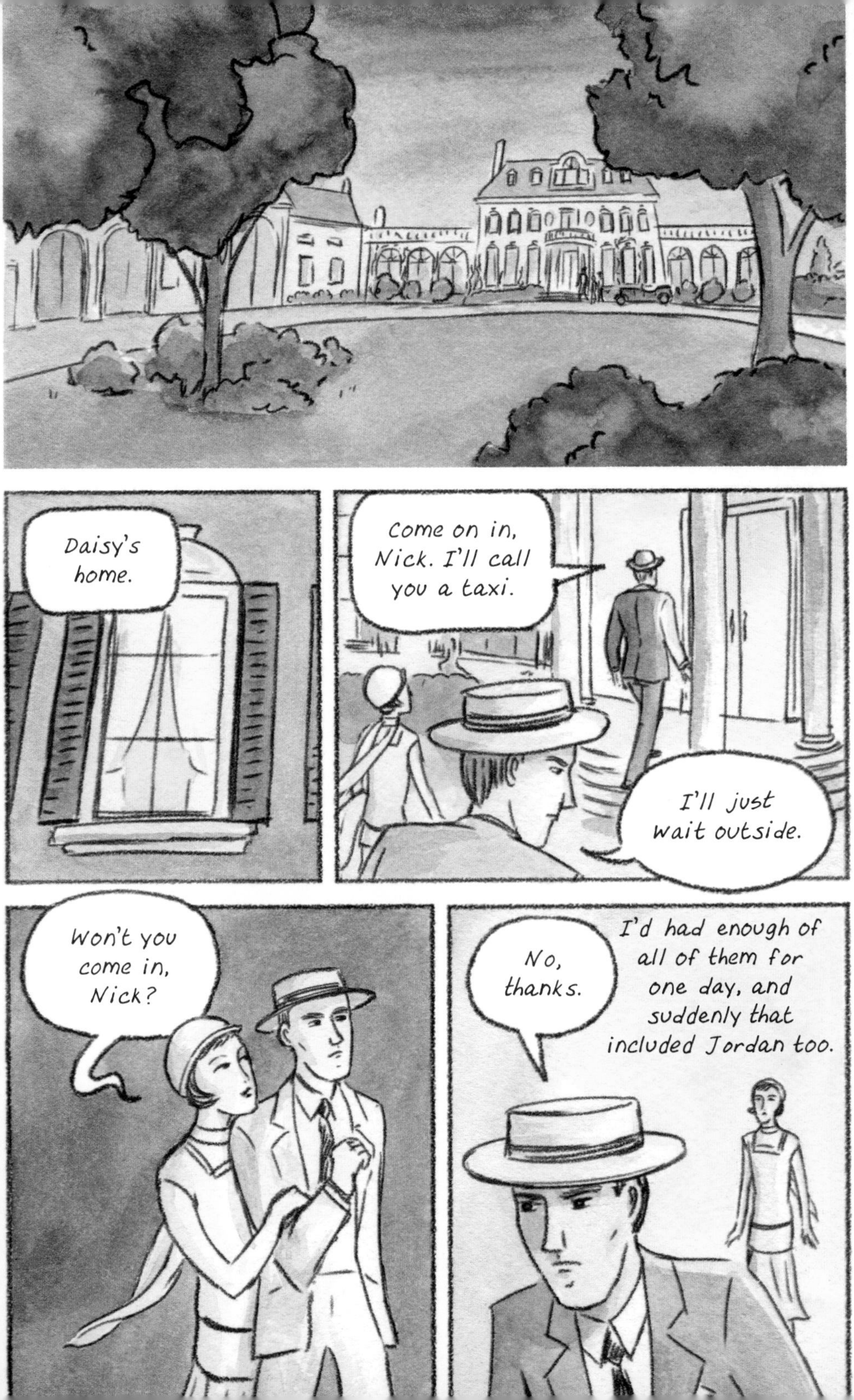
Daisy's home.
Come on in, Nick. I'll call you a taxi.
I'll just wait outside.
Won't you come in, Nick?
No, thanks.
I'd had enough of all of them for one day, and suddenly that included Jordan too.

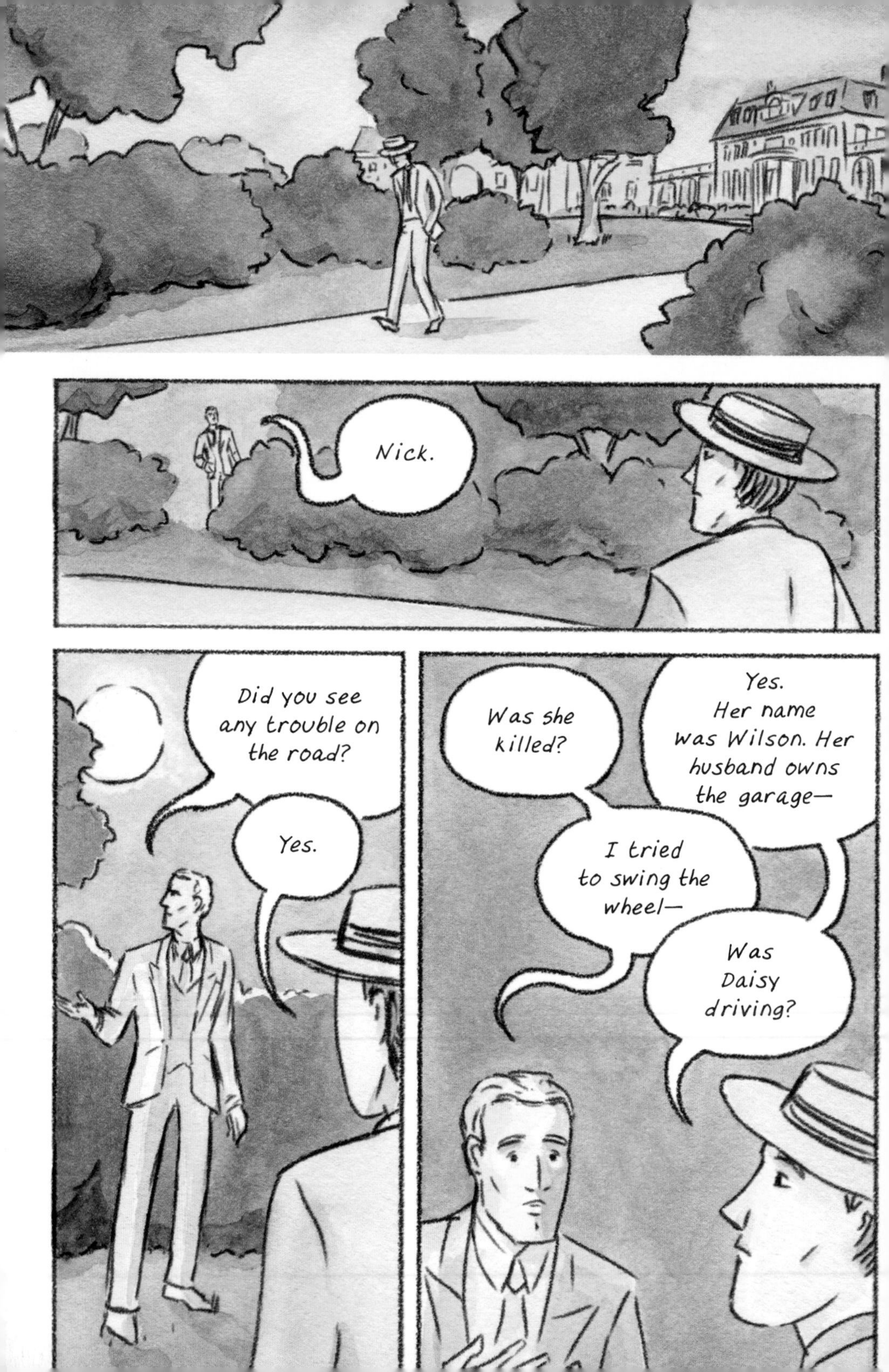
Nick.
Did you see any trouble on the road?
Yes.
Was she killed?
Yes. Her name was Wilson. Her husband owns the garage—
I tried to swing the wheel—
Was Daisy driving?

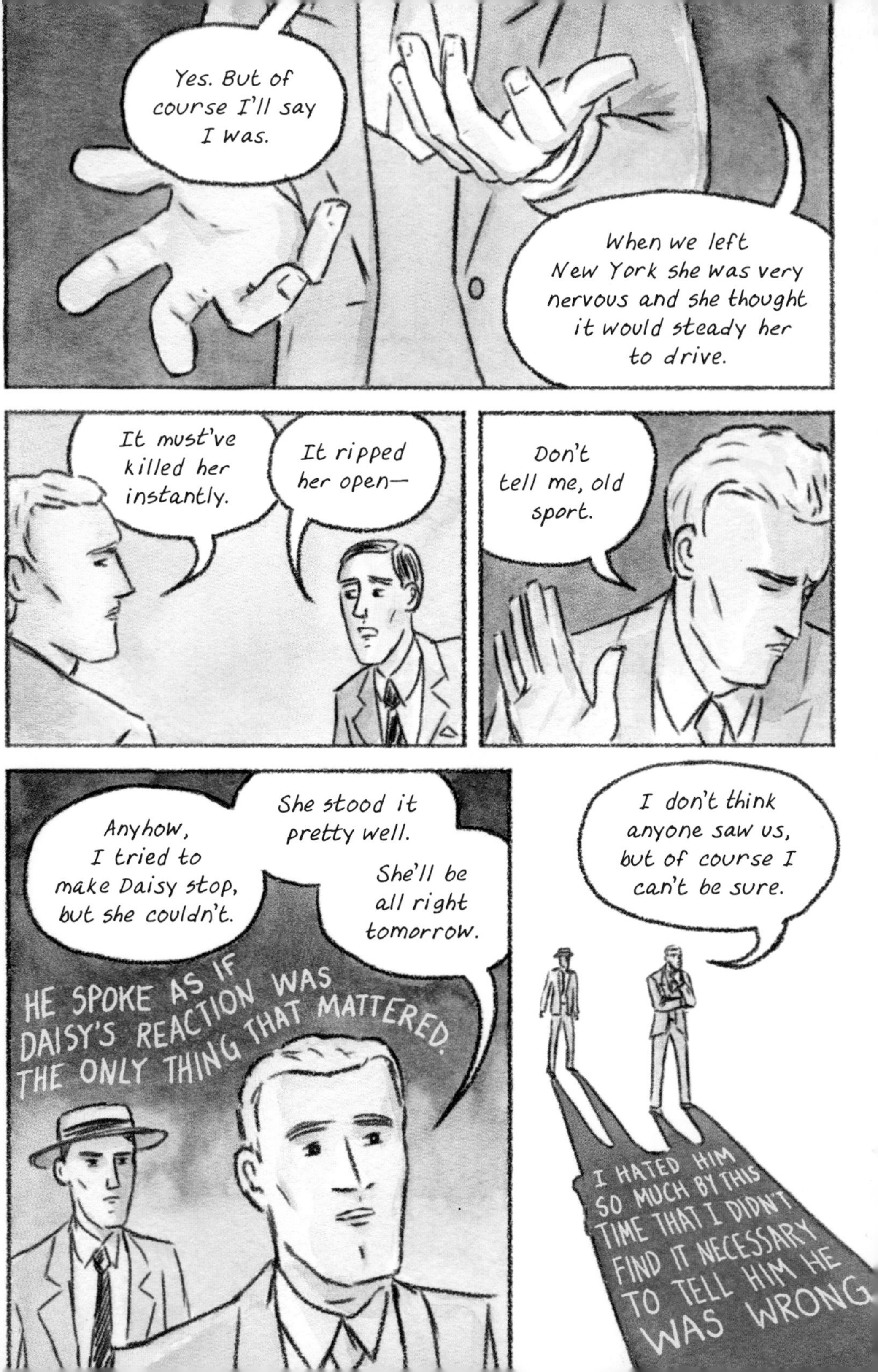
Yes. But of course I'll say I was.
When we left New York she was very nervous and she thought it would steady her to drive.
It must've killed her instantly.
It ripped her open—
Don't tell me, old sport.
Anyhow, I tried to make Daisy stop, but she couldn't.
She stood it pretty well.
She'll be all right tomorrow.
HE SPOKE AS IF DAISY'S REACTION WAS THE ONLY THING THAT MATTERED.
I don't think anyone saw us, but of course I can't be sure.
I HATED HIM SO MUCH BY THIS TIME THAT I DIDN'T FIND IT NECESSARY TO TELL HIM HE WAS WRONG

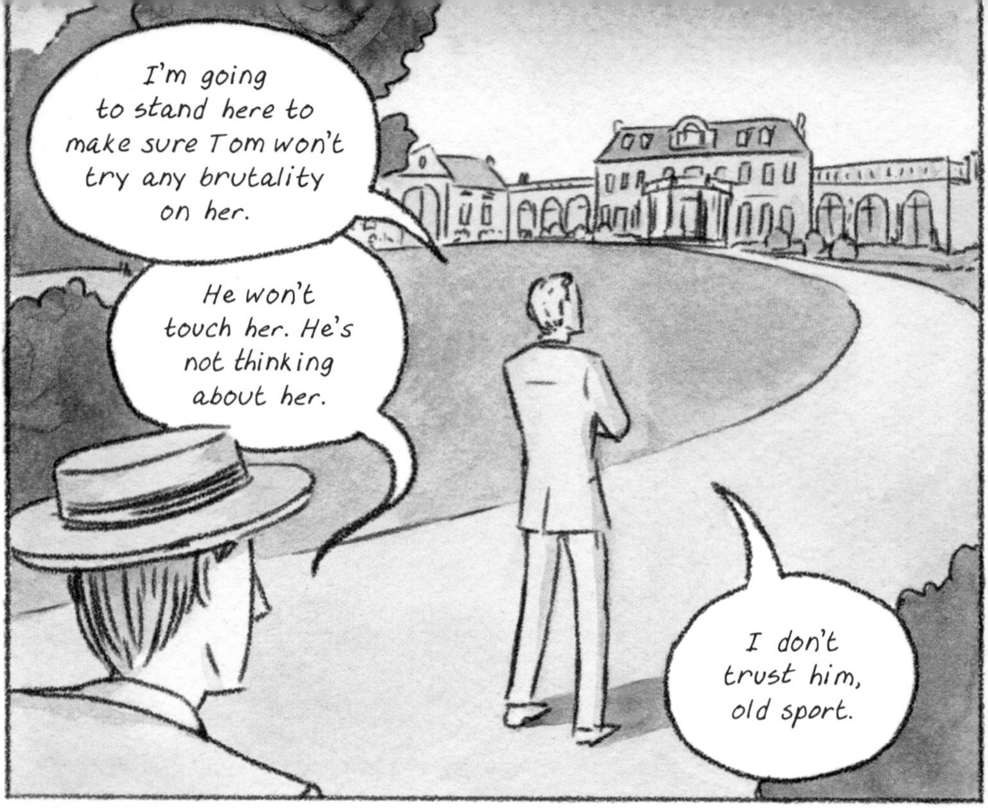
I'm going to stand here to make sure Tom won't try any brutality on her.
He won't touch her. He's not thinking about her.
I don't trust him, old sport.

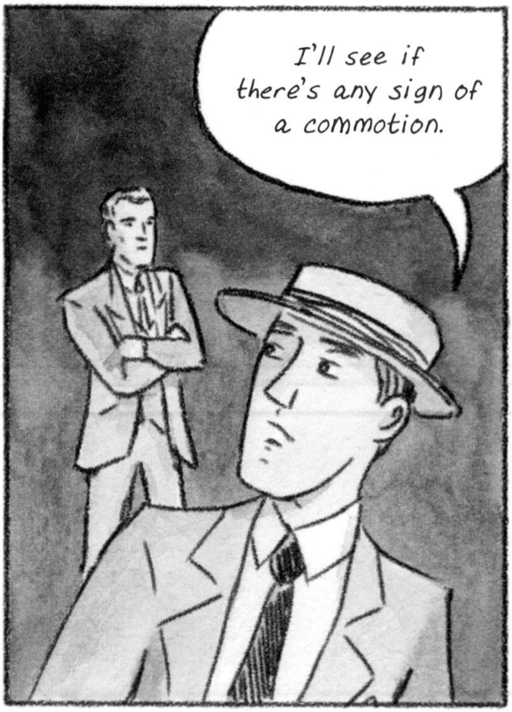
I'll see if there's any sign of a commotion.

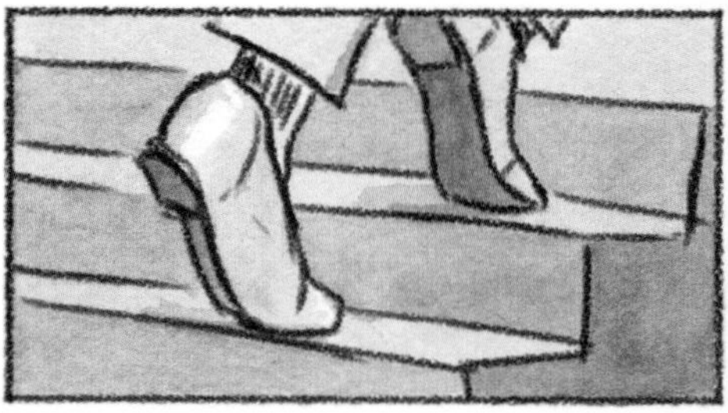

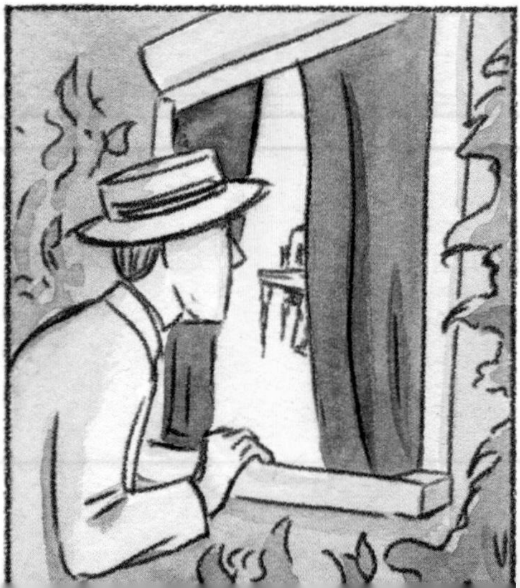

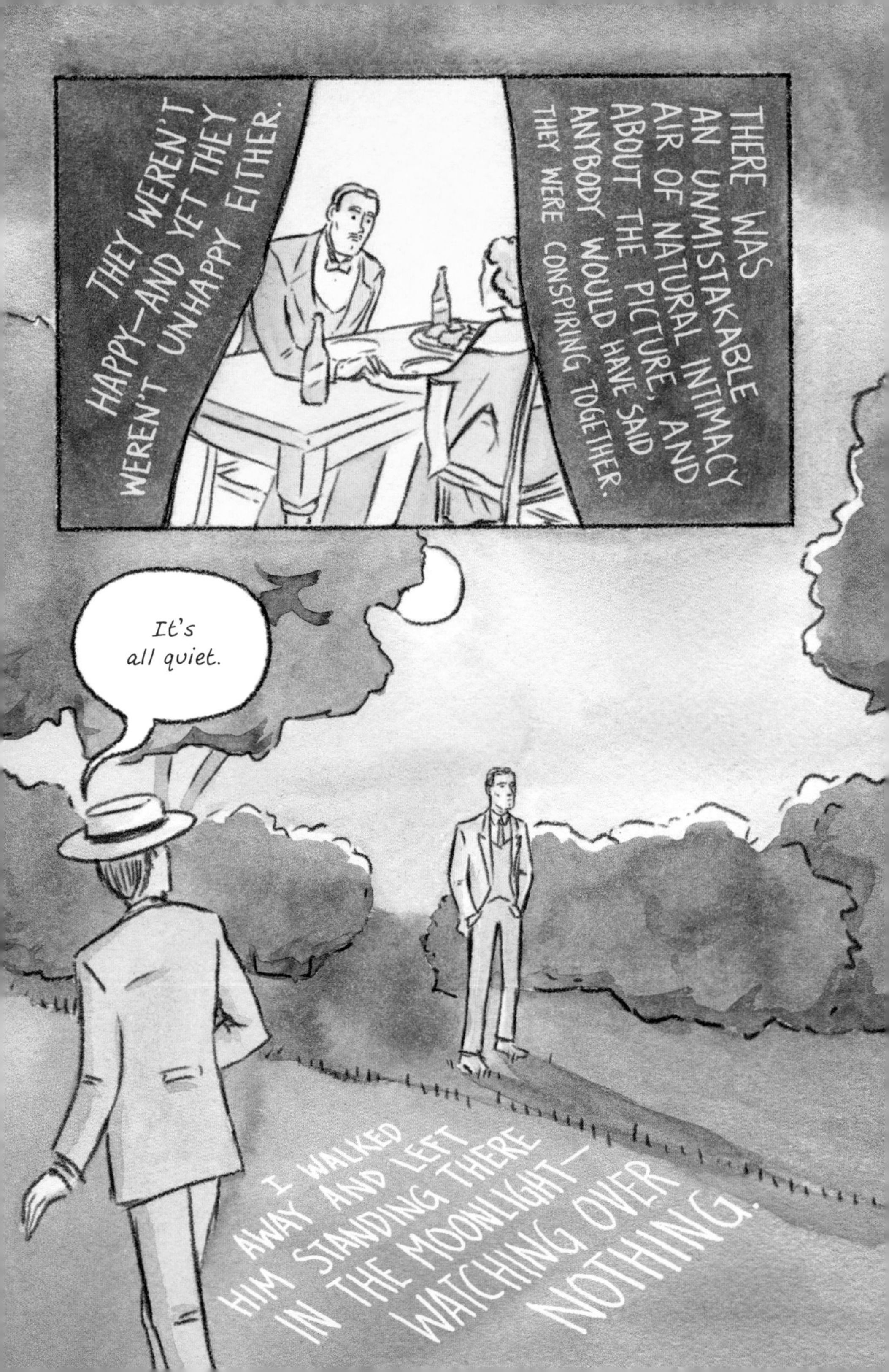
THEY WEREN'T HAPPY—AND YET THEY WEREN'T UNHAPPY EITHER.
THERE WAS AN UNMISTAKABLE AIR OF NATURAL INTIMACY ABOUT THE PICTURE, AND ANYBODY WOULD HAVE SAID THEY WERE CONSPIRING TOGETHER.
It's all quiet.
I WALKED AWAY AND LEFT HIM STANDING THERE IN THE MOONLIGHT—WATCHING OVER NOTHING.

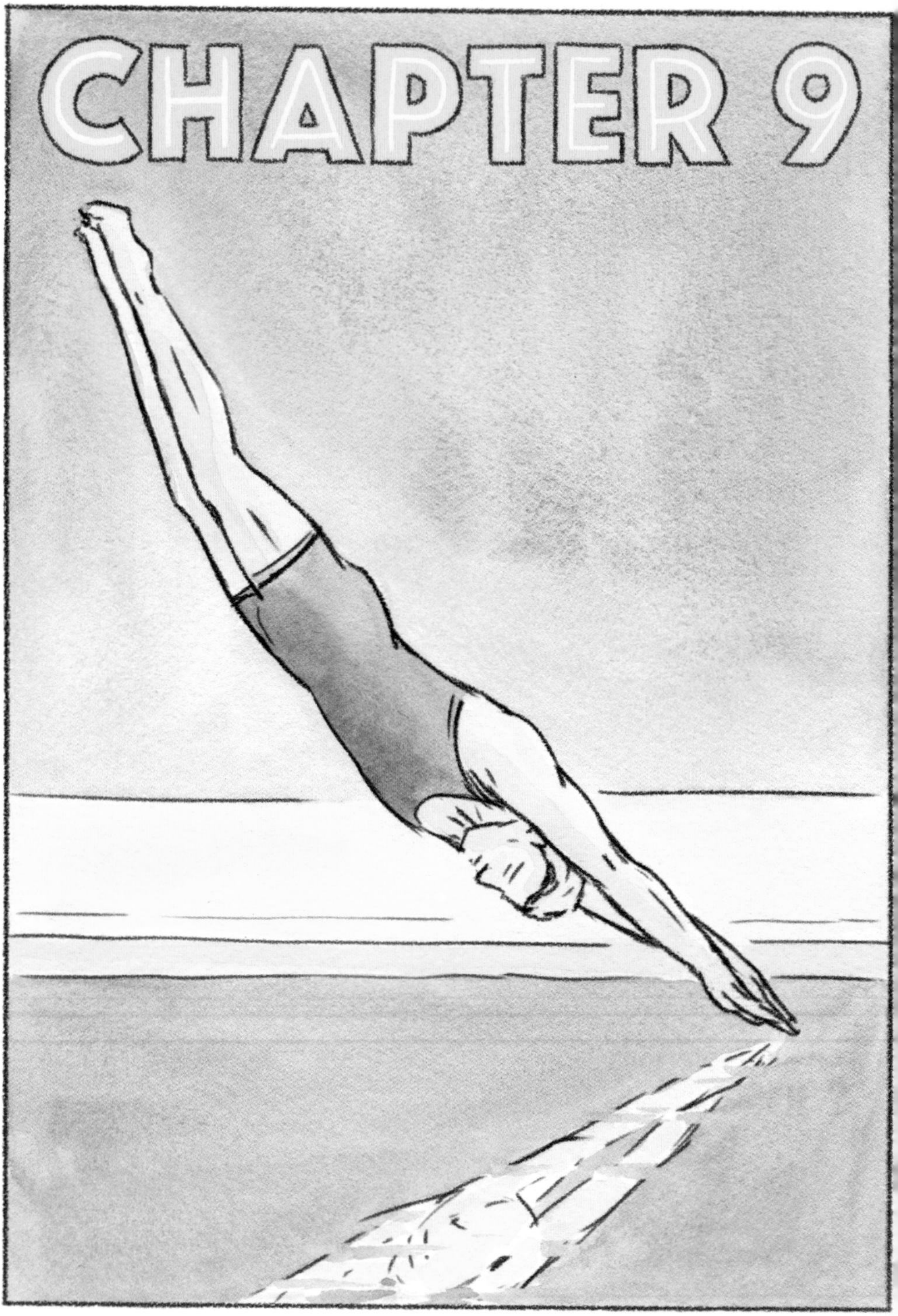
CHAPTER 9

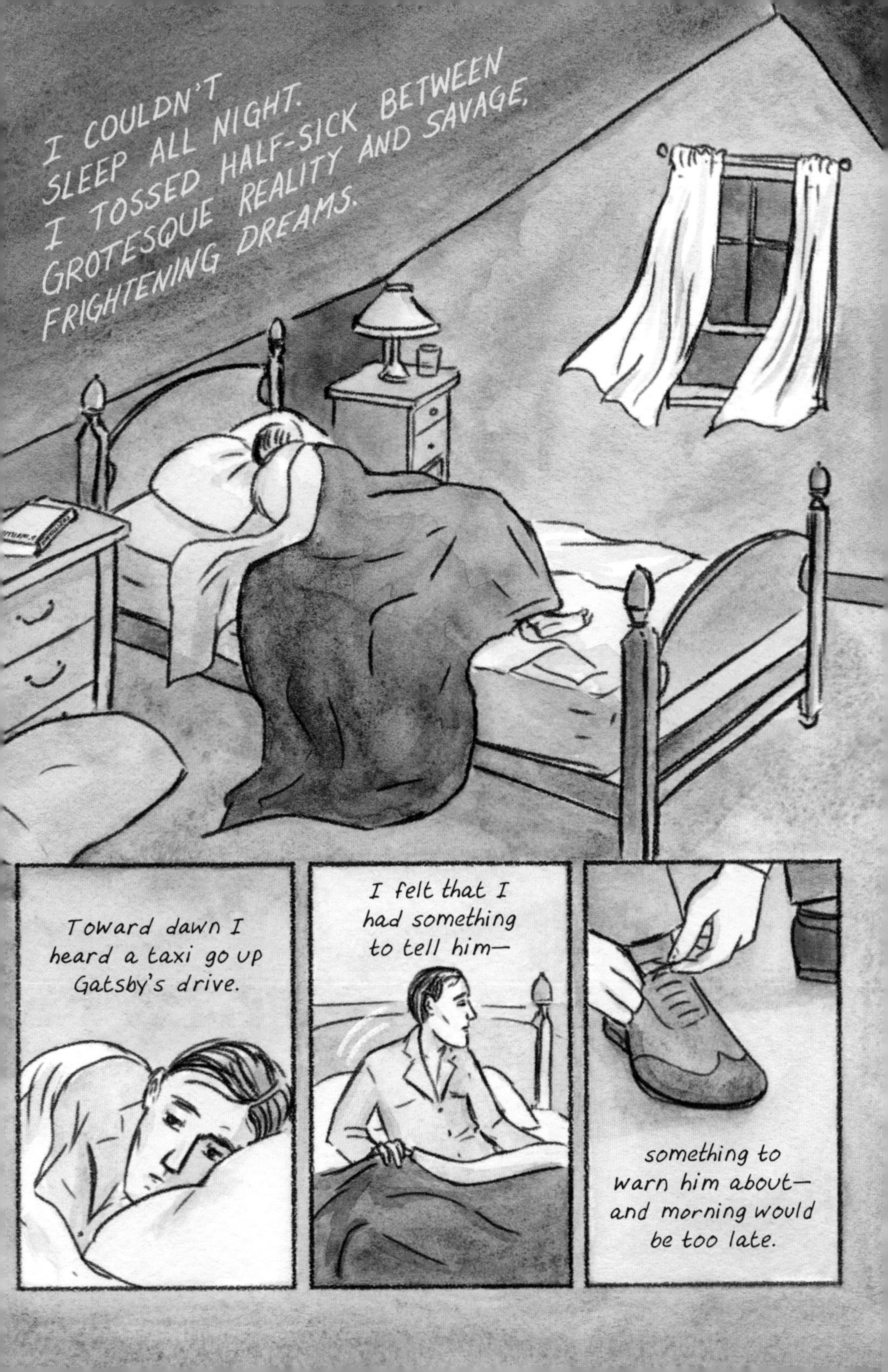
I COULDN'T SLEEP ALL NIGHT. I TOSSED HALF-SICK BETWEEN GROTESQUE REALITY AND SAVAGE, FRIGHTENING DREAMS.
Toward dawn I heard a taxi go up Gatsby's drive.
I felt that I had something to tell him—
something to warn him about— and morning would be too late.

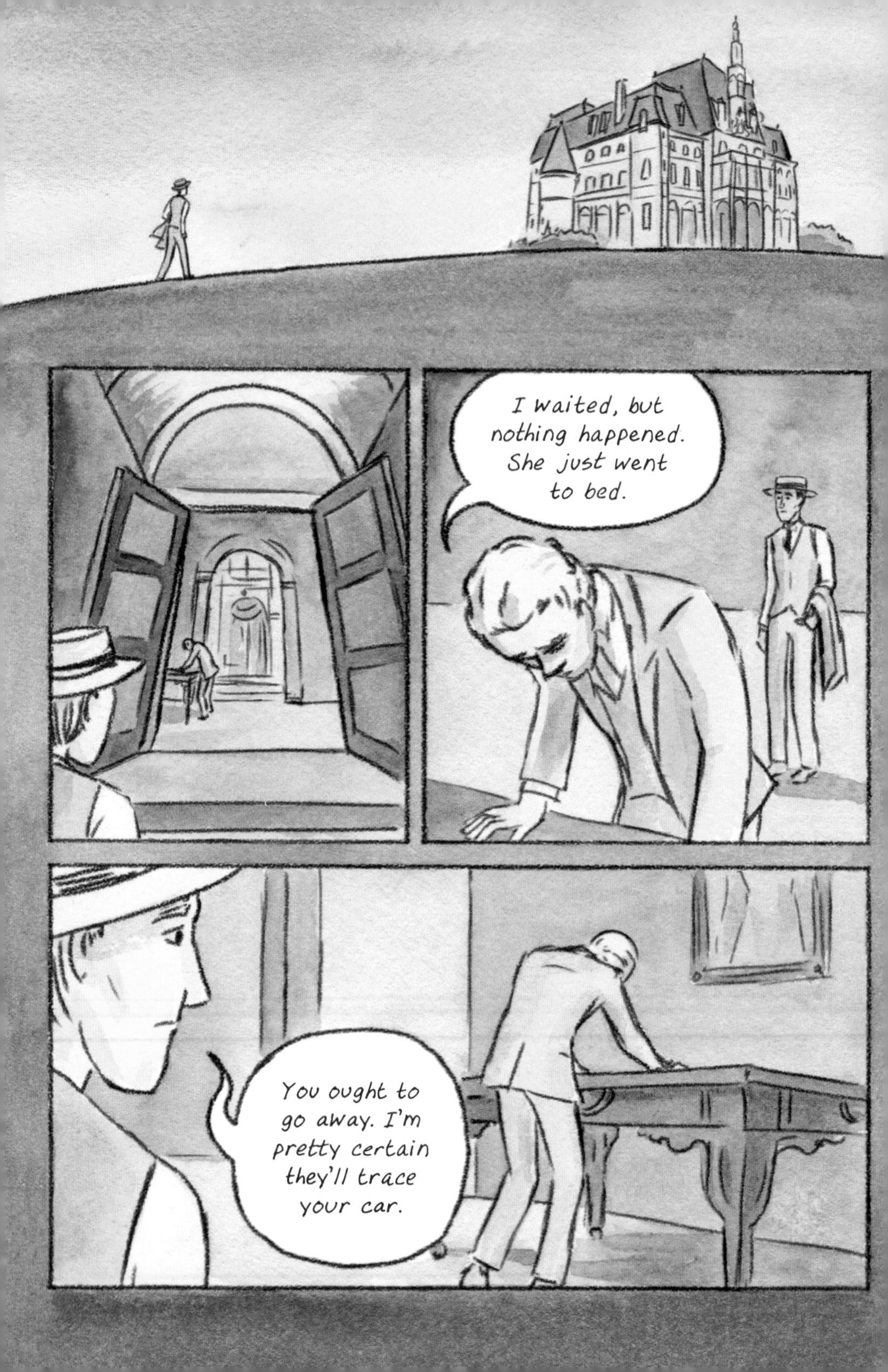
I waited, but nothing happened. She just went to bed.
You ought to go away. I'm pretty certain they'll trace your car.

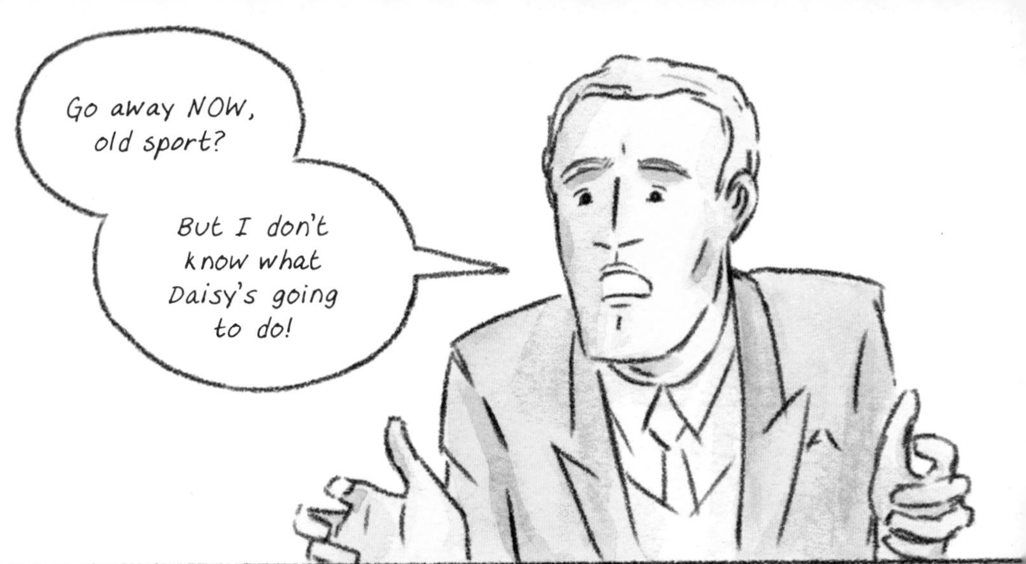
Go away NOW, old sport?
But I don't know what Daisy's going to do!

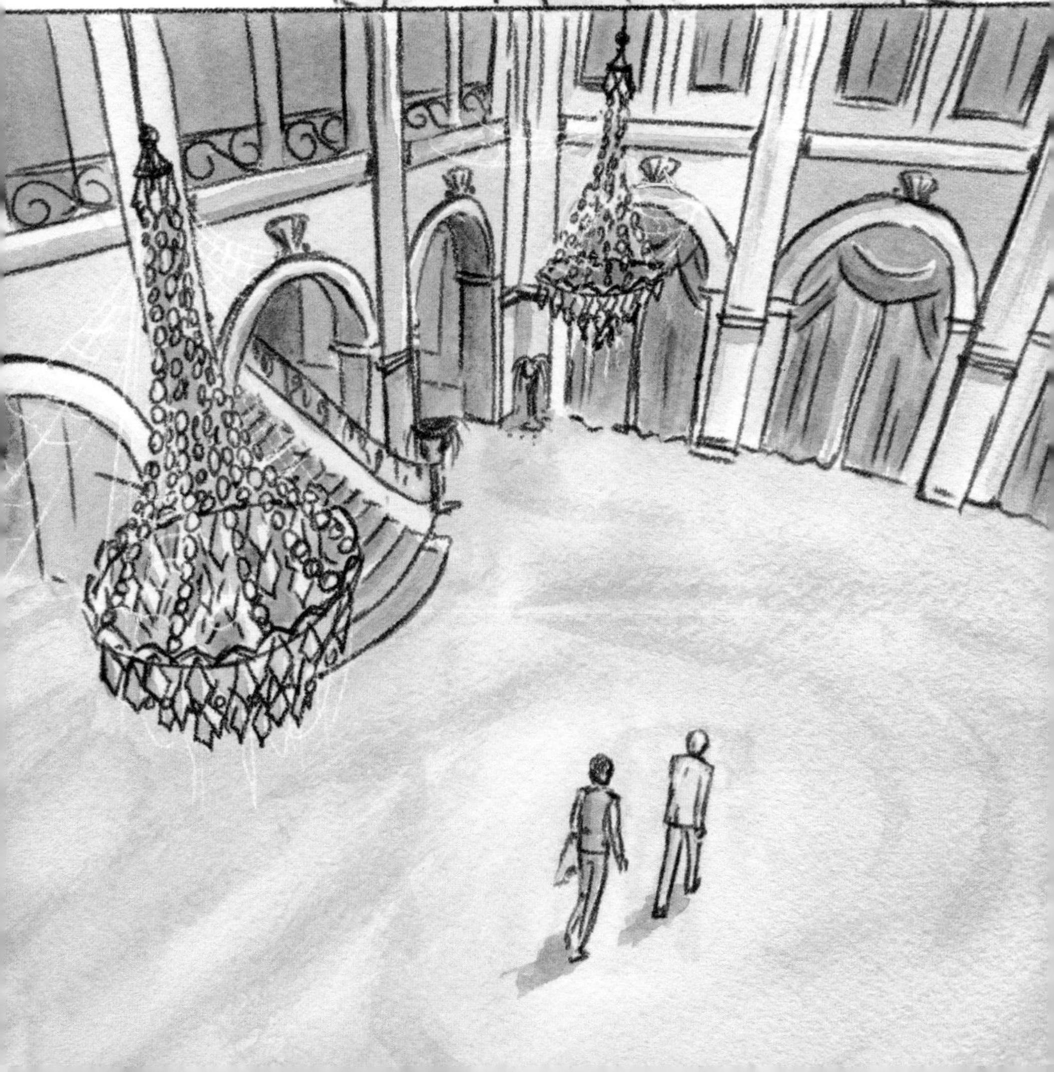

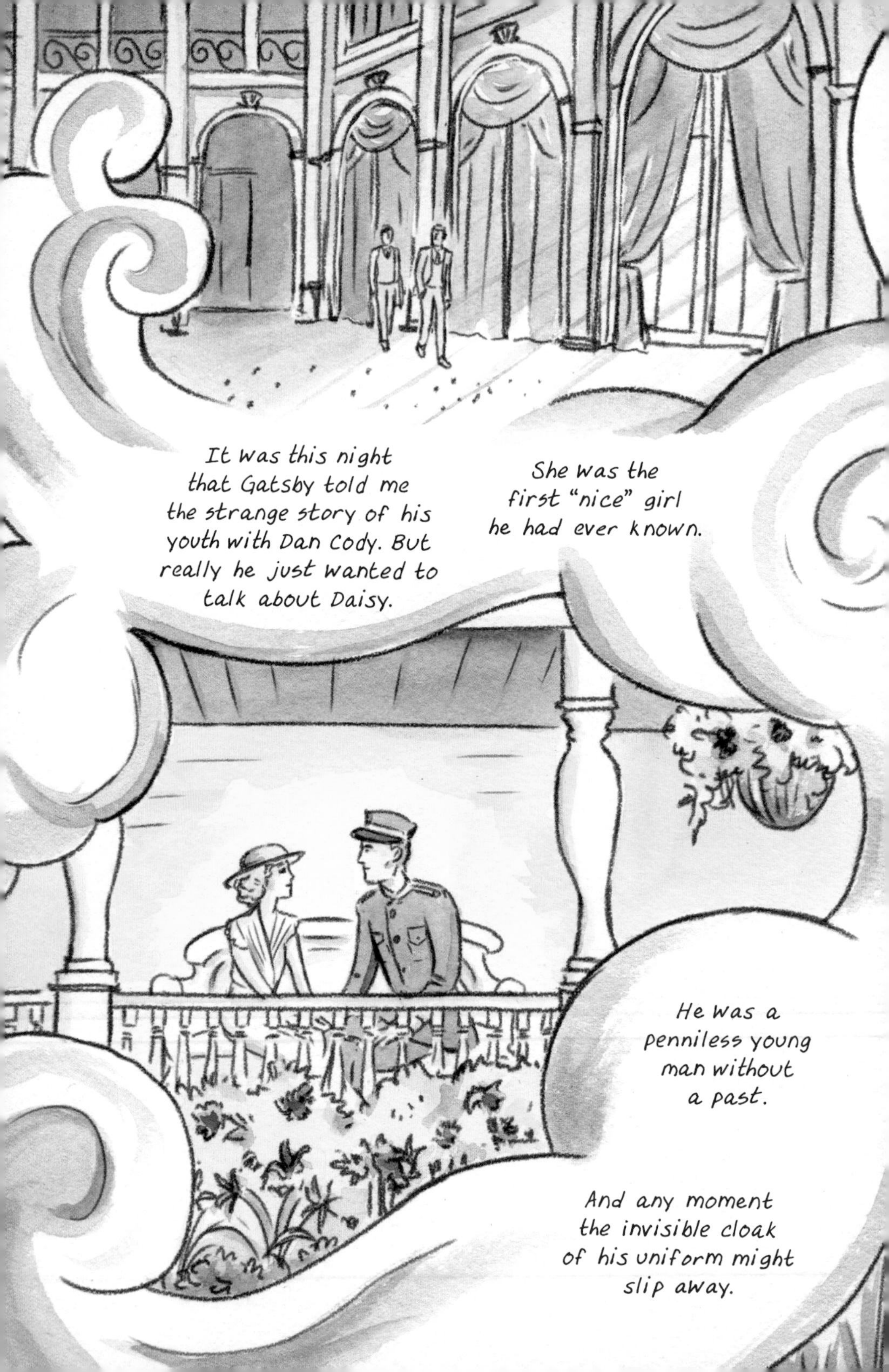
It was this night that Gatsby told me the strange story of his youth with Dan Cody. But really he just wanted to talk about Daisy.
She was the first "nice" girl he had ever known.
He was a penniless young man without a past.
And any moment the invisible cloak of his uniform might slip away.

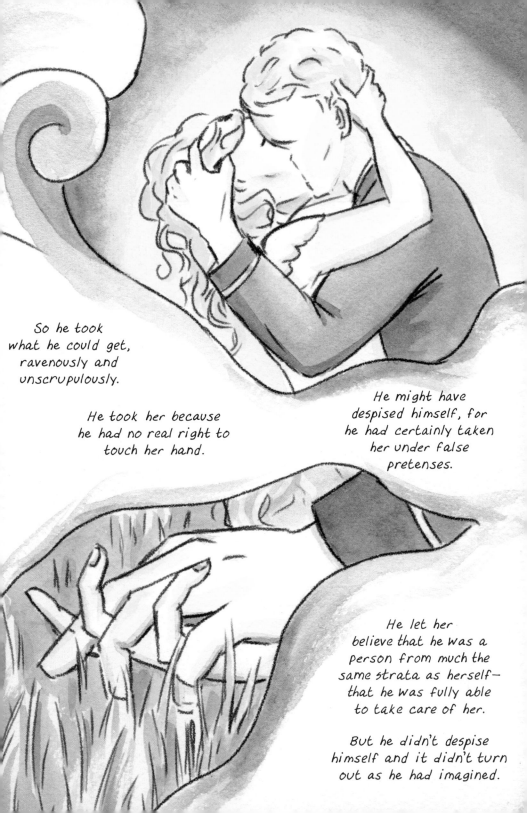

So he took what he could get, ravenously and unscrupulously.

He took her because he had no real right to touch her hand.

He might have despised himself, for he had certainly taken her under false pretenses.

He let her believe that he was a person from much the same strata as herself— that he was fully able to take care of her.

But he didn't despise himself and it didn't turn out as he had imagined.

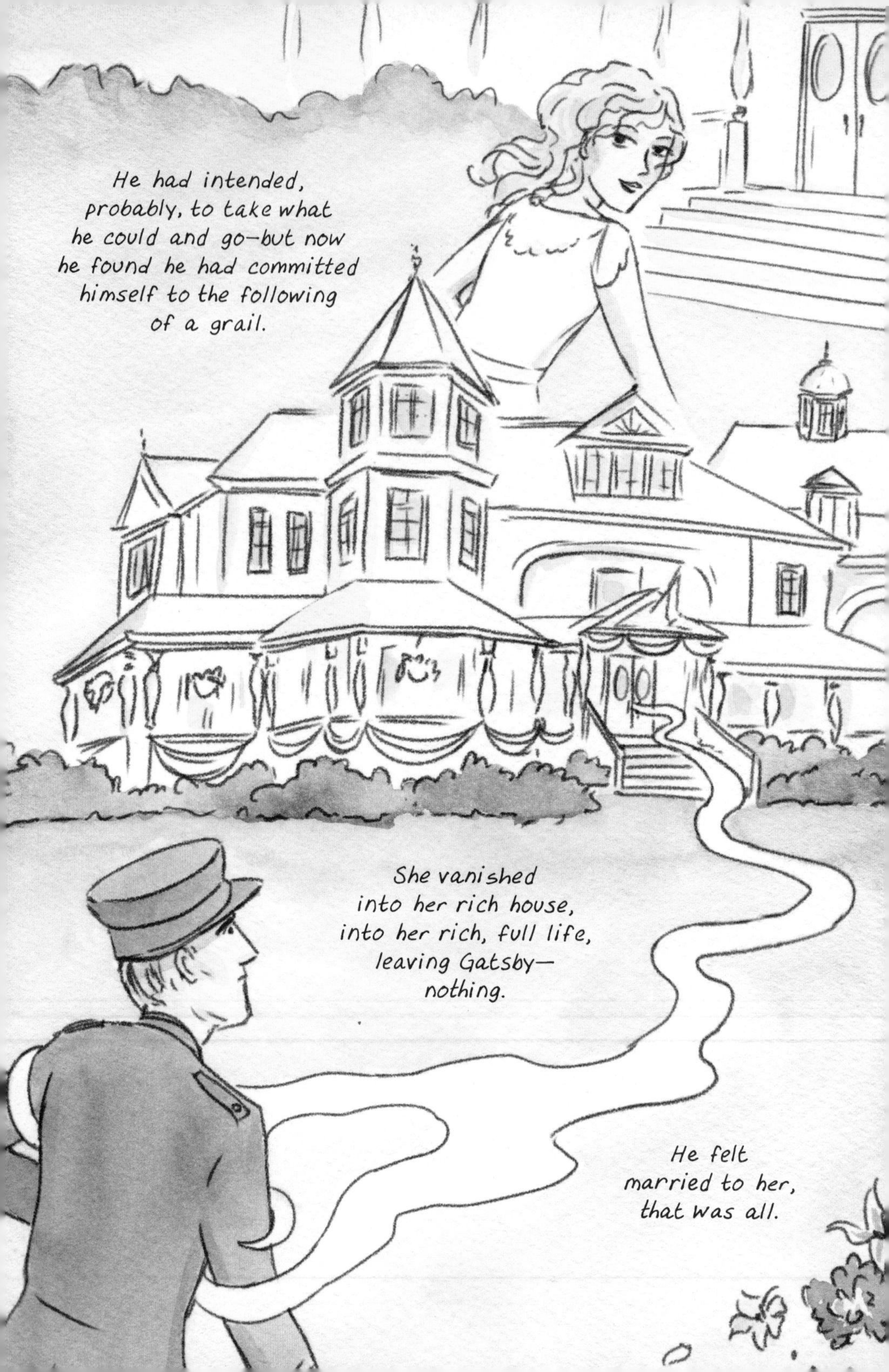
He had intended, probably, to take what he could and go—but now he found he had committed himself to the following of a grail.
She vanished into her rich house, into her rich, full life, leaving Gatsby—nothing.
He felt married to her, that was all.

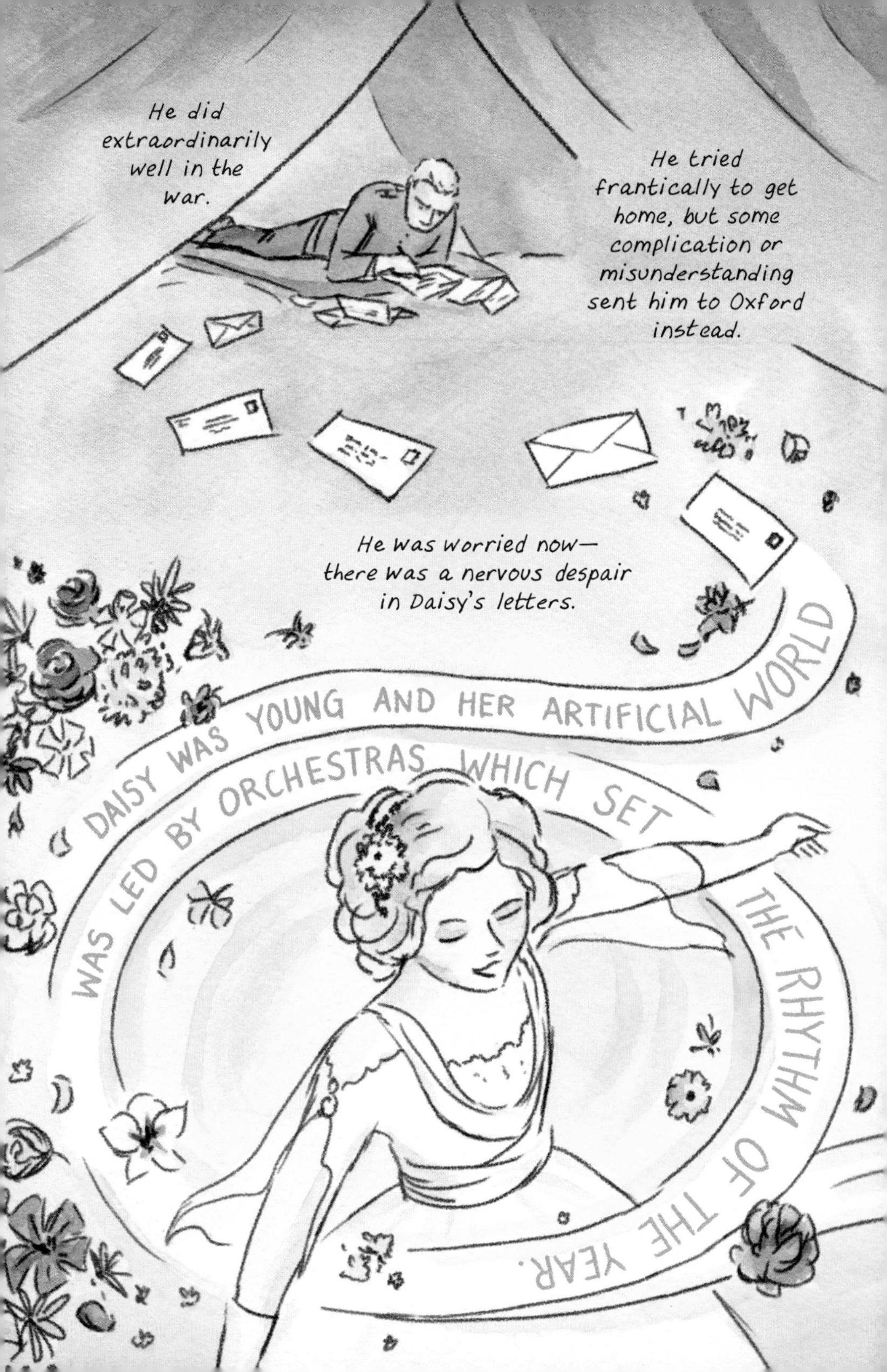
He did extraordinarily well in the war.
He tried frantically to get home, but some complication or misunderstanding sent him to Oxford instead.
He was worried now— there was a nervous despair in Daisy's letters.
DAISY WAS YOUNG AND HER ARTIFICIAL WORLD
WAS LED BY ORCHESTRAS WHICH SET THE RHYTHM OF THE YEAR.

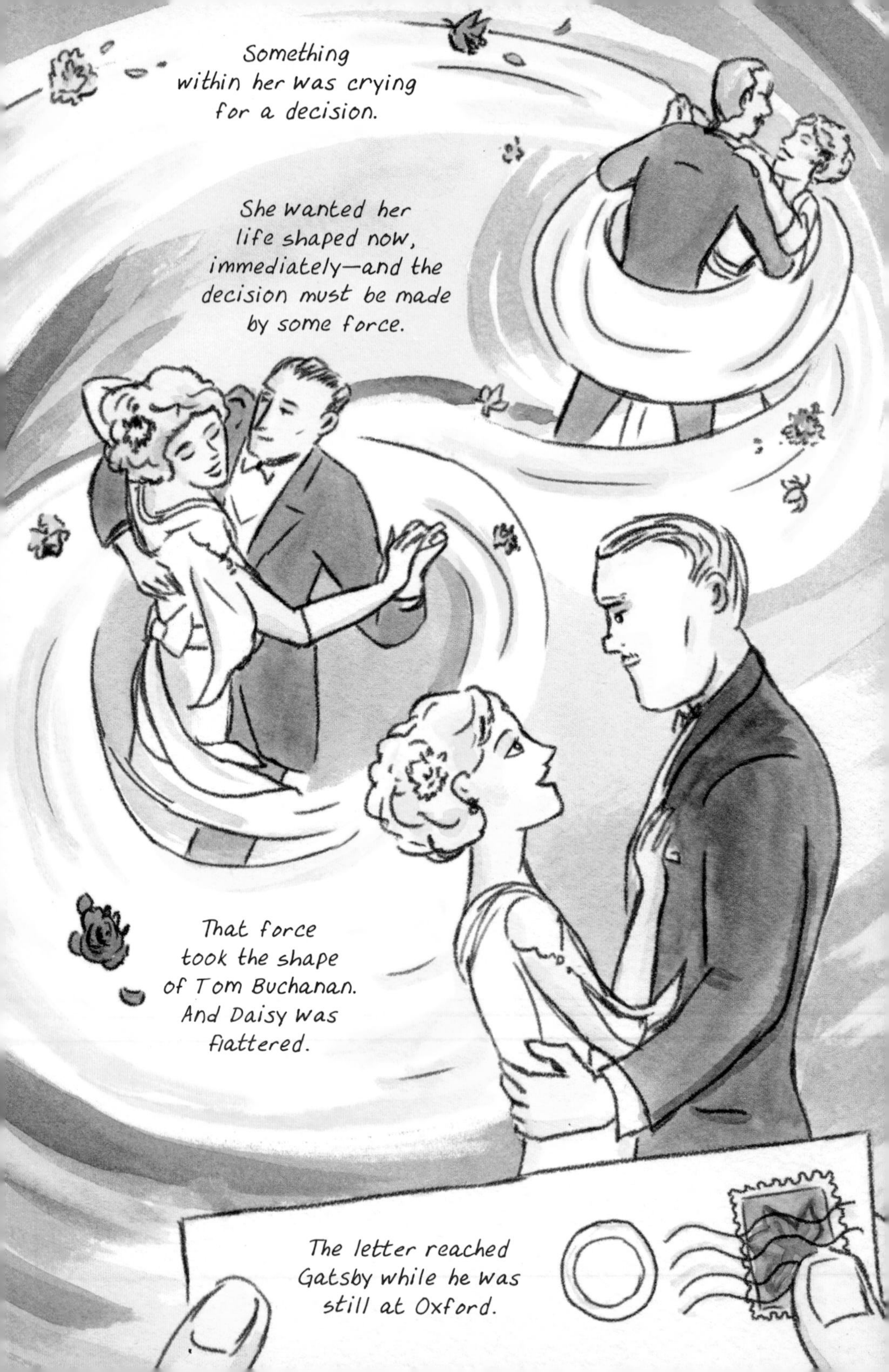
Something within her was crying for a decision.
She wanted her life shaped now, immediately—and the decision must be made by some force.
That force took the shape of Tom Buchanan. And Daisy was flattered.
The letter reached Gatsby while he was still at Oxford.

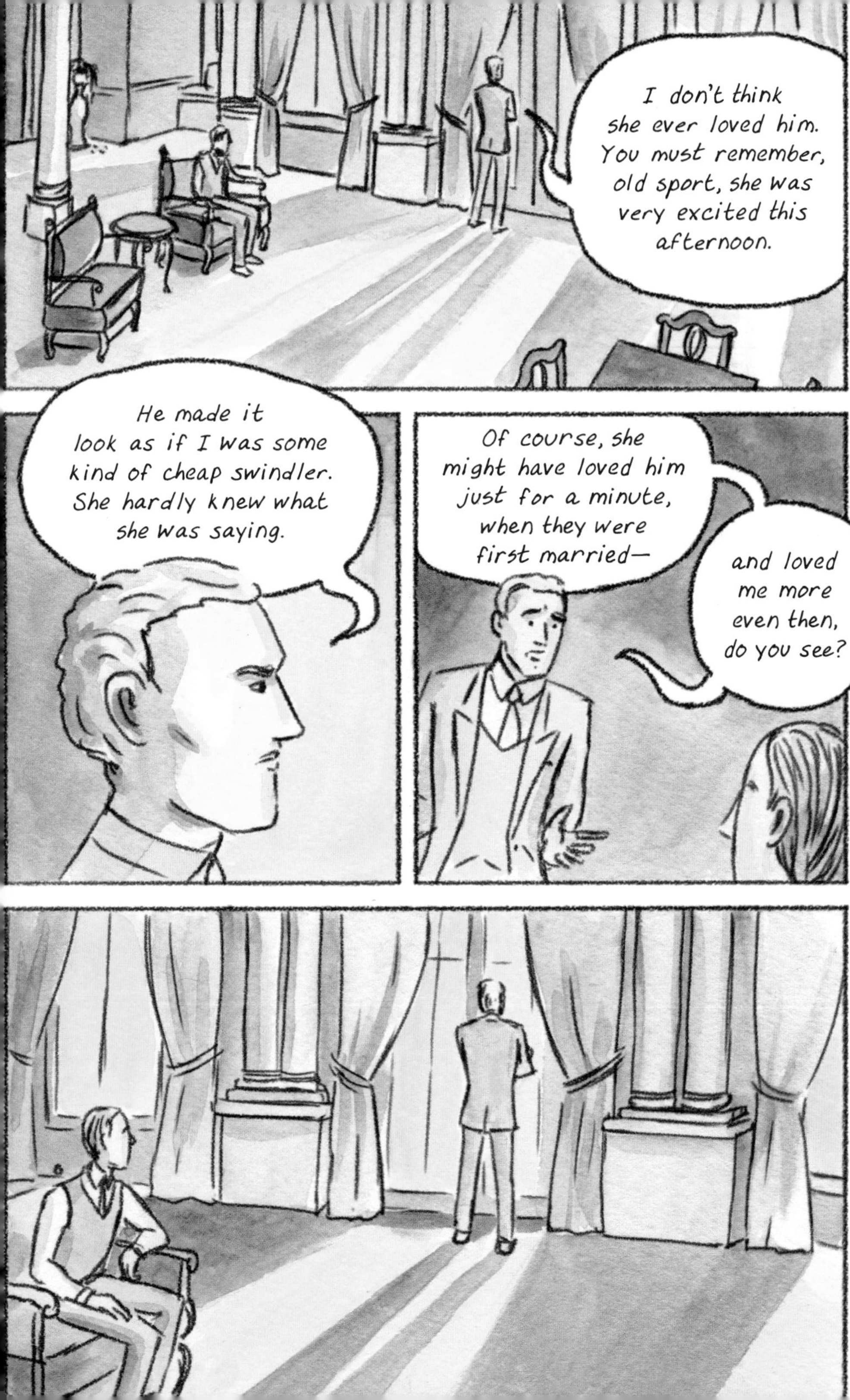
I don't think she ever loved him. You must remember, old sport, she was very excited this afternoon.
He made it look as if I was some kind of cheap swindler. She hardly knew what she was saying.
Of course, she might have loved him just for a minute, when they were first married—
and loved me more even then, do you see?

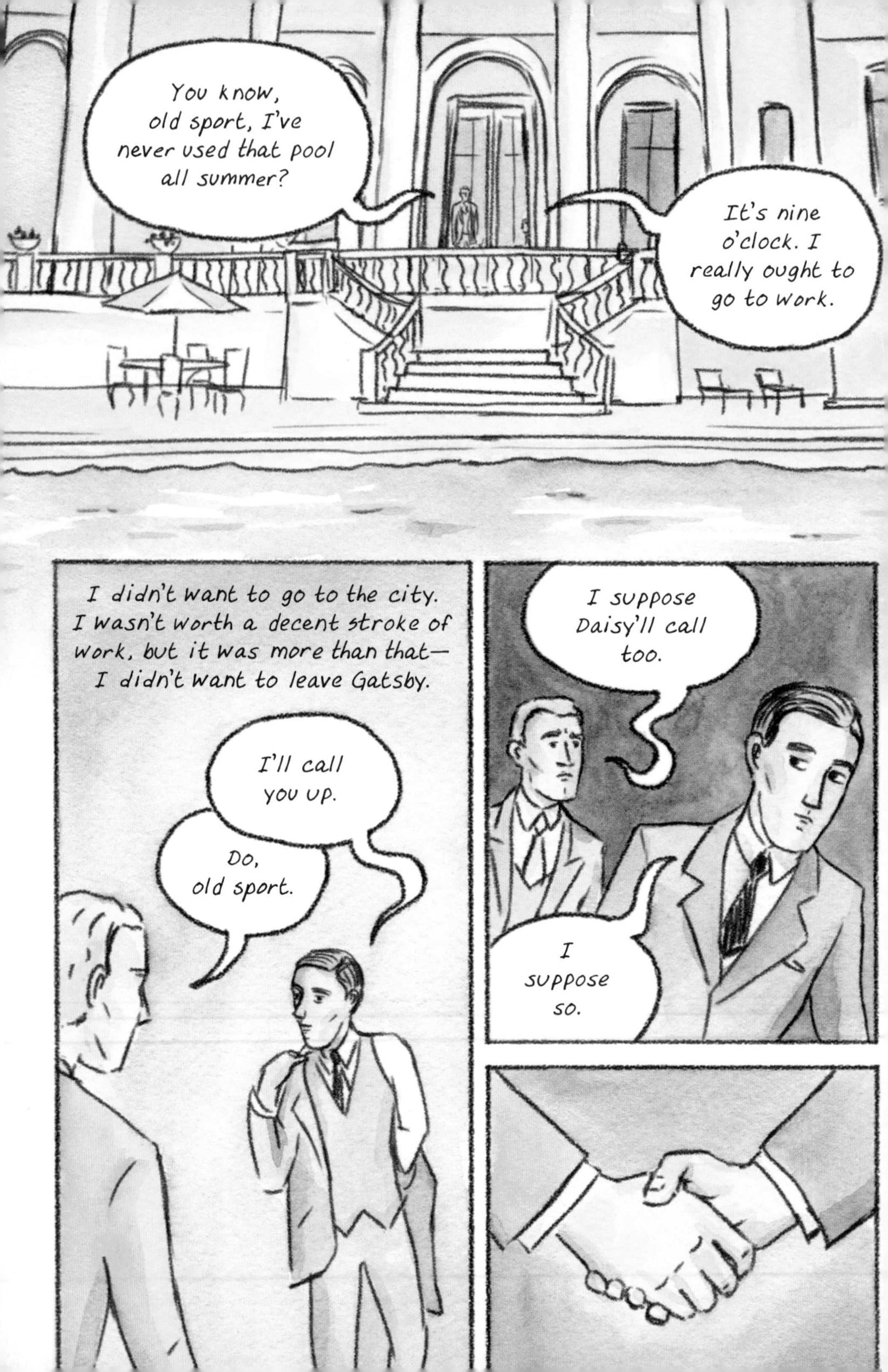
You know, old sport, I've never used that pool all summer?
It's nine o'clock. I really ought to go to work.
I didn't want to go to the city. I wasn't worth a decent stroke of work, but it was more than that— I didn't want to leave Gatsby.
I'll call you up.
Do, old sport.
I suppose Daisy'll call too.
I suppose so.

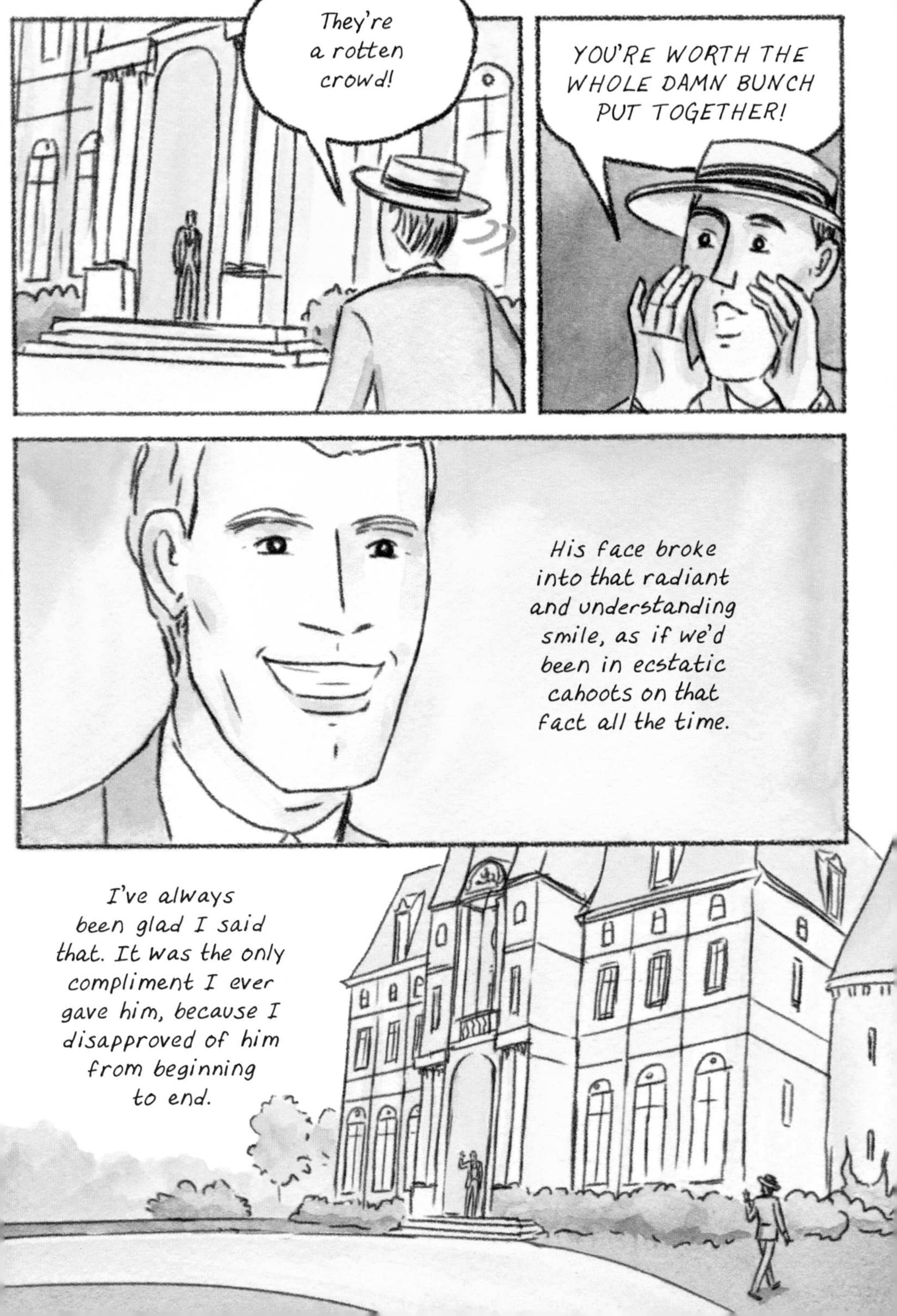
They're a rotten crowd!
YOU'RE WORTH THE WHOLE DAMN BUNCH PUT TOGETHER!
His face broke into that radiant and understanding smile, as if we'd been in ecstatic cahoots on that fact all the time.
I've always been glad I said that. It was the only compliment I ever gave him, because I disapproved of him from beginning to end.

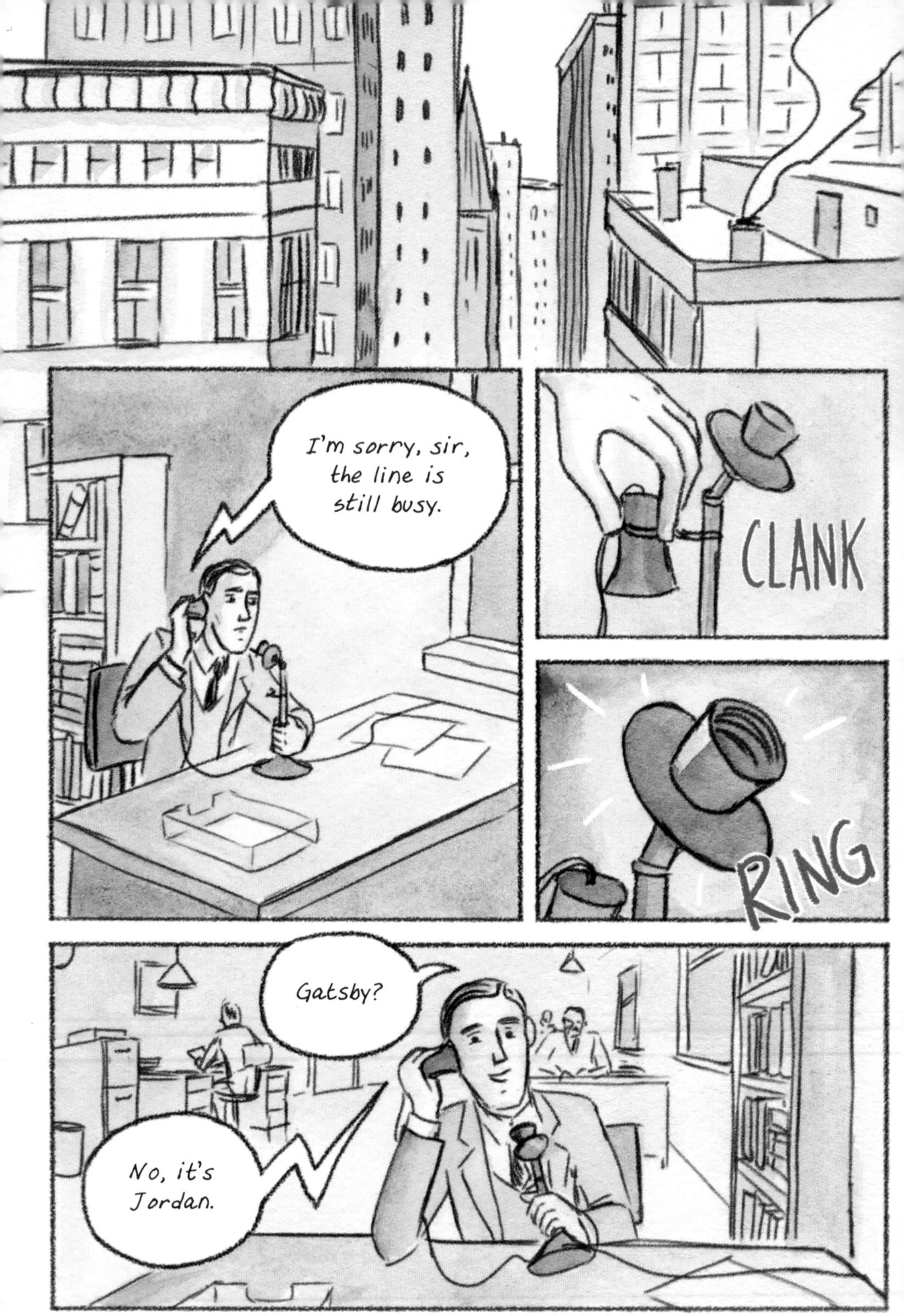
I'm sorry, sir, the line is still busy.
CLANK
RING
Gatsby?
No, it's Jordan.

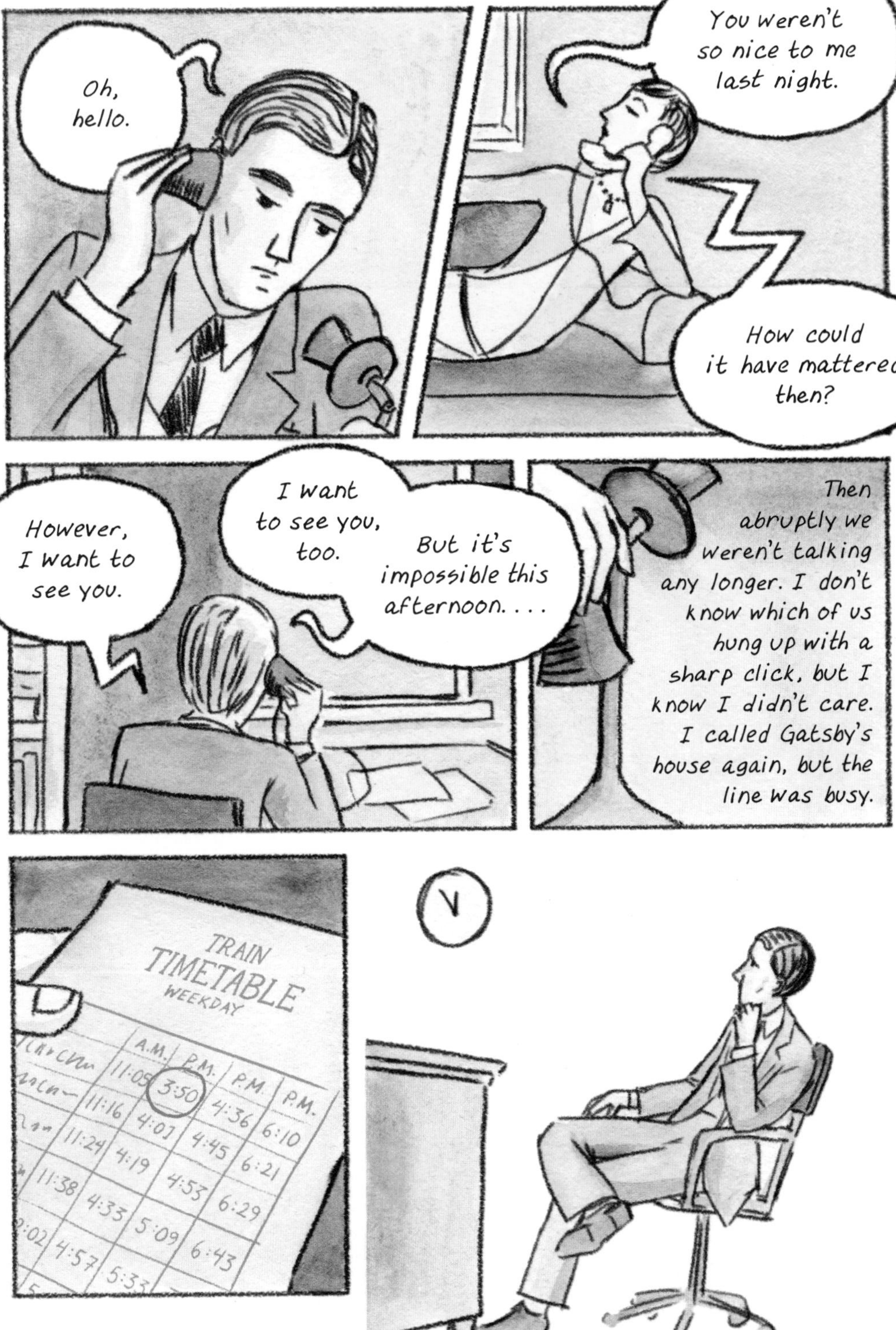
Oh, hello.
You weren't so nice to me last night.
How could it have mattered then?
However, I want to see you.
I want to see you, too.
But it's impossible this afternoon. . . .
Then abruptly we weren't talking any longer. I don't know which of us hung up with a sharp click, but I know I didn't care. I called Gatsby's house again, but the line was busy.
TRAIN
TIMETABLE
WEEKDAY
A.M. P.M. P.M. P.M.
11:05 3:50 4:36 6:10
11:16 4:07 4:45 6:21
11:24 4:19 4:53 6:29
11:38 4:33 5:09 6:43
4:57 5:33

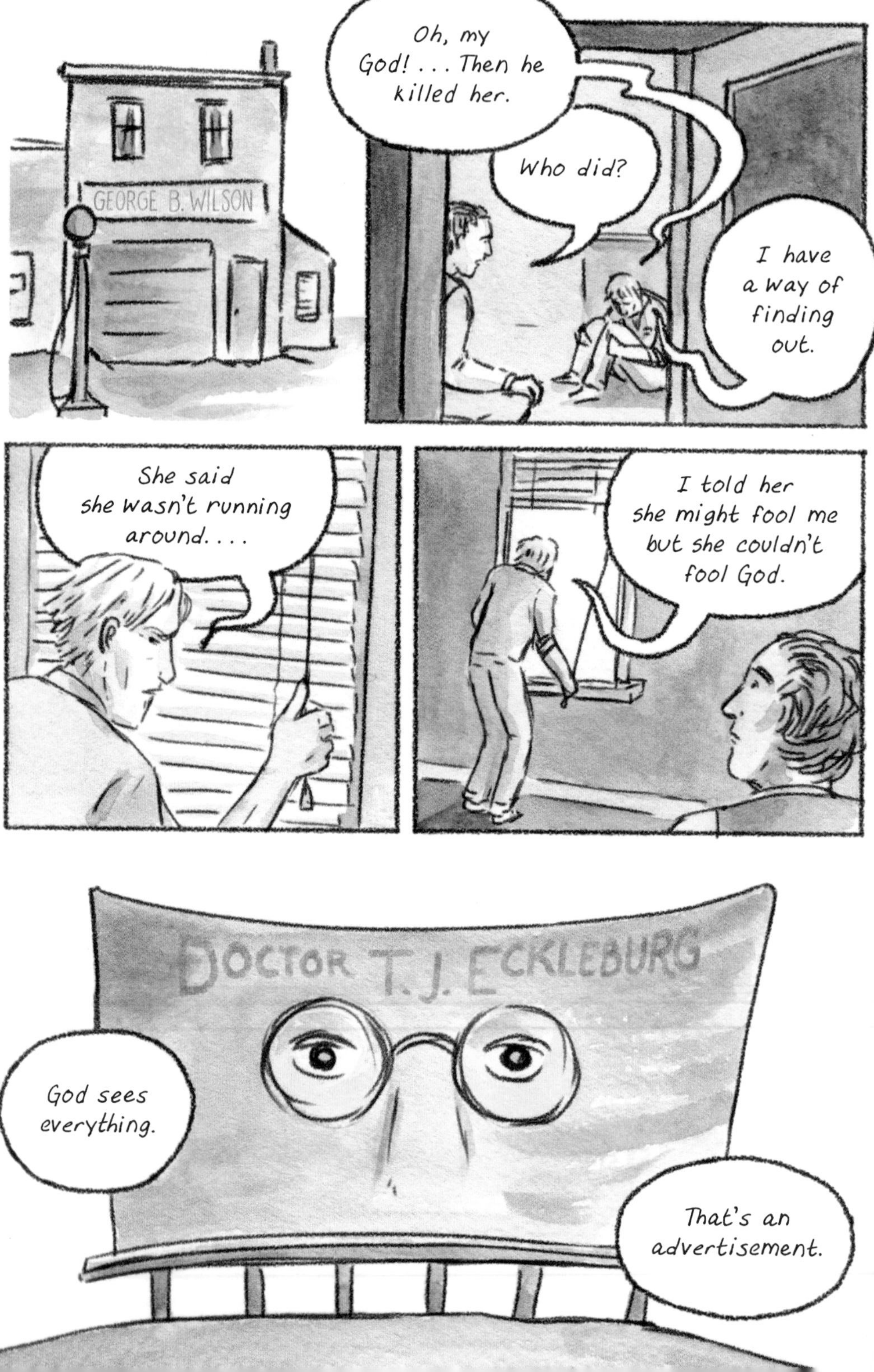
GEORGE B. WILSON
Oh, my God! . . . Then he killed her.
Who did?
I have a way of finding out.
She said she wasn't running around. . . .
I told her she might fool me but she couldn't fool God.
DOCTOR T. J. ECKLEBURG
God sees everything.
That's an advertisement.

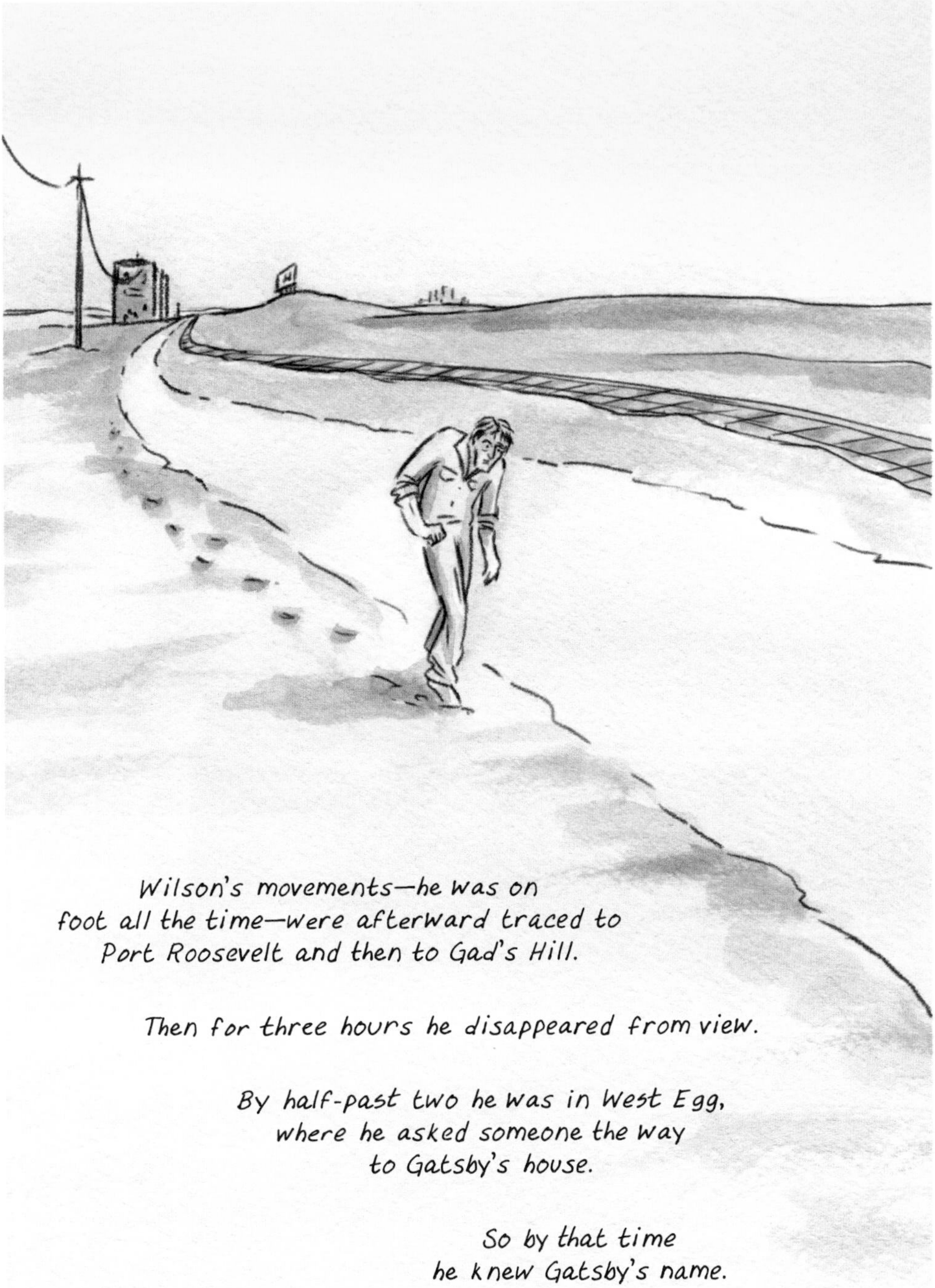
Wilson's movements—he was on foot all the time—were afterward traced to Port Roosevelt and then to Gad's Hill.
Then for three hours he disappeared from view.
By half-past two he was in West Egg, where he asked someone the way to Gatsby's house.
So by that time he knew Gatsby's name.

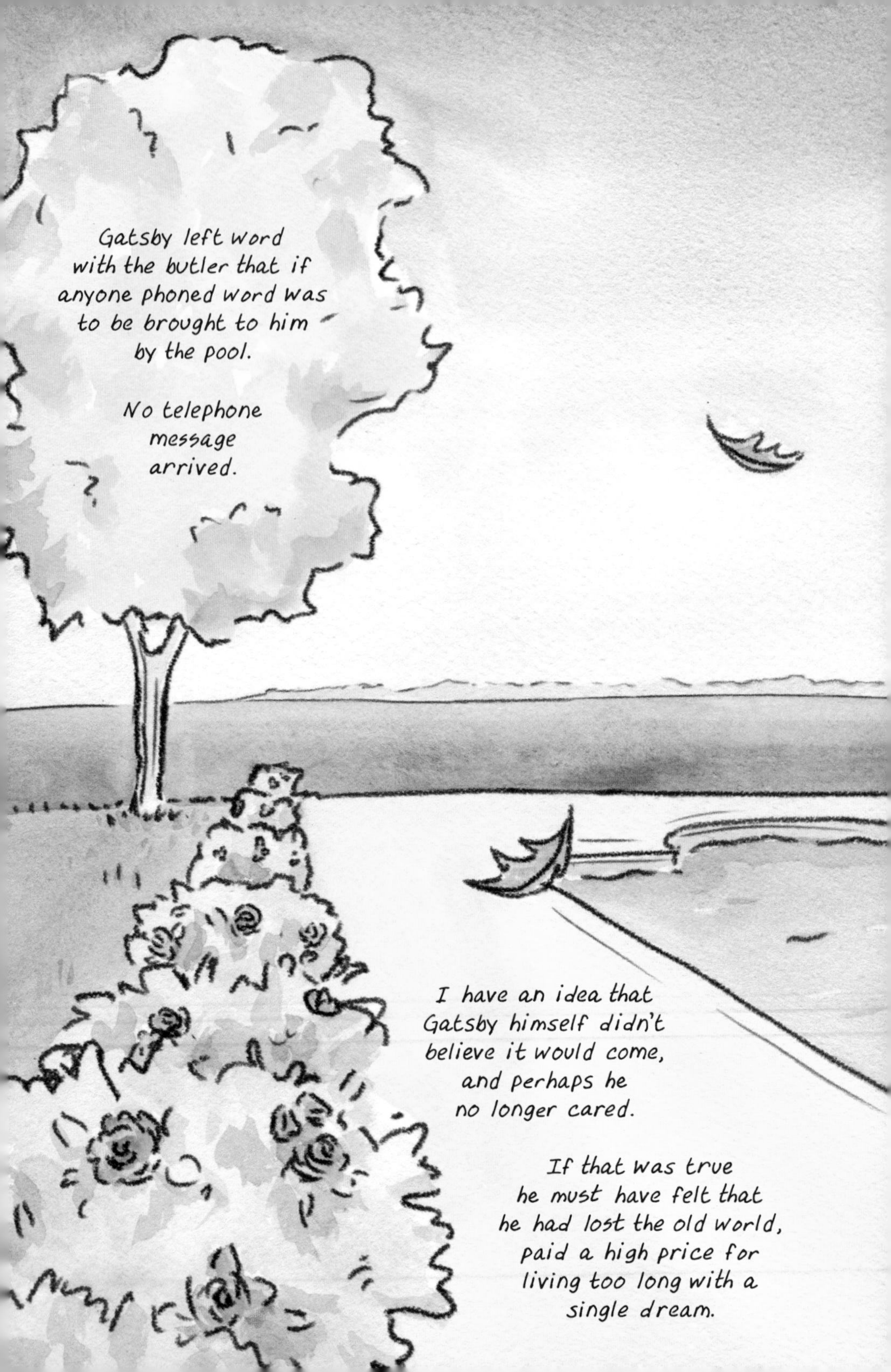
Gatsby left word with the butler that if anyone phoned word was to be brought to him by the pool.
No telephone message arrived.
I have an idea that Gatsby himself didn't believe it would come, and perhaps he no longer cared.
If that was true he must have felt that he had lost the old world, paid a high price for living too long with a single dream.

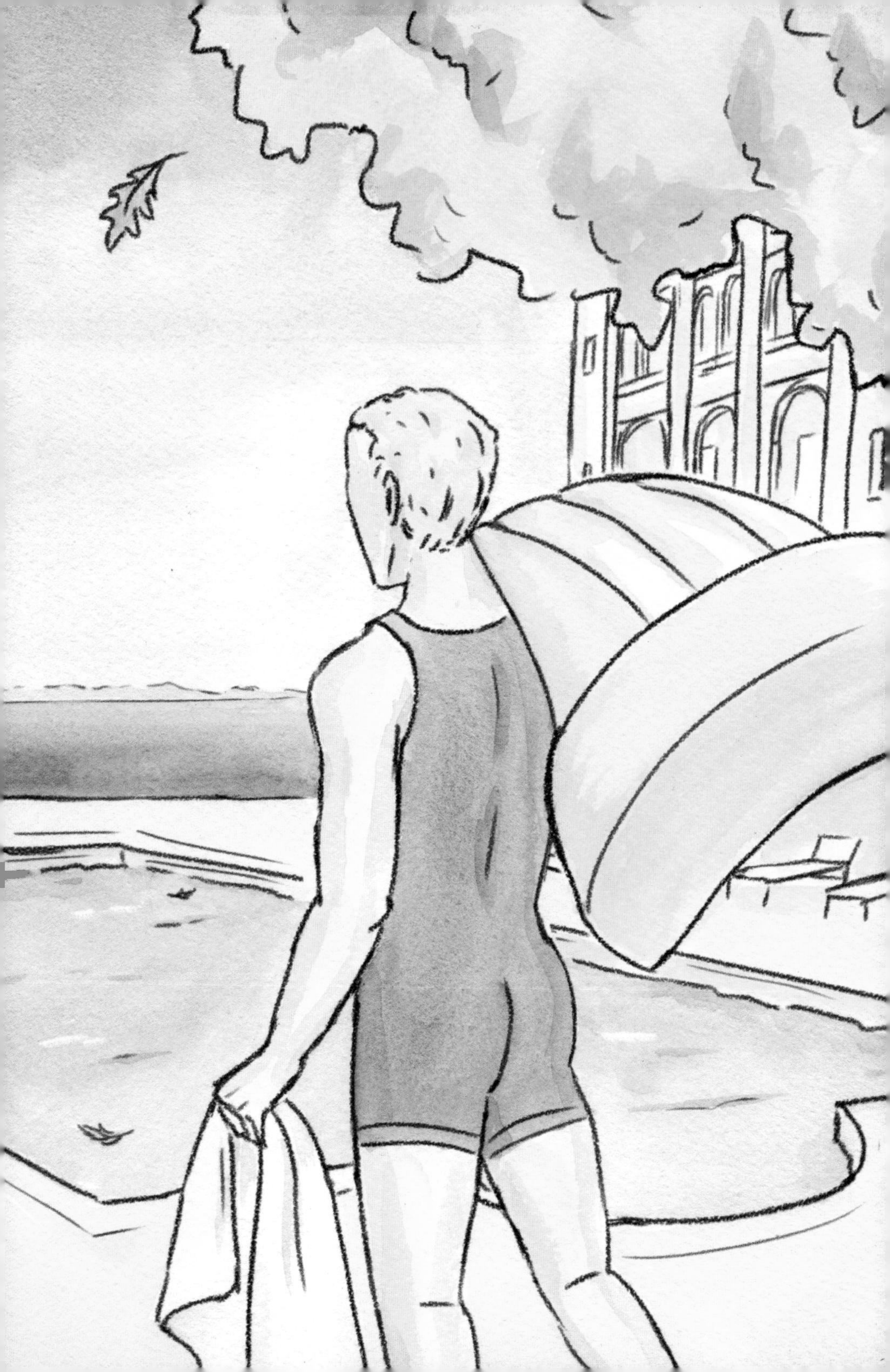

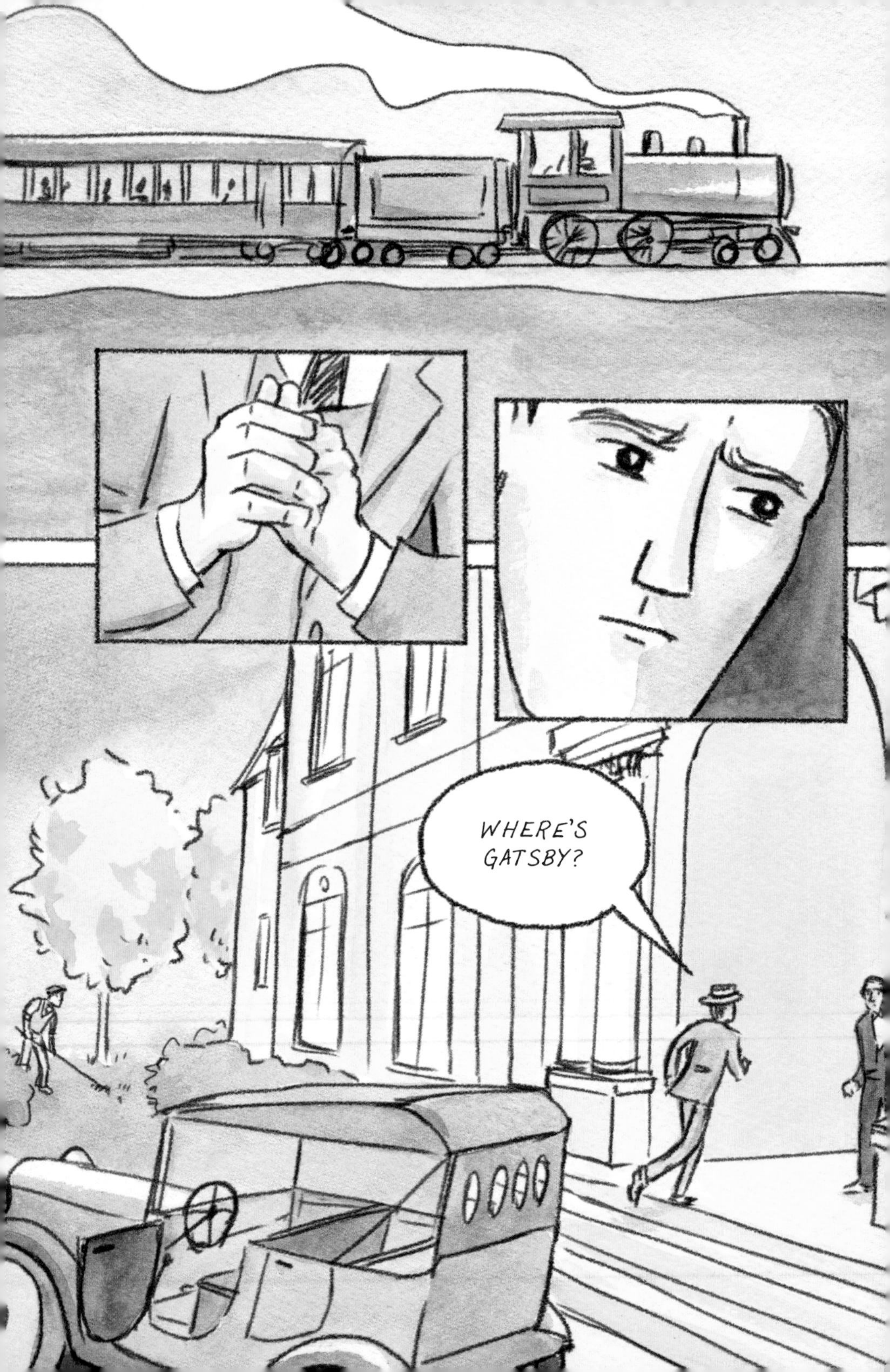
WHERE'S GATSBY?

At the pool . . .

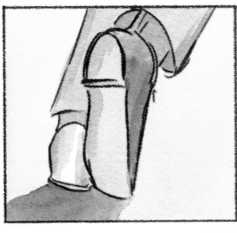

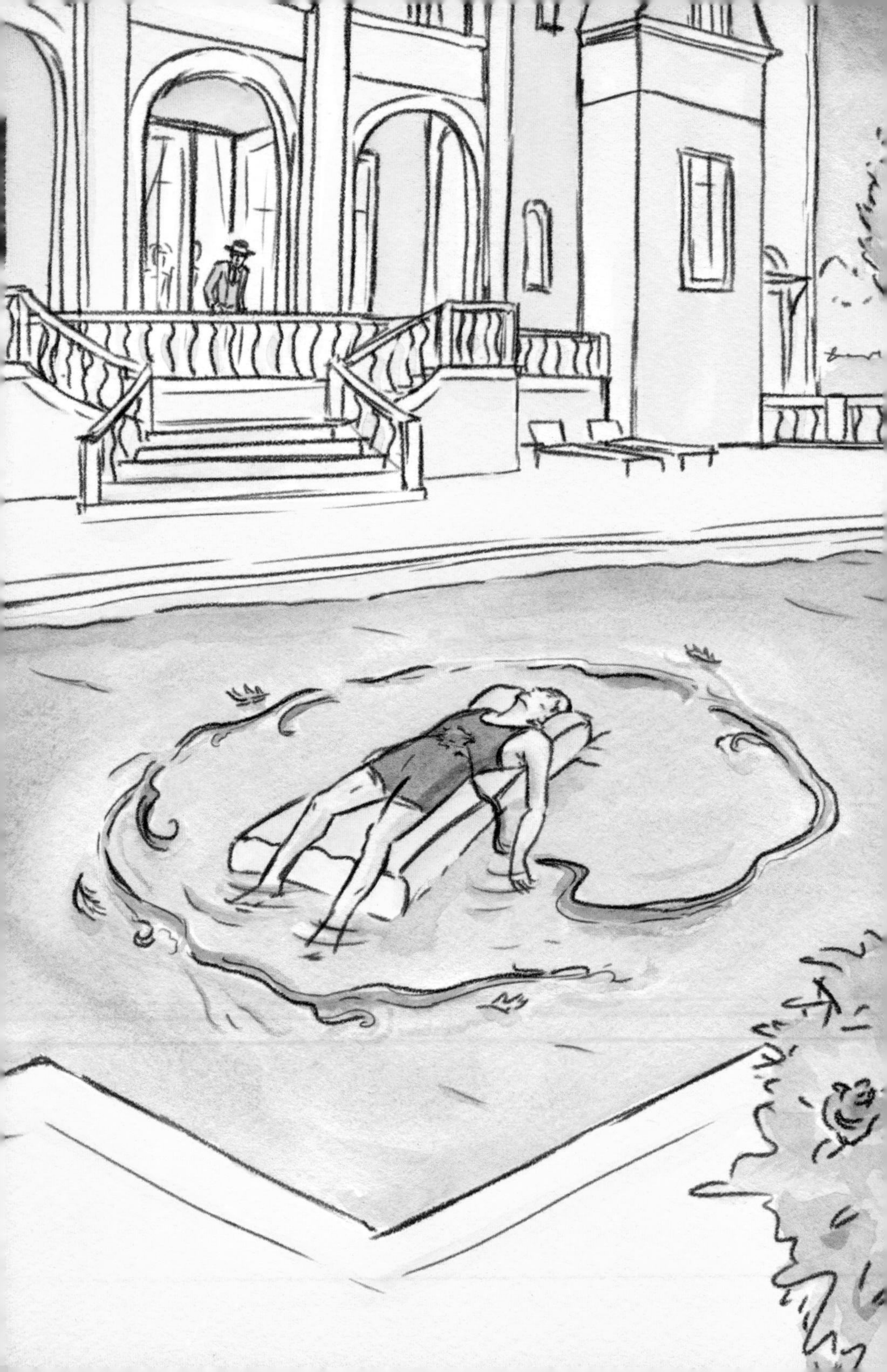

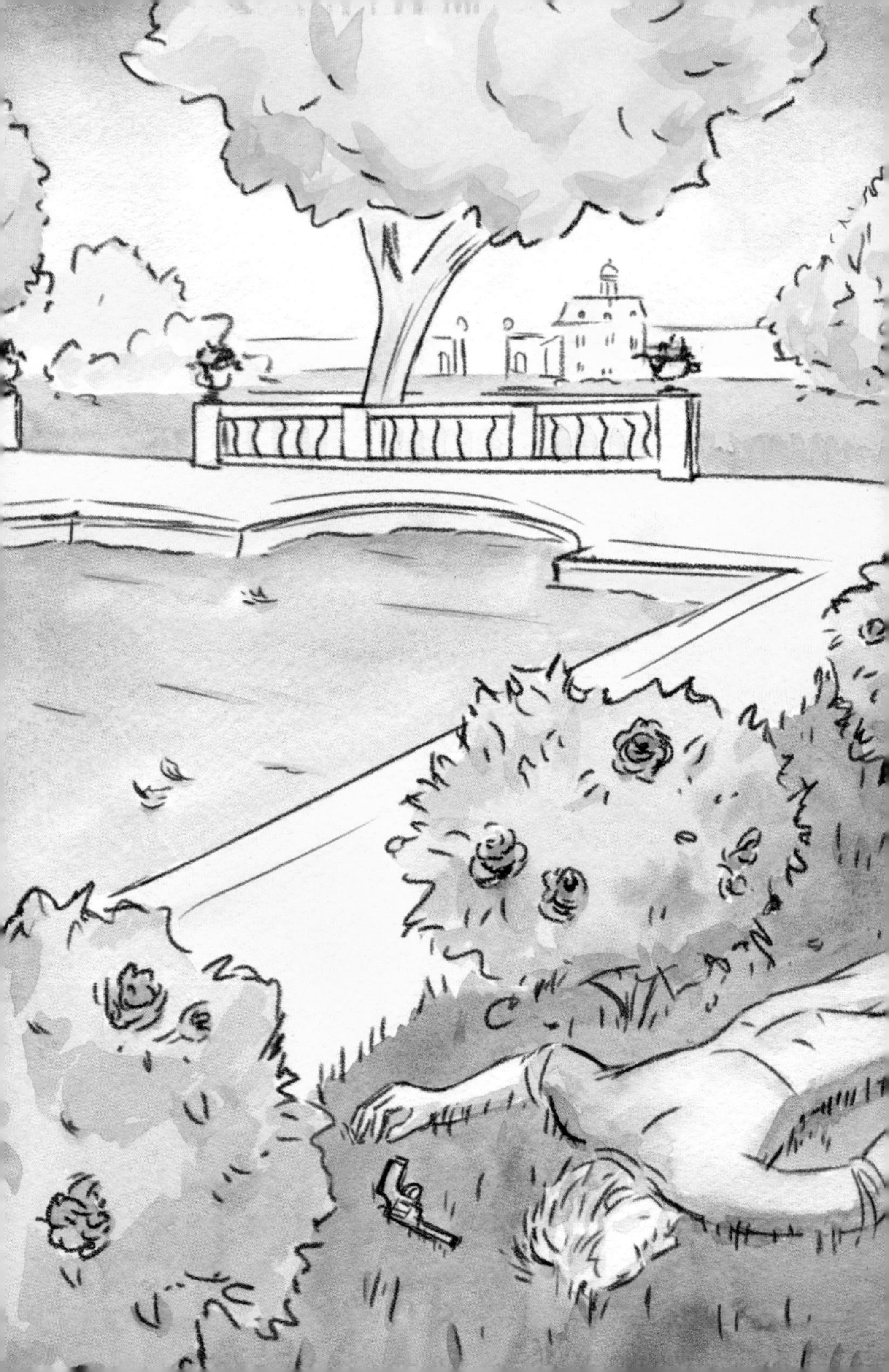

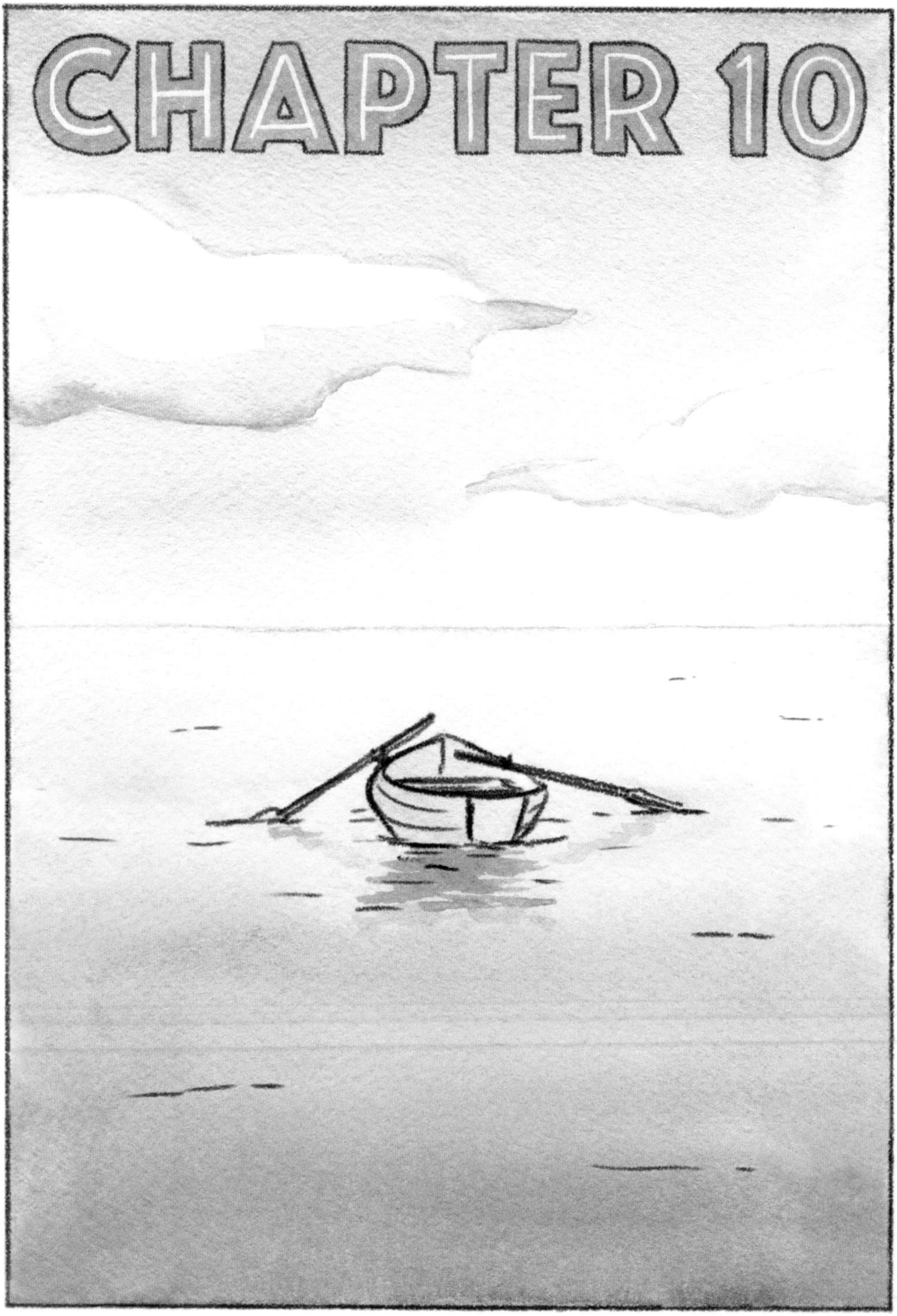
CHAPTER 10

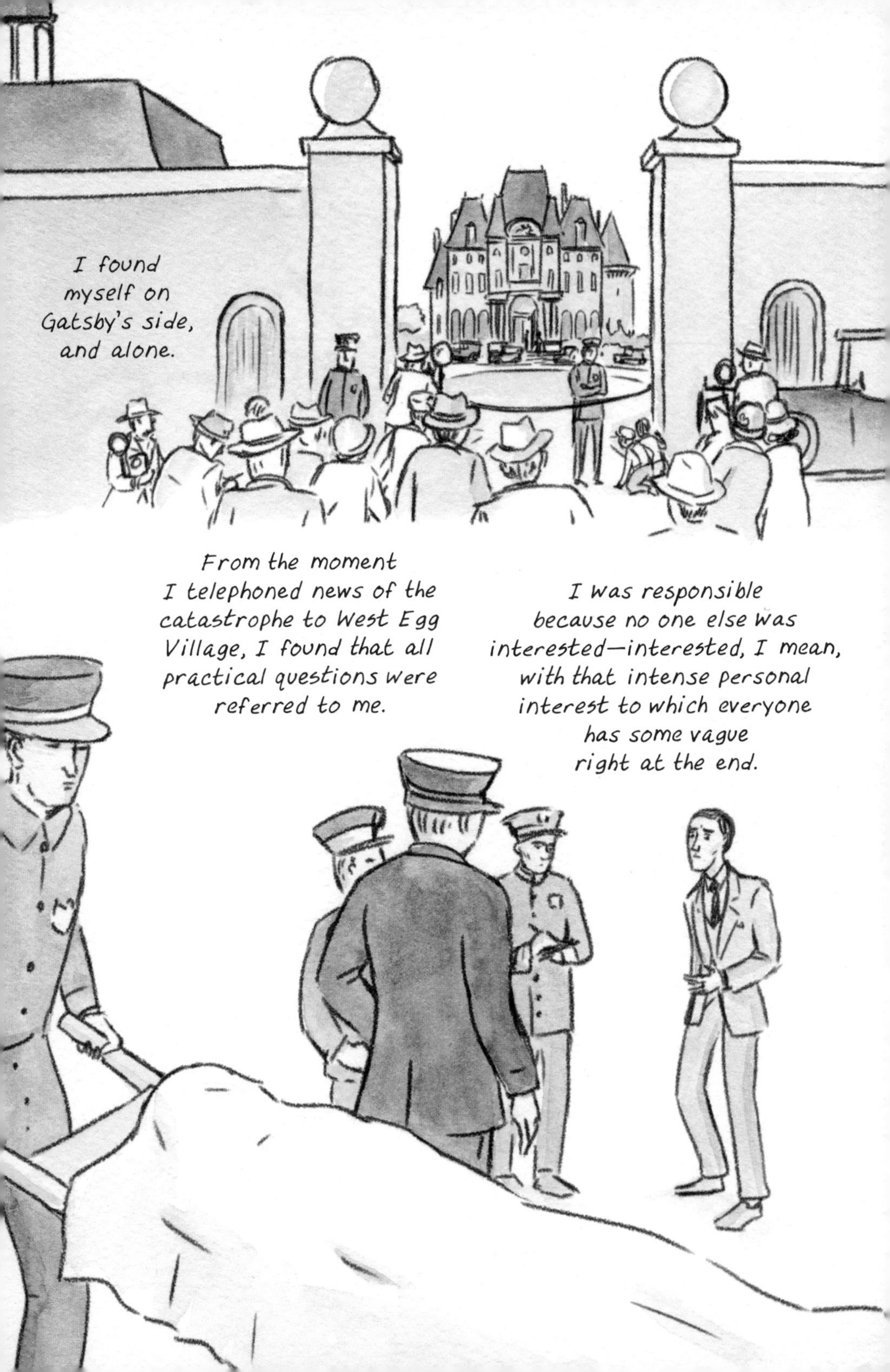
I found myself on Gatsby's side, and alone.
From the moment I telephoned news of the catastrophe to West Egg Village, I found that all practical questions were referred to me.
I was responsible because no one else was interested—interested, I mean, with that intense personal interest to which everyone has some vague right at the end.

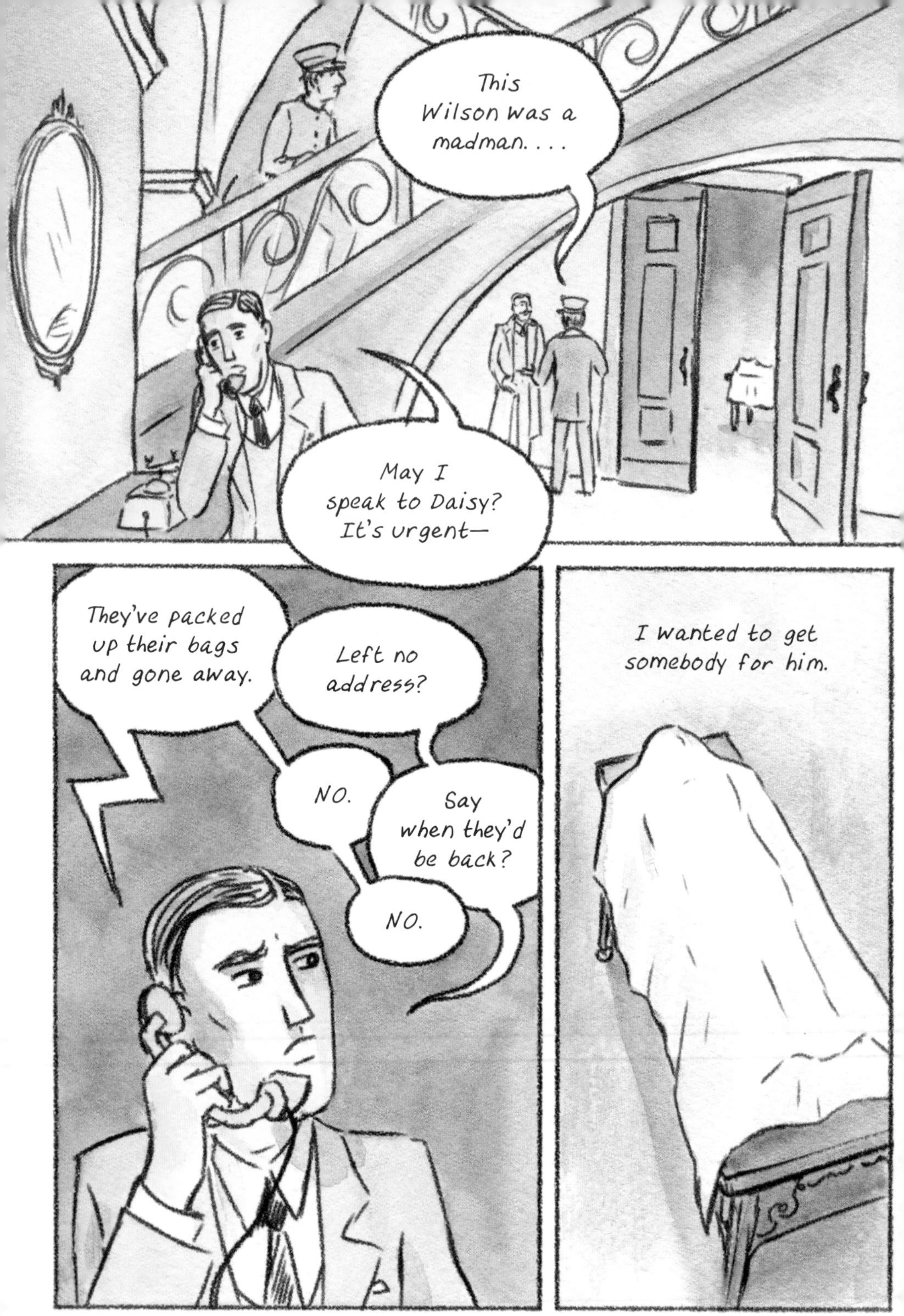
This Wilson was a madman. . . .
May I speak to Daisy? It's urgent—
They've packed up their bags and gone away.
Left no address?
NO.
Say when they'd be back?
NO.
I wanted to get somebody for him.

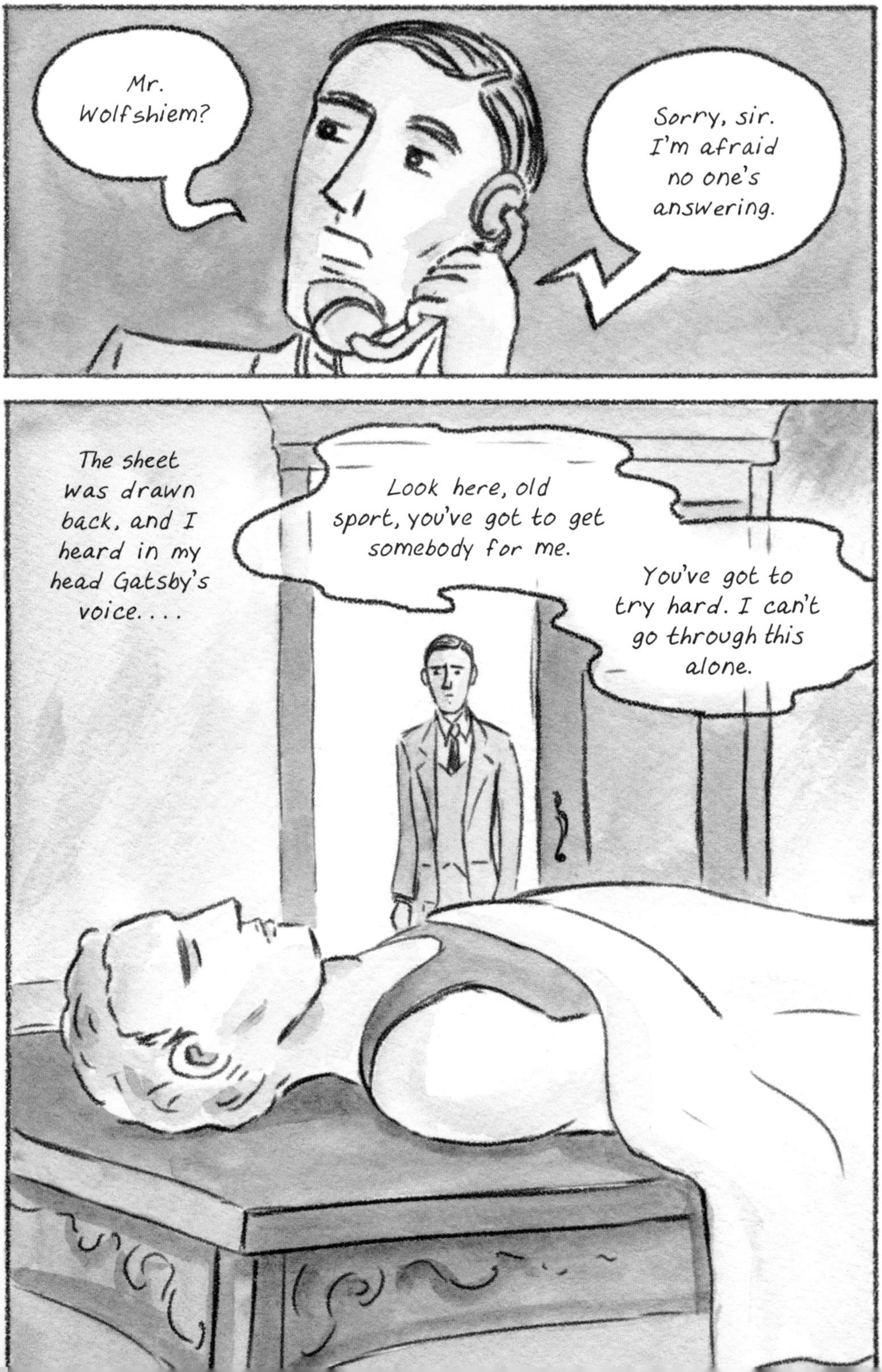
Mr. Wolfshiem?
Sorry, sir. I'm afraid no one's answering.
The sheet was drawn back, and I heard in my head Gatsby's voice. . . .
Look here, old sport, you've got to get somebody for me.
You've got to try hard. I can't go through this alone.

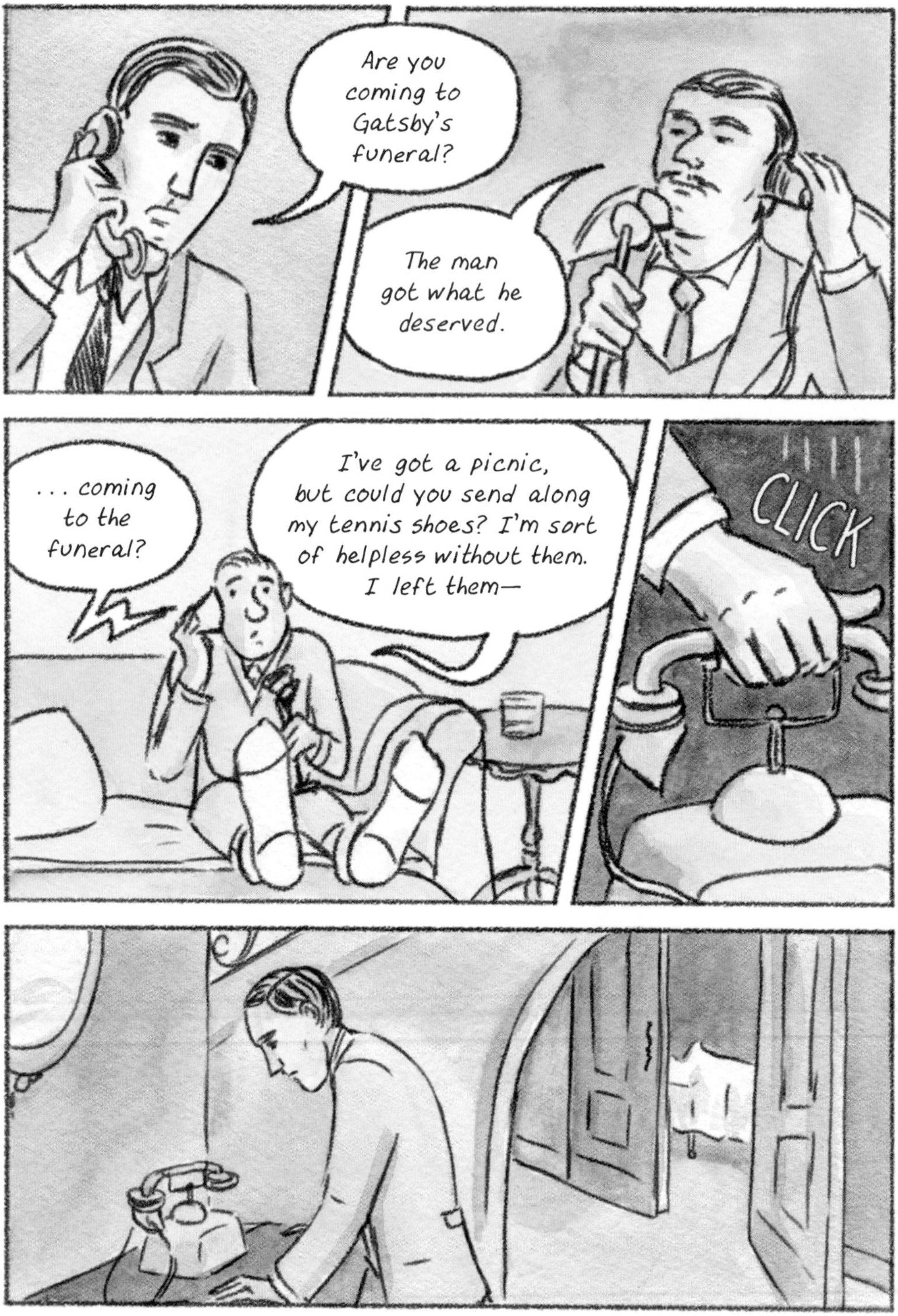
Are you coming to Gatsby's funeral?
The man got what he deserved.
. . . coming to the funeral?
I've got a picnic, but could you send along my tennis shoes? I'm sort of helpless without them. I left them—
CLICK

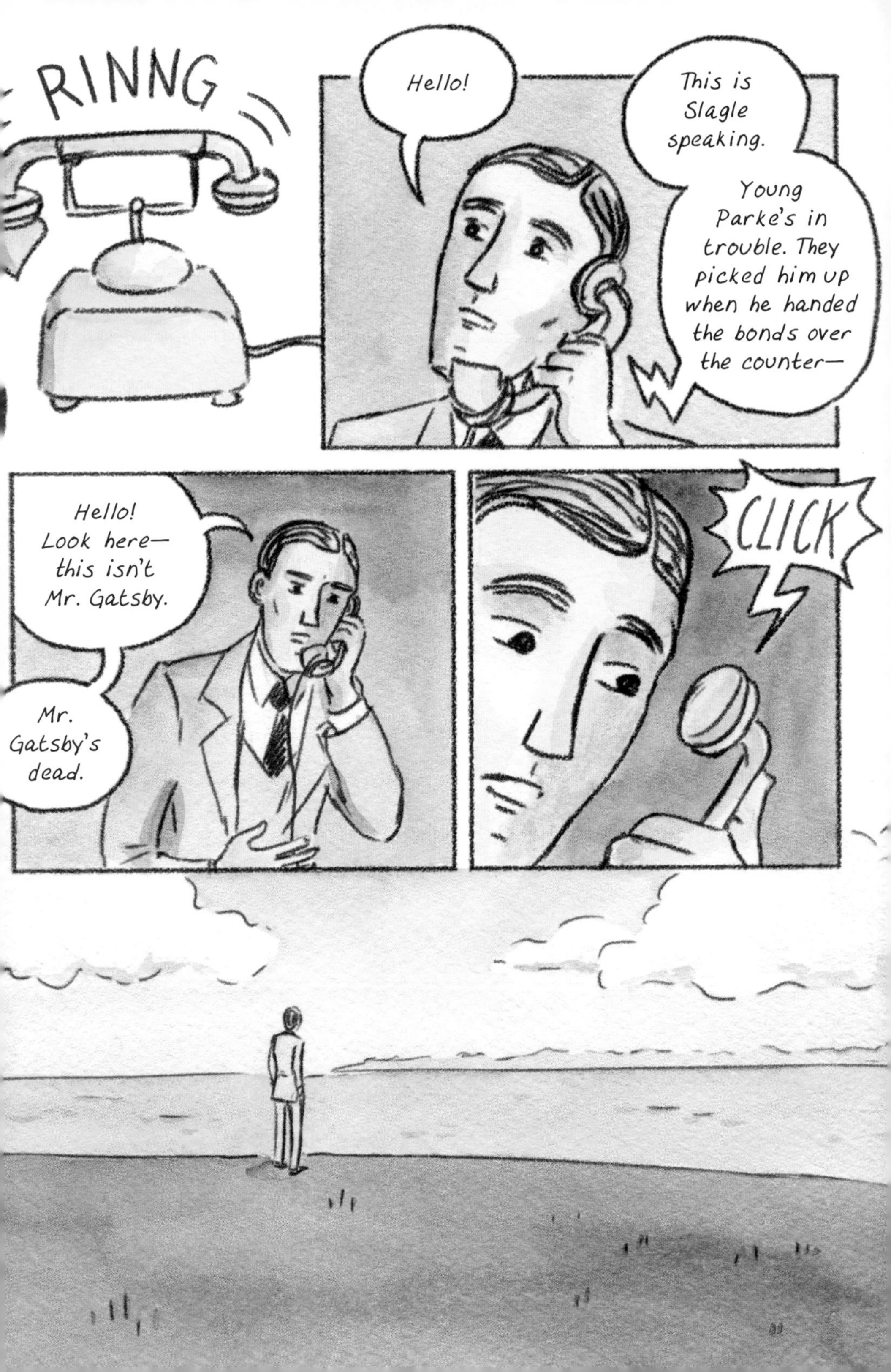
RINNG
Hello!
This is Slagle speaking.
Young Parke's in trouble. They picked him up when he handed the bonds over the counter—
Hello! Look here— this isn't Mr. Gatsby.
Mr. Gatsby's dead.
CLICK

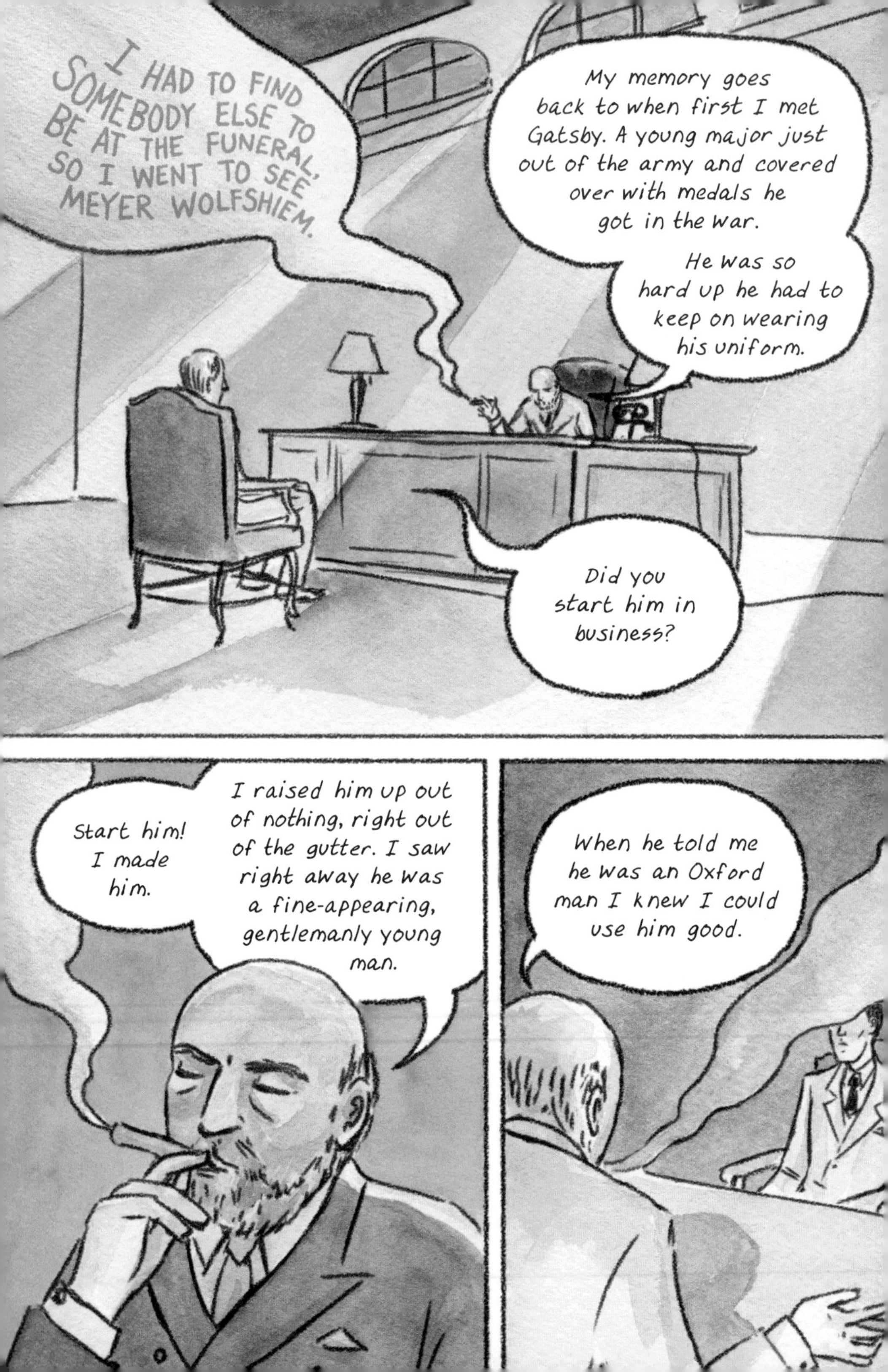
I HAD TO FIND SOMEBODY ELSE TO BE AT THE FUNERAL, SO I WENT TO SEE MEYER WOLFSHIEM.
My memory goes back to when first I met Gatsby. A young major just out of the army and covered over with medals he got in the war.
He was so hard up he had to keep on wearing his uniform.
Did you start him in business?
Start him! I made him.
I raised him up out of nothing, right out of the gutter. I saw right away he was a fine-appearing, gentlemanly young man.
When he told me he was an Oxford man I knew I could use him good.

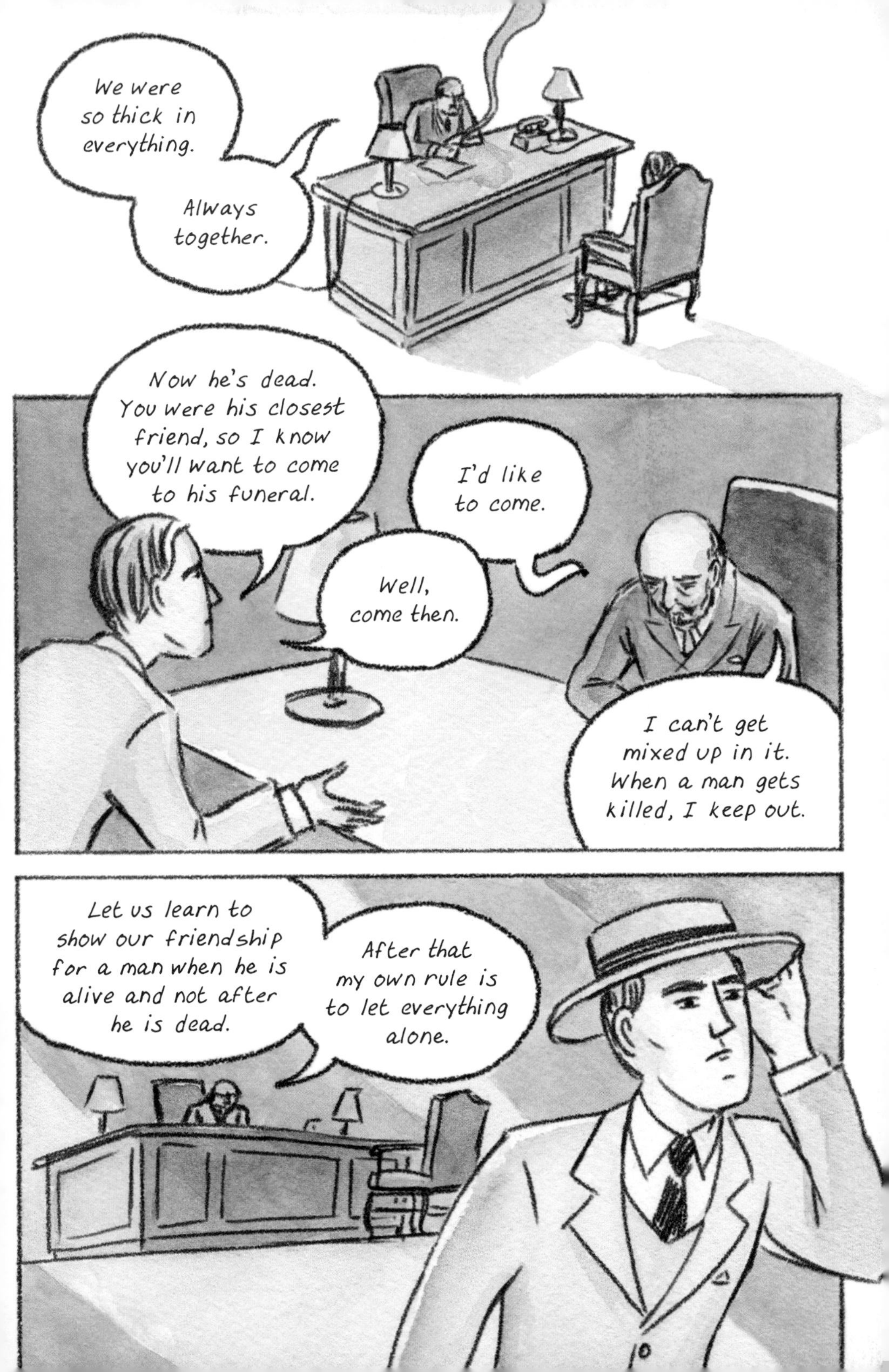
We were so thick in everything.
Always together.
Now he's dead. You were his closest friend, so I know you'll want to come to his funeral.
I'd like to come.
Well, come then.
I can't get mixed up in it. When a man gets killed, I keep out.
Let us learn to show our friendship for a man when he is alive and not after he is dead.
After that my own rule is to let everything alone.

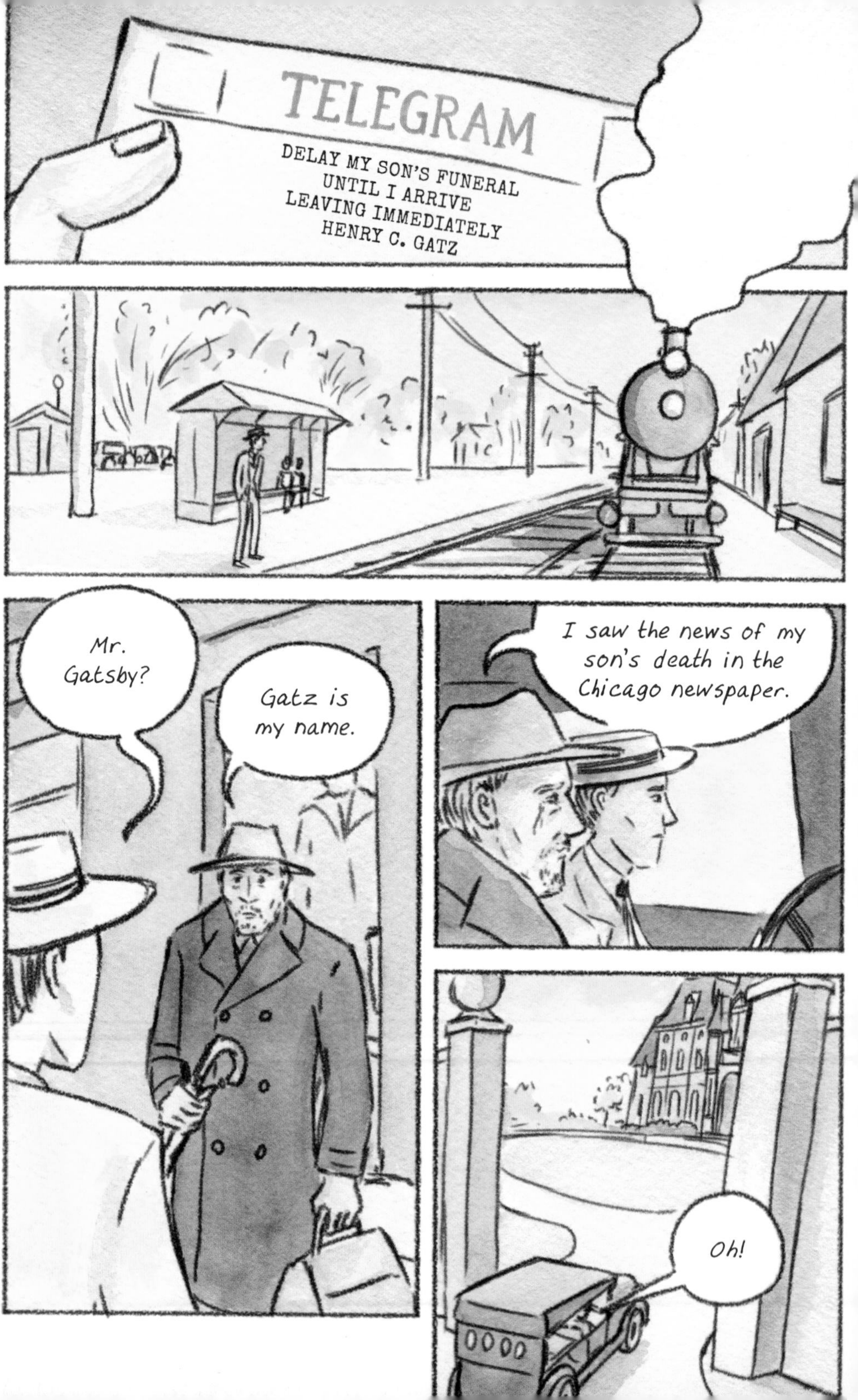
TELEGRAM
DELAY MY SON'S FUNERAL UNTIL I ARRIVE LEAVING IMMEDIATELY HENRY C. GATZ
Mr. Gatsby?
Gatz is my name.
I saw the news of my son's death in the Chicago newspaper.
Oh!

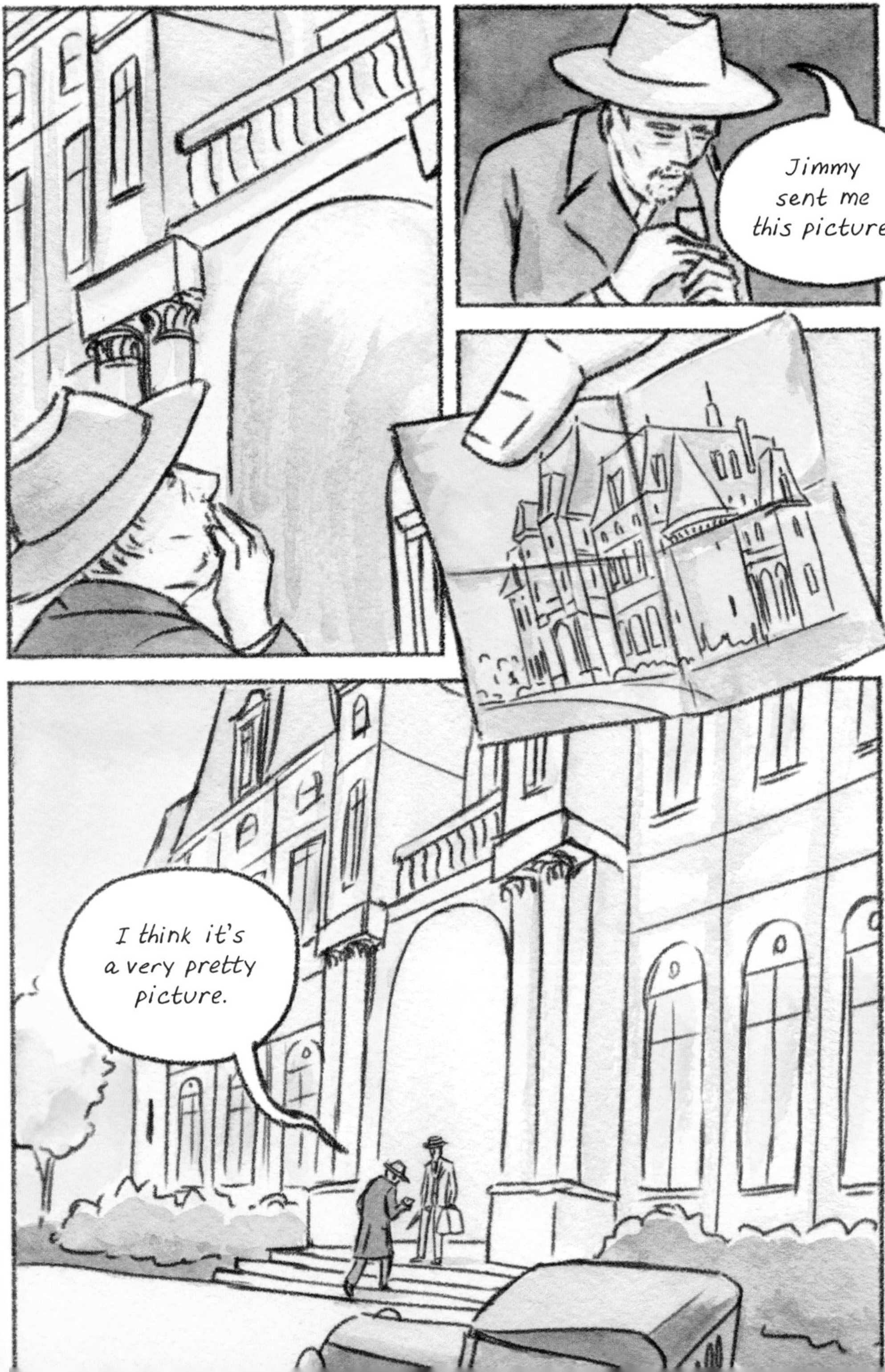
Jimmy sent me this picture.
I think it's a very pretty picture.

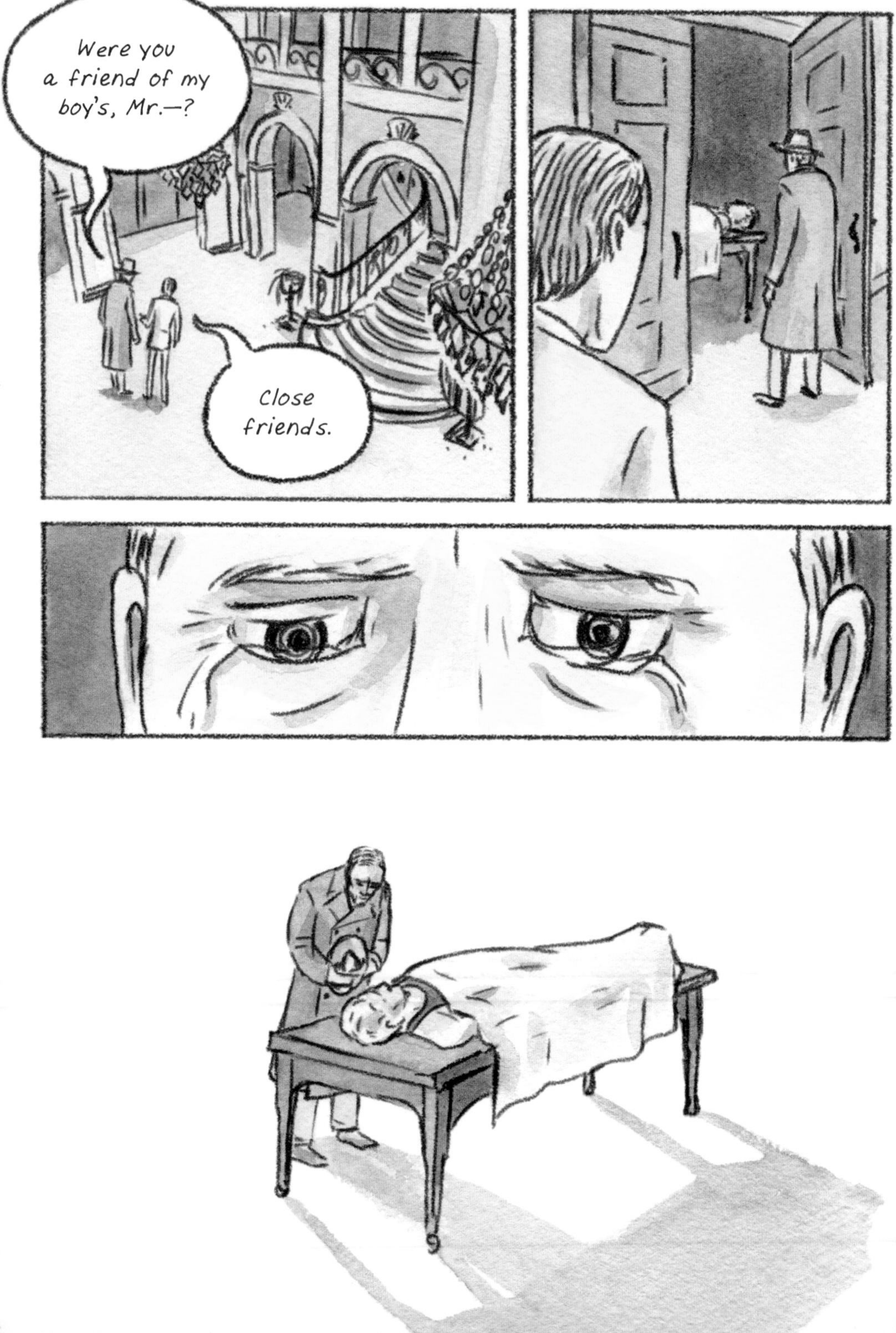
Were you a friend of my boy's, Mr.—?
Close friends.

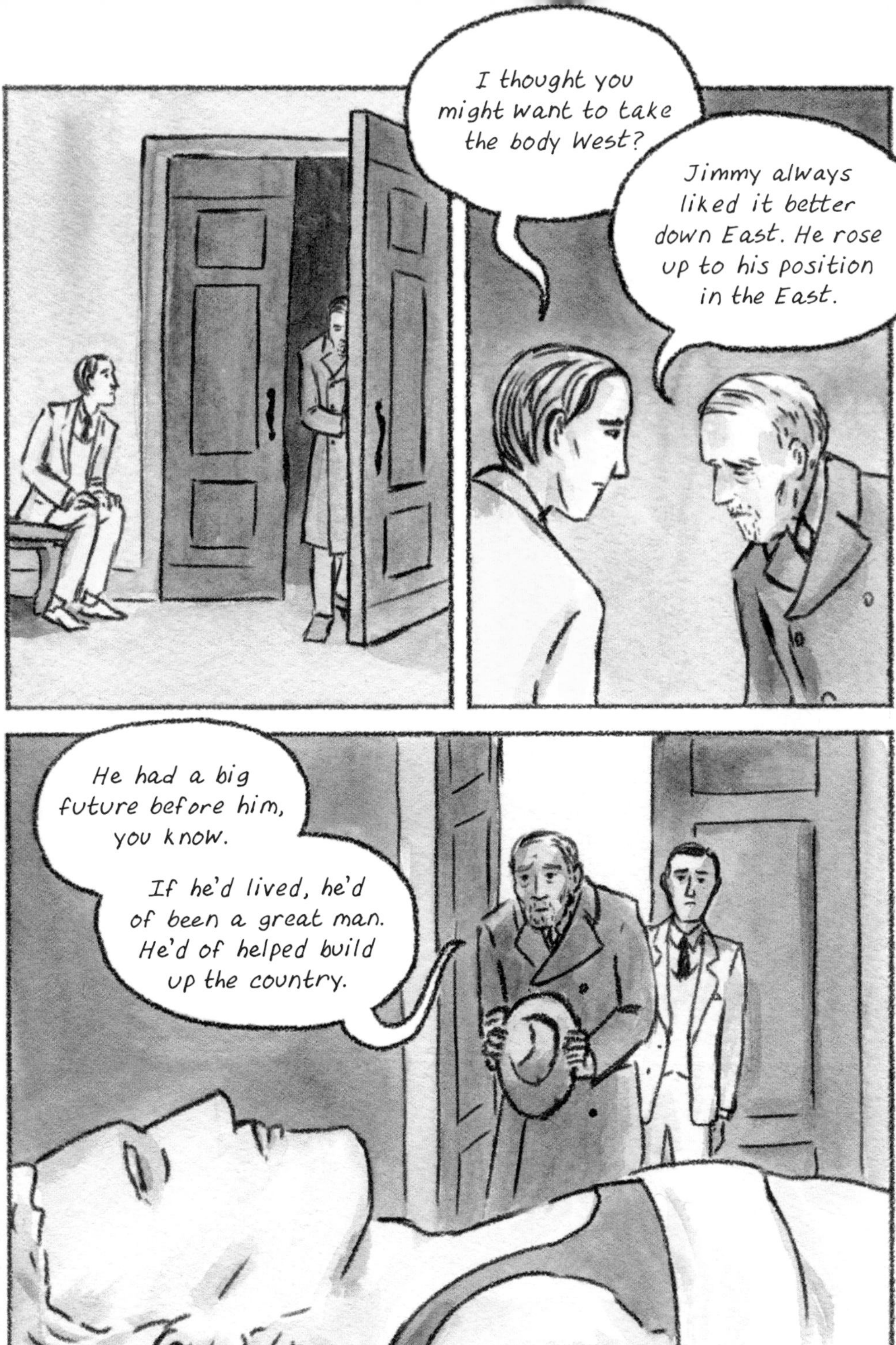
I thought you might want to take the body West?
Jimmy always liked it better down East. He rose up to his position in the East.
He had a big future before him, you know.
If he'd lived, he'd of been a great man. He'd of helped build up the country.

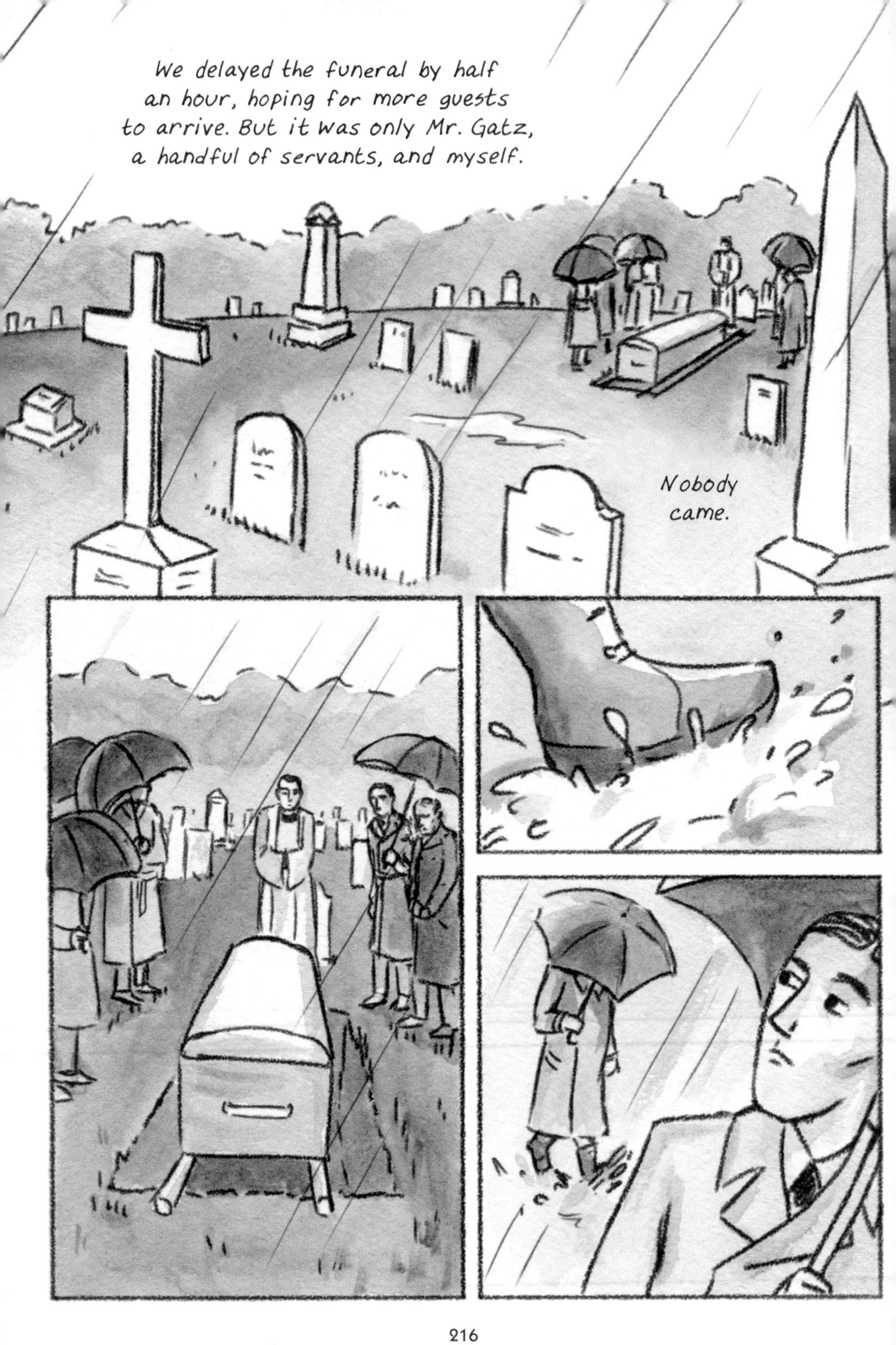
We delayed the funeral by half an hour, hoping for more guests to arrive. But it was only Mr. Gatz, a handful of servants, and myself.
Nobody came.

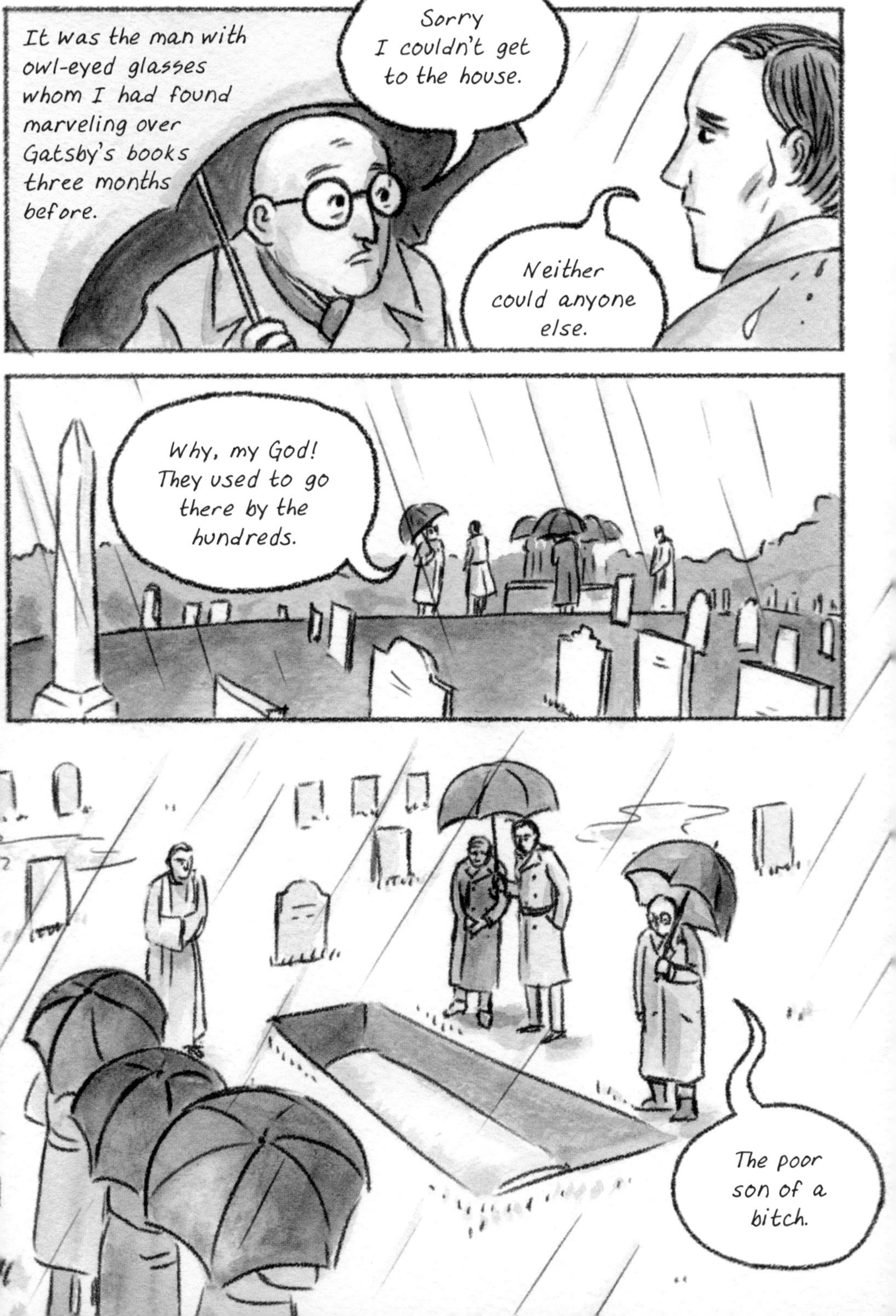
It was the man with owl-eyed glasses whom I had found marveling over Gatsby's books three months before.
Sorry I couldn't get to the house.
Neither could anyone else.
Why, my God! They used to go there by the hundreds.
The poor son of a bitch.

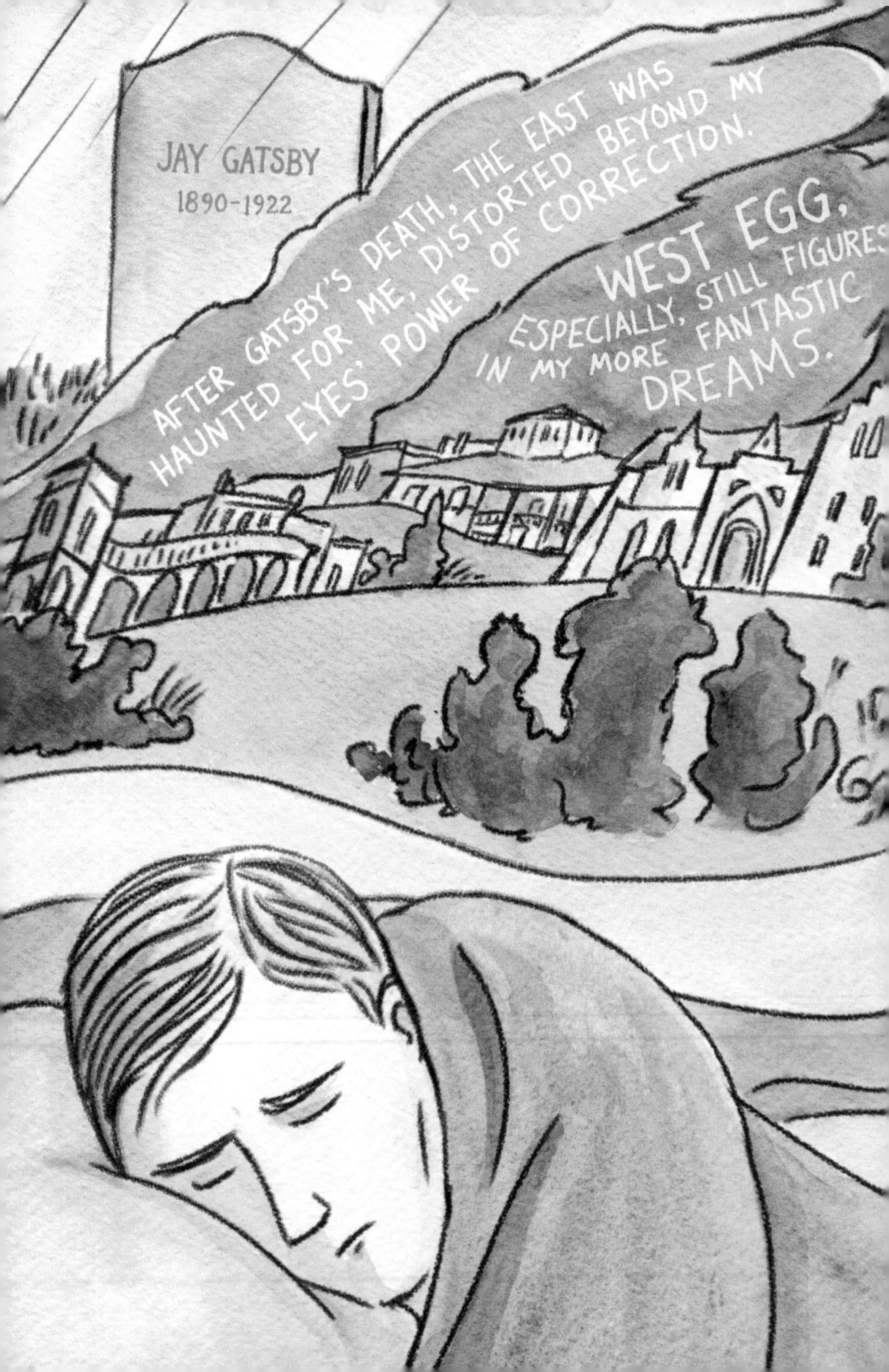
JAY GATSBY
1890-1922
AFTER GATSBY'S DEATH, THE EAST WAS HAUNTED FOR ME, DISTORTED BEYOND MY EYES' POWER OF CORRECTION.
WEST EGG, ESPECIALLY, STILL FIGURES IN MY MORE FANTASTIC DREAMS.

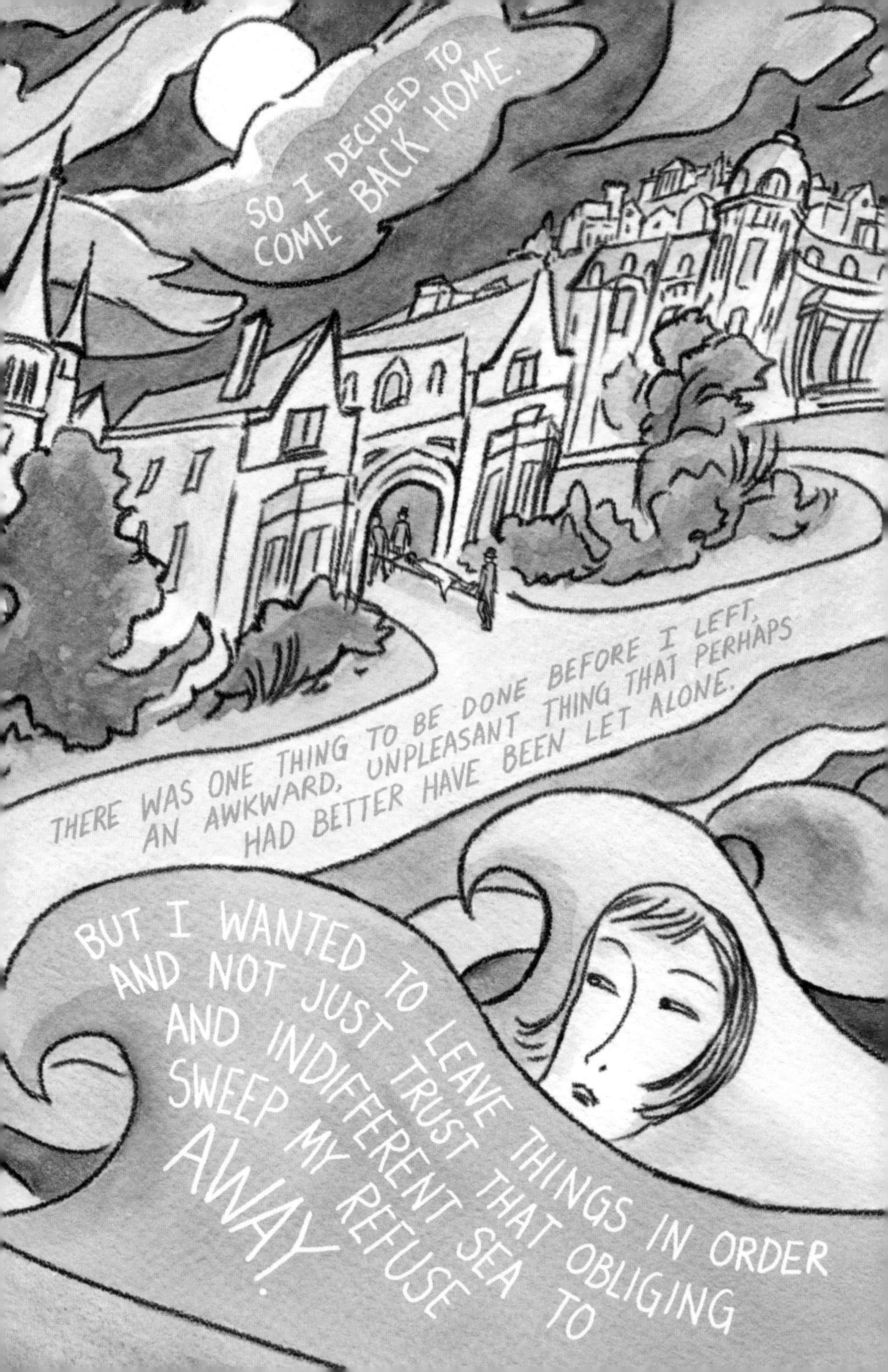
SO I DECIDED TO COME BACK HOME.
THERE WAS ONE THING TO BE DONE BEFORE I LEFT, AN AWKWARD, UNPLEASANT THING THAT PERHAPS HAD BETTER HAVE BEEN LET ALONE.
BUT I WANTED TO LEAVE THINGS IN ORDER AND NOT JUST TRUST THAT OBLIGING AND INDIFFERENT SEA TO SWEEP MY REFUSE AWAY.

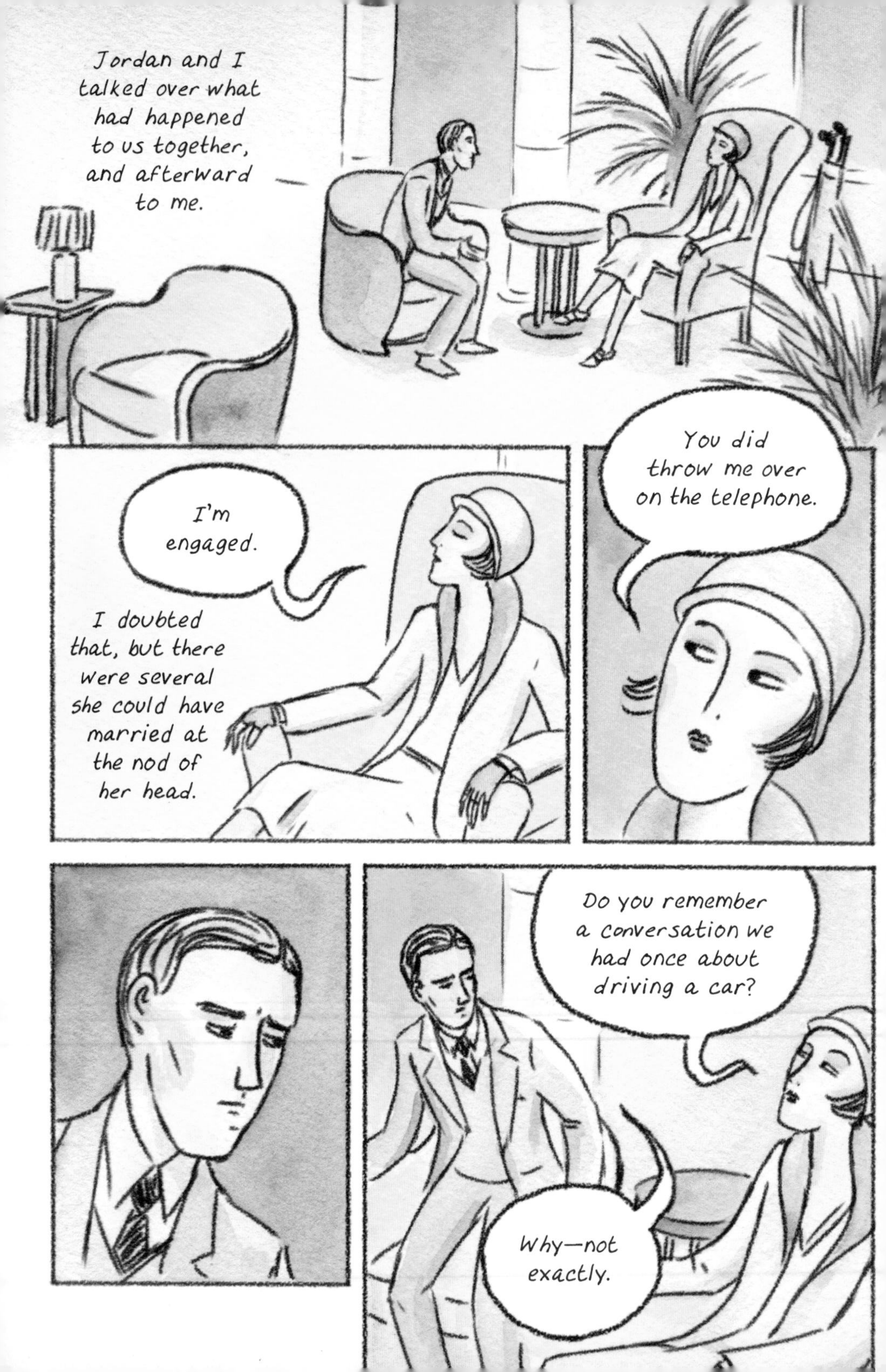
Jordan and I talked over what had happened to us together, and afterward to me.
I'm engaged.
I doubted that, but there were several she could have married at the nod of her head.
You did throw me over on the telephone.
Do you remember a conversation we had once about driving a car?
Why—not exactly.

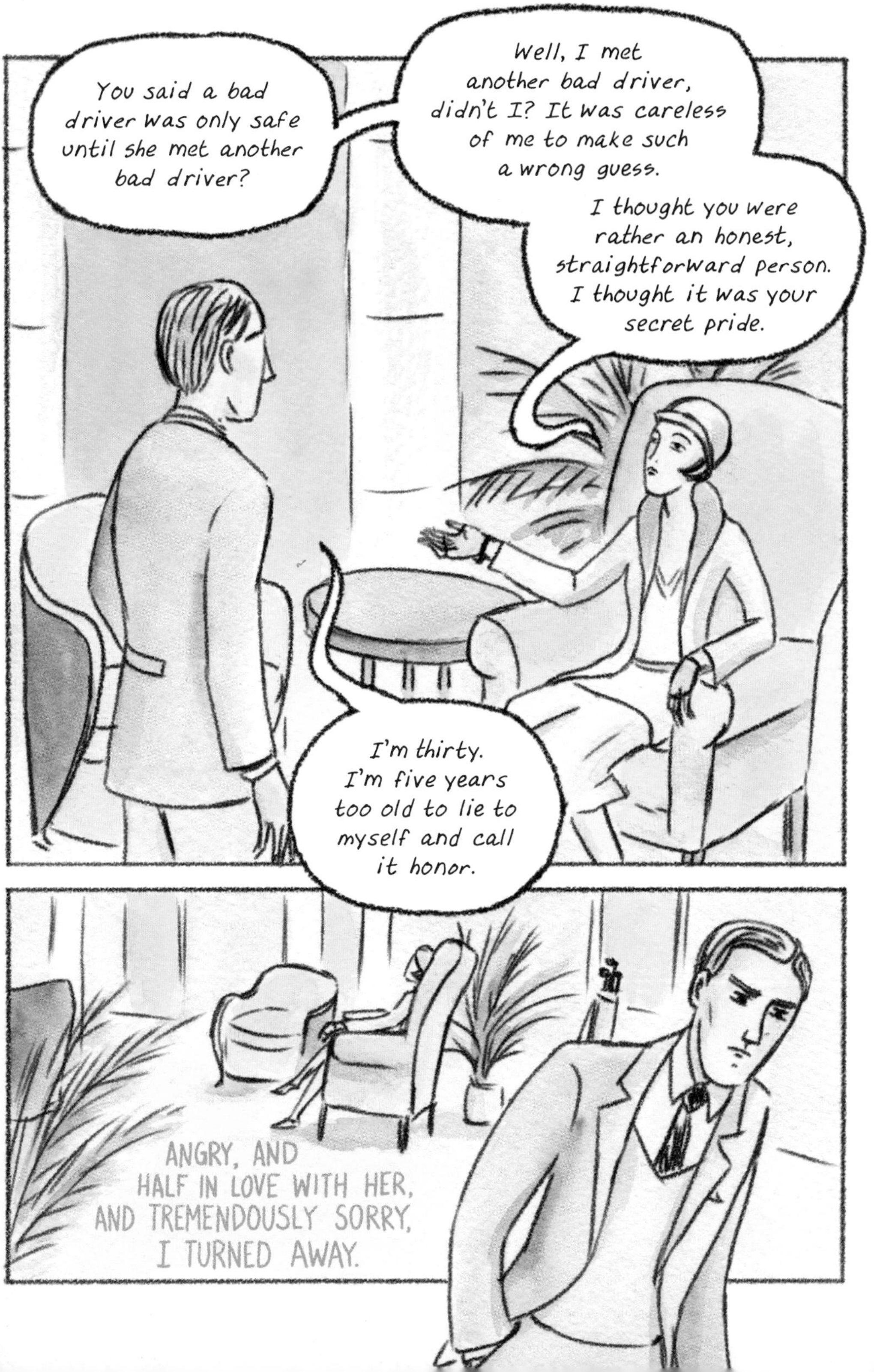

You said a bad driver was only safe until she met another bad driver?
Well, I met another bad driver, didn't I? It was careless of me to make such a wrong guess.
I thought you were rather an honest, straightforward person. I thought it was your secret pride.
I'm thirty. I'm five years too old to lie to myself and call it honor.
ANGRY, AND HALF IN LOVE WITH HER, AND TREMENDOUSLY SORRY, I TURNED AWAY.

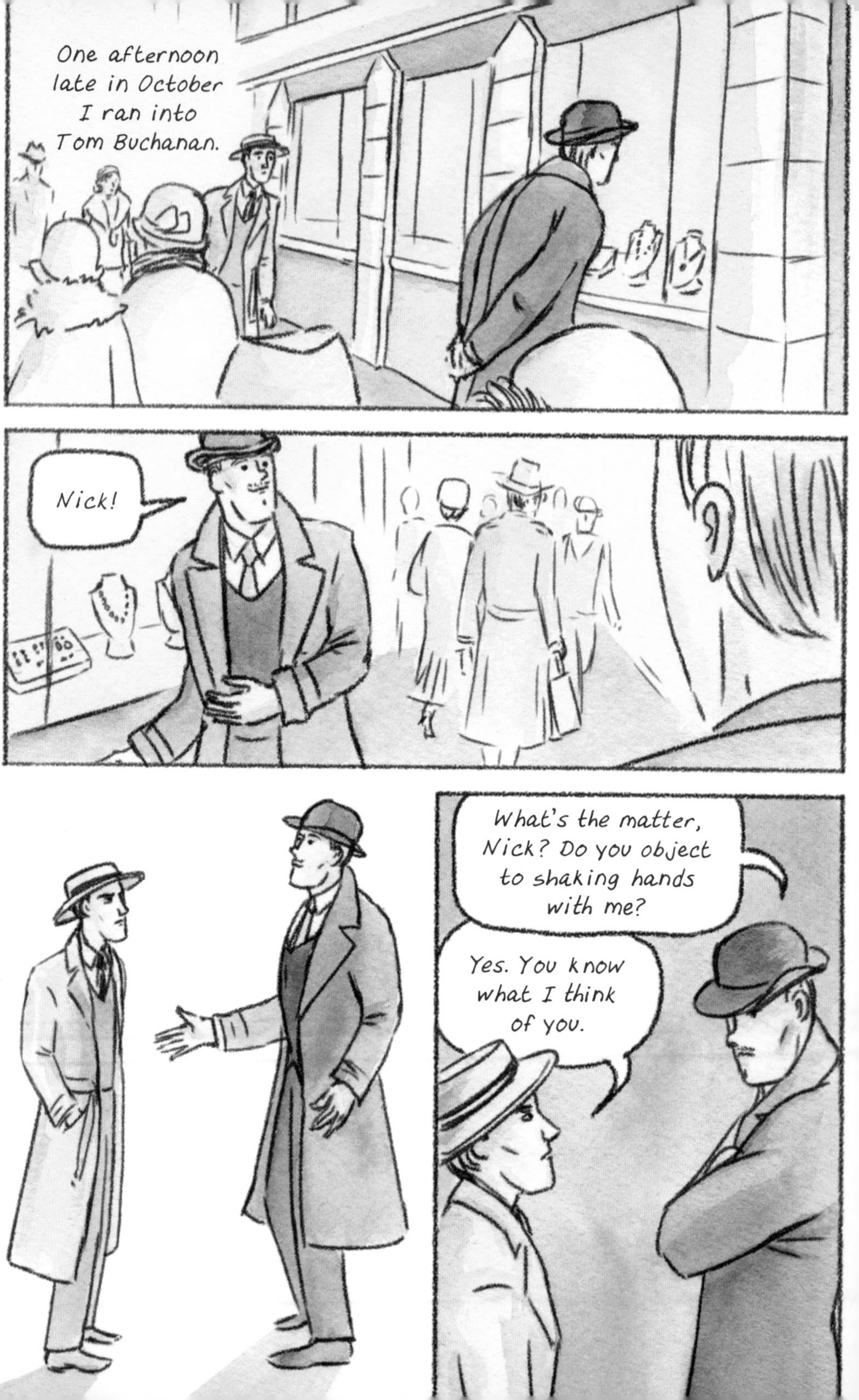
One afternoon late in October I ran into Tom Buchanan.
Nick!
What's the matter, Nick? Do you object to shaking hands with me?
Yes. You know what I think of you.

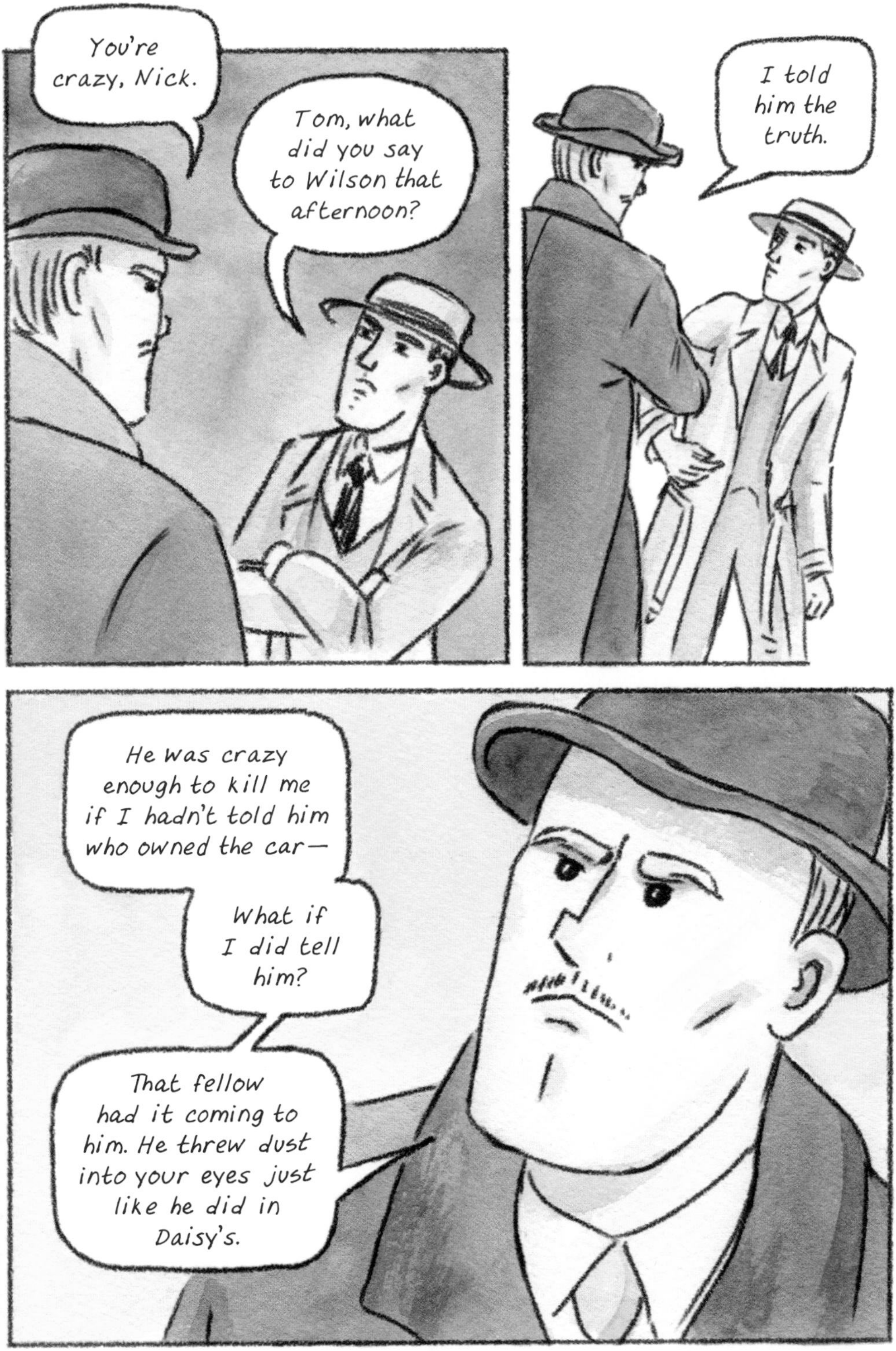
You're crazy, Nick.
Tom, what did you say to Wilson that afternoon?
I told him the truth.
He was crazy enough to kill me if I hadn't told him who owned the car—
What if I did tell him?
That fellow had it coming to him. He threw dust into your eyes just like he did in Daisy's.

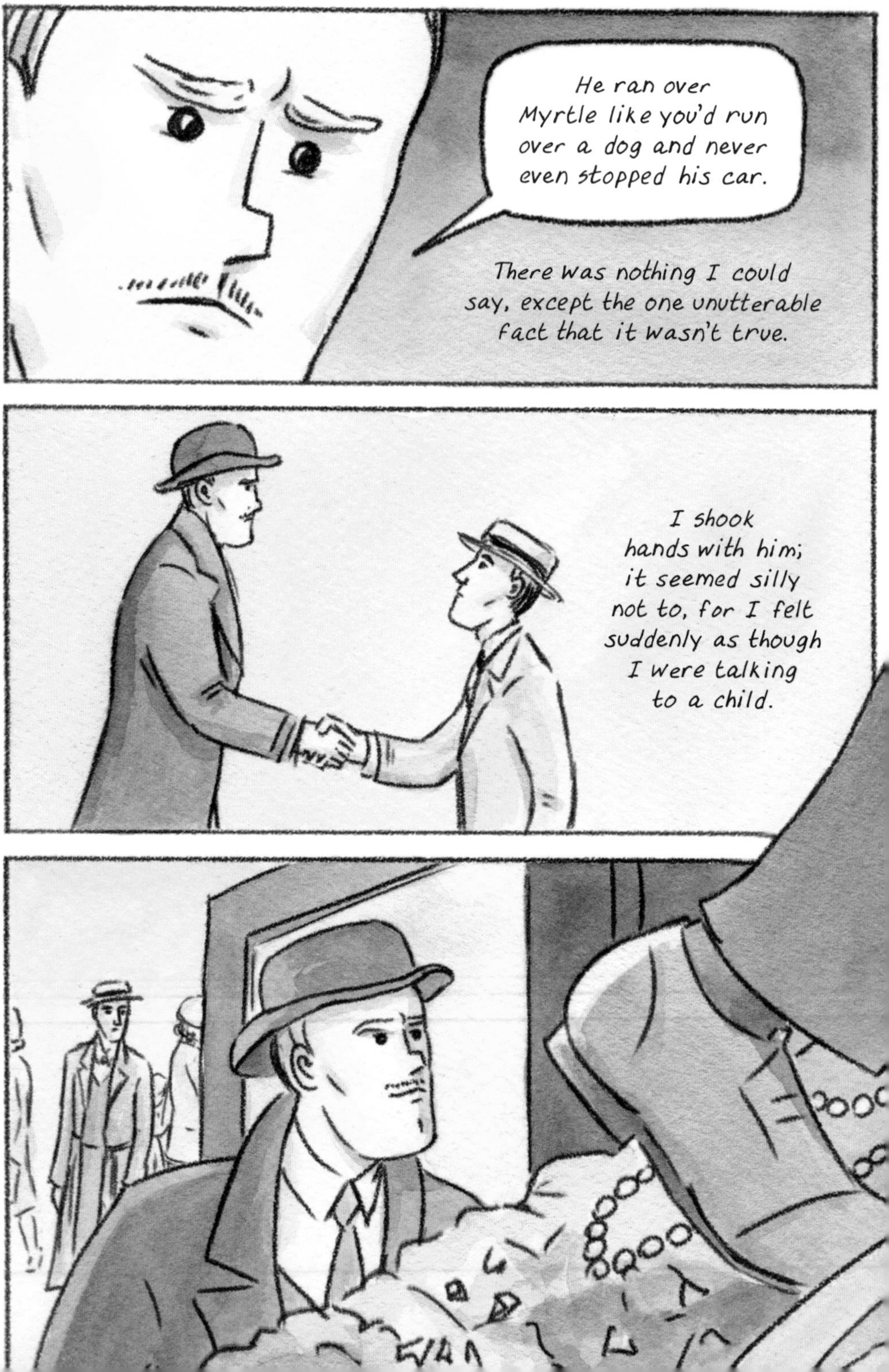
He ran over Myrtle like you'd run over a dog and never even stopped his car.
There was nothing I could say, except the one unutterable fact that it wasn't true.
I shook hands with him; it seemed silly not to, for I felt suddenly as though I were talking to a child.

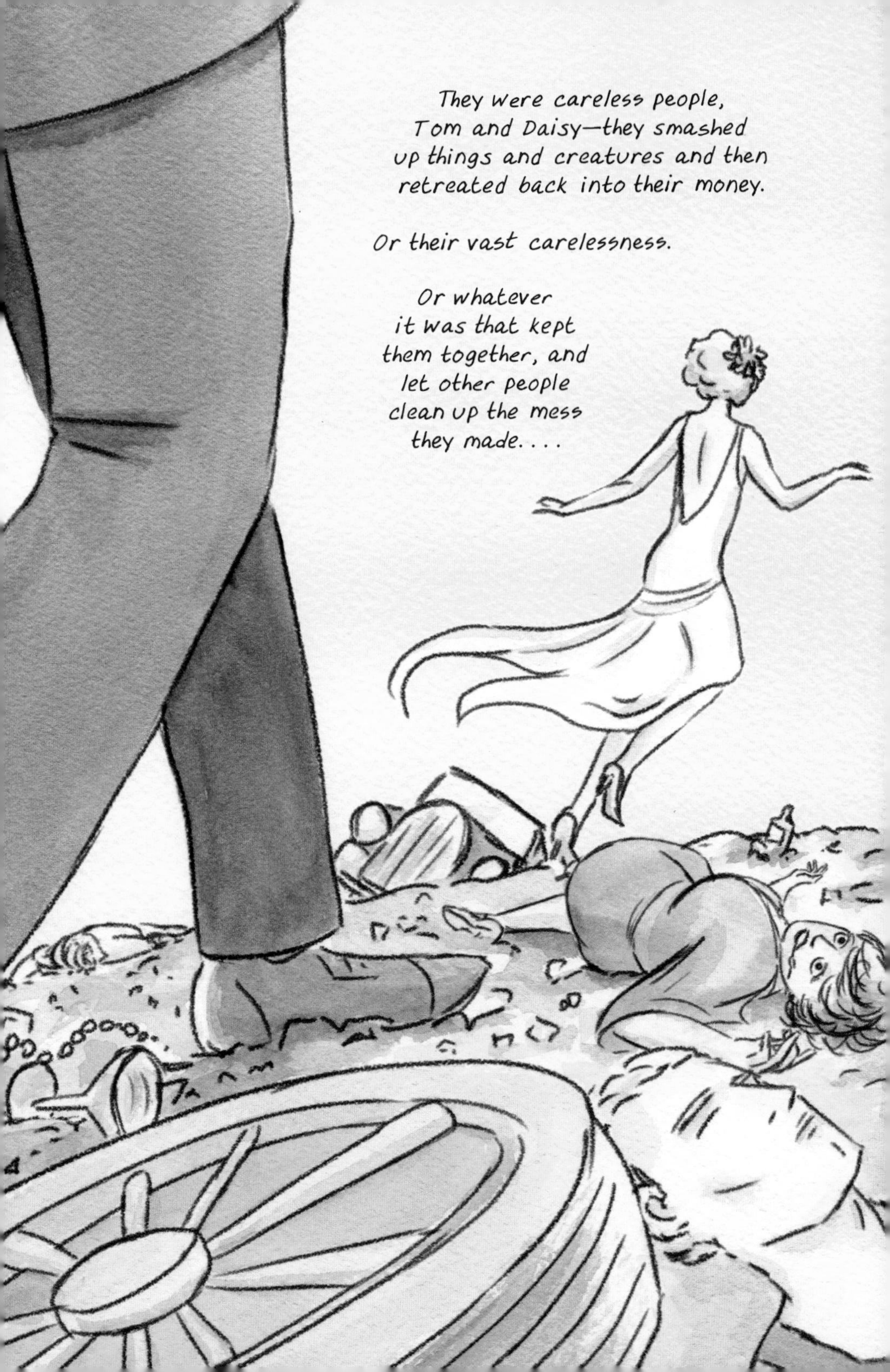
They were careless people, Tom and Daisy—they smashed up things and creatures and then retreated back into their money.
Or their vast carelessness.
Or whatever it was that kept them together, and let other people clean up the mess they made. . . .

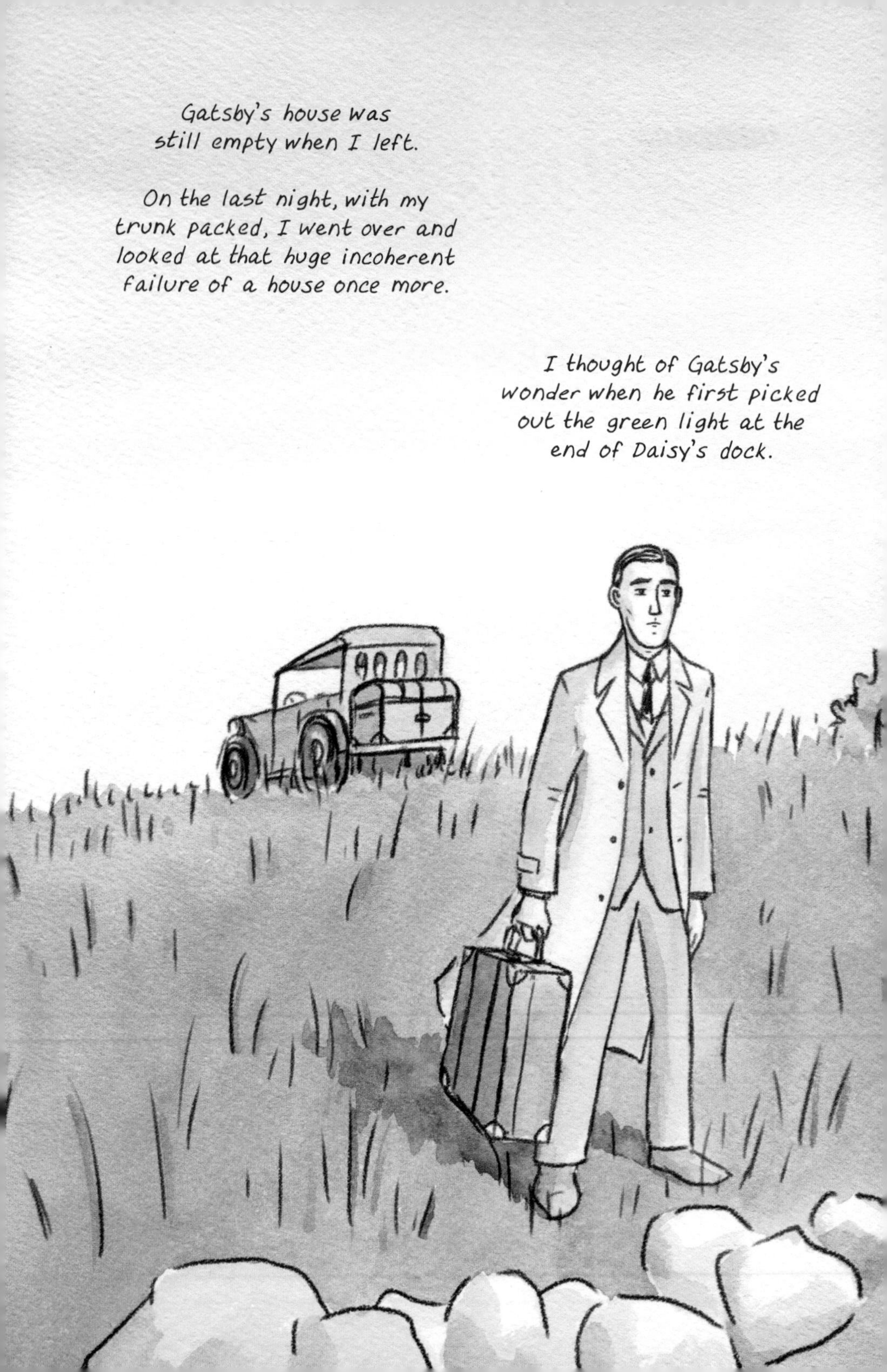
Gatsby's house was still empty when I left.
On the last night, with my trunk packed, I went over and looked at that huge incoherent failure of a house once more.
I thought of Gatsby's wonder when he first picked out the green light at the end of Daisy's dock.

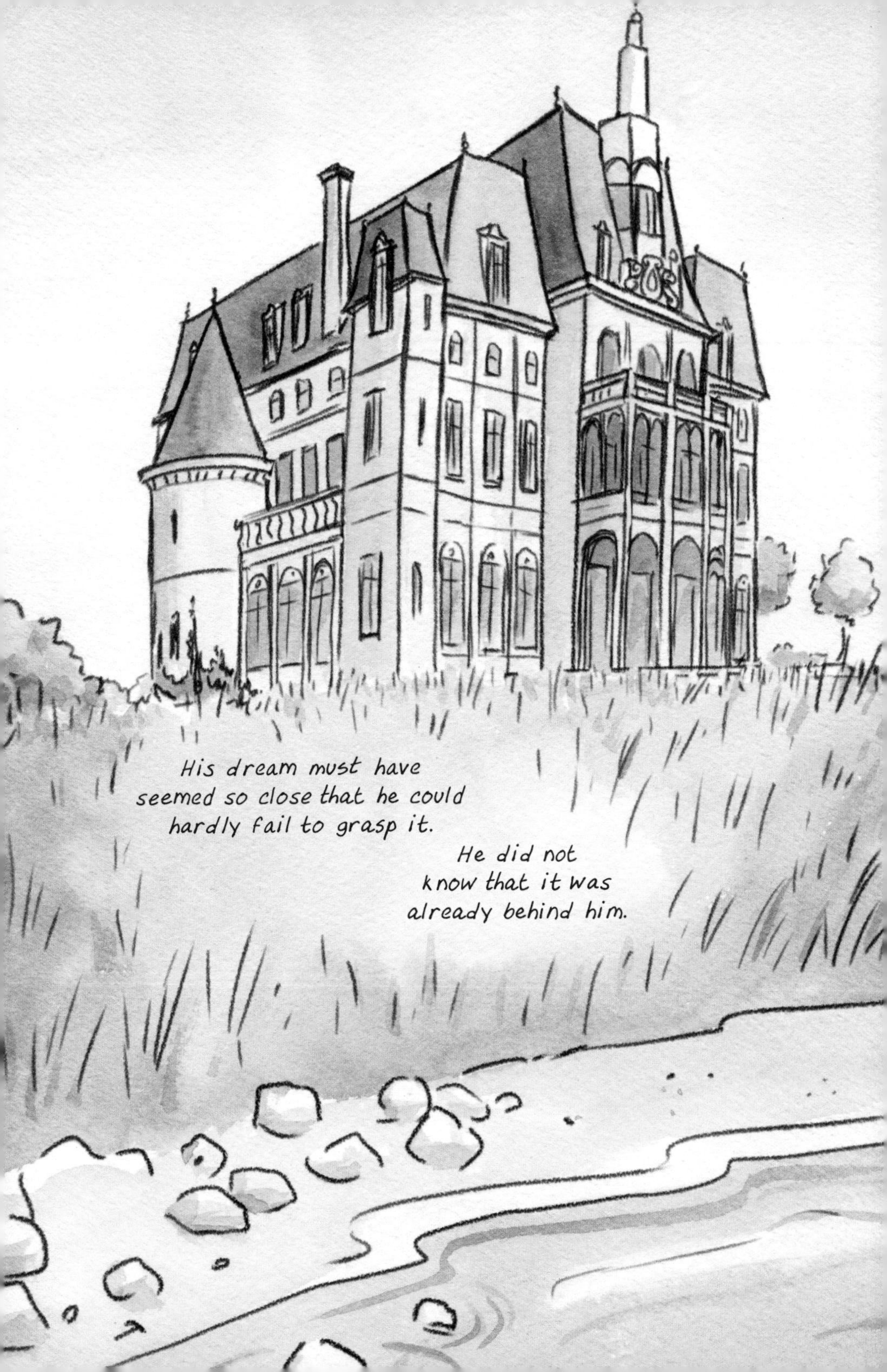
His dream must have seemed so close that he could hardly fail to grasp it.
He did not know that it was already behind him.

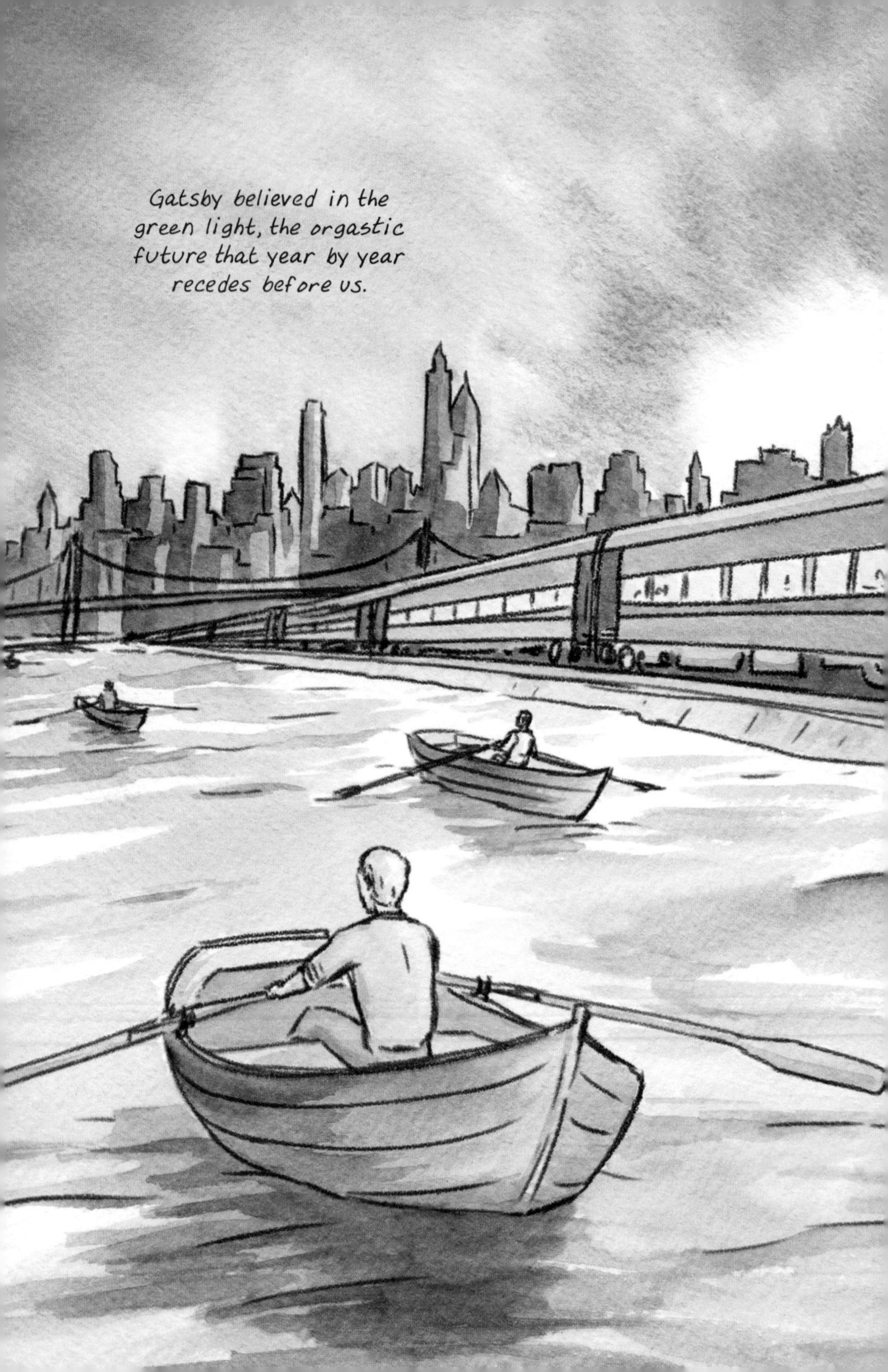
Gatsby believed in the green light, the orgastic future that year by year recedes before us.

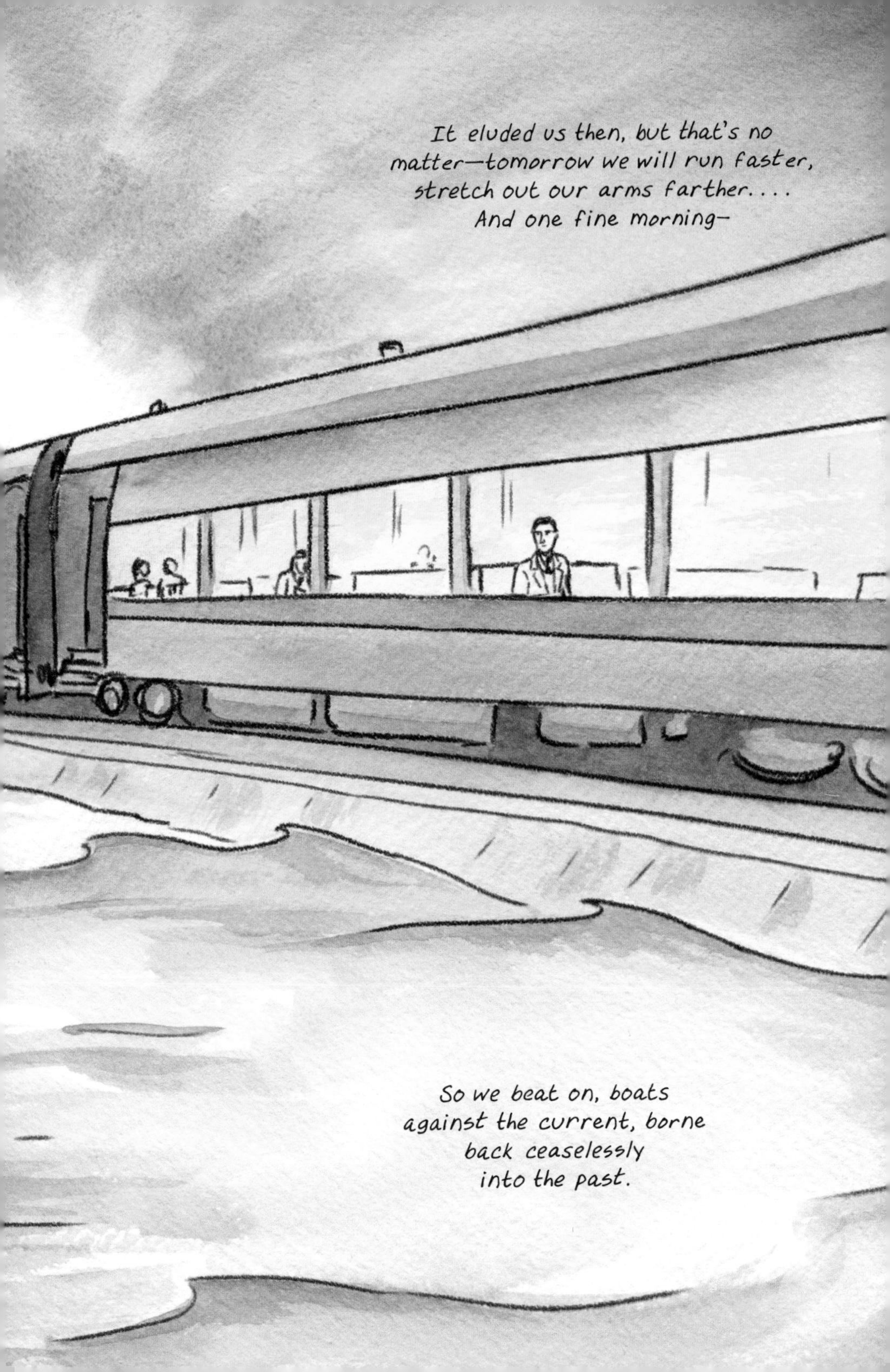
It eluded us then, but that's no matter—tomorrow we will run faster, stretch out our arms farther. . . . And one fine morning—
So we beat on, boats against the current, borne back ceaselessly into the past.

AUTHOR'S NOTE

Like so many others, I first read *The Great Gatsby* in my high school English class. I was initially struck by the gorgeousness of F. Scott Fitzgerald's language and the opulent world he depicted. But then my English teacher used the book to discuss metaphors and symbolism, and it was the first time I truly understood the power of metaphors. The book stuck with me, as some books do, and I have read it countless times over the years, making different observations and connections to my own life with every reading.

When I was contemplating adapting *The Great Gatsby* into a graphic novel, it was again the metaphors that drew me to it. I was excited by the idea of showing Daisy and Jordan literally floating over a couch, a treatment that I believe encapsulates the fantastic nature of Gatsby's world. This kind of surreal interpretation is ideally suited for the graphic novel medium, since illustration is not bound by the laws of gravity or the reality of the human form.

I never intended this graphic novel adaptation to be an exact literal interpretation of the novel. My goal was to capture the mood of *The Great Gatsby*, and so there are a few areas where I took more artistic license than others. For example, I reordered certain scenes so that they better suit the pacing of the graphic novel, such as Gatsby's throwing his shirts into the air. Furthermore, some text has been modernized or changed for clarity's sake. During this adaptation, I attempted to balance being true to the text with what I felt would work in the graphic novel medium and what would be easily understood by a modern reader.

One of the challenges of adapting *The Great Gatsby* is that the readers are seeing the story through Nick's eyes, and he is not a reliable narrator. From the first page we see that Nick's perspective cannot be fully trusted when he says, "I'm inclined to reserve all judgments, a habit that has opened up many curious natures to me and also made me the victim of not a few veteran bores." Nick claims that he doesn't pass judgment, but then in the same sentence pronounces a judgment, and he continues passing judgments throughout the book. So the question for the reader (or in my case, the adapter) is, how much can we trust his descriptions of events or people? I tried to highlight Nick's unreliability as a narrator in Chapter 6 when he says of Gatsby and Daisy that "They sat on the steps for half an hour, while I kept watch." I drew Daisy and Gatsby intentionally incongruent with the text—they disappear into the woods together. Nick's unreliability certainly allows for artistic freedom but also generates challenges.

Nick's depiction of Meyer Wolfshiem is especially difficult. Although both Wolfshiem and Gatsby engage in illegal activity and are essentially gangsters, Gatsby is described as a mythic and beautiful character while the depiction of Wolfshiem is an anti-Semitic caricature of a Jewish mobster. I wasn't comfortable depicting Wolfshiem in this way, but I kept him intimidating and mysterious by showing him as backlit and in shadow.

I also changed Meyer Wolfshiem's words in Fitzgerald's work from "gonnection" to "connection" and "Oggsford" to "Oxford." I vacillated about this change. On one hand, I wanted to be true to the text, and these well-known lines are often used by English teachers to discuss anti-Semitism. On the other hand, I had removed the visual caricature of Wolfshiem as well as the other accents in the book. In the end, my editor and I decided not to use text that is offensive and does not drive the story forward. Furthermore, accents indicated places during Fitzgerald's time; however, accents are no longer anchored to locations.

In developing the character design for the rest of my cast, I first looked at their descriptions in the book and then tried to design the characters to reflect their personalities. For Jordan and Daisy, I based their slender figures on 1920s fashion illustrations where the women have an airy otherworldliness that suits Daisy and Jordan. I couldn't reconcile Daisy with being a brunette, as she is described in the text, so I made her blond. For Tom Buchanan, I drew him much larger and more muscular than the other characters to emphasize his bullying nature and also how he dominates any room.

Jay Gatsby is actually described with very little detail by Fitzgerald. In seeking inspiration for his character design, I discovered the art of J. C. Leyendecker, who depicted his partner Charles Beach as the "Arrow Collar Man" in advertisements of the 1910s and 1920s. Charles Beach, classically handsome, was similar to the Gatsby I saw in my head, so I used Beach as inspiration. Later, I learned that scholars think that Daisy actually compares Gatsby to Beach when she tells Gatsby, "You always look so cool . . . you resemble the advertisement of the man . . . you know the advertisement of the man." I took this happy coincidence to be a sign that I was on the right track with Gatsby's character design.

Although I wanted the clothing, cars, and furniture to evoke the 1920s, again I was not going for exact verisimilitude. I did not restrict myself to designs from 1922 or earlier and allowed myself to be inspired by designs from throughout the 1920s, 1930s, and my own imagination. That being said, I spent far more time than I ever thought I would poring over 1920s women's fashion and luxury cars.

If this is your first encounter with *The Great Gatsby*, I encourage you to read Fitzgerald's masterpiece. Limitations of the graphic form prevented me from highlighting all of the themes that appear in Fitzgerald's work. In addition, I did not want to weigh down the graphic novel with too many words. However, Fitzgerald's language is unbelievably beautiful, and fans of this story should not miss one word. I think Maxwell Perkins, Fitzgerald's editor, stated it best when he told Fitzgerald, "The amount of meaning you get into a sentence, the dimensions and intensity of the impression you make a paragraph carry, are most extraordinary. The manuscript is full of phrases which make a scene blaze with life."

For those of you who love Fitzgerald's *The Great Gatsby* as much as I do, thank you for entrusting me with your eyes in reading this. I know it's difficult to see another's visual interpretation of something you love. I hope you found it enjoyable to see *Gatsby* through Nick's and my eyes.

ACKNOWLEDGMENTS

A huge thank-you to my husband, Mike Schowalter, who first read *The Great Gatsby* after my insistence in the early days of our relationship. Little did he know that he would become so closely acquainted with the story as I worked on this book, always patiently offering his feedback and support. I'm especially appreciative for the time he spent researching the legal aspects related to *The Great Gatsby* entering the public domain, as well as drawing in all my panel borders and scanning my art to help me reach my deadline.

I'm grateful to my readers, who offered me valuable feedback and advice: Carl Mefferd, Taylor Reynolds, Louise Deitrich, and Anna Christine. And I'm grateful to my high school English teacher, Michael Bazzett, who taught *The Great Gatsby* so compellingly and also gave me feedback on early versions of this adaptation.

I'm truly appreciative of Paul Karasik, Tillie Walden, and Jo Knowles for their excellent workshops at Center for Cartoon Studies that put me on the path to creating better graphic novels, with a special thanks again to Paul for being a great comics mentor.

Thank you to my parents for their love and encouragement of the arts from a young age.

I am especially grateful to Margaret Klein Salamon, Laura Powers, Ashleigh Parsons, and Ann I. for their understanding and ongoing support.

Thank you to my excellent literary agent, Bernadette Baker-Baughman, for her belief in this adaptation and wise guidance throughout. And another huge thank-you to my wonderful team at Candlewick Press for their thoughtful editorial and design guidance and enthusiasm: Kharissia Pettus, Maggie Deslaurier, Martha Dwyer, Sherry Fatla, and Lisa Rudden.

Finally, I am grateful to F. Scott Fitzgerald for writing a book in the 1920s that lives so vibrantly today and has given me, and many others, so much joy in reading it.

For my husband, Mike

Illustrations copyright © 2021 by Katharine Woodman-Maynard LLC

Originally published as a novel in 1925 as *The Great Gatsby* by F. Scott Fitzgerald
First edition 2021

Library of Congress Catalog Card Number pending
ISBN 978-1-5362-1301-0 (hardcover)
ISBN 978-1-5362-1676-9 (paperback)

20 21 22 23 24 25 CCP 10 9 8 7 6 5 4 3 2 1

Printed in Shenzhen, Guangdong, China

This book was typeset in WPG KWoodmanMaynard.
The illustrations were done in watercolor and digital media.

Candlewick Press
99 Dover Street
Somerville, Massachusetts 02144

www.candlewick.com

MIX
Paper from
responsible sources
FSC® C008047

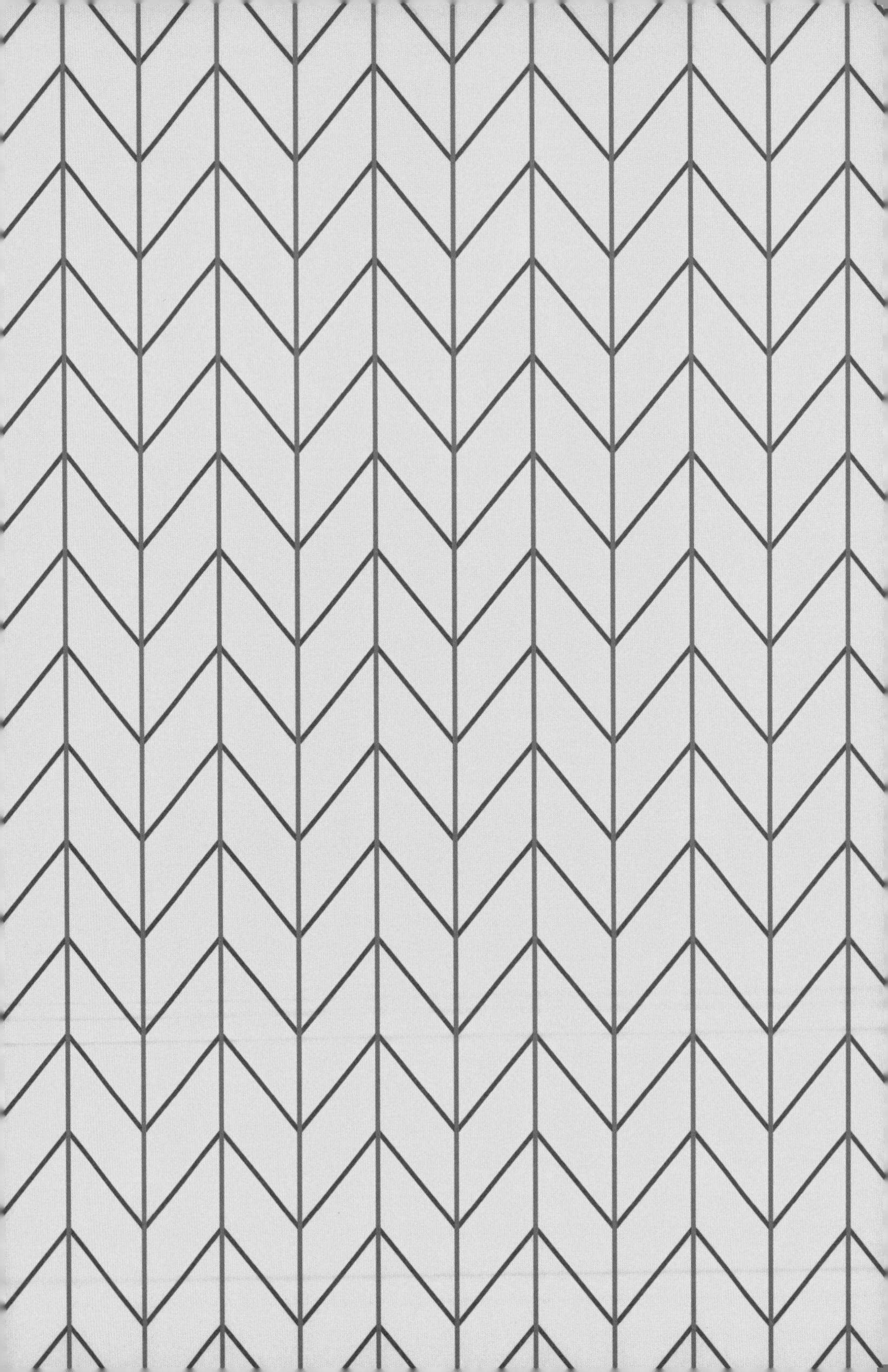

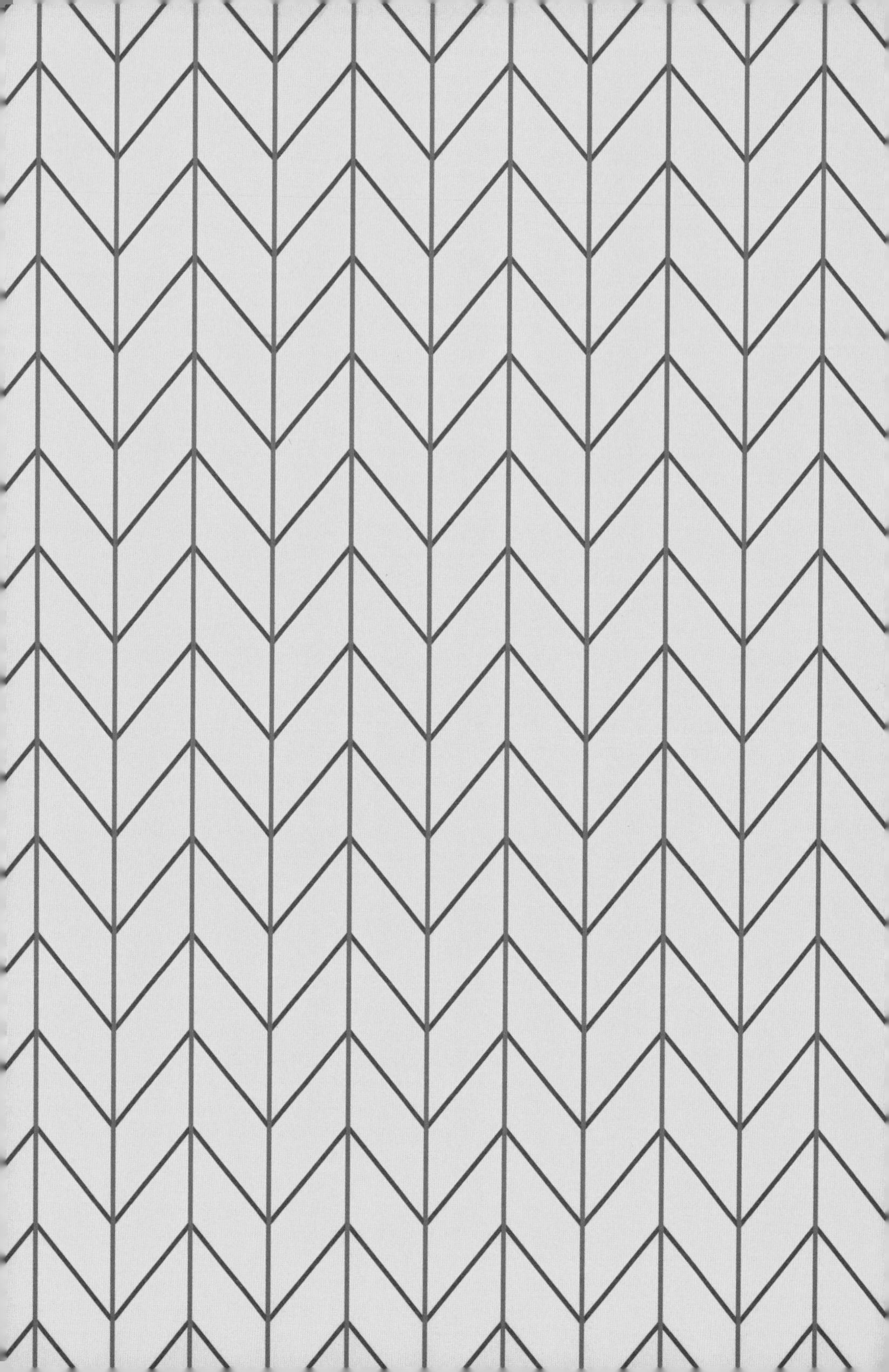

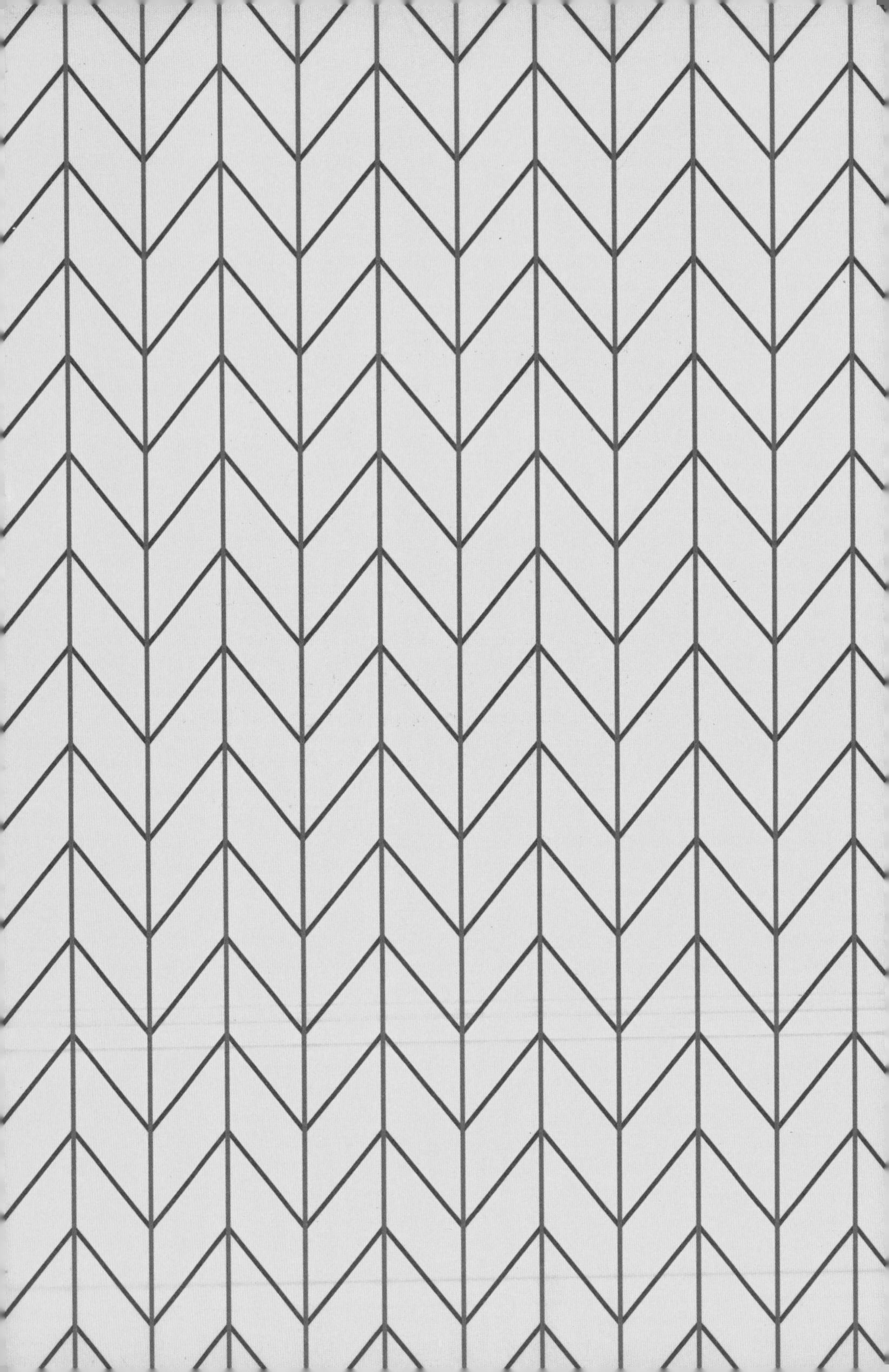